the silent *fall* of a magpie

a cove novel

ASHLAN THOMAS

The Silent Fall of a Magpie
A Cove Novel
by Ashlan Thomas
Ashlan Thomas Edition 2021
Copyright © 2016, 2021 Ashlan Thomas

This is a work of fiction. Names, characters, and incidents are the product of the author's imagination and are used fictitiously for entertainment purposes. Any resemblance to actual persons, living or dead, is entirely coincidental. The author is responsible for any artistic license used in erroneous portrayals or terminology of medical conditions. The graphic slogans/taglines within either originated from or were inspired by www.cafepress.com and www.zazzle.com.

ISBN: 9781533598554

also by ashlan thomas

THE TO FALL NOVELS
To Fall
To Hold
To Love

THE COVE NOVELS

THE MAGPIE SERIES:
The Silent Cries of a Magpie
The Silent Fall of a Magpie
The Silent Flight of a Magpie

author's note

Dear Reader,

Please note that this is a revised and expanded edition of *The Silent Fall of a Magpie*. Due to graphic scenes and language, the stories in this series are intended for a mature audience only. If you prefer not to read spoilers or be informed of sensitive subject matter prior to reading, please stop here. The *Magpie* series includes elements of, but not limited to, substance and alcohol abuse, grief, brief talk of suicide, sexual assault, and physical and mental abuse. Some scenes of assault/abuse are graphic but by no means romanticized and never between the hero and heroine. For an extensive list of the subject matter in this book, visit my website: AshlanThomas.com. Please do not continue if you find this subject matter unsettling, as I only hope to provide you with an escape from reality, never a return to one. If you or anyone you know is suffering from abuse, contact the National Domestic Violence Hotline at 800-799-7233 or chat online at thehotline.org. And if you or anyone you know is a victim of sexual violence, contact the National Sexual Assault Hotline 800-656-4673 or online by visiting rainn.org.

If you are returning to *The Cove*, this expanded version doesn't stray far from the original plot, but you will need to read the new edition of *The Silent Cries of the Magpie* to complete the *Magpie* series. This version does include needless shirtlessness, men in very short tutus, bad produce jokes, more questionable RAM shenanigans, and an older brother with a worsening case of anatidaephobia: a fear of ducks.

I hope you enjoy and I haven't let you down. Thank you for sticking with me.

XO,
Ashlan

dedicated to the believers of
true love…

Once upon a time there was a kingdom
shadowed in lies and darkness.
Hidden deep within the forest was a magpie,
imprisoned by a dragon that silenced her
cries.
His fire scorched her feathers, and when she
tried to fly, she could only fall.
This is a love story, but it isn't a fairy tale.
Knights in shining armor don't exist.
The dragon won't be slain.
And this doesn't end with a
happily ever after...

Maggie

chapter one

maggie

The light of a thousand suns blasted through my eyelids, ripping me out of what had been an all too brief sleep. I shielded my face with a pillow while attempting to comprehend why Jamey was dancing what could best be described as the sprinkler at…two a.m.

"God," I pleaded into the void. "Please end the horror." Groaning, I shoved a pillow over my head, but it didn't muffle the jerk's feet tapping across the planked floors. "You do know that you're the *worst* best friend ever, right?"

Jamey scoffed, tugging my light shield out of my grip despite my protests. "I'm the *best* best friend ever because you will be the first to hear my happy news."

"Jamey," I yawned his name. "There are few acceptable reasons for waking a person, and none of them include extreme joy. Only tragedies or deaths warrant a middle of the night wake-up. Happy news has to wait for the sun." Everyone knew this. Everyone but freakishly tall boys with silver tipped hair begging for a world of hurt. Like a kick to the man parts or a well-timed throat punch. Nothing he said at two in the morning could possibly—

"I'm ninety-nine percent sure I have an exclusive make out partner, which in gay translates to serious boyfriend."

Licking my chapped lips, I cracked an eye. "Okay, I'll let you live." Voice full of sleep, I croaked, "I'm a hundred percent happy for you."

The most I could do was raise my arms and make grabby hands, but the ache along my ribcage made a reappearance, reminding me of yesterday's events. Chuckling, Jamey met me the rest of the way. I snuggled in close, scenting Ben's cologne and what might be...Lemonheads?

Twisting slightly, my line of sight was smack dab in front of—

"Is that a hickey?" My eyes widened. It so totally was. *Oh, my God. Benjamin Scott gave Jameson Hayes a hickey.* And why my inner monolog was in full-name mode, I'd have to blame on sleep deprivation.

A sinful grin spread across Jamey's plumper than usual plump lips. "You think this is something? You should see—"

My hand slapped over his mouth. "That qualifies as TMI. I told you, I don't want to see, hear, or have you pantomime it to me."

Laughing, Jamey made an irritable gesture at my sprawled limbs to make room for him. I more or less flopped over as he settled in next to me on the mattress.

"I have to admit," I said, kicking the sheet free from my foot. "I'm a little disappointed. Don't gays usually move a lot faster than this? I thought you were supposed to shack up together by the second date and adopt a cat, so you had something to dress up in a tutu."

His eyes danced with mischief. "Well, in true gay fashion, we're skipping the pussy and going straight to the adoption agencies. But I'll make an exception for you if your heart is set on being our surrogate."

I craned away from him. "I don't have to have sex with you, do I?"

Jamey's face screwed up to near comical levels. "Ew! Gross, Mags! No, we'll use turkey basters and shit."

I shot him a bland look. "A simple no would have sufficed."

Grinning, Jamey tucked a mass of tangled hair behind my ear, his fingers skimming the depression on my left temple. It didn't hurt, but I fought the urge to cringe from him, nonetheless.

"You're due for a trim. I can do it in the morning if you want."

"No," I yawned, covering my mouth mid-way this time. "I have to get out early. Lots to do."

Frowning, he picked the tangle apart, careful not to pull on the roots. "Did Mason drop you off from the bowling alley okay?"

How could such an innocent question feel like an elephant had plopped onto my chest?

I didn't know how to answer that. It hadn't been a simple drop off because nothing about Mason Scott was simple. From the moment we'd met, he'd been complex and confusing, blurring boundaries that only he'd set.

Last night, after weeks of refusing to touch me, Mason had done the very thing Jamey had. He'd swept my hair away from my face, and when he got too close to my left temple, I freaked out that he'd feel the rutted stretch of bone there, see my scar. And in that moment, Taylor Price's acidic words had invaded me.

Simply put, Mason Scott should be with someone of equal pedigree.

And she'd been right. I wasn't of equal pedigree. I didn't have a pedigree at all. I was a poor townie. A freak. A spaz. *Worthless garbage...*

Yet, when Mason had asked for my friendship, my trust, I had agreed. But I couldn't allow my heart to feel anything more than friendship. I'd been hurt by him, fallen for his honeyed words too many times. Mason Scott was a force far more powerful than me, and if I wasn't careful, he'd ruin me.

"Yeah, Mason brought me back okay," I answered. And by okay, I meant *eventually*. I didn't want to go into the detour that Mason had taken between the bowling alley and Jamey's house.

Jamey hummed, his mouth forming a smile. "Mags," he sighed dreamily. "I think you have to give Camden a whirl. Those Scott lips are decadent."

"I'll take your word for it."

"There's always Matt," he lilted.

"Matt treats me like a little sister, which I am totally fine with." Being careful not to stab his eye out with my shaky fingers, I played with his hair that was less gelled from before as if someone had their hands in it all night. A Ben Scott someone.

"I think Mason would be down," he offered with a nudge.

Stretching my legs, I moaned. "Please. Do I need to remind you of the date that never was? Mason Scott is not interested in Maggie Davis."

He flipped onto his stomach, hazel eyes unnaturally bright for this time of night. "I would beg to differ with that assessment because I lost count of how many times he wasn't *not* interested in your ass last night."

My heart thumped, but I narrowed my glare to throw off Jamey's human lie detector. "He was probably looking for the perfect spot to kick."

"Wrong, Mags. So *very* wrong." He vaulted off the bed. Seriously, what kind of Ben-high was he on? "By the way, you didn't say you didn't want to kiss him."

That's because I do. "I don't want to kiss Mason Scott."

"You can't even look me in the eye, you dirty liar!"

"Shut up and go to bed." I chucked the pillow at him, and it hit the wall. I was aiming for his head. "Isn't Ava dragging you to San Francisco in, like, four hours for that hair convention? Why are you home so late?"

"Because when you're making out with a mouth like Benjamin Scott's, priorities shift. Being a zombie tomorrow will be so worth it, and Mom won't care. Hell, she'll give me a high-five and then ask for the uncensored deets."

Yes, Ava Hayes would totally do that. She was the most supportive, loving mother, and there had been plenty of times I'd been jealous of their relationship. Though Ava and Jamey had done everything possible to include me in their lives, I couldn't stem the pang in my chest that appeared with every hug, kiss, and silly moment I witnessed between them.

Sometimes it wasn't easy to be around them.

Opening a drawer, Jamey peered inside and began rifling through his clothes. "By the way, Ben has a seriously talented tongue. He does this little swirl move—"

"Jamey."

"—and it's so true what they say about the size of a man's hands in correlation to his man parts. Have you *seen* the size of Ben's hands?"

I muttered, "I'm asleep now. Can't hear a thing you're saying."

He pulled clothes out of the drawer and shut it. "Huge. Enormous. Mind-blowing."

Leaning up on my elbows, I spoke louder, so there wasn't any confusion. "I'm going to hurt you in your sleep, and I won't feel bad about it. Not one—" Something forced my attention down. To the bed. I squinted, slanting my head. Then leaned closer, struggling to decipher the printed images. He didn't. He wouldn't. "Are these *penises* on the sheets?"

A sly grin curved one side of his mouth.

Squealing, I launched off the mattress, slapping at the invisible cooties swarming my body. "I've been sleeping on penises this whole time? What is wrong with you?" They weren't even cartoon dicks. They were *actual* dicks. With balls and veins and—

They were all erect.

"Cock does a body good, Mags. You should get some. And soon. You're rocking some serious sexual frustration."

Mid smack of my arm, I paused to glare at him. "As if I'd know what to do with one if that miracle ever happened."

"That's the beauty of it. You don't have to do much." That was when he picked the pillow off the floor. The pillow my face had been smashed into. Right there, in bold black letters, it read, IT'S ALL FUN AND GAY UNTIL SOMEONE FORGETS THE LUBE.

I swallowed sourly. "I really should have turned the light on before coming in here."

Chuckling, Jamey sauntered into the bathroom with his pajamas in hand. "Heads up. You reaaaally shouldn't look in my nightstand."

My gaze crawled toward said furniture, zeroing in on the top drawer. All kinds of bad thoughts took over my brain.

That was when the bathroom door shut, and I could still hear the jerk laughing behind it.

"You sure you're gonna make it to Crescent Lake with all of this, Mags?" A snowy white eyebrow lifted on Henry's forehead as he helped hook the grocery bags onto my Schwinn's front basket. "Maybe I should call Two Dimples to drive you there."

Irritation stiffened my jaw. Only one person would fit that moniker.

"*Two Dimples?*" I asked, exasperated. "What is with the nicknames in this town?" Mumbling to myself, I jerked the zipper of my backpack closed, but it took two tries to complete the job. My lack of sleep this weekend was officially showing in my tremor.

Henry's ruddy palms faced me. "You can thank Darlene for that one. The woman hasn't stopped talking about him, and I quote, '*His yummy tushy,*' since you brought him here last week."

Last week. Right. The day Mason begrudgingly drove me to Henry's Market, nearly knocked Darlene on her ass with just a smile, made Henry his new BFF, and then Eric Ryan cornered me in the café's alley to make sure I wouldn't tell the Scotts that I'd witnessed him and his friend gang rape a girl two years ago. A girl who died a month later. Two horrible events that I could have prevented if I hadn't been such a coward.

If I'd only fought them off Jenna that night instead of running for help, if I'd only spoken up for her, reached out to her, she might still be here. But Eric's father was a powerful man. So powerful that he'd made her rape disappear completely. Marcus had somehow persuaded Jenna and me to be silent. Only for her, I suspected a hefty sum of money had been involved. For me, all that was needed was a leather belt wielded by my father's hand.

But something had been bugging me since last night. What Eric had said…

Don't tell me you don't know how dirty the hands that tuck you in at night are.

Eric was aware that I knew my father had covered up what he'd done to Jenna by telling people that I'd been mistaken. I must have had one of my "episodes" and hallucinated. Eric and Jenna's story had become the real story. Just a boy breaking up with a girl as he consoled her.

When I'm done with you, off yourself. Like everyone thought Jenna did.

And there was that. We were told Jenna had taken her own life, but— Had Marcus done something to her instead? And had my father covered up more than her rape? How far would Marcus go to protect his son?

That probably wasn't a question I wanted answered.

As I untied my backpack from the basket to make room for more groceries, a gust of briny air snuck past the thin layer of my hoodie. I wished I'd worn jeans rather than shorts, but it was supposed to be warm later today, and the ocean breeze didn't quite make it as far inland as the Scotts' home.

"Well, Two Dimples and his *yummy tushy* are probably still asleep at the fraternity house. It's not his job to cart me around town." Nor did I want it to be.

"Speaking of cart." Henry used a stubby finger to tap the bike frame. "New lights? Where'd ya get 'em?"

My mouth thinned. "Two Dimples. He'll be more than happy to tell you all about them and then screw them onto your bike every time you unscrew them." And the ass had done that at some point during Ben's party. Seriously, I had no idea when he had time to do that.

Or why.

Okay, I did know why. Mason had a hero complex that stemmed from not protecting his little sister the way he believed he should have. This whole thing started because Mason felt guilty for breaking my light the night we crashed into each other. At the time, I loved that he'd been thoughtful enough to buy me a new set of lights and had come all the way into town to surprise me with them. I loved it so much that I agreed to go on a date with him even though I didn't know what he looked like because the storm had caused a blackout.

It had been the ultimate blind meet cute.

But the cute went to shit once Mason was no longer blind to what I looked like. And though he'd apologized, I wasn't sure I'd ever forgive him for walking out on our date.

Correction. *Running* out on our date.

And after acting like a complete dick and trying to bribe me to quit working for his parents, Mason was now back to playing my hero. A hero I didn't want or need. So as soon as I could get my hands on a screwdriver, these lights were gonna go.

Henry attempted to hold back a laugh, but not well enough. "Ah, you're being too hard on the guy. It's sweet."

"You only think that because he likes your jokes."

"Everyone likes my jokes." I lifted a brow at that. "Okay, *most* people," he amended.

Shaking my head, I hung the last two grocery bags on the handlebars. "I'll be by tonight to get Poker's food." Finished with the bags, I paused. "Did you...have a chance to do a check this morning?" After all these years, I still hated asking that question.

"Oh. I did." Henry shuffled inside and returned with a bag at least five pounds heavier than it should be.

I peered inside, then looked to Henry. "I think you grabbed the wrong bag."

"No, that's yours." Squinting at a sooty shearwater aiming for his trashcan, he sniffed. "Didn't like how the Grannies looked today."

Frowning, I drew out one unblemished, firm green apple from the bag, noting his plump red counterparts along with a few oranges and grapefruits. "What are you talking about? There's nothing wrong with— Is that a summer sausage? Henry! There's…" Digging through the items, I tallied things up in my head. "There's gotta be thirty dollars' worth of groceries here."

Grunting, he shoved the bag into my arms, so he could clap at the encroaching menace. The fat brown bird hopped off toward Cove Cleaners.

Attention returning to me, he said, "I found roaches in the delivery box. Can't sell the stuff, Mags. Put them in your basket."

"This won't all fit, Henry. I—"

Hold up. Was I seriously complaining right now? About having *too much* food to feed starving people? I thought he was being ridiculous, but I never had a haul this good. Usually, the produce Henry gave me was one minute away from the dumpster, and any kind of protein was on life support.

I hugged the bag close to my chest. "Thank you. This is very generous."

Shrugging, he groused something that sounded a lot like, "It's not me you should be thanking."

"Huh?"

Henry's clear blue eyes widened behind his rimless frames as if at a loss for words when he wasn't a second ago. "What? Oh, nothing. Sorry. Just remembered something the wife told me about a bank deposit."

My brow pinched. That didn't sound at all like what he'd said. "Okay, well, thanks again."

He nodded, but it was stiff, and a thread of unease slipped through my belly. "Sure thing, Mags."

As soon as Henry cleared the door, the shearwater tipped its head and waited a beat before hopping back over to inspect the market's trash. I shook my head at it. "You wouldn't be doing that if you knew how many of your cousins he's got lined up on ice in there."

Ignoring me, the bird shoved its head into an empty Ruffles bag.

After making sure my bike wouldn't topple over with the new weight of the basket goodies, I shouldered my backpack and winced as it slammed into my side. I'd done a number on my ribcage yesterday when I'd tried to duck Eric's attack. I briefly wondered what his face looked like this morning. It couldn't have been any match for Mason's fist. That thing had mad strength. And good aim.

While I waited for the pain to ebb, I squinted against the sunlight, studying the alleyways and finding a lump resembling a human body tucked between Trudy and Rick's buildings. I rolled the Schwinn toward the café and collected a few items from the grocery bag.

I crossed the street, making noise by scuffing my Chucks on the uneven pavers as I approached the ratty brown blanket that I knew had been red plaid at one point in its lifetime.

"Ronnie? It's the Princess."

Ronnie had a nickname for everyone, and I wasn't sure if that was part of his illness, or he had a penchant for nicknames like everyone else in Crescent Cove. I, for whatever reason, had the only name that made no sense.

The blanket shifted, stirring up an odor that could be bottled for biochemical warfare. Ronnie used to bathe and wash his clothes in the beach showers, but the final one had broken six months ago. Like everything else downtown, the repair date remained indefinite.

I crouched next to him along with the remnants of the orange that Etana—*the Sun God*—must have given him yesterday. Ronnie's mental state had been questionable lately, and over the last few weeks, he'd been isolating himself more and eating less. The only way I could get him to eat now was to leave food at the surf shop or hand deliver it.

"Ronnie, I have an apple today. It's red."

Ronnie only ate food and surrounded himself with things that had warm tones. Many a blueberry and key lime pie had died a gruesome death before I figured that out.

The top of a brown boot that was missing half a sole peeked out of the blanket. The bottom of his big toe had been cut recently, and it didn't look as if he'd taken care of it.

Concern trickled through me. "I also have sliced turkey and cheese. The good deli kind. Henry was very generous today."

The blanket didn't move.

I worried my bottom lip. "You don't feel like talking?"

The outline of a head shook back and forth.

"That's alright. You don't have to talk if you don't want to. But will you let me look at you?"

The blanket shook again, faster this time. I didn't take offense to that, but I'd feel better if I could have visual confirmation that he was okay. Ronnie was prone to inflicting self-harm, mainly to his head and especially when his paranoia was heightened. Ronnie really liked Trudy—*Flora*—and with her florist shop going out of business, combined with the fact that I'd been coming around less, could have caused his regression. His life was unstable at best, and the little stability he had was being taken from him.

"Ronnie, I'm going to leave the food here and something to help your toe. Will you use them for me? They're safe. I promise."

He nodded that time.

From the front pouch of my backpack, I pulled out a first-aid travel kit that I bought last week after a vertigo spell in the university library caused me to fall and scrape my knees. I set the kit and the food on what looked to be the cleanest part of his blanket.

"Ronnie, if you're still hungry, come over to the café. Maybe we'll have some leftover sourdough for you." I waited another beat for him to speak, and when he didn't, I stood and turned.

I took one step off the curb.

"Brownies."

His rusted voice stopped me cold, and a slight grin pulled at my mouth. Every time I drew him out of himself, I felt as if I'd climbed Everest. Ronnie lived for the café's brownies. I wasn't sure if it was the sweet treat he liked or that they were easier to eat. He didn't have the best dental hygiene, and the last toothbrush I'd given him hadn't been used for its…intended purpose.

"Brownies, huh? I'll see what I can do."

With that, I crossed the street. Unhooking Henry's bag from my bike, I stepped around the two-top table on the walkway. The front door of the Crest Cent Café was already propped open, so I didn't have a clanging bell to announce my arrival.

I crossed the dining room, detecting the scent of cookies baking. Candi jutted her chin my way as she served table three their breakfast plates.

"Hey, girl! You just missed the boys, but they asked about you."

Disappointment etched through me, causing me to stop. "Oh."

Though I saw them yesterday before Ben's birthday party, I'd hoped to talk with the boys again this morning. I'd been a little harsh with them after discovering they were going to meet with my father to…

God, I still couldn't believe it.

Nothing's been decided yet, but if Marcus wants us to enforce the vagrant laws, we will. And you already know the why of it.

Yeah. Yeah, I did. Mayor Marcus Ryan treated people like Ronnie as if they were rats who needed exterminating. He wanted to gather them in cages and dump them anywhere that would make them someone else's problem. These were human beings who needed help, someone to give a damn about them, not to be carted off to wait out their death from starvation or the elements.

It didn't have to be this way. I never minded putting the basket together every morning, but the entire community should be involved. It was long past time Crescent Cove addressed the serious issues plaguing the underprivileged. While this town was populated by some of the wealthiest families on the California coast, others had to choose between paying their mortgage or eating dinner. People didn't choose to live in filthy alleyways, wear dirty rags, eat garbage. It was how they survived when those who could help them shut their eyes to the *unsightly*.

"How, uh— How did your date go last night?" I didn't want to ask this question because Candi was all about the details. Details I'd already cleaned up after stopping by the house this morning to take care of Poker. I supposed I'd asked so I could gauge the look in her eyes, waiting for the inevitable day my father revealed what he was to her. By the way her amber irises practically glittered, today was not that day.

"Soooo fun! After dinner, he took me dancing. Did you know your father could dance?"

"No, I didn't."

Her caramel curls bobbed with an enthusiastic nod. "That he can. You should ask him to show you sometime."

"I'll have to keep that in mind."

Pleased with herself, Candi freshened table ten's coffees, and I fought back a twinge of guilt. I had hoped this thing between them would fizzle quickly, that he'd tire of her and move on. It didn't seem as if Candi was that lucky.

Sliding past the kitchen doors, I set my bag on the prep table and waved to the gray head bent over the second fryer. Frankie still hadn't called the technician to fix it. I frowned, thinking back to that overdue notice I'd found in the office weeks ago. Considering how Frankie had been extra grouchy lately over the lack of customers, increased food waste, and repair costs, I suspected that notice was for the café. After Trudy had put up a going-out-of-business sign in her flower shop window, it was a reasonable assumption.

"Morning, Frankie."

"Mags." He more or less grumbled my name in greeting while I inspected the cookies in the oven. The very batch of dough that I'd prepped yesterday. I then peeked at the tray of brownies destined for the pastry display once they were cut. Unfortunately, I didn't see any rejects or crimped edges that I could use for the basket.

I began to put the cling wrap back into place when Frankie's gruff voice filtered over. "G'head. Take two."

My eyes shot up in surprise. "Really?"

"You honestly want me to reconsider?"

He was right. I wasn't sure what was making everyone so generous today, but I shouldn't question it. This had been exactly what I'd been hoping for.

"Nope!" I made quick work of cutting the tray and wrapped up two of the smallest brownies. I organized the basket, so they were on top. "Thank you, Frankie." Lifting to my toes, I pressed a kiss to his stubbled cheek as he met me at the prep station.

"Yeah, yeah. Don't get all..." His focus rotated toward the kitchen cutout, bushy brows furrowed low and tight. Shoulders nearing his ears, Frankie's gnarled knuckles bleached white on his spatula.

I slanted my head as I studied his expression. "Frankie? What's wrong?"

Glaring at the cutout, his upper lip curled back. "Nothing. Just spotted a rat in my dining room."

"What?" Confused as to why Frankie stormed out through the double doors wielding a pancake flipper like a battle-ax, I collected the basket and sped off after him. One step out of the kitchen, I came to an utter and complete halt, letting the doors smack me in the back. I didn't even flinch from the surge of pain along my side because in that instant, every molecule of oxygen whooshed out of my lungs and white-hot rage swirled in.

Indeed, we did have a rat.

A rat that greeted me with a chipper, "Good morning, Miss Davis."

chapter two

maggie

Frankie growled something that didn't sound at all welcoming, but I wasn't paying attention because I was focused on the all-encompassing need to launch my fist into a facial feature of the man standing on the opposite side of the counter. To be fair, the dude could tempt God and all the Archangels into committing what was perhaps the most heinous of the Ten Commandments.

Marcus Ryan was as I remembered him, as was my consuming desire to rearrange the placement of his nose and chin. Eyes that were a flat and lifeless shade of brown swung away from Frankie, locking onto me. A few more wrinkles had marred his polished features from the last time I had seen him; otherwise, he hadn't aged. Maybe his ugly soul was finally chipping away at the beautiful façade.

"Mayor Ryan," I gritted out, setting my basket on the counter. I was quick to hide my trembling hands from him. Like most, Marcus assumed that my essential tremor was a sign of nervousness, a weakness of character. He would use that to his advantage.

Frankie sidled up next to me. "To what do we owe this displeasure?"

Marcus' lips slid up on one side, smiling as if he were hiding a secret. He was. More than one. "Mr. de Ruvo." Placing his black blazer onto the stool sent the intended message. He wasn't leaving anytime soon. "How is Mrs. de Ruvo these days?"

"Not well after you increased our small business taxes last year to build your marina. And approving the licenses of big corporations to buy out our buildings only to raise our rents and force good people into bankruptcy hasn't done much for her blood pressure. But I'm sure you upper-class folk are just fine. Seeing that the city council recently gave themselves a raise and all."

My stomach churned painfully. I'd been right. The café was in trouble.

Marcus cleared his throat, casting an uncomfortable glance over his shoulder. He needn't concern himself with drawing any negative attention. Candi had ensured her tips by entertaining her tables and talking well above an appropriate decibel level.

"I understand how that must concern you, Mr. de Ruvo." Brushing a dark blond curl back from his forehead, Marcus' gaze was deceptively soft. Nothing about this man being here was innocent. Nothing he did was without motive. "We'd love to hear your voice at the next city council meeting."

Frankie snorted. "Would you now? Because you didn't seem to love the sound of my voice during the last five meetings, and you especially weren't loving it when I spoke against your decision to cut funding on city repairs and beautification programs. Now, if that's all, you can see yourself out."

"Actually, Mr. de Ruvo…" One palm lifted, the gold band of an obnoxiously large ring winking in the morning light. "I came here to see Miss Davis." His head tilted in my direction. "Do you have time to enjoy a cup of coffee with me while we discuss a few things outside?"

Frankie crossed his arms, the spatula twirling in his hand. "I think you'll find the answer to that is a hard no."

Frankie wasn't wrong. I'd rather clean out the café's grease trap with my tongue than talk to Marcus Ryan, but if I didn't voluntarily speak to him now, my father would make me do it involuntarily later.

Frankie was now one second away from snapping the spatula in two and shoving each broken end up Marcus' nostrils when I said, "It's fine, Frankie."

Frankie's steady glare grazed over to me. "You sure, Mags?" I nodded. "Alright. I'm right here if you need me." The flippy part of the spatula pointed to our unwanted guest. "Watch it with her."

I waited for Frankie to slip into the back before I checked the time on the wall. Then I gave Marcus my undivided attention. "Have you come here to listen to my reasons to reconsider enforcing the vagrant laws? Because I have quite a bit to say on that subject. For instance, rather than wrangling up innocent people and shipping them off like animals, it's possible to treat them humanely and with respect, and I even have a solution that would both help them become productive members of society *and* increase your popularity. If your political aspirations go beyond mayor, that is."

It wasn't until the last part did his eyes take on a hungry gleam. "Go on."

"There is a plot of land on the south side of Baywoods Forest that is discreet enough for at least a dozen semi-permanent trailers that could provide private housing, which would give the homeless a community of their own, and in return, have them work for the city. They can keep the beaches clean, maintain downtown, or help with the city's infrastructure. If someone could donate a vehicle it would make their commute much easier. This would give them job experience, a resume to rebuild their lives, a chance to earn money, and after some time, they will no longer be dependent for assistance. In the meantime, for those who need medical aid, I'm sure we can find therapists and doctors who would volunteer their time to help. Community gardens could be built, and if we reach out to local hardware stores and nurseries for supplies and maybe a few contractors, their food costs would be next to nothing. It's possible to give these people hope and dignity, Mayor, and with you running a program like that, it would certainly gain you approval ratings."

Truth be told, he was the last person I would want involved in any part of that program, but I had to work with what I was given.

Playing with his ring, he considered me for a torturous moment. "That is quite the proposal, but unfortunately, my constituents, the *taxpayers*, have a different vision for Crescent Cove that does not include...impracticalities."

"You mean decency."

For a second, Marcus adopted an unpretentious look. "Margaret—"

"Unless you want me to start calling you Marco or Marky, it's Maggie or Miss Davis." I didn't know when he decided to use that godawful name, but it wasn't helping his chances at not getting his balls bashed in with a meat cleaver.

A tanned hand loosened the top button of his dress shirt as if to ease his discomfort. He wasn't uncomfortable. It was an act to convince me he was human. He wasn't.

"Of course. My apologies, *Miss Davis*."

Marcus' gaze drifted over my head to the kitchen. I didn't have to look to know Frankie was glowering at Marcus this very second. I could feel the heat of his eyes on the back of my neck.

An insincere smile graced Marcus' lips. "I had time before church this morning and hoped you would grant me time to speak with you regarding a personal matter."

"You attend church? Is that safe for the other parishioners? Doesn't your blood start to boil and skin turn to ash?"

The smile vanished as his mouth pursed, hands clasping together on the counter to give the illusion that he was deep in reflection, channeling his piousness as if he'd actually read the *Bible* at any point in his life. I recognized that tactic from the many speeches he'd given over the years. He wasn't reflecting on shit. He was calculating. Always. I really should not be pushing his buttons, but the man just... God, I loathed him.

"Miss Davis, you are eighteen and in college now. Perhaps you can raise your maturity level and keep this conversation civil?"

"You're here because you need something from me. Perhaps I'm not the person you should be patronizing today." Hooking my arm under the wicker handle, I strolled past a smirking Candi.

I set the basket on the two-top outside and aimed toward my bike, quickly remembering that I'd left my backpack in the kitchen. I wasn't going to stop and turn around now, give Marcus another opportunity to speak with me. Maybe I could circle the block—

"You and Mr. Hayes are both planning to attend OHU once the repairs are completed, are you not? It would be a terrible shame if something happened to those scholarships." He paused for dramatic effect as my forward momentum came to a halt. "Or to the ones you currently maintain at Warrington."

There he is.

I swiveled to face him. To threaten me was one thing, but when he dared mess with Jamey was another. He was a cobra and I the mouse, waiting for me to tire, slip, and then sink his teeth into me.

"You do know my vote in next year's election is at risk, don't you? As you pointed out, I am eighteen now."

"I didn't realize I ever favored your vote, Miss Davis." Amusement shone in his eyes as his dress shoes slapped along the ground between us, forcing me to tilt my head back. "I only need five minutes of your time."

I shoved my hands into my back pockets. "The clock stopped ticking when you blackmailed Jamey. If you want me to listen, you will not bring his name up again."

He nodded once before slipping on his blazer. "Fair enough. How about we start over?" A manicured hand waved across the lot to a blacked-out SUV that could very well be housing a bunch of scary G-men ready to disappear my body. "May I give you a ride to the Scotts', so we can talk privately?"

It didn't surprise me that he knew about my scholarship to OHU or that I was headed to the Scotts'. This was information my father could and would have given him. But the longer I was in his presence, the more he unnerved me, and willingly locking myself in a car with a man as dangerous as Marcus Ryan was not going to happen.

"No, you may not. Especially being that you're armed."

Giving me what I was sure was a disapproving look, his head slowly swiped side to side. "I'm not armed, Miss Davis."

"You forget that I'm a cop's daughter, Mayor Ryan. I not only take care of my father's uniforms, but I clean and ready his gear every night. Your trousers are cut wider to accommodate your holster. It's on the inside of your left ankle. It's where my father keeps his, but you don't strike me as a Glock man. No, with your panache, I'd guess that's a Smith & Wesson revolver with a snazzy flair. Pearl grip, maybe?" I didn't give him a chance to lie again. "So what kind of business is the mayor of a town like Crescent Cove involved in that makes him nervous enough to carry a concealed weapon?"

A glint of appreciation shone down at me. "Very astute of you, Miss Davis. Most impressive. But as to my business… Sometimes it's necessary to perform duties that pretty, little brunettes rather not know about." He studied the street as if to ensure we were alone. Once upon a time, this road would have been bustling with people, townies and richies alike. Now, the only occupants were the people he and his constituents didn't include in their vision of Crescent Cove. Whatever that meant. "I will speak to you here if I must."

"You must." I waited, knowing there was little doubt the man would follow me across town and then nudge my body into ditch with his fancy Caddy. But since I wasn't into dramatic pauses… "Spare me the windup and get to the point."

He studied my features an insufferable moment, my skin tightening as if it, too, wanted to get away from him. "You are your father's daughter."

"I'm nothing like him," I hissed.

There was that secretive grin again as if he wanted to refute that but thought better of it. "You will speak to the Scotts on my son's behalf today. Tell them you were mistaken about his intentions at the party. You were talking, and the argument got heated. You overreacted. After some reflection, you now realize that Eric never meant to harm you and ask that his RAM pledgeship be reinstated."

Now I was shocked, and my gaping mouth spoke to how much. "Your precious little boy tried to assault me last night after he threatened to shove his cock down my throat."

The mayor's lips became a firm slash, displaying the first sign that I'd struck a nerve. Not many dared to be openly hostile to him, but not many had the history we had either.

"It was an unfortunate event fueled by alcohol—"

"He wasn't drunk, and we both know Eric is prone to unfortunate events when he's sober, as well."

Marcus didn't react that time, keeping his politician mask in place. "Eric regrets his actions and assures me his intention was to speak to you. He didn't mean to raise his hand and startle you."

I crossed my arms. "You mean like how he *startled* Jenna?"

Drawing his shoulders back, Marcus placed his hands inside his pockets. Perhaps to stop himself from strangling me. "That girl was sick and troubled. What happened to her was quite sad. It doesn't do her family or her memory any good to keep bringing up your version of the past. The two situations are nothing alike."

Somehow, and I was going with an act of God on this one, I clamped my jaw tight and restrained my tongue. Sort of.

"Every situation involving your son is alike because you raised a psychopath. He was a bully throughout high school, and his serial rapist tendencies haven't been curbed in the slightest. And from what I understand, you and the Scotts have some ugly history between you. Yesterday didn't help matters since they were there to witness what happened. You should be thanking me because *I'm* the only reason the CCPD wasn't called. Not that it would have mattered, seeing that my father has been shielding you and your son for years."

"Miss Davis—"

"Did Eric tell you about the *unfortunate event* with another sick and troubled girl at the RAM house a few weeks ago? You're not dealing with just the Scotts here, Mayor. You're dealing with an entire fraternity of men who dislike your son. This isn't high school anymore. You can't buy the school library all new computers when he fails a class. Or gift the principal a Mercedes after Eric trashes his office. Eric is the sick and troubled one. Instead of traipsing around town, cleaning up your son's messes, how about you deal with the problem. Your *son*. He needs help. Real help. Like the intensive psychiatric kind."

Making an awful tsking sound, his head shook in admonishment. "Oh, Miss Davis. I did hope I wouldn't have to resort to this. I am sorry, but I did ask nicely." Drawing a small manila envelope from inside his jacket, his voice dropped to just above a whisper. "Now that I've seen your gift for debate firsthand, I don't believe it will be difficult for you to articulate a convincing argument. After all, Daniel's youngest seems to be quite taken with you, which I have to admit, I find most intriguing given the situation. And something I will use to my benefit. Because once you persuade Mason, you'll sway the rest of the fraternity."

…given the situation. What?

I didn't have a chance to ask before Marcus opened the envelope and out slid what looked like photographs. The glossy kind. He held them in front of me, and when the first image came into view, a chilling stab of fear drove into my lungs, seizing the air in my throat.

His lips twitched in delight. "Lover's Inlet isn't very original for a midnight rendezvous, but neither of you seemed to mind."

My skin itched as though a thousand poisonous spiders were crawling across my skin. He'd had someone...watch us last night? *Photograph* us? We must have been followed from the bowling alley in Pacific Cliffs because there was no way to know that Mason would have taken me on an unexpected detour to the beach so we could talk. Which was all we did.

This...was fucked up.

"This is all you've got?" I challenged, steeling my voice in what I hoped was a bored tone. "Mason's hands on my cheeks? He looks like he's ready to choke me."

"Hmm."

Spinning the photographs around, he flipped through the pictures slowly, each one documenting Mason's movements as he got closer to me until he had me tilted back in his arms, our mouths a mere breath apart as he'd said, *Challenge accepted, Sticks.*

"Though crude of me," Marcus murmured, "I'd say he's ready to choke you with his tongue in this one. What do you think?"

It actually did totally look like that. If I hadn't been there, lived it, I would have thought that man was about to devour that woman in the picture. But that wasn't what happened. Mason lifted me back up, helped me in the truck, and drove me to Jamey's house. Nothing more.

"Do you have that picture, Mayor?" Without answering me, he slipped the photographs back inside the envelope. "What was it that you were hoping to accomplish here?"

He swiftly worked the clasp on the envelope. "A romantic relationship between you and Mason Scott is less than ideal. I want to keep that leash short and his hands off those pink cheeks. As soon as this business between us is finished, you will distance yourself from him."

This was interesting. What was it about the Scotts that made the Ryans so nervous? "You only want me to stay away from Mason?"

He sighed. "In a perfect world, it would be all the Scotts, but I know Daniel and Eve well. Too well. There is no way they would let you walk out of their lives that easily, especially with you still in town."

I didn't know why he believed that, but the questions that sprung to mind were silenced when his gaze slithered down to my worn Chucks and back up to study my face in the most unsettling way possible.

"Stick to the plan, Miss Davis. Earn as much money as you can and leave Crescent Cove once OHU opens back up. Cutting ties with this town will be much simpler for everyone involved."

The way he said so much and so little at the same time really was disturbing. "And I don't suppose destroying those pictures is part of the deal."

The envelope went back inside his jacket as his gaze latched onto mine. "No, it's not. It would be wise to remember that I have them and that I'm watching."

Well, that was all kinds of creepy.

"Believe it or not, I meant this to be a courtesy visit to you, Miss Davis. My son will be reinstated, and you will make sure that happens. Though I'm sure it's unnecessary, I'll be generous and give you until Wednesday evening. Might I suggest you speak directly to Brady Hale? I think you'll find his ear to be sympathetic to our cause."

Our. Since when were Marcus Ryan and Maggie Davis an *our*? And what was Brady's connection to Marcus? Mason had told me that Brady had wanted Eric in the fraternity, and he had brought him to Ben's party yesterday...

"If I don't?" I asked.

"Then you force my hand. As you so put it, your father is especially invested in my affairs. If memory serves, his methods of persuading you have been effective in the past. I doubt he'll need convincing, but if so..." His buffed fingertips patted the breast pocket where the pictures hid. A fine tremble settled over me. "You see, I really am thinking of you. I'd hate for you to be *persuaded* again."

It took a great deal of effort to keep my shit together. There was not a doubt in my mind that Marcus knew exactly what kind of monster my father was and that he so casually threatened me, spoke to his own hidden beast.

"I really would be careful when you step into that church, Mayor. That suit looks flammable."

Canting his head, he was quiet for a long beat, and then the corner of his mouth curled into a frightening smile. "You've got a hell of a lot more backbone than your father, but you will bend just the same."

"I told you. I'm *nothing* like my father."

That smile was back, but it didn't reach his eyes this time. "We'll see, Miss Davis. Anything can break given the right conditions."

chapter three

maggie

I grunted as my backpack smacked against my spine for what had to be the thousandth time. And my ribs weren't all too thrilled either. I knew the trip to the Scotts' would be tricky, but I didn't realize how tricky until I almost fell over. Twice. I hated that I was late to work; however, I had no choice but to walk my bike most of the trek to Crescent Lake Estates.

The fact that I was late, though, didn't matter to the disinterested wall of muscle lingering in the doorway of the guardhouse. Behind him, paused on the flat-screen, was what looked like a rabid woman in a green gown ready to flip over a table.

Quality entertainment.

"You look especially ready to pummel someone today, B."

Bernard's eye twitched, and I was secretly thrilled by it. I'd invested quite a bit of time cultivating this relationship of ours, and I'd become hell-bent on making this man speak to me. The day I interviewed for Mrs. Scott to work as her house assistant, I had confirmed the dude owned vocal cords but had yet to be blessed by them. Our interactions thus far consisted of leers, grunts, brow spasms, inaudible grumbles, sighs, and one nod.

I'd been quite proud that day.

From the front pouch of my backpack, I procured the fresh cookies Frankie had baked this morning. Cookies that I'd paid for and the exact recipe that Bernard liked.

A brow lifted, and the black globes within his orbital sockets narrowed on the paper sack dangling from my wobbly grip. Bernard was hooked on my cooking. I knew it. And he knew I knew it.

Typically, Bernard was a grab-and-go kinda guy. Today, his dark fingers plucked the bag from my hand and shook it as if to make sure I hadn't hidden explosives inside. The next thing I knew, the gate swayed open. He neither moved nor touched a button.

I needed to figure out how he did that.

Hitching my bag over my shoulders, I grinned. "One day, you're gonna speak to me."

Then it happened. Bernard's head jerked to the side to wave me on.

I somehow found the power to not smile at him like an idiot, but as I pedaled away, I called over my shoulder, "Have a great day, B!" I couldn't be sure, but I swore that was a mumble just before he slammed the door.

As usual, I parked on the side of the Scotts' house to hide my eyesore Schwinn from offending the neighborhood and thusly bringing down the property values. Once I loaded my arms with as many bags as possible, I lugged them up the stairs to the front door, passing Mason's electric blue Raptor in the circular driveway. Without a clue why he was here or what rules of his I'd be playing by today, I set the groceries down, unlocked the door, and then went through the process of looping all the bags onto my arms once more.

Then immediately realized my mistake.

I sighed, staring at the closed door that I neglected to open while I had my hands free. One of these days, I would use my brain as nature intended. I really didn't want to unload and then reload all the damn bags for the third time, so I decided to woman-up.

Hand quivering from the weight, lack of sleep, fun times with Marcus Ryan, and the million issues wrong with my neurological system, I struggled to grip the door handle. Without any finesse, my fingers simultaneously slipped off the hardware, unintentionally shoving the door so that it rocketed open and struck the rubber stopper with a *bam*!

Eyes rounding wide, I watched as the five-hundred-pound chunk of wood came flying back toward me, and I threw my sneaker out to stop it before my face did. The door bounced off my foot and sailed back the other way, hitting the stopper with a thud this time.

Loosing a haggard breath, my gaze lifted to find that I had an audience. An audience standing in the living room with his brows as high as I'd ever seen them. Mason. Great. Just great.

"Sorry," I offered lamely, shuffling my way into the foyer.

Holding the weight of the bags, I knew shutting the door like a normal person would be a joke. As I toed the door shut, something warm and wiry grazed my other calf. I spun, my ass bumping the door, and I sucked in a sharp breath along with a spiced chocolate scent so rich I could taste it on the tip of my tongue. Eyes the color of new spring leaves locked with mine, and in that instant, Mason Scott became my world.

"Good morning." His voice was husky with sleep, and my traitorous lady parts went all flippy and warm, ignoring the heartache and utter muddled state he'd left me in time and again.

My lady parts needed an eviction notice. Stat.

The weight on my forearms had vanished, and it took me a second more to notice that Mason was now holding all the grocery bags. Lord, how long had I been staring at him?

Heat steeped into my cheeks, trickling down my neck. "Th— thanks."

He held my gaze with such a strange intensity, air stalled in my lungs. "My pleasure."

Desperate to put some space between me and that gravelly voice, I made use of the few inches between us that Mason wasn't occupying and ducked outside to haul the rest of the bags back to the house.

Balancing the last of the groceries and with my focus directed no more than a foot ahead, I spotted two black Nikes blocking the stairs much too late. I tried to correct my course but misread the weight I was carrying and tipped backward. I couldn't flail my arms to regain my equilibrium because I was weighed down by a cantaloupe, a gallon of milk, hazelnut coffee creamer, a box of Lucky Charms, along with the load stuffed into my backpack.

I was going down, and worse, I was going to split my skull wide on the pavers. Brains would splatter. The cantaloupe would crack wide. The milk and creamer would spill all over the lawn. Tiny marshmallow rainbows would scatter.

This was the third time Mason Scott could have been the cause of my untimely death.

Huh. I thought having my head bust open would hurt. *Note to self:* It didn't. In fact, death felt kind of nice. Warm and hard and a lot like…

"Am I dead?"

A deep chuckle rumbled through me, and a wisp of air got stuck in my throat as my heart rammed into my sternum.

I peeled my eyes open.

Oh. Holy. God. What in all the nine circles of Hell was happening? Bulky arms were wrapped around me, an iron chest smooshed my boobs flat, and a thigh as thick as a tree trunk was lodged between both of mine. This went well beyond touching. This was body melding.

Angling my chin back, my rounded gaze crawled up a square jaw covered with three days of stubble, a blindingly perfect set of teeth between a pair of sinfully full lips, a single dimple begging to be licked, a nose that was slightly crooked yet had the ability to make him more perfect, along with the most entrancing set of green eyes on this planet, a brilliant shade of peridot banded in slivers of citrine. And they were staring right at me.

"You are very much alive, Sticks."

I gathered he wasn't dropping the nickname anytime soon. There were worse things to be called rather than my penchant to have at least two ChapSticks on me, but still.

"How...?" I was at a forty-five-degree angle, and he was somehow holding me, plus the weight of all the groceries attached to me. And...wow, that thigh of his was all up in there.

The other dimple made an appearance, deep and infuriatingly sexy. "I have the reflexes of a jungle cat, that's how. If it weren't for me, you'd be dead. You're welcome." The boy did have exceptional skills because he'd caught me in a blink of an eye.

My brow rose. "If it weren't for you, I wouldn't have needed your jungle cat reflexes."

That only made his smile kick up a notch, and I was certain his thigh shifted. Or maybe that was me. Either way, the friction caused all the muscles in my belly to coil low and tight, which wasn't a reaction that was welcome in the slightest.

"You may have a point." All ten of his fingers flexed, four of which were mighty close to my aforementioned squished boobs. Tantalizing heat zinged through me, my heart peeling itself off my ribcage to gallop within the confines of my chest. "You ready to get vertical?"

Not in the slightest. "Like yesterday."

He had me upright with the last of the bags off my arms before I could take a full breath.

As I steadied my feet, I swallowed, struggling to calm my pulse. Didn't work. "Thanks again."

He winked an enviable set of dark, thick lashes. "My pleasure. Again." With that, Mason sauntered back into the house.

Touching you has never been the problem, Maggie. It's the letting go part I can't deal with.

He seemed to be over both of those issues today. I had not one clue what to do with this new development, so I followed him inside to the kitchen island and set my backpack on the floor.

Dragging his attention to me, Mason's gaze coasted down my body and then back up, stopping at my eyes. It flitted in my mind that my ponytail felt loose, and Mason could see the scar on my temple. A thread of cold panic chased away the remnants of heat in my veins. The longer he stared, the harder it was not to sprint to the closest mirror and check.

"I didn't hurt your side more, did I?"

My side did hurt more, but I wouldn't tell him that. "No, I'm okay. Thank you."

Mason's brows slammed low, turning to scowl at the contents of the bag in front of him. "Don't thank me for that. If I hadn't gotten there when I had, that fucker would have hit you and—" After a brief pause, his voice adopted a vicious edge. "Eric is lucky I let him walk out of my aunt's house."

Because once you persuade Mason, you'll sway the rest of the fraternity.

Yeah, I didn't see that happening. Ever. Mason hated Eric Ryan more than Jamey and I combined, and that was saying something. Eric was our high school nemesis and bullied us every day for four years, but Mason had a history with him. A history that dated back to when Eric had broken his little sister's arm and then…

I…blacked out and woke up to Cam and Dylan holding me down. Eric was unconscious on my room floor. There was blood everywhere. On him. And me. Too…too much of it.

Eric had only been at Ben's birthday party because Brady had wanted him there. No one else. Convincing Mason wouldn't be an uphill battle.

It would be a climb to outer space.

I released a weary sigh. Had Ocean Hills not been destroyed by a mudslide during the summer storm, I wouldn't have to deal with this shit. Instead, I'd be one hundred and fifty miles north of here with Poker and Jamey, living in bliss, far removed from the Ryans and my father.

"How did you get here with all of this?" Mason's question snapped me out of my visions of a cramped studio apartment in Ocean Hills and three-day-old leftovers. He eyed the jug of orange juice and granite cleaner in his hands as if deliberating which went into the fridge.

"You're not the only one who possesses special powers." They were called I-need-this-job powers. A job that Mason had helped me find and then later tried to bribe me to quit.

Emptying my pockets, I dumped the change in the cookie jar and placed the receipt on the counter.

As we finished putting the groceries away—Mason finally asking where things went after the fourth misplaced item—Mrs. Scott rounded the corner. Her crystal blue eyes landed on me. "Good morning, Maggie! We thought we heard you."

Confusion swept through me as to her choice of pronouns. "We…?"

"Morning, sunshine!" Not one but two blondes emerged from the hall next, and while both Price sisters were equally primped for a casual Sunday morning fashion shoot, only one of them was happy to see me.

I gathered by the glare I was receiving, Taylor hadn't forgotten that she'd found Mason and I in a compromising position in his cousins' basement yesterday. I assumed she was still under the impression I'd tried to steal her sister's boyfriend—*pretend* boyfriend. Whatever.

Speaking of sister, I wasn't sure when this hugging thing had become a standard greeting for Charlie, but I had two arms in a vise lock around me, planting my face right where I'd be the envy of most men.

The scent of sweet florals mingled with rich coffee, and I was sure she had squealed when she hugged me tighter. "We've been waiting for you! What took you so long?"

Mason jumped in to answer before I could. "What took her so long was this." He gestured to the empty grocery bags on the island. "Mom, you have to stop giving her these long lists. She's gonna hurt herself getting here."

"Oh, did I do it again?" Cheeks losing color, Mrs. Scott's fingers fluttered to her mouth. "I'm so sorry, Maggie."

Hell, Mason made it sound like I'd complained to him. "It wasn't a problem, Mrs. Scott." I withdrew from Charlie, shoving my hands inside my hoodie pockets. "Really, it's okay. And I'm sorry for being late."

"Stop apologizing." That peridot gaze pinned me to my spot. "I'm driving you next time. Mom will give me the list, and I'll pick you up from home, then take you to the store."

"Whoa. No. *Pick me up?* That's—"

"Ridiculous?" That came from the blonde who would not and never would be hugging me in greeting or otherwise. "What's wrong with your car that you can't drive yourself?"

Yeah…this was so not something I wanted to explain to Taylor. I took a breath. Then another. "I—"

"She doesn't own a car," Mason butted in again. "Which means she just brought an entire week of groceries across town on a bicycle." His voice may have been inflected with pride but oddly only served to humiliate me, especially when Taylor's lips curled up on one side like an evil Dr. Seuss character.

"You know, Maggie. Dan and I were just discussing that." Mrs. Scott played with the diamond stud in her ear, a habit of hers I noticed. "What if you got your license? We could buy something for you to use, kind of like a company car. You'd be free to drive it when you're not working, too. And we'll cover the cost of the insurance. It's the perfect solution."

Well, it would be if the state of California would allow me to drive.

Canting his head, Mason jutted out his bottom lip, all plump and boyish. "But BB's gotten so attached to Sticks. They've bonded. There was petting. *Heavy* petting. BB will be jealous if another takes her place."

Oh, dear. I risked a peek just in time to see Taylor's eyes roll, and when Charlie caught her sister's reaction, she cringed ever so slightly.

Mason was so not helping.

"Anyway…" Mrs. Scott peered into her coffee mug only to frown when she found it was empty. "Think of it as a perk, Maggie. Or a promotion!"

The more eager she sounded, the drier my throat got. "Uh, that's—"

"I'm sorry. I must be missing something here." Taylor spun her Starbucks cup around, so the ruby red lipstick marks on the lid faced her. "She doesn't have a car or a license, and yet the job requires her to do the shopping? If she can't get from A to B with the supplies you require on time, as per her duties, then why does she have the job?"

Charlie's mouth sprang wide along with her eyelids. "Taylor!"

Taylor shrugged, her black and white striped crop top inching higher up her tanned ribcage to reveal the lacy red bralette beneath. "It's a valid point. In the end, it costs Eve and Dan for her to work here. It makes no sense. And come on, could you imagine Amahle pedaling a bicycle around Sea Haven with our groceries? We'd be the laughingstock."

Christ. I felt my head go light, but my cheeks went hot as if all the blood in my body had been transported to them.

A broad palm landed on the small of my back, causing me to jump in surprise. Taylor's eyes narrowed on that blue inked arm reaching behind me. And I swore that was…hurt sweeping across Charlie's features.

I squirmed a little, and as if determined to torture me, Mason's hand curled around my hip, keeping me planted right where I was.

Though the heat of each finger seared past every layer of clothing, Mason's deep voice was so cold, it cooled me right down. "Thank God Crescent Cove isn't anything like Sea Haven, then. I would have to teach my neighbors some manners."

Huffing, Taylor folded her arms. "It's like that here, Mason."

God, was it? Had I embarrassed the Scotts? Was that why Mrs. Scott wanted me to have a car?

"Taylor…" Mrs. Scott began, her voice was calm, but her tone was framed with a maternal admonishment that I hadn't heard before. "Maggie has the job because she earned it, excels at it, and has made my life immensely easier. I've learned that when you have an employee like Maggie, you should value them and do what you can to make *their* lives easier."

While her expression resembled something that could be described as contrite, one had to question if Taylor was capable of feeling the emotion. "Of course, Eve. I'm sorry. I wasn't trying to tell you your place. I'm only looking out for your family. I've known you since I was in diapers, and I think of you as an aunt. Sometimes a mother, even. It's hard for me not to feel protective of you."

Wearing a small smile, Mrs. Scott wrapped an arm around Taylor. And just like that, everyone was at ease. Mason's hand fell away, Charlie plucked up the other Starbucks tanker off the counter, and when Taylor's repentant gaze met mine, I could only watch those honey eyes squeeze into slits, the shine on her ruby lips pulling into a triumphant sneer.

Seriously? Everyone bought that load of crap? I mean, I got the attitude. I did. But... *seriously*?

Biting my tongue, I gathered the fabric grocery bags into a pile. "Would anyone like anything? More coffee, Mrs. Scott?"

"Oh." She cast a longing look to her empty mug as I shoved the bags into my backpack. "I shouldn't, since I've already had three, but I will. Thank you. Dan didn't get in until four, and he's not exactly light on his feet after he's been on them for forty-eight hours. So, I've been up a while."

"Okay, I'll get right on it." I shouldered my backpack and placed it inside the hall closet before grabbing a clean mug from the cabinet. "And breakfast?"

"Oh, no thanks, sweetie. We finished off those chocolate muffins you made the other day. And they were absolutely sinful." Laughing, Mrs. Scott nodded to the girl her arm was still draped around. "In fact, Taylor wanted to know what bakery they came from so she could get more. You should have seen the look on her face when I told her you made them."

Yeah, I bet it was something. "I'm glad you enjoyed them."

Taylor's eye twitched right before that too saccharine-sweet smile split her lips. "I *so* did. Maybe you could make Charlie and me a batch? We're not leaving for a while. If you have the time between cleaning, that is."

Well played.

"None for me, thanks." Charlie set down her cup. "I'm consuming my daily allotment of calories in the form of caramel macchiatos."

Crossing his arms, Mason cocked a brow at her. "You are joking. Right?"

As I started the Keurig, I watched one of Charlie's shoulders rise in an identical movement to her sister's. It was unnerving how alike they appeared on the surface, yet what was beneath that unblemished skin was so different. "The meal last night was heavy, and I have an editorial shoot on Wednesday, Mase."

"Charlie—"

"Oh, that reminds me, Eve!" Charlie spun toward Mrs. Scott, dismissing Mason, and it seemed all too intentional. "I must show you the ah-*mazing* Dior gown Tay found last night. It would be simply gorg on you for the gala!"

Taylor gasped, clutching her chest. "Paired with those Jimmy Choo pumps you saw this morning? Oh, Eve! You. Will. Die!"

Mrs. Scott's amused gaze met her son's. "I guess I must."

"Good," he said, moving aside as I carried the mug to her. "And while you ladies are doing that, I'm gonna borrow Sticks. Mom, do you mind?"

"Not in the least. Hmm, thank you, Mag— Whoops." Right then and there, steaming brown liquid sloshed over the sides of the mug and plopped onto the floor and my shoes, staining my already stained sneakers. Awesome. Even holding a cup with two hands like a toddler, I could spill.

Though my eyes were glued to the mess I'd created, I could feel Taylor's glee leach into the air from here, and my cheeks went hotter than the highest Keurig setting.

"I'm so sorry, Mrs. Scott. I'll clean that right up." I set her coffee on the island, but before I could do anything else, Mason snatched both of my wrists up in his hands and began twisting my arms around in their sockets. "What are you doing?"

"Looking for burns." He now had both of my quivering hands eye level, examining my fingers. "You're the only person I know who could sever a limb and think that asking for a Band-Aid was too intrusive."

"I don't have any burns, but I am experiencing blood loss from the steep elevation," I replied dryly. I appreciated the concern, but Mason was bringing more attention to my tremor. "May I have my limbs back now?"

Slanting his head to the side, the corners of his eyes crinkled. "Magic word?"

"Snollygoster."

Laughing, Mason released me and stepped to the sink. "It's uncanny how well you know me."

"Told you I had special pow— No, don't use the…sponge." Too late. Mason was already working that green rectangle along the floor.

"Why not?" Then he swiped the sponge across my shoes as if it would improve their appearance.

I spoke to the top of his dark head. "Because I use that to clean the counters. Where food is prepared. You can't clean the floor with it."

"Seems like I can. And I just did." In what felt like slow-motion, Mason stood so he was right there in my airspace. Keeping his eyes on me, he chucked the sponge over his shoulder, and of course, it landed inside the sink. And the jerk knew it. His grin was pure boyish arrogance. "Maybe it's time you took a lesson from me."

"That time will never come."

A single brow rose. "Is that a challenge?"

"No, that's a fact."

He squinted, his head weaving a bit. "Mmm...that sounded like a challenge."

"I—"

A throat cleared, and I startled, realizing a bit too late that Mason and I were way too close to each other to be deemed appropriate, and to make matters worse, at some point, I'd risen to my toes to get even closer.

Flattening my feet and taking a healthy step backward, that awful heat swamped my cheeks again. I glanced over to see Mrs. Scott was holding back a laugh, and Taylor was imagining me in the oven with the broiler on, but it was Charlie that worried me the most. That was definite hurt in her eyes.

Mason had said they were just friends and their relationship wasn't real, but was that how she saw it? Were there deeper feelings on her side? I liked Charlie, and the last thing I wanted to do was upset her.

"Sorry again about the spill, Mrs. Scott." Scurrying to the sink, I relocated the sponge to the trash and got a new one from the cabinet.

"It's fine, sweetie." She ripped off a paper towel and swiped the side of her mug dry. "I'm only grateful you didn't get hurt."

"Yes, and I'm grateful you spilled the scalding coffee on the floor instead of Eve's hands," Taylor added, jamming her hands onto her hips. "She needs them to perform *surgeries*, you know."

A thick lump of humiliation flopped over in my stomach. Taylor wasn't wrong. This was why I never directly handed anyone anything that could spill.

"Thanks for the unwanted commentary, Taylor." My gaze flew to Mason to see the hardness in his tone matched the clench of his jaw, and it only made my stomach twist around that lump now. "Anyway, I was about to say that Sticks needs a change in her duties."

That didn't sound good. "A change in my... W—what change?"

Mason folded his arms across his chest, the white T-shirt stretching the cotton fibers at his shoulders and biceps. It was a miracle the fabric didn't rip. "Like you are now running with me on Sunday mornings."

I couldn't have heard that right. "Did you say *running with you?*"

"Yup." The P popped on his perfect lips, eyes glittering with mischief.

No. This...couldn't happen. Spending time with Mason was the exact opposite of distancing myself from him. "And why are we doing this?"

"Better question," Taylor snipped. "Why *aren't* you taking your *girlfriend?*"

That was a better question. And, apparently, the only thing Taylor and I would ever agree on outside of that Mason was crazy hot was that he was also just plain crazy.

"Well, it seems as if my *girlfriend* already has plans this morning and is not properly nourished." Mason tore his eyes away from Taylor, planting them on me. "Coach Watkins has been on my ass about my endurance training, and now that I know you love running so much you do it for fun, I figured you'd be the perfect person to help me."

"Wait." Charlie's nose squinched. "Maggie runs? *For fun?*"

"I know." Mason nodded emphatically to her. "Weird, right?"

"So weird," she replied, nodding back.

"I'm standing right here. And it's not weird."

Mason slid a grin my way.

But Taylor wasn't smiling. Instead, she wheeled on her sister, one beautiful hand splayed in my direction. "You cannot be okay with this!"

Shifting uncomfortably under Taylor's glare, Charlie brushed her ponytail off her shoulder. "Mase knows I hate cardio of any kind. And Maggie likes it. I don't see the problem."

"Me neither." Mrs. Scott opened the fridge door. "I support this one hundred percent."

This situation was getting exponentially worse by the second.

Standing there scrambling for words, my gaze bounced between mother and son. "Well, I don't support this."

"Finally, she says something somewhat intelligent," was muttered by the younger Price, but I think I was the only one who heard.

Mason scoffed. Loudly. "You'd rather clean than spend time with me?" He waved over himself and then scoffed again. "Please."

"Yes, I would. Besides, I..." I went over the mental to-do list that I'd been making since I'd walked in the house. "I have to start the laundry. The dining room table desperately needs a polish. The gym is in serious need of—"

"It can wait." Mrs. Scott opened the top of her Coffee-mate. "I think it's a great idea. You love running, and Mason sucks at it. I call that a win-win." Smirking, she added a healthy plop of creamer to her mug.

"See?" Mason's expression was full of innocence, and I didn't trust it. Not one bit. "One out of one doctors agree. We should get going before it gets too hot."

How was this happening? Mrs. Scott wanted to buy me a car, Taylor was convinced I was the man-stealing Antichrist, Mason was paying me to run with him, Marcus' photographer was lurking out there somewhere to document it all, and…Charlie wouldn't look me in the eye now. It was impossible to deny. She wasn't okay with this.

"I don't have my running shoes," I blurted. "So, it's a lose-lose."

Mrs. Scott eyed my tread-worn Chucks over the brim of her mug. "What size do you wear?"

Shitballs.

"Eight," I squeaked. I might as well tell the truth. I didn't put it past Mason to remove my shoe to check the label.

"Perfect." After setting down her coffee, Mrs. Scott pranced upstairs, leaving me with Mason and the Price sisters. Because things weren't awkward enough.

"Charlie," Taylor hissed. "Are you really going to let this happen because I wouldn't let my boyfriend hang out with another girl, even one that looks like *her*."

Okay, ouch.

"*Tay*." Gaze reluctantly meeting mine, Charlie paled. "Maggie, I'm sorry. You don't deserve that."

I waved her off. "It's fine. I don't—"

"The hell it's fine," Mason growled, glare set. "Taylor, apologize or go back to the office."

The huff Taylor blew out was epic. She could actually teach a MasterClass on the Art of the Huff. "For reals? How am I—"

"I'm not going to fucking say it twice."

Lips hinged open, Taylor scowled at him. Then, after a fantastic display of how loose her ocular orbits were, she literally stomped down the hall. And slammed the office door.

Mason's eyes slid shut, expelling a frustrated breath out of his nose. "Charlie, this is exactly why I asked you—"

"I know." Her hand banded around his wrist, panic contorting her face. "I know I promised. Please, just for—"

"Here we go!" Mrs. Scott appeared, arms full of purple gear. "You're in luck, Maggie. I wear an eight." Which I already knew because I was inside the woman's closet five days a week.

Sneakers that looked fresh out of the box and workout clothes that were sure to be too big for me were piled into my arms. Everything she'd handed me was far too nice. I would scuff the shoes to hell, fall, get mud on her clothes...

"Mrs. Scott, I—I can't."

She rotated me to face the hall Taylor had just gone down. "You can. Go change." As she pushed me along, her tone changed to something younger yet cultured, what I imagined a princess would sound like. "*You're my only hope.*"

"*Star Wars?*" Mason chuckled behind me. "Subtle, Mom."

Okay, I had no clue what that was about, but figuring it out would have to take a backseat to the position I'd been forced into. Grumbling to no one in particular, I slid into the guestroom. Based on the heavy clomps shaking the walls, Mason must be going upstairs to his room. I placed the gear on the bed, exhaling a shaky breath. How did I get myself into these situations?

I rubbed at the ache spurring to life in my temple. I could do this. Marcus said to distance myself *after* our business was finished. And a run was only a run. It certainly wasn't anything romantic because Mason didn't want that. He wanted friendship and friends...ran together. Right? Maybe during the run, I could talk to him about Eric. Or perhaps later tonight before I left.

Once I changed and made sure my scar was concealed, I left the guestroom and came down the hallway, fiddling with my sleeves as they billowed around my elbows. Stopping in the foyer, I gave up on trying to make this shirt fit and looked up. My mouth went completely dry. Waiting by the front door, Mason leaned against the wall, gaze casually pointed in my direction. It wasn't his stare that had my mouth go all Sahara on me. It was Mason's state of shirtlessness. Now, I knew he owned a plethora of shirts because I washed them all the time, and he'd just been wearing one.

But, to be clear, I wasn't complaining.

Along with that body, his left arm was nothing short of a work of art, full of detailed ink from his wrist, up to his shoulder, just kissing his neck, and then dipping down to his chest. Five butterflies in shades of blue from midnight to bright teal and specks of purple fluttered along his arm and chest, designed in 3-D as if they were ready for flight. Black and gray swirls played around their wings, ending in an infinity symbol over his left pectoral. The bottom right link bore his sister's name Faith in elegant script.

The art on his skin was beautiful and tragic, yet the entire meaning was still a mystery that I wasn't sure I'd ever uncover. But I wanted to.

That moss-rimmed gaze slowly traveled over me from the tips of my toes to the top of my head, an unwelcome warmth lingering in its wake. But that warmth cooled as soon as his pink lips curved up on one side, pushing away from the wall with a shake of his head.

"You look like a grape puked all over you."

Mouth sloping down in the corners, I gathered the loose material of the borrowed shirt in my hands. Mrs. Scott was more than a half-foot taller than me and had the body of a woman. Not one that often shopped in the children's section.

"Do I look that bad?"

He gave me another once-over as his head cranked from one side to the next. "If this were a bad nineties' music video, you'd fit right in."

This would be a superb time to go check out the bottom of the lake for twenty minutes. Deflating under his gaze, I studied the swirly floor tiles, Taylor's words like daggers in my brain.

"Sorry. We don't have to go. I'm sure you don't—"

Suddenly and without warning, Mason was all up in my orbit, and oxygen couldn't seem to get past my windpipe. His fingers skated over my skin—touching me. Really, his goal was to roll up the sleeves I'd given up on, but each brush of his skin made my heart skip a beat as if he were shocking me with a jolt of electricity.

Mason's long lashes hid his eyes from me, but he wasn't smiling anymore. He cleared his throat, and when he spoke, his voice sounded thicker, rougher. "Stop apologizing. I should have told you to bring your gear. I'm the one who should be sorry." Shifting over, he rolled my other sleeve so that it now looked like I was wearing a sleeveless dress.

Standing back, his dark hair flopped across his brow when he gave me an approving nod. "There. Less tent-like. Try not to trip over it with your huge feet."

I shot him a withering look. "I'm not that short, and my feet are not that big. I'm actually quite average."

He made a point to stand up straight so that I was eye to nipple. Before my mind delved into naughty thoughts that I was on the verge of having, I forced my eyes away from all the muscley goodness. I wasn't entirely certain, but I would guess that was amusement crinkling his eyes. "Uh-huh."

I ground my molars, and his grin grew to confirm my suspicion. He was teasing me and enjoying it. Was this a normal friend thing? Because this felt different from when Jamey and I razzed each other.

Reaching past me, Mason opened the door and gestured me to go ahead.

I accepted. "Thank you."

"My pleasure, but really I was only saving my doorstopper from being traumatized again."

Rounding on him, my jaw slacked wide. "I didn't hit it that hard!"

With one flick of his finger, the wraparound Oakleys that were perched on top of his tousled hair landed on his nose. He peered at me over the frames. "I'd really appreciate you not taking your aggression out on my house."

My hands curled into fists. "How about I take it out—"

"Mase?" Charlie's voice drifted over from the living room, and just like that, the playfulness in Mason's eyes vanished along with his relaxed posture. "Can we talk a sec?" she asked.

I looked over to see the emotion from earlier was back in her eyes. Like her favorite stilettos had just been thrown into the sewer. Clearly, something was off between them, and I couldn't help but feel as if I were responsible for it.

"Yeah, one sec," Mason clipped.

Her head bobbed, as did the curls in her ponytail. "Thank you."

Mason returned his focus to me. Mouth pulled into a grim line, he said, "I won't be long."

I assumed that meant I was excused, which was fine by me. Grabbing the door handle, I stepped over the threshold. "Take your time."

I shut the door behind me, the latch catching right as I heard Charlie croon Mason's name. A twinge of jealousy sparked, but before it could become more, I doused it with a good dose of reality. They had been friends long before Mason and I were. Since the age of diapers, evidently. Charlie and Taylor were a part of Mason's life, and no matter what role I played, be it friend or maid, they were more important than me.

Treading across the front lawn, I squinted as I slid on my sunglasses. The morning light slowly became more tolerable. Tolerable enough to see there was an Audi convertible parked in the street. I hadn't a clue how I missed it before since it was the same color as Taylor's lips. And bra.

I faced away from the house and planted my butt on the grass to start my leg stretches. I heard the door behind me open as I took the stretch deeper, gripping my foot as my forehead met my knee. Feet pounded across the lawn, and then I had a six-foot-three golden god looming over me. That also wasn't something I'd complain about.

"Get your lazy ass up," he ordered.

I released my foot and lounged back on my palms. By the return of the happy bounce in his step and the tease of one dimple, I gathered everything was back to normal with Charlie.

34 | ashlan thomas

When my brow arched, Mason's grin expanded to include two dimples. I warned, "You're gonna regret calling my ass lazy."

"Doubtful." Mason offered a hand to help me up, and I refused it. Instead, I shot to my feet, and he laughed, dropping his arm.

I had no clue what was so funny, but he really was going to pay. "We'll see about that." I fixed my sunglasses that had slipped a little. "Three miles along the trail around the lake? Can you handle that?"

He threw out a dismissive shrug. "Easy."

Now it was my turn for my grin to widen, and his confident mask slipped a little. He had no clue what he was in for.

chapter four

maggie

"I am totally regretting this decision!" Mason hacked, then spit onto the side of the running trail. "Sorry. Wouldn't normally...do that in front of a woman, but— God, I'm an asshole. I was...so wrong. Why did I think— Three miles... *Jesus.*"

I had demolished him by the first mile. It felt fantastic. I was sure I was glowing with something other than sweat. Victory maybe.

"If we go any slower, the snails will beat us," I called over.

He made a noise like the lung tissue was being stripped out of his chest. "I really am an old biddy. Watkins was right."

"You get points for trying."

"My face is on fire!"

"A razor would take care of that problem."

He heaved a breath as if he were reaching for the top ozone layer. "I'm also regretting our lack of water."

I shook my head. "Do you always complain this much when you exercise?"

"Yes. I'm a— A delicate flower." Another round of hacking. "So, Sticks...what got you...into running?"

Wow, he had no clue how deep that conversation went. "I just like it."

"Right, but you told me it was a stress reliever." *He remembered that?* "Do you...have a lot of stress? Two jobs and...college. Seems like— A lot."

Nodding, I licked my lips as the wind dried them, regretting that I hadn't grabbed my ChapStick before leaving the house. "It can be a bit much at times."

"Have you been…working at the café…a long time?" Glimpsing over to him, I swore his nylon shorts had dropped even lower. He had the kind of body that looked as if it had been painstakingly chiseled from the finest marble. I tried to keep my eyes off those indents of his Adonis belt, but not even the Greek gods themselves could stop me. His endurance may suck, but I had no doubt he could take me in a cold sprint. He was built for short bursts of massive energy and strength.

"Since I was thirteen." Officially. Unofficially, I'd been working odd jobs around town much earlier than that.

"That's— Shit." Mason stumbled over a puddle, taking him a few steps to recover. "Why so young?"

All these questions were making me itchy. "How else would I support my Beanie Boo obsession?"

"Ah…yeah." Mason could barely get the words out as he took long swipes at his forehead to clear his eyes of sweat.

"You need a break?"

Shaking his head, his feet swerved with the movement. "We've already taken three."

"Four." I didn't feel the least bit bad for correcting him.

The racket in his throat suggested he disagreed. "That second one didn't count! I really did need to retie my shoelace."

"And we just *had* to check out that tree after?"

He gaped at me. "Come on! How could we not? It looked like it was growing a dick out of its trunk." He was right. It did.

I put my palms up innocently. "I'm not judging you. If you want to take a break to look at tree dicks, we'll take one."

Mason barked a hoarse laugh. "Okay. In the future, if you see any more trees with dicks, I want to stop and look."

"What about boulders?"

His fingers made a *scritching* sound as they rubbed along his jaw. "Abso-fucking-lutely."

"Are you open to oddly shaped gourds?"

He chuckled again. Then wound up coughing. "Yes. Definitely, any dick-shaped food…would be on that list."

"Duly noted." Our feet ate up more of the trail, and I took those moments to admire the cloudless sky as the sun warmed my skin between the breaks in the canopy of trees lining the path.

"You're a good runner, Sticks."

"I'd like to be better, but I don't have the time."

"That's a crime, you know. To not…have time for the things you love to do." Another string of coughs had me staring at him. Who knew a body could look so sexy while hacking up bronchial tissue?

"Okay, my turn to ask something," I said.

He made a rolling motion with his hand. "Shoot."

"Why are we doing this? And don't give me that bullshit about training you. You could easily do this on the treadmill."

He was silent for a dozen or so steps with only the sound of leaves tinkling together in the wind. I turned my head to find Mason looking at me, brows knitted tight above his sunglasses. "I think we can both agree that I fucked up phase four through twenty. Right?"

I didn't know how I kept up with his mind at times. "For the sake of argument, let's pretend I know what the phases are, and I agree with you wholeheartedly."

"Good." He slowed to a stop beneath the shade of an ash tree, and I did the same not far ahead, turning toward him. Coughing a breath, his hands went to his hips. "Last night, I told you I wouldn't make any promises except that I wanted to earn your trust. I hoped today could be…the start of an altered phase four. Where we get to know each other, build that trust. A real start to our friendship. How does that sound?"

"It sounds terrible, like every other idea you have."

Head kicking back, a frown shaped his lips. "I have the best ideas."

I scanned the surface of the lake as if someone with a camera would pop up any second to snap our picture—which was all too likely—and closed the distance between us, voice low. "Really? Because I'm essentially being paid to spend time with you."

He was quiet for far too long, and through his shades, I could see the shadow of his repeated blinking. "That's not true."

"You may not think that, but that's exactly what this is."

"No. I— I wanted to do something for *you*. Something to relieve your stress. I thought you'd enjoy it."

I shook my head. "You thought I'd enjoy taking advantage of your parents? Who pay me? To work? This," my arms gesticulated to…everything, "is not working, Mason."

His shoulders fell, palms facing me. "You're right. I'm sorry." Mason's hands went down to his sides as one corner of his mouth tilted up. "But you've gotta admit. You're having fun."

God, I was. "I'm so not."

His head swayed side to side. "Oh, Sticks. I'm disappointed in you. We agreed to no more lies."

Setting my hands on my hips this time, my voice flattened. "Fine. I'm having fun."

The other side of his mouth curled into a wicked grin.

I squinted at him through my sunglasses. "What is that smile for?"

"Just imagining you at the next RAM party. Because that? *That's* gonna be fun."

I was no longer having fun. "Me. You want me at a RAM party?"

"Yeah, why not you?"

"Please." I snorted in the most unladylike way possible and restarted my run. "You and your family don't have to feel obligated to invite me—"

"Whoa." It took him five leaps with those logs he called legs to catch up to me. He tugged on my wrist, stopping me. "*Obligated*? What are you talking about?"

I shrugged out of his grip and kept going. "What I'm talking about is that your dad felt sorry for me yesterday and suggested you take me to the next RAM party. So I'm guessing that was his idea. Let me know where I should park my Schwinn, will you? Between the fleet of Porsches or Mercedes? And what are we going to do when I'm there? Play shadow puppets? Guess how much I paid for my thrift store T-shirt? Because something tells me fraternity parties are all about fraternizing, and let's be honest, a guy like you doesn't fraternize with girls like me."

There was an absence of feet drumming and air puffing next to me. Concern for him wove beneath my irritation, and I stopped to turn. Mason was a good seven paces back, and that was not a happy look on his face.

"You done stuffing me in that tiny box of yours, or do you want to keep going?"

I thought about that. "I'm done."

"Good." In three strides, he was right up in my face. "One, my dad didn't say shit to me. Two, a Schwinn is German, so you park it next to the Mercedes. Three, I'd be so down for shadow puppets. I can create a swan that would make you weep. And four, I fraternize with whoever the fuck I want to fraternize with. I actually prefer talking to a girl wearing a thrift store T-shirt over something straight from New York Fashion Week because that tells me she has a different perspective than mine, and I might learn something from her. So are there any other assumptions you have about me that I can address?"

Rather than answer him, I kicked a rock toward the bank. And missed.

"Is this about that bullshit Taylor said? Because I—"

"No," I lied, stopping him before he could defend her to me.

Honestly, if he and Charlie would figure their shit out, Taylor might not be so hostile toward me. She was protecting her sister, and part of me respected that. Didn't make her any less evil, but my focus needed to be on the Ryans, not Mason's faux-girlfriend drama.

"I'm sorry," I said. "I've had a long morning, and last night I slept on penis sheets. Before you ask, they were all very realistic and far too happy. And you're right. I shouldn't have assumed all that stuff about you because when it comes down to it, we don't know each other. While I appreciate the gesture, if you genuinely want me to train you, I will, but not when I'm working for your parents. It's not right."

Head dropping, his chest deflated with an exhale. "So, what you're saying is...you slept on a bunch of boners last night?"

My mouth pulled into a grin, so thankful that whatever this was ended quickly. "Yes. Every shape, size, and ethnicity was represented."

Tipping his chin up, his lips lifted. "Were they cut?"

"Not all of them."

"See?" Mason scratched at his beard. "How else would I learn penis sheets existed if not for you? And now I know what to get my mother for Christmas. Thanks, Sticks."

My smile fell. "Oh, God. Please don't. You're joking, right?"

"Come on!" The next thing I knew, my ponytail kicked up in the air that his sprint stirred around me. "Stop lollygagging! I have an ass that needs kicking!"

Since it was there, I took a moment to appreciate what a fine ass it was. Too bad I wouldn't have this view for much longer. Once the first cough hit the air, I shook my head and took off. Then passed him.

So that Mason's respiratory system remained intact, I kept the conversation minimal to directions and an occasional odor that neither of us could identify. We made a loop through the trails around half the lake and ended up on his street.

As I hit the cobbled road, I asked, "Do you have a sprint in you?"

"We weren't already sprinting?" That was a near yell.

I laughed. "Hardly."

"Fuck," he gasped and then hacked up his diaphragm into his elbow. One swallow of air later, he said, "Tell me when."

I didn't hesitate. "Now."

I sped off, leaving him with a line of curses coming out of his mouth that would singe off his mother's ears. Based on the trampling of feet and heaving going on behind me, he was gaining. I pushed harder, flying past his house with my arms up for the win. I'd only won because I'd exhausted him first, but I was going to enjoy this anyway.

"You really do suck, Scott!"

Coming to a grinding halt, Mason coughed out, "You're gonna— Kill...me." I twirled as he folded himself in half, finally losing a part of his lung to the ground. Mission accomplished. But my goal wasn't to end his life, and his posture wasn't helping.

I shoved his sweaty and hella heavy arms up. Wow, he smelled good. How was that even possible? "You gotta keep moving."

He began to walk—or stagger—with his arms draped over his head. Each breath rolled and popped through his eight pack, and if his shorts didn't fall off soon, there was seriously something wrong with the laws of gravity. "Thanks. That was…fun."

Fun? Really?

"You're welcome?" I offered.

He attempted to smile at my questioning tone, but it wound up as a grimace, so his hand motioned over me instead. "I noticed that you're not one of those…glistening girls. You *sweat*. A lot."

I assessed my borrowed clothes, splotched with wet spots in the most unfortunate places. A bead of sweat slid off my temple and smacked off the top of the purple sneaker. I was gross.

Kicking my hip out, I struck a pose. "Jealous?"

His broken laugh was deep and loud amid the lake water lapping the shore. "Completely. It's impressive."

Now that I was sure Mason would live, I could focus on our surroundings and realized something was missing. A big red something.

"Charlie and Taylor left?" I asked.

"Must have." He tried to swallow but wound up spitting again. And apologizing again.

"I thought they were going to be here awhile. I was supposed to make muffins."

He shrugged, but there was something off about the movement. Wrong and stiff. Had Mason…did he ask them to leave?

"Hey." He tugged my ponytail, fingers skimming down my neck. A pleasant shiver coursed over my spine that had me stumbling now. "Seriously, thanks for this. I know today was for you, but I didn't realize how much I needed it, too."

Thank God you're not boring. You have no idea how much I needed that right now.

I didn't know it at the time, but he'd said that to me the night he'd stopped Eric from sexually assaulting Charlie. And he said it now after a tense morning with Charlie. I didn't know how to define what Mason and I were but becoming his Charlie-stress-reliever wasn't on the top of my list.

I had nothing to offer other than, "Sure," before heading up to the house.

Meeting me step for step, Mason's arm brushed against mine. I noted there was plenty of room on the walkway that he could have avoided touching me if he wanted.

He popped the door open, waiting on the threshold for me to squeeze past him. "You're welcome to use the guestroom shower if you want."

"Thank you. I think I will." I would normally refuse the offer, but I was sure the Scotts would appreciate me not dripping sweat all through their home.

Back inside the kitchen, Mason grabbed two bottled waters and held one out for me.

"Thank you."

"My pleasure."

Emerging from the hall with a mug of coffee, Mr. Scott eyed us. "Hell, Son, what did Maggie do to you?"

Mason couldn't extract the bottle from his mouth fast enough. "She pulverized my ass and then threw the scraps in the lake. I think a momma duck is regurgitating it to her ducklings right now."

Mr. Scott nodded his approval. "Good job, Maggie." Then he hugged me, not caring that I was leaking from every pore.

I dragged my mouth off the rim of my bottle and swallowed the icy water as the chill coated my throat. "It was only three miles."

Mason straightened as if I'd thrown down a challenge. "Okay. Next time, four."

"And only two breaks." I had to suppress a grin that there would be a next time. *A shirtless next time.* I probably should *Webster* the meaning of friendship. Pretty sure it didn't include ogling your friend's naked body.

"Fine, but we're bringing water," he said. "I was tempted to risk dysentery from the lake."

"Please. That lake is cleaner than an Antarctic glacier."

Still wrapped around me, Mr. Scott laughed.

I pulled away to set my water in the fridge for later. "If you don't mind, Mr. Scott, I'd like to take a moment to wash up?"

Mason didn't give him a chance to answer. "Believe me, he's cool with it. He doesn't want you to sweat in his pie."

Aiming toward the coffeemaker, Mr. Scott shot back, "Wouldn't stop me from eating it."

After five glorious minutes, I took one last rinse in the shower and regretfully turned off the faucet. I knew then and there, that was the best shower I'd ever have. Not only did they have one of those rainwater showerheads, but the water had heated to the perfect temp in all of two point three seconds. Truly astounding. As were the luxurious soaps of golden amber and sandalwood that I wouldn't mind another five minutes with.

But I couldn't.

I was here to work, and my gut was already chockful of guilt from wasting an hour of my shift under the pretense of training Mason. Though it touched me that he cared enough to do something for me, it put me way behind this morning.

While finger brushing my hair—because I'd forgotten to grab my brush from my backpack before showering—my ears perked to the rumble of a Harley Sportster outside. Giddiness bubbled in my chest. I shouldn't feel that way at the prospect of seeing Matt. It was silly. Utterly ridiculous. And yet, I tore out of the room.

I'd left Mrs. Scott's gear and shoes in the guestroom to wash later, and once my sneakers met the kitchen tile, strong arms swept me against a rock-hard chest that smelled like a cookie laced with a hint of something I couldn't identify. I soaked it up. There was just something about Matt's hugs. They were exactly like how his parents hugged me. As if…this was where I was meant to be. As though the cosmos had screwed up big time, and they were trying to make it up to me now.

"There she is." Matt's voice vibrated against my forehead. "I heard you were going after Watkins' position as Coach Sadist."

"Hardly."

Leaning back, his emerald eyes glittered down at me, a darker shade of green than his younger brother's. They were just as breathtaking but didn't affect me the way Mason's did. "Taking a Scott down a peg is good for our egos. Feel free to do that for Mase every fucking day."

"Matt!" From out of nowhere, a hand smacked the back of his head, but he didn't even flinch.

Matt laughed at his mother, then corrected himself. "Every *freaking* day."

"Fair warning, Eve," Ashley said, walking past me on the slate deck as I was hit with the scent of coconut and spring flowers from her fancy sunscreen. "Will and I discussed it. We're kidnapping Maggie today."

Will nodded, his pool float bobbing with the movement. "Rope's in the car."

"Try all you want," Mrs. Scott challenged, "but you have to go through Matt, Mason, and Dan to get her."

"Cam and I can take them." Ben popped back a slice of pineapple from the fruit platter that I'd organized. On my second trip out here, I noticed that the leather bracelet Jamey had given him last night was with the rest of everyone's belongings on the kitchen counter.

"Just give up now. You'll embarrass yourselves." Rocking board shorts, Matt dove into the pool, and Ashley jolted backward as chlorinated water hit her legs.

Rearranging the veggie platter after Camden had attacked it, I listened to Ashley chew out her nephew, but by Matt's wide grin, I'd say he was planning a second assault.

"Maggie," Ashley grabbed a towel from the stack by Mrs. Scott, "why don't you join us? Eve has extra suits in the guestroom."

Here we go again.

I would love nothing more than to dive in like Matt had. I'd only been out here for fifteen minutes and already needed another shower. But no one...no one wanted to see that much of this body.

I spoke a smidge louder, so she would hear me over the babbling waterfall. "I couldn't but thank you."

From the shaded lounge chair, the corners of Mrs. Scott's mouth tipped down. "Of course, you can. Take a break and have some fun. You've earned it."

It was such a nice invitation, and today was unseasonably warm, but I had to think fast to get out of this one. "I have an apple pie to make."

"Eve, leave the girl alone!" Mr. Scott splashed her, and something that sounded suspiciously like the F-word flew out of his wife's mouth. "She's making me a pie, dammit."

She lobbed a pool noodle at her husband's head. "It's for everyone, Dan."

"That's what I meant." Immediately, he shook his head and mouthed to me, *No, it wasn't.*

I thought it best to make my escape before someone decided to throw me in the pool. The same someone who had just gotten out of the water and was aiming toward me. *Prowling* toward me, to be more accurate.

My eye line dropped directly to Mason's chest as chlorinated drops glided past the blue and black ink of his tattoos, and onto his dusky, flat nipples, and then lower onto the dusting of hair that disappeared below his waistband. Gawking at a man's happy trail wasn't something I'd thought I'd ever do, nor wonder how it would tickle my lips as I kissed my way down it. Mason had that power to make me notice things about a man's body that I never really took notice of before. He made me feel things that I hadn't felt before. That body was what I imagined next to mine when the loneliness crept in. Those green eyes were what I thought of in the dark instead of the nightmares that came for me.

I forced myself back inside the house, and from behind the French doors, I studied everyone with a careful eye.

They all seemed content, and Mason, it turned out, had been aiming for the pile of sub sandwiches. That made sense. Since we'd gotten back to the house, it seemed as if he had distanced himself from me. The lingering looks and unnecessary touches had stopped. Completely. An insidious voice in the back of my head wondered if he'd been using me to make a point to Charlie, but…what that point was, I didn't know.

Shaking off the thought, it dawned on me that the opportunity I'd been waiting for all morning had come. Everyone was outside and distracted, and I was inside…alone.

I all but raced to the hall closet, tearing it open. A grin sprang to my lips as I took out my surprise from the front pouch of my backpack. With another peek at the pool, I snuck upstairs. I didn't have to sneak anywhere, but I had never done anything like this before, and it felt like sneakiness was required.

Three steps from the upstairs landing, a chill crept across the nape of my neck. It was a sensation I'd felt before many times. As if I were…being watched. I whirled around on the ball of my foot, spinning faster than I intended. My head went light, hand flying out to grip the wrought iron banister to keep myself from tumbling down the stairs and face-planting on the travertine floor. It took a moment for my vertigo to settle before I scanned every room, corner, and shadow. Huh.

Shaking off the feeling as a misfiring of neurons, I continued upstairs and slipped into Mason's bedroom. I assessed my surroundings like I had the first time I stepped in here. Only now, I could see the furniture. And the carpet. Well, mostly. The state of chaos had greatly improved, anyway.

Now where to hide this? Nightstand? No, I didn't want my surprise anywhere near where the Trojan Dude used to reside. My gaze skipped around… Bingo. The closet. I smiled at what Mason's reaction would be when he—

A creaking noise startled me. I froze, stomach flipping and flopping like a fish out of water. That sound had come from downstairs. Panic raced across my skin, leaving goosebumps in their wake. My breaths came choppy, heart pounding so hard I swore it would leave an imprint on my ribcage. I forced down a somewhat steady breath and craned my neck as if that would help me hear any better. Nothing.

I shook my head. I was gonna have to add paranoia to my ever-growing list of neurological symptoms. I kinda understood now what my origami gifter went through every week.

I drew the closet door open and chose a hanger in the exact center. I hung the yarn necklace in such a way that he'd see the front of my surprise when he opened the door. I almost didn't want to be here when he did. Maybe this was a bad idea. Actually… *This is so stupid.* Whatever. Mason would either laugh or think I was a total creeper.

"Mags?"

A godawful yelp came out of me, doing some kind of spin move that made me dizzy all over again. My elbow banged into the door, effectively shutting the closet and sending a spark of fire up to my shoulder and down to my fingertips. Once the world righted, I focused on Ben's raised hands and bulging eyes.

Oh, thank God. I wasn't paranoid or hallucinating. Ben must have been downstairs.

"Sorry. I didn't mean to scare you while you…" His brown eyes bounced from one wall to the next. "…were in my cousin's closet."

"It's uh—" Gulping, I hooked a thumb over my shoulder. "Inside joke. What's up?"

"Oh. Well, I wanted a private moment with you to, um…" His cheeks pinked a little as his head ducked. "I wanted to make sure we were cool."

"Sure. Why wouldn't we be?"

"Because of last night."

I shook my head in the universal sign that conveyed *I don't know what the hell you're talking about.*

Ben's throat worked. "Jamey and I were so wrapped up in our thing, I felt like we excluded you. I didn't even realize what time it was or how tired you must have been until Mase said something, and it— It wasn't that I didn't want you to stay or take you home, but I hadn't ever been anywhere like that before, and it was… For the first time, I felt like I belonged. And I—Jamey thinks the world of you, and the last thing I want is to come between you. So if you ever feel that I'm doing that or—"

"Ben, take a breath."

He did, and that damn thing tripped through his lungs.

"I never felt excluded or thought you'd come between us. I only hoped you'd make Jamey happy and be my friend if you wanted to be."

"I do, Mags." True honesty rang in his tone.

"Good, because that was the happiest I'd seen Jamey in a long time. I'm not going to do the cliché thing by threatening your life if you hurt my best friend because…well." I waved over my minuscule stature, and that produced a grin on his end. "But please, don't break his heart."

He looked away, cheeks flushing again. "It's not just his heart that I'm worried about."

"I'm glad to hear it, and— Hang on. Jamey was the one who suggested it was time to leave. Not Mason."

"Ah…" Glancing to me, a cringe stamped across Ben's defined features. He folded his arms across his bare chest, the thick Celtic tattoos on his left arm and chest rippling with the movement. "Actually, no. Mase was the one who noticed how tired you were. He didn't think you'd listen to him, so he had Jamey bring it up. It was Mase's idea to take you home. I may have been…a little eager to go along with that plan so I could stay longer."

Wow. Okay, didn't see that coming. "Ben, you don't have anything to worry about here. Honestly, what you should worry about is Ava's cooking. Never, and I mean *never*, accept a dinner invitation. And for the love of God, stay away from her baked goods."

He somberly shook his head. "Too late. I had the—"

"Don't say the oatmeal raisin cookies."

He nodded, grimacing. "And the sweet tea. I think it took a week for my intestines to recover."

Jesus, that woman was going to kill someone. "I'm sorry. Truly."

"Yeah," he sighed the word. "Anyway, I'll let you get back to…" Smirking, his head swung a little. "Whatever you're doing."

My face warmed as I rocked on my heels. "Thanks."

Chuckling to himself, Ben headed downstairs, and thirty seconds later, the door chime skipped through the house. Odd. I didn't hear it when he came inside. Either I hadn't been paying attention, or the alarm contact was going bad like the one over the garage door. The former was likely since I was exhibiting preictal symptoms. Still, I should let Mrs. Scott know.

Once I tidied Mason's room, I checked the other bedrooms. I put another load in the laundry, prepped the ribs for dinner, and made dessert. Being in the kitchen most of the afternoon, though, sucked. I refused to look out the windows, but I couldn't turn off my ears. Listening to everyone splash and play with each other amid varied peals of laughter wasn't helping to curb that deep desperation to be a part of the Scotts' life.

I wasn't and never would be. No matter how many warm hugs and smiles they gave me, this was as close as I would get to being inside their world. I had to remind myself there was a line drawn between us, but that line was getting thinner and harder to see every time I came here.

Back upstairs, I busied myself in the laundry room as the door chime sounded off every five seconds. It must be time for bathroom breaks and drink refreshments. I should get down there before someone thought I was slacking, but before I could do that, Mrs. Scott appeared in the hallway. Her head rotated as if searching for something.

I poked my head out of the laundry room. "Mrs. Scott, do you need anything?"

Finding my voice, she turned, and all at once, every molecule of oxygen was sucked out of the atmosphere.

I'd never seen her look like this before. Her natural ease and composure were utterly shattered by what looked to be the tail-end of a panic attack. Or the beginning of one. Hair frazzled and face drawn, Mrs. Scott clutched the panels of her cover-up, fingers bleached white. Her blue eyes were swollen and red, lashes clumped together.

"M—Maggie," she sniffed. "Did you happen to move my earrings?"

I didn't have to ask which earrings because I'd only ever see her wear the diamond studs that she had on earlier today. "No, Mrs. Scott. Where did you leave them?"

If possible, disappointment paled her even further. "I swore I put them in that little dish on the counter. The one you set out, but when I came inside to use the restroom, they weren't there. Then I thought maybe I put them by my glass outside, but..." Lips quivering, she knotted her fingers together. "I just don't remember. Maybe I was wearing them, and they came off somewhere outside or in the pool? I...I—" Her cold hands covered mine and begged, "I know you're busy, but can you help us find them? Maybe a fresh set of eyes would help."

"Of course."

I shut the dryer door and followed Mrs. Scott's frantic flip-flopping outside to where everyone was already searching. Towels were picked up and shaken out. Cracks in the slate were studied with a careful eye. I scoured the area where she had been lounging, finding nothing. I remembered her playing with them this morning and suggested they might be in the office since she had spent the morning in there with Charlie and Taylor. Because Mrs. Scott's hands were trembling more than mine at this point, Ashley and I went inside and searched the office, her bureau upstairs, and then every inch of the kitchen.

They weren't anywhere.

By the time we made it back outside, Mrs. Scott was near inconsolable, and I couldn't help but hug her this time. "We'll find them, Mrs. Scott. I know we will. The skimmer? Did anyone check?"

"Twice." Mr. Scott released a resigned sigh. "Boys, why don't you scan the bottom of the pool again."

Mason and Matt didn't hesitate to slap on goggles and dive in. Ben and Camden checked the steps and loveseats.

"How could I be so stupid?" Mrs. Scott choked out, shuddering in my hold. "I never should have had them on today. I knew we were going swimming and— How can I not remember when or where I took them off?"

"Because your brain is occupied with a million other things. They'll turn up. They always do, Eve. Don't beat yourself up." Mr. Scott sat down on the other side of her and took over for me.

Unsurprisingly, the guys didn't find the earrings. If they were in the pool, I doubt a team of search and recovery divers could find them. The news didn't help Mrs. Scott's fragile condition.

Matt ran over to the outdoor bar and returned with a full tumbler of amber liquid. He handed her the glass that smelled of sweet rum. "Mom, it's fine. We'll find the earrings, and you'll be laughing about this tomorrow. You'll see."

"And if we...don't? What if we don't find them this time?" she pleaded, eyes spilling with tears. "They were..."

Kneeling before her, Mr. Scott rubbed her bare legs with a look of deep devotion in his eyes. "Then we move on, and that's okay for us to do."

I didn't think she agreed with whatever he meant by that. Mr. Scott encouraged her to take a sip of liquor, the liquid sloshing against her lips as she drank from the rim. Pulling the glass away, Mrs. Scott cringed like it was filled with battery acid but then drew another long pull of liquor.

Since there wasn't anything else for me to do, and I was sure the family would rather not have me hanging around, I went back inside and finished the laundry.

It wasn't but ten minutes later when Mr. Scott found me hanging his shirts in his closet. His face... Oh, God. He was wearing an expression like he was about to tell me I had five days left to live, and it would be an excruciating death.

"Mr. Scott?"

"Maggie." My name came on a ragged breath. "I'm sorry to even... Eve loses those earrings about three times a year, but it's never taken this long to find them. I— Ben is almost certain the earrings were on the counter when he took his bracelet off."

A weird feeling wriggled in my chest, making its way into my stomach. It didn't sound as if he were asking me to confirm what Ben had said, and I didn't know how to respond.

"I'm sorry, Mr. Scott. I noticed Ben's bracelet earlier with the wallets and phones, but I didn't pay attention to anything else on the counter.

The last I remember of the earrings was before my run with Mason, and Mrs. Scott was wearing them."

He nodded slowly as if absorbing my answer. My fingertips absently curled around the velvet lining of the hanger. "Ben also said you were doing something in Mason's closet earlier. And I'm sure— No, I *know* you have an explanation for that, but I have to ask. Maggie, did you take the earrings?"

The hanger and button-down shirt in my clammy grip fell to the floor, my stomach going down with them. "No! Mr. Scott, I would never…*never* take anything of yours."

"I know. I know you wouldn't, but I—" His gaze dropped, no longer able to look me in the eye. "Maggie… God forgive me. Could I check your bag?"

Those words took a solid minute to sink in. And when they did, my voice came out so very small and thin. "Of course."

I quickly collected the shirt and hanger off the floor, and I hung them on the rack, all sloppy and crooked. It would wrinkle if I left it like that.

"S—sorry." I reached to fix it.

His voice was gentle yet firm. "Maggie, let's take care of this first. Then we can be done, and I— Please."

Head angling back, I met his green eyes and nodded. "Right. I'll take care of it later. I'll fix it. I promise."

"I know you will." Mr. Scott moved out of the doorway and waited.

Swallowing, I slipped past him, and it didn't take but a few heartbeats to feel the heaviness of his stare weigh on my shoulders. When I realized what he was doing, the back of my eyes seared with heat.

He was watching me.

He watched me exit the master bedroom, a mere step behind me as I took the stairs. He watched my hand slide on the knob when I twisted it to take my backpack out of the hall closet. He watched my hand shake when I handed the bag over to him. He watched me as if he wanted to say, *innocent people's hands don't shake.*

I heard a sniffle, and I glanced over to find everyone in the living room. Everyone was watching me and thinking the same thing. Well, everyone but Mrs. Scott because she was huddled on the couch with a box of tissues, and she had Ashley do the watching for her.

Then it was my turn to watch.

My bag bounced on the outside of Mr. Scott's thigh as it swung from his blanched knuckles. With tentative feet, I followed him, Mason and Matt flanking me as though they were primed to bust out a Wolverine tackle move and take me down when I ran.

I wouldn't run. There was no reason to.

Mr. Scott set my bag on his desk and kept his grip on it, waiting for the click of the office door to close us in. After that, the only sounds in the room were the tinny *zips* of pockets opening and closing, material shifting. I clung to the knowledge that once he found that I was innocent, he would relax and give me a hug and smile that Scott smile. He would laugh this off. He would tell me how sorry he was, but he had to be sure, and I would understand. The earrings were important to his wife.

The moment that I had been waiting for never came, and it never would.

Mr. Scott's shoulders dropped as he reached into the front pocket and dragged out his hand. His palm splayed open. Laying there were two sparkly diamond earrings.

The world went to a slant, and I was sliding off it. "No. No! I didn't! I…would never!"

Mr. Scott shook his head, refusing to look at me. "I'm so disappointed in you, Maggie."

My heart bounded into my throat the exact moment my stomach plummeted toward my feet again. "Mr. Scott, please. I didn't take the earrings. Someone put them in my bag. It—"

Cringing, he held up a hand to silence me. The hand that wasn't holding the two diamonds that he believed I'd stolen. "I won't listen to this, Maggie. The proof is right here. You've given me no choice but to let you go."

No.

No. No. No.

This couldn't be happening. This couldn't be real. Was I seizing somewhere in my room, hallucinating, having a nightmare?

"Please, I'm begging you to listen. I—"

His once kind, gentle face twisted into something unrecognizable as he yelled, "*Stop, Maggie!*"

I flinched, and everything inside me withered, inching away from him until the back of my knees hit the couch. His gaze filled with darkened rage, and the back of my eyes stung with a riot of emotions, blurring my vision, thickening my throat.

"We trusted you! We welcomed you into our home, into our lives, and you broke our trust. How dare you do this? And then *lie* to me!" His anger became a jagged blade, cleaving into my heart.

"I…did…n't." I fought to get those syllables out, doubtful he could understand me. The trembling in my hands was like a tidal wave that had broken free of a levy, bursting through my body. The office walls closed in, dread squeezing at my chest, making it impossible for my lungs to breathe and my heart to beat. "It wasn't…me."

Mr. Scott shook his head, repulsed by my words. By me. "I had hoped you would at least have enough integrity to admit it." His hand curled around the diamonds, lips pulling away from his teeth as he seethed, "These were my daughter's. How dare you take something that belonged to her." After leveling me with a hateful glare, Mr. Scott twisted away to jerk open a drawer in his desk and pulled out a manila folder. He paused long enough to look right at me. "Never in my life have I been more wrong about anyone. You *disgust* me."

I'd been called every nasty name, including those that should never be uttered to a child by my own flesh and blood as I was beaten to the point I would pass out. But to hear Mr. Scott say that I *disgusted* him, hurt more than any belt, any hand, any word ever could.

The *slam* of the office door shook every bone.

My last shred of composure splintered, and I let it, something I never did. My father would punish me more if I ever dared to allow one tear to escape, but he wasn't here now, and any kindness I had ever been shown by this wonderful family had been ripped away from me by whoever put those earrings in my bag.

My thoughts collided into each other, and I couldn't concentrate on any one of them. There was nothing I could say to clear my name. No evidence. I had no defense other than my word, and he wouldn't allow me to give him that.

Someone had done this, but why? What had I done to deserve this?

Lost in a fog, the pounding in my ears cut off when Mr. Scott barked my name, and I jumped, having no clue how much time had passed since he stormed out of the office.

"I've called your father," he snapped. "He's on his way over here."

No. I didn't even think of that. That was why he had the folder. It was *my* folder. My folder with the paperwork I had filled out for Mrs. Scott. The paperwork with my emergency contact information. My father's number.

"Please no, Mr. Scott," I whimpered, begging for anything but that. "I'm eighteen. I can…"

"You can what? Make this right? Fix it? There is no fixing this." His eyes were so cold that it was like a blast of ice to my chest. All the compassion and warmth they once held for me, gone. I had no idea he had this kind of cruelty in him. I had no idea he was capable of hating me to the same depths that my own father did. "You've done this to yourself, Maggie."

I'd been wrong. So very wrong. All men were the same. Beneath the smiles and gentled words, a true monster hid, and it was only a matter of time before they revealed the dragon within.

chapter five

mason

I'd never felt like a bigger asshole than I did in this moment. And there had been plenty of moments during the last twenty years to use as comparison to validate that statement. I thought I was a decent judge of character, not the best, but not so terrible that I'd miss something like this. Never occurred to me that Maggie was capable of it. In fact, my brother and I had spent the last ten minutes defending the girl. I was even pissed at Dad for questioning her character, for daring to *think* she was guilty. Maggie wasn't that kind of person.

Plain.

Simple.

Next.

It took a special kind of sickness to steal. To come to our home day after day, be around, look at, touch our shit, and then swipe it right out from under us. Maggie didn't have it in her. I would have waged my soul on it.

Good thing I hadn't because…big asshole.

Why? Why had she done this? What thoughts had run through her head before taking those earrings? What did she want with them? Sell them, earn a quick buck? Did she want them for herself, or did she get off on the high of stealing?

I had seen the earrings on Mom this morning, but like most everyone else, I hadn't a clue when she'd taken them off or where she'd put them. It wasn't something I kept track of. But Maggie had.

And thankfully, so had Ben.

Had Maggie perched by the window, laughing to herself while we scrambled to find them? Had she felt a speck of remorse when my mother shed her first tear? Did she think Mom wore those earrings every day because they were worth a small fortune? Not even close. Mom wore them because they had been Faith's. *My sister's.*

If Maggie was looking to strike where it hurt, mission fucking accomplished.

Right up until I had seen those diamonds splayed out in my dad's palm, she had me completely fooled. Last night, I'd even concocted a plan to run the lake trails together, so I could spend one-on-one time with her today and nearly popped a lung this morning over said plan. For fuck's sake, I'd had a hard-on for most of our run, and if it hadn't been for severe muscle cramps and lack of oh-twos, I would have been rocking a nylon tent the entire time.

The real kicker?

I liked the man I was with her. Since losing my sister five years ago, I hadn't been able to say that. Not until I met Maggie. Around her, I didn't want to drink and fuck and numb out. When I was with Maggie, the last thing I wanted to be was numb. I wanted to *feel*. She made me want to be a better man. Someone my dad would be proud of.

All for a girl who was a liar. A thief.

Hell, just this morning, I'd been furious with Charlie when I found out that she still hadn't told her family that the ruse between us was over. Especially since she'd promised that she'd tell Taylor the truth last night. It had been close to a week now that Charlie had dragged her feet on this. I should have broken the news myself, but Charlie had PR to worry about along with social media and her controlling parents. So I let her do it her way.

What I didn't expect was the building resentment. And it hadn't been pretty. I'd openly flirted with Maggie in front of Taylor, something that was deliberate and spiteful. I wanted to send a message to Charlie that I was done, but it had only caused Taylor's catty blowback.

And after all that, after finally finding a girl who my heart did the pitter-patter shit for, that fucking organ got flipped on its ass. Here I stood in my parents' office watching that girl fall apart.

'Cause she got caught.

She's the town pariah for a reason. A pathological liar. Watch your back with Mags the Spaz.

Those words coming from Eric Ryan had meant nothing to me last week. But they had a history, went to high school together, and then…

Jenna said she was crying because Eric had broken up with her and that I was a liar, looking for attention.

Yeah, there was that. Either Maggie had witnessed that girl being raped by Eric, and Jenna had been too scared to speak up, or Maggie had made up the entire thing. That was possible because Maggie was good. So good, I actually thought she was destined for sainthood. She put everything into her performance, from the oversized and tattered clothes, the disintegrating Chucks, and even that rusty bicycle parked out front. It was likely the girl could really drive. She could be the next Danica Patrick for all I knew. Maybe Maggie could bowl, too, and last night the fumbling feet, misplaced fingers, and gutter balls had been all to suck me in. The hand tremors, unbalanced walk, and for fuck's sake, even feeding the homeless…

Bravo to her.

Cue another sob wrenching out of Maggie's throat. Another tissue balled up in the trash. Real tears or not, Dad was right. She brought this on herself. She took something of my sister's, and there was no forgiving that.

Looking at those earrings, anger hollowed my gut, threatening a reprise of all the crap I'd stuffed into it this afternoon.

Whatever her reason, Maggie didn't understand how this would destroy my parents. I'd been responsible for keeping her in our lives. She had been out. Right after Maggie had stormed into the RAM house and announced she was quitting, I was the one who convinced my brother not to let her go. I allowed myself to care about her, and the real bitch of it all was that I knew this would happen one way or another.

I let this girl in, and she broke us.

If it hadn't been for one freak summer storm, I never would have heard about her and Dad's secret meetings at the café. She never would have taken the job at our home. She wouldn't have been in Crescent Cove at all. She and her doppelganger face would have been one hundred and fifty miles north of here, and I wouldn't have been the wiser that she existed.

One storm had fucked us over and swept heartache onto our doorstep. She was an opportunist. A grave robber. A leech.

Disgusted to my core, I left the office as Uncle Will and Aunt Ashley made their way to the front door with my cousins in tow. The disappointment in the air was so thick, I could choke on it. They'd been fooled by her, too. They had adored Maggie for the same reasons I had. Because once I'd gotten over the shock of how much she resembled my late sister, the ache that had a permanent residence inside my soul didn't have as much real estate anymore. From the dark hair to the striking blue eyes, freckles dotting her button nose, petite frame… I'd seen Faith every time I looked at Maggie. And then I…didn't. Yesterday, I had seen *her*. Maggie Davis. Sticks. Mags…

A thought so dark and disturbing made my heart turn over heavily. Maybe Matt had been right.

Because I'm not convinced this girl is as innocent as everyone believes. It takes one Google search to find Faith's obituary.

Had she known this entire time that she resembled Faith? Taken the job at the Crest Cent Café, waiting for one of us to return? Dad had done just that. And then, for four years, he'd kept Maggie—Mags—a secret from us. Maybe she knew exactly who he was, what she meant to him, then saw the ad Mom posted for the house assistant and made her move, taking advantage of a mourning family.

A family in so much pain that they were blind to the red flags.

For all I knew, she'd played Dad about OHU. After the university had been destroyed by the mudslides, had she cried her crocodile tears, hoping he'd pay her way? Ah, he'd done much more than that. He'd convinced Warrington's board of trustees to grant the Cove's displaced students scholarships until OHU was restored. And I had suspected his intention was to pay the rest of her four-year tuition to keep her in town.

Slipping on his flip-flops, panic had seated deep into Ben's voice. "Text me. After." The *when Uncle Dan is done losing his shit* went unsaid. I figured Ben would want to talk to Jamey before Maggie got to him.

With a nod, I swallowed my plea for Ben to cut ties with Jamey before he was in too deep. While it may seem unfair to lump Jamey and Maggie together, I had serious doubts that Jamey didn't know what she was. The cliché *as thick as thieves* came to mind. But if Jamey was innocent in this... Damn, that sucked.

Way to go, Maggie. You fucked over your best friend, too.

The girl was a tsunami. She'd risen from the ocean depths, her undertow drawing us deep below the water's surface, and when she had us exactly where she wanted, she came crashing down, obliterating every heart in her path.

Mom was still curled up on the couch with a box of Kleenex as echoing footsteps forced us to turn toward the hallway. Dad emerged from the office for the second time, leaving Matt to watch Maggie. Thank God he closed the door, so I didn't have to hear every pathetic whimper and sniffle.

Settled on the couch, still in their swimsuits, Dad tugged Mom to his chest and pressed a kiss to her head. "I'm sorry, Eve. So damn sorry. I—"

The doorbell cut him off, and by the plummet of Dad's shoulders, I guessed who was behind the door. Bernard hadn't called the house because Dad had already given permission for the visitor to come.

Sighing, I went to the foyer and rubbed my palms down my board shorts before grabbing the bronzed handle. Pulling the door wide—

I, uh... Fuck me. Just as my body recoiled, the air surrounding me was sucked back into my chest.

Okay, so I admit, when Dad had called Maggie's father, I expected to open the door to a man resembling a Hobbit with graying hair, sporting pleated slacks, a polo, and an undershirt suffering from a mean case of bacon neck. He was definitely gonna be rocking a pair of worn loafers, maybe even a comb-over, possibly topped off with a set of gold aviator glasses straight from the nineties.

The man on the other side of this door was none of that. I would know. I saw him yesterday outside the café with his four cop friends.

"Can I help you, Officer?" I asked.

Irises near void of pigment drilled into mine, the kind of eyes that could size up a man's soul in a blink. "Son, I'm here for Margaret Davis."

Margaret?

Dad was at my side before questions could gather in my gray matter. "Officer, I called her father. My intention was to handle this parent-to-parent. I understand she's legally an adult, but I was concerned about the choices she was making, a path of self-destruction she could be on. She has a future with Warrington that I don't want her to ruin. I am not pressing charges. I don't want this on her record. I never intended to involve the police."

The cop dipped his head once in acknowledgment. "And I appreciate that, Dr. Scott. However, my being here can't be helped. You called me. I'm Chief Nathan Davis, Margaret's father."

A cop? Her father was a cop? And not only that...the fucking chief of police?

Holy shit. When I'd introduced myself yesterday, explained that Maggie worked for my parents, he'd said nothing to indicate that he was Maggie's father. And Maggie had done nothing to acknowledge that she even had a father.

This was all kinds of fucked up.

"May I come inside, Dr. Scott? I don't believe you and Mrs. Scott would care for the attention this might bring." Though his tone was soft, the man looked like he was ready to take down anything that moved, using whatever means necessary, and I supposed he had to from time to time.

Dad didn't budge from my side. Not right away. After a glance to the hall as though he could see Maggie's slouched form through the walls, Dad gave the chief a hesitant nod and moved aside. "Yes. Yes, of course."

"Thank you." All boots and barrel chest, a wall of navy blue stormed in as if he wanted to yell, "Claimed," and stake ownership of the house and everything inside it. My eyes went right to the gun on his hip, the same hip wearing a belt loaded down with scary ass shit meant to incapacitate scary ass people, and the body armor hulked him out even more.

Yesterday, he'd been dressed in a button-down shirt and tie, but today he looked every bit lethal as I suspected he could.

Dad paused at the edge of the foyer, gesturing to Mom. "Chief Davis, my wife, Dr. Eve Scott."

At some point, Mom had stood from the couch with a balled-up tissue in hand. Confusion, much like what Dad and I were experiencing, fused to her features. "Y—you're Maggie's father?"

"Yes, ma'am."

Dad cleared his throat, apprehension tensing his frame. There was…something about this guy that didn't exactly make one feel like his objective was to protect and serve.

"She's right this way, Chief. If you'll follow me." Dad began the trek down the hall, but the cop's head swung the opposite direction as though he were expecting an ambush of gangbangers hiding behind the drapes.

The sun streaming through the foyer's windows highlighted his hair that was the color of a night sky absent of stars, cropped in a brush cut, a startling contrast to his stark eyes when his head whipped back my way. His gaze scanned over every inch of the house that could be seen and possibly unseen because the guy may actually have X-ray vision.

Dad advanced again to get the chief moving, and every pound stuffed into that uniform echoed on the stone floor. I half expected him to slam me into the wall like this was Pamplona. He was the bull, and I was the idiot sporting a red bodysuit with a matching cape.

Matt bolted to his feet when the office door opened, his cold glare dissipating into shock. "Dad?"

Yeah, we weren't the let-the-authorities-handle-our-problems kind of people.

From the corner, the sniffles and tears stopped as if someone had just turned off Maggie's faucet. Act over, curtain down. The trash bin by her feet was piled to the rim with Kleenex, and she yanked out a handful of tissues from the box at her side to mop up her splotchy face. Maggie was no fool. She knew who those tears would work on and who was a complete waste of saline.

RoboCop fell into the latter category.

Dad continued the introductions with, "Matt, this is Chief Davis, Maggie's father."

My brother's lips parted and stayed that way, blinking without words. I couldn't blame him. Even with them in the same room, I still couldn't comprehend that this man was of any blood relation to Maggie. Aside from possessing a similar shade of hair, he looked nothing like her. Even the blue of their irises seemed to be from a different color spectrum. Everywhere Maggie was soft, this man was stone from the cut of his jaw to the sharpness in his gaze.

"These are the earrings?" Thumbs tucked into his belt, he studied the shiny stones on the edge of Dad's desk. It struck me odd that he hadn't asked for any details or offered an argument to defend his daughter. There wasn't a defense, but still…

"Yes." Dad shifted restlessly when the cop's gaze didn't budge. "I know they don't look like much, but they are important to my family."

"Whether they are five or five thousand dollars, your feelings are justified, and on behalf of my daughter, I hope you can accept my apology. I can empathize with how it must feel to entrust a stranger with your belongings and then have them break that trust." The chief's eyes flicked to Dad and then to Maggie. "Margaret, did you take anything else of the Scotts'?"

A long moment passed where she didn't respond, but then one gulp heard 'round the world later, she choked out, "No…sir." Maggie struggled to keep her voice even, but her quaking body made that impossible. Again, hard to tell what was real with her.

Forehead drawn, he faced away from Maggie. "Dr. Scott, have you checked the rest of your home for missing items?"

"No, I haven't," Dad answered. "If there is, I will contact you."

Nodding, the chief cast Maggie a sideways glare. "If I may ask… How much have you paid her in wages?"

Turning rigid, Maggie angled her head back to him but said nothing.

"What do her wages have to do with this?" Mom questioned from the doorway.

The chief's lips formed a flat line, mouth losing color. "Since you called, I've been struggling with a way that would make this right by you. You're under no obligation to do so, but I hoped if you could treat her time here as compensation, you would be gracious enough to leave what happened today in this room. I think you can appreciate that as chief of the CCPD, I do have a reputation to uphold, and this— It's a small town." A breath teased the capacity of the Velcro binding his vest. "Margaret has made her fair share of missteps. It's no excuse, but I'm a single father, and my work is very demanding of my time. I believe— rather, *pray*—that her acting out stems from needing my attention."

"Chief Davis, thank you, but it is not necessary," Dad protested. "We won't speak of this, and I don't want her wages back. She's done the work and earned it. We've been very happy with her."

"Yes. I can see that." The cop's gaze scrolled over Mom's swollen lids and raw nose as if to say, *bullshit*. "Margaret, how much?" It was a command but a weary one. When she refused to answer, his dark brows inched toward his hairline, expectant.

Then Maggie's lips moved around what I assumed was an answer.

Apparently, he was part hound, too, because he followed that up with, "And that was one paycheck?"

She didn't answer as he transferred his weight to the other boot, a metallic clang coming from his belt. A chill of dread worked down my spine as an image of Maggie in cuffs entered my head.

"Margaret, how much do you have on you?"

Though her eyes were bloodshot and puffy, they widened with disbelief. "S—sir?" Her father stared on, impassive, time stretching as though he could wait out a statue. "A hundred, but it was for poker."

Poker? Did she...? Did she really just say that?

Whatever micron of warmth I had left for Maggie was obliterated by her answer. Who was this girl? What had we allowed into our lives?

The chief sighed, and it sounded like a practiced event. "Give the Scotts their key, and you can pay them back on Monday."

Maggie took a moment to digest that, and once she nodded, she stood on legs that were as sturdy as a buoy in a tropical storm. Maggie stepped over to the gray backpack that may have been used since before her age hit double digits. Dipping her trembling hand into the frayed material, she removed our house key from a worn blue leather wallet. When she shoved the wallet back inside, I heard the muted *crinkle* of the blister pack in a hidden compartment that Dad had revealed when he had rifled through her bag.

Birth control.

I'd had a suspicion that she was a virgin from her awkwardness around me, the way she looked at me, responded to me. The flare of pink in her cheeks every time I teased her, a hitch in her breath when I touched her, and the shudder that rocked through her when I dragged my tongue down her throat—

Had that only been yesterday?

That little blister pack was another reminder that I knew nothing about Maggie, Margaret, Mags—whoever the hell she was.

As it took the girl five tries to zip her bag closed, Dad folded his arms across his chest, the jewel-toned hues in his eyes hard and hollow. "Do you have anything to say for yourself, young lady?"

Not answering, she stared at her feet, refusing to give my parents the decency of looking them in the eye.

"Apologize to the Scotts, Margaret," Chief Davis pressed.

The only sound made was from the grandfather clock in the other room, and it must have made sixty goddamn *ticks* before two simple words were uttered by a wooden voice, void of apology.

"I'm sorry."

Nice. Real fucking nice.

"Go to the patrol vehicle, Margaret, while I finish with the Scotts," her father ordered.

Bag clutched to her chest, Maggie shuffled out of the room, head down, eyes low, shoulders rolled in. This was the first time that I was happy to see her this way. At the very least, she should pretend to be ashamed of herself.

Watching her leave, Chief Davis loosed a strained breath. "Again, I am sorry for any anguish she has caused your family."

"Thank you," Dad said. "I admit, I did lose my temper with her. I shouldn't have said the things I did. I was—*am* angry and deeply disappointed in her actions. In her. Maggie's a highly intelligent girl with a bright future. I think if she can overcome whatever she's struggling with right now, I have no doubt that she'll be successful in any career she chooses. If you'd like some referrals for a counselor, I'd be happy to give you a recommendation. My wife and I...we wish the best for your daughter."

"I might do that. And allow me to give you the same advice I'd give anyone else in this situation. Change your alarm code, rekey your locks, and alert your community guards to her employment status. Please don't hesitate to call if you find anything else missing."

Dad offered him a nod, and Mom was a little busy relying on the wall to keep her upright to acknowledge the conversation or that the chief was leaving.

From the office window, I watched the chief load the clunky Schwinn into the back of a black and white Tahoe. Then the vehicle dipped under his weight when he slid into the driver's seat.

Somewhere between the bars and mesh in the backseat sat a girl with the uncanny likeness of my baby sister. The thought of it unnerved me down to the bone, and I had to turn away.

Once SUV pulled out of the drive, we blew out a collective breath.

"What the fuck was that? Her father's the chief of police?" Matt's eyes still hadn't returned to their standard size.

"Believe me, I'm right there with you." Dad flopped onto the leather couch and eyed the overflowing trashcan with a wince. "All these years... I had no clue."

Dragging in an unsteady breath, Mom scooped the earrings off the desk and held them to her heart. With her head bowed, another sniffle hit the air, and Matt swooped over to comfort her before Dad could.

The promise I'd made earlier was at the forefront of my mind, and I left my family in the office as I drew out my phone, skimming past the five apology texts from Charlie. I found Ben's number and then filled him in on everything.

It didn't go well.

"Mase, I can't believe this." Ben's voice warbled in the earpiece. "I know I kinda started this entire thing when— I told Uncle Dan that I wasn't completely sure about the earrings. I swore I saw them when I took off my bracelet, but... Jesus, I can't believe Mags actually did it."

"Not only did she apologize, but her father is making her pay us back her wages."

"Fuck." The word came out on an exhale, then swallowed. "What am I supposed to say to Jamey?"

I chewed my lip. "The truth, Ben."

A few seconds ticked by, Ben's breaths coming harsh through the earpiece. I imagined he was pacing in his room, wrecking his gelled hair with frantic swipes of his hand. "You don't understand, Mase. Jamey talks about Mags nonstop. She's his entire world. Things almost went south between us when he discovered how you and Matt treated her weeks ago. I can't tell him something like this over the phone, and I have no clue when he and his mom will be home from that convention in San Francisco."

"I'm sorry, Ben. I am. But maybe...it's for the best." As the words left my mouth, I cringed. If Ben had been standing in front of me, he would have swung without warning.

I would have taken it.

"Jamey's. Not. Like. That."

"And we thought the same about Maggie." The line went dead.

Eyes sliding shut, I stood there in the living room, somewhat numb. But not near numb enough to stem that bitter taste in the back of my mouth. I brought this pain on my family and hated myself for it. I'd been so focused on seeing Maggie as I needed her to be instead of who she was. And now we were all paying the price.

Turning, I aimed for the basement bar to drown each and every sin in whiskey and find utter and complete numbness.

chapter six

maggie

I knew why we lived on the outskirts of Crescent Cove. I knew why only abandoned homes surrounded ours. I also knew why we were the only ones who lived in the motherfucking woods. No one would be scandalized by the abhorrent things he said to me. No one would peer into our windows and witness the horrors of what he did to me. No one would hear my screams when he inflicted his *lessons*.

Bounding along Verde Way, dirt clouded the road as we proceeded deeper into Baywoods Forest, the dense redwoods concealing us from the last slices of sun that peeked through the canopy overhead. As the world closed in and darkened around me, I weighed my two options.

Stay or run.

If I stayed, I needed to get it before he broke out the JD. The drunker he was, the worse the beating. The whiskey ate through the sliver of control that kept him from becoming the full beast. And it was a *sliver*. But if I ran, I had to time it right. I'd have to escape and somehow contact Jamey—

Wasn't that just perfect. Jamey was still in San Francisco, and he wasn't sure when he'd be home tonight. I couldn't hide at the Hayeses' because that was the first place my father would search for me. The second was the café. I needed wheels and calling a ride was out of the question. He'd have every badge on the taxi and rideshare companies, searching the bus depot in Pacific Cliffs, and alert every precinct in Cove County that the chief's daughter was missing. He'd make up some story about mental illness, throw in the fact I had epilepsy, and he'd have the sympathy of the entire West Coast. There might even be a part of him that hoped I'd go missing because there would be plenty of women ready to console his...grief. Candi not necessarily at the top of the list, as she might believe.

As I stared at my trembling hands, the stirrings of a headache flared in my temple from all the stupid crying. I inwardly chastised myself. I couldn't believe I'd lost control over my emotions like I had, but again, I'd never been accused of theft before. Nor had I ever been yelled at by anyone but my father. My thighs and calves were starting to twitch with cramps in the luxurious six inches of legroom I was allowed. The hard bucket seat bit into my shoulders, and my spine ached, the plastic burrowing against every bone. I couldn't imagine how someone as large as my father fit back here.

The bars on the windows were a nice Alcatraz touch, and the bulletproof partition sandwiched between the mesh grilles gave dear ol' Dad a prime view of me squirming. There was at least one camera on me, and on either side of the front console was a shotgun and a rifle locked in their vertical gun racks, along with enough technical gear to man a spaceship. But he wasn't running an astronaut program; he was running my life. And he did it well. So very well.

Fallen limbs and leaves crunched under the tires as the PPV rolled to a stop in the carport. He cut the engine and made me wait while he checked that his weapons were secure.

After shutting down the MDT, he flung the door wide. The Tahoe bounced when his weight lifted, the cabin becoming entrenched with the suffocating scent of pine and stagnant earth.

He slammed the driver's door, then opened mine. Poker stood feet behind him, ears low and locking his wary brown eyes on my father. As my shoes met the cracked concrete, I had one final thought that Poker and I could run, hide in the woods for a little while. It would take at least an hour to assemble the Pacific Cliffs K-9 Unit and SWAT team, which would give me enough time to figure something out, maybe break into one of those empty apartments on Sands and squat for a while.

As if Poker had read my mind, his front paw lifted. The blue wrap on his foot had unraveled, skimming the ground, a reminder that his injury from the fishhook was far from healed. Poker would never make it. The wound would split wide halfway into our escape.

I'd have to carry him. I would. I would carry him to the ends of the earth and back. But I wouldn't be fast enough to save us. And just like that, my choices narrowed from two to one.

Stay.

Without a word, my father unlocked the front door and stepped inside the house. I didn't dare remind him that my bike was still in the trunk as I glimpsed another look to the Tahoe; the front bumper butted almost all the way against the side door. There was only one reason he parked that close, and it wasn't to keep his vehicle tucked beneath the safety of the carport.

Following him in, I shut the front door behind me, and while he connected his phone to the charger on the kitchen counter, I set my backpack inside my room and gathered the supplies to change Poker's bandage. He leapt onto the bed for me, and I made quick work of the wrapping and gave him his antibiotics. It was too early for either, but…something told me to take care of him now. Strangely, I never heard my father's boots clomping down the hall to his room, but I must not have been paying attention like I hadn't with the door chime earlier.

Once I finished with Poker, we returned to the kitchen, but my feet lurched to a stop. I hadn't heard my father go down the hallway earlier because he had never left the kitchen. Hadn't taken off his uniform nor his armor yet. And he'd already shot back a double, maybe more. That was unusual. And unusual for Nathan Davis was never a good thing.

It was too early for Poker's dinner, but again, nothing about this day was going as planned. As I dumped the last of the kibble into the dog bowl, guilt gripped my heart. I was supposed to pick up his food after work today. *Along with the uniforms.* If I couldn't get them tonight, I'd have to get out early tomorrow.

Not a word had been spoken since we'd left the Scotts', nor had my father looked at me. As my sore eyes lifted to his broad back, I swallowed past the dryness in my throat. "Sir, I—"

"I don't want to talk to you or see you right now." The bottle tapped against the rim of his glass with a clink as he filled it. "Go to your room."

Though I'd never been accused of theft before, I'd been through this enough times to know what that meant.

Go to your room and wait. Wait until I'm ready to beat the ever-loving shit out of you.

He was going to keep drinking until his brain was swimming in whiskey, until the control melted away, and then he'd come for me. I had to do this now while he was still human enough. I had to provoke him before the dragon was completely unveiled.

He downed another gulp as I said, "Sir, I didn't do it. I know—"

"I didn't stutter the first time!" He hammered the glass on the counter, ice cubes smacking together as one flew out and cracked onto the linoleum, skating across the floor and beneath the fridge. "Go to your room."

I faintly heard the rattle of Poker's tags as he charged over, stopping to act as a barrier between my father's back and me. Hackles raised, his nails were protracted, every muscle rigid and poised to attack.

"Please, sir, hear me out. I was set up. I never touched the earrings."
Shit, my voice was shaking, and in his mind, that meant one thing.
Only the guilty sound guilty.

"Stop with the lies," he growled, shoulders rising. His head swayed side to side so slowly, it chilled my very core. "You think you're so clever, don't you? You've been working for two doctors this entire time and thought you could hide that from me? It didn't occur to you that I would run a background check the second you gave me their name?"

No, it had occurred to me, and I knew he wouldn't like it. But he never brought it up until now, and I… Well, I figured he'd permitted me to continue working for the Scotts because he knew they'd be paying me decent wages that he would eventually try to steal from me. But after meeting with Marcus, I was no longer sure that was true.

…I know Daniel and Eve well. Too well. There is no way they would let you walk out of their lives that easily, especially with you still in town.

I didn't know what he meant by that, but Marcus may have been the reason I'd been allowed to stay at the Scotts this long. Made me wonder who the most powerful players were in this game.

"Sir—"

"Then I saw their little bastard lurking outside the café yesterday." He lifted his drink, turning to drill me with a frigid, measured glare. "The very one I told you to stay away from. You didn't tell me that he'd be at that party. You conveniently left that part out, too."

Mason? God, what…? "Sir, I assumed you…"

There was something in his expression that killed every word on my tongue, something I didn't quite recognize, and cold dread poured through me. Rooted to my spot, I could only watch as he shot back another glass. Then another. He was drinking a lot faster than usual. This was a bad idea. This was such an epically bad idea, but there was no looking back now. I'd awoken the beast.

I picked up Poker's bowls and ordered him to follow me. He didn't. His stare had locked onto my father, muzzle twitching, canines slowly being bared.

"Poker, *now.*" My command was assertive enough to get his paws moving in my direction, but there was a part of me, a dark and small part that wished it had been an order for something else entirely.

Cowardice choked me as I pushed the side door open, the PPV leaving just enough room to fit the bowls through. While I shoved Poker outside, I inhaled a desperate gulp of air that was tinged with the beginning layer of fog as the sun began to set. I prayed it wasn't my final taste of freedom.

I shut myself inside with him, the heart-wrenching sounds of Poker's nails digging into the wood as he pawed at the door.

I stood in the doorway of the laundry room, my toes technically in the kitchen with my legs quivering as much as my hands.

My throat spasmed as I worked to clear it. "Do you think I'm stupid enough to steal? Do you think I don't know what you would do to me if I got caught? Why? Why would I take those earrings? It makes no sense."

With an eerie calm, he canted his head. Eyes that held the warmth of the Arctic met mine, dropping the temperature by twenty degrees with just that look. "Oh, it makes complete sense. We both know why you did it, and your dumb ass fucked it up."

He held up another pour and sipped it down as though he was savoring this moment, thinking of all the ways he would hurt me, inflict his wrath. It was so slow and methodical that all my blood pooled to my feet.

The tumbler withdrew from his mouth, lips glossed with whiskey. "And to answer your question, yeah, I do think you're stupid. Too fucking stupid to realize what I'm going to do to you."

No, after eighteen years of this, I had a pretty good idea. It was simply a question if he'd use his hand or his belt.

He shoved off the counter and set his glass down like it was a fine crystal goblet, as if he wanted to make a point that he could be gentle, and it was a choice that he would not afford me.

Boots thudding closer, vibrating the floor beneath me like foreshocks before an earthquake, he jerked at his duty belt, wrist flicking out and to his side. That quiet *click* blasted through my ears like a cannon. My gaze tracked to what he was holding—

It was then I understood I'd never been more wrong or more fucking stupid in all my life.

Sweet Mother.

Every muscle in my body froze, eyes refusing to move from the blanched knuckles wrapped around a black baton. His police baton.

He...he had never used that on me before.

My mind switched to survival mode, allowing me a moment of clarity. He was standing near the mouth of the hall, blocking my room, blocking me from my backpack with my IDs and what money I had.

Fuck it.

Spinning, I sprinted to the front door, knowing he'd parked that damn Tahoe too close for the exact purpose of limiting my escape routes. No more than a foot away from reaching the knob, an incredible force snapped my head backward, and the rest of me went off-kilter.

The room whirled, sharp needles driving into my skull as he yanked on my ponytail. His grip tightened, bowing my spine to an unnatural degree. If I'd only let Jamey trim my hair this morning, it would have been too short for him to grab.

Balance failed me, and out of fear of losing a chunk of my skull, I wrenched my head, forcing him to lose his grip. Then I scrabbled, clawing at the air, fighting to stay upright. My palm landed on the door handle, but before I could grip it, his hand was around my bicep, painfully squeezing my muscles. With an incredible force, he spun me, air rushing in and around my ears. He slammed me into the wall, the back of my head taking the brunt of the blow. The impact ricocheted down my spine and then back up, the fiery blaze pooling in my temple.

Something hard was then jammed into my cheek, pressure building in my eye socket with every pounding drum of my heart, and I briefly wondered if he would blind me. Maybe he thought the scars marring my entire back weren't enough to remind me of his power.

There was never a question. He had all the power. I had none.

"You think you can run from me?" he seethed.

I met his eyes beneath the strands of dark hair obscuring my vision. My bottom lip trembled. "No...s—sir. I'm...s—sorry."

The end of the baton dug in even harder. "We both know how much of a lie that is. Because that's what little whores do. They *lie*."

The pressure beneath my eye vanished, and his body shifted to pin me in place. I felt all of him against me and was wholly terrified to move for fear of rousing parts of him that were pressing into my hip. No reason to test my theory of what those recent looks at my breasts had meant.

"You don't learn. You *never* learn." His breath was cloyingly sweet as it swamped my face. Stomach churning, my skin flushed with heat, throat closing as if trying to protect my airway from the toxic scent. "I would find you. I would have every badge, private dick, and dog in the state hunt you down. No one would believe you, Margaret. No one would take the word of a fucking head case over me." Leaning closer, his breath stirred the hair at my ruined temple. "*Everyone* knows me. *Everyone* in the Cove loves me. They feel sorry for me because I have you as a burden. If it weren't for their sympathy, I would have been rid of you long ago."

The only thing worse than the cool delivery of his threat was that every word rang true.

He moved too fast for me to track, his hand clamping around my throat like a steel band in the next breath. He angled my head back, exposing my neck to him like a predator before the kill. My lungs burned for oxygen as the hills and valleys of the popcorn ceiling swam together.

Darkness crept into my vision, and I opened my mouth wider, but the air never made it down my throat. I slapped at him blindly, my own choking noises filling my ears. Terror scratched at the edges of my consciousness, which was starting to fade...

Suddenly, he released me, and I dragged down gasps of stale oxygen between coughs, slumping between the wall and his hard frame. At some point in his drunken haze, he must have realized he'd leave marks that I couldn't hide. And if he cared about the visible bruises...

A thin thread of relief eased between the panic cinching my chest that today wouldn't be my last. Didn't mean he wouldn't make me suffer, though.

His fingers formed a vise on my forearm, heaving me to my feet. He towed me forward, feet fumbling and tripping over each other. The walls blurred as he wheeled me around, grip releasing. Gravity welcomed me as I tumbled to the kitchen floor and splattered facedown onto the dingy gold pattern of the linoleum. Next thing I knew, he had my wrists restrained behind me, driving a knee into my spine.

Like I was a criminal.

A meaty hand shoved my head to the side, cheek and jawbones digging into the hard floor. My sternum bore his weight, air rushing out of my lungs, my chest compressed and blocking its return. It occurred to me far too late that there was nothing to soften the blow. I'd feel this front to back and in between.

"You embarrassed me in front of the richies," he fumed. "*Stole* from them." He repositioned himself, knee screwing into my spine. I tensed, readying for his attack. "Did you really think I'd let that go unpunished?"

Whack.

Strange enough, I heard the dulled thud before anything else. That may have been because my brain couldn't process the degree of pain screaming across my shoulder blades and upper arms. Once it did, though... He may as well have taken a serrated knife to me, sawing, shredding, tearing through my skin, muscles, nerves, and bones. I only knew my mouth was open because I felt the drool puddle under my cheek, but my cries were so loud they were silent.

"I put a roof over your head. I pay for your water, electricity, and food. And this is the thanks I get? You take and lie just like that bitch whore mother! Do you know what she did to my good name? Did it ever cross your damaged brain how this would affect me?" Spit dotted my face when he leaned over me to hiss, "No. You selfish bitches never do."

My vision swam, and I fought to get two words out. "Ple...ase... St— Stop."

"Stop? No, I'm not going to stop. Not until I beat her out of you." His knee ground into my vertebrae when he shifted again, but I didn't have time to prepare for the next hit.

Whack.

A stuttered and deafening scream ripped free of my throat, stars bursting behind my eyelids. Fire lashed at my lower back, and there was no stopping the rush of tears from my eyes. His hold on me tightened, my arms like twigs that he could snap with his sheer will. I had no strength to fight, free myself, his weight crushing me from the inside out. Dear God, I'd never been in this much pain.

Somewhere in my scrambled brain, I heard the barks and scratches as Poker battered the door to get to me. "Please, it's...too...much. Use your...belt. P—please. I'm sc—ared."

His knee lifted away, as did the pressure restricting my lungs. Though a few pants of air rattled their way down my windpipe, the mere effort it took for my tissues and muscles to expand reverberated pain throughout my torso.

I was vaguely aware of the dull hum pinging against my eardrums, but it was impossible to focus on where it was coming from.

"You should be fucking scared." Hot breath reeking of bitter Jack washed across my damp cheek, and either his words were slurring together, or my hearing was going. "Did you really think I'd let you run from me? I would find you, Margaret, and I would fucking *kill* you. And I wouldn't stop with you. That little faggot and his bitch mother would be next. Right after that retarded mutt."

The musky scent rolling off him vanished, and my skin no longer prickled from his nearness. It was over. Done. I wilted into the floor, my lids too heavy to keep open. I let them slide shut.

"Do you know what it was like listening to that rich fuck tell me his sob story about the stupid girl who stole his dead daughter's earrings? How much he detested you. Wished you out of his life and his posh school, the shame you bring to them all because you're nothing but a failure. And because of you, *I* had to apologize. *To a richie!*"

My shoulders were suddenly lurched backward, a spark of heat tearing through each arm and down to my fingertips. He still had my wrists pinned behind my back.

Oh, dear Lord. *He's not done.*

"Please, stop. Please. *Please.*" My words were nothing more than a pathetic whimper. My heart rate spiked. I had a genuine fear that he was going to cripple me.

Bark-thump. Scratch-bark-bark.

"I'm so sorry, Dr. Scott. My deepest apologies to your family!"

Whack.

Bright flashes took over my vision as flames screamed across my backside and blasted my tailbone. It was the most brutal blow yet, the shockwave rippling up my spine and into my brain.

The low humming noise abruptly became a thunderous ringing sound that rattled my ears. My mouth flooded with saliva so fast, I couldn't spit it out before choking on it, the froth blocking my airway. A metallic taste stretched across my tongue, my stomach roiling with acid.

No. No, not now.

The ground shifted to a tilt as though I'd slide right off, and somewhere within the ringing, I heard her. The woman's voice that came before the darkness took me. My vision blackened, and another surge of fear drenched my insides. Over and over, I heard her words, possessing my mind, forcing me to listen to her frantic voice.

My world fell away, and I was swept into hers. It was a different kind of hell, one that I was just as terrified of.

Hush, Magpie. Don't make a sound...

chapter seven

maggie

A putrid stench tunneled into my nose, stirring the bile in the pit of my stomach, drawing my consciousness out of the murky depths of my mind. With every inhale, the act of breathing became more challenging as if I were sinking underwater, the pressure and weight preventing my lungs from taking a full breath. A dense haze surrounding my brain lingered as my eyes peeled open to nothing but darkness and shadows. My lids were as dry as sandpaper, scraping my eyes as I blinked. Slowly, the deep grooves of the kitchen chair legs came into view.

Beneath me, the linoleum floor was hard and unforgiving against every bone and joint. My focus swam together to see that inches away was the mess from my stomach, the acrid taste still thick on my tongue, coating my lips. I thought I heard dulled scraping sounds echoing all around me, but it was impossible to identify what it was or where it was coming from.

I'd had a seizure—that much I could guess. But before that? Not a clue how I'd ended up in the middle of my kitchen.

I couldn't determine yet if I was wearing clothing, but to be fair, my nerve receptors seemed a bit scrambled. I sometimes pulled at them when I had a seizure, but there were times…there were times that I swore he'd removed them.

With a shift of my hip, each and every one of those nerve receptors came back online all at once. A firestorm blazed across my back, burning, searing into me with such force that I was on the brink of unconsciousness again. My vision blinked out, and another wave of nausea slammed into me. I was somehow able to roll onto my side, and before I could stop it, a hoarse cry ripped free from my throat. The broken sound bounded through the house, cracking off the walls that couldn't absorb one more cry, one more tear, one more secret. These walls had seen and heard too much.

Bark! Slam-bark-scrape! Bark!

Poker.

Every muffled bark on the other side of the door, scrape of his nails down the wood, and slam of his body elicited the memories to flicker in my brain like a movie that had been spliced together all wrong.

The baton.

He'd beaten me with his fucking police baton. I distinctly remembered the three strikes of the metal rod before I blacked out, and there was no telling how many more he'd given me, but every micrometer of my body from my shoulders to the backs of my thighs felt destroyed. The sick bastard even had the forethought to beat me in the kitchen, so I wouldn't stain the carpet again.

I was wet all over, inner thighs sticky, the scent of ammonia mingling with the odor of sickness. My gaze trailed up to the clock on the stove, the numbers blurred and dull. *Ten hours.* I'd been lying in my own piss and vomit for ten fucking hours.

It said a lot about my pain threshold that I was tempted to lay here another…year.

I knew now, without a doubt after today, God didn't exist. How could He allow this to happen to me? Allow me to be born into the hands of a monster? How could He be without any mercy? What was the point of giving me a life that wasn't worth living?

Sucking down any spare molecule of oxygen my lungs could hold, I pushed off the floor by a mere inch. The movement sent another blast of heat through me, pain driving into my brain that was throbbing, swelling to the point it couldn't possibly fit in my skull.

The headache alone was enough to incapacitate me.

My arm violently shook as I reached for the kitchen chair, eternity passing before I could curl my hand around a spindled leg. When I gathered my knees beneath me, I'd discovered that not one muscle in my torso had gone unscathed. By means I couldn't fathom nor remember, I'd pulled myself up and over the seat. Resting for a minute, my gaze found the bottle of Jack on the counter, a mouthful or less of liquid left inside. He didn't finish it because it was my silent reminder to get more.

Between Poker's barks and scratches, snores sawed the air from behind my father's bedroom door. My only hope was that one day, he would give himself alcohol poisoning and die in his sleep, choke on his puke.

That was the same fate he'd left me to. It was only fair.

Using the chair as a makeshift walker, I knee-walked my way across the kitchen, my movements measured, going no faster than I could tolerate. A slug could lap the Earth before I made it to the sink and back with my supplies. As I lowered myself to clean my vomit off the floor, pain washed over me in unrelenting waves. Even depressing the nozzle on the Lysol bottle sent a shock of heat up my arm, lumping all the nerves in my shoulder into a tight knot. My vision blurred again.

The mess was clean, and I had to stand at some point. Since the chair was right next to me, now was the ideal time. It took five attempts to get vertical, and by then, I'd bitten my tongue so hard, the metallic tinge of blood was thick in my mouth. I gripped onto the back of the chair, the floor shifting under me.

I gauged the room, determining that I was halfway between the kitchen counter and the laundry room. I was desperate to let Poker inside, take care of him, but if he accidentally knocked me over now, I didn't think I could get back up. Using my chair-walker, I shuffled my way to the trash—

Son. Of. A. *Bitch*.

There were dirty dishes in the sink. Dishes dirtied from the small white boxes littering the counter. The same takeout boxes that had been in the fridge after his date night with Candi. I wondered if he sat at the table and ate his leftovers as if the unconscious girl on his kitchen floor was part of the new décor, or if he took his meal into the living room because the stench of my vomit was too bothersome.

I slunk to my bedroom, relying on the counters and walls to stay upright. From the doorway, I could see that my curtains were pulled back from the window as I had left them this morning. Or technically, yesterday morning. Outside, the moonlight glinted off the thin redwood branches as the breeze tapped them against my window. I flicked on my lamp.

Fuuuuck.

The mattress had been thrown off my bed, the sheets lumped into a corner of my room, and the clothes from my dresser were splayed all over as if a tornado high on crack had torn through here. The few items that had been hung were now at the bottom of my closet, along with a mangled heap of wire hangers. My laundry basket had been upturned and emptied.

He'd ransacked all my hiding spots. The ones he knew of.

And the proof of that was neatly sitting on top of my dresser in the form of a pile of money that looked far too meager. My chest hollowed as my heart slid down to my feet. I knew what I would find before I counted it. He'd left enough to pay back the Scotts and had taken the rest. My stomach burned with anger. It hadn't been much, but that had been *mine*. I had scrimped, saved, worked, and bled for that money. It was my escape from him.

For a future free of *this*.

Hot rivers streaked down my face from either the physical pain or something that hurt infinitely more. I didn't want to think about the latter yet.

Cleaning my room would have to wait, just like the dishes and the trash. I had tried to bend over, but I ended up toppling down to my hands and knees and then crawled to collect what clothes I could. I made it into the bathroom and gasped when the light illuminated the bruises on my wrists.

Shutting my eyes, I closed and locked the door as quietly as I could. I nearly bit through my already swollen tongue when I stripped off my soiled clothes.

Dragging my eyes up to the mirror, I stilled as shock inundated me. He...he'd never marked me like this before.

Dark pink and purple smudges like the handprints on my wrists encircled my neck from where he'd choked me. And my back... Five distinct lines stippled in blood-red branded my skin, the purple shadows of each one bleeding into the next. Along the edges of the baton strikes, my skin looked black as if necrosis had set in. My entire back was bruised, including the back of my arms, and my backside was the worst.

How he didn't break my spine, I'd never know. But he— He had hit me twice more *after* my seizure. When I was unconscious. Helpless.

There wasn't a shred of humanity in that monster.

Emotion crested, stinging the back of my eyes. I shifted my attention to the filth in my hair and the stickiness between my thighs. With little to hold onto, it took some nimble footwork to get over the lip of the tub without falling. Once in, I turned the faucet to C. The chilled water sputtered as it choked its way through the pipes, then spat out to pelt my battered body. Letting my eyelids drift shut, I rested my forehead against the wall as another rush of tears threatened to come. I fought it. Crying wouldn't help me. The only thing that would help me was a pool of ice.

And a hospital with an IV drip of morphine would be swell, too.

Pain consumed me as I tried to wash myself, giving up after the second swipe of the pouf. Shaving was out of the question and so was shampooing. I ended up air-drying to avoid moving more than necessary. Even brushing my teeth was an impossible task.

I popped the medicine cabinet open and located my secret stash of Vicodin. These had been prescribed to my father after he'd rolled his ankle from a joint training exercise with the CCFD. Seven years ago. I doubted they were still effective, but I was glad I had the forethought to swipe them from the trash when he'd thrown them away. They'd gotten me through some of the harsher beatings, but none had compared to this.

I opened the box of yeast ointment that had been a successful deterrent thus far to hide the pills and slid out the tissue paper lodged in the bottom of the box. As I unrolled the paper, my heart sank all over again. I had six left. I swallowed one, knowing it wouldn't be enough for this level of pain and rolled up the rest. I set them aside to take with me later.

Somehow, and to this day I didn't know how, I pulled on a long sleeve black turtleneck and jeans. It was going to be hot today, but I had to cover everything that he'd done. If anyone saw this, I'd wind up six feet under long before an investigation could even start.

He told me that. He *promised* me that.

And then he would go after Jamey, Ava, Poker...

I tried to brush my hair but decided it wasn't worth passing out over. The sensible thing would be to go sleep in my room, but he was here, and though I would be in complete hell, I couldn't be anywhere near him now. Just breathing the same air as that sick fuck soured my stomach. Or maybe that was the Vicodin. Probably both.

I managed to stick my dirty clothes into the washer and gave a half-assed attempt at assembling a lunch. I set aside a stack of bread on the counter to give to Poker on the way out. It would upset his stomach, but he was out of his hypoallergenic kibble. It was this, or he'd go hungry.

I collected the cash from my room, tempted to feed it to the garbage disposal. Making me give it back to the Scotts was another *fuck you* from my father.

I checked the time to see that it was already six o'clock. It had taken me almost three hours to finish what should take thirty minutes, and I still hadn't cleaned those fucking dishes or taken out the puke and piss-filled paper towels in the trash.

And I wouldn't. It was my silent *fuck you* to him.

Slinging my bag to my chest, I checked the pockets and then my wallet. I blew out a faltered sigh. Everything had remained untouched, Poker's money included. Maybe the JD had saved me this one time.

It was nothing short of a miracle that I arrived at school, but I gauged I was late by the number of cars in the lot. I spotted Jamey milling near our oak tree, and it took a solid minute of watching him march back and forth to see that his pacing had created a bald spot in the grass. Questions sprung to mind, but then I saw the phone at his ear.

Shit. Was he talking to Ben now, listening to his lies? Would Jamey believe me, or would he be loyal to the Scotts? The thought gutted me, but I...would understand. I had no defense other than my word.

Cheapo aviators were suddenly aimed my way as if he heard my thoughts across the quad, and then his long legs charged forward, eating up the distance between us. I must look worse than I thought. Like, ready for a chilled, sliding drawer in the morgue.

Jaw clenched, Jamey dropped his bag at my feet while pulling mine off my arms to do the same. "I knew it. I fucking knew he did something. You didn't come to my house this morning. Frankie said you didn't stop by the café to take care of the basket. You—"

Something drew his attention down, and I figured it was my trembling hands, until I felt the cuff of my sweater draw back. Jamey inhaled sharply, shifting his focus to my neck, pulling down my collar. Tearing his sunglasses off, his hazel eyes brimmed with tears, and he did nothing to hide it.

"What did he do to you?"

My lips were stuck in wobble mode, the words lodged somewhere around my collarbone.

"Mags." Before I could stop him, Jamey flung his arms around me. A sound best described as a dying animal erupted from my throat. It was as though I'd been pushed into a broiler, straight on the rack. Jamey released me, moving his hands to gently cradle my jaw, thumbs sweeping across my cheeks. I gathered I was crying again, but I couldn't divert that many brain cells to confirm it.

"Mags," he urged, "you need a hospital."

"C—can't."

He held me closer, and I caught the scent of cherry Starbursts. That wasn't helping the fact I was ready to vomit the nothingness in my stomach.

"*Why?*" he demanded.

"He..." *And I wouldn't stop with you...* I pinched my eyes until spots appeared, and when I shook my head, I swore every nerve in my back fissured apart. "I can't."

Stooping low, his eyes pleaded with mine. There was so much pain there, so much ugliness tangled between us. "I can't do this. I can't watch this and do nothing."

The words came out in a strangled whisper. "If you say anything, he'll hurt you, too." I fisted his T-shirt that read, IS IT GAY IN HERE OR IS IT JUST ME? "He'll hurt Ava, Jamey. Please, you can't."

We'd been over this so many times. The first time my father threatened Jamey's life, he left me with ten belt marks because I was late coming home from his house. He'd given me one strike for every minute.

"Tell me why he did this," Jamey insisted, shifting his sunglasses that he'd hung on his collar at some point.

Though it took a while, and I wasn't sure Jamey could understand anything I said, the story spilled out, starting with Mayor Ryan and ending with waking up this morning.

"I'm sorry," I sniffed. "And I wouldn't blame you if you didn't believe me. I—"

"Of course, I believe you. I'll always believe you." His gaze darkened, frost edging his words. "And don't you dare apologize. There is nothing you should apologize for." Shaking his head at the sky, he barked a dry laugh. "This was what Ben was freaking out about. That's why he left all those messages that he wanted to talk to me before class. He was trying to get to me first. Thinking I'd ever take his word over yours." Head dropping back down, he bit out, "Look at what they've done. Those fuckers."

They were fuckers, but after thinking it over, it didn't make any sense for Ben to frame me unless he was jealous of my relationship with Jamey. He had insinuated to Mr. Scott that I had been doing something suspicious in Mason's closet, and it was possible he'd kept me talking in Mason's room while someone slipped those earrings in my bag, but I...didn't believe he'd do that.

"I don't know who it was, but I don't think Ben—"

"Stop," he ordered. "Do not defend him to me. I don't care about Ben or his goddamn family. You are all I care about."

My gaze fell to the strawberry bruise on his neck that was shaped like a mouth, the very contradiction to that statement. Until ten minutes ago, Jamey did care about Ben. He cared about meeting his parents and wore a hideous collared shirt to Ben's birthday party just to impress them. He cared that Ben's father had called him *James*, and Ben had introduced him as his *buddy*. He cared about that moment Ben had kissed him, and all the ones that followed it. He cared that Ben had wanted to sit in the backseat all the way to Pacific Cliffs to hold his hand. He cared that Ben wore the bracelet he'd given him and all the little touches between them when they thought no one was looking. He cared about showing Ben that there was a place for him in this world, and he didn't have to feel alone and isolated. Until ten minutes ago, Jamey had cared.

"Don't say that," I pleaded. "You don't mean it."

In the sunlight, flecks of amber gleamed within a bed of mint green in Jamey's irises, flashing something so rare for me to see in him. Cold rage.

"Yes. I. Do."

Honestly, right this second, I didn't have the strength to argue. I barely had the strength to stand upright. "I need a favor. In my bag…there's money. I have to pay the Scotts back."

It took a pained moment, but once the meaning sunk in, his eyes turned hard again, and he punctuated every word. "Pay them back for what?"

"My wages."

"No." Head swiveling side to side, a muscle jumped at his temple. It wasn't until then that I realized he'd freshly dyed his hair a silver platinum, hiding the dark roots. "No fucking way."

Sniffing in an unladylike way, I used my sleeve to clean up the river of snot my nose was hosting. "Jamey, I have to. If I don't do what my father says or what Marcus wants… Please, don't fight me. I can't—" My words ended as a sob paralyzed my throat.

Oh, so slowly, Jamey nodded, his lips pulling away from his teeth. "Fine. Do you mind if I use it as toilet paper before I shove it down their throats?"

I pretended to think. "There weren't any stipulations on the condition of the money or how it was to be delivered. Can you eat a Union burrito first?"

"Blue Eyes, I'll eat ten and load 'em up with ghost pepper sauce." Leaning down, he pressed a kiss to my forehead, lips lingering.

Wilting against him, I mumbled into his chest, "He stole my money again, Jamey. All I have is what's left at your house. If those deposits from OHU aren't refunded, I'll never be able to leave. I'll be stuck here."

His frame stiffened. "Did he find the origami money?"

I think I shook my head, but it was difficult to tell at this point. "No." By the state of my dresser, I knew it was still there. There was no way he could find it unless he moved the furniture. There were roughly a thousand dollars hidden behind my dresser, but I had never planned to spend it. I didn't consider it mine. I wanted to return the money to whoever was leaving it at the café every Saturday morning. It was one of the boys, but I had yet to catch them in the act.

Jamey withdrew the cash from my bag and chucked it inside his. He shouldered both our backpacks, lacing his fingers with mine. "Did he find your birth control?"

"I wouldn't be here if he had." He was far too quiet, and I flicked a glance to see his expression.

I wouldn't doubt if Jamey had just cracked a molar.

Lady Gaga's voice blared from his pocket, which wasn't helping the enamel on his teeth. With impressive speed, his free hand shot down, and the song stopped.

Shaking his head, he gritted out, "Motherfucking richie."

"Jamey—"

"Did I miss something?" He wheeled on me so fast, I was shocked his sunglasses didn't fly off his collar. "Like an integral part of the story where Ben defended you, protected you? 'Cause I was pretty sure you said he stood by and watched as you were marched through that house after insinuating you were doing something questionable in Mason's room. Even if he didn't hide those earrings, and even if he doesn't know who did, Ben still instigated this. Then he turned his back on *my* best friend and walked out." Jamey dipped close, his nose squishing mine. "Fuck. Him."

I had nothing to say to that. He was right. If the roles were reversed, I would have had the same reaction. Though I knew he wanted to storm away, kick a tree, yell at a few inanimate objects, Jamey continued toward Finch Hall, keeping a slug pace with me.

Entering my Public Speaking class, Jamey guided me to my seat, up a bazillion stairs. I didn't look anywhere other than my feet, but I knew Mason was here, or rather, I could sense those cruel peridot eyes tracking me. He was my top suspect for setting me up, and that hurt almost as much as the bruises on my back. Okay, maybe in a month it would hurt almost as much.

It took everything I had not to scream at him, demand answers as to why they had done this to me. Was the entire weekend all a ploy in their twisted world? The final move in their elaborate game to be rid of me? Were Matt's hugs, Camden's jokes, Ben including me all part of it? Were Mason and Charlie hiding those earrings while I waited on the lawn for our run?

"Daaaaayum, girl." From his seat, Dylan let out a low whistle as his dark eyes followed my movements. "What kind of rager did you go to last night, and why didn't you invite me?"

Flattening him with a glare, Jamey set my bag on the floor. "What kind of hot mess are you used to waking up to that you think this says, *Last night was fucking epic!*"

Dipping back in his seat, Dylan's palms went up in surrender. "Fair point."

Muttering a curse, Jamey curled a hand around my elbow to help steady me as I sat. The pain along my tailbone was more than I thought I could handle, and the Vicodin sent up a reminder it was still in my stomach, but not for much longer.

"Uh, seriously, man," Dylan leaned in. "Should she be here?"

"No, she shouldn't." Jamey held his hand out to Dylan expectantly. "Phone."

Without asking why, Dylan handed his phone to Jamey. One side of his mouth curled up. "No name exchange, first? Kinky."

"Something tells me I'm not the first." Dylan snickered as Jamey typed something into the phone, then set the device on the desk. "I'm Jamey Hayes. You're Dylan Ward, my best friend's class partner, RAM, wide receiver for the Wolverines, and from what I understand, not a complete prick. So, Dylan, if anything, and I mean *anything* happens to her, you call me. Don't text. *Call.* Got it?"

Dylan's brows crept together. "You want to narrow down what *anything* means?"

Jamey's eyes hardened. "You'll know it when it happens."

"Nice," I grumbled, and now I was on the receiving end of that hazel glare.

"Your ass better be right here when I come back to get you for your next class. Dylan's going to make sure of it. Aren't you, Dylan?"

"I, uh…" Looming over us, Jamey's head swiveled, giving Dylan a look that made him nod emphatically. "Yeah. We'll be right here. Two peas, one pod, man. Promise."

Jamey pressed a kiss to my left temple. Said quite a bit about my current state that I hadn't even cared to check if my scar was covered.

He spoke only loud enough for me to hear. "You're loved, you know."

Before I could respond, Jamey pulled away, and along the journey out the classroom, his scowl was fused to one point in the room. Mason Scott. Oh, and he added two middle fingers to boot.

"So, Jamey seems…"

"Careful," I warned, and because I couldn't move my head, I let my eyes trail to my side. "I happen to know that he owns a glow-in-the-dark Green Lantern Funko Pop."

"Like I was saying." Dylan slid his phone back inside his pocket. "Jamey seems like he could be my next best friend."

"Yeah," I groaned the word as I shifted in my chair. "And he'd be the *best* best friend you ever had."

I didn't remember the rest of the day, how I'd made it to my classes, or even the topic of discussion. It was all muddled in a blur of pain and pain meds. There had been a decent attempt to eat the crappy lunch that had taken me an hour to assemble this morning, but the late August heat and the drugs swimming in my gut killed my appetite. Jamey took pity on me and let me use his lap as a pillow. He told me I'd fallen asleep, but my body disagreed.

At some point, Jamey said that he would pick up Poker's food from Henry's. I wanted to refuse the help, especially since Ava had taken the car to Pacific Cliffs for a supply run, which meant Jamey would have to transport fifty pounds of kibble on his bike across town. But if I did, Poker would suffer. I had no choice but to swallow my pride this time.

Turned out, I had to swallow a hell of a lot more than pride. Each step home sent a jolt of lightning up my back, pulsating my brain. And each step was a reminder of what the Scotts had done to me. Each step was a stab of regret that I'd allowed them into my heart, that I'd begged Mrs. Scott for a chance, called for the job, and pulled that damn want ad off the pinboard. That I had spent every Saturday of the last four years hoping to see a man who detested me almost as much as my father and thought I was a stupid failure, bringing shame to this school and town.

My biggest regret? Mason Scott.

If it hadn't been for that fucking storm, I never would have known the Scotts. With each day that passed, this nightmare of a life had only darkened, pulling me so far down that the light would never reach me.

I decided to take the back roads home along Laurel, to the trails that lead to the woods. It wasn't a shortcut by any means and never one I would attempt if it wasn't daytime, but Canyon Boulevard went right by the CCPD, and I didn't want any of the boys to see me like this. There would be questions, and those questions would only piss my father off more.

Hobbling along, mind fuzzy from my last Vicodin dose, beads of sweat dripped between my shoulder blades, and a few more trickled down between my breasts. My turtleneck was stuck to my skin, chaffing my back as if the fabric was constructed from steel wool. I hadn't even made it a half-mile when car tires rolled to a stop next to me. I looked over and winced as the sun gleamed off the hood of a familiar beige Taurus.

Jamey flew out of the passenger seat and scooped the backpack off my shoulder. "I knew you wouldn't stay in the quad like I told you. Thank God you didn't make it much further."

I snorted. "I'm actually quite proud I did make it this far."

He frowned, lowering his voice. "I was going to come back with an Uber. Frankie spotted me first."

"Oh. Well, that was nice of him to offer."

"Yeah," Jamey sighed and reached over to open the door for me, but I couldn't do much more than dead flop into the backseat.

Which was a mistake.

Closing my eyes, I waited for the pain to yield enough so I could lift my legs into the cabin.

"Here, drink this." I pried my eyes open to find Jamey holding a bottled water dotted with moisture. He even unscrewed the cap and drew a sip off the rim so I wouldn't spill it all over myself. It was a small gesture, one of millions. And each meant the world to me.

You're loved, you know.

Fighting the emotion strangling my voice as I took the bottle from him, I croaked, "Thanks." The cool water slid down my scratchy throat, and though the upper half of my digestive tract was happy, the lower half was not.

"Mags?"

I'd forgotten Frankie was even here until he'd said my name. I drew the lip of the bottle away from my mouth to find him in the driver's seat. Frankie's brow was bunched, so it looked as though a furry gray caterpillar had copped a squat above his eyes, but those brown eyes were different today. They weren't warm or soft. They were distant and hard. Assessing and damning me all in one look.

His tone wasn't any softer than the look in his eyes. "Jamey said you threw your back out again."

Threw my back out. That was my go-to excuse for when my father had been too rough with me.

I nodded, grunting as I lifted my feet onto the floorboard one at a time so Jamey could buckle me in like a toddler. After I mumbled a weary thanks, he shut my door. I thought about taking another sip of water but saw half my sweater was wearing my last sip.

Using the back of my hand, I wiped the dribble on my chin as another lie niggled its way into my mind. "Yeah. Poker spilled his water on the kitchen floor, and I slipped."

Frankie's jaw worked like he was trying to digest that reason and didn't like the taste of it. He gestured to Jamey as he slid into the passenger seat. "Well, I saw this stick walking around with a bag that weighed more than he does, and I couldn't let him pay to get to your house when I could drive him."

The jab would typically have been made with a smile, but there was none of that today. Not even a hint.

My gaze dropped to the label on the bottle as something unpleasant curled in my gut. It wasn't the water this time. "Thanks, Frankie."

His stare lingered on me for what felt like an eternity before Frankie turned forward and put the gear in Drive. "Sure, kid."

That made me pause. I was no longer *hon.* I was *kid.* And that was when I understood this for what it was. Frankie wasn't here to help either of us. He was here because he wanted to confront me. He *knew.* And if Frankie knew what had happened, everyone must have heard by now.

Resting my head on the seat, the back of my eyes seared with heat, betrayal thickening my throat. The Scotts had tainted what little good there was in my life.

During the ride home, I didn't speak or open my eyes. The migraine did a decent job at blocking out Jamey and Frankie's chatter but did nothing to distract me from the pain slicing into my brain like shards of glass.

Once I felt the car come to a complete stop, I opened my eyes to find we were parked outside of my house. Jamey got out to run the bag of food and my backpack inside. I watched from behind the window as Poker followed Jamey without his usual peppy gait or wag of his tail. His stomach had to be hurting from the bread, and it would take days before he'd feel better.

I guess I hadn't heard Frankie get out of the car, but he met me on my side and opened the door. I couldn't get my fingers to disengage the damn belt, and Frankie had to reach in and do that for me, too.

I gripped the doorframe and worked my way out of the car, struggling to find a modicum of balance. I lifted my chin as Frankie looked away.

"Thanks again."

He nodded before bringing his eyes back to me. His gaze didn't linger.

"Mags." He more or less coughed my name. "Look, I'm not going to pretend that I don't know what's going on. Nate stopped over this morning and filled me in. He thought I should know being that…" His gaze flicked to mine before dropping to his black Rockports. "Well, being that you have access to the safe and all. Now I haven't seen any discrepancies in the deposits, so I— I'm not going to ask why you did it. I've always had a soft spot for you and could use you around the café if you want your Sunday shifts again. Maybe pick up some more during the week when you feel up to it."

That was like another hit of the baton. Right to my legs, taking them out from under me. This man who I had known most of my life, the man who I had worked for—without pay—for years, and it took one conversation with my father for him to turn on me.

I'd never done Frankie or Paula wrong. I'd admired him for how he doted on his wife, for never looking down on me, treating me no different. He never even had to tell me what needed to be done around the café. Sometimes words weren't even spoken, we worked so well together.

And now that was all gone.

I should have told him to fuck off for believing my father, for not bothering to even ask me *if* I did it. But I was up against the Great Nathan Davis, after all. Crescent Cove's personal Superman.

No one questioned the hero when they pointed to the villain.

I was not disillusioned to the fact that the only reason Frankie had asked me to work was that no one else would demean themselves to work for nothing but tips. The café was at risk of closing like Trudy's flower shop, and he was only worried about *his* wife, *his* bills, *his* restaurant, and not the broken girl barely able to stand in front of him.

But I had…nothing and nowhere to go.

No one else would hire me now. My father had made sure of it.

Hiding the bitterness and the hatred building in my blood, the words grated out of me. "That would be great. I'll see you Friday."

chapter eight

mason

I shut off my morning alarm, a muscle in my neck straining as I struggled to a sitting position. At some point between going from horizontal to vertical, I realized it was Tuesday. Squeezing the butterfly pillow to my bare chest, I stared out Faith's bedroom window as the sun chased away the midnight sky and cut through the fog blanketing the lake. I stretched, the ache in my thighs still present from my Sunday run, my sister's floor had done a number on my spinal cord, and yesterday's drills with Coach Watkins took care of the rest.

Good ol' Watkins didn't believe in using dummies during practice because it made for "soft players." Instead, I was voluntold to mow down half the defensive line during jump cut drills as Adam, Noah, and Jordon tackled me from behind, all while I was tethered to a tire. A real motherfucking tire that I suspected had human blood in the tread. Coach called it "RLOT." Real Life Offensive Training. I wondered if he made his Marines use live grenades. Reassessing my bruised kidney and fractured vertebrae, I'd go with a yes.

As my bones did the Snap-Crackle-Pop routine, I placed the pillow back into its designated spot on the bed and headed to my room for a proper defunkification. Mom had enough problems and didn't need to smell the JD oozing out of my pores. I shouldn't have stayed here last night and honestly didn't know why I had.

After a hot shower and a quick dry, I wrapped the towel around my waist. I was in a Henley mood today, and they were all hanging in my closet instead of earning wrinkles in my drawer. Just one of the hundreds of reminders of who had been in my house, organized my things, touched my shit.

As I opened the closet door, I immediately stumbled back.

What I saw was a shot to the gut. My hand rose and then dropped to my side as if it were filled with wet sand.

With everything going on, I'd completely forgotten that Ben had said he'd found Maggie poking around in my room. I'd shrugged it off at the time because it was her job to be in here. And I had trusted her. But this...

Damn her. Damn her for putting that there.

When had she hung this in my closet? Before she stole from us? After? Was the hand that touched this thing the same hand that had touched my sister's earrings? Did she smile to herself, thinking I'd want this shit?

Fuck her.

I snapped it off the hanger, breaking the yarn necklace as the oval foil crumpled in my palm. I balled it up until it was nothing more than a speck of red, so I could no longer see the black sharpie seeds or the green rim that resembled a watermelon medal.

I hated it.

I *hated* her.

Dressed now, I had that fucking thing in my grip as I took to the stairs. Penetrating through the house were dulled clinks of ceramic along with the dense aroma of coffee melding with something not nearly as pleasant. I stepped onto the landing to the sight of Matt draped over the island, having spent last night at the house, too. He looked like he'd rather face-plant into his cereal than eat it. Mom was at her spot at the kitchen table, having spent another night with a tissue box, and Dad's posture suggested he was hauling invisible rocks on his back.

It was as though we'd lost Faith all over again.

I pulled open the trash drawer, lungs stilling as my fisted hand hovered there. Right on top of the garbage was the uneaten apple pie Maggie had made on Sunday. The entire thing plus the glass dish had been thrown away. Beneath that was the corner of one of Matt's sketchbooks. He'd ripped it in half. It looked like he had tried to shove it to the bottom of the can, and I briefly wondered if it was full of Maggie's image.

Shame that he'd wasted his talent on her.

I dropped the yarn and foil into the trash and slammed it shut. Unfortunately, we had soft close drawers, so I didn't have a satisfying *slam* to accompany my anger. Instead, the quiet *swoosh* prickled my skin.

Deciding I'd try something other than liquid calories today, I opened the pantry door to fish out the box of my favorite breakfast cereal, Lucky Charms. But as soon as I saw that leprechaun, my hand itched to launch a punch right between his stupid orange eyebrows. *Rainbow Run.* Fucking hell.

Since it was either this or what may have been scrambled eggs on the stove—it was hard to tell around the charring—I chose the whole grain magical deliciousness. It wasn't until I chewed the first spoonful that I remembered Maggie had bought this. Plus the milk. Well, she'd bought them with our money.

I then remembered startling her Sunday morning when she came up the front steps, and that had been an accident. I had also saved her from cracking her head open on those steps by wrapping my arms around her and holding her body against mine, and that *hadn't* been an accident. No, I recalled enjoying that quite a lot, along with the feel of those petite curves against mine, holding her longer than necessary.

The crunchy marshmallows did nothing to help get the oats down my throat. I may as well be eating sawdust. As I shoveled in another bite, my gaze lifted to the jar of money on the counter. The jar of money that Maggie had put the change into. Or…had she?

After two bites, I dumped my bowl into the sink and emptied the jar onto the island. Had to say, I was surprised when coins went rolling every which way, and a heap of green bills plopped onto the granite. While I counted, my family remained quiet, only allowing the *pings* of metal and *pffts* of shifting paper to pervade the room.

"Four hundred and sixty-three?" I asked Mom when I was done.

She considered me for a moment. "That's probably right after her grocery trips. I…wasn't checking because—" Mom loosed a sigh that was as weary as her soul. "I trusted her, so I threw out the receipts."

"Taking cash slowly would have been smarter," Dad muttered, poking at the congealed blob on his plate. "We wouldn't have known, and she could keep stealing."

Matt set down his coffee mug after a sip. "Yeah, but earrings are fast money. They're small and could be lost easily. She just chose the wrong damn ones to take."

Sinking into her seat, Mom rubbed her temples. "I don't get it. I thought she liked us and was happy here. Why would she do this? She let me think I was crazy and even helped us search the house." Shivering, Mom wrapped her arms around herself.

Looking to her, frown lines framed Dad's mouth. "Who knows why she did it, Eve. When it comes down to it, what do we know about her? She works at the café. She can cook and clean. That's it. We saw her as she wanted us to. A façade." Dad focused on me as I stuffed the cash back into the jar. "Mason, you seemed to be spending a lot of time with her lately. Did she ever say anything odd to you?"

I thought that over, picking apart every conversation we'd had, including the ones my parents still didn't know about. The way we'd met during the blackout, our date that never was, when I tried to buy her out of our lives…

And what I want now is money, and I'll do whatever I must to get it.

That she had.

"Everything about her was odd. She was so closed off. I didn't learn much about her, but there was—" I shook my head as a memory crawled to the surface. "I honestly don't think it's worth mentioning considering the source."

"What is it?" he prompted.

My stomach tightened, and I wanted to think that was its plea to eat more, but I knew it stemmed from that warning. One that I should have heeded. "It was something Eric Ryan had said. That Maggie was the town pariah, a pathological liar, and…" I gritted my molars. "I refused to give that asshole any credibility, except after Eric attacked her, Maggie had said the same thing about herself. They had a history, went to CCH together. She claims that she witnessed Eric and his friend gang rape a girl during their junior year, but no one believed her. Even the victim denied it. I had no reason to doubt Maggie, but…who the hell knows. She lied to me about where she lived, never mentioned her father was a cop, and you heard Chief Davis. It sounded like he's run the gauntlet with her. And then there's the poker…."

"Christ, I forgot about that." Matt scrubbed a hand through his hair. "I can't believe we let her into our house."

What he really meant was our hearts.

Mom pushed her untouched toast across the kitchen table. "Well, no more want ads. I learned my lesson. I'm so sorry, guys."

"Mom, it's not your fault. She fooled all of us." The corners of Matt's mouth flipped down as he crossed the room to give her a hug. After a long embrace, he flicked his wrist to read the time, and it was then that I spotted the charcoal stains on his hands from sketching. As Mom sagged against him, he pulled away regretfully. "I'm gonna be late, and I have to swing by the RAM house before our morning meeting."

Leaning up, she pressed a kiss to his cheek. "Okay. Be safe."

"Always. I'll see you guys later." Matt gave Dad a hug next and then one for me. Drawing back, he stared at me dead on and whispered, "Eat something, Mase."

"I will," I lied.

After a meeting consisting of Coach Bell's film analysis and Watkins' promise of hosting freeze drills on an active minefield, I stepped out of the Athletic Complex doors, shut my eyes, and greedily sucked down a lungful of air that wasn't laden with the stench of moldy wood or feet. My moment of solitude was broken by an auditory assault of whirring drills and thwacking hammers as crews worked on repairing the mold damage from the roof leak during the summer storm.

The campus had been without a gym for weeks, with the team still rotating workouts between our home gyms and the fraternity houses. I was over it and ready to have my life return to normal. And I certainly didn't want to field the inevitable questions from my teammates as to why a certain someone no longer worked in my home. Still didn't know what I would say to that. No matter what reason I gave, the guys were going to take it hard. They'd become strangely...attached to Maggie in a short amount of time. Everyone had.

A familiar hand landed on my shoulder, stopping me. "You didn't lose your shit. I'm proud of you."

Cocking a brow, my gaze slid to my cousin. "You wouldn't say that if you knew the thoughts running through my head, Cam."

Hand falling to his side, he shrugged. "You sat in the same room with Eric for an hour and didn't add more bandages to his face. I'd say that's progress."

"It wasn't out of lack of wanting," I muttered, scanning the lot. Idling a few lanes over was a dark gray Rover, the driver letting his head hang low.

Nothing about that was good.

Ben was in complete shutdown mode. He'd refused to answer my calls and texts, wouldn't speak to me when I'd stopped by his house last night, and word was, he skipped both Coach Zawasky's meeting and practice yesterday. I wasn't even sure if he'd gone to class.

"How is your brother?"

The corners of Cam's mouth sloped down as he tracked my gaze to the SUV. "No bueno." He took a step, then stopped. His hands curled into fists then shook them loose. "Can you take point? You're better at reaching him."

I wasn't so sure about that. Ben and I were the closest out of all cousins, but that might have something to do with us being the broodier of the bunch. Matt and Rich deflected their shit, Cam and Ethan partied away their shit, and Ben and I wallowed in our shit. Ben had been so deep in it this summer that he'd contemplated suicide, and I— I didn't have a clue he'd gotten to that point. So, if I was Ben's best shot, the poor bastard was fucked.

With purpose, our steps closed in on the SUV, but a silver i8 Roadster purred to a stop in front of us, blocking our intended target. I sighed.

"You deal with this yet?" Cam asked.

"No," I groaned with a rub of my eyes. "Been a little busy."

"With…?"

Dropping my hand, I cranked my head around to glare at Cam, and he glared back without apology. If that was a shot at how I'd spent the last couple of nights, I was so down to kick his hypocritical ass.

The door to the BMW scissored upward and out stepped long legs covered in knee-high black suede boots, a miniskirt revealing a tantalizing stretch of skin, and as the rest of the five-foot-nine-inch body emerged, blonde curls floated over a gray sweater that bared one tanned shoulder. Plump pink lips stood out against the cat-eye Miu Miu sunglasses that were no doubt photographed in at least fifty-eight selfies before one was chosen to feature on all her social media this morning as if it were a casual afterthought.

Charlie left the car door open as her thin heels snapped toward us, the sweater falling low enough to indicate there was nothing beneath.

Staring at her, Cam slanted his head to one side. "Why is it again you two aren't hitting it on the regular?"

Charlie answered, "Because Mason couldn't handle me."

"Miss Price, my cousin doesn't represent the Scott name properly." Grin curling one side of his mouth, Cam threw her a wink. "I'd be more than happy to demonstrate my *handling skills*."

"I'm sure she's heard about your skills from half the Zeta house," I stated drolly.

"More like three-quarters," Charlie corrected, and Cam's smile broadened. Her dark shades faced me. "Mase, could we…talk?"

I tipped my head to look past her. Ben could bolt any second. "Now's not a good time."

It was subtle, but she inched over to block my view of the Rover, and my jaw hardened. "Please, Mase. You've been putting me off for days. I know you're pissed and with good reason. I swear I'll take care of it. But it's just that Tay and I were getting along so well this weekend, and I didn't want to ruin it. I mean…Sunday was all her idea. She wanted to drive down the coast and then help plan the gala with Eve and me.

She *wanted* to spend time with me. That hasn't happened in years, and it's thanks to you. And, yes, she went too far with Maggie, but—"

"Charlie—" Cam butted in, but she kept rolling.

"No, I know!" Her purse—that probably cost as much as a mid-sized sedan—swung down to the crook of her elbow as both palms went into the air. "It was coming from a good place. I know that's hard to believe with Taylor, but she meant well. I mean, it's impossible not to see that you and Maggie are getting close. She was protecting me. That's all. And I was going to tell her the truth about us after we left your place on Sunday, but she suddenly canceled our plans when she dropped me off at the Zeta house. I can't exactly tell her this in a text—"

"Charlie, I don't give a fuck if you tell Taylor or not. It doesn't matter anymore."

Her hands lowered, the luggage purse slipping off her arm and landing on the asphalt. Pretty sure that was a sin of the eleventh commandment or something.

"What does that mean?" she asked.

"That Maggie is a nonissue, so do what you want. Just tell me where and when you need me to play my part."

She tore off her sunglasses, thick fringes of lashes batting at me. "What happened to Maggie?"

"Charlie..." I counted to three, and that was as high as I could get. "I don't want to get into this now, but if you see Maggie, steer clear of her. Okay?"

Her brows drew together. "Um, yeah, okay. But what—"

"Like I said, now's not a good time." Without another word, I diverted around her, the purse, and the Roadster. Dickish? Yeah. And I knew just how much because even *Cam* was apologizing for me.

I opened the passenger door of the Rover, instantly overtaken by the stale scent of leather mixing with rank whiskey sweats. Jesus. Ben wasn't usually this heavy of a drinker, but I wasn't going to pull a Cam and open my trap about it.

I slid into the seat as Cam took the spot behind his brother. As if in sync, we shut our doors, trapping all of us plus that odor inside. Ben had yet to move. Or blink. If his wrinkled clothes weren't shocking enough, his jaw was peppered with thick stubble, his hair wasn't shellacked into place, and there were dark circles around his eyes.

This was bad.

I slid my palm over his shoulder and gripped tight. "You talk to Jamey?"

Fingers raking through his hair, the braided leather bracelet Jamey had given Ben on his birthday shifted, the rainbow clasp catching the light.

"Well..." He sounded like he gargled with broken glass. "Until today, his vocabulary hadn't expanded past *fuck* and *off*, so not a lot of talking has occurred." Still refusing to lift his gaze, Ben handed me the bulging yellow envelope sitting on his lap. "But he did throw this at me. Literally. At my head."

I opened the envelope to see the thing was filled with quarter-sized olive balls that were...one-dollar bills. That was dedication right there. I didn't want it, but I knew Ben wanted it even less, so I shoved it into my bag.

"Ben, give him some time. He'll come around," I reasoned.

A choked laugh erupted out of him. "I don't see that happening, considering he would like us all to go to Hell and for our limp dicks to, and I quote, *'Desiccate and rot off our bodies.'*"

Cam mumbled, "Well, that took a dark turn."

"You should have seen the way he *looked* at me." Ben's voice cracked, and that sliced me wide open. "It was like...he loathed me, and I— Fuck!" His fist slammed down on the steering wheel, punching the horn, and a dude walking by flipped us off. Pretty sure it was my TA from Bio Chem.

Cam reached over from the back of the cab. "Ben, chillax."

Ben turned to face him, his swollen eyes bright with fury. "*Chillax?* My life is turning to shit, and you want me to *chillax?*"

"Yeah, I do," Cam barked back, leaning forward in his seat. "Man the fuck up. You can't act this way every time your ass gets dumped."

Ben's face screwed up, pounding the console this time. "Get the fuck out! Get the fuck out of my fucking car! And take that fucking money with you!"

We wisely exited as Ben beat the shit out of his dashboard next.

Looking on, Cam observed, "Who knew ass fuckers were so emotional."

Rotating to face my cousin, my palm clipped the back of his head. "What happened to me taking point?"

Shouldering his bag, Cam sniffed. "I didn't realize you were going to turtle it, Coz. I got shit to do today."

"Turtle..." I shook my head in astonishment. "Where is your sensitivity? That's your little brother!"

Cam's eyes bugged out of his head, pointing to the SUV. "You listen to a grown-ass man whine for two days straight and tell me where your sensitivity level is. I've been locked up with him since Sunday because

94 | ashlan thomas

Mom won't let me go back to the RAM house until he eats a damn meal and takes a fucking shower. She even made me drive to Pacific Cliffs to get him that coconut curry crap he loves, and not only did the asshole *not* eat it, but he drank all the fucking whiskey. Even Dad's Lagavulin. So how about some sensitivity for me?"

I blinked down at him. "There is no way the Scott genes run through your veins."

"Listen. Just because—"

Buzz. That vibration came from both of our phones, and a cold shot of awareness tingled along the back of my neck. Text blasts only came from one person and for one of two reasons: Wolverine business or RAM business. And since we just came from a Wolverine meeting...

Cam drew his phone out the same time I did. "I only need one guess what this is about." After reading the text, he grunted and shoved the phone into his front pocket. "It's both a pleasure and a curse being me."

Though I already knew not only who had sent the text but what the subject matter was, I swiped my thumb across the screen.

Adam: *Mandatory RAM mtg tmw nite.*

"Shit."

Cam aimed a raised brow my way. "You knew he wasn't going to let it go. Brady has a hard-on for Eric. Hell, the two were practically sitting in each other's laps a few minutes ago."

They had been, and I didn't miss the look Brady shot me when I had walked into the lounge. Frowning, I disappeared my phone inside my pocket, wishing I could do the same with that text.

Cam studied me for way too long, causing unease to creep along my skin like an itchy blanket. "Mase, I gotta ask. How sure are you that Eric was going to hit Maggie?"

I met his gaze and stated, "A hundred."

He inhaled through his nose. "Is it? Because I didn't see shit. Uncle Dan and I came in just as you rushed the room, and Maggie was already on the floor. You know I've got your back no matter what. I want that fucker out as much as you, and if this is how we do it, I'm good with that. There's no way in hell I'd ever forgive him for what he did to Faith, but he claims he didn't touch Maggie, and she overreacted. I have to admit, Coz, that jives with what I saw. And, sadly, Maggie's lost all her cred with me."

Lowering my head, a steady stream of air left me. Truth was, I wasn't sure. I was somewhere around...thirty percent. Maggie was down when I came in, and Eric had been towering over her, but his intent could have been to help her up. That scenario was highly unlikely since I had witnessed their interaction in my foyer last week when Eric *had* threatened Maggie. I'd kept my cool then, but at Ben's party, I was close to losing it. The only thing that kept me on this side of sane was the memory of that day when Eric had broken Faith's arm. I'd come to, saw Eric unconscious on my floor, blood covering my hands and clothes, waiting to hear if I'd killed him.

I told Maggie that I hadn't regretted what I'd done, but…I never wanted to lose control like that again. And I hadn't since. There was a line between humanity and darkness, and the instant I knew he'd broken my sister's arm, I'd left the light without care or thought.

"Alright then, we need to get ahead of this." Cam paused, deep in thought, which was a rare look on him. "We should get our stories straight in case Brady calls Maggie in to testify."

The two bites of Lucky Charms I'd had earlier went rancid in my gut. "God, I hadn't even thought of that."

Cam scanned the lot and then nodded to the i8 parked a few spaces down from my Raptor. "What about Charlie? She can prove a history of assault, attempted rape."

I gripped the back of my neck, working out a knot that promised to turn into a headache later. "She has a shoot up north tomorrow. Even if she didn't, she doesn't want to bring any attention to what happened at the RAM party. She wants to bury it." *Like everything else.*

He let out a low-pitched whistle. "Okay. Then one of us needs to talk to Maggie. Find out if Brady contacted her and what her story is. If we go into that meeting saying that you reacted because Eric was attacking her, and she decides to fuck us over again and says different…it's not going to be good for you, Mase."

I cursed under my breath. Talking to Maggie… Cam was right. This needed to be dealt with, but letting him talk with Maggie might turn out as well as our talk with Ben had, which meant, *I* needed to deal with her.

This was what I got for playing a hero.

chapter nine

maggie

I was ready to slam my pounding head against my locker by my fourth failed attempt to open it. My luck, I'd bust the thing open but knock myself out in the process. And had I been anywhere else on planet Earth, I might be worried that someone would steal all my worthless crap as I lay unconscious on the ground, but since I was in the land of the richies, that was a nonissue.

Because, apparently, richies only stole diamond earrings.

That belonged to their own mothers.

The metal door rattled as I lined the dial to twenty-four, and…flew right past it for the fifth time.

A fresh wave of fire licked down my back from holding up my arm, and all at once, my vision blurred together, stomach dipping as the ground did the same. My mouth flooded with saliva as bile tinged the back of my throat. I swallowed it down.

Today, my symptoms had been an interesting mixture of preictal, postictal, and imminent death. The cooing doves in the courtyard sounded like squawking pterodactyls in my ears, my skull might be shrinking, and someone was stabbing the back of my eyeballs with hot needles. I squeezed my eyes to shut it all out and gripped that combination lock so hard it left an impression in my palm.

Between this monster migraine and the makers of Master Lock doing their job too well, I wanted to scream and throw down like a toddler right here and now. And it was only Tuesday afternoon.

Where was Jamey? He was supposed to meet—

Oh, right. I'd forgotten. He told me he had to stay late today and tomorrow to complete a photography project. I hated that I didn't even know what he was working on. I hadn't even thought to ask him.

Awesome friend you are.

Jamey was, though. I didn't know how he did it, but he'd been there after every one of my classes to carry my bag, walk with me, and keep me from falling over. And here I was, forgetting something he'd repeated to me three times during lunch, all so I wouldn't wait for him outside of Crenshaw's lecture hall for ten minutes. A lecture on exponential and logarithmic functions that I must have slept through because the only thing I'd gotten out of it was an imprint of a spiral notebook on my forehead. Thankfully, Adam took pity on me and let me borrow his notes, and my only thought when he handed over his notebook was that he must not have heard I was a grave robber yet.

All I wanted to do was crawl into a corner, swallow the last Vicodin that I'd been hoarding and then pass out. Or die. Whatever. I wasn't picky. That wasn't going to happen, though, because I'd half-assed my chores this morning and still had to make dinner, not to mention study for two tests and start my essay for a psych paper due on Monday.

I couldn't even think about how I would work at the café this weekend, stand at the cooktop, bus tables, lift…anything. I hadn't been downtown since Sunday, and considering that Frankie thought I was pond scum, I didn't hold out much hope that he and Henry had done anything with the basket—

The back of my neck suddenly prickled with awareness, and my eyes flew open. I rotated my head, my vision swimming together as I locked onto an all too familiar peridot glare. Dark and narrowed, those eyes speared right through me. I hadn't a clue how long Mason had been standing at the end of the tunnel, watching me fail at life. He must be enjoying the show. Actually, strike that. He didn't look as if he were enjoying anything, which confused me because this was precisely what he wanted. To break me.

The sun warmed Mason's hair, copper strung through the thick, dark strands, inviting my hands to play with it and ruffle the colors together, but the same sun hardened the planes of his face, the shadows glancing off his cheekbones, features harsh and cold. The wide breadth of Mason's shoulders were heavy and stiff like a pair of cinder blocks had taken the place of his bones, the fabric of his shirt was taut across his chest, and the muscles of his forearms bunched as he held his fists at his sides. His thighs bulged against his tech shorts, calves equally strong and holding a stance that suggested he was ready to charge.

His reason for being here couldn't have been anything other than me. There were a total of twenty lockers on campus, and only two of them were occupied. Jamey rented the other. This underpass wasn't a shortcut to anywhere, and I doubted more than three people on campus knew this place existed. Even the bookstore clerk had to ask two custodians where the locker bay was. So, Mason finding me was either a complete accident, or…he wasn't done breaking me.

His lips parted. Shut. Maybe a miracle happened, and he would admit to that he'd put those earrings in my bag, or perhaps the Scotts had discovered they had a ghost in their house. A jewelry thieving ghost.

Mason lingered there, disgust seeping into his features. One side of his mouth slowly curled before he spat, "Fuck it."

As soon as he turned away from me, the words flew out of my mouth. "Yeah? Well, fuck you, too, asshole!"

I didn't care to see if he had any reaction. I released the grip on my locker, giving up on my books and notes and starting my phobia paper. There was no way I could concentrate long enough to even write down my topic: geniophobia, the fear of chins. Which was not to be confused with genuphobia, the fear of knees. Or genophobia, the fear of sex.

I didn't have any experience to base this on, but that last one might really suck.

Leaning over enough for my fingers to curl around the strap of my bag, I dragged the thing out of the locker bay and toward the courtyard. The shitshow that was my life was about to get a whole lot shittier. I just didn't know it yet. Not until the other thorn in my side blocked me from leaving.

I sighed.

"What do you want." It wasn't a question, more like a demand that he apologize for existing.

Eric's gaze slithered over me, his lashes bending around the thick bandage across the bridge of his nose and up his forehead. "I imagine the same as what my father already spoke to you about."

"Oh? You'd also like to threaten my best friend and me with getting kicked out of Warrington?"

It could have been surprise that flickered in his blood-shot eyes, but the bruising and general swollenness made it hard to tell. I had to admit. I was a wee bit jealous Mason got to hit him, and I didn't.

Since standing was haaaard, I leaned a shoulder against the wall and released the pathetic hold on my bag. "What's wrong, Eric? Daddy left out that part of our happy convo? Does he not share all the dirt with you?"

His nostrils flared, and I imagined that had to hurt. Good. "I didn't mean for what happened on Saturday to get out of hand. I had too much to drink and was just reacting to the things you said. We both know I never hit you."

"Wow." I wanted to shake my head, but the muscles in my neck were knotted in agony. "Forgive me, my hearing is a little off. Did you seriously say it was my fault that you threatened to assault me? Is this what they're teaching boys these days?"

His chest rose sharply, his restraint precarious at best. "It's Tuesday. Time's running out. There is a mandatory RAM meeting regarding my pledgeship tomorrow night. Fix this with the Scotts before then."

A sad laugh bubbled out of me. "Well, sonny. You're shit outta luck on the Scott front. They're not going to listen to me."

His lids tapered low, pulling at the thin scar above his eye—the one Mason gave him five years ago. "They think the sun shines out of your ass. Of course, they'll listen to you."

"I don't work for them anymore, Eric. Turns out they're just as corrupt and evil as your family. Truly, I don't see why you all aren't swapping Thanksgiving recipes and Christmas cards."

"Bullshit."

I released an exasperated breath. "You're right. It's bullshit. We done?"

His dull brown eyes pierced into mine. "I need to be in that RAM house, Maggie."

"I'll get right on it," I drawled. "You're my top priority."

"I should be." Hand landing on the wall an inch from my face, Eric slid closer, voice dripping with malice. "Contrary to what you believe, I do know all the dirt. Specifically, the piles of it covering the buried bodies." A gleam shone in his eyes, unsettling me to my very core. "And I know how they got there. So don't make the wrong choice here, *Spaz*. Nothing good happens to those who do."

With that, Eric pushed off the wall and stormed away.

Though Eric didn't know it, this meeting was a waste of his time. I had every intention of making the wrong choice. But it did make me wonder what secrets Marcus Ryan had shared with his son. And if those secrets really did include buried bodies.

chapter ten

maggie

On Wednesday, at the speed of a three legged-sloth, I headed toward a building I never wanted to be in again, looking for a guy I didn't want to speak with, all to convince a group of men I didn't care about to allow a complete douche who I absolutely loathed back into their brotherhood.

Fuck my life. For reals.

I swiped at what had become a semi-permanent sheen of sweat on my forehead as my feet swerved. I decided to deviate from the sidewalk altogether and dragged my ass across the lawn instead. I figured if I fell, I'd have a softer landing zone. I peered up to gauge how much further I had to go. Good news, I wasn't far from the four-story mansion.

Bad news, I wasn't far from the four-story mansion.

Rather than think about how much this sucked, I concentrated on my psych paper that I'd yet to start because after making dinner last night, folding my father's laundry, getting his uniform ready—that I'd later discovered he had picked up from the cleaners before my beating—and taking care of Poker, I was done. But I hadn't slept. I'd laid on my bed, staring at Adam's class notes as if learning by osmosis was a thing. Ironically, the most sleep I'd had in three days had been during calculus class yesterday.

"Hate to tell you this..." I paused my shuffling when Jamey's voice spoke behind me. "But you're nowhere near your house."

"How did you know—" I resumed my forward momentum. "Whatever. I'm beyond caring."

"How did I know you'd be here?" he finished my thought. "I didn't. I finished in the photo lab early and saw you leaving. In the wrong direction." Jamey caught up to me, pushing his bike alongside him. I sighed. I missed my bike. I missed sitting without almost passing out more. "So, what are we doing here, Mags?"

"Wanted to check out the architecture."

"No." His hand shot out in front of me like one of those security arm gates at a parking garage, effectively stopping me, but my reflexes were discombobulated. My back tensed, every nerve lighting up as if my muscles were boobytrapped with TNT. Stars burst behind my eyelids as my stomach bottomed out. I teetered on my feet, the earth swaying beneath me.

Cursing, Jamey caught my elbow, letting his bike crash to the ground. "*Christ, Mags.* What made you think you could do this?"

I scraped a wad of hair out of my mouth with my free hand as Jamey kept me steady. "I didn't, but it's not like I have a choice. My messages for Brady have gone unanswered, no one will give me his cell number, and I even gave Dylan a note that I needed to speak to him, but the guy hasn't called me back. And while it sucks exponentially that I had to physically come here on the off chance that I could speak to Brady face to face, I figured it would suck way less than another beating."

"Mags—"

"I'll be damned if I'm the reason Marcus takes your scholarship away. I will do everything in my power to stop that from happening." I didn't put it past Marcus to do it regardless, just to spite me. He was that evil.

Jamey's hazel eyes softened. "Don't do this. There's—"

"There is no other way. You know there isn't. I need to do this, Jamey. Please. Don't let me live with the guilt of not trying."

A wave of dizziness surged, and I released a jagged breath as it passed. I turned my focus to the gray brick building ahead, fuzzier than I remembered. The white columns looked extra shiny in the late afternoon sun, forcing me to squint. The lawn was as lush and green as the grass on campus, but the earthy scent roiled my stomach. I forced my focus to the PAM on the pediment, black and soulless, representing everything I hated about Crescent Cove.

The richies.

There were more vehicles in the gated parking lot than what had been here the last and only time I'd come to the RAM house, and I figured the meeting planned later tonight had something to do with that.

Marcus had organized this. His chess pieces were aligned to strike, awaiting my move.

"Did they put in more stairs? I don't remember climbing so many." That was more of a wail than actual English. Warrington sure did like stairs. I had to go up or down a flight for just about every class.

Jamey shouldered my bag and spared his Huffy one last glance, leaving it on the lawn. "Come on. Let's get this over with."

After trekking up all of eight stairs and having to stop twice to give me a breather, we were on the porch. Jamey hit the doorbell. Last time, Adam and Camden had answered the intercom as soon as I pressed that button.

Today…silence.

"Jamey?" Apprehension squeezed my chest as we neared the minute mark of just standing here. "What if they don't answer? What if they refuse to let me talk to Bra—"

The door flew wide, causing both of us to jump. Ben stood there gripping the doorjamb, huffing as if he'd sprinted from the top floor. He tore his widened gaze away from a disinterested Jameson Hayes to me.

Then he recoiled. "Holy fuck."

I lifted a brow. "Am I having an aura, 'cause I feel like we've done this before."

"You have," Jamey drawled, inspecting the blue stain on his nailbeds. "But this time, feel free to kick him in the balls. If you can find them."

Ouch.

Cringing, Ben's chocolate eyes bounced to Jamey and back to me. "Mags, you…you don't look so good."

"You're not one to talk." Seriously, he seemed to have aged ten years in a matter of days.

"Ben? What's wrong? Who's at the…" Mason's voice trailed off when he appeared in the doorway, and everything about him from the concern in his eyes, the slack of his jaw, and even the low position of his shoulders changed in an instant, turning stiff and cold with rage. He gripped Ben's forearm as if he needed to protect him from us, pinning me with a glare. "I really don't need to ask, but what are you doing here, Maggie?"

Ah, I was no longer *Sticks*. So this was what it took to shake the nickname.

"The Kappas are hosting a wicked caber toss competition. Thought the RAMs would like to join in. As the cabers."

Mason's gaze tapered to shards of peridot.

Cursing under his breath, Jamey rolled his eyes. "She's here to speak to Brady."

A voice I recognized and equally disliked asked, "And why would she need to speak with Brady."

Oh, fun. I guess two Scotts weren't enough to guard the RAM entrance. A third had come to join the blockade. This one was a virtual twin for his younger brother, but I knew the differences only too well. Matt stood no more than two inches taller than Mason, a little bulkier, his hair a bit shorter but the exact same shade of deep brown, and though they both had green eyes, Matt's were a rich emerald split by blades of sapphires. Where they were exactly alike?

They both looked at me as if I were a bag of shit on their porch.

"*She*," I snapped, aiming a glare at Matt, "doesn't answer to you."

Matt blatantly stared back. "If this is regarding RAM business, you sure as fuck will."

"*Matt*," Ben snarled, shoving his cousin aside. "Back off. You, too, Mase." Pushing the door wider, Ben gestured us inside, voice gentle. "Come in."

Exhaling as if taking three steps was a feat akin to crossing a frozen tundra, I staggered with Jamey's help to get me over the threshold. I swore my symptoms were getting worse by the second. And by the muttering going on around me, I'd say I had an audience to verify that.

"Do you guys need water or something? J—" Ben reached for Jamey.

Keeping his grip on my arm, Jamey's head whipped around. "Unless you're getting Brady for her, fuck off."

Arm falling to his side, Ben did nothing to hide the hurt in his eyes. And I knew…God, this had to be hard for him, concealing his feelings for Jamey from his fraternity brothers.

Ben's voice broke around one name. "Cam."

On command, Camden surfaced from out of the crowd and took the left staircase, leaping up two stairs at a time. He wove between the lingering audience like they were obstacles on the football field.

Someone shut the front door, and while I concentrated on staying upright, Jamey's gaze wandered to the trophy room to our right, up to the domed skylight above, the expansive double staircase, and finally on the black and gold PAM inlaid on the gray and white marble flooring just in case we forgot which fraternity house we were in.

Funny thing, Jamey knew a lot about wealth and what things cost, and never once did it impress him. If anything, the display of riches only pissed him off. I'd have to examine the reason another time. A time that hopefully didn't include me trying not to puke.

A voice tinged with a southern drawl drifted down from the landing above. "I heard my fiancée was here. How are you, darlin'? I've been trying to…" Trailing Camden down the stairs, Brady's blond hair was rumpled as if he'd just woken from a nap, but his blue eyes were alight and filled with mischief. Until he saw me.

Last time I was here, Brady had gone out of his way to make me feel welcome. He'd helped me. And though I didn't trust him, I didn't need to. Not for this.

Jamey leaned down and whispered just loud enough for me to hear. "*Fiancée?*"

I was going to answer him, but I thought... I swore I'd heard a faint hum playing in my ears. It was so fast, I couldn't be sure. I directed my attention back to Brady. "We need to talk."

"Yes, we do." Brady glanced behind him, to the person responsible for me being here. My gaze latched with Eric's. There was absolute triumph in that bastard's face. Beneath the bandages, of course.

Ruffling his hair with one hand, Brady's blue T-shirt lifted to reveal a tan stomach, ridged with muscle. I gathered a six-pack and golden skin were the base requirements to become a RAM. Brain cells and ethics be damned. "I've been trying to reach you. I asked Dylan to let you know— Darlin', are you alright?"

Hold up.

Dylan? Dylan was supposed to let me know Brady had wanted to speak to me? Son of a bitch. The fact that Dylan hadn't said a damn word shouldn't surprise me; he was Mason's bestie. But that...hurt. He was my class partner, and I thought my friend, too. I searched the room for Dylan and found him as his gaze diverted to his feet. But he wasn't the only one who refused to look me in the eye.

Assholes.

"No, I'm not alright." I figured I might as well be honest. I knew what I looked like. "I've tried to get in touch with you, too."

Sparing a glimpse to the room of men, his jaw hardened. "Have you now."

"Yes. So, since my efforts failed, I decided to come here in person. I need a moment with you in private. Please."

Nodding, he kept his blue eyes fastened with mine. His were soft and kind, and I felt a spark of what suspiciously felt like hope in my chest. "Not a problem."

"It's a problem for me," Matt growled, facing off with Brady.

Brady zeroed in on the older Scott. "And why is that exactly?"

Matt's eyes cut to me. Hard. "She's here to discuss Eric and what happened between them on Saturday. I don't want her poisoning anyone else with her lies. Because that's all she is. A liar."

That...*God.* There was nothing about Matt in this moment to remind me of the man who had given me those hugs, smiles, taught me to bowl...

"And she's a thief," Jamey added, giving Matt the glare to end all glares. "Can't forget that one."

"Well, technically," I interjected, "I only steal from the dead, so everyone here should be good."

"Right. I forgot."

As utter confusion overtook Brady, Matt's eyes filled with every ounce of hatred he had for me.

"Enough," Mason ordered. "Matt's right. Maggie isn't a reliable witness. She's here out of spite because my parents fired her. My entire family can speak to her poor character. Hell, even Eric thinks she's a liar. Two witnesses have corroborated my testimony. We shouldn't even be having a vote tonight."

"Really?" Brady challenged, coming onto the landing to square off Matt and Mason. "You want to know why we're having that vote, Mase? Because the moment Eric stepped one foot onto RAM property, you've been trying to kick him off it, using your past grudge to justify it. Then you tried to use your girlfriend to do your dirty work, and even she wanted nothing to do with your vendetta. And your witnesses? They were your cousin and your father. Who also want Eric out. This is the first and only witness whose testimony isn't biased, and you and your whole goddamn family are maligning her before she can even open her mouth. Not only that, but it seems as if our efforts to speak to one another have been sabotaged. I find that *very* interesting."

Matt folded his arms across his chest, stretching out his Henley, so the tip of a teal butterfly wing on his collarbone appeared. "If we're doing this, then I want to hear the shit she tells you. In fact, every brother present should hear her testimony. There's enough of us here for a quorum."

"Matt." Brady's jaw clenched, staring him down dead-on. "She asked to speak to me in private for a reason. We should respect that."

Matt's shrug conveyed his I-don't-give-a-shit stance quite well. "What she says and how you relay it could affect our vote later. And I reserve the right to ask questions." Brady opened his mouth to object when Matt said, "No brother above the brotherhood. This is the RAM's core value, isn't it?"

Closing his eyes, Brady inhaled deeply through his nose as if he needed every particle of air to keep calm. I gathered this wasn't the first time these two had butted heads. He looked to me. "Maggie, are you comfortable with that?"

I assumed this meant I was about to sit on trial. "Whatever gets me out of this house faster is fine with me."

"Good, it's settled." Matt twisted enough to address Jamey. "You're joining us?"

"It would be a travesty to deny you my presence."

"Right." Matt gave him an irritated nod and then shouted, "Adam!"

"Dude," Adam answered. "I'm literally standing right next to you."

Matt's dark head snapped to the right. "Oh. Do your thing."

"On it." Adam whipped out his phone, fingers flying on the screen. Chirps, buzzes, and what might have been a woman moaning suggestively reverberated in the grand foyer. Doors opened above, below, and all around me, feet proceeding deep into the never-ending maze that I'd gotten lost in the last time I was here.

With a few people left in the foyer, Mason's eyes flicked to mine, mouth nothing more than a white slash of flesh. "This isn't going to end the way you want it to."

"No. But it's going to end the way I expect it to."

chapter eleven

mason

N*o. But it's going to end the way I expect it to.*

What the fuck did that mean? Whatever. I wasn't going to waste precious brain cells trying to decode Maggie Davis. She wasn't worth my time. Speaking of time…

At most, it was a ninety-second trip from the foyer to the dining hall, and yet, it took Maggie a year. Plus a day. I hung back and watched as Jamey and Maggie walked, or whatever it was they were doing. He was all but carrying her, and I could see why. She definitely looked worse than Monday. Hell, she looked worse than this morning, and I didn't think that was possible until now.

This was bad. Like something off the set of *The Walking Dead* kind of bad.

Maggie's hair hung around her chin in an oily, tangled heap like it hadn't ever seen shampoo. Or a brush. What little of her skin I could see was waxy and ashen, and she was wearing another thick sweater and jeans as if she had her seasons mixed up or her internal thermostat was faulty. Her lids were swollen and pink, eyes half-mast and focused no higher than two feet off the ground.

The girl looked like she was on drugs. And not the fun kind.

Not halfway to the dining hall yet, I checked my watch. Then sighed. There were another three hours left before the RAM meeting—the scheduled one. Then another four, maybe five, before I could crack open the amber bottle I'd been staring at before the doorbell rang. I'd been so desperate to get wasted, I'd been willing to do anything to make the time go faster, and that included listening to Cam and Adam compare their ball hair count. Again.

The bitter scent of burnt garlic and despair from Vic and Pete's recent cooking failure singed the air with a cloud of awful as we neared the kitchen, and my stomach sent up a reminder that the only solid thing I'd had in days were two bites of cereal.

I glanced to Ben beside me as he dragged himself along. He looked like shit, but I wasn't one to judge. I was still hungover from last night and certain that I could sweat pure JD with the amount I'd had to drink. Seeing Maggie yesterday had fucked with my head. I had meant to talk to her but wound up standing there, watching her and that tremor as she tried and failed to open her locker.

That need to help her, be her hero, invaded me. And before I allowed myself to feel an ounce of sympathy for her, I forced myself to walk away, drive here, and then damn near broke the treadmill's belt. Then I killed a bottle of whiskey. But this…

I doubted two bottles of the stuff would wipe this image of Maggie out of my head.

Ben's weary eyes latched onto Jamey once more. Since I had extensive knowledge of what heartbreak looked like, I'd say Ben was in the thick of it. I knew he'd been going to Jamey's every night, parking outside his house for hours, hoping for a chance to see him. They did have one class together, and Jamey threatened to drop it if Ben attempted to talk to him again. Didn't know if that threat had much sway because since minute one of this fiasco, Jamey had blocked Ben's phone number, and Ben had resorted to borrowing everyone else's phones.

So, my cousin pretty much qualified for restraining order status.

I elbowed him, the guy not showing any signs he'd felt it. "You hanging in there?"

"Sure," he rasped, dropping his head again, but those eyes didn't let go of Jamey. Not for a second.

We'd finally spilled into the dining room, the brothers having shifted the rectangular tables around as if to recreate something out of King Arthur's court, with one difference. A table and chair were placed in the center of the circle directly across from Eric's seat. He hadn't been here when my father and Cam gave their testimony, and he shouldn't be here now.

Maggie would have to recount her attack while facing the very asshole who she claimed attacked her. And though she more than likely had lied about the entire thing, nothing about this was sitting right with me.

Still keeping a hold of her arm, Jamey lowered Maggie to her chair. There was an audible whimper the moment she touched down on the hard seat, and I swore my heart lurched at the sound. I cursed it and thought back to the moment my father showed her the stolen earrings and the lies she told, the fake tears she'd cried, welcoming the anger to encase my heart like a shield against her.

Pinching her eyes shut, Maggie's knuckles went white on the edge of the table as though it were taking every bone, tissue, muscle, and cell in her body to sit. Around a limp curtain of hair, I could see her grimace as if the chair had been lined with barbed spikes.

Once she was settled, Jamèy dipped low and pressed a kiss to the top of her head. It occurred to me that this could all be part of the act, but honestly, even Meryl Streep couldn't keep that up.

Scanning the room once more to the setup, unease settled across my shoulders, bunching them into tight knots. As usual, the televisions were muted and set to various sports channels, including football, tennis, soccer, and I believe that was...curling? Only half the RAMs were present, and I imagined any woman would feel as if this were still an overwhelming amount of men in one room. One brother after another took a spot within the outer circle, and as Adam's text blast reached the rest of the RAMs, they would filter in and get caught up.

Jamey hovered in the back of the room as if he'd rather endure a full body wax than get any closer to Ben than he had to. On the opposite side of the circle from me, Ben took a spot between Matt and Cam. I grabbed a seat that wouldn't give Maggie a direct view of me, but I could still watch her, gauge her emotions. I didn't know why I bothered.

Pulling out my chair, I glanced over as Brady whispered something to Quince. The Wolverine's safety nodded and whipped out his phone. That unease I'd felt earlier reignited, crawling down my arms and into my hands as I curled them into fists.

"Maggie, do you mind if we record this?" Brady asked as he gestured to Quince, already propping up his phone to face her. "This way, we can have the video of your testimony to show the brothers who aren't present."

"Fine," she murmured, slumping down in her chair the same time as that unease made its way to the center of my chest, ripping through that shield like it was made of paper.

I didn't want Maggie here, and I especially didn't want her defending Eric; that was true. But this...this needed to stop.

"It's not fine," I said to Brady, pushing my chair back under the table. "This shouldn't happen. Not today. Not like this."

"Jesus." Taking his seat next to Eric, Brady shook his head, glaring at me. "Mase, your objection was noted. Just like your unilateral decision to expel Eric from the RAM brotherhood without so much as a discussion with me. You claim he committed assault. He says otherwise.

He has the right to defend himself, and when this is done, this committee would like to hear the reasons that you and Dylan prevented a witness from speaking to me."

I had nothing to do with that.

I kept that little ditty to myself. If D had stopped Maggie from contacting Brady, then he was acting out of loyalty to me. Wasn't right, and I'd never ask him to do that, but I sure as shit wasn't going to roll on him.

"That's not what this is about," I argued. "You can see for yourself. There's something clearly not right with her. I'm simply suggesting we postpone all of this until—"

"I'm not postponing shit." That came from the lone female in the center of the room, but her voice sounded off. The innate rasp of her throat rougher, drier than usual. Her words not quite slurred but slower and not as crisp as they should be. Without lifting her head, those dark lashes flicked up enough to reveal her eyes. What should be a brilliant array of azure and teal irises were muted and flat, rimmed in an angry red, abnormally empty as they bore into mine. "If you can't handle what I look like, then look elsewhere. I'm not leaving until I'm done, and I sure as hell am not coming back down here to do this with you assholes again. So, ask your questions already."

My mouth parted on a sharp inhale. I was used to the bite of her tongue, the sting they left behind, but something about her had become unnaturally hard.

Brows inching together, Brady shifted in his seat. "Right, ah…" His gaze dropped, lingering on what the rest of us were now staring at.

Though Maggie's hands were in tight balls on the table, they looked as though she were getting stuck with a cattle prod. I thought I'd seen her tremor at its worst. I was so wrong.

Brady cleared his throat, cracking open a black and gold notebook stamped with the RAM logo on the front. I wasn't sure what its purpose was since he didn't have a pen and this was being recorded anyway. "You don't have to be nervous, Maggie. Please, tell us why you're here."

"I'm not nervous," she spat beneath a mass of hair as she shoved her hands beneath the table to hide her tremor. Until now, she'd been somewhat agreeable with Brady. I'd say he was now on the outs of her good graces like the rest of us. "I'm here because I want you to reinstate Eric Ryan's pledgeship."

Her words surprised no one but still had the power to cease ten crinkling bags of potato chips, twenty thumbs punching at phone screens, and stopped Jamey from pacing a hole in the floor. Since this shitshow was going to happen regardless of what I said, I took my seat.

Brady slid to the edge of his chair, bracing his elbows on the table. "And why would you like us to do that?"

It was too low and quiet, but I thought she grumbled, "I don't." Tipping her chin up, her eyes squeezed shut for a long blink as if the slightest movement of her head was painful. "Eric never hurt me. We were talking, and...the argument got heated, and— Um..." Closing her eyes a bit longer that time, Maggie's throat worked over and over again as if she'd forgotten how to swallow. Jamey crept closer.

"So, Eric never attempted to hit you?" Matt's words were accusatory and sharp. "You just, what? Flopped down on the floor when Mason happened by and played the victim?"

Frowning, Brady twisted around in his chair. "Matt, let her—"

"Let her what?" My brother cut him off. "This is bullshit! Either Eric attacked her, or she wanted Mason to think he did. Her admission speaks to which one it is. She's sick. This is all part of her little game—"

BAM!

Every single person jarred at the noise, Maggie having flipped her table on its side. "Would you shut the hell up already?" It was then her slumped form and absent stare evolved into...something else. Something that I didn't recognize as Maggie.

"Mags?" Jamey called from the back of the room.

If she'd heard Jamey, I wouldn't have known. If she saw anything outside of one foot in front of her, I wouldn't have known. Maggie's quivering fingers formed into claws as she pushed to her feet, legs wobbling at the knees as though she'd tumble over if someone breathed too hard. It...it wasn't pretty.

No high was worth this.

"You," Brady snapped, pointing a finger at Jamey who had impressively vaulted over a table between Noah and Jordon. "I will not allow—"

"Mags!" Disregarding Brady's command, Jamey skidded up to her side. He was wild-eyed, hands reaching out but not touching her. "Mags, lie down. Please. I need—"

"No!" Maggie's hands flew to her head, gripping tight, hair springing up between her fingers. Concern for her, true and deep, was at the forefront again. "Stop the ringing. I can't hear anything over the fucking ringing, goddamn it!"

Losing her balance, Maggie dipped to one side as Jamey whipped his arm around her waist, barely catching her. We all stood stunned as he pulled her away from the toppled desk, as well as from the chair he should be sitting her ass in.

What the hell was wrong with him? Better question, what the hell was wrong with her?

"Don't touch me!" *Smack!* With what may be her last drop of strength, Maggie wheeled, slapping her best friend like he was a cockroach. "Get away from me!"

Instead of being shocked and dismayed like the rest of us, Jamey took five more hits to the arm, not phased in the slightest.

"Get your fucking hands off me!" she shrieked, shoving him away so hard they broke apart, both stumbling backward to catch their footing.

Maggie swallowed convulsively, drool pooling in the corner of her mouth. "I don't…deserve this! I didn't do anything wrong!"

Off to my side, I thought I heard Eric drolly say, "And here comes the spaz attack."

I wasn't sure what that meant, but it kinda seemed like Maggie was in the middle of a nervous breakdown. Whatever it was, we were all transfixed, watching this unfold in the middle of the room like a horror show we never signed up to watch.

"I'm not going to hurt you." Jamey inched his way closer to her. "Mags, lay down, please. It's Jamey. I'm your friend." He reached for her again, but she spun, crashing into Jordon and Owen's table.

"Mags."

Jamey neared her again, but when he took a palm to the face, Quince cried out, "What the hell, man? Is she rabid or some shit?"

Without bothering to look behind him, Jamey kept his eyes fastened on the tiny brunette. "She can't help it, fuckwit." Jamey continued to creep closer to her. The dude really didn't value his balls. "Please, Mags. Lie down."

"NO!" she screeched, fingers flying up to her hair again, clawing at her scalp, yanking on every strand, and when she tilted her head back, I had to blink a few times to comprehend what I was seeing. Her eyes… There wasn't any blue left. They were black.

Jamey's voice shook, stretching his hand out for her. "Mags."

As though the Invisible Man had stunned her, Maggie went rigid, and then someone had put the world in slow-mo because her limbs began to coil, twisting her spine, forcing her face to rotate toward the ceiling. Her jaw opened, widening until a guttural noise thundered out of her that chilled me right to the core.

I swore if two priests shot through the room right now screaming, *The power of Christ compels you*, I'd shit my pants. No lie.

Jamey was able to get one hand around her wrist, and the other held her cheek. "It's Jamey. I'm right here, Mags. You're safe. I'm not leaving you."

Yeah, wherever she checked into had turned on the vacancy sign.

Maggie's frame had warped to the point she couldn't stand, and like a tree falling, her body tipped backward, stiff and without mercy. I heard a distinct *thump*, and I didn't remember moving or how I'd gotten in the middle of the room, but suddenly, I was there looking down at her.

Dear God.

With her back bowed, Maggie's limbs were now stretched out, aberrantly taut, but her fists had curled in so hard, she had to be shredding her palms. Grunts spilled out of her locked jaw, and her eyes had rolled back into her head. Then her body began jerking at the shoulders and hips like that Invisible Man was now shaking different parts of her in multiple directions. Her muted sounds eventually quieted, and there was only Jamey whispering to her as the violent shudders thrashed her around.

I knew first aid, but for a moment, my mind went blank.

Utterly blank.

It took a couple of tries before Jamey successfully got Maggie on her side. Spittle dotted her lips, the convulsions at their worst now.

She could choke, bite her tongue, chew through her lip, hit her head…

Breaking out of my daze, I fell to my knees at Maggie's back to support her. Out of nowhere, Jamey's arm snapped up, and with a strength I didn't know he had, I took a blow to my chest. I fell on my ass, the back of my head hitting the leg of the table Maggie had overturned.

Dazed and wide-eyed, I said, "What the fu—"

"Stay away from her!" His hazel eyes held so much hatred that I now understood what Ben had meant. I didn't think anyone had ever looked at me with that much loathing. "This is your fault!" he hissed.

I knew that made no sense, but I kept my distance. Unmoved, I watched Jamey rub his hand down her arm and soothe her with words, but it only seemed to make her tremors worse. I hadn't ever seen someone have a seizure, and it felt like days passed before she stilled, body slumping as the shocks wrung their way out of her limbs.

The moment the convulsions were over, Maggie went limp. Quickly moving and with purpose like the guy was a trauma nurse, Jamey wiped the dribble off her face and leaned down to put his ear to her lips at the same time his fingers went to her jugular artery.

Before my eyes, the color in Jamey's face leached out, turning almost as white as the tips of his hair. "NO!" In the next blink, he had Maggie on her back, chin tipped up, mouth covering hers.

The ground left me, my vision going spotty. In the space of one heartbeat, I was transported to my room, my bed, the unnatural blank stare reflecting at me, my throat raw from screaming, my hands shaking that fragile body, begging her to come back—

A strong hand gripped my bicep, Ben bringing me to the present. "Mase…"

I couldn't move, didn't think I'd blinked.

Jamey's ear was poised over Maggie's mouth, waiting. He breathed for her again and paused once more, keeping his fingers on her pulse point.

Fear wrenched me out of my stupor, waking me up. I crawled to her side. "Let me help, Jamey. Two people—"

A quiet, relieved breath left Jamey as Maggie's chest rose and fell on her own. I wish I could say the relief was reciprocated.

"…an overdose, I think," Brady said into his phone behind us.

Jamey's head twisted, and if eyes could become flamethrowers, Brady would be inside a ball of fire. "She has *epilepsy*, you ignorant fuck! She doesn't take drugs!"

Face turning ruddy with embarrassment, Brady corrected himself with the 9-1-1 dispatcher.

The next thing I knew, Jamey had Maggie cradled in his arms, but he was struggling to lift her. The guy was more than capable of picking her up, but after what he'd just been through, I gathered the surge of adrenaline was wearing off and wreaking havoc on him.

"I'll get her," I offered, reaching out.

Glowering at me, he tucked Maggie to his chest, possessively. "Don't touch her."

Brady inched closer with the phone to his ear. "Emergency crews are delayed. There's a bad accident on Cove Highway."

Translation: Maggie and anyone else in Crescent Cove who needed the FD/paramedics/EMTs—our *emergency crews*—were fucked. By the time they dealt with the accident, battled the congestion of rush hour, delivered the wounded to Pacific Cliffs Hospital, and then drove back down here, we might as well call a coroner.

That was a lesson I knew far too well.

As instinct kicked in, I reached for Maggie again, and Jamey snarled, "I told you not to touch her."

I fixed my glare on him, doing my best to dim the glimmer of anger brewing beneath the surface of my skin. Maggie was Jamey's best friend, and he'd just held her while she'd gone through something terrible, breathed air for her, brought her back to life. That would fuck anyone up, and he wasn't thinking straight right now. But if I didn't act, everything he'd done would have been a wasted effort.

"Try to stop me again, Jamey. See what happens." I pushed him aside enough to evaluate her vitals.

Noah crouched next to me. "The University Clinic is closed for the day, but I'm on hold with the clinic manager. She's trying to get a nurse practitioner over here."

How in the fuck was this happening right now? Her pulse was far too thready, breaths shallow, and color…scary.

"I'll take her to PCH," I heard myself say.

"Mase," Brady drew the phone away from his mouth, "just wait. Help is on its way."

"No." I cranked my head around to him. "*Help* is stuck in traffic *helping* other people. Her vitals aren't good, and she may not have any at all in the next minute. I'm not going to sit on my ass while she lays here on the fucking floor to die."

I scanned the crowd, looking to my brother for backup. It wasn't like I needed it from him, but I quickly realized I wasn't going to get anything out of Matt other than a vacant stare and questions as to where all the blood in his face went to. I didn't have time to ask.

I threw my keys to Ben, and he sprinted out of the room. Jamey backed away enough to allow me to get my arms beneath Maggie. As I drew her frame against mine, it hit me then how very little she weighed, how slack her body felt, how fragile and vulnerable she was in this moment.

With her face tucked against my chest, the purple shadows smudging the delicate skin around her eyes made her look gaunt. Her peaches and cream complexion had been washed out, darkening her freckles, and her cheeks and eyes were far too hollow. Dread swelled inside me and crushed my heart.

Now, more than ever, Maggie reminded me of Faith and everything that had happened during my last moments with her.

Like I was carrying nothing but air, I ran through the house and out the back lot with Jamey trailing me to my Raptor that Ben had idling by the steps. He opened the back door, and I slid her inside, careful not to bang her head, arms, legs… This wasn't good.

A litany of the worst-case scenarios came to mind as I left her with Jamey and Ben. Once I was behind the wheel and all the doors shut, my foot punched the accelerator, tearing out of the gates Ben had opened, tires squealing along the asphalt.

"Take her to my house," Jamey ordered as I pulled onto the main road.

I couldn't have heard that right. "*What?*"

Ben implored, "Jamey, I—"

"She doesn't need a hospital for a seizure," Jamey cut in. "I didn't argue back there because I didn't have any other way of getting her home. She just needs to rest."

"*Rest?*" Keeping my eyes on the windshield, I growled, "She's not resting, Jamey. She's fucking unconscious!"

"And whose fault is that?"

My fingers clenched the wheel, bleaching out as I took a road few knew existed. My luck, men wearing overalls and strumming banjos owned this land. The speedometer tipped to eighty, and I prayed the entire CCPD was at that accident since I was breaking about ten different laws right now.

"Arguing about fault is not going to help her," I said.

Pulling his cell from his ear, Ben muttered a low curse. "Uncle Dan and Aunt Eve aren't picking up."

"Mom's probably in surgery, and Dad silences his phone when he's on the floor." I spotted the narrow road that would take me north and spun the wheel. "Try the back line. It's in my contacts." Without looking, I threw my phone behind me.

A minute later, Ben cursed, louder this time. "I'm on hold, and Neil Diamond is 'Coming to America.'"

At that, my stomach did a full three-sixty.

And much to my surprise, I learned that he's a professional Neil Diamond impersonator...

That had been Maggie's way of getting under my skin during Public Speaking class on our first day. She had also insinuated I was a weasel. The dig had been well deserved. Both of them.

My leg tensed, the speedometer kissing ninety. "We'll be there soo— Fuck!" Cranking the wheel, I saved us all from being chewed to bits by John Deere's finest. "Hang on!"

I corrected the turn a little too hard, and Ben's hands shot out, nearly ripping the oh-shit bar out of the roof. I was pretty sure Jamey called me a *dumb fuck*.

Fair enough.

"How is she?" I asked as the guys situated Maggie back across their laps.

"Fine, like I said she was ten minutes ago," Jamey snapped.

Flicking my eyes to the rearview, I caught the bright red handprint streaked across his cheek. "I think someone with a medical degree should assess if she's *fine*."

His gaze blazed into mine in the mirror. "Fuck you, Mason. If you haven't been clued in yet, this is not the first time she's had a seizure."

"Yeah? And how many times have you had to resuscitate her after?"

Rather than answer me, Jamey planted his forehead against the window and stroked Maggie's hair.

"That's what I thought. So regardless of what you or Maggie want, we're going to the hospital. Because no matter what she's done, I'm going to fucking make sure she's okay. Got it?"

If he had a response to that, I didn't hear it.

With a little 4WD action and cutting through my third field, I'd made it to the outskirts of Pacific Cliffs faster than I expected and didn't let up on the gas until I skidded to a stop behind an ambulance unloading a guy who looked like he'd be down a limb by the end of the day. When I flew out of the truck, I was sure that was an artichoke jammed in my wheel well.

Oddly, Jamey didn't put up a fight when I took Maggie from him or have a snappy retort for me. Maybe he was finally coming to his senses, or…nope. Strike that. He was ready to hurl on my floorboards.

Ben hopped out, meeting me on Jamey's side of the Raptor. As Jamey staggered out, Ben cringed. "I'll find you a ginger ale. It'll help with the carsickness."

Hunched over, Jamey spit onto the asphalt, giving us an impressive side-glare. "What would have helped was if you pricks took us home like I asked, instead of pulling a *Mad Max* routine throughout the fucking county."

My faith in his assholery was restored.

I ignored the invitation to go at Jamey again as I readjusted my hold on Maggie. Tension formed around my mouth and then seeped through the rest of me as I cradled her. She didn't stir in the slightest, show one sign that she was coming around. I wasn't an expert on these things, but it couldn't be normal to be knocked out this long. Panic replaced the tension in my legs as I rushed her through the emergency room doors. The sterile, medicinal scent was the first thing to greet me, stinging my nostrils, overtaking my senses. For the second time today, I was catapulted back to a time that eviscerated my very soul.

Ben raced around me and made it to the ER window before I did, his voice echoing through a room of bodies hacking and moaning. "Let us in, Manny."

Behind the glass, the ER manager's smirk grew, crinkling the deep olive skin around eyes the color of rich espresso. "It's early. I don't usually see the Scott boys until after midnight."

Glowering, I shifted for him to get a good view of Maggie. Lids flying wide, Manny's dark curls sprung as he launched out of his chair.

The ER doors swung open, and I charged in, meeting Manny in the hallway. "She had an epileptic seizure and had to be resuscitated. Get

Mom or Dad, please. And, Manny." I lowered my voice, looking to him. "She's a friend."

Okay, Maggie and I weren't friends, but it was enough for Manny to know to keep this on the down low. I didn't need the entire hospital throwing around conspiracy theories as to why the Scotts' son had brought an unconscious woman to the ER.

Manny pointed to an empty curtain, and I aimed for it. "Your mom is finishing up with a multiple rib fracture, and I'm sure the guy in the ambulance bay will need her next. What's her name? Age?"

"Maggie Davis," I answered. "Eighteen."

While Manny took a quick assessment, Ben helped me lay Maggie on the bed, and as soon as her back hit the mattress, the quietest of groans escaped her lips, her eyelids flickering but not opening. It was enough to stop my gut from hollowing out completely.

Drawing my arms away, I chased the movement of her head. "Maggie?"

Still clutching his stomach, Jamey shoved me aside and swept back her hair. "Hey, Blue Eyes. It's Jamey. I'm right here, Mags. You're okay."

"Jamey, is she on any medications that you know of? Taken anything?" Manny slipped the pulse-oximeter on her finger.

"No. Nothing."

The blood pressure monitor appeared next as Manny called out, "Dr. Scott!" So much for keeping this on the DL.

A curtain five beds over shifted, and Dad's head appeared, eyes filled with confusion when he saw me. "Mase? What are you...?" His gaze dropped to the prone body on the gurney, and he rushed forward in some strange Dad-Doctor mode. It was usually one or the other, not both. "What happened?"

While Manny opened packs of monitoring wires and began attaching them to Maggie, Jamey stroked her cheeks. "She had a grand mal seizure about twenty minutes ago. She doesn't need or want treatment, but no one will listen to me."

Dad paled, ignoring the last statement. "Seizure...? Has she had them before?"

"Yes, she's epileptic." And though Jamey's tone was harsh, the touch of his fingers on her skin was gentle.

Staring down at the bed, Dad muttered, "She didn't tell me when we—" With an abrupt shake of his head, he was back in doctor mode, finding her radial pulse. "How long was the seizure?"

A year.

"Seventy seconds." As Jamey answered, Maggie's hands shifted toward her midline, her fingers finding the fabric of her jeans. Grunting, she pulled and tugged at her pants. Jamey plucked her fingers away.

"This is all normal for her," he protested, setting her hands by her sides. "She doesn't need to be here. If she could speak, she would decline treatment."

My head whirled to Jamey, and before I could yell at him, Ben said, "Uncle Dan, she stopped breathing. Jamey had to give her mouth to mouth."

Dad's lips parted, and whatever he was going to say was cut off by Manny's question to Jamey. "Are you her proxy?"

As Manny waited for a response, Jamey's nostrils flared.

"Her father is the chief of the CCPD," Dad answered for him, and his focus swung to whom I assumed was the case manager standing at the end of the bed with his tablet. "Have Yvette call for Nathan Davis, and until I speak to her family or a legal proxy, we're treating."

Staring at my dad, Jamey leaned over the bed, upper lip pulled back from his teeth. "Her father will tell you the same thing. Don't. Treat."

Dad aimed a stern glare to Jamey. "Then I look forward to hearing it directly from his mouth." Bringing his attention to Maggie, Dad assessed her pupils as Manny gave him an info dump of numbers and stats. "Maggie," Dad spoke in a soothing voice, "you're at Pacific Cliffs Hospital. It's Doc, and you're safe. We're gonna take good care of you, okay?"

Her lids fluttered some more, and her arms lifted, hands pushing, fingers pulling, seemingly at odds with what she wanted.

Jamey caught her wayward hand as it flew toward him. "It's Jamey. I'm here. You're okay, Mags."

Dad slid his stethoscope over her turtleneck that I could have sworn was the same one she had worn on Monday. The one with the tiny hole in the collar.

Ben nudged my arm. "Your truck is still parked out front. I'll move it."

"Oh, shit. Thanks." Handing my keys over, I jutted my chin toward Jamey. "The nurse's station has a fridge that's usually stocked with ginger ale for him on your way back."

Still a little green, Jamey grumbled, "Don't bother. I won't take it from you."

Exhaling through his nostrils, Ben's mouth thinned. "You're being ridiculous, Jamey. It's a soda."

"And I really don't give a shit what you think, *Ben*," Jamey announced over his shoulder, then snapped his head right back to my dad when he drew the stethoscope off Maggie. "Haven't you done enough? She doesn't want you or any Scott touching her."

Dad cocked a dark brow at him and used a voice that was so very rare. Kinda always scared me a little. "My patience is wearing thin with you. Continue to interfere with my care, and I'll throw you out of the ER myself."

At some point, another nurse had joined in the fun, holding a clipboard with a paper and pen. Even she looked a little scared for Jamey. "I can call her mother if that would help," she offered.

"Yes, that would be oh so helpful *if* she had a mother." Molars gnashed, Jamey snatched up the clipboard and slammed it down onto a nearby cart with a *clap*!

The noise agitated Maggie, her hips lifting as if to sit up, but her shoulders weren't coordinating. Wriggling, she made more grunting noises, not forming any definable words.

While Manny stilled her head, Dad held her legs from kicking out and bruising her shins. "Maggie, you're not ready to get up yet. And you." He looked to Jamey. "Talk to my staff like that one—"

"Did she hit her head during the seizure?" Everyone's focus whipped around to Manny, who had Maggie's face turned to the right, the hair on her left temple parted, exposing…

What in the hell?

Like everyone else, I crept closer, but that did nothing to answer the questions amassing by the second.

"She didn't. I caught her," Jamey answered, jaw so tight, I was shocked he could speak.

"He's right," Ben confirmed. "I saw it. He protected her head. She never hit anything."

Manny and Dad combed through those black strands, fear and panic unraveling my thoughts, straining my breaths. Slowly, they exposed a path of rutted, depressed bone stretching from her temple all the way to behind her ear with a thick scar parting her hair.

Good God. That…didn't look new. And so much more than a superficial flesh wound.

I was suddenly catapulted back to all the times Maggie's fingers had run along her temple to fix her hair, rub her head as if it hurt. And Saturday night in the parking lot, when I'd tried to sweep her hair back, she'd swatted me away. The night I gave her the bicycle lights, my lips had been there, and she'd abruptly shifted out of my reach. I thought I'd pushed her too fast, but that wasn't it at all. She hadn't wanted me to know, touch, see…

She'd been hiding that scar from me.

Dad's focus reeled around to Jamey. "How old is this? What happened to her?" When Jamey's lips mashed together, my father's eyes narrowed. "What happened—"

"I'm Chief Davis." Behind us, a familiar voice echoed throughout the ER. "My daughter, Margaret Davis, was just brought in."

I turned as Yvette directed the chief our way, his feet pivoting toward us before his head could swivel. His paces were sharp, frame brutal and bullish. It was still such a mindfuck to think this man was Maggie's father.

His eyes were rimmed pink to suggest he'd been on shift for a while but were keen as he surveyed and measured every person and object surrounding his daughter's gurney as if walking into an active scene. "The university called and told me she was brought here, but I was dealing with the accident..." Pausing feet from the bed, his gaze landed on that strip of scarred skin on his daughter's scalp.

He pulled down a rough breath. "How is she?"

"Her vitals are stable, and she's beginning to regain consciousness but hasn't been able to verbalize yet." Dad didn't move his hands away from the hollowed bone on Maggie's head. "Chief, what is this trauma from?"

Shaking himself, the chief stepped to the end of the bed and lowered his voice. "It's an old injury. It's nothing to concern yourself with."

"Chief, your daughter suffered a tonic-clonic seizure and had to be resuscitated. This trauma to her skull could have affected her temporal lobe and quite possibly her cerebellum. This is absolutely my concern, especially if it's the cause of her epilepsy and tremors. Has she been diagnosed with PTE?"

PTE...? I filed that away to research later.

Dad was in full doctor mode now, and I knew he *hated* anything that delayed a patient's care. And when the chief refused to answer my father, he did just that.

Dad's mouth flattened, his attention back on Maggie. "Manny, I need a CT, EEG—"

"I won't agree to that." The chief cut him off.

Dad's brows slammed down, and his voice took on that tone again as he looked at Maggie's father. "Bloodwork then. A CBC, chem—"

"No." The chief's jaw moved as though he were grinding several layers of enamel away. "I appreciate your boy for being concerned for my daughter and bringing her here, but she doesn't want medical treatment. These seizures are common for her, more so when she's under stress. And as you can imagine, she's had a lot of that lately."

"Who is her neurologist? What medication is she taking?" Dad demanded, and the chief didn't make any sign that he would answer. The same frustration showing on my dad's face was now beginning to flare in my gut. "How frequent are her seizures?" he prompted again.

After a controlled breath, Maggie's father gently stated, "None of this is necessary."

Dad's head jerked back. It was a rare thing to shock my dad, and this dude had done it. "With all due respect, Chief, this is the very *minimum* of what is necessary. Sudden Unexpected Death in Epilepsy, or SUDEP, is the leading cause of death in young adults with uncontrolled seizures—"

The chief held up his palm. "Margaret has been through enough. You are correct about her diagnosis. She has PTE, and she doesn't want treatment."

I didn't think Dad could get any paler, but he did. "I understand how difficult the road for her has been, and while Post Traumatic Epilepsy can't always be treated, it can be managed. There are new breakthroughs and trials to consider. Our neurology department has one of the country's leading epileptologists—"

"With all due respect, Doctor, it's impossible. She has tried every medication there is, and we bought the hype about them all. The only thing medicine did for her was make her sicker and break her heart each time they failed. She has learned to live with her condition and has accepted it. And even after everything she's put your family through, I thank you for the concern."

"Everything outside of these walls is irrelevant, but we all still care about her welfare, as you can see." Dad nodded to Ben and me. "I'm speaking as her doctor, advocating for her care. We can help her do much more than *live with* and *accept* her diagnosis."

Chief Davis' eyes flicked to Manny and the other nurse poised to apply EEG electrodes to Maggie's scalp. "My daughter is to remain untouched." His tone suggested Manny and his cohort were serial killers instead of trauma nurses doing their jobs.

Jesus. Okay, I got that he may not be our biggest fans, but the hospital staff had nothing to do with this.

His gaze steeled until Manny and his partner complied, backing away. "I'd like to take her home now."

Dad's lids flared wide. "Maggie's not even conscious—"

"I'm taking my daughter home. Now." The chief's eyes flashed like frosted glass a moment before softening into a pallid blue. "She was brought here against her will. I'm trying to right that wrong now, do what she would want. I'm sure you, most of all, can understand and respect a patient's wishes."

Dad's shoulders tensed, and for a blink, I swore his hands fisted. "Please, Chief Davis. Give her time to come around. I may be able to get through to her, present her with options she wasn't given before. And while we're waiting, we can observe her, at least let us run an EEG. It'll give us a better picture of what we're dealing with. I'm not offering treatment, simply tests and monitoring. A second opinion could make a world of difference."

The chief sighed, his patience waning. "Dr. Scott, I'm taking Margaret home."

"Ja— Jamey?" As if her father's command had the power to wake Maggie, her broken voice drifted up from the bed.

Sliding closer, Jamey laced his fingers with hers. "I'm here. You're okay."

Her sleepy eyes strained to focus on him. "W— Where's here…?" Gaze roaming over the strangers in scrubs surrounding her, understanding swept over her features, and as her lids slid shut, she groaned again. Before I could comprehend what she was doing, her other hand wrapped around the sheet and heaved herself up with a faltered whimper.

Dad reached for her again. "Maggie, sweetheart, lay down."

Eyes flying open at his voice, a look of shock and horror streamed across her features. She abruptly twisted away from Dad, letting out a small cry as her entire body cringed in what looked like absolute agony.

Dad winced on her behalf, palms out. "Please, Maggie, let me examine you. You may have hurt yourself during—"

"It's her back," Chief Davis interjected. "She wrenched it Sunday night, and I'm sure this incident didn't help."

Wrenched it? More like obliterated it the way she'd been hobbling all week.

Dad pressed, "Maggie, let me make sure you can leave here safely. You had a seizure—"

"I know…exactly what happened." Without moving her head, her eyes raged with azure flames beneath her lashes. And though her speech was sluggish, there was no mistaking the hatred in her voice. "I know exactly what…is wrong with me. I don't need your help, and I don't want—" She swallowed with some work. "I don't want anything to do with you or your family… *ever again.*"

The look on my dad's face spoke to how much Maggie had shredded him. I got that she was still very much out of it, and her words were reactive, but dammit, Dad didn't deserve that. He'd done nothing wrong by Maggie. It was the other way around.

The chief took a healthy step forward, pushing the second nurse out of the way. "Come on, Margaret. Let's get home so you can rest."

"She should rest here," Dad reasoned. "She's postictal and could hurt herself further."

His cool gaze slid back to my father. "I'm more than capable of caring for my daughter, Dr. Scott." And there it was, in his tone, unyielding and rigid. There would be no dissuading the chief. "This was not her first seizure. And you are not the first doctor under the delusion they can help."

Determined, Dad spun to face Maggie. "Sweetheart, I don't have to be your treating physician. Dr. Wes—"

"Dr. Scott," the chief said crisply. "My daughter is not interested in what you or this hospital has to offer."

Dad twisted back to her father. "Please. There are treatments to consider. Medications, surgeries, homeopathic options, even diets that can improve her quality of life. This isn't a terminal—"

Chief Davis leveled Dad with a glare. "Dr. Scott, I am not only her father but her healthcare proxy. Both your patient and I have expressed our wishes. But if you prefer, we can discuss this further back at my station. In handcuffs."

The fuck...?

Working his throat, Dad's gaze shifted to Maggie, and I knew what he saw there on that bed. *Faith.* A frail girl who was all bones and pale skin with only patches of hair, a girl who was his whole world and would do anything and everything he could do to fight for her. And he had.

Nodding, Dad said, "If you'll come with me and sign some paperwork, Chief Davis."

After a long stare down, he grunted his assent and followed Dad to the nurses' station. "Very well."

Manny attempted to remove the monitoring equipment, but Maggie stopped him. "I'll do it. Can I...have some privacy, please?"

Manny took an extended pause, his gaze traveling to me before agreeing. "Of course."

As soon as Manny and the other nurse I had yet to learn the name of cleared the way, Jamey snapped the curtain closed, the division clear. We were not welcome in their world.

I knew Ben wouldn't leave the ER now because this was the longest Jamey had allowed Ben to be around him in days, but my feet didn't seem to be moving either.

Bodies shifted behind the curtain, Jamey's voice too quiet to distinguish his words. I stepped closer.

"No one saw, right?" Maggie asked, and when he didn't say anything, she urged, "*Jamey.*"

A pause. "Mags…"

She whispered, her words cracking, "Don't be mad at me. Please."

"No, *you* please," he hissed back. "This is your one chance and—"

"Oh, my God. Did I— Did I do that to your face? Oh, Jamey. Jamey, I'm so sorry."

A shorter pause that time, but his words were clipped. "It's fine. It doesn't hurt."

Over the rustling sheets, her voice broke on a choked sob. "I didn't…mean to, Jamey. I swear. I would never—"

"Of course, you didn't mean to. I know that." He sighed. "Come on. Let's get you out of this bed. Okay?"

A second later, her strangled whimper sent panic surging through my veins like a pulse of electricity. Because respecting boundaries had never been my thing, I yanked the curtain back.

Jamey had Maggie in his arms, not fully lifting her off the bed yet, but he was fully scowling at me. I scowled right back without one fuck to give because Maggie looked like she was on the brink of coding. Her face was buried in Jamey's chest, but what little I could see of her complexion was near gray. Her chest heaved as she struggled for air, fingers blanched of color, nails leaving crescents in Jamey's forearms.

Ben was quick to sidle up on the other side of Maggie. "Here. I'll help you."

Jamey's face screwed up even more, his grip on Maggie tighter, and her entire body flinched in reaction. Jamey didn't seem to notice. Nor did he notice that he had her back in the worst possible position.

"Jamey—"

"When are any of you going to understand that none of us want you?" He cut me off, seething. "How many times do we have to say it?"

I clenched my teeth as I swallowed my response to that.

Thank God Manny rushed over, rolling a wheelchair to the side of the bed. "She shouldn't be walking. She could slip. Please."

It took a minute plus a look that said he'd rather fellate a screwdriver, but Jamey conceded. "Thank you."

Ben and I stood by as Jamey and Manny got Maggie down off the bed and into the chair, and that didn't happen without the four of us grimacing as if we collectively felt her pain. The girl had the mobility of an elderly woman with two broken hips and a calcified spine.

I hadn't realized how quiet the ER had gotten until a phone rang, cutting through the silence. I glanced behind me to Chief Davis signing Maggie's e-documents with the case manager as Dad looked longingly to Maggie like he'd just lost a patient.

Like, the forever kind of lost.

Regardless of what they wanted, Ben and I followed Jamey and Maggie through the exit doors. The way her head lolled, eyes sliding shut…it hurt to watch her.

Ben managed to stay in step with them as we maneuvered through the crowded waiting room. "Jamey, please let me help."

"Go. Away," Jamey growled as he wheeled Maggie outside to where the black and white PPV was parked along the curb. The engine was still running, and that fact made me want to punch something.

I could be wrong, but I got the impression that her father came here with the sole intention of taking Maggie right back home, regardless of what her condition was.

Jamey tried the passenger door, but the chief had locked it. He grumbled something under his breath as he ran an irritated hand through his hair.

Ben shot a glimpse to me, and I shook my head in warning. He didn't heed it. "Jamey—"

"Why are you here?" Jamey whirled on him as every ounce of anger that had been building up since the moment he stepped one foot inside the RAM house was primed to explode.

Drawing back, Ben's eyes shone. "You really don't know? I'm here for both of you. I care about both of you. Please, can you give me—"

"Give you what?" Jamey raged. "*A chance? A minute to explain?* Did you give Mags the same courtesy? Any of you? No. You didn't do shit for her. She was a servant. She was your entertainment. You used her for your sick game and then threw her away once you were done. Fuck you, Ben, and fuck your family."

Lips trembling, the first tear trailed down Ben's face. It was taking everything inside me not to step in and stop this.

"That's not true. That's not fair. Jamey, please."

In a blink, Jamey moved from standing beside Maggie's chair to his nose being a mere inch away from Ben's, teeth bared. "It is true. And your family will do the same to me that they did to Mags. We don't fit in your richie world. You shit all over us and expect us to take it with a smile. Well, I'm so *very* done taking shit from people like you. It wouldn't have worked out anyway, Ben. You're better off finding some equally rich asshole who's happy to live in the closet with you and your designer tags and expensive cars."

Ben exhaled a rough breath. "You know I don't care about any of that."

Narrowing his lids, Jamey's eyes darkened. "Yes, you do. You care about your image more than your own happiness. That's the one thing that really disappointed me, Ben. To know that you're like all the rest. So good fucking luck with the weak dick willing to put up with that."

I couldn't stand to see Ben go through this, and more so, Maggie. They were forcing her to endure this as sweat dotted her forehead in her too warm clothes, aching back, her breaths far too fast and shallow, barely able to keep her eyes open.

As much as I didn't want to, as much as it shattered me, I cared. God help me…I still cared about that girl.

"Let them go, Ben." I gripped his arm, drawing him away.

Ben fought me. "Mase—"

I jerked to a stop and made him look at me. "Pissing Jamey off is only distracting him from helping her. This isn't what Maggie needs right now. She needs help. She needs a goddamned friend. Let. Them. Go."

Looking back to the pair, it was a long, tense minute before he agreed. I barely got Ben into the truck before whatever was left of him fell apart.

chapter twelve

maggie

"Are you okay?"

Lifting a brow above his sunglasses, Jamey pushed off the oak tree in the university courtyard and quipped, "Yeah, I'm walking upright without baton bruises all over my back. I'm fucking dandy."

Okay, that had been a stupid question, and the sarcasm was deserved.

It was Monday, and I had another headache that rivaled all headaches like it was trying to win the Migraine of the Year award. And to say working this weekend was the worst thing ever was the understatement of the century. I hadn't been downtown in almost a week, but Jamey had assured me that Henry had been setting the basket out daily. However, I'd come to find out on Friday night that he'd not only been setting the basket out every day but had filled it to the brim with food.

Which in and of itself was odd, not to mention the other thing…

When I stepped into the market, Henry hadn't asked me how I'd been, how school was going, didn't invite me behind the counter to look at Billy's catch of the day, and he didn't share any new or old jokes with me. Instead, he shadowed me around the store as though I'd shove cucumbers down my pants, and it wasn't just Henry who had acted that way.

Not only had my regulars sat in Candi's section, but when she tried to have me serve the Jensens, they left. They legit gripped their children's hands and scurried out the door. Before yesterday, I'd never seen anyone scurry anywhere.

So, after five years of laughing at Mr. Jensen's corny puns, listening to Mrs. Jensen's stories about her grandmother's award-winning barbecue sauce, and making Mickey Mouse pancakes for their two children, I was as well-liked as Smallpox.

After that, Candi stopped trying to get me tables, and I spent a few extra minutes out by the dumpster, wondering how much it would hurt if I kicked it.

I was too chicken to find out.

Jamey and the boys were the only ones who hadn't treated me any differently, and when I found an origami penguin stuck between the ketchup and Tabasco bottles, I had to bite the inside of my cheek to stop from tearing up.

Now a week after my beating, I was rocking the winter wear in eighty degrees during a freak autumn warm front, standing outside of the cursed school in this cursed town as my back screamed for one more hit of painkillers that I was out of. I wasn't above raiding a meth house in Sunset Bay.

And while asking if Jamey was *okay* seemed ridiculous, I wasn't blind to the fact that I wasn't the only one hating life today.

Reaching for his face wasn't possible, so I gestured to mine that was covered in a semi-permanent sheen of sweat. "Why do you look like you were just told you could never dye your hair again?"

"Because the prick came to my house again last night."

Oh, and Ben was now known as *the prick*.

"What did he say?" I asked.

Jamey's scowl deepened. "He told me there's a video of your seizure online. He doesn't know when it was uploaded exactly, but it's on TikTok, Instagram, Twitter…"

If I could drop my shoulders, I would, but they wouldn't go any lower. "Shut up."

"The IP address is anonymous, and they used dummy accounts, but obviously, one of the RAMs did this. I don't know how much you remember, but they were filming you." Disgust twisted his features. "You agreed to it, Mags."

"I did? God, I… I'll be honest. I don't remember much after Ben opened the door." A wearied breath left me, and there wasn't anything else to say other than, "My life sucks so hard, Jamey." He held my cheeks, thumbs caressing tenderly as my eyes lifted to his. "Did you watch it? Is it bad?"

"Yeah, but it's not *bad*. It's a lot like what's out there already. It's cut in such a way that only people who know you can tell it's you. They were smart to blur everyone else's faces, including mine. I…I'm sorry I didn't stop it. I didn't think you'd have another seizure so soon after the last one, but when I realized what was happening, I wasn't focused on anything but you. And though you agreed to have your testimony filmed, you didn't agree to have your seizure—"

"No." I could see where that train of thought was going, and I needed to derail it. "I am not going to my father with this. You told him we were at the RAM house to meet with our partners for a Public Speaking project. A fake project I didn't have his permission to meet with my partner on for a class that you're not even enrolled in. And if he sees that video, he'll find out you lied. He'll find out about Eric and Marcus and those pictures… He'll beat me for sure."

Jamey's dark brows flew up. "You may not have a choice. The deans have already started to act. They don't want to be associated with this video any more than you do. They want to find out who posted it."

A sad laugh left me. "Don't kid yourself. They want me to think they're trying to find out who posted it, so I won't go to the cops. They'll sweep it under the rug like nothing happened. This university has one interest. Money. And whoever's responsible for that video has a family that contributes a shit ton to this place on the regular. The last thing they want to do is cut off their cash supply for a girl who is literally leeching off them. Face it, as long as I keep my mouth shut, no one will care."

Jamey filled his cheeks with air, letting them deflate slowly. "Well, I care, and the more time that passes, the harder it will be to shut it down. Especially now that it's viral."

I squeezed my eyes shut, turning over that word. *Viral.*

Realistically? What good would it do me to get upset over something I'd never see? I didn't have any social media accounts, didn't even own a device that could access them, and the chances of my father seeing it… Candi or one of the boys would have to stumble across it first, which was a possible outcome. But there was only so much I could handle, so much I could take. This wasn't a battle worth fighting. Not today.

I shrugged. "It's not like I made a porno, and you're right. There are a ton of them already on TubeYou. I've watched some on Frankie's computer only because I wanted to know what I looked like during a seizure."

"YouTube," he corrected.

I angled my head back, the nerves in my shoulders finally not protesting so much when I did. "Did Ben say anything else?"

"Same shit, different day. *Hear me out. Take me back. We can work through this.*"

"You should, Jamey. I don't think he had anything to do with it. He wouldn't be going to your house every night, begging you to take him back if he did. You're punishing yourself."

"I threatened to bust out his headlights the next time he came over," he stated with an air of pride.

"Jamey—"

"Don't." Taking the bag off my shoulder, he said, "He doesn't matter. You're what matters. He was too good to be true anyway. I should know better by now." I filed that last part under the some-other-time-when-he's-not-so-pissed category. Jamey grasped my hand and immediately shot me a stern look. "Mags."

"I know," I muttered before he could say anything else.

Closing both Friday and Saturday didn't lend a lot of time to sleep, even if I physically could. Every position hurt. On the plus side, I had plenty of time to catch up on the classes I'd skipped Thursday and Friday, but now my hands were vibrating like a hummingbird on crack. My only hope was that my next seizure would strike on my way home, a bear would turn me into a Maggie Snack Pack, and my misery would be over.

As I took the stairs one at a time like a toddler, Jamey paused on a step halfway down, probably because he thought I was going to tumble and go *splat* on the concrete.

"I'm okay, Jamey. You can keep—"

I stopped talking when his fingers squeezed mine in a silent order to *shut it*. My gaze flicked up. Charlie was at the bottom of the stairs, mirroring our frozen stance, her intention to go up the stairs rather than down. Without assistance. In heels. Just thinking about wearing those things gave my vertigo vertigo.

"Hi," I said.

Her honey eyes flared at my greeting as if shocked I would dare speak to her. Then, for some reason, she scanned her surroundings before bringing her gaze back to us. "H—hey."

She hadn't moved yet, so I figured today's reception wouldn't be followed by a hug. I left things a little shaky the last time I'd seen her at the Scotts, but this was shaky enough to register on a Richter scale. Guess her girl crush was over, and I only needed one guess as to why.

Mason.

My eyes narrowed. "We're coming down, so you may want to hold onto your jewelry. It looks expensive."

She frowned at that, glancing to her coffee cup. "I, uh— I shouldn't be…" Biting her lip, she did that quick recon thing again, and then it dawned on me why.

Charlie was making sure no one would see her speaking to me.

"Wow." I wasn't much for rolling my eyes, but I made an exception this once. "Is it that you can't think for yourself, or is your reputation really this fragile?"

Avoiding the answer, Charlie's throat rolled in a swallow, thick lashes hiding her eyes. I nudged Jamey to get us moving, and he did.

Stepping aside, Charlie waited for us to hit the landing before speaking again. "Maggie, I'm sorry."

I glared at her, daring her to look directly at me, to speak louder than a mumble. "No, I'm sorry. I'm sorry, I thought you were different. I'm sorry I saw you as someone I'd like to be friends with."

She flinched, and I had to admit, I got a little satisfaction out of that.

As I entered the lecture hall of my public speaking class, a few students were mingling in the upper rows, but their hushed whispers went silent as they averted their eyes the moment I appeared. God only knew what rumors they'd heard or what interesting nickname they'd made for me. It would be a challenge to outdo my high school senior class. As a prank last year, anytime a senior passed by me, they would throw themselves on the ground and pretend they were seizing.

Good times.

Grumbling to himself, Jamey helped me scale another set of stairs to get to my seat. He grimaced as much as I did when my ass hit the chair. I was glad my appetite was shit because the bathroom situation? Not good. I was now on a diet catered by Jell-O and Mott's.

With a kiss to my pounding temple, Jamey took my classwork from my bag and placed it on Allen's desk for me. He turned to leave as Dylan and Mason walked in. Passing between them, Jamey not so subtly shouldered both men on the way out. Shockingly, they took it without so much as a dirty look in his direction. That either had something to do with their loyalty to Ben or Addison's choice of miniskirt today. She flaunted past the men with a wink and a flirty flip of blonde hair, but I doubted they noticed either since their eyeballs were attached to the denim fabric that was so short, it could defuse WWIII. I couldn't blame her. If I had a body like that, I wouldn't cover it up either.

Clipping to the front of the class in her low heels, Professor Allen held a mug that read, WITH EACH TYPO YOU MAKE, A PIECE OF MY SOUL FIGURATIVELY DIES. "Take your seats, people. Today, we're practicing interviewing skills with your partner, and I wrote down a list of topics to cover." With a push of her hand, the whiteboards slid apart to reveal her elegant handwriting.

Bummer. I was hoping today would be a solo act.

My gaze rose as Dylan was about to take the first step up the stairs, stopping when Mason clamped a hand on his shoulder. The two men exchanged a quick conversation, and then both of their gazes lifted in unison to connect with mine. So not interested in what that was about, I focused on finding a notebook with enough available real estate for my scribbles.

Movement on the stairs a few rows down caught the edge of my sight, and though I knew it was Mason heading toward his seat, those damned disloyal eyes of mine took it upon themselves to look anyway.

But it…wasn't Mason. Why was Dylan going down the wrong aisle, headed straight for—

Oh, I didn't have a good feeling about this. At all. Dylan's smile was near blinding against a canvas of rich umber skin with a twinkle in his eyes that I'd seen more than enough times. When he stopped, my belly took a tumble. Dylan's large hand landed on the desk above, using it to lower himself while he whispered in Addison's ear. He couldn't have said more than five words to the girl before she collected her bag and followed him right out the door.

Asshole. This was the second time he'd bailed on me for a hookup.

Dylan Ward was soooo on my shit list. Taking the number two spot under the dude who just occupied the seat next to mine.

"Mr. Scott." From the lectern, Allen's glower shot over the rim of her glasses and targeted the unwelcome man at my side. "You're in the wrong seat."

All the shuffling in the room stilled at once. Clearing his throat, Mason then projected that deep voice loud enough to travel across Finch Hall. "Yes, Professor. Neither Maggie nor I have a partner today. I thought I would remedy the problem. *Like adults.*"

Oh, Christ.

Inclining her head, the helmet of auburn curls didn't so much as move. Allen's lips pursed. "Should I take this to mean you've also remedied your…*issue?*"

The *issue* being complete and utter bullshit. A lie Mason had made up to get out of being my partner to begin with. That he was a sex addict and petite brunettes were his trigger.

Mason shifted in his seat, throwing a quick glance in my direction. "Yes, ma'am. I have."

That over-the-frames glare came my way. "Miss Davis? I suppose you should have a say here."

Nice. Hell if I was going to be the non-adult in the room. "Who my partner is, Professor, doesn't make a difference to me as long as they can stay on task."

A shadow of a thin brow shot up in what could be construed as approval of my response, but the moment passed as fast it came. The brow sank back down, her tone dry. "Couldn't agree more. Very well, let us proceed." With that, she tipped her head down to look through the glasses perched on the tip of her nose, scrutinizing the paperwork in front of her as though she were editing a manuscript and hated every word. I prayed that wasn't my writing prompt from Friday.

The pairings began to turn in their chairs to face each other, and I refused. Immature? Probably. But hell, I was in agony. Mason could not only turn his seat toward me but hoist men off the ground with one hand.

And the former, he did.

Rotating his chair, Mason inched closer. So close that he was all up in my bubble, those flippers he called feet on either side of my chair, legs spread as if to act like a barricade, fencing me in.

Quite the change from the first time we had done this.

I didn't bother acknowledging *my partner*, but he was about to see another one of his brilliant plans burst into flames.

I let my hair act as a shield as I tucked my hands into my hoodie sleeves to complete the Unabomber look.

Mason leaned in, his minty breath stirring the air around me. "Sticks...?" *Ah, we're back to the nickname.* "How are you feeling?" I let my silence answer that dumbass question. "You don't... You're not looking so great."

I lifted my lashes, and without moving my head, I slid my eyes to his direction, our gazes crashing together. There was a time those mossy eyes could have stopped my lungs from drawing air, quickened the beat of my heart, halted the world from spinning. He no longer had that power over me.

"Is that your way of saying I look like shit?" I asked.

A single dimple teased an appearance. "In a much nicer way, yes." He then took my response as an invite to touch my sleeve. I lurched away from him as heat sliced into my shoulder. He sighed as the almost-dimple vanished. "How's your back? Is it any better?"

I released a terse breath as the fresh wash of pain ebbed. "It's fantastic. So good even, I'm going salsa dancing after school."

Invading my orbit even more, the bitter scent of stale whiskey enveloped me. I drew strength from that, using it to brace my walls, a reminder that he was no different than my father.

"How did you hurt it?"

How did...? "I wrestled a shark. Your nana was right about staying out of the ocean during my time of the month. Too bad she didn't warn me about the ones on land."

Defeat folded down the corners of his mouth, twisting slightly to study the list on the board as though it were a portal that would swallow him up and transport him to another dimension. I wished the same thing.

"Is there a religion you practice?"

Of all the damn topics on the board, this was what he chose? Was this some sort of segue into saving my soul from committing more sins?

I scoffed. "Please."

"What?"

"I don't subscribe to fantasy."

"You think religion is a fantasy?" Cocking his head, that stupid, thick hair tumbled over his brow. Apparently, I'd decided his hair was stupid at some point. "How do you believe we exist? You think it's all happenstance?"

"I believe in science," I stated. "You're religious?"

Without hesitation, he nodded, and I had to admit, I was surprised. "I mean, I don't go to church, but I believe there's something greater than me at play. Maybe *spiritual* would be a better term."

"So, you're telling me some mystical, all-powerful being out there said, 'Let it be,' and poof, *this* was the best it could do?" I shook my head, the ache in my temple reminding me that wasn't medically advised. "God doesn't exist."

His dark brows drew together in question. "Why do you believe that?" Mason didn't sound offended or that he was even debating religion with me. He seemed as if he genuinely wanted to know my thoughts, which only pissed me off more. Why did he want to know anything about me now? Why did he orchestrate being my partner today? Had he not tortured me enough?

"Because your Almighty is supposed to be kind and just?" I didn't wait for his acknowledgment. "How do you explain what He did to Faith?" Mason winced at his sister's name, and I knew that hurt, but for some sick reason, I kept going. "Was her disease kind, Mason? Did she deserve it?"

I still didn't know how she had passed away or when, but I did know it was a long, drawn-out illness that had stripped her life away painfully, leaving the Scotts hollow and broken.

Mason's entire body withered as he eased back a millimeter.

My insides twisted with guilt. "I didn't say that to be cruel, but you have to see how ridiculous it is to worship a being that allows an innocent child to suffer while the real monsters of the world walk free."

Lashes fanned his cheekbones, hiding his eyes. After a long, torturous moment, Mason's Adam's apple shuddered, releasing a strained breath. I kinda hated myself now. "I *have* to believe there's a greater purpose. A reason for it all. Otherwise, I'll go insane."

"Greater purpose?" A sad laugh bubbled out of me. "That's a good one. I'll have to remember that next time."

Lifting his gaze, the citrine bands in his eyes shone bright as they locked onto me. "Next time what?"

The next time I'm beaten within an inch of my life for doing… "Nothing," I murmured.

As we sat quietly, he chewed his lips, emptied his ballooned cheeks, and tapped his pen to some rock tune that I'd heard during one of his workouts.

He broke first. "I'm sorry about your epilepsy. What is it like when it happens?"

Staring at him, my mouth dropped open. "Are you for real? Was the floor show not enough for you? If you need a reminder, I'm sure you can catch that shit again on Facegram or whatever the hell it's called. Thanks for that, by the way."

Before I could blink, Mason was way up in my personal space, eyes as dark as the forest at dusk. "You have got to be shitting me. You think *I* uploaded that video?"

I angled my head back to give him a proper glare. "You set me up by hiding those earrings in my bag. Of course, you uploaded that video."

"Me…?" His eyes expanded with shock. "What could I possibly gain from doing that?"

"You've been fucking with me from the very beginning, Mason. I couldn't even hazard a guess as to how sick your head is."

"You… You're unbelievable. You're actually trying to spin this." With a disgusted shake of his head, Mason's fists clenched, and then his palms went flat on his thighs as though he were restraining himself from throttling me. "I would never do something as fucked up as uploading a video of anyone having a seizure, which is the very reason my family's private investigator is trying to find out who did."

Ah, okay. I didn't know that part.

Leaning in, he pressed on. "You and I both know there was one person in that RAM house who is demented enough to do that. The person you lied for, for reasons that are beyond my comprehension. But regardless of what you've done, I don't want that for you. It's not right."

I couldn't say anything to that because he had a point. Eric would totally do something like that. And why would the Scotts go through the trouble of hiring an investigator if it had been one of them?

Unless it was another lie.

Mason exhaled through his nose. "I meant, what is epilepsy like *for you?*"

Nodding, I kicked my chin forward. "You want to know what it's like? So do I. I want to know what it's like to have everything you want and more and never have to work for it. What it must feel like to be one of the privileged. Did you grow up knowing you were superior to all of those around you? Tell me, is that trait taught or something you're born with?"

Jaw hardening, a muscle in his temple jumped. "I never thought I was superior to you or anyone else."

My head reared back. "Wow. I almost believed you." Eyes flashing, his nostrils flared, and I kept hitting that nerve. "Truth is, you did. You took one look at me and realized I was so far beneath you, not worthy of *the* Mason Scott. You really should stop going on blind dates and stick to the girls in your class. Might I also suggest you view them in good lighting first so you can grade them properly before wasting your time?"

Hurt and what might be disbelief flickered across his face, and I honestly doubted anyone had called his self-righteous ass out before.

"Maggie, you have been wrong about me from day one. I am not this shallow man you keep making me out to be."

"No, it's you who has been wrong about you. You're not equipped for anything but a privileged life, Mason. Stop trying to slum it down here with the have-nots. Your hands are far too pretty to dirty."

His lips parted and then snapped shut. "And is that what your hands are? Dirty after you tried to steal from us?"

A scream built in my throat, and it took everything inside me to keep it there. My knee tensed, ready to punt kick him between the thighs. I wanted to chuck my backpack at his head and hit him with it until he saw the truth.

I did none of that.

I was silent. That was all there ever was when it came to the truth. *Silence.* I had to keep it buried far and deep because it was too ugly for anyone to see or hear.

It was easier to believe that evil only existed in fairy tales. It lived in stories that could be shut away and never be seen until the book was opened. That evil could never touch them until they invited it to. Little did they know, they were the ones living in the fairy tale. True evil was all around us, waiting for the right moment to tear away the pretty cover, rip through the pages, and reveal the ending where the dragon destroys the castle, kills the prince, and crushes the princess under the rubble. Those of us living in the darkness and shadows knew the ending all too well.

Pity filled his eyes, his tone matching. "You've done this to yourself, Maggie."

Point for Mason. He won this round and may as well have socked me in the gut. "Aren't you a big boy, using your father's words." I fought like hell to keep my head high, refusing to show him how much that hurt. "The only thing I did, Mason, was believe I could—"

Don't fuck things up with those richies. Don't embarrass me. I don't want to hear that you can't even handle scrubbing shitters temporarily.

With strength coming from somewhere unknown, I stood before *my* father's words spilled out of my mouth. "Professor Allen, I've changed my mind. Turns out, my standards for a class partner have changed drastically."

Without bothering to hear her response, I was out.

With another day done and my head ready to implode or explode, I slogged my way across the quad to meet Jamey. My sole focus was taking one small step at a time to get through a mile of grass that seemed to be growing longer by the second. So, when male voices shouted my name, their freaked-out tone didn't fully compute.

Nor did my flight or fight response.

Out of nowhere, a semi-truck barreled into my side, whirling me like one of those damn fidget spinners that were all the rage. The sky reeled around me until gravity decided to have its fun. My tailbone landed first, and then the back of my head slammed into something a tad softer than concrete. An immense weight pinned me to the ground, squeezing all the air out of my chest, and my vision went black. My back felt as if I'd been submerged into an active volcano, every nerve scorched by the lava. I think I screamed, but it was impossible to hear over the blood roaring in my ears.

Pain was my world.

Slowly, like eternity passed kind of slow, whatever was on top of me lifted away. "Oh, no. Maggie? Jesus, I'm so sorry." The voice sounded familiar, but I couldn't divert that many brain cells to figure out his name.

Another voice I couldn't pin a face to said, "Dude, she looks bad."

I wanted to say something along the lines of, *No shit*, but I couldn't move, let alone form words.

"Sticks!" Well, only one person on this godforsaken planet called me that, so I knew who one of the three assholes was.

Someone was shaking me, and for the love of all things holy, I took back everything I said in class this morning and prayed to whomever was up there that they stopped. Each shock against the ground was like another strike of the baton.

I couldn't open my eyes, but the sunlight filtered through my lids, so they looked like sheets of blood. It was all too possible my eyes were bleeding.

"Sticks?" Something warm and comforting cradled my face. "Maggie, breathe."

I would have loved to, but my back throbbed with every heartbeat, and a sob had stalled somewhere in my throat, blocking my air, but I think my mouth was as wide as it would go. The shaking was only getting worse, and it loosened two tears as they leaked from my pinched eyes.

"Maggie, breathe!" Mason commanded, and when I didn't—or couldn't—he whispered, "Oh, God."

Oh, Satan would have been more fitting.

"Get Jamey!" Mason hadn't whispered that time. No, he yelled like a megaphone was attached to his mouth. "Maggie, come on. Take a breath. Try."

I did, and the damn thing nearly ripped me in two. I had no idea how much time had passed before I forced out, "St—stop...sha...king...me."

The warm thing on my cheek stroked softly. A thumb, maybe. "I'm not. It's you. You're shaking."

Well...damn.

"Maggie, I'm so sorry. I— I didn't see you." I swore I knew that voice from somewhere.

"Mags!" Feet pounded toward me, and the ground vibrated as Jamey toppled to my side. Or I assumed it was him because I could scent all the colors in the Skittles' rainbow. "Get away from her!"

"No! Jamey, don't move—" Mason's warning fell on deaf ears.

I was yanked up and twisted to a degree that sent a flash of white-hot fire down my spine, and the cry finally ripped free from my throat.

"Shit! I'm sorry!" Jamey set me down as I buried my face in some unknown body part, praying to pass the fuck out.

"What were you thinking, Vic?" Mason boomed.

Ah, Vic. I only needed one guess who the other nameless asshole was.

"I...I didn't see her. I would never hurt Maggie. You know that, Mason. I was trying to catch the disc—"

"It's my fault," the last nameless asshole said. "We just started this frolf thing, and I shanked it."

Frolf? I was flattened to a pancake because of the stupidest sport ever invented? Motherfucking *frolf?* Actually, strike that. Bathtubbing was the stupidest sport ever invented.

Mason's voice became a vicious growl. "You need to leave. And I mean *now* before I rip your throats out and feed them to you." I wasn't totally sure how one could eat their own throat, but Mason made it sound all too believable.

"We're so sorry, Mag—"

"Pete," Ben urged, having stopped by at some point. "You and Vic should go."

I finally peeled my eyes open to see a blurred image of Jamey hovering above me. By the invading earthy scent of grass and dirt, I could guess this wasn't Hell but Warrington's courtyard. Same difference.

"Get me home," I begged. "Please."

"Let me help you." Mason wrapped a hand around my knee, and I tried to pull away, but it only caused a frisson of pain to spark again.

"Stop touching her!" Jamey barked.

Ben reasoned, "Jamey, she needs a hospital."

I did. I really did need a hospital.

Go ahead and cry, Margaret. Cry to the world and watch me take everything you love away from you.

My grip tightened on the unicorn pooping out a rainbow on Jamey's T-shirt. I had thought it was kinda funny earlier, but that was back when I wasn't dying.

"Jamey, please," I implored, voice choked and thick with misery. "I wanna go h—home."

I refused to look, but I sensed we had amassed a decent gathering of observers while Jamey helped me to my feet. Once he was sure I wouldn't fall back down, Jamey took my bag from Ben. Next to us was a discarded plastic disc that Jamey kicked out of the way, but it only rolled three inches before flopping back on the lawn. For what could possibly be his first and last time touching a frolf disc, it was a decent attempt.

Two excruciating steps later, Mason appeared in front of us, eyes fraught with concern. "Sticks, you need a doctor. Please, I'll take you."

"No, and stop calling me that stupid name," I bit out and took five more steps. Pissed off was good. Pissed off got my feet to move faster. Less primordial ooze-like anyway.

"At least go to the University Clinic. They'll give you painkillers."

In order to get those, they'd require a physical exam. I couldn't risk it.

Ben tried next. "Jamey, reason with her. She can barely hobble. Let us help."

Jamey tucked me closer to his side. "You can help by getting out of our way."

Mason caught my hand. "Sticks, please."

"Why?" I jerked out of his grip and gritted my teeth at the sharp, stabbing blaze rippling through my back. "Why do you care what happens to me? I stole your sister's earrings, remember? Aren't I without any integrity? A disappointment? Don't I *disgust* you?"

Mason cringed at the last one. Good.

"You were right, Mason. I did all of this to myself. This was exactly what I had in mind when I took those diamond earrings and was stupid enough to put them in my own damn bag. Felt so fucking good that I wanna rob some more dead people. In fact, Jamey, can you drive me to Pacific Cliffs Cemetery right now? I think I can dig up three graves tonight."

I turned away from him and those sad green eyes and parted lips that were ready to say the next moronic thing that would only fuel my tirade. Whatever Mason Scott had left to say didn't matter.

I didn't want to hear it. I didn't care.

Jamey walked me home, barely making it before sunset. At his insistence, he took care of Poker's paw that I prayed only needed another week of wraps. Then Jamey made my father's dinner while ten icepacks and a medley of frozen vegetables thawed on my back.

Coming into my room, Jamey wore a face I was all too familiar with, eyes far too focused, trying to stay out of his head and stave off whatever was bothering him.

"Make room, Tripod." At Jamey's command, Poker shifted so Jamey could lay down facing me. He tucked my head beneath his chin, twirling my gross hair between his fingers. I should ask him to help me wash it, and I was surprised he hadn't offered already.

"I'm sorry, Mags." His voice sounded empty and robotic, and before I could ask why he was apologizing, Jamey answered me. "I should have taken you to the hospital today. I shouldn't have argued with Mason's dad when you were at the hospital. I should have shown them— *everyone*—what they did to you. What *he* does to you."

"Jamey..."

His entire body shook, but it was the kind that I couldn't tell if he was laughing or crying. By the swallowing movement rolling on my forehead, I'd say the latter.

His words came out in not much more than a pained whisper. "I feel so fucking helpless."

I inched up so I could look him in the eyes, and the anguish pulling at his features split apart all four chambers of my heart. "You're exactly who I need you to be."

"No, I'm not. We both know it. You need a superhero, not a plucky sidekick."

"I hate to tell you this, but I don't think you're all that plucky."

A sad smile curled one side of his mouth. It was the same tortured smile he wore when trying to convince himself that life didn't suck.

I lifted my hand to his cheek; the slight stubble that had grown since this morning poked my palm. "Do you miss him?" I didn't need to clarify who I was talking about. He knew I was asking about *the prick*, who I didn't think was a prick.

"I miss the idea of him."

"And you don't think you could ever forgive Ben?"

Shaking his head, Jamey's thumb traced the scar on my temple. "You're my family, Mags, and they hurt you. I can't be with a man who doesn't care for you, love you like I do."

Well, gee-whiz.

"I'll get over him, eventually." Lashes lowering, his gaze met mine. "In the meantime, I might go through some strange hairstyle choices, so you'll have to lie and tell me that I look fabulous. Just don't let Ava start waxing my brows. That shit looks weird."

"Done."

chapter thirteen

maggie

With the help of an ill-advised amount of Excedrin and a menthol gel that Jamey applied to my back four times a day, I'd made it to Thursday. Not only that, but I earned bonus points for taking a proper shower. I even shaved. Well, mostly.

And yesterday, a miracle happened. Allen didn't reprimand me for walking out of her class on Monday. Though I couldn't ride my Schwinn yet, I was finally able to unscrew the lights from the frame and left them sitting on Mason's chair when he arrived. When he discovered the lights, his shoulders had slumped, and then Mason looked up to find me. There was a moment—a brief one—where I thought he was dumb enough to try to speak to me again. Thankfully, he grew at least one brain cell and thought better of it. Also, my old weasel of a partner was back from his hookup hiatus. Not that I was speaking to him, either.

Dylan Ward still had the number two spot on my shit list.

Dean Evans had met me in the hallway after class to check in with me. Apparently, there were emails I hadn't responded to, and she wanted to make sure I knew the university was aware of the video and had opened an investigation to find out who was responsible. I honestly wanted to forget about the damn thing, but that was easier said than done when a particular best friend kept giving me hourly status updates on all the hits and shares and something about retooting. Or was that retwitting? I didn't care.

What I cared about was that I'd passed my calculus test and that my psych professor hadn't laughed at my paper. I might even get a B on it. Typically, anything less than an A would make me completely freak out, but my priorities had changed of late.

Another surprise of the not-so-fun kind came in the form of Jamey insisting we immerse ourselves in the college experience. I figured that desire stemmed from his non-boyfriend status or that he'd been kicked off the cross-country team for lack of participation. I kinda owed him since I was a shitastic friend and hadn't realized all those walks home coincided with his team practices. He'd never told me.

And I'd never asked.

So when Jamey suggested we attend a pep rally, I didn't argue. Even though I had no interest in the reason for the rally—which was to announce the football team. And my lack of interest could be because of who was on the team, or that I didn't know anything about football, or that I knew after this year I would no longer be attending Warrington. But there might have been a small part of me—no bigger than a micron—that believed Jamey and I really did deserve a normal college experience.

The college experience I wasn't jazzed about...? Sitting on rock-hard plastic seats in the Cave, Warrington's basketball arena.

My butt was not a happy butt.

What I needed was one of those padded courtside chairs currently occupied by some fancy suits. I assumed they were university staff, considering President Bowler and Dean Evans were among them.

Leaning over in her seat, Bowler spoke to a woman whose diamonds could be seen all the way at the top of the bleachers where we happened to be. The all-white getup she was sporting seemed a bit much for a professor, but the man next to her was equally posh and dapper. The dude even had a pocket square.

"It's Thursday," I complained as the guy next to me blew into a noisemaker that looked like it came straight from a five-year-old's birthday party. "Kind of a weird day for a rally, isn't it?"

"I—" Jamey winced as the chick next to him tested the range of her vocal cords, singing along to the band's rendition of 5 Seconds of Summer's "Youngblood." Being that we were in an enclosed space, every sound was amplified. "Yeah. Word is, they're doing electrical work in here tomorrow. Updates or something."

I arched a brow. "Or the electrical is fine, and they don't want to tell us we're really breathing in black mold from next door."

A grin sprang to his lips. "You're probably..." Simultaneously, twelve students stood up on their chairs five rows down and ripped off their shirts to reveal the blue body paint that spelled out, GO WOLVERINES. "You're probably right, but— Hey, is that *Taylor*?"

"What?" Angling my head to look between the letters L and V, I tracked Jamey's line of sight to the courtside chairs I'd been admiring earlier. Sure enough, sitting right next to Pocket Square was a head of icy blonde hair, every strand styled to perfection. Her complexion was bronzed, and her body...well, only sixty percent of her skin was on display, so it was natural to question if this was, in fact, Taylor Price. But no one else could retain that look of general distaste for the human existence like her.

It was definitely Taylor.

"What is she doing here?" I asked.

"Not a clue," he murmured, and as if Taylor had heard us then, her head swung up, jolting a little as her gaze collided with mine.

I didn't break my stare as I waited for the narrowed eyes, puckered expression, upturned lip... Huh. Didn't get any of that. Instead, her skin tone went from I-spent-a-week-in-the-Bahamas to I-could-use-a-blood-transfusion-stat.

After a solid five seconds of that, her chin cut away, putting all her focus into her phone.

Oh-kay. "That was..."

"Weird?" Jamey finished, and I agreed with a mindless nod of my head.

Once the band finished, the crowd settled into their seats, and President Bowler adjusted her blazer as she stepped to the podium. Introducing herself first, she gave a welcome speech to the students and then named off the university CFO, COO, a few more acronyms along with what seemed like a hundred deans, each receiving lengthy applause.

Finally, she announced, "And please help me extend a warm welcome to our special guests joining us today, Warrington alumni, Vivian and Leo Price!"

Well, Taylor's attendance made a bit more sense now.

As if she'd introduced Beyoncé and Jay-Z, a cacophony of clapping exploded, students leaping out of their seats to cheer. Down on the court, Bling Lady and Pocket Square stood in unison as if it had been practiced and signaled to the crowd with their beauty pageant waves. Now that she was standing, I could see the resemblance. Vivian possessed the beauty and graceful attributes that Taylor and Charlie had, but there was something else...something dark lingering beneath that her daughters didn't possess.

"Jesus." Hunkered low, Jamey nursed his left ear that could have permanent hearing damage by the end of today. "I know she's a supermodel and all, but—"

"How did you know that she's a supermodel? I never told you that."

"Me?" Pointing to himself, Jamey's brows hiked up his forehead. "I know all things useless in pop culture. Question is, how did *you* know that?"

One shoulder lifted. "Charlie told me her mother was a model. I didn't know about the super part."

"She was, and as you can see, still could be." Looking on, Jamey squinted. "She must bathe in the tears of newborns every day to look like that."

More than curious, I asked, "What else do you know about them?"

"Well…" Jamey craned his head for a different angle to gander at the couple. "Leo, the guy bedecked in a Brioni suit, is an über rich hotelier. He's the founder of the Exalted Resort chain, and he started dabbling in nightclubs a few years ago. The Prices own Sinister in Pacific Cliffs and Deviant up in Sea Haven."

"Interesting name choices," I muttered, still a little shocked at how up to speed Jamey was.

"Meh." He made a face to match the sentiment. "I went to Sinister on one of their underage nights. The place was grossly overpriced, the music dated as fuck, and not only were the bartenders rude, but they even watered down their virgin drinks. I mean…that's not only cheap but pathetic."

As the arena quieted, Bowler stepped to the microphone again. "And lastly, joining us today is someone who is no stranger to this campus. An alumnus of the Rho Alpha Mu fraternity and graduated summa cum laude…Mayor Marcus Ryan!" She gestured to the tunnel beneath the bleachers, and the Devil appeared.

While not receiving quite the enthusiasm as the Prices, Marcus crossed the court, smiling and waving to the crowd. The navy suit he wore was impeccably tailored, paired with an orange tie that was the perfect accent to his striking good looks. Dark blond hair curled naturally around his ears in a style that softened his appearance, giving the façade that he was approachable and friendly.

"Thank you, President Bowler." Nodding to her as she stepped aside, Marcus adjusted the microphone to his height, the ginormous ring on his right hand catching the glare of the fluorescent lights in the rafters. "And thank you, Warrington, for having me today. It's an honor to be invited back home, a place where my son, Eric, also now calls home."

Applause erupted, Marcus taking a step back from the podium, nodding and smiling while he relished the moment. Cue the return to the microphone with a somber, reserved expression in three…two…

One.

The audience took their prompt as the applause died down, Marcus clearing his throat before surveying the crowd pensively. "But we mustn't forget how fortunate we are. As you're all aware, with the constant sounds of construction on campus, the summer storms were not kind to Crescent Cove. Families were without electricity for days, road closures that limited our resources took weeks to clear, and homes and businesses suffered significant damage. But none of that compares to the tragedy that our neighbors to the north suffered. Ocean Hills was struck by a massive flood, displacing half their city, not to mention closing Ocean Hills University. I'd like to extend my deep gratitude for the professionalism and compassion the first responders of the CCPD and the CCFD have shown by volunteering their time and expertise to help in a time of crisis. And I'm happy to report, Ocean Hills is starting to rebuild!"

As the crowd reacted, Jamey slid me a knowing look. The politician's act was as slick and shiny as his shoes. My stomach churned as I watched him soak up the adoration.

"I'm not only proud of our town but of my Warrington family, as well. Please accept my appreciation for making our home a welcome environment to those OHU students who otherwise wouldn't have been able to attend college this year."

Again with the ovation.

"I'm surprised he didn't call us down there, so we could tell our sob stories," Jamey grumbled, digging out the Swedish Fish from his backpack.

I nodded in agreement and declined a red fishy when he offered it to me.

"Now." Marcus' tone was lighter, glancing all around him. "I do believe you are all here for one reason. The presentation of your Wolverines?"

Suddenly, the arena exploded with masculine *boos* and *nos*.

Jamey and I shot each other matching confused stares.

Marcus' brows drew high, eyes widening as if bewildered by the crowd's reaction, as well. "No? Have I been mistaken? W—" President Bowler made a show of crossing the podium to whisper in his ear as Marcus muffled the mic, and then he made the universal sign of understanding. "Ah, right. Thank you. I almost forgot about… The Warrington Cheer Squad!"

Like a blast hit us, the walls ricocheted with every male voice and pounding foot, vibrating my seat and eardrums.

Yelling over the crowd, Marcus' arm swung in an arc, like a game show model. "Without further ado, here to present your squad, the stunning and talented, Charlotte Price!"

From the same tunnel Marcus had emerged from, Charlie bounced onto the court, shaking a pair of blue and silver pom-poms, all golden curls and perky boobs, wearing a short navy skirt and what looked to be a football jersey that was knotted below her bust to reveal a flat stomach.

Charlie twirled once, and my throat went tight. On the back of the jersey, in bold silver letters, was the name SCOTT. I didn't know Mason's number, but it wasn't a leap to assume that was his.

It would be so much easier if Charlie were like her sister. Then I could hate her without feeling so guilty.

Prancing onto the podium, Charlie did something that confused the hell out of me. She gave Marcus a kiss on each cheek in greeting. The very man whose son had sexually assaulted her.

I shook my head. I would never understand the richie world.

While Charlie situated the microphone, Marcus stepped down and took the empty chair by Vivian Price.

Once the catcalls and hollers died down, Charlie took over the stage as if she were born to be on it. Considering her DNA, she might have been. All pearly whites and perfect enunciation, Charlie began rattling off a long list of cheerleaders' names, each one rushing the court in an assortment of flips, cartwheels, and tumbles, and in between each, the baritone voices got louder. I wasn't paying much attention because my focus was on those padded chairs below.

"That's interesting," I commented.

"Whad?" Jamey swallowed his candy. "The fact that Warrington has apparently never heard of the Me-Too movement and are well on their way to a class-action sexual harassment suit?"

"Well, that, too. But I was referring to *that*."

Dipping into my airspace, Jamey's gaze followed mine to watch Marcus get mighty chummy with the Prices.

"Hmm…" he mumbled. "Maybe they're reliving the rich ol' days?"

As Vivian threw her head back in laughter, her palm landed high on Marcus' thigh, and Leo wasn't exactly throwing out a jealous vibe. He looked…

"Or maybe they're planning their next threesome?" Jamey drawled.

Yep. That was it. I cringed because it so totally did look like that. "Gross."

I forced my attention back to the court as the cheerleaders formed two lines, creating what looked to be a thoroughfare for the players to strut down as pom-poms shook over their heads. Charlie began announcing the team, but I didn't recognize anyone until Adam sauntered down the line. He did a curtsey. And when Jordon blew kisses to the audience, one chick might have legit fainted.

"And Number Forty-one, Running Back, Eric Ryan!" As Charlie clapped with the same enthusiasm she had for the previous players, one had to wonder if this was the same guy Mason had saved her from. I got that she was putting on a performance and all, but still… The entire thing was wrong.

Jogging down the lineup, Eric didn't bother waving to or looking at the crowd. He settled himself next to Noah as the men created an even longer runway. Camden was announced next, and he proceeded down the line…skipping, wearing a getup similar to Charlie's. Skirt and all. As the crowd showed their appreciation, I hated to admit that Camden looked cute, but it was impossible to ignore.

When Ben hit the court, waving to the crowd, Jamey grumbled something under his breath. It didn't sound complimentary.

Charlie brought the microphone to her mouth again, a demure gleam in her eye, stance a hint flirtier. "I'm a bit biased presenting the next player, but he just so happens to be the cutest Wolverine ever! My boyfriend, Number Thirty-two, Running Back…Mason Scott!"

I swore my stomach shriveled.

Jamey's sticky Swedish Fish fingers threaded between mine. "You wanna go?"

Before I could answer with a resounding, *YES*, Mason rushed out of the tunnel, and though it was quick and small, my heart stalled an entire beat. Just one.

"I hate him, Jamey," I rasped around an unknown emotion crowding the back of my throat. I couldn't stop my eyes from tracking that muscled body as he glided across the court beneath the river of blue and silver sparkles.

Jamey polished off his last fishy and threw the empty bag into his backpack. "No, you want to hate him, like I want to hate Ben. It would be easier."

My elbow launched into his side. "Can't you be one of those placating gays who agree with whatever I say?"

Recovering quickly, Jamey smoothed a hand over his KEEP CALM AND LISTEN TO WHAM! shirt as if he needed to reinforce his point. "I'm already so very stereotypically gay, I can't deviate now. My role is to think with a dirty mind and act bitchy at all opportune moments."

Choosing not to respond, I watched Mason cross the gleaming wood floor, his thigh muscles straining against those black tech shorts that he preferred to wear and the jersey over his gray Henley that was tight around his biceps. Though his beard was thicker than I'd ever seen, it did nothing to diminish the bright smile he flashed at the crowd. He really should be in a toothpaste commercial, strutting on a runway, modeling underwear all at the same damn time.

Scowling, Jamey shook his head. "Why are all the hot boys such dicks? It's like a naturally occurring defect in their DNA. The hotter they look, the more dickish they are."

My gaze swung over to him. "You're hot, and you're not a dick."

"Awww." Tilting his head to rest on my shoulder, he batted his lashes, locking his hazel eyes with mine. "You might be my favorite person today."

I grinned, but the moment of brightness dimmed quickly as Mason accepted the microphone, Charlie curling her arm around his, creating a seal against his body like two Legos snapping together.

The perfect vomit-inducing couple.

Mason's deep voice rumbled out of the speakers and possibly rattled my chest a little. "Thanks for the intro, Charlie. I must say you are the cutest girlfriend ever." Charlie reached up and gave him a kiss on the cheek in appreciation. Acid soured and burned through my belly.

I glared at the genius next to me. "I'm revoking your planning privileges for the next month."

Jamey sighed. "Noted."

Arm gesturing toward the shaking pom-poms, Mason asked, "Can we give it up one more time for the Wolverine Cheer Squad?"

And the crowd obliged. Hoots and hollers broke out, and I think dogs were barking at one point.

Mason looked to the two rows of cheerleaders and players lined up along the entire length of the court. "So? Are we ready for him, guys?"

While the cheerleaders shook their pom-poms, all the men on the football team howled. They actually *howled*.

"What about my Wolverines?" he asked the crowd. "Are you ready for him?" Mason cupped his ear, and then the crowd began howling.

"Do wolverines howl?" Jamey wondered.

I shrugged. "No clue, but I've learned they are closely related to weasels."

He threw me a cheeky grin. "That explains a lot."

Facing away from me, Mason said, "For the man who needs little introduction, give a warm Wolverine welcome to Number Seven, your starting quarterback...Matthew Scott!" He signaled toward the dark corridor, and even from here, I could see the bright ink on Mason's forearm that looked strong enough to lift three of those cheerleaders making eyes at him.

As Matt appeared with a light jog across the court, screams burst through the arena as if the place had transformed into Chippendales.

Studying the lineup, at the men who used to fill Mason's basement, the men who joked with me, smiled at me, told me I got the best ice water…my heart seemed to wilt. Even the smallest joy I'd gotten from that had been taken from me.

Matt made it to the podium, and Mason handed the microphone to his near twin. Matt grinned a sinful smile to the crowd. "Okay, so Charlie is completely biased because we all know that *I'm* the cutest Wolverine ever."

An arena of women and a good amount of men confirmed his declaration, and his teammates did the same. Someone threw a jockstrap at the podium. Chuckling, Matt scooped the thing up like a prize and stuffed it into his back pocket, then waited for the crowd to settle.

"As you know, Coach Bell has your Wolverines working hard, and our first game is a little over a month from now. The schedule's a bit delayed due to the damages along the coastal campuses from the summer storms, but that means we have more time to prepare to kick ass, right?" Cheers broke out. "So, here's where I'm gonna ask for everyone's help. The guys and I sure do need it."

The entire football team hollered their support. Well, Eric gave an unenthused clap, but whatever.

"I'm asking you, Warrington…do we have our claws out?" Taking the microphone, Matt flipped it toward the crowd, and everyone cheered. His head kicked back with a pained flinch. "Wow, that…kinda sucked. What do you think, guys?"

Nods of agreement went through the squads on the court, both football and cheerleaders.

"I'll ask again," Matt began. "Warrington, do we have our claws out?" The cheers came louder, but Matt shook his head, disappointment drawing down his shoulders as he turned back to the court. "I don't know, guys. It doesn't sound like they want to get their claws out for us. I think…I think we need the Wolverine." The screams were deafening, and Matt's brows shot up, turning to face every angle of the crowd. "Oh, is that what you want?" He held the microphone up again, and the shrieks confirmed it. "Are my girls gonna help?" Matt looked at the cheerleaders, and they shook everything they had.

With a slow turn back to the crowd, a sly grin tipped the corner of Matt's mouth. "Gentlemen…you're welcome."

Baritone voices were eager to give their thanks.

The cheerleaders were evenly distributed throughout the basketball court and all the tripping hazards were removed before Matt ordered, "Release...the Wolverine!"

Steppenwolf's "Born to be Wild" played from the speakers, and a person in what I could only guess was dressed in a wolverine costume sprinted out of the passageway. The combination of a rabid bear-dog-weasel chased after the cheerleaders, and the football players tried to catch the ugly thing.

Once the Wolverine touched a cheerleader, she had to run up into the bleachers and jiggle her pom-poms, all while wearing a skirt that barely covered her ass. It didn't take a genius to figure out that the football players were clearly trying to miss the mascot, forcing all the girls into the stands, but I hadn't realized Charlie was still down there until Mason sprinted across the court to rescue her.

Mason, of course, ever the hero, got to her before the mascot did. And as the *cutest girlfriend ever* was hoisted onto Mason's shoulder, the Wolverine wound up at the bottom of a dogpile of football players. The crowd detonated, and the cheer squad shook their boobs harder.

I groaned, "Kill me now, Jamey."

"How do you want it?"

"I don't care. Just start with my eyeballs first, would ya? I never want to see anything that stupid again."

Walking through the courtyard, my steps paused when I thought I heard my name. I perked my ears and—

"Miss Davis! A word if I may!"

An obnoxious groan escaped my throat as the voice and who it was attached to registered. With Jamey halfway across campus retrieving a notebook that he'd forgotten in his locker, I was yet again alone to face off with Marcus Ryan. Well, I was alone if I didn't count the crowd exiting the Cave and heading toward the parking lot.

Dumping my backpack on the grass, I turned as my quivering hands went behind me. "Technically, that was seven words, Mayor."

Sticking to the sidewalk so as not to soil his pristine loafers, Marcus clipped closer. Clipping sounds included. I noted how his pant legs were tapered at his ankles with no indication there was room for a holster.

Didn't mean he wasn't carrying, though. Not that I was worried, being that we were out in public, but it was ingrained in me to notice these things.

"So it was." He came to a stop, eyes shielded by sunglasses. An amused grin tugged at his mouth. "How are you, Miss Davis? I heard you had a rough go lately."

"Yeah, I'm sure you were super concerned. Look, I did what you wanted—"

"That you did. And very well, may I add." As he tucked his hands into his pockets, the sides of his blazer splayed open to reveal a belt buckle that coordinated with the rose gold frames of his sunglasses. "You'll be happy to know that soon, Eric will be inducted into the Rho Alpha Mu brotherhood."

The corners of my mouth lifted, but it wasn't a smile. "*Happy* doesn't quite describe what I'm feeling, Mayor."

The hidden meaning to that did nothing to deflate his cheery mood. "I have to admit. I had my doubts you would follow through."

"Well, imagine what I could do with matters that are actually important. Like caring for the town's homeless. People are starving on the streets, mere miles from the very place you call *home*. You have the power to help them. The plan I outlined for you—"

"Miss Davis." Taking a moment, his chest rose and fell with a heavy breath as if he wanted to consider his words to spare my feelings. "We've been over this. The fate of the Cove will be prosperous, and the investors I've brought here don't want their streets strewn with rubbish."

Rubbish. He seriously just referred to human beings as *rubbish*. I licked my lips, the skin rough on my tongue. "And would these investors happen to be the Prices? I couldn't help but notice how chummy you were with them."

He chuckled under his breath. "*Chummy*. Yes, I suppose we are." Another pause. A tilt of his head. "I'm pleased to see you took care of my other request. Not only did you distance yourself from Mason, but you managed to annihilate that Scott bridge in the process. Well done."

My fists curled behind me as my jaw tightened. "You and your creepy pictures were a great motivator."

Each side of his mouth curled, and... *Oh, that was disturbing*. I really did not want to know what he was doing with those pictures of Mason and me at Lover's Inlet.

"I am curious about something," he said, and I swallowed as his next thought percolated. "Your father doesn't seem to know anything about the issues between my son and you."

"Was that a question?"

"An observation. It's—" The letter W of GO WOLVERINES came streaking by, and Marcus drew his right hand out of his pocket to adjust his tie while he waited for the guy to pass. "It's such a shame we aren't on the same side of things, Miss Davis. Your skills and sharp mind would be of great use to me. I can appreciate someone who…recognizes the importance of discretion."

"You pronounced extortion wrong, Mayor," I said dryly.

"That I did." Again with the creepy smile. "It's been a pleasure, Miss Davis. And if you reconsider your position, let me know. I can make a slip of morality well worth your while."

"No amount of money would be worth it to me."

He hummed. "We'll see. Just in case, I'll keep a special spot open for you when I become governor. Right next to your father."

chapter fourteen

mason

"Best rally ever, Mase!" As I trailed Charlie through the parking lot, she twirled on one Stella McCartney sneaker to face me, scuffing the tread, which might be a sin of the twelfth commandment. "You were ah-*mazing*!"

"Yeah." My voice sounded detached, almost like it hadn't even come from me. Doing the one foot in front of the other routine, a drop of sweat trickled down my brow and along my jaw. I ran a palm over my scruff to swipe it away, surprised at how thick my beard felt. When was the last time I had shaved? Monday? No, last Friday. That explained the Yeti joke Owen cracked this morning.

I couldn't wait for this warm front to push through. Practice had not only sucked all week, but yesterday was Drill Day Fun Day with Watkins. And by the way, DDFD? Not fun. At all. I briefly wondered how Maggie could deal with this weather wearing those heavy sweaters and jeans. That had to be hotter than a bi—

"Did you hear that crowd when you put me on your shoulders? Genius! Pure genius! Guaranteed it will be trending all over social media by tonight!" Charlie's honey eyes danced in the sun as she sidled up next to me. "Even Mother looked pleased. I think. It's hard to tell since her smile lines have been filled. Sorry she gave you the third-degree about missing the dinner party weeks ago."

Reaching up, she pinched my cheek, and I pulled back from her touch. Hurt shuttled across her features, but she was quick to smooth it away.

"Anyway," she said, smiling, "we have plenty of time to change before dinner, but we need to be at the airstrip by…"

Her words slowed to a trickle as a matte black tank rumbled to a stop in front of us. Dylan lowered the window. As expected, he was riding solo because if anyone so much as breathed on his baby, he broke out in hives. Not an exaggeration. The dude got literal hives.

Pulling up behind the Conquest Knight XV was Mike's Hummer, the thing looking like a baby following its momma.

Dylan peered over his sunglasses. "You coming back to the house for a post-rally drink, Miss Price?"

Charlie nodded eagerly. "Possibly after—"

"She can't." I hijacked the convo, feeling not one qualm about it, and that look Charlie gave me moments ago returned, but it didn't disappear this time.

D's dark gaze switched between us. "Oh-kay. Uh…maybe we'll see you tomorrow night then?"

Glancing to me awkwardly, Charlie worried her bottom lip. "Yeah, maybe."

Pushing his shades up, Dylan's chin ticked my way. "What about you, Mase? You on your way back?"

I nodded my answer, and with a quick goodbye to Charlie, D guided his monster out of the parking lot. The Hummer stuffed with RAMs was close behind.

Once the vehicles cleared, two figures across the quad caught my attention. I squinted to find it was Maggie and…Marcus Ryan? That was a pairing I'd never thought I'd see. Perhaps that was stupid considering what she'd done for his son, and thinking about it, maybe she'd gotten a payout from it. But something about her stance was off, wrong.

Though a good distance away, I could see she had her hands tucked behind her, chin jutted out stubbornly, glare defiant. I knew that look all too well. She was pissed and ready to take out a knee. And Marcus looked—

"You know, Daddy and Mother offered to let us take the jet back from Pacific Cliffs after dinner. It's a twenty-minute flight, so we could meet everyone for drinks later." Head dipped to the side to enter my focus, a curl from Charlie's intricate side braid-ponytail, courtesy of her stylist, shifted over the top of the number three on my jersey. My jersey that was nothing more than a prop.

Just like me.

And each second that passed that I had to see her in my jersey and play the part I was sick of, frustration burned hotter in my blood. I bit back a plea to take it off.

I hated that she'd called me last night to tell me her parents would be in town for business. I hated that she'd asked me to pretend to be madly in love with her and promised this was the last time. I hated every moment of that rally, every word that had come out of my mouth. Most of all, I hated that I had done nothing to stop it.

And if Charlie thought shutting down that invitation to the RAM house had anything to do with my desire to stay in Pacific Cliffs with her family longer than necessary? Uh, hell no.

In fact…

"I can't, Charlie. I know I told you I could do this tonight, but I can't." Shoving off, I targeted my Raptor, stealing another glance to the courtyard.

"Mase?" Her cool fingers wrapped around my bicep, tugging me to a stop. I did. "Please. It's just—"

"Just what?" Weary, I turned to her. "Another insufferable night with your father as he not so subtly offers me the position in one of his many companies once we're married? Or listening to your mother give you a macronutrient breakdown of everything you put into your mouth? Or listening to Taylor's snide comments about how you slept your way to your last gig, all while I sit there holding my dick with a fake ass smile? I can't fucking do it tonight."

Or ever again. But I kept that to myself.

Her fingers curled tighter. "I know. My parents are awful, but Tay's been better, Mase. I swear. Maybe…a night away from everything would do you some good."

A dry laugh escaped before I could stop it. "*Me?* No, Charlie. It would do *you* some good."

Hand dropping to her side, Charlie's brows teased together. "What does that mean?"

"It means that with me, you have free rein to hit the X anytime life gets too real because I will be there to clean up your mess. It means the next time your parents threaten to extend the terms of your conservatorship, I'll be there to convince them not to. It means I've gotta be careful about who I talk to, who I'm seen with, who I fuck because if I'm within a mile of a pair of tits, I'm branded the cheating asshole. Nothing about this arrangement was, is, or will ever be about me. It's all about you, Charlie, and what you need and what you want."

She visibly paled, eyes brimming with tears faster than she could blink them away.

"Shit. I'm sorry. I didn't mean that." I ran a frustrated hand through my hair. I apologized not because I didn't mean it, but because making her cry was the last thing I intended right now. "I don't know where that came from. I haven't slept more than a couple of hours in days, and I've got a wicked hangover."

Lids in rapid-fire mode to clear them, she swallowed. "Well, I don't feel so bad now telling you that you smell worse than Sinister's floor after Friday night, and a brick wall is better company." She gave me a tentative smile, but it was wobbly.

Looking away from Charlie, those fucking mutinous things in my eye sockets went right back to the quad as Marcus practically skipped away from Maggie with glee. And Maggie looked...

"Mase?"

"Hmm?" I watched Maggie take her hands out of her back pockets to rip out her ponytail only to shove her hair right back in it, meticulously combing the hair at her left temple. How? How had I missed something so obv—

"What is going on with you?" Charlie asked. "It's like you're..."

I tore my gaze off Maggie. "Like I'm what?"

Discomfort pinched her pretty features. "Like you're mourning Maggie." She glimpsed the courtyard, shaking her head. "I don't get it. You know what she did. You were the one who told me to stay away from her. And yet, you're the one who can't let her go. You're constantly looking for her, thinking about her. Why?"

"*Why?*" I recoiled. "Because she almost died, Charlie. Less than a foot away from me, I watched Jamey give her mouth to mouth. I carried her into the emergency room, and then I had to stand by and watch her leave in a wheelchair. She went home when she was in a state that she couldn't even get out of a bed by herself. Her epilepsy was caused by *brain trauma*, and Dad thinks her tremor is connected to it. I can't even wrap my head around how difficult her life must be, and worse, she and her father refused all treatment and acted like a near death experience was a completely normal occurrence. And if that wasn't bad enough, there's a video all over social media documenting every horrible second of what she went through without her consent, and she thinks *I* uploaded it!"

"Mase... None of that is your fault."

"Yes. It is."

Her head swiveled side to side. "She stole from your family, deceived you. She took advantage of you."

I shook my head. "I read that stress can make her condition worse. And I knew she was having a hard time. I *saw* it that day at the RAM house. Her hand tremor, her staggered walk, even her speech was off. She wasn't okay. And I didn't help her. Not like I should have. Then someone—*Eric*—took advantage of her when she was vulnerable and used her disorder for his own sick pleasure. I know what Maggie did, and

I'm pissed at her for it, but she was fired. She lost her job. That's punishment enough. She...she doesn't deserve *this*."

Nodding, Charlie's gaze veered away from mine to observe the parking lot occupied by a few students and faculty leftover from the rally. "I know. That video is awful. It even got around to Tay. Surprised the hell out of me when she asked how Maggie was doing, which...showing concern for *anyone* has never happened before. She really has been different—"

"Charlie." Head snapping up to my sharp tone, her parted lips closed. "I think it's great that you and Taylor are on better terms, but please don't use Maggie to bond over." The thought caused an oily taint to cover my skin, suffocating me.

"Right. No, of course. I only meant..." Twirling a curl around her finger, Charlie's lashes swept up to mine. "So, since you don't seem to be in the mood for being trapped in a confined space with my family tens of thousands of feet in the air, how about I order a pizza, and we can binge *Ozark*? Or that *Flash* show you like."

There were times like these that I wanted to shake some sense into this girl. What wasn't she getting here? I needed her to be honest with her family, release me from this chain I'd placed around my own fucking neck. Did she not understand that, or did she not...care?

Maggie would care. Maggie would never put me in this position. No, she would take that chain and drag it behind her until she collapsed.

Clenching my jaw, I stopped that thought before it could go any further. Those were fantasies, hopes that had died weeks ago. That was not who Maggie was. That was who I wanted her to be.

Rather than deal with everything that needed to be dealt with, I outright lied. "I'm beat, Charlie. I'm just gonna crash."

After a quick and rather angry drive back to the RAM house, I walked inside from the back lot as my stomach churned and tightened like the thing was desiccating from lack of use. Try as I might to remember the last meal I'd had, I couldn't. It was a toss-up between a slice of cold Hawaiian pizza or what may have been week-old Kung Pao leftovers. There was a scent in the air that was vaguely appetizing, so I followed it.

I really shouldn't have.

Coming to a stop in the middle of the kitchen, my brain couldn't quite comprehend what my eyes were seeing. Honestly, even if I'd spent a lifetime in this fraternity, I still wouldn't have been prepared.

"Please do not tell me you're doing what I think you're doing," I said.

Adam—and I only knew it was Adam because of the tattoo on his bicep depicting a mermaid wielding a sword against a squid army— peeled a cucumber slice off one eye. "Dude, you gotta try this. Check it. It's a beer foot spa!"

Sprawled out next to the oven in a lounge chair, Noah scratched at his head. Well, he scratched at the pink swimming cap on top of his head. "A week of these, Mase, and your foot fungus will be no more! I swear!"

Against my better judgment, my throat rolled in a swallow. Immediately regretted it. "And you're using our pots and pans to soak your fungus feet? The pots and pans we use to cook our *food?*"

Vic drank from his Corona as a chunk of unmashed avocado slid off his cheek and onto his bare chest, getting caught in the few wiry hairs he had there. "We wash 'em when we're done!" He then proceeded to dump the rest of his beer into a saucepan.

I was suddenly grateful for my current state of starvation.

Pete sat up in his lounger, and I was just now noticing his left brow had grown back. Mostly. "We were gonna get those pedicure fish and put them in a tub, but the logistics of ordering them were a fucking nightmare."

I nodded slow and measured, still trying to take this all in. "And you didn't consider doing *this* in a tub?"

Removing the cucumbers from his eyes, Jordon blinked up at me. For whatever reason, his head was coated in a thick layer of mayonnaise. And I knew it was mayonnaise because the empty jar was on the island next to a line of scented candles, avocado skins, eggshells, and…turmeric?

"We're working with food here, man. Food belongs in the kitchen. We're not troglodytes." With an irritated shake of his head, the cucumber slices went back on Jordon's eyes— Oh, nope. They were on his nipples now.

"Of course," I drawled, my gaze dropping to the music playing on Mike's phone. "Obviously, a group of grown men who have a spa day in the kitchen while listening to Sade's 'No Ordinary Love' are anything but troglodytes."

"Diss it all you want, man," Adam murmured, settling back onto his lounger. "This is cleansing my soul."

"Well, that shit's the only thing *cleansed* around here." My eyes bounced over the wax drippings on the counters, the sinks filled with water and rose petals, and the three empty bottles of honey strewn on the floor… "When— No, *why* did you start doing this?"

"Ah, funny thing about that." Pete poured sugar onto a lemon slice. "You kind of inspired us."

My brows drew low and tight. "How exactly?"

"Remember when Pete turned my skin orange?"

I twisted my head around to Vic. "I can't *not* remember that."

"Well— Ah, thanks." Vic accepted the sugared lemon from Pete. "I started using these lemons to exfoliate and shit, and while they didn't do anything for the stain, I noticed my skin had never felt so fucking smooth. Seriously, my elbows were like a baby's ass cheek. So then, of course, I wanted my entire body as smooth and soft as a baby's ass cheek, but reaching my back was a bitch."

"I can imagine," I muttered.

"So then Pete's girl gave him this oil mixture to help regrow that eyebrow I removed, but he kept getting that shit in his eye."

"Thought I'd go blind." Pete handed out two more lemon slices to the group.

Vic rubbed the lemon along his thigh, matting the hair. "Well, when you told me to spend more time with the Irish Spring rather than looking like a leprechaun, it clicked. Pete could help get my back baby-ass-cheek smooth, and I could help save his eyesight."

"Win-win, brotha!" Pete clinked lemon slices with Vic.

Mike sipped from a mug that had…four different tea bags steeped in it. "Things kinda snowballed from there."

"Uh-huh." I reluctantly took another look at the jar of coconut oil with a…hair in it. "Do me a favor and don't repeat that story. Ever. To anyone."

"You got it!" Noah promised, and then the hand holding his sugared lemon went somewhere a lemon nor sugar should ever go.

I took that as my cue to leave. Unfortunately, the next room I entered wasn't much better. I blamed the two men occupying it.

As Brady was about to head up the stairs, he stopped and slanted his head at me, eyes narrowing. "Let me guess. Spa day?"

"Apparently."

"Damn," he grumbled. "Hope they didn't use all the eggs this time."

My brows shot up. "If *that's* your biggest concern, I need to move out of here. Stat."

Brady's sidekick and all-around pain in my ass sniffed. "That'd be fine by me."

My gaze slid over to Eric. "No one cared enough to ask you."

"Alright." Shifting over, Brady planted himself between us. "I'm not going to play referee between you assaches." His blue eyes landed on me for a beat. "Mase, get over your shit and quick. And Eric—" Brady turned to his little friend. "You have some adjusting to do, as well."

"The only adjusting Eric knows how to do is when he's recording a video," I commented.

Eric's upper lip curled. "You suggesting something there, Scott?"

"Oh, I'm doing more than suggesting, Ryan."

Brady cursed. "Mason, stop. We don't know who posted it."

A sharp laugh cracked out of my throat. "You're going to legit look me in the eye and say that you think it's possible one of *our* brothers posted a video of a girl seizing in the middle of the dining hall? Bull. Shit. The angle it was filmed from wasn't from Quince's phone, and in case Eric didn't enlighten you, allow me. He and Maggie have a history. She witnessed him gang-raping—"

Eric lunged for me just as someone put me in a full nelson and whipped me around, so I was facing the opposite staircase. I wasn't sure who was holding me yet, but it wasn't Matt. No, he was standing a foot away like a sentry, his cold glare drilling past me.

Brady ordered, "Get him to chill the fuck out, Matt."

"How about you do your job, *President* Hale," Matt lobbed back. "You know Mase isn't wrong about Eric. It's why you haven't done shit to investigate yet."

Brady scoffed. "No. I haven't done shit yet because it has to be done through proper channels. By the university. With a search warrant. You want to tell every brother in here to hand over their devices and hard drives along with their constitutional rights? You may want to reconsider prelaw as your major."

"Fuck off. You know I'm talking about keeping the investigation in-house. You haven't asked one goddamned brother if they posted that video because you already know who did it. I told you, Brady. No matter his last name or how much money his family has, Eric Ryan isn't one of us. Never will be."

With half my body still in a pretzel, it was Dylan who whispered in my ear. "Can I let you go, or are you gonna punch my junk?"

"I'm good," I grunted as Dylan released his hold only to have Matt take over by cuffing a hand around my neck to drag me into the next room.

"I got him, D. Thanks."

"No prob. It was either wrangle your brother or see that fucked-up shit going on in the kitchen again," he mumbled, taking the stairs. "Ain't nobody right after seeing that."

Matt didn't stop walking me until my ass was firmly planted behind the bar, and he continued to the other side of the counter to feed me the amber liquid I'd been craving. Since the earring incident, he'd been getting as wasted as I had, and tonight would be no different.

As the drinks were poured, we didn't talk about my performance at the rally or the fact that I should be thousands of feet in the air on a private jet, sipping champagne while the Prices wooed me with their wealth and their daughters.

In no particular order.

Not a syllable was spoken until my voice hit the point of slurring. I let the words I'd been holding in for days tumble out. "I miss Sticks."

Matt's lids tapered until I could no longer distinguish the sapphire threads in his emerald eyes. "You miss the illusion of her. Everything about that girl was a lie. While what Eric did was wrong on so many levels, I don't even think that seizure was real."

Mouth filled with JD, it remained in a holding pattern between my lips and throat. I couldn't have heard that right. This wasn't the first time he'd thrown a Maggie conspiracy theory down on me. Before Matt had even shaken Maggie's trembling hand, he thought she was some kind of mastermind grifter.

Swallowing, my head took wide swipes, making the room go a bit wonky. "What? Why would you think she faked a seizure?"

Fingers began to spring up with every sentence out of his mouth. "Jamey didn't want you to take her to the hospital. Then she just so happened to wake up when her father walked in. Then he denied treatment and wouldn't even let her stay for observation. Sounds like they knew exactly what the tests would show. That she was faking it. And if I were the chief of police with a kid like that... I'd do the same and roll her out before anyone could call her on it and embarrass me."

Whiskey stirred in my gut, souring it. "She wasn't faking it, Matt. I would know when someone is really unconscious." It could have been my blood alcohol was tipping to a dangerous point, but I swore he flinched at that. "You...weren't there for all of it. You didn't see that scar on her head. And you didn't see how much pain she was in when Vic tackled her days later."

Staring me down, his head bobbed. "Another event you happened to be front and center for. It wasn't a coincidence, Mase. By driving her to the hospital, you showed her sympathy, and she knows she's close to getting you on the hook again." Matt emptied the last few drops of whiskey into his tumbler and reached for a new bottle. "It's all part of her game."

Flashes from the last couple of weeks played over in my mind where, yeah, everything that he was suggesting was possible. There was something, though, call it hope, belief in humanity, or blind instinct, but I rejected Matt's theory.

"I don't think so. She hates us. And it's a deep-seated hate like *we're* the ones who wronged her. And maybe we have. I mean—"

Hands on the bar, Matt leaned over it, meeting my eyes. "We have done nothing wrong by her. And in return, she's done nothing but fuck us over. Because of her, Eric will be in this house in a matter of weeks. Brady made the announcement last night when you were upstairs getting shitfaced. Little that there was, Maggie's testimony got him absolved of all charges and reinstated as a pledge. And if Cam and I hadn't argued on your behalf, your ass would be in the shitbox now."

I thought back to the courtyard today. At the way Maggie had glared at Marcus like he was her mortal enemy.

But it's going to end the way I expect it to.

Maybe she hadn't wanted to testify on Eric's behalf. What if she...was forced to? But why?

Mulling that over, I spun my glass on the counter, watching the ice smack against the sides. "What if there's a reason for all of it? A reason she stole the earrings."

"Such as?" Matt cracked open the new bottle.

"Such as maybe she needed money for her medical bills. What if she has crappy health insurance, and that's why she refused treatment at the hospital. I don't know, but I don't believe she took them for the thrill of it or to hurt us."

Leveling me with a stare, his knuckles went white on the bottle. "Don't go down this road, Mase. She tried to take a piece of Faith from us, and she did hurt our family. It's as simple as that. Let her go and walk away." His gaze skipped over my head to the blonde who walked into the room. Matt dispensed another double for himself that went down faster than it took to pour. "Just in time, Lexi."

Her stilettos carried her over to the bar. "When Matthew Scott calls, I come."

He chuckled deep and low at the innuendo, the weight of our conversation clinging to the edges of his laugh. "And that you will, baby."

Jesus. How could he get hard with that word coming out of his mouth? *Baby.* Never understood the endearment. It only brought Pampers to the forefront of my mind and had always been a boner killer for me.

I wasn't sure how long I stayed at the bar or how much I had to drink, but I crashed in my room sometime later, thoughts fuzzy and muddling together.

Let her go and walk away.

With all that Maggie had done, it should be that simple.

I dragged my phone out of my pocket and did what I had done every day since I'd seen it in person. I pulled up the video and hit Play.

Jamey's voice warbled out of the speaker, the people and scene blurred around her. His words were clear, though, as he begged Maggie to lay down. Then came her screams at the invisible person tormenting her. Her guttural cry. The shaking. The stillness.

Hitting Pause, my finger drew along the screen over her limp body. "Why'd you do it, Sticks? Why'd you ruin everything?"

A drunk text was never wise, but my finger drifted down to the fuzzy messenger app anyway. I ignored the ten texts from Charlie with her minute-to-minute drama updates, finding the only person I wanted an update from. I couldn't sleep until I knew.

Me: *How wz she feeling 2day?*

chapter fifteen

mason

B*uzz.*

A familiar vibration shuddered against my thigh, and I dragged my phone out of my pocket as I crossed the quad toward the Athletic Complex. At first glance, the glare from the Friday afternoon sun made it impossible to read the screen. Once the phone auto-adjusted the light settings, disappointment settled across my shoulders as I read the text on my screen.

CB: *Tay is @ ur house planning the gala with Eve. Do u mind driving me after practice? I'd like to help.*

I exhaled a harsh breath, resisting the urge to ask why she couldn't drive herself. In her own car. I already knew the answer. Yet again, this was another ploy to reassure the Price family of our shipping status by not only being together but arriving together, and she knew I would do it because…that was what I did. I gripped the phone harder. When did I adopt such a cynical view of a friend I'd had since diapers?

But you know you're right.

I shut down the insidious voice in my head. It was getting harder to do that by the day, and if I didn't deal with this soon, I'd blow to a degree that put yesterday's outburst to shame. Maybe that needed to happen because I didn't like what I'd become, someone who was simply going through the motions, getting from sunup to sundown, rinse and repeat.

Buzz.

Without looking this time, I jammed my phone back inside my pocket and headed down the shadowed corridor, my mind drifting back to class this morning when I watched Maggie struggle up the stairs. She was still so damn stiff—

Buzz.

I gritted my molars, gnashing them together until my jaw ached. Then I slammed through the double doors to the men's locker room. A voice I recognized echoed against the tile walls, bringing me to a pause.

"You fuck! It was you!"

I didn't know him very well, but I'd say Jamey was ready to bleach assholes using real bleach and steel wool.

"Hold up. That's a serious accusation." *Brady?* Why was Jamey talking to Brady Hale? "What proof do you have?"

And then a third voice scraped against my eardrums. One I both recognized and loathed. "Ignore him. That homo doesn't have anything but a crusty dildo in his ass."

Oh, hells yeah. I was going to test my throat eating theory right now. On Eric Ryan.

Flying through the lockers, I found Eric and Brady changing out with Jamey standing by, red-faced, fists balled at his sides.

Jamey seethed, "Take it down, Eric."

Inclining closer, Eric lowered his voice. "The only thing going down is your spaz girlfriend. To suck my dick like she begged to."

Jamey opened his mouth, but he didn't see what I did. Eric's stance suddenly shifted, and before I could warn him, Eric's arm cocked back, and then Jamey's neck was hinged at an unnatural angle. Jamey's head collided with a locker, and a *bang* echoed through the room.

Rage swelled to the surface, red overtaking my world. I was sure Brady had yelled something to the tune of a warning, but the roar in my ears blocked it out. Charging in, not seeing anything but that damn sneer and his shit-colored eyes, I rammed straight into Eric. Flying backward, Eric's spine met the metal latch on a locker door. That had to hurt.

While I was focused on the now displaced bandage from the last time I'd hit Eric's ugly puss, a hand clamped down on my shoulder. On pure reflex, my elbow cranked back into what felt like a facial feature.

"Son of a bitch!" Brady cried out.

Aw, shit. I twisted around to apologize right when Brady decided that wouldn't be necessary. His upper lip pulled back, exposing a mouth full of blood, and then his fist drove into my side to tenderize my kidney. Pain shot across my back and down my leg. There wasn't much thought, if any, after that.

I snatched up his collar with my left hand while my right drove between his eyes with a sickening crack. The blood was immediate. A beat later, Brady was sprawled on the floor, holding his nose.

Bringing my attention back to Eric a second too late, a blur came at my face, but I didn't spin my head away fast enough. Pain ricocheted like a pinball around my orbital socket. As I shifted onto the balls of my feet, his right shoulder rolled and swung for me again. I angled back, his own weight throwing him off-kilter. That was all I needed.

Uncle Aaron had told me the number one rule to fighting was to shut off your feelings. Emotions made you sloppy. Emotions put you in the hospital or got you killed. He was one of the smartest men I knew. Respected the hell out of him. I wasn't listening to that sage advice right now, though. Because this? This felt too fucking good.

This little bitch had it coming to him.

Right after left, my fists met his stomach, sides, jaw, and face. Crimson dotted the floor and leather benches, spraying the lockers. He was still standing, so I was still giving. There was no tapping out of this. There was no white towel—

"WHAT THE HELL!" Ah, but there was Watkins.

I stilled, fist hovering and ready to deploy another blow, and before me, Eric wobbled. Not a second later, he stumbled backward and flopped on his ass, collapsing onto the floor next to Brady.

Okay, I may have been wrong about his ability to stand.

Whoops.

His face… Well, all the essential pieces were where they should be. *Kinda.*

Double whoops.

Those black marbles in Watkins' sockets shifted from one body to the next, assessing if an ambulance or a coroner was needed. "Whoever doesn't have a broken jaw better start singing."

Nursing half his face, Jamey made a waving motion to Eric, still on the floor. "That asshole videoed a student having a seizure without her permission and then posted it to social media."

"Aye idn'd pohd id!" Or I think that was what Eric said behind his hand and a gallon of blood.

Jamey bared his teeth. "Yes, you did. Are you that stupid that you thought it was completely untraceable?"

Watkins was far too quiet to be considered human, those beady eyes of coal skipping over a moaning Brady before cutting to me. Syllables were barely definable outside of his growl, but it sounded like, "And why are you involved?"

I shrugged one shoulder, rediscovering my bruised kidney. "It was two against one. Odd numbers make me crazy."

Eyes narrowing, Watkins' jaw clenched like he was trying to grind his molars down to nubs, and then he barked clear as fucking day, "University Clinic, all of you!"

Somehow having heard about the fight, Cam, Ben, and Charlie were waiting for me outside the clinic doors.

Dropping his messenger bag in the grass, Ben's eyes popped wide as he shot toward me. Correction, he shot toward the guy walking next to me.

"What did you do?" Ben reached for him, but Jamey drew up short, not allowing Ben to touch him. Examining the distance between them, Ben cringed. "Fuck, Jamey. I didn't send you that text, so you'd go after him!"

Jamey was quick to divert around Ben, moving as if he were on a mission to speed walk across America.

Leaving his bag, Ben chased after Jamey. For some reason, perhaps the lack of boundary issues, we all followed. "Jamey, are you okay?"

"What do you think?" Jamey snapped, pulling the icepack off his eye. Though he was pointed away from me, I didn't have to see his face to know that things hadn't improved during the last hour. His eye was swollen shut and a scary shade of *oh my hell*.

Ben cringed again. "Let me take you to the hospital."

"I don't need a hospital." Jamey tried to step around my cousin once more, but Ben interceded this time.

"Please. Let me drive you home then. I just want to talk this out. It doesn't have to be this way."

At this, Jamey stopped as his good eye narrowed at my cousin. "Listen up because I'm getting really fucking tired of saying this. Maggie would never steal. *Never*. Everything that she has, she has worked for. She has killed herself for. She has more heart and integrity than anyone I've ever known. She's kind and sweet and wonderful. You want the truth, Ben? You're not worthy to even know her name, which means you're not worthy of me. So, yes, it does have to be this way."

Ben's chest shuddered with his next breath. "Ja—"

Jamey held up his hand, stopping him. "Look, I appreciate everything your family has done. I do. And thank you for letting me know what your investigator found, but I won't do this anymore. Stay away from me. Stop coming to my house. I don't want you there. I don't want to see you. I don't want to talk to you, and I don't want you talking to my mom. I don't want to have anything to do with you. It's over, Ben. I'm done."

Watching Jamey walk away, Ben kept his back to us, shoulders as low as I'd ever seen them. Though my heart broke for my cousin, I felt a twinge of gratitude that Jamey hadn't abandoned Maggie. Throughout all of this, he had stood by her side. He was loyal, to a fault, but I understood that. I respected him for it.

Wincing, Charlie's fingers skimmed my cheek. "You need to put ice on that."

I scoffed and waved to my face, ignoring the ache in my knuckles as the bandage pulled taut. "This is the least of my problems."

Her brows pinched together. "What does that mean?"

I glanced to her and then refocused on Jamey as he took his frustration out on his bike lock. "It means I'm suspended from football."

Cam spun toward me, mouth agape, and at some point, had picked up his brother's messenger bag. "Are you shitting me?"

"Nope. In one month, I can hope to get it lifted. Eric was expelled. Brady's punishment is coming in the form of extra drills. Coach Watkins has laryngitis, and subsequently, Dean Evans might have permanent hearing damage. So, there's that."

I almost laughed at the memory of the tiny woman weaving around piles of bloody gauze on the clinic floor to meet us bedside because Watkins refused to wait until we were medically cleared for the dean to deal with us.

Cam blinked once and then did it again. "Fuck, Mase! *One month*! Why?"

"Why?" I waved to the disappearing Jamey as he sped out on his bike. "Eric posted the video of Maggie, and Jamey's stupid ass confronted him without backup. Eric got the drop on Jamey in one hit, and God knows Brady wouldn't have stepped in!"

"So why did you get suspended?" Cam argued. "It was in defense of another student. That's not right. We need to fight—"

"I may have taken it a smidge too far."

He popped a brow, voice gritty and tight. "Define a smidge?"

I squeezed the back of my neck, working out a knot. "Like…sending two men to PCH for possible broken faces and definite concussions too far."

He stared at me. "Mase! What the fuck? Did you not learn from the last time?"

My shoulders lifted and fell. "Guess not."

Cam gripped his hair in both hands. "Jesus, this has… *Fuck*!" He whirled on the source of all the sniffling. "Would you stop crying already!

I can't take it another goddamned second! Go get your ass fucked and forget about Jamey."

With a speed and fury so rare for Ben, he charged into Cam, fisting his shirt and dragging him close enough, so their noses smashed together. I was honestly a bit worried for Cam.

"*Forget about him?* Jamey was my first boyfriend, and I really wanted him to be my only boyfriend. So, no amount of *ass fucking* or *cock sucking* or *jacking off* is going to miraculously erase the fact that I lost the man I fell in love with."

Whoa.

Cam recoiled, but his shirt was still attached to his brother's fist. "Ben... I didn't know. I didn't know you felt *that* way. I just thought you were having fun."

"That's because your head is stuck up your ass. It's got a permanent residence there. Why the hell do you think I've been miserable for two fucking weeks? Why do you think I've been going to his house every night, begging him to take me back?"

"I—" Cam's throat rolled in a thick swallow. "I'm sorry. I didn't know you were in love with him."

Ben released Cam's shirt, glaring down at his older brother. "Why would you know? You, Matt, and Mason...you don't understand. Dad doesn't understand. Rich and E— Hell, Papa doesn't even know that I like dick. You all only want me to be attracted to women." Ben threw out a disgusted gesture to Charlie as though she represented the entire gender. "Believe me, life would be so much easier. I would fit in. I would be one of you." His voice cracked, breaking me along with him. "But I'm not. This is who I am. The assfucker. The cocksucker. The f—"

"Shut the fuck up," Cam growled, shoving Ben's chest, so he stumbled back this time. Cam prowled forward. "You are one of us, Ben. I never thought you weren't, and I *never* wished that you were any different. It has never mattered to me who you were attracted to or where you put your dick. And just because you're gay does not mean I'm going to pussyfoot around you, afraid I'll hurt your feelings. I don't hold back because gay, straight, bi, pan, or transgender...you're a Scott, and you can handle it. I treat you the same as I've always treated you. You're my equal. I know exactly who you are, and I'm fucking proud to be your brother."

Ben blinked. "Well...shit. When did you start sounding like an adult?"

Cam threw out a shrug. "Don't get too excited. I'm sure it's just a phase."

"God, this is such a mess." Charlie curled her fingers around my bicep since my hands were a little busy with Johnson & Johnson. It skated along the back of my mind that if Charlie didn't know Ben's status before, she sure as hell did now. "Come on, let's get you home. Your mom will fix you up."

Ben took his bag off his brother's shoulder as we aimed toward our rides. "Can we come, too? We'll order a pizza and celebrate Cam's brief stint into manhood."

"Can I call Crystal instead?" Cam suggested. "I'd rather my manhood was celebrated inside a vagina."

Charlie repositioned her bag as her face screwed up. "Gross."

Cam yelled over, "If Ben had said that, you would have been cheering for him."

I shouted back, "He likes dick! Get over it!"

"Yeah, but what if we could convert him to be bi? Think about it. He'll double his pool. Maybe it just takes the right pussy."

Ben groaned. "Can we please stop shouting about dicks and pussy in public?"

Cam eyed his brother. "You started it."

I nodded. "You did, actually."

Shaking his head, Ben popped his door handle. "No, Cam did when he told me to get my ass fucked."

"Oh, right." I held the door open while Charlie climbed into BB.

"Hey, Mase…?" Ben hedged.

With Charlie's pins tucked away, I closed the passenger door and turned to my cousin. Whatever moment of levity I'd just glimpsed of the old Ben was gone. He shut down again as his eyes drifted to my bandaged hand and stayed there.

"Thank you for helping Jamey." As his throat worked a thick swallow, a heaviness weighed down my shoulders like someone was stacking invisible bricks on my back.

"I'm sorry I didn't see your texts earlier. I thought it was— Anyway, if I had looked at my phone, I might have gotten there faster."

"No, I should have waited. That was my fault. I didn't think Jamey would do something so dumb." He tipped his gaze to the sky, giving a long blink as if to let the sun dry out his eyes. "And I know you would have protected him no matter what, but…uh— Shit."

This was gutting me to watch him go through this. I drew him in for a hug. "I'm sorry, Ben. For what it's worth, I'm sorry it didn't work out for you."

"You know, I don't think I realized I loved him until I said it just now," he rasped. "I kept telling myself that it was purely physical, and no one could fall in love that fast. I thought insta-love was a nicer way of describing lust. But then he was gone, out of my life, and—" Ben pulled away from me. "I know I'm nineteen, but I...I really can't see myself with anyone else. Is that weird?"

"No," I assured him, and I meant it. "It's not weird at all. I saw you together." At the memory, warmth grew in my chest, only to turn cold a heartbeat later. "I was kinda jealous of you on your birthday."

The corner of his mouth teased a smile. "If you're switching to my team, don't tell Cam."

"Too late! I can hear everything," Cam's muted shout bled through the Rover's windows.

I squeezed his shoulder, leaning in. "You looked happy that night, and I've never..." I whispered the rest of my thought in case Charlie could hear us, too. I wasn't that much of a dick. "I've never felt that."

"Yeah, well. It's overrated. Look at me. I'm a fucking mess."

"You're in better shape than me."

He nodded ruefully, giving me a quick scan. "I am. I really am."

"Ass." I chuckled and turned toward the Raptor. "See ya at the house."

"Yup."

Along the drive to Crescent Lake, Charlie wasn't occupied with her social media accounts, which was shocking enough, but she also didn't ask for every gory detail of the fight, nor did she discuss Ben. She was probably more worried the story would be leaked to the press and didn't know how she would spin it.

I stopped the truck right outside of the guardhouse. My window lined up with the door down to the millimeter because the remote only worked at this very spot. Not a foot behind or ahead like it used to work back when Phil manned the guard post. No one else I knew with a gate remote had this issue. I wasn't much for conspiracy theories, but this had Bernard written all over it. He forced me to wait right here until the gate swung open.

Only they... Shit, they weren't opening.

On the third press of the button without so much as a twitch in the wrought iron, a bad feeling churned in my gut. Either the wiring in the remote was going bad, or someone was preventing it from working. Whichever the reason, if I wanted to get past that gate, I'd have to speak to the person on the other side of that door.

I cursed something foul enough to earn two head slaps.

"This can't be happening." I frantically stabbed the button overhead, but as the door to my left creaked open, a chill crept across my neck.

My arm froze.

"Doesn't he ever take a day off?" Charlie whispered at a decibel level I could barely hear, but I knew *he* could.

Keeping my head straight, I remained unmoved with my arm up, finger still on the button. "I think he lives beneath the ground. That's my current theory."

As Bernard turned sideways to slip out of the guardhouse doorway, the skin on my neck went from freezing to burning as though this dude had laser beams for eyes.

Swallowing, I lowered my hand to the wheel and risked a peek over to him. "Bernard."

His dead glare was giving me all kinds of Jason Voorhees vibes. No hockey mask required. Even had the creeper slow-walk down solid. Look, I wasn't a small guy by any means, but Bernard... Bernard worked for *Jagger*, which meant he was the type who had a very particular set of skills. Skills that made him a nightmare for *everyone*.

As he slid a look over to the passenger seat, I refrained from launching across Charlie, opening her door, shoving both of us out, and then running for our lives.

"Anything I can help you with, Bernard?" I offered.

Those black orbs took a trip back to me as every drop of moisture in my throat evaporated. "Tell the other one she better not forget anything. Last time, I was polite. I don't do *polite*."

Holy shit. Bernard could speak? During the last four months, I figured the guy had either taken a vow of silence, or had sliced his own vocal cords as an anti-terrorism tactic. His voice sounded rusty. Like there was actual rust knocking loose in his throat. But the fact he could speak took a backseat to the content of his words.

I had no clue who *she* was or what she better not forget, but I completely agreed with the last bit. *Polite* and *Bernard* didn't mesh like chocolate and peanut butter.

I nodded. "Sure."

A scar that I'd never noticed before distorted his upper lip when the thick flesh twisted back. Charlie audibly swallowed.

"Anything else?" Did my voice just crack?

His lids narrowed, disappearing the whites of his eyes, leaving nothing but black pits. As if tapping into his telekinetic powers, the gates moved. Okay, that was...creepy AF.

When my foot lifted from the brake, he spoke again. "I didn't mind that annoying one, you know."

Pressing the brake pedal all the way to the floor, my head rotated toward him at a similar pace to the gates. Slow and measured. "What did you say?"

"*Mase*," Charlie warned, tugging on my arm. "The gates are open. *Go*."

Eyes locked with mine, the veins along Bernard's bald scalp throbbed. "I didn't mind her. She was n— Nnn—" He grunted, jowls and neck straining. "Nnniii…"

I stared as that damn scar on his upper lip stretched with whatever word was scraping its way out of his clenched teeth. Sweat dotted his forehead as he tried again and failed.

"Tolerable," he finally growled, and with that, Bernard stepped backward, squeezed his massive body through the door and slammed it.

"What the hell?" I muttered to myself.

"Mase, it's gonna close!"

"What— Oh, shit!" I stomped my foot down on the accelerator, and as Charlie flew back into her seat, something—lipstick maybe—rolled around on the floorboards. As soon as I cleared the gates, I threw her a cringe. "Sorry."

"It's fine." After situating her things, Charlie sat up and tugged down her skirt. "What was he talking about? What *annoying one*?"

Taking the next turn, I shook my head. "No idea."

That wasn't true, and I didn't know why I lied. Or why I was still protecting a girl I shouldn't give two shits about.

I'm ahead of schedule with Bernard. I've got that scowl down to two seconds.

Maggie. Everything fucking came back to Maggie. She'd not only been going downtown every day to fill the basket to feed the homeless but had also brought treats to Bernard. That was…so her. She had a way with people. Saw what most didn't.

I guess that was what made her a great liar.

I swung past Tay's cherry red Spyder and parked BB in the drive. Charlie waited patiently in the truck for me to get out and open her door. For whatever reason, as I passed the front bumper, my mind catapulted me back to the time I drove Maggie to Henry's Market and that odd look she'd given me when I held the door open for her. As if no one had ever done that before. And she certainly hadn't waited for me to open her door. She hadn't even waited for me to park before launching herself out of my cab because there was no way in hell that girl would ever sit and wait for anyone to do anything for her if she could do it herself.

I may not be normal, but I'm not weak, Mason. It might take me longer, and I may not get the job done as well, but it's important to me that you let me do things my way.

I shook my head as if that would get her voice out of my head. Charlie was right. I had to let this go. *Her* go. A virtual stranger shouldn't affect my every waking moment like this. It wasn't normal.

Stepping into the house with Charlie, I announced us with a, "Hey!"

"We're in here," was the return greeting from my dad somewhere near the kitchen.

"I wasn't expecting you, Mason," Mom called out. "Is Matt..." Her words died off as I rounded the corner.

Taylor's ruby lips fell open in shock as Mom's gaze narrowed in frustration. Grumbling under her breath, Mom got up from the island to rummage together bags of frozen peas that were probably only in the freezer for the sole purpose of providing first aid.

Dad's approach was a tad different.

Examining my face for fractures, he asked, "How does the other guy look?"

"Dan!" Mom's irritation was well noted as the first bag of peas met my face a bit too hard. She had two—no, three more Jolly Green Giant bags in her doctor arsenal.

My grin to Dad was wide, left cheek pulsing from the effort. "I fucked them both up."

Mom's free hand rose to hit me for the F-bomb, but then it fell. She was probably afraid I had a concussion.

"Two, huh?" Dad's eyes gleamed with pride as the front door chimed with Ben and Cam's arrival.

"Honestly, Dan," Mom scolded him, slapping the next bag onto my bruised hand.

"What?" he asked with mock innocence. "I'm sure there's a good reason he got into a fight. Or, at the very least, a good story. I bet Taylor would like to hear it."

As Taylor's brown eyes took a nosedive down to the pile of pictures and fabric samples on the counter, she swept a lock of blonde hair behind her ear that was bedazzled with three different silver cuffs. "Um, no. I don't need to know."

Cam's sneakers squeaked to a stop on the way to the fridge, head swiveling back to Taylor. "Since when aren't you down for the tea?"

All eyes diverted to Taylor. It was a valid question. Charlie wasn't the only Price obsessed with her social media and PR.

Tay shrugged, the collar of her camo V-neck gaping wider. "It seems personal."

Again with the dumbfounded looks by us all.

"Well, it wouldn't be personal"—Cam cracked open a Coke and shut the fridge—"if Mase hadn't been suspended from the team for a month."

Mom's eyes rolled to the ceiling, groaning. "Mason Alexander Scott."

Ooh. Full name. That wasn't good.

"It was for Jamey, Aunt Eve," Ben explained. "Jagger found out who uploaded the video of Maggie, and without thinking, I texted Jamey that it was Eric Ryan, and he went to the locker room to confront him. Mase got there right as Eric threw the first punch. If he hadn't stepped in…" Looking away, Ben shook his head.

"*Eric Ryan* uploaded the video?" Mom's blue eyes went wide while she waited for us to confirm. She made a sound of disgust in the back of her throat. "I mean, I know that boy has serious issues, but what the hell is going on these days? Do parents really not know how to instill a conscience in their children? I thought Maggie stealing my earrings was a bad indication of where our youth was at, but this…"

"Tay, you okay?" Charlie asked, taking the stool next to her sister. "You're unusually quiet."

Taylor busied herself with organizing the mess of fabric samples on the island. "Hmm? Oh, yeah. I was, uh, thinking about the chair sashes. Chiffon or satin."

"Oh, no contest, Tay-Tay. Chiffon all day." Cam slurped his soda. "Satin wrinkles and will show every greasy fingerprint. Ain't nobody got time for that." Now it was his turn to garner all our attention.

Dad cranked his head to the side to study his nephew. "That was oddly insightful of you, Cam."

Cam's grin widened. "Why, thank you, Uncle Dan. I know that was meant to be a backhanded compliment, but I'm gonna tuck that away into my already inflated ego, nonetheless."

Dad patted him on the back. "I'm sure you will."

"Anyways…" I gave up on managing four bags of peas and went with two. "What the hell is up with Jagger anyway? It took him almost a week to find the IP address. I thought he was some super hacker genius."

"Dude!" Cam cast a cagey glance to the ceiling and then to the windows as he mouthed, *He could be listening.*

Gulping, Ben nodded emphatically and said much too loud, "He *is* a super hacker genius, Coz!"

Okay, I doubted our house was bugged, but their concern was warranted.

Ben woke his phone, using his indoor voice. "Word is Jagger and his team—whatever that means—have been in a Honduras jungle or some shit for the last week. Communicating with him hasn't exactly been eas—"

Bang!

The front door swung open, and Matt's boots pounded through the house until they skidded to a halt once we were in full view. His emerald eyes went large, palms shooting up to face us. "I didn't walk in on a come-to-Jesus meeting, did I?"

Dad shook his head. "That's tomorrow. You're the guest of honor."

Cam left the room to shut the front door since my brother had an issue with the closing and locking aspect of doors.

Matt peeled the veggies from my face, hissing with a wince. "Damn. How's Jamey?"

"Worse." Frowning, Ben snatched up a package of Oreos from the pantry and slid them onto the counter.

"Ooh! Yum-o!" Making his way back into the kitchen, Cam dove right into the Oreo package a popped a cookie into his mouth. He looked to my mom. "Oo ee hab ilk?"

Mom tried to repress her smile, but she could never resist a male Scott getting his munchies on. "Yes, *we* have milk. I'll get it."

Matt inspected the cookies before nabbing three. "Hey, whatever happened to that Oreo Dipr? That thing was the bomb. I never got the cookie mush on my fingers."

Mom's hand paused on the milk cap with a far-off look as if remembering something, and it didn't seem like a pleasant memory. She moved to the cabinet to grab the glasses. "Uh, not sure."

"Jesus, Cam." Dad ripped the last paper towel from the roll and handed it over.

"Dahnkz." Cam used the towel for the one black crumb on his face rather than the hundred that littered the island.

Ben slung the pantry door open again, searching the shelves. "Where do you keep the extra rolls? You're all out in here."

"Garage. I'll grab 'em." Setting all my peas in a pile, I got off my stool and headed down the hallway.

Lowering the handle on the garage door, I opened it and… That was odd. I shut the door and then opened it again. Reaching up, I fiddled with the sensor above the door and then tried again. Nothing.

"Mom, the alarm sensor on the garage door isn't working."

"Oh. Yeah, I know. I keep meaning to call Richard to send over someone to fix it."

"Shit, I kept forgetting about it, too." I heard Dad say. "I'll shoot him a text right now before I forget again."

Disregarding why I needed to go to the garage in the first place, I returned to the kitchen, concern niggling at me.

It wasn't as if we'd ever had a break-in or that our neighborhood wasn't patrolled by Bernard seemingly twenty-four-seven, but I didn't like this. Mom was home alone often, and she had Matt's penchant for not closing and locking doors. And if the alarm sensor was glitching, she may not hear anyone come in through the garage...

"How long has it been loose?" I asked.

Mom shrugged. "Um, I noticed it—" She looked to Taylor. "What would you say? Four weeks ago?"

For some reason, Tay thought over her answer. "Around that."

I blinked at Taylor and then Mom. "Why would Taylor know?"

Pouring the last glass of milk, Mom waved me off. "When Taylor stopped by to help plan the gala, she happened to pull up as I arrived home. We came in through the garage. That's when I noticed the chime didn't go off. It was the day before I interviewed Mag—" Shaking herself of the thought, she capped the milk and put it back in the fridge. "Anyway, it's been a while."

"Why didn't you tell me?"

Dad threw a wet sponge at Cam so he could wipe up his crumbs. "You don't use the garage. Just slipped our minds, Son."

Four weeks. Had it been that long since I'd met Maggie? I guessed that was right. And it was true; I never needed to go into the garage, especially since I wasn't home much, and Maggie had been here taking care of our every need...

My gaze drifted away from the Oreo mess on the island and landed on the porcelain jar on the counter. That jar had never known what a cookie, Oreo or otherwise, looked like. It had only ever been used to hold cash. I wondered if Maggie had a cookie jar. If she thought it was weird that we kept money in ours.

And look, she even left the receipt for the groceries and put the change in the jar.

I'd never questioned Maggie's character. None of us had. That was why my mom handed over the keys and alarm codes to the house without batting an eye the first day she'd met her. Why my dad kept going back to the café for four years and fought so hard to keep her in town. Why my parents wanted to buy her a car and pay for her insurance.

Taking cash slowly would have been smarter. We wouldn't have known, and she could keep stealing.

That would have been smarter, and Maggie was smart, resourceful. She'd had a job at the café since she was thirteen. She would have learned how to skim off the register, hide money. She had a good thing going here, and I didn't doubt my parents paid her better than the café did.

Maggie didn't have much, but she took pride in what little she did have because she had earned it. She actually got pissed at me when I gave her a hard time about her rusted bike, oversized clothes, the need for two jobs.

None of it added up. Never had.

My mind played back the thick tears falling from those Caribbean blue eyes. The look of pure shock on her face when Dad drew the diamonds out of her bag.

I didn't take the earrings. Someone put them in my bag.

Okay, so who would? It wasn't a question I'd entertained before because there wasn't a soul in my family who didn't like—

Are you really going to let this happen because I wouldn't let my boyfriend hang out with another girl, even one that looks like her.

Alright, Taylor would never be accused of stanning Maggie Davis. And that was one of many swipes Taylor had taken at her that morning. Her aggression was the very reason I told Charlie to take Taylor home before I lost my shit.

And I was going to tell her the truth about us after we left your place on Sunday, but she suddenly canceled our plans when she dropped me off at the Zeta house.

Hold up. My head rotated to the side, just as Taylor glanced away from me with something pulling her features taut. Something I couldn't identify yet.

Surprised the hell out of me when she asked how Maggie was doing, which…showing concern for anyone *has never happened before.*

As I mentally tumbled over the different scenes from the last day Taylor and Maggie were in this room together, dread lanced my chest.

Tell the other one she better not forget anything. Last time, I was polite.

Last time… Last time was—

Oh, God. *Please, no.* My heart pounded so loud I couldn't hear anything else. That look, the one Taylor had been wearing since I came home, made complete sense now.

"You came back to the house," I said.

Taylor's smooth brow creased, batting her thick lashes. "Me? What are you talking about?" Her voice sounded off, hesitant. So unlike the girl I'd known all these years.

A girl who knew far too much about how we lived. Our habits.

"You knew the sensor wasn't working." My throat was almost too dry to talk. "And you know the code to the garage door opener. It's Faith's birthday."

The rustling of the Oreo bag stopped, and Taylor's throat dipped.

Matt set his cookie down on a napkin. "What are you getting at, Mase?"

I didn't break my stare from Taylor. "Coming here after Ben's birthday, wanting to spend the day with Charlie…that's very unlike you, and yet, it was *your* idea. I thought it was weird that you chose to get up that early to pick up Charlie, but I wanted to believe that maybe you two were finally turning a corner." A sad laugh broke free. "That wasn't it all, was it?"

It was slight, but Taylor squirmed a little in her stool. "It was. You were the one who told me to get along with her. And…we are. I was doing what you suggested."

"No." I shook my head, seeing her for what she was for the first time. And she wasn't as pretty as she looked. "You don't like Maggie and did nothing to hide it. You didn't like that she was invited to Ben's party or how she and Charlie hit it off, and you really didn't like that I defended her after you repeatedly tried to shame her for working for my family. You also knew she would be here working the day after the birthday party. That's why you were here that morning. It wasn't to help plan the gala. It was to put Maggie in her place as a *maid*. Someone who makes *basic look posh*."

Standing up from her stool, Charlie put a hand on my arm. "Mase—"

"You canceled your plans for the rest of the day and dropped your sister off at the Zeta house. What did you do after, Taylor? Where did you go?" When she didn't answer, I took care of the details for her. "Bernard said you came back here that Sunday because you forgot something."

Okay, I was taking some liberty with that, but Taylor didn't deny it, so I pressed on. "You didn't forget anything. You knew we'd be at the pool later. You came back and heard us outside. I'm guessing you checked before you left that morning that the sensor hadn't been fixed yet, so you had a clear path to sneak in without being noticed. You know my mom always takes her earrings out and puts them somewhere on the kitchen counter. And you were there that morning to see Maggie put her backpack in the hall closet."

"Oh, God." Mom clutched her chest with one hand.

Charlie's clammy fingers fell off my arm, shaking her head. "Mase, that's…"

"Not possible? You really think that? After years of treating you like a mortal enemy, it didn't strike you odd that all of a sudden Taylor wanted to be your best friend?"

Charlie paled, glancing away from me.

"It never added up. In that cookie jar, there's a stack of cash that Maggie could have stolen from, and there's jewelry upstairs that she had access to every single day. Most of those pieces cost a hell of a lot more than those diamond studs. Why only *those* earrings? Why that day with everyone here? Right under our noses?" My face screwed up as my head took slow swipes side to side. "You knew they were Faith's. You knew it was something we'd notice was missing right away. What better way was there to get rid of Maggie? Because you knew that was the one thing we couldn't forgive."

"Motherfucker," Matt growled.

Taylor licked her lips. "You're crazy. I didn't do any of that. Besides, I didn't even know those earrings were Faith's."

"Yes, you did," Charlie corrected her, stepping back from the island. "We all knew those earrings were Faith's, Taylor. And you… You did open the door to the garage that morning, and when I asked where you were going, you played it off like you forgot where the powder room was."

Inching closer, Mom gripped Dad's arm. "Taylor, is any of this true? Did you do this?"

Eyes flicking to her sister, Taylor shrunk in the stool. "N—no."

My back tensed, forearms trembling. "Stop. Lying."

"I'm not. I—" I wasn't sure what that sound was coming out of me, but it made Taylor lurch back and gulp. "I— *IdiditforCharlie.*"

That took an entire minute to process. It took sixty seconds for the world to come to a screeching halt, for me to hear and understand those words, for the mere gravity of what she'd done to sink in. Every tear Maggie had cried had been real. Every word she had spoken had been the truth.

Maggie was innocent.

"You did it for *Charlie?* Oh, I doubt that. I doubt that very much." Anger rose with every strained pump of my heart. "But tell me your reasons anyway because I'd love to hear why you think ruining someone's life was for anyone but Taylor Price."

Her chin kicked up defiantly, eyes turning hard. "You want my reasons? Fine. You were flirting with that girl. Right in front of my sister and me. So, no, I didn't like that. And I shouldn't. Especially not after what I saw in Cam and Ben's basement. Would you like me to share that with everyone or just your *girlfriend?*"

A breath halted in my throat. I didn't know Taylor had seen that. Her aggression toward Maggie made sense now, but it didn't excuse a damn thing. And I wasn't going to let whatever shame my family would feel stand in the way of what was right.

"If you're about to share that I almost kissed Maggie, and the only reason I didn't was that we were interrupted, go ahead. I'll even give the play-by-play when you're done."

If my parents had any reaction to that, I didn't see it.

Taylor's eyes narrowed. "So you're admitting that you cheated on my sister with that townie slut—"

"He didn't cheat on me," Charlie choked out, and Taylor opened her mouth to argue when Charlie stopped her. "He didn't cheat on me because we're not together. It's fake. The whole thing. We've been pretending this entire time. I was going to tell you, I wanted to tell you, but... Oh, Taylor. What have you done?"

Taylor glared at her sister. "You're lying. You're—"

"She's not lying, Tay," Ben stated, leveling her with a stare. "Not about this."

Her eyes bounced around the room, to all the faces revealing the same knowledge. They'd all known what she didn't. Because I could trust them. Not her.

Hurt, true and deep flooded Taylor's brown eyes.

Face turning pallid, she inhaled a faltering breath. "You knew? You all knew? Why am I the last to know something like this?"

"Young lady, you should focus on what's important here." Dad bit out each syllable, his rage on the brink of breaking free. "Do you have any idea, any clue what Maggie has been through? I accused her of being a thief as she cried, begging for her innocence! She pleaded with me to listen, and I refused her. Do you have any idea what I said to her?"

When she didn't answer, Dad's fist pounded the counter, and Taylor jumped off the stool in utter shock. Dad had never raised his voice to her or around her, had never even so much as used a harsh tone.

"You lied for two goddamned weeks!" he shouted. "Maggie had a seizure because of this and had to be resuscitated. If that had happened when she was alone, she'd be *dead*! Do you not get that?" Veins popped in Dad's neck that I didn't know existed. "It's sheer luck that she's alive! How do you have such little value for another human's life?"

Backing away, Taylor's head shook. "I didn't know any of that would happen. Who would?"

"Is that seriously your defense?" Matt barked, shoulders bunched tight. "You didn't know there could be consequences, so that makes it okay?"

"No! It's— How would I know it could get so out of hand? I didn't know about the seizures or that Eric would post a video and Mase would get suspended. I just wanted—" Twisting up her face, she spat at me, "If you hadn't lied, none of this would have happened. I was looking out for my sister. From what I thought was a cheating boyfriend."

"Then why didn't you tell Charlie?" I challenged, my tone deceptively calm. "Huh, Tay? If you cared so dearly for your sister, why not tell her right when it happened or the weeks since?" When she had nothing to say to that, I scoffed. "Don't bother trying to think of another lie. I already know the reason. You didn't tell Charlie because *you* wanted to be the one I cheated with."

"Dayum," Cam muttered, eyes rounding. "This just took a pivot of Ross Geller proportions."

"That's not true," Taylor argued, hands balling at her sides.

"Oh, it's true. Because wasn't it you who said that Charlie's perfect and no matter what she does, she gets everything she wants? Admit it, Taylor. You feel nothing but jealousy and hatred for Charlie because you're still under the delusion that she ruined your career. Deep down, somewhere in there, you know she didn't. But rather than admit that, it's easier to play the victim, blame her. Hurt her. And what better way to do that than by taking me away from her? Humiliating her publicly?"

Backing away from me, Taylor shook her head, and I was quick to close the distance again.

"As soon as Charlie left for London, you were at the RAM house looking for me, but Matt sent you back to Stafford. When the tabloid pictures leaked, you didn't hesitate to share every shocking angle of her. You even checked in with me to make sure I was okay, but not your sister. And after, when you thought Charlie and I were still together, you came back to the RAM house, thinking you could make me jealous by flirting with Wyatt. And it was at Ben's party that you realized your next attempt wouldn't work either. Because someone else was in your way. *Maggie.*"

"God, you're so blind to her. All of you." Taylor aimed her scowl at me for a long beat, and then everyone else was on the receiving end. "Charlie was the jealous one. She was scared I would threaten her career. Vinsant wanted *me* to walk for him. I was supposed to be the new face of haute coutour. Not her. And she couldn't handle it. She sabotaged me, ruined any chance of me getting another editorial shoot or runway. It's not fair."

"Fair?" I mocked. "Do you want to hear what's not fair? To be called a liar. A thief. To lose a job that you deserve and you're good at. To have people turn against you. To be so stressed that you have a seizure and stop breathing. Maggie almost died because of your unjustified hatred for your sister. And you know the ironic part, Taylor? What Charlie did was out of love for you. She saved you from paying the price for the very career you resent her for, even though it ruined your relationship. And knowing the consequences, she would do it again to protect you."

"Puh-lease," Taylor shot back. "Charlie's no different than me. What she did was to protect her career, and you know as well as I do that Maggie's not innocent. She made a play for you. That's the only reason she was so buddy-buddy with Charlie. To get closer to you."

"She knew, Taylor," I argued. "Maggie knew the truth. She did nothing wrong. And her friendship with Charlie was real."

Taylor fumed for a solid ten seconds. "Whatever. She's a freak anyway," she sneered.

I wanted to believe Taylor was simply hurt, ashamed of her actions, humiliated for being so wrong, but the longer she glared at me, the clearer it became. There wasn't an ounce of remorse in her for what she had done to Maggie. There never would be. And for the first time, I felt only one thing for her. It wasn't pity or empathy. It was rage, dark and ugly, flooding my world with red for the third time in my life.

chapter sixteen

maggie

Saturday morning, I pulled my bike up to the café, clumsily sliding off the seat. Today had been the first time I'd been able to ride my bike. Well, *ride* was being generous. I more hunchbacked my way over here, and while my butt wasn't thrilled, the rest of me was happy to cut my travel time in half.

As I pushed the Schwinn around the corner of the back alley, I slowed to a crawl, and my heart…sank. Frankie's Taurus was parked there, the engine still ticking. He had the back door propped open, and as I neared, I heard the shifting of coins coming from the office. Sharp betrayal hollowed out my chest, causing my eyes to burn.

Frankie never used to arrive so early. He never used to recount my closing drawer or deposits either. Until a couple of weeks ago, I had his complete trust. But yesterday, I had to ask him what the new password was to log onto the computer. He wouldn't give it to me. Said he couldn't remember, which was bullshit. The man didn't even trust me to Google.

Last night had been dead, and if this kept up much longer, Frankie would fire me. I could see it in his face every time he looked at the empty dining room.

Not only had my regulars stopped coming to the café, but Darlene and Chuck's light banter was absent when I dropped off my father's uniforms. When I went to find Ronnie, Etana pretended not to hear me as he inspected the surfboard he was refinishing, and Trudy and Rick didn't wave back when I spotted them chatting across the street. And the bag with Henry's generous daily basket donations now sat outside the market door, so he didn't have to speak to me.

Everything I was to them had been ruined. I was no longer their little Mags.

I was a liar.

A thief.

A disgrace.

Exactly what my father wanted. For everyone to see me as he did.

While I loaded the pies in the oven, the front door chimed, and Candi swept through the double doors to meet the table. I stayed where I was. There wasn't any point in going up there unless they were tourists passing through.

Moments later, the bell over the door chimed again, and I heard my boys, their voices calling out numbers, boots thudding, and gear clanging. For the first time in what felt like years, I smiled. Well, more like the corner of my mouth twitched, but it was the most I could muster.

I wiped my hands dry before going up to greet the boys when Candi popped back through the door, her cheeks pinker than usual and slightly out of breath.

"Mags," she all but exhaled my name as she gripped my arms, shaking me slightly. "There is a table of the yummiest men I have ever seen. I mean...*Jesus.*" My brows rose when Candi leaned dramatically against the wall, fanning herself with her manicure. "It's like they stepped out of *GQ*. The one with dimples asked for you by name."

The tug on my lips, the twitch of my mouth, the minuscule smile I'd scraped together crashed to the floor. *Dimples?* I glared past her as if I could tap into a mystical power of telekinesis, unhinge those doors and use them to smack each one of those bastards in their *GQ* faces. What were the Scotts doing here?

Frankie peered through the kitchen window, squinting. "I don't get it. What makes them yummy?"

"What *doesn't* is easier to answer," Candi quipped. "Nothing."

I had to give it to Candi. While she hadn't exactly been herself around me recently, she hadn't denied me tips on the rare occasion they came around. But this wasn't one I would take her up on.

"Candi, thank you, but I'm gonna get my boys and come right back. I don't want anything to do with that table. You can have it."

I ignored her gaping mouth as I swept up front and loaded a tray with a fresh pot of coffee, creamer, and sugar. I went straight to the four navy blue uniforms and sent up a, *thanks,* to whoever was up there that Logan had sat in his usual spot. I leaned against his chair with my back facing the Scotts, but not before glimpsing who was here. Mr. Scott, Ben, Camden, Matt, and Mason all tracked my movements with a mixture of green and brown eyes. There was a prickling sensation at the top of my spine, and I refused to believe that peridot gaze had anything to do with it.

"How are my favorite boys?" Because my tremor was bound to give someone third-degree burns today, I used the next table over to set down my tray and pour their coffees. On the second cup, I looked to the kitchen for that head of caramel curls that should be in the dining room right now.

"I'm fifty dollars closer to my Camaro." Robert relaxed into his chair, hands sliding behind his head.

I nodded, fighting to steady my voice. "Nice!"

"You know, Magnifico, Camaros are overrated." Logan grinned that California boyish smile up at me as I set his mug in front of him. "Now a motorcycle? That's a fun ride."

Robert pointed a dark finger at Logan. "Chief catches her anywhere near your Indian, you're gonna have to go deep underground."

"You're right about that one." I nudged Logan's arm with my hip before pouring the last cup for Gil. I flicked my gaze back to the kitchen again, and dread began to itch the back of my throat. I was so not taking that table.

A set of amber eyes finally appeared in the window, and I signaled Candi to get her ass out here already. A second later, the doors were shoved open, and she sashayed past the counter with her pot of brew for the table's refills. I didn't have to ask what had taken her so long; I could see it. Her lips were shinier and plumper than a minute ago, and the apron was no longer obstructing the girls.

I received a wink as she glided past me.

Good grief.

It wasn't like I could blame her. My tips had been non-existent, and Candi was feeling it, too. I was sure she hadn't missed the dozen or so luxury brands attached to those centerfold-worthy bodies and assumed they would tip well. She was right.

I directed my attention back to my table as I placed the creamer and sugar between Robert and Keith. "What'll it be, boys, four plates?"

"Gentlemen, is our Egg Mag Muffin implying we are…predictable?" Logan's eyes twinkled at me when my lips pressed together at the second nickname he'd dropped.

Gil reached for the sugar. "I think you're right, LJ. Maybe we should shake it up and order something else."

"Like what?" I challenged. In almost a year since the boys had been coming here on a routine basis, they had only ever ordered our breakfast special.

"How about a plate with whipped cream," Logan offered.

My brows pulled together. "That's shaking it up?"

"Yeah. Don't you have to shake the can?" His hands wrapped around an invisible cylinder, and his bulky mass shook up and down.

"Logan." I smacked his bicep, and my palm stung. Damn, he was solid.

He blinked at me. "What?"

"I make my own cream."

It was then that his chestnut eyes widened along with three other pairs. Someone choked. It must have taken me a solid minute to understand why.

I swore someone had jacked up the thermostat because I flushed to the roots of my hair.

"I meant *whipped*. With heavy cream. And sugar. And a mixer." As my cheeks flamed hotter, four deep chuckles filled the dining room. "Drink your coffee," I snapped and aimed to the back, my steps getting heavier as I shoved the doors wide. "Four plates for the boys," I muttered to Frankie.

Candi slipped through the door after I did, and she chased me to the sink as I set the emptied carafe aside to wash later. "They won't order from me, hon, only you. I think Dimples has a thing for you."

I swung her a side-glare as I gathered four plates off the rack. "He's probably thinking about the next way to screw me over."

"More like screw you." Candi's perfectly crafted brows danced at me.

"Not likely," I muttered. "They can rot in Hell."

"*Mags.*" From the other side of the cooktop, Frankie scolded me. And that was officially the first time he'd ever done that.

I swallowed to his harsh tone, gripping the plates until my fingers ached. "I—I'm sorry, Frankie, but those are the Scotts."

At their name, recognition deepened his wrinkles. "Oh." Gray head dropping to focus on the griddle, he asked, "Do you...want me to ask them to leave?"

I hated that I was taking money out of his pocket, but yeah, I did want them to leave. I wouldn't mind the rotting in Hell part, either.

My hope was thin and fragile as I asked, "Please?"

He stared at me a long moment before giving me a reluctant nod Frankie set the spatula down, the corners of his mouth tight. He trudged through the doors, and I scurried over to man the hash browns and bacon Frankie had started.

"Need a hand, Frankie?" Logan's deep voice took my flimsy hope and pounded it into dust. Over the pops of bacon grease, I heard four chairs scrape across the wood floors, and I went to my tiptoes to see there was a wall of navy blue surrounding the Scotts' table.

Shit on a stick.

I shot into the dining room before a brawl broke out, or Frankie's precious floors got scratched. I squirmed between Logan and Keith. "Please, boys, sit. Frankie, it's fine."

Frankie's brown eyes cut back my way, and they were filled with…disappointment. Another reminder as to how much of a letdown I was. I should quit today.

I waited for Frankie to nod, and then he disappeared into the kitchen. I turned to Mr. Scott, channeling my frustration and anger toward him. I had to admit, he looked kinda pathetic. Good.

"You can wait until I'm ready."

"We'll wait as long as you need, Maggie."

I was on the verge of saying, *Damn straight*, when Logan cut me off.

"Mag Top?" His voice rumbled above me, and I twisted around to find he was wearing his cop eyes, and they were fixated somewhere over my head. "Are you cool with this? 'Cause if not, say the word, and they're gone."

THE WORD!

"It's okay. Thanks, Logan. Sit and I'll get your breakfast." I pressed on his chest, but it was like a fly trying to move a brick. I gave up and slunk back to the kitchen.

I had no idea where Candi was, but I grabbed the whipped cream from the walk-in, scooped up a dollop and plopped it onto Logan's pancakes. The exhale that left me might have been shakier than my hands. I loaded my tray with plates and brought out the food to the dining room. The boys were back at their table, and Logan shot me a wink when I set down his plate.

Dragging in a lungful of air and finding courage from places unknown, I crossed my arms and faced Mr. Scott, focusing nowhere else. "Find a lint ball missing and want to blame me for that, too? Conveniently, there are four cops here who can take your statement."

"Be happy to!" Gil offered behind me.

Keith grunted. "We have some lovely accommodations at the station for just the thing."

Mr. Scott stood, his eyes red-rimmed and sad, reminding me of all those late Saturday nights not so long ago. How different things were then. Simpler.

"No, Maggie. We would like to speak to you and your father. We were hoping you both could come over for dinner tonight."

Clearly, one of us had woken up in an alternate universe or ate some hallucinogenic 'shrooms today. I didn't think it had been me.

I gaped at him as my arms uncrossed. "Considering my employment has changed recently, dinner won't be possible. We have to work for a living, and I'm pulling a double today."

A small crease appeared between his eyes, lips turning downward. "Tomorrow night, then?"

I didn't need to disclose that I was planning to quit so that I'd save Frankie from an ulcer and possible bankruptcy. "I work doubles on Sundays, too. So if that's all you came here for, a dinner invitation, you can leave now."

Mr. Scott stepped closer, so I was forced to tip my head back. It was to make me feel smaller, weaker. Men knew how to do that. They used their size, their physical power to get what they wanted.

"Maggie, it's important that we speak with you. I can talk to your father later. Please sit and hear us out."

My molars ground together, kicking myself for having stopped the boys from breaking their chairs over the Scotts' heads. "Do you have no shame? I'm working. At the only place left in town that will employ me. And you come in here, snap your fingers, and expect me to do your bidding? Haven't I been debased enough? How much more are you going to take away from me?"

His palms flew up like he was corralling a wild animal, and to be fair, I probably resembled one. "I understand you're angry with us, and rightly so. Please. This won't take long." He motioned for me to sit, his words spinning around in my head, never quite landing.

Had he implied my anger was justified?

Glancing over my shoulder to the boys, they hadn't touched their food yet. They were facing our direction, giving the Scotts the fuck-with-her-and-we'll-fuck-with-you stare down.

I steeled my spine. With them behind me, I could do this.

I pulled out the chair and sat, refusing to look at anyone but Mr. Scott.

Returning to his seat beside me, Mr. Scott plugged his elbows on his knees and folded his hands together in front of him. He was a little too close to me, but I wouldn't back down.

"Maggie..." Swallowing, his gaze met mine. "Taylor put the earrings in your bag. Mason figured it out yesterday and confronted her. She confessed. And I can't express to you how sorry I am for accusing you and everything you've endured because of this."

Somewhere in those last ten seconds, my blood had been replaced with cement, clogging me up from the inside, hardening, and weighing me down so I couldn't move, breathe. As I tried to compute what he'd already said, Mr. Scott began talking again.

"Sweetheart, I feel…we all feel terrible for how we treated you. I didn't believe you or listen to you. Eve and I are so incredibly sorry. There's no way we could ever make it up to you, but we…" I was still struggling to latch onto what this all meant as he slid to the edge of his seat. "We hope that you can forgive us. Someday. We all miss you so much, and we want you to come back. I'll compensate you for the last two weeks, give you a raise— Whatever you need to make this right. Just come back."

One strained heartbeat later, the cement liquefied into an ocean that filled the back of my throat and brimmed in my eyes. I blinked to keep the tears at bay, but they were determined to invade my vision.

It had all been so…pointless, and worst of all, avoidable. Every horrible word spoken to me, every nasty look, every blow of that baton…

"You're *sorry*? *You* feel terrible? Do you have any idea what *I've* been through?" My bottom lip quivered, and I hated it, hated that I couldn't fake control like I had countless times before. After keeping my walls up for so long, I hated that he was responsible for creating another crack, and it was breaking right in front of him. "People who have known me my entire life don't trust me. They watch me like I'm a thief. A grave robber. They watch me like *you* watched me. Like your sons did, and your nephews. You paraded me through that house, and you had no intention of letting me leave until I was found guilty."

His hand lifted as if to reach for me. "Mag—"

"No." I choked down a sob and drew my shoulders back as if that would help stop my voice from trembling. "Do you have any idea what you've done? People stopped coming to the café because of me. I'm the town pariah. Even Frankie—" I dragged in a choppy breath that seared my throat. "The boys are my only regulars who will let me serve them. Besides Jamey, they're the only ones who never treated me any differently, whether or not they thought I was guilty.

"Why would I come back? So you have a scapegoat the next time one of you gets bored? You all meant something to me, and in a blink, you turned on me. You've known me for four years! And never once did I give you a reason to distrust me. Was it really so hard to believe that I could be telling the truth, just because I wasn't of your class?"

Something a lot like disbelief flitted across his features. "Oh, Maggie, that wasn't why. It had nothing to do with that."

"But it did. It had *everything* to do with it. You couldn't give me the benefit of the doubt. You denied me the chance to defend myself. We all know that it wouldn't have mattered what you found. I had to be guilty. In your world, it was the only thing that made sense."

I stood, or I thought I did because now Mr. Scott's chin had tipped back, and yet I was still the same small, weak girl.

"Don't come back here." My voice came out as a strangled rasp, and I wasn't sure if he would understand any of what was said next. "Nothing you do…will ever make it up to me. You said—" I fought around the thick lump in my throat. "You said I *disgusted* you." If he reacted to that, I couldn't see it. Hell, I was really losing my shit, and my vision was getting wonky. I forced the words out. "Some things can't be forgiven. Some things can't be forgotten."

Large hands cupped my shoulders from behind, and until then, I didn't realize how badly I was shaking. Logan's chest pressed against my back, anchoring me, supporting me, and the more he gave, the more I took.

"I want you to go away and forget you were ever a part of my life."

Deep hurt flared in Mr. Scott's eyes, and he reached for me. "Maggie—"

It happened so fast, I wasn't sure how Logan did it. My face was buried in his armor as one arm bound my shoulders, and his other hand was free. Free to take out every Scott asshole in here, all before his coffee went cold. I had no question that Logan could pull it off.

"It's time you left," Logan commanded. "After all you've put her through, the very least you can do is what she's asked and leave."

"Sticks…"

I sucked in a gasp at Mason's voice and pinched my eyes shut, burrowing into Logan as hard as I could.

"I. Said. *Leave.*" Logan's growl vibrated through his vest as he held me tighter.

There was a long pause, and I didn't doubt there had been an exchange of glares. I remained where I was in Logan's arms, and with my back to the door, I heard bodies shift across the room until the bell clanged for the last time. The pathetic grip I had on the sob in my throat slipped, and though I tried to muffle the pain, it broke through the silence.

I had no idea how long Logan held me before my tears eased, how many times his hand rubbed my sore back. I didn't care how much it hurt when he grazed over the baton marks. It was nice. Nice to be given affection. Nice for someone other than Jamey to have looked at me no differently these last two weeks.

"Mags, I'm—"

"Frankie, give her the damn courtesy of looking in her eye when you apologize." Whoa. I'd never heard any of the boys speak to Frankie like that, and Keith's tone was scary enough to make me want to piss my pants.

As the last shudders worked through my chest, Logan smoothed down my hair, and he whispered, "You gonna be okay?"

"No."

No, I wasn't okay, and I wasn't going to be okay. I was different. I had changed on some level. I hated the Scotts had shown me any warmth, hated that I'd felt wanted and cared for. I hated them for giving me a glimpse of what a family was like and then thrusting me back into this hell.

Logan gently lifted my chin and frowned. His brows sank low over his kind eyes. Using his thumbs, he wiped my cheeks, but two new tears replaced the old ones.

"Richies are different than us, kid." Gil's voice wasn't edged with the rough gravel I was used to hearing. "They don't have to work for everything like we do. They don't value what they have when they have it."

Robert shoved his chair back and settled down in his spot. "I'm sure your father will have a word or two with those asshats. I would love to be there for that."

I almost laughed; the only reason my father would be angry was for the mere fact that the richies had embarrassed Crescent Cove's chief of police.

When I looked back to Robert, he had his fork ready to impale a clump of eggs that didn't look appetizing in the least.

"Don't eat that." I dragged my hands away from Logan, immediately missing the comfort of his embrace. "I'll make you a fresh plate. Everything's on me today. Thank you. It meant more than you know that you—" I couldn't even lift my head to look at them as the tears crawled back in. "That you had my back."

There was a long moment of quiet before Logan tucked a lock of hair behind my ear, his touch lingering. "Anytime, Mag Cakes. You need us, we'll be there. You're one of us. Always."

chapter seventeen

mason

The door to the café hadn't even opened yet when the aroma of buttery crust from this morning's pies, salty bacon, sweet syrup, and rich coffee hit me like slamming into a wall at a dead run.

My heart collapsed, and my lungs struggled to take in a breath as if the air had memories that would claw up my insides, making the pain unbearable. One more breath…yep. I was there.

Excruciating agony.

Five years and this place felt the same. Smelled the same. Looked the same.

Except it wasn't.

Faith wasn't with us. She wasn't sitting on Dad's lap. She wasn't going to smack my hand away when I tried to steal a sip of her hot cocoa. She wouldn't take a bite of Matt's peach cobbler after he'd "sampled" half her lemon meringue. She wouldn't giggle at Dad's whipped cream mustache and cover half her face trying to imitate his.

None of that would happen.

I followed Dad's lead as he walked past the WELCOME! PLEASE SEAT YOURSELF sign by the entryway. Without a word, we avoided our old booth and settled into a front table, but Ben's knee was shaking the entire damn thing. Since last night, he'd been acting like a starved lion prowling behind a herd of plump zebras. Somehow, we'd convinced him to wait to talk to Jamey until after we were done here. It hadn't been easy, but Maggie deserved to be the first to know the truth. She deserved to hear it from us.

Not long after taking a seat, a pair of breasts were shoved between Matt and me, followed by a fruity perfume that itched my throat. "My, my, handsome. Are they all yours?" The question was aimed at Dad. I glanced up to find a name tag that couldn't have fit that miniskirt any better.

Dad gestured to Matt and me first. "Those two are, and the other two are my nephews."

She made a sound that reminded me of my great aunt Matilda's cat right before it would bite my hand for trying to pet it. "God sure blessed all of you with the right genes." As her hands caressed my shoulders, her fuck-me eyes adhered to Matt.

I had enough of this woman. "Is Maggie working?"

Before she could answer, the old bell got to ringing again, followed by heavy boots scraping the wood floors. Baritone voices in four dark uniforms muttered their way past us, but one paused long enough to pin me with a stare. Well, he attempted to.

The cop. The cop with gorilla arms who thought he could intimidate me with that same stare weeks ago. Didn't work then. Didn't work now.

The pain in my chest abruptly morphed into something else. I couldn't put a name to it, but it made me think thoughts that caused my muscles to spasm and fists to clench.

His unwanted attention got his three buddies to turn around. It didn't take but a second for them to recognize me. Yeah, they knew exactly who I was.

Gorilla Arms' upper lip curled back, and I'd bet good money he'd spent hours in front of a mirror practicing that look. Kinda wanted to bring him to Bernard so he could learn how to sneer properly.

He growled, "You *really* shouldn't be here, kid."

Kid. Such a dick. "Yeah? Why—"

Matt's hand went to my chest to put my ass back in my chair, and Dad stood, blocking my view. "Officers, good morning. I'm guessing you know who we are."

"You'd be guessing right but don't have a lick of common sense among you." The one with eyes as soft as steel fastened a glare on Dad. "You know she works here. Haven't you done enough?"

Dad flinched at that. That was the second time someone had said that to him. "I'm only here to talk to her. Please. You can sit right there and listen. I'm not here to cause her any more problems."

A guy who looked like he spent more time in a tattoo parlor than a uniform snickered. "We didn't need your invitation to listen, *Doctor.*" With that, he took a chair at the next table over. Facing us.

The fourth one didn't speak. He sat next to his buddy, but his job was to put the sweats into my cousins. Cam pursed his lips and blew him a kiss. Surprisingly, the cop didn't take the bait. But he did...*smile*. Okay, that was creeping me out.

"One wrong word is all I'm waiting for," Gorilla Arms started, gaze sweeping across each of our faces. "And you'll know what that wrong word is after you've said it." Tearing his death glare off us, he settled into his seat, the wooden thing creaking beneath the mound of roided muscles. Though his back faced me, he positioned himself like he had delusions of being the next Jackie Chan and could take out our entire table using three moves, a spoon, and the chair his ass was parked in.

Steel Eyes—possibly the only one sane enough to possess a gun—stared down Dad. "I really would be careful. Even tasers don't stop him."

Okay, so I might have been a bit hasty on that sanity assessment.

As Steel Eyes took his seat, Gorilla Arms said to the cops, "It's three today."

Snickers snorted. "Please, like you're saving anything with the winnings, LJ?"

LJ? Stupid ass nickname. Mine was better. And did *LJ* think he was in the Corps or something? What was with the high and tight? Did women really want a guy who had stubble all over his head? He probably went to Watkins' barber.

Shoulders that didn't look capable of shrugging did just that. "She's gotta pay for her books."

That...that made me pause. *Books?* My stomach soured. They were talking about Maggie. Had to be. No offense to Tits McGee here, but she didn't strike me as the *War and Peace* type.

I almost forgot Candi was still lingering at our table until she bumped me with her breast for the fifth count. Any other time I would have taken her up on the invitation to look, but not today.

She filled my coffee mug even though I didn't drink the stuff. "Yeah, sugar, Mags is here. She's busy, but I can get your order started until she's available."

"We're not here to eat." I realized after I spoke that my tone had a hint of asshole attached to it. I managed a weak smile and attempted to adopt a pleasant attitude to avoid embarrassing my dad any further. "We came to talk to Maggie. If you don't mind telling her for me?"

"Sure," she chirped with a squeeze to my arm. "Anything for those dimples." Curvy hips swayed on over to the cops, and she threw herself into Gorilla Arms' face. He also didn't look, which shocked the shit outta me. "Boys, you causing trouble this early?"

"Good morning, Candi," mixed in with a, "You know it," along with one, "Hells yeah."

She leaned down, placing a hand on the back of Gorilla Arms' chair. "Who's winning today?"

"Like you have to ask?" Steel Eyes grumbled, unrolling his linen napkin. "Wunderkinds over here."

Laughing, Candi straightened. "LJ, I'd be shocked if you lost. What's the streak now? Nine weeks?"

Grinning, the bastard shrugged again. She shot him a flirty wink and kept on to the back.

"Yeah, you really should cool it, LJ," Snickers warned, leaning on his elbows with a stern look.

Sliding me a side-eye, the corner of GA's mouth tipped up. "I'm always cool."

My fist itched to punch that smirk—

The double doors swayed open, diverting my attention. I instantly forgot about the near bald hulk with initials for a name, who I prayed was gay, and I'd only imagined him flirting with Maggie weeks ago. As my eyes took in the tiny form emerging from the kitchen, I swore I went rock still.

Maggie.

She had her hair down today, raven silk swaying around the soft angle of her jaw, and her blue eyes were the perfect mixture of tropical water and the sky. A lavender shirt hugged her beneath a black apron dusted with flour, tied high around a flat waist. She was wearing shorts, so I could see her long, toned legs from the top of her thighs down to her worn Chucks. She looked like the quintessential all-American girl next door who earned smiles of adoration.

And four of those adoring smiles were coming from the table she was heading toward and didn't even so much as glance in my direction.

Maggie sidled up next to that so *not* gay, near bald hulk with initials for a name, and it turned out, he did like breasts; they just had to be attached to Maggie.

Blood roared in my ears as heat tore across my chest, coiling around my shoulders. And when she smiled at him, my stomach dropped, twisted, and churned all at once, and then rolled out the door to play in traffic.

I then imagined pummeling that very *straight*, near bald hulk with initials for a name. In the face. Maybe launch my knee into his gut. Snap a few ribs. I wouldn't mind throwing an elbow into his back. Bruise a kidney—

Holy shit. I hadn't realized what this was until now. This all-encompassing feeling was as if I'd been hollowed from the inside out.

I was…jealous.

So that's what it felt like.

Huh.

Candi returned to our table, but I wasn't listening to whatever she was babbling on about. My glare was on that cop, waiting for him to do something stupid that would give me an excuse to do something even stupider.

With his stare still locked onto Maggie as she walked back to the kitchen, the situation in my stomach worsened. He wasn't much older than me. Maybe…twenty-five.

I couldn't remember the last thing I ate, but it was ready to evict the premises and remind me.

"LJ!" Steel Eyes scowled at the younger officer. "Did you take one too many trips into the gas chamber during boot? Your *Indian?*"

He blinked, somewhat offended. "She'd be safe with me."

"Doesn't matter." A mug clinked on the table from the one who had yet to speak until now. I'd dubbed him Creeper at some point. "He will castrate you the moment you roll up."

I liked the sound of that.

Gorilla Arms leaned in, the Velcro of his body armor pulling with a crackle. "I told you I was going to talk to him."

Snickers chuckled. "You'd be lucky if you get the first sentence out."

Creeper's hands slid together. "I give the rookie five words before the screaming begins."

"Let's make it interesting. Twenty—"

"Not on this, guys. Please." Gorilla Arms cut off their chatter with his plea, and he shifted uncomfortably. "By the way, we're up to two. One more."

I couldn't even guess what that was all about, but if they were betting on how to land Maggie, the fact that he was a cop wouldn't stop my violent, albeit satisfying inclinations to take him down.

The kitchen doors parted again, and the man stepping through them wasn't throwing off a welcome-to-the-Crest-Cent-Café kind of vibe. The gray head of hair looked familiar. That was the owner. Fred…Floyd… Frankie. His wife used to work the tables. She'd been so nice to Faith.

Meeting us, the creases lining his face were deeper than I remembered, hair more salt than pepper, stature a bit more slumped. Discomfort shuttled across Frankie's face as he rubbed those liver-spotted hands down his immaculate apron. "I'm sorry, fellas. I have to ask you to leave."

"We're not here to cause problems," Dad explained. "We're here to speak with Maggie."

"I appreciate that, but..." The owner sighed, words reluctant. "You're making her uncomfortable."

And that was all the four Jack in the Boxes needed. They launched from their chairs like their springs had been cranked too tight.

"Need a hand, Frankie?" Though not speaking to me, Gorilla Arms' brown marbles drilled a hole into my forehead. His hands flexed, black ink peeking out beneath his collar. I was surprised his uniform didn't crack from the five cans of starch he'd used.

Before things got interesting, Maggie reappeared and said she would talk with us, but I had the feeling we'd see Santa Claus skinny dip in the Pacific before that happened.

Eyes latched onto me, Gorilla Arms waited for the swinging doors to shut before he spoke. "If that girl suffers a seizure from the stress you put her under today, you and I are gonna have a big problem."

Matt held up his palms, trying to draw the focus away from me. "It wasn't our intention to upset Maggie."

Snickers snarled, "And what gave you the impression we cared what your intentions were?"

"Officers," Dad interjected, "we're here to make things right and apologize. We're only asking for a few minutes of her time, and then we'll leave. Let us stay for her sake. Please."

Gorilla Arms' gaze scrolled over the five of us as if we were nothing more than ants, and he was the boot of life. When the muscle in his jaw ticked, I had a sneaky suspicion that Steel Eyes was correct. A taser wouldn't stop him.

Maggie returned with their food, and the cop resumed gawking at her. As he smiled a well-practiced, panty-dropping grin, the asshole even shot her a wink, and she ate it up.

Flashes of that hulk running his thick hands along her delicate skin invaded my brain. Shit, I needed to pour scalding coffee in my ear in hopes of it burning my gray matter and destroying that image.

The conversation with Maggie went so much worse than I had feared. When the first hint of tears emerged, I should have gouged my eyes out with the fork Cam had been twirling since we sat down. Every instinct screamed for me to leap across the table, beg for forgiveness, apologize for acting like a dick so many times, for not listening to her, not believing her.

But I didn't, and she went right to the cop, right into his arms.

The pain and hurt I'd caused her was like a riptide slamming me into the ocean floor, knocking me against the razor-sharp coral.

My voice cracked around her name. "Sticks—"

"I. Said. *Leave*." Gorilla Arms ground out every word. Cinched around Maggie, the uniform stretched, revealing the bottom of a tattoo on his right bicep.

The high and tight now made sense and was completely justified.

It was then that I saw it in his eyes. My violent, albeit satisfying inclinations, weren't just mine. Yeah, he had some of his own. Like that badge didn't mean as much to the Devil Dog as another code he lived by. A code he'd learned from things he'd seen…and done.

The code of a warrior.

And he was holding Maggie.

Five fingers gripped my arm, tugging me backward. "Let's go, little brother."

Realizing that I was getting further from Maggie, panic entrenched me, my body tensing and fighting the distance. "No, Matt—"

More hands were on my chest, the floor was moving, and suddenly, an ocean breeze was skating along my heated skin. I blinked to find that I was standing outside in the café's parking lot. As the door closed, I swore I heard her cry bleed into the air.

My feet shot forward, but I wasn't getting any closer to her. "Sticks…" I struggled, fighting a losing battle. "She's crying, she's—"

"She's had enough, Mase." My dad entered my vision, obstructing the café door. "We're not helping her. The officer was right. I don't want to cause Maggie any further stress. It's not good for her. Give her time, and we can try again."

"He's right, Coz." Cam's hand firmed on my shoulder, holding me back when I tensed again. "We're making it worse."

When I didn't back down, Matt got me going in reverse toward the SUV. "Come on. Let's go grab some breakfast."

My sneakers dug into the asphalt. "No, I have to fix this. It's my fault, I—"

Dad's hand came to my chest, my heart pounding beneath his steady palm. The corners of his mouth were pulled down, failure stamped into his eyes. "We'll try later. I promise."

I believed him, but I knew I'd see that look in his eyes again.

After grabbing breakfast, my brother and cousins went to the RAM house, and I went home with Dad. I started my laundry and cleaned my room. Even with the assistance of Google and YouTube, I didn't do nearly as good a job as Maggie. She had a way to make my bathroom counter shine, and the mirror wasn't spotted with all the crap I'd flung onto it. My room used to smell like lemons and laundry detergent instead of feet and sweat. My clothes were folded and organized and not lumped in piles of dirty and questionable.

Our kitchen was messy again, the pantry cluttered with crap. The fridge was filled with Styrofoam containers from various takeout joints around the Cove. Dust layered the furniture, and the exercise equipment was covered in fingerprint smudges.

It was the little things...

That was what hit me first when Faith had passed. Her stuffed toys weren't strewn about the house, and her pill bottles weren't cluttering the counter. Her Legos had been assembled and put back on her shelves. The hospital scent was replaced by Glade Plug-Ins and Febreeze. Her fuzzy blankets weren't bunched on the couch, and the multiple trashcans for her to get sick in were put away.

Everywhere I turned were reminders of the two girls who were no longer a part of my life.

Coming up empty with things to keep me occupied, I knew if my parents weren't home right now, I would have started drinking regardless that it was ten in the morning. That knowledge was more than disturbing. Instead, I slid on my gear and went for a run. I didn't know where I was running to, but I had to leave the house, the lake, the running trail...

I ended up downtown for the second time today, which was moronic of me because that meant I had to run back home, and the breakfast burrito I'd Hoover'd an hour ago wasn't loving that fact.

I stopped across the street from the café as a mother and her two kids rifled through the splintered wicker basket on the small table outside. She took a large cucumber and plump apple, and made her son put back something that resembled a brownie. But when he pointed to the cookie his little sister had, the mother gave up and let them keep their treats. She rummaged through the basket once more, almost longingly, as if she wanted to take more but resisted the urge. Concern swarmed me. She was thin—too thin. So were the kids. And they looked as if they shopped wherever Maggie did. Their clothes were not much more than rags, shoes riddled with holes.

Once the family moved on, I spotted Maggie in the window. My heart lurched behind my sternum like the thing wanted to remind me it was still present and functional.

Her head was down, keeping to the other side of the dining room, cleaning off the empty tables. She didn't speak to anyone, didn't smile, and the two customers inside only glimpsed her way when Maggie's back was turned.

People stopped coming to the café because of me. I'm the town pariah.

It killed me to know what we had done to her. This town had adored their little Mags. The raven beauty with a soft grace who could quietly work her way into your heart and warm it without ever realizing you had let her in. I remembered the day I'd taken her to Henry's Market and how everyone lit up like she'd brought the sun with her and they were desperate for her light. I'd taken that away from her. I'd made her life harder and dragged her deeper into the darkness.

You've done this to yourself, Maggie.

When I had said that, I was surprised by the depth of hurt in her eyes. And the truth was that the only thing Maggie had done wrong was trust us.

I could go into the café now and talk to her. Maybe without the cop there, I'd convince her to listen. Or...knowing my mouth? I'd make it worse.

Maybe everyone was right. She needed time. Chances were good that I'd push her further away, and she'd go back into the cop's arms. Would he treat her right? Had he already taken her on a date? Did he spend twenty minutes on the phone with a florist trying to get her the right color roses? Admire her every curve in a borrowed, skintight dress, imagining what was beneath? Did he bring Maggie back to his place, feed her disgusting kale chips? Did they end up in his room? On his bed? Did he touch her with those thick, greedy hands, pop the front clasp of that navy striped bra, put his mouth on her, fuck her—

I clenched my eyes until small white dots danced behind my lids, the images going nowhere, torturing me. And I should be tortured. If I hadn't put my fate in someone else's hands, Maggie could have been mine to hold, touch, kiss...

Shoving off my sneaker, I headed further down the street, spotting a lump or two in the alley by the barbershop. Stepping over the fresh orange peels littering the ground near a dingy brown blanket, I crossed the street when I was no longer within sight of the café's window.

As soon as I hit the market's threshold, a head of prematurely white hair lifted from a game of Sudoku, blue eyes widening. "Mason. How're you doing?"

"Henry." I nodded once and drew out the two bills I'd tucked into my pocket before leaving the house. "Been better. You?"

"Same." Setting his pencil in the middle of the book, Henry accepted the bills with a rough cough, and I was smacked with a hit of déjà vu. This conversation was going exactly like it had last week, except…those bills didn't go into the drawer this time. They stayed in Henry's calloused mitt. "I, uh— Listen, I don't know if I can keep accepting your money."

I shoved my hands into the pockets of my shorts, leveling him with a glare, jaw hardening. "And why is that?"

His eyes dropped away from me, and my fists clenched. I already knew what he was going to say before he even opened his mouth. "It doesn't seem right. I know this food isn't for Mags, but—"

"No, the food was never for Maggie. The gesture was. To make her life easier. But if you're looking to punish her because you somehow feel deceived, then you're only punishing the starving homeless or the families in dire need by turning my money away."

Henry's thick shoulders sagged, and I wanted to yell at him for being so hurtful, close-minded. He'd known this girl all her life, a girl who had come here every day for years to collect scraps for the neighborhood vagrants, and he was treating her no differently than I had. Maybe it wasn't fair to judge him for that, but I wasn't exactly in a fair frame of mind.

I shook my head. "It should ease your conscience to know that Maggie didn't steal a damn thing. I discovered yesterday that it was a family friend who put the earrings in Maggie's bag. Maggie's completely innocent. We told her the news this morning."

His gaze lifted, the bags beneath his eyes suddenly heavier and darker. "Oh. I…hadn't heard."

No, I could tell he hadn't. But it shouldn't have mattered. To either of us.

"Now you have." And with that, I did leave him with the same sendoff I had the last time I was here. "See you next week, Henry."

Fueled by an ugly rage, my feet pounded all the way back home. Turned out, that was what I needed to get me from B back to A, but I might die from the ache in my muscles and lack of oxygen.

Being pissed off was like a one-way ticket to Stupidville.

I punched in my code to the gates, and thankfully, Bernard didn't give me any shit today, and when I turned onto my street, I learned why. Parked in front of my house was a black and white Tahoe, and the ache in my legs instantly vanished. I sprinted the rest of the way.

Flinging the front door wide, I faced a formidable body neatly tucked inside a pressed police uniform on our couch. He was wearing the button-down and tie combo today, pins on display, sporting a pair of shoes with a reflection that could rival a mirror.

He cast his icy gaze over to me and didn't move. "Mason."

Giving a decent attempt at controlling the breaths slicing their way through my bronchial tissues from running over here, I shut the front door.

I repeated his cursory greeting. "Chief."

As I crossed the room, Chief Davis' eyes took a stroll along my bruised cheek and then down to my swollen knuckles. I did nothing to shield them, mainly because it wasn't a good idea to hide your hands from anyone with a gun.

"Your father was just telling me about your girlfriend's sister."

"Ex," I corrected him, and if he needed more confirmation, the news of our *breakup* was splashed across every goddamned gossip rag. Charlie's publicist made sure of it.

The chief studied me as though he didn't believe me, or it was a temporary situation. There was nothing temporary about it.

Those near colorless eyes held mine, his mouth compressing into a flat line. "If people could only understand the ramifications of their actions. Word spreads fast in a small town like ours. Not only was my daughter affected, but Frankie's café and my good name have also been dragged through the mud despite my best efforts. The people of Crescent Cove look to me as a role model, a leader of the community, and for weeks, they believed their chief of police raised a criminal."

"I assure you, we knew nothing until yesterday, and neither my family nor I are responsible for spreading those allegations. But I am sorry for what Maggie has suffered through, and we have made sure the video was taken down."

His sharp gaze narrowed at the latter of my statement. "Video?"

My brain stumbled over his confusion. How...? How did he not know about that? Was he fucking with me, or had Maggie not told him? I would have thought he'd be the first she'd told, being that he was her father *and* a cop. Weird.

"The video of her seizure. Eric Ryan recorded her and uploaded it to social media without her permission or knowledge. She didn't tell you?"

Surprise flitted across his face before the chief's jaw solidified into stone. "She failed to mention it. I'm sure it slipped her mind. She has been rather preoccupied lately."

Yeah, I called bullshit on that.

"Mason is right," Dad said, drawing the chief's focus. "It's not going to be a problem for her any longer. Our family employs excellent cyber security specialists. They've done right by you and your daughter. And as for Eric… He's been dealt with."

"Has he now," Chief Davis murmured. "I seem to be at a disadvantage today. How exactly was Eric dealt with?"

"Yesterday afternoon, he attacked a student, Jamey Hayes," I supplied. "Eric's been expelled from Warrington for that and the video."

Whatever his reaction was to that news, he kept it on lockdown.

Dad shifted on the sofa cushion. "If you don't mind me prying, were there any repercussions for Maggie? At home, I mean."

Chief Davis cocked his head. "What kind of parent would I be if there hadn't been? Put yourself in my position. Wouldn't you punish your sons?"

I honestly couldn't remember the last time I was "punished," but then, the only thing I'd ever done was get into fights. Even then, they were in defense of others or for my own protection.

"My sons are twenty-one and twenty, Chief Davis. I think we're long past that point, but…" Dad nodded thoughtfully. "When they were younger, yes."

The cop shook his head. "And yet, I fail to understand why you would try to convince me not to bring up charges against Miss Price."

Dad considered his words. "I understand your frustration, but a minor infraction with the law won't teach her what you'd expect. Taylor is a self-centered girl from a privileged home. I know the Prices well. Their primary concern isn't raising their daughters, only making sure the right kind of news makes it to the public. They can take an overdose, a breakup, or a DUI and bounce back with an even stronger public image. But the same won't apply here. There's no viable spin, so the only recourse will be to do everything in their power to make this go away, and they'll spare no expense. The only thing Taylor will learn from this is that money fixes everything."

"You'd be surprised what a little time at the station in the right room can do, Dr. Scott."

Dad's gaze held steady. "Which brings me to my next point. I know the situation is different, but I never intended to involve the authorities with Maggie. I would be a hypocrite if I encouraged you to do so with Taylor. Don't get me wrong. I'm not saying there shouldn't be consequences, but I think community service and a year's suspension from the Stafford Cheer Squad would serve as a better punishment for Taylor. The reasons can be kept quiet, and her parents can twist it to their benefit. They can paint Taylor as a maturing, young woman who cares about her community more than her own self-interests. She'll become an Instagram inspiration and win public adoration. I think if you presented Mr. Price with that option, you'd get a much better response."

Tearing his eyes off my dad, Chief Davis drank the water in front of him, ice clinking together as it slid against his lips. He sighed. "You have no idea how much it bothers me that you are right. I see it a lot in…" His gaze wandered around the room, and I swore that was resentment in his eyes. "In our community."

"Chief, we would like Maggie to come back and work for us." Mom's voice was full of hope, gripping onto Dad's arm. "We loved having her here."

I knew my parents weren't asking for Maggie to come work for them again, though they did want that. They wanted her here, to see her, talk to her, make this right.

The chief set his glass on the coffee table. "No. I'm not comfortable with that."

Mom inhaled a startled breath, and I didn't blame her. I hadn't expected such a blunt response, either.

Taking a moment to collect herself, Mom urged, "I understand your hesitation, Chief Davis, but she told me she loved it here."

"She may have, but a lot has changed since, hasn't it?" He watched a drop of condensation slide down his glass before lifting that cool gaze to my mother. "She loves the café, Dr. Scott. Frankie and Paula are dear friends of ours, and the girl you believed was a thief has been working only for tips for the last five years to help them with their medical bills."

She was *what*? Who the hell worked just for tips? No wonder she needed another job. Scratch that. Two more jobs. And…where was this character defense when he came here the first time? Why didn't he tell us this then?

He leaned forward, elbows resting on his thighs, planting that steady gaze on my parents. "One job is enough for her to handle. Sometimes too much. And to be brutally frank, I don't want my name associated with yours."

Jesus. Okay, I got why he'd feel that way, but…damn.

Dad paled as he ran a hand over his stubbled jaw. "If it's alright with you, Chief, I would like to try to talk to your daughter again. I didn't like how I left things with her."

At that, the cop stood, drawing my attention to the four stars on each collar, the pins decorating his chest, every inch of his uniform starched and lint-free.

He looked down at Dad, and maybe the guy had enough of us and wanted to make his way to the door, but it seemed more deliberate to me. Like he was trying to…intimidate us.

He didn't know us well. At all.

"Dr. Scott, you left things fine. You spoke your piece, and I don't believe anything good can come from you going to the café again. I do not want to hear from my officers or Frankie that you've upset Margaret again."

I didn't like how he said her name. It didn't fit her. She was Sticks, Mags, or Maggie. A cute name like she was. *Margaret* was the name of a woman who wore muumuus and ate haggis.

Dad stood, meeting the chief in the eye. "Of course. I was only trying to set things right."

Eyes and shoulders softening, the chief's thumbs curled around his belt. "We're all very protective of her. Our team is like a family, and they care for Margaret like a daughter."

Yeah, I highly doubted Gorilla Arms would check out his own daughter's ass, but I kept that comment to myself.

The chief nodded his farewell to Mom. "Thank you for the water, Dr. Scott."

As he walked out, the chief's gear clanked with his movements, heavy boots echoing in our silence until the door shut.

From the window, I watched the SUV turn around and rumble down the street. "You called him?" I asked Dad.

"No. I was going to go down to the station, but he showed up here first. He explained that his officers relayed our…morning to him."

With a quiet moan, Mom wrapped her arms around her stomach. "Dan, I know what he said, but we have to make this right. Do what it takes. Get her back." Tears welled in her crystal blue eyes. "I can't imagine what Maggie's been going through because of us."

"We will, Eve." Dad swept her into his arms, pulling her close. "I'm going back tonight. She'll be closing, and the place will be empty."

And I had every intention of tagging along.

chapter eighteen

maggie

Sometime in the afternoon, that blond I'd had my mind on all day appeared and collapsed into a corner booth. He didn't announce himself by shouting an embarrassing declaration like the color of his neon underwear or twirling his way across the floor or singing the lyrics to "Baby Shark." Something was definitely amiss.

"Frankie, do you mind if I take five?" I asked.

Brown eyes full of remorse, his voice came rougher than I was used to hearing. "Take whatever you want, hon."

Ah, I was officially back to *hon*. Oh, and not long after the boys had left, Frankie apologized, looking me in the eye and all. Candi had even caught me in the walk-in and apologized for believing the gossip. I thanked them, but I didn't forgive them. They didn't deserve it.

I brought over a chocolate milkshake for Jamey and slid into the opposite side of the booth.

"Thanks," he mumbled, playing with the straw.

I tugged on his bare wrist that had been absent of his leather bracelet for the last couple of weeks. It was weird to see him without it, and I knew he'd taken it off because it had only served as a reminder of Ben.

"You haven't answered your phone all day," I said. "I left a message with Ava. She told me you were playing with Khal Drogo's *arakh*, and that was where I stopped the conversation."

The corner of his mouth twitched, but the smile didn't take. "It's not what you think it is, but I wouldn't mind playing with Khal Drogo's—"

"We really need to stick to those TMI boundaries, Jamey."

Keeping his head low, Jamey pinned his lips together. "I know you called. Sorry. I wasn't ignoring you. I...needed to clear my head."

I curled my legs under me and leaned across the table. "What's going on under the sunglasses?"

After an exaggerated exhale, he tugged them off.

"Holy swollen eyeball!" Gasping, I grabbed the side of his face that didn't look like it had met a Mack Truck. "What happened to you? Who did this? Tell me you filed a report!"

He patted the hand still gripping his face. "Slow down. You know I can't jump to the end like that. You need to hear the drama from start to finish." He dragged in a breath, really ramping up for this story. "I got a text from Ben after class yesterday. His family's cyber security guy traced the video back to Eric. In what I will call a blond rage of stupidity or the effects of too much hair dye leaking into my bloodstream, I confronted Eric in the locker room. Only, he was there with that Brady dude, too. Eric swung at me, and that's when Mason showed up. I don't think Brady was going to hit me, but he wasn't exactly helping either. Didn't matter because Mason kicked both their asses."

I stared at him. Jamey simply shrugged and continued to play with his straw.

My eyebrow flicked up, waiting. "Please don't make me keep saying *and then* like that stupid *Dude Car* movie you forced me to watch."

He pouted at me. "You're no fun."

With that, Jamey tenderly touched his bruise as if he needed to test his pain threshold. Turned out, it was pretty low.

Letting the straw go, he said, "*And then*, Coach Watkins broke up the fight, and we all ended up in the clinic. The video has been taken down, but there's no guarantee that it won't pop back up. Ben said to let him know if it does, and they will take care of it."

Unease twisted sharply in my gut. "I don't have money to pay them back for that, Jamey. A cyber security guy? That had to cost a lot."

"Then I guess it's a good thing the Scotts are rich, so they can clean up their messes."

"Jamey—"

"There's more, Mags." His hazel gaze was fixated on the tall glass forming beads of sweat between us. "Eric was expelled, in large part because I threatened to call the cops and charge him with a hate crime. I said I would let it go and keep quiet if they kicked him out. With that, plus the video...they didn't have a choice."

"Christ." My eyes darted to the window as if expecting Marcus to be standing there, ready to have another happy chat with me.

"You may not want to hear this, but Mason was suspended from the football team for a month, and he's got one of these. It just looks way sexier on him."

My focus returned to Jamey, gaze narrowing. "Why was Mason suspended?"

His good eye met mine. "Though I wholeheartedly disagreed, Watkins and Evans felt Mason took things far beyond the point of defending me. After the doctor evaluated Eric and Brady, Watkins had to drive them to the hospital for concussions and broken faces."

I let that news settle a moment. "Mason was here today, but I was too pissed to even look at him, let alone care he had a black eye."

Pulling the milkshake toward him, he sucked down a thick gulp. "Did they tell you what happened?"

I nodded, my mouth loathing the words. "Yeah. Mason's girlfriend's sister set me up."

"*Ex*-girlfriend's sister with all caps and three exclamation points."

My brows pinched. "How do you know that?"

"Ben and Camden. They said that Mason figured it out after the fight yesterday. Evidently, Taylor's got some major beef with big sis and wanted to take Mason away from Charlie as an act of war, but that plan was derailed when she saw you in the basement with Mason—which after this, we are so going to kick it in reverse, 'cause I need to hear that story."

Jamey gave me a pointed stare until I relented.

Satisfied, he continued. "Anyway, you landed in Taylor's revenge sites, and you were the entire reason she was there that morning because she needed you out of the way. So, after dropping Charlie off at her sorority house, she returned to the Scotts', snuck inside through the garage door, and hid the earrings in your bag. From what the guys said, Mason went nuclear on Taylor when he Sherlock'd it out. Mason and Charlie's fakemance breakup has been all over the social media and the gossip rags as an amicable we're-better-as-friends kind of thing, but from what I'm told, it wasn't friendly. At all."

A few weeks ago, I might have cared about that. Now? Didn't have one fuck to give. "What else did Ben say?"

"The gist through all of the groveling? He wants me back. He wants—" Jamey's lashes swept down, shielding his eyes. "It doesn't matter what he wants."

Frowning, I made tiny tears in his wilted cocktail napkin. "Doesn't it, though?"

One shoulder lifted and fell. "He wants things to be how they were before. Ben said he'll wait as long as I need until we can have that again." Jamey's one working lid flipped up to mine. "But it doesn't matter."

"Why? Have your feelings for him changed?"

"That's what doesn't matter."

Reaching over, I laced my fingers with his. "Jamey, you know I only want you to be happy, and you've been miserable for weeks. Ben made you happy."

His brows drew together, wincing from the effort. "How can I look at him and not remember what they did to you? How can I ever expect you to be okay with our relationship? Mags, you're as much a part of my life as Crazy Ava is. I can't keep my best friend and my boyfriend in separate boxes. I won't do that. I need you to love whom I'm with as much as I do, and you're not ready to be around Ben right now. You might never be."

"Let me figure that out. Take him back, Jamey."

Shaking his head, his gaze fixed on me. "They said Logan practically threw them out this morning after they made you cry."

"I didn't cry," I said defensively.

His brows sprung high and then flinched again. He really should learn to stop moving his face.

"Okay, maybe I did," I conceded. "But only *after* they left."

Jamey nibbled his bottom lip. "Well, Ben and Camden kinda sorta asked me to tell you that the Scotts really do want you to come back to work. They seemed desperate." He paused as if waiting for me to suddenly care about how the Scotts felt. "Are you? Considering it?"

"No." I shook my head as though the word wasn't enough. "I can't go back to them."

A sad smile notched one corner of his mouth. "Blue Eyes, you might have convinced me if you said you didn't want to."

Closing came faster than I wanted, and I wished I didn't have to lift the chairs to clean the floors because that was a bitch. I started earlier than usual since it took me so long these days, and the last customer had left hours ago, anyway. Frankie offered to take the closing shift, but that meant I'd have to go home early. So, here I stayed.

I'd just wrangled the mop bucket into the dining room when the bell chimed behind me, and a messy pile of dread flopped over in my stomach. I knew who it was before I turned around.

His lean, muscular form filled the doorway, startling handsome in the same black T-shirt and distressed jeans that he had on earlier today. He knew he was the only one who came on Saturday nights. He'd waited all damn day to corner me.

Without a word, Mr. Scott took his usual seat in the booth by the Wall of Death and gave me those eyes, the ones that made me feel pity for him and do stupid things like not kick his ass out of here four years ago. "How's your back?"

"What do you want?" My fingers curled around the mop handle, a dry splinter pricking my palm. I hated that the first thing out of his mouth had been concern for me. And I hated that I was too defeated to sound as angry as I was.

His voice was gentle and kind like it used to be for me. "To talk to you."

The tears were thick in my throat, but I swallowed them down. "When I tried to talk, you refused to listen. Order something or leave."

Hurt scored his features, and we both knew the reason. Only once in the four years that he'd been coming here had I'd asked what he wanted to order, and that was the first night I'd met him. Since then, it had been a weekly game of mine to guess what he'd like and then watch him enjoy what I'd picked for him. The fact that I had to ask spoke for how much I didn't care anymore. That was his fault. He had done that to himself.

His emerald gaze swung to the pastry display and then back to me. "Apple pie."

"They all went bad."

"Coffee."

"Machines are broken." I was kinda digging Mean Maggie.

With an unsteady breath, his lids slid shut in resignation. When he opened them, Mr. Scott stared at me like he was trying to memorize each of my features as though he knew he'd never see me again. I wanted to look away and deny him, but before I could, he stood, his hand lifting to the pictures on the wall. The photos of those who had passed of Frankie and Paula's friends, relatives, and customers. He hesitated before removing a frame off the nail. When I realized which one it was, a chill slithered around my gut, and the anger encasing me began to chip away.

The family.

Mr. Scott sat back down in the booth as his fingers reverently outlined the frame. "This is us." His gaze drifted up to mine. "I'm guessing by the look on your face, you didn't know that."

I rested the mop handle against a tabletop and risked a step closer. "I don't like this wall. I...don't like to look at it." Even to my own ears, my voice sounded fragile.

Swallowing, his focus returned to the photograph. "I'd hoped... I thought maybe if I sat in *this* booth, in the very booth that's in this picture, underneath the very spot that it was hung, you would have seen the connection. The reason I kept coming back here."

Oh-kay... I was utterly lost.

"This was taken years ago, only to me, it feels like yesterday." He spun the frame around to face me, but I didn't accept his offer to look. Undeterred, he explained, "That's Matt, Mason, and...Faith. Eve was at work that day, and Paula did her best to take a steady picture with her arthritis, but I wanted... We wanted to celebrate that day. It was the first time Faith went into remission."

My heart bottomed out. "The...first time?"

His nod was tentative and choppy. "Faith didn't want to celebrate the rest of them."

Oh, God.

Though I wanted to know, I was too much of a coward to ask how many remissions there had been, to hear how long his little girl had suffered.

"This was our super-secret place, me and the kids." Mr. Scott spoke to the photograph as though he were talking to his daughter, and I listened because that was the least I could do for her. His sins didn't belong to Faith, and she didn't deserve my anger.

"I would wink, so they knew we were coming here and not to tell Eve. We made a game of it, sneaking out of the house to ruin our dinner. And every time we came, we would bring home something made of chocolate for Mom so she wouldn't be mad." A ghost of a smile flickered across his face and then crumbled. "Eventually, the café became...something else. A distraction from life and not a celebration of it. Between the chemo, surgeries, trials...our trips came fewer and farther between. The last time we came here, Faith ordered her favorite, apple pie with vanilla ice cream and hot cocoa. She couldn't—" His words cut off as his lips began to tremble.

"She'd been having problems swallowing from the tumor in her—" Abruptly looking away, he covered his mouth with his fist as if he wanted to spare me the horrid details. Or perhaps they were too horrid to speak of. I realized he was staring down to his side in the booth, and with the way his chest shuddered and skin paled, it was as though he were stuck inside a memory. And maybe he was. It was all too likely that was where Faith had sat when he brought her here.

Mr. Scott blinked as a single tear slipped down his face, splashing onto the tabletop. It wasn't until then that I understood how hard it must have been for him to come back here time and again. Return to the place that once held happiness for him and his family. And now...all that was left was pure sorrow, the kind that decimated the soul.

A part of me wanted to offer him comfort, ease his hurt in some way, but the voice in my head reminded me of how he had looked at me, followed me through his home, spoke those awful words that broke me. So I stayed standing, unwilling to show him that kindness.

After a hard swallow, his fist rested on the table, voice hoarse and thready when he spoke. "One night, about a year after Faith had passed, I...had a case come into the ER, a little girl around five years old. She was lethargic, feverish, her belly hurt. Like most parents, they thought she had a virus she couldn't kick. Only it wasn't. They couldn't know that she was tired because she was anemic. They couldn't know the pain in her belly was really from an enlarged spleen. They couldn't know that her fever stemmed from their worst nightmare because no parent ever expects to be told their child has leukemia."

Mr. Scott shut his eyes for a long moment, another tear escaping. "And as much as I could empathize with those parents and the pain that family was about to face, it was too damn much too soon. I had to excuse myself from the case because that family needed a doctor, not a broken man."

He stopped to swallow thickly. "I left work, but I couldn't go home because *home* was where my little girl *wasn't*. So, I drove around for hours until I ended up here, and I'm still not sure why. But when I looked inside the window, I saw a girl walk out of those doors." His chin jutted behind me to the kitchen, gaze lingering there. "She had dark hair, a sweet smile, and the brightest blue eyes. And for a moment, just a flash...I swore it was my Faith. Like I'd woken up from my nightmare, and she was really alive, here, waiting for me that whole time."

His head ducked back down as if the memory weighed too heavily on him. "It wasn't, of course. It was you, Maggie."

Hand shaking, he pushed the photo across the table, and as my brain assembled the image facing me, every piece of this sordid puzzle snapped together. I inched closer to that picture, my gait becoming loose and wonky.

Matt had his arm slung around his brother's shoulders. The boys couldn't have been older than ten, eleven maybe. Even in black and white, I could distinguish that Scott smile and kicked myself for never noticing it before. But there on the other side of the booth, wrapped up in her father's arms, snug in his lap, Faith had—

I gulped as I picked up the frame to see her closer. There was something not quite right about her face. Her cheeks were swollen, painfully so. Her head was covered in a scarf of cartoon bears, eyes hollow and empty, body far too frail. But that wasn't the reason I stopped breathing.

A sense of numbness washed over me, my knees ready to buckle, and I had no choice but to sit down across from him in that booth. Faith was young here and visibly ill, but what I was seeing was impossible to deny.

"I— I thought I bore some resemblance to her after Nana confused us, but..."

Closing his eyes, Mr. Scott's head swayed. "No, Maggie. It's not a resemblance. You could be her. So much so that it's *painful* to look at you."

Suddenly, everything and every moment with the Scotts made sense. Nothing Mason had said or done had been because he hated me.

It was to protect his family and himself.

From me.

From a ghost.

That was why he'd ran out on our date. That was why he wanted me to quit. That was why he needed me out of his life.

"Are we..." The words scraped out of my throat. "We're not—"

"No. We're in no way related if that's what you're asking." I think I nodded, but he kept on. "I tried to stay away, Maggie. I did. But I wasn't strong enough. It doesn't make a lot of sense but seeing you, talking to you even for a few minutes a week made me feel as if she'd somehow sent me to you, to ease my pain." His throat bobbed on a heavy pause. "In all those years, I never told anyone I came here. I didn't think Eve or the boys would understand. Just like I didn't think they would understand why I went to the university and asked them to honor your scholarship."

I gasped, clutching the frame tight. "What?"

Mr. Scott's watery gaze collided with mine. "I did that. For you. To keep you here in town. Regardless of Warrington's answer, I would have paid your tuition, but considering the circumstance, I thought it was best you didn't know it was me. I thought it was best you didn't know that I couldn't stand the thought of you leaving. Eve did the same thing when you came to the house for the job. She opened the door and saw Faith. As painful as it was, Eve couldn't let you walk out of her life either, and like me, she didn't know how to tell us about you. But it didn't take long to figure out she'd hired you, and I was ecstatic.

"But that was our mistake. We hide our pain, refuse to share it, terrified of burdening each other with it. Because of that, Matt and Mason thought we were trying to replace Faith with you. They felt we were betraying her memory. They were furious with us. But that wasn't what we were doing. We didn't know how to heal, how to move on. When you lose a child...it's the worst kind of hell there is, and when you're lost in that darkness, it's human nature to reach for any speck of light you can find."

Two more tears tracked down his face as he held my gaze. "Slowly, Matt and Mason forgave us, and at different points, we all welcomed you into our hearts. Waking up and seeing that closed bedroom door down the hall, sitting next to the empty chair at the kitchen table...hurt less. We began to heal. Move forward. I'd been so desperate for that, but until you came into our lives, we hadn't been able to." His gaze settled back on the picture in my hands. "That day with the earrings, Maggie... It was like losing my daughter all over again. Like all the wounds you helped us stitch back together were ripped open. We've been mourning whatever hope you gave us. Eve cries herself to sleep every night, Matt's angry, and Mason's painfully withdrawn, slipping into himself again. When we lost Faith, it nearly broke us, broke my marriage, my family apart. The boys don't know how close Eve and I came to it. We clawed our way out of hell, and I can't... I'm not strong enough to go through that again."

His head shook once more. "You were right about everything, and we don't deserve you. What Taylor did was so wrong, so terrible. But *I* carry the sins of that day by not stopping for a second to listen to y—"

"Stop." My voice cracked beneath the weight of an emotional overload as I swung from one extreme to the next. I *wanted* to be angry. I *wanted* to hate him. The more he spoke, the more he explained...he was whittling down my defenses, stone by stone. I couldn't allow that to happen. "Your family hurt me, the hate you had for me..."

He leaned in, arms stretching toward me. "Maggie—"

"No." Placing the picture between us, I drew back. "The only reason you're here is for you. To assuage *your* guilt, not the trust you broke. Not the hurt you caused. You came here all those years ago for yourself, to ease *your* pain. And that's why you're here now. You don't care about me. You never did. You don't see me. You never have."

A breath rattled his chest, tears making multiple trails down his face, catching in his thick stubble. "I am here for you. I do see you, Maggie."

"You *used* me."

Lowering his gaze, he didn't deny it. "If I could change it all, I would."

"It's an easy sentiment, isn't it?" I bit out. "We'd take a different path if we could. We apologize, express regret when we realize our actions have caused hurt. But the only thing that you regret is that the truth came out because we both know that you would have kept lying to me. You had four years to tell me the truth, and you didn't. And what's worse, in those four years, I didn't give you one reason not to trust me, not to give me the benefit of the doubt. And now you haven't given me one reason to forgive you."

Mr. Scott drew in a razor-sharp breath, and before he could say anything else, I pressed as far back into the booth as I could, welcoming the pressure to ignite every mark on my back.

"You need to leave."

We stared at each other amid a stretch of silence that seemed eternal, until he finally nodded. He tugged something out from behind him and placed it next to the picture. "You're right. About all of it. And you deserve so much more than an apology, so much more than I can convey with words. Before I go, I want you to have this. It's your pay for the month you were with us, the last two weeks, and a little extra."

He made the next mood swing pretty damned easy. "You're unbelievable," I spat. "That makes it all better, doesn't it? Throw enough money at your sins, and your soul will be cleansed? Sorry, Doc. You're gonna have to live with this one. I'm not like *you*."

His lids flew wide, palms facing me. "This is yours, Maggie. You earned it. I'm not trying to buy your forgiveness, but I have to— I want to make this right. I meant it when I said that we all want you to come back."

I refused to touch the envelope. "No."

He blinked a few times as if he didn't understand the word. Like he'd never heard it spoken to him before and couldn't process the meaning. "If you change your mind…you are always welcome." He reached for me again, and I coiled into myself, staying out of his reach. His fingers withdrew. "Is it alright if I— Can I come back next Saturday?"

"No, it's not alright."

He blinked hard. "Okay. I won't come back because you asked me not to, not because I don't want to." With slow movements, as if he were giving me time to change my mind, he rehung the picture. I refused to lift my gaze until the bell chimed, and the door slid shut.

Unmoved from my seat, I stared at what he left behind. A stack of guilt and remorse tucked neatly inside a crisp, clean package. All the pain, anger, frustration, loss that I had suffered flooded me. The Scotts, the beating, Jamey...none of it had to happen. None of it would have happened if it weren't for them.

Mr. Scott was right, in a way. This was my fault. I'd let my defenses down. I'd forgotten whose story this was, who would get their happily ever after.

The dragon.

With a swipe of my arm, the envelope flew across the room, and a scream tore out of me, releasing all my secrets, all the bitter darkness inside me, all the years I'd been forced to be silent into the sugar-scented air of the café.

chapter nineteen

mason

Every time I looked at the clock, I swore time was moving backward. Since dinner, I'd been in the gym doing lifts, squats, burpees, jumping rope, more lifts, more squats, spinning the hamster wheel, and 'round I went. I had to sweat more, burn more, keep moving because once I stopped, regret would choke the shit out of me with Maggie's words on an endless reel.

Some things can't be forgiven.
Some things can't be forgotten.
You said I disgusted *you.*

I knew that tore my dad up. Those words had come from a place of anger, and he hated himself for it.

Nothing burned through your soul deeper than guilt, knowing you were the one responsible for destroying another.

And with one gesture, a few words, I could have saved us all from this. Her from this.

I had done the unforgivable and hurt her. It was the one thing she'd asked me not to do, and I had time and again. The worse part? My gut instinct about Maggie had been right, and I'd ignored it.

I had a speech planned for tonight, then scrapped and rewritten it a hundred times. And I still didn't know what I was going to say to her. I wanted Maggie to go for a cheap shot, slap me, punch me, kick me in the balls. Do anything but cry. I didn't think I could handle seeing that again.

Somewhere around my third water break, footsteps crossed the room above, and I stilled. The steps were headed further down the hallway. I swiped the sweat from my eyes and heaved a breath, finding the last drop of energy to fly up the stairs in time to see Dad opening the garage door.

"You're leaving?" I asked, suddenly seven years old again, trailing my dad to the door with a half-eaten Oreo in my hand as he left for his ER shift.

He stopped at my voice. Shoulders nearing his ears, Dad's hand curled tighter on the hardware. "I...don't think I'll be long."

My stomach plunged at his use of pronoun. *I* not *we*.

"I thought we—" As the moments ticked by with Dad refusing to look at me, I realized he had no intention to include another person on this trip. "Can I come?"

It seemed like forever before his gaze met mine, and if I wasn't already gutted, the pain in his eyes would have done it. "I don't think that's a good idea, Mase."

"I'll stay in the car. I promise." I didn't care how desperate I sounded.

Dad considered me a long while, and just when I figured he would shoot me down again, he nodded. "If you stay in the car."

"Okay."

A quick drive later, without a word spoken between us, Dad parked the GX across the street, facing the café. He killed the lights. Through the windows, we watched Maggie place the chairs onto the tables. Face drawn and tense, her arms shook with each lift, cringed with each bend of her back, but she kept going until all the chairs were up.

"If she had only let me examine her," Dad murmured, more to himself than me. "Just a few goddamned tests. Figure out what meds she'd tried, if her back pain was related to her head trauma, the essential tremors, her balance... She *shouldn't* be off meds."

Watching her from the parking lot, something dawned on me. "This is when you would come."

His gaze reluctantly shifted to mine. "Yeah." Glancing away from me, Dad lowered the heater. "And you know, even after working nineteen hours straight, she kept that door unlocked for me. Every week."

I made a point to look down the road that was sporadically lit by street lamps, thinking back to the night we'd met. The blackout, the storm... A large shadow slunk into one of the alleys, and I wondered if it was the same person who had left those orange peels on the walk earlier.

I added, "And then she went home, *alone*, in the middle of the fucking night without a helmet on a piece of shit bike." A bike she shouldn't be riding with her poor balance. The same bike that didn't have lights because she refused to accept anything from me. The day that she'd left them on my desk in class had been her final *fuck you.*

"Yeah." Dad chased the word with an exhale and reached for the handle. For whatever reason, that was the moment I decided to word vomit all over him.

"I almost kissed Maggie."

He stilled, not so much as a blink for ten seconds. Illuminated by the dim blue lights of the dash, I saw his head nod once. "I know."

Shame wrenched my chest, constricting it so hard I could feel it in my throat. "But you don't know that I lied to you and Mom."

He twisted to face me. "How so?"

"I met Maggie before Mom hired her. It was... Hell, I don't know what it was. Fate? Coincidence? Dumb luck?" Swallowing, I concentrated on the gearshift as if I could slam it in Reverse and take back the last thirty seconds. "We met during the storm. The blackout after Matt's birthday. The details aren't important, but I was ashamed to tell you that I had developed feelings for her before I knew what she looked like. And after... I tried, Dad. I did. I didn't want this. I didn't want to feel anything for her. I tried to push her away, forget her, but it didn't work. It was like the harder I tried, the more I needed to know her. And no matter what I told myself, I knew that I wanted to end the farce with Charlie, so I could be with Maggie. Regardless of how wrong it was or what you would think of me, Maggie was who I wanted. But I was too late, too wrapped up in not hurting Charlie, and it was Maggie who got hurt. Because of me."

"Mase, no." His hand curled around the back of my neck, gripping tight. "It's not your fault. Don't shoulder that. This is on me. There's no way you could have predicted Taylor would go to such extremes."

"Maybe not, but—"

"No." Dipping lower, Dad's gaze snared mine. "I did this. I couldn't see past my own anger. The words spoken to her were mine alone. And it's up to me to make this right."

Movement in the café brought our attention back to Maggie as she dragged the mop bucket out of the back. As the wayward wheels veered in the opposite direction than she was pulling, her lips must have dropped at least five F-bombs.

Sighing, Dad gave my neck one more squeeze before he climbed out.

I lowered the window as though the absence of glass would help me hear their conversation. The tinge of ozone chilled the cab, faint crashing waves the only sound in the otherwise still night. I crossed my arms to keep warm.

As Dad went inside, Maggie's frame instantly hardened, her eyes narrowing with fury. That was the fire I had liked about her. The spirit that I wished this once didn't exist, give us the chance we never gave her. Sad thing was, I wasn't sure if Maggie could have changed our minds. I knew Taylor was manipulative, but to go to the lengths she did to hurt my family, saying nothing after Maggie's seizure... I never would have guessed she had that kind of cruelty inside her.

No matter what Dad said, I had created this mess. I'd gotten so caught up in being Maggie's hero that I had unwittingly become her villain.

My gaze cut back to the café as Dad removed a photo from the wall. I knew which one it was because I had avoided looking at it this morning. By Maggie's softened stance, I was sure he was telling her about Faith. Hope bloomed that she would keep the door open to the possibility of forgiving us. But once that envelope appeared, that hope went straight to the shitter.

Revulsion drew across her face. The fire was back, blazing with rage. With an exchange of a few more words, Dad ambled back into the fog, dragging himself toward the car. Once he slipped inside, he slumped into the leather seat, rubbing his sore eyes.

The air felt dense with failure.

I gave him a solid minute before I asked, "What happened?"

Dad let his hand fall to his lap. "I didn't have a reason for her to forgive me. Not a damn one."

As if she heard him then, Maggie shoved the envelope of money off the table, her mouth opening in what looked like a scream. Then she pulled her knees to her chest, tucking herself into a ball for what felt like an eternity. What little that was left of my restraint broke.

"I can't sit here anymore." I reached for the handle.

Dad grasped my arm. "Don't, Mason. I've said all she can stand to hear right now. She's angry, and she deserves to be. I would be more worried if she didn't have any reaction at all."

Considering that, my hand relaxed, the rest of my body slowly following. He was right. She hadn't put up a wall, hadn't slapped on an impassive face, hadn't tried to pretend that she was okay. She was hurting, and as much as it pained me, she was *feeling*.

"What did she say?"

Dad's focus didn't stray from the girl in the booth. "That she wouldn't come back and asked that I stay away. I said I would, but she was welcome back anytime she wanted."

I scoffed weakly. "I think Mom will learn to cook before that happens."

Dad faced me, the dim light sinking into the shadowed tolls the last two weeks had taken on him.

"I wouldn't be so sure about that. When I spoke to her about Faith and told her why I started coming here, she gave me that time. She didn't have to. She did what I had refused to do. Listen, show compassion. Maybe she never comes back, or maybe she does. But I do know one thing. Maggie's heart is too good to hold on to hate."

It was another quiet trip back home, doing nothing more than watching the moon ghost through the clouds, the silhouette of Baywoods Forest growing and shrinking before disappearing into the night. As we pulled further away from the ocean, all I could think of was my run earlier. Taking this same path in the light of day and how much hope my heart held, and now in the dark, that hope had become despair.

Dad parked in the garage, and I followed him to the kitchen. "I've got an early shift," he said, setting his keys on the kitchen counter. "I was gonna head up unless you want to talk, have a beer with me."

Pushing my body to the extreme had started to have its desired effect. And, honestly, I had drunk myself into a stupor every night since *that* night. I really should give my liver a break.

"Nah, I'm good. Go on. You've had a long day, too."

I caught his frown a split second before I was in his arms. He squeezed me tight, pushing the remainder of the air out of my chest. "You're a good man, Mason. I'm proud of you."

I wanted to laugh, but my heart ached too damn much. Here I was at my absolute lowest, and he was telling me he was proud of me.

"For what?"

Standing back, he held onto my shoulders with a firm grip. "It takes strength to do one of the hardest things a man can do. Admit he's wrong, ask for forgiveness. That's why I'm proud of you." With one more hug, he said, "Get some sleep."

As I stood alone in the kitchen, I knew if sleep came for me tonight, it wouldn't be in my bed. There was no point pretending. I went straight to Faith's room and laid down on the fuzzy blue rug with her favorite pillow tucked to my chest. And for the first time, a different girl's voice played in my mind, and a different kind of pain laced the link over my heart.

I want you to go away and forget you were ever a part of my life.

I woke up to an unmistakable scent drifting through the cracks of the door, enticing me to open my eyes. *Butter.* The sprig of hope that I'd had last night blossomed again. I tore off the blanket, tripped over the pillow, ripped open the door, and sprinted downstairs, nearly falling on my ass when I skidded on the landing.

Dad did it. He got through to her.

"Sticks?" I flew into the kitchen and found Dad at the island. He was wearing his scrubs and holding a spatula. The spatula in his hand could only mean that he was helping Maggie with breakfast, like when they put the barbecue back together.

My head swiveled. "Where...?" There was batter splattered all over the counter, a stack of charred discs on a plate, the sink piled high with dishes, but the raven beauty was nowhere in sight.

My heart kinda...disintegrated.

"Sorry." Dad studied the pat of butter leaving a streak of sizzling black on the griddle. "I, uh, bought some of that just-add-water-pancake-mix and decided to give it a whirl. It sounds foolproof, but evidently, even I can screw it up."

My lungs collapsed next and then my ribs. "Oh. I thought..."

"I know. I'm sorry." His gaze held mine. There were dark smudges around his eyes, red lining the irises. I couldn't be sure if he looked better or worse than yesterday. "I didn't mean to make you think she was here. I wanted..." He sighed, letting the words die there.

I eyed the lumpy, pale glop in the mixing bowl I didn't even know we owned. I guess it had been easier for Dad to find because the cabinet housing all our Tupperware was still organized. By size and shape. By Maggie.

"Fuck it." Dad chucked the spatula into the sink and grabbed two bowls from the cabinet.

I got the cereal.

chapter twenty

maggie

So I took the money. Sort of. I couldn't exactly leave an envelope of cash on the café floor, and I couldn't keep it at home; therefore, it was in my backpack. I wasn't sure what I'd do with it yet, but the money changed nothing.

It had fixed nothing.

The silver lining to the dumpster fire that was my life was that working more at the café meant I hadn't seen my father for three days.

And while the news I was innocent had eventually made its way through Sands Drive, it took far less time to reach everyone than when they had thought I was a thief. I guess that headline wasn't as entertaining. On Sunday, the rest of the shop owners trickled by the café to tell me how they knew I wasn't guilty, which was an outright lie. Suddenly, I was their little Mags again.

But I wasn't the same. I never would be.

There was a jagged edge around my heart now, one that grew sharper the more I was expected to forgive and forget. The Scotts broke what had been left of an already broken girl.

I wanted to run to school this morning since I hadn't been able to in weeks, but I needed to stop by Jamey's house today and didn't want to push my recovery too fast. The time to train before the Rainbow Run had dwindled to two weeks, and gauging the burn in my thighs as I pedaled up the Hayeses' driveway this morning, two weeks was not nearly enough. But Jamey said I'd be fashionable, at least. He'd already picked out a teal tutu for me and a chartreuse one for himself. Both were laden with glitter.

With a swing of my leg over my bike, I knocked down the kickstand. There was a new gnome on the lawn, and while this one wasn't riding a unicorn, he was naked. I shook my head. The Hayeses had an unhealthy obsession with all things weird.

Speaking of…

I sighed, bending low with my arms splayed wide to lift the ginormous cardboard box on the porch. Expecting it to weigh at least fifty pounds, I put way too much *oomph* in my lift and wound up smacking myself right in the nose. What in the…? I shook the box, and the object rattling within suggested it was no bigger than my hand. Amazon really needed to get their packing shit together.

I drew back the screen door, propping it open with my hip. As I wrapped my fingers around the knob, it slipped out of my grip, the door swinging open like I'd just announced a going out of business sale at Hot Topic.

Hazel irises blinked at me, one eye still a horrible shade of *yikes,* but the hair almost distracted from it with his natural dark hair buzzed on the sides, dyed silver platinum on top and a little root growth beneath. Not many could pull off that look. Jamey could.

"It can't be. It looks like Mags, but…" His arm lifted, hand reaching toward me, two fingers poised with the intent to pinch me.

"Do it, and I'll tell Ava where you hide your Milk Duds."

His hand snapped back and yelled over his shoulder, "It's her! It's definitely Mags!"

Ava's voice carried out from within, "Told you that rain dance we performed last night would bring her back!"

My brows inched up my forehead. Though I hoped Ava was joking, it was all too believable. "Jamey, it didn't rain last night."

His gaze returned to me, an impish smile playing on his lips. "I know. We improvised with the lawn sprinkler." As I gaped at him, Jamey grabbed the box from me. "Get your cute ass in here."

I did, but one step past the threshold, I came to a screeching halt, going no further. My eyes burned. Nose…immediately started dripping.

"W—what is that smell?" I didn't recognize the stench as being anything the salon could be responsible for. Nor did it seem natural.

My feet reflexively took me back to air that was both clean and wouldn't singe nostril hair.

Jamey must have sensed my retreat. His head twisted around, eyes growing wide, narrowing half a heartbeat later. "Oh, no, you don't." His hand snapped up to grab me.

"Watch out!" came out of my mouth at the same time as Jamey's, "Gah!"

Too late. The corner of the Amazon box smacked the cabinet. The cabinet with a bazillion precariously placed PEZ dispensers. Frozen in place, Jamey and I didn't so much as blink while PEZ Spiderman teetered dangerously close to a green lizard-man. Or was that a fish-man? Either way, he was fugly. And if Fugly Lizard-Fish-Man went down, they'd all go like Dominoes.

After an eon passed, good old Spidey remained upright and stable. Crisis averted.

Risking a breath, I complained, "Can't we glue them down or something? There's a gotta be a better way."

"Yeah, there is," he grumbled, moving inside. "Setting fire to them when she's asleep. That's the better way."

Grinning, I trailed Jamey to the kitchen as the scent of burnt spices mixed with embalming fluid got stronger. I coughed as I searched every nook and cranny for the culprit. Easier said than done in this house.

"What is th—" The sting in my throat cut off my words, which was just as well. I changed my mind. I didn't want to know what bowels of Hell that stench had escaped from.

A squealing platinum blur flew at me, and before I could stop her, Ava's arms were wrapped around my body, squeezing as if she were trying to fuse my spine to my sternum. "It's been for-evah!"

Had it really been that long since I'd been here? "Sorry, I—" A wad of hair landed in my mouth, and it tasted like...the tangerine color of Ava's dress. Which oddly matched the retro kitchen appliances. Twisting my head, I dislodged the hair from my tongue, but then it stuck to my ChapStick. "I haven't been feeling well."

"Oh, I know." Pulling back, Ava smooshed my cheeks in her hands. "I wanted to come by your house with this utterly fantastic cannabis I tried, Hairy Wookie, but *someone* wouldn't let me. Seriously, it's life changing. Organic, too! The THC level—"

"Woman, I have told you a million times," Jamey blustered. "Mags doesn't—"

"Have a prescription," Ava finished with a snap as she turned to him, smooshing my face even tighter. "I *know*. I wanted her to try it before she went to the trouble. See if it helped with her tremor, at least. But it's not like it's hard to get a prescription, Jamey. I have one."

"Because you're legally insane!" He slammed the hollow box onto the kitchen table, glowering at his mother. "Do you seriously not get that you're peddling drugs to the police chief's daughter! What do you think is going to happen when he sees her high on marijuana? Mags, *tell* her!"

Yeeeeeah. That would not go well.

Ava huffed, releasing half my face to throw a hand onto her hip. "Well, if you'd only let me explain it to Nate before—"

"Ava," I squeaked, holding onto the hand still on my face. "Jamey's right. My father wouldn't be okay with that." Because he wouldn't be okay with anything that could help me. "But it's sweet of you to think of me. I appreciate it."

"Ugh! Fine!" Flinging herself away, Ava mumbled as she tore through the kitchen until she procured a mug of hot water and a tea bag. The mumbling increased in volume and clarity as Ava proceeded to the salon. "But this is exactly like the time I bought those placenta capsules, Jameson. And do you remember how firm my skin was? The cure to our ailments lies in nature. The sooner you—"

"And scene," Jamey announced as he flung the salon door shut with Ava's rant going strong.

I blinked at Jamey. "Did she say placenta—"

"*Yes.*" Jamey's jaw turned to stone as he leveled me with an equally hard glare. "It was a dark time in my life that I don't want to relive. Please never mention it again."

My gaze wandered back to the salon window. Ava was on the other side of the glass, arms flailing, mouth moving as if she were lecturing her stools or...nope, it was her hair dryer. "Is she okay? She seems..."

"Extra Ava-ish?" He grabbed a box cutter from the writing desk in the corner of the kitchen. The little desk that was the same blinding orange shade as everything else in this room. "She got an AARP letter in the mail yesterday, and the woman has been intolerable since."

I didn't doubt that was possible since Ava was fanatical about looking exactly twelve years younger than her age, and an AARP letter would definitely set her over the edge of sanity. Still, there was a strange tension in the house that wasn't normally here.

"Oh, thank Adam Levine and Baby Jesus."

My attention was drawn back to Jamey as he unearthed two small objects from the box. I craned my head. "Who are they?"

A single brow flicked up as he worked the candy into each of the dispensers. "Why am I still surprised by you? It's SpongeBob and Patrick." He wiggled the tiny yellow sponge and pink starfish PEZ.

"Oh-kay." I took one from him. "They're cute, but why are we so happy to have them?"

He snorted. "Because it will distract the Hairy Wookie in there from getting her ass thrown in jail by your father." His chin kicked toward my hand. "Open him up."

I pulled back on the smiling little star as pink candy shot out of his pants like... *Oh.* I glanced at the sponge's equally happy expression, a yellow candy popping out of his underwear, as well.

"Does Ava know these PEZ have peckers?"

Chuckling, Jamey snatched Patrick from my hand to position the cartoon characters in a compromising position on the counter. "Why else do you think she bought them?"

As we set our bikes into the rack at school, Jamey was more occupied with staring at the courtyard than stringing his lock together. I followed his eye line to find the object of his focus. Or rather...person. Intently staring in our direction, Ben stood under our oak tree. The same tree the three of us used to eat lunch under. Before Mason had joined us to make it a foursome. It seemed like years had passed since then.

"Just so I understand the rules," I began as I got my bike lock in place, "are you still referring to him as the prick?"

"Ye—" Jamey sighed and finished with his lock. "I don't know. I wouldn't stop you, though."

I gave him a look. "You know I haven't and would never call him that."

"I know. You've been annoyingly unsupportive throughout this process." Pinching his bottom lip between his teeth, Jamey's gaze strayed back to the tree. "He hasn't let up, you know. Not once. Shows up at my house every night, no matter what I yell at him. I heard he even volunteered at Cove Pride Community Center last week."

"Maybe there's something to be said for persistence." I nudged him, but his stare didn't break. "Jamey, if you didn't mean something to him, he wouldn't have tried at all."

"God," he groaned, scrubbing a hand down his face. "You sound like Ava."

"Come on." I tugged his hand. "He looks pathetic."

"And hot," he grumbled. "He's the hottest pathetic asshole on the planet."

Begrudgingly, Jamey crossed the courtyard with me and stopped when there was a football field between him and Ben. Not great, but it was a start. And a good sign, considering Jamey wasn't shouting obscenities and throwing things at the guy.

"Hey." If Ben noticed I was here, I wouldn't know. His attention belonged to Jamey. "Your eye is…looking better."

Jamey's brows quirked. "No, it doesn't."

A faint smile graced Ben's mouth. "No. It doesn't." Gaze floating to me, wariness etched into his features. "Hey, Mags. I, um… I wanted to apologize. If that's okay. I never thought Taylor would do something like that."

Wow, he went right in. Not even a warmup.

My feet carried me backward. "Ben—"

Not clued in yet, he stepped closer. "Mags, I'm sorry I didn't stick up for you. I'm sorry I didn't believe you. I assumed, and that was wrong of me. At the very least, I owed you the benefit of the doubt."

Looking at him now, the crack in my heart widened, remembering his cold glare as I crossed the living room. Turned out, Jamey knew me better than I did. He'd been right the other day. I couldn't do this. I wasn't sure if the three of us would ever coexist under this tree again.

"Ben." This time, we were both aware of the healthy step I'd taken back from him. "I'm not…"

Nodding, Ben held his palms up in surrender. "I'm sorry. I'll go before I make this worse. I know you don't want to hear it now or maybe ever, but you deserve an apology when you're ready."

"No, Ben, you stay. I have to stop at my locker anyway. But know that whatever happens here"—I waved a finger between them—"I'm cool with it. Okay?"

Ducking his head, Ben swallowed loud enough to drown out the squawking birds overhead. "Thanks, Mags. That…means a lot."

I gave Jamey a somewhat hopeful smile before I headed off. After swinging by my locker, I went to my Public Speaking class and took my seat. Since it was early, I pulled out a notebook and pen to doodle until class started. The door opened and closed a few times as bodies shuffled their way in, and the tingles along the back of my neck were a good enough indication as to whom one of those bodies belonged to.

A chocolaty spiced cologne drifted over me as soft as a whisper. Mason knelt in the aisle next to my seat, and as much as I wanted to ignore him, it was impossible.

"Hey, Sticks."

Impossible because he was talking to me.

Releasing a sigh, I turned, my gaze first catching on his swollen knuckles that were laced with tiny cuts and fading purple splotches that had begun to turn a sickly green. I drank in the rest of him from his long fingers, corded arms, heavy shoulders, dark hair that was due for a trim, and his chiseled profile that made my heart drum a little faster. With his head bowed, only the right side of his face was visible. His near black brows were furrowed tight, gaze suspended somewhere around my knees, and that tiny crook in his nose looked darker somehow.

He was bruised and battered, skin marked with the beauty and sorrow of battles that he'd won and lost. A modern-day knight in a life of nightmares.

"I have to know something," I said. "And I want the truth."

Mason nodded solemnly, voice rougher than usual. "I'll give it to you if I can."

I swallowed past a sudden knot in my throat. "How did it feel…to hit Eric?"

A long moment passed before the tension in Mason's frame eased. One side of his lips edged up, dimpling his cheek. There wasn't an ounce of regret in that smile. "Really fucking good."

"Man, I'm jealous," I breathed as I slumped in my chair. "You not only got to do it once but twice."

Twisting toward me, he was closer, scent stronger. Our gazes collided, and my breath caught. His eyes…reminded me of springtime. The newness of life, the promise of hope and light, and all things *good*. They traced my features one by one, and I couldn't help but wonder if he saw his sister now. If he had ever seen me.

His gaze dropped to the floor as if answering my unspoken thoughts, the humor dissipating. "I could teach you how. To defend yourself. You've got the ball-busting knee move down, might as well have a fist to match."

Rather than agree to that, I revealed my trembling hand. When my fingers met his scruffy chin, he inhaled sharply at the same time my heart skipped a full beat. It may only be on my end, but there was an undeniable pull between us, a connection, one that I thought had been severed. But it had been there the entire time, and I'd just been trying to deny its existence.

My palm skimmed his jaw, the thick growth prickly but softer than I thought it would be. I tugged his face to see the other side and cursed. Jamey was right. Even a bruised cheek looked sexy on him. It was already turning the same color as his knuckles, the swelling minimal.

I returned my hand beneath the desktop. "Thank you for helping Jamey. I'm sorry you were suspended from the team. I know it's important to you."

His penetrating gaze didn't break from mine. "Football is a sport. For enjoyment. Does it mean something to me? Yes. Do I love being around my teammates and the work we put in? Yes. But it doesn't even come close to what I would consider important. My family? They're important. Standing up for what's right? That's important. Protecting someone from the bullies and assholes who pick on the weak? That's important. And it's important to me that you know I never looked down on you or thought less of you. Me walking away from you that night was never about that. I saw…" His eyes closed as if he couldn't bear to say the words neither of us wanted to hear.

His sister.

I knew Mason was struggling with that. It would be cruel of me to deny how difficult this must have been for him. To have any type of attraction to me, whatever that meant for him. It wasn't physical, at least not for him, but he was ashamed of it, regardless.

What happened in the basement shouldn't have. I'm sorry that it happened, that I let it get that far. I know this is the last thing you want to hear right now, but I need to say it. I wasn't thinking about the consequences. Honestly, I didn't care, and I should have. I wasn't fair to you.

"I'm sorry. I know those two words mean shit to you right now, but I don't know what else to say or do. I don't know how to make it right. If it's even possible." He paused, waiting for me to acknowledge that I could forgive him, and when I said nothing, a deep crease appeared on his forehead. "I hope you took the money."

I focused on the shaky stick figures I'd drawn. A three-year-old could do better. "I didn't want it. I still don't, but I—" The words came out before I could stop them. "I need it." There was so much shame in my voice.

Because I am ashamed.

I was ashamed that I was unloved. Ashamed of the scars I'd been given in place of that love. I was ashamed that when I faced the dragon, I never once reached for my sword. I wasn't strong or brave. I was weak and cowardly.

I was ashamed because I needed that money to do the only thing I had ever done. *Run.*

"Why?" He dipped low to chase my gaze. "Why do you need it?"

The truth punctured my skin with sharp stingers, and with every reason that played through my head, agitation flared brighter in my blood.

I kicked up my chin, steeling my gaze with his. "It's none of your business, Mason."

Lids widening, he drew back, but no more than a centimeter. "You're right. I'm sorry."

Okay, maybe I was being a bit touchy, but he had no right to ask me anything.

When I faced forward in my seat, I could feel Mason's eyes trace the side of my head. The stretch of ruined bone and skin concealed beneath my hair that I meticulously combed into a ponytail to hide. Just like the other scars hidden beneath the overlarge shirts I wore, long enough that they wouldn't show my lower back with a neckline tight enough that it didn't gape wide and reveal my upper back.

I wore shields not to fight my horrors but to conceal them.

"How are you feeling?" he hedged.

Feeling far too exposed to him, I slid my hands beneath my legs. "Tired."

He shifted, taking back that centimeter he'd relinquished moments ago. "Because you pulled doubles all weekend?"

How did he...?

I spun my head sharply toward him as lightness swarmed my brain, stomach plummeting to my feet. I shut my eyes, working my throat until the vertigo eased.

"Yeah," I answered, opening my eyes again.

A frown drew his mouth down in the corners, those startling green eyes pleading with mine. For what, I wasn't sure. "Sticks—"

"Mr. Scott? Have you decided *yet again* to disturb my seating arrangement?"

We jarred to Allen's voice cutting across the room, neither of us realizing every chair but Mason's had been occupied at some point, and there was quite a bit of snickering going on. Especially from the chair to my right.

I slid a sideways glare to Dylan wiggling his fingers at me, then he tacked on a wink. Mason cleared his throat. Obnoxiously. Dylan's grin expanded.

Standing, Mason grabbed his bag, voice as stiff as his shoulders while he went down the staircase. "No, Professor. My apologies."

Allen straightened a pile of papers on her lectern with an over-the-glasses glower as she watched Mason take his assigned seat. To my knowledge, she was the only professor on campus who had a seating chart. And required permission to use the restroom.

Her interruption was for the best. If that conversation had continued, I might have ended up saying something dumb to Mason, like *I forgive you.*

I didn't forgive him. I couldn't.

I wasn't sure if I hated him still, but I was nowhere near forgiveness.

With my mind on the Scotts all morning, I fumbled my way through the rest of my classes. By lunchtime, it felt like I had a little man dancing the Zumba on my gray matter. Wearing spiked heels.

I was more than over these headaches.

Jamey offered his lap for a pillow again and massaged my temples while I put my earbuds in and attempted to shut off the world. After what seemed like seconds, I was being shaken awake. I pulled my buds out to see the sun wasn't overhead anymore.

I blinked at my human pillow. "I fell asleep?"

"As soon as you shut your eyes." Jamey smoothed a hand over my head. "Mason and Ben came by to check on you. When I told them you had a headache, they sat about ten feet away like little guard dogs." His head tipped toward our grassy area where the shade of the oak tree ended, the blades still bent from their weight. "It was kinda cute."

"*Cute?*" I shot him a look of death as I sat up, brushing the grass off my clothes. "It's called guilt, Jamey."

Reaching for me, his voice softened. "It's more than that."

A wisp of betrayal unfurled in my stomach, reaching up into my chest. "Have you forgotten everything I went through because of them?"

His brows slammed down, and I could have sworn he muttered, "It wasn't all their fault."

Around my teeth, I seethed, "You did not just say that to me."

His hazel eyes met mine. "They didn't know you had epilepsy, Mags." Leaning closer, he whisper-hissed, "They didn't know what your father would do to you."

"Oh!" I feigned shock, that wisp of betrayal solidifying into something cold and sharp. "Well, that makes it okay then. I feel so much better now because this entire time I'd assumed they had known."

I moved to stand, but Jamey was faster, cuffing both wrists to stop me. Not wise on his part. "That's not what I meant, and you know it. Sit and hear me out."

I did, but that didn't mean I would and not scowl at him.

"It would be a hell of a lot easier if the Scotts were heartless bastards, but you and I both know they aren't. They're good people, and they care about you, Mags. Even when they thought you were guilty, Ben asked about you every day. In fact, that was the first question out of his mouth. And in case you forgot, it was Ben and Mason who helped when you had a seizure. Mason legit threatened me, so he could make sure you were alright.

"*He* carried you to his truck, *he* drove you, and *he* then carried you all the way to a hospital bed and didn't leave your side for a second. Mr. Scott was there, too. Remember? He did everything he could to help you and only backed off when your father threatened to handcuff him and press charges." Jamey shook his head, aggravated. "I wasn't going to tell you this, but I think it's time I did. Mason's been calling and texting me since that day. *Every day.* Just to know you're okay. Even when he thought you took the earrings."

Jamey opened his phone and shoved the screen in my face. Sure enough, there was a long line of messages.

ScottFucker2: *Plz. How is she?*

ScottFucker2: *I get it. Ur pissed. Not asking u 2 talk. Just want to know how Maggie is.*

ScottFucker2: *She wz limping in class today. Did she see a Dr. yet? I could drive her to school tomorrow.*

ScottFucker2: *Maggie looked pale at lunch. Did she eat anything?*

ScottFucker2: *How wz she feeling 2day?*

ScottFucker2: *Her tremor was bad, J. I can drive her home. She should be resting.*

ScottFucker2: *Did she make it home OK? Her backpack wz loaded down. A few guys on the team offered to drive her home if she'd rather them. Plz tell her. We're all worried.*

There were more. A hell of a lot more.

After scrolling past three more screen lengths, I handed the phone back to Jamey, voice reed thin. "How many Scott Fuckers are in your contacts?"

"Eight."

I didn't have a clue how he kept them all straight or assigned their numbers. "Why are you showing me this now? I told you that you could be with Ben if you wanted—"

"This has nothing to do with me. I'm not trying to convince you to forgive them, but I want you to see that it's not guilt. Cam, Matt, Ben, Mason's parents, Ben's parents…they've all tried to get in touch with me. Mason…well, he's more persistent than Ben, so that should tell you something. They genuinely care about you. I think you deserve to know that."

"Deserve to know?" My spine stiffened, irritation renewed. "I don't care if they care about me. I don't care about them at all. You, Ava, the boys, and Poker. You are all I care about."

I swore he deflated. "That's not true. What about Frankie, Darlene, Henry—"

"You mean all the people who turned their backs on me?"

His shoulders definitely fell that time. "Mags, I get the anger, and you have every right to feel it. But this isn't you. You're the forgiving, compassionate one—"

"Not anymore."

Frown lines bracketed his mouth. "Don't do this. Holding onto this hate will eat you up from the inside. That's no way to live, Mags."

One side of my mouth drew up in a sad smile. "You think I'm living? I'm not. I never have been. I'm surviving. It's all I know how to do, and it's gotten me this far."

Jaw set, Jamey's eyes flashed an array of amber and jade. "Here's some truth then, whether or not you want to hear it. You're doing a shit job, and you haven't gotten very far at anything."

My molars gnashed together. "I think it's best you and I stop talking."

"And I think it's best you turn your father in."

"Yeah? Well, here's what I think about that." After a rather excruciating ascent, I got to my feet and went to class.

"I love you!" he called after me.

Man, now I couldn't be all pissed off like I wanted to be. I angled my head enough to shout, "I love your annoying ass back!"

"Son of a bitch," I muttered as my head rotated, looking for said son of a bitch, AKA ScottFucker2. I made a complete three-sixty. When I didn't see Mason or BB in the parking lot, my gaze went right back to my bike. More specifically, those two assholes attached to my bike, reflecting in the sunlight. He'd screwed the lights back on. When in God's name did Mason find the time to do this? And was that…? I sped up, nearing the front of the bike. Oh, hell to the no.

A helmet?

He *bought* me a helmet?

Stringing a few curses together, I received some interesting looks as I strapped my bag to the basket. Once I had my lock undone, I rolled the bike out of the rack and stopped ignoring the thing dangling off the handlebar. Robin's egg wasn't a shade of blue I would typically go for, but it was feminine without being overtly so. The white leaf design etched on the side was delicate. Pretty. And along the back of the helmet was a strange notch. Like it was designed for someone with…a ponytail.

"Son. Of. A. Bitch."

It didn't matter how high or treacherous I built that wall around me; Mason found a foothold and kept climbing. And by taking that money, I'd invited him to keep trying.

And that had to stop.

Perhaps the Scotts did care about me, but I couldn't let them back in. I had armed myself. I rebuilt my shields. Now I had to be patient. I'd waited eighteen years; I could wait a little longer. It was all in the timing. I'd leave this place and never look back.

I left the helmet tied to the handlebar, mounted the bike, and shoved off. On the ride home, I hit the point along Canyon Boulevard where the weeds grew out of the cracks in the sidewalks and potholes pockmarked the asphalt. The painted lines were no longer crisp and bright but dulled and pitted, narrowing from four lanes to two. This was the line that separated the townies from the richies. One did not belong on the other side.

When it was no longer comfortable to keep riding, I dismounted my bike. My backside was aching, and that bike seat offered zero padding. I lifted my front tire onto the sidewalk as my ears perked to the sound of a car slowing to a crawl behind me. An eerie thread wove down my spine, the hairs on the back of my neck rising.

I was well attuned to the sound of my father's PPV, and this was a much smaller vehicle. One I didn't recognize. Up ahead was nothing but empty roads, not a house for at least another mile, so there was no reason for anyone to slow down. Either they were lost, or they had found who they were looking for.

Me.

My palms felt clammy and slick on the handlebars, knowing precisely who had followed me out to the middle of nowhere, not a witness in sight. I'd be lying if I said that I hadn't expected this. Though I'd done everything that had been asked of me, it hadn't mattered. Marcus would get his revenge.

Tense anticipation hummed through my muscles, beads of sweat blooming on my forehead as I readied myself. When the vehicle pulled to a stop, I reacted. I whipped my head around to face my attacker, but the rest of my body had other ideas. I went completely off-kilter. I didn't know how I could forget about my vertigo, especially when my brain reminded me daily.

My feet stumbled like my joints had been welded together. My ankle rammed into the curb, and when I tried to catch myself, the handlebar spun around, slamming into my belly. I went down. Hard. I fell directly on the end of the handlebar, lodging it into my gut. Gravity finished the job, ribs cracking against the metal frame, white heat engulfing my side.

The world went black.

chapter twenty-one

maggie

Shit.

Shit. Shit. *Shit!*

Hold up. Was I cursing repeatedly or—

"Shit! I don't know. Sh—she just fell. I think she had another seizure or something. And her head... There's something not right about her head— *I don't know!* ... How? I—I've never checked anyone's vitals before!"

The sound of clacking heels vibrated my addled brain, and I swore that voice belonged to...

"*Charlie?*" Peeling one eye open, a car that resembled an oversized bullet idled in the street. A pair of black stilettos cut into my vision and came right for me at a speed they were in no way designed for.

"Oh! I think sh—she's coming around! Her eye is open. Does that mean she's conscious? Do I still need to do all that pulse and breathing stuff?"

Ah, crap. If Charlie was on the phone with 9-1-1, breaking half my ribcage would be the best thing that happened to me today.

I tried to get up but laying on a heap of metal with my stomach exploding didn't make for an easy exit. I was certain the few bites of peanut butter and jelly I'd had for lunch were about to make a reappearance.

"I'm o—" Another wave of dizziness settled in, and I shut my eyes to stop the world from spinning. Didn't work.

"Mase, hurry! I...I don't know if I should move her! She's *incoherent!*"

Was I? I didn't think so. This was not at all like a postictal state. More like I'd blacked out, and it couldn't have been for long. If anything, Charlie was the incoherent one, and by all that pacing she was doing, I'd say she was emotionally ill-equipped to handle emergency situations.

A moment later, the squeal of tire versus asphalt competed with the sound of rushing blood in my ears.

"Sticks!" Feet pounded toward me, and it took all of one second for Mason to extract me from my own stupidity. He'd somehow untangled me from my bike and had me in his lap before I could take a breath. "Say something, Maggie."

I grunted with another painful churn of my stomach. "I think... I'm gonna puke."

Mason swept the hairs off my face and smoothed them back in a soothing, rhythmic motion. "Take deep breaths and concentrate on that. Did you hit your head?" As if spurred on by his own words, his fingers began searching for any cracks in my skull, protruding vertebra, oozing gray matter.

"N—no. I don't think so. It's...my stomach." Another wave of nausea crested as I groaned, "I landed on my stomach."

"Okay, just keep breathing like you're doing. It'll pass." His search continued along my left temple, and if I weren't in so much pain, I would care more about that. "What happened?"

"I told you!" Charlie cried. "She—"

"From Maggie," Mason growled, voice quite the contrast to his gentle touch. "I want to hear it from *Maggie*. It's important that she tell me in her own words."

Mason sounded pissed, but there wasn't time to analyze that, either. The things happening in my abdominal cavity couldn't be normal. I think my liver traded places with a kidney.

His voice softened as he caressed my cheek. "What happened?"

"Vertigo. Faulty feet. Poor life choices. Pick one." I hacked out most of that.

Releasing a breath, Mason curled me into his chest. I wasn't sure whose heart was thumping so loud, but one of us might need an ambulance. I prayed we wouldn't have to rely on Charlie to call one.

I sensed Mason's gaze on me, and I lifted my lashes to find that he wasn't just looking at me but rather staring at me intensely. "Sticks, where is your helmet? The one I got you. I need to inspect it for breaks. Did it come off?"

"Ah. No. It's um...was on the bike. Where I left it."

"Where you…?" His gaze flicked over my head, and right when his brow smoothed, his jaw went tight. Those peridot eyes returned to mine, hurt replacing his confusion. "Why? Why are you so fucking stubborn?"

My lips parted to answer when a car horn cut me off. More tires squealed, but I was facing the wrong direction to see who those tires belonged to.

"What happened?" That was Ben, and by the sound of slamming car doors, I'd say he brought two guests.

Mason didn't tear his glare away from me when he answered Ben. "Poor life choices."

"Ha-ha," I coughed out, and he gave me a look in return.

"Mags!" Jamey landed in our fun huddle. "How long was she out for?"

"I— Uh…" Charlie sputtered. "A few seconds? She turned and staggered and then just fell on her bike. And her head, Mase. Did you see—"

"Charlie," he cut her off, sliding his palm over my temple as if to hide the dent in my skull. A bit late for that, apparently. "What were you doing out here? Were you *following* her?"

"No! I— Well, yeah. Kinda. I wanted to apologize. For Tay. A— and me. I wasn't… I didn't know that Maggie would fa—"

"Taylor should apologize for her fucking self. And you…" Shutting his eyes, Mason's lungs heaved an exhale. "Charlie, I think you should go."

The pause was not only awkward but hella long before Charlie spoke. "Mase, I—"

"Please." His eyes and jaw were fixed hard on her as if his patience would evaporate with his next breath. "I need to focus on Maggie right now. Okay?"

My stomach roiled viciously, and I fisted Mason's shirt as I burrowed into his chest. "You so lied. This isn't passing."

"Yeah, I may have." Holding me tighter, his breaths swept across my forehead. "By your position, it looked like you took a blunt hit to your upper abdomen. I'm honestly a little worried you're in shock. You're pretty pale."

"That's because I'm diligent with my daily SPF application. I seem to be the only one in the Cove concerned that melanoma is the most common form of cancer in the United States."

I peered up at him as the corner of his mouth tipped high on one side. "Paler than normal," he clarified as he shifted me, so we were chest to chest. "Cam, get her head. Guys, help out. I'm gonna set her down."

Oh, goody. Camden was here, too.

Hands cradled the back of my head, and two more sets were at my sides. Mason placed me on the sidewalk as if my bones were nothing more than matchsticks glued together.

Mason scanned my body as his warm fingers dragged my sweater up over my hips. "Let me take a look."

Of all the times and places I had imagined this very thing to happen… I pushed the thick cotton down. "No, Camden will see my daisy bra."

"Fuck yes!" Camden cheered.

Mason's lips broke into a broad grin followed by a deep chuckle. "I'll save the breast exam for another day. I'm only checking if you have an innie or an outie." His gaze met mine, smile flattening into a serious line. "Mom and Dad taught me a few things. I'll be quick, I swear."

"That's not normally something you wanna boast about, Mase," Camden commented, but Mason and I ignored him.

After a long, agonizing moment, I relented and let Mason lift the material away. A breeze licked across my damp skin, the hot concrete burning my sensitive back. It was then that I realized if he rolled me an inch in either direction, he'd see the bruises.

As I plastered myself against the scorching ground, Mason trailed his hand across my stomach, and butterflies began to flutter around the painful waves. Mason's gaze drifted over my exposed skin, eyes darkening beneath a set of dense lashes. He was close enough for me to count the citrine shards flecked between the bed of mossy green.

Lost in his eyes, I was vaguely aware that his fingers were kneading the muscle beneath the band of my bra. My breaths hitched.

He stilled, worry bunching his brow. "Did that hurt?"

Hurt? God, it totally hurt, but I didn't want him to stop. No one had ever touched me there and certainly not like that. "Yeah, if you hadn't heard, I just had a Schwinn lodged all up in there."

Shooting me a bland look, Mason's hand splayed out over my exposed belly again, bare skin hot against mine, and with each centimeter that his fingers discovered, warmth grew between my thighs, and yep, either I was sweating in the oddest of places or my panties were…

Wow, this so wasn't the time for *that* to happen.

"How's your headache?" Jamey asked, combing my hair to the left, covering up my scar.

"Strangely overshadowed by the recent stabbing pain in my stomach."

Ben smiled. "Sarcasm is a good sign, Mase."

"On anyone else, yes, but Sticks' first language is sarcasm." Those green eyes tore away from mine as the tips of his fingers slid under my jeans, pressing down, exploring past my navel. Suddenly, even through the debilitating pain, I could sense my breasts growing heavier, nipples stiffening like two traitorous bastards giving a salute. His hand shifted even *lower*, fingertips teasing the waistband of my panties, warmth tingling beneath his touch. On pure reflex, my legs were begging me to part them wide. I was so swollen and needy, and if I weren't dying of a perforated stomach, Mason's touch would kill me.

"I think you'll be fine." As his fingers slid out of my waistband, his voice sounded like it had been roughened with sand. When his gaze glided back to mine, his eyes were... Huh. Kinda reminded me of the time in his cousins' basement when I thought he was going to—

Didn't matter.

"I, uh—" Tearing his gaze away, Mason cleared his throat. "I could call Mom or Dad to be sure. They wouldn't mind."

"No."

Nodding, Mason drew my sweater down, the back of his knuckles tickling my belly, those warm tingles intensifying. His hand curved around my side, which was large enough to get acquainted with my meager boobage. My heart stuttered.

"Okay, I'm gonna get you vertical," he said, dipping low. "Put your arms around my neck."

I slid my hands around his heavy shoulders as he placed a hand behind my head. The other hand...all but cupped my ass.

"We'll go slow." Shifting, Mason's minty breath danced over my cheek. I was questioning how he had the time to get his Colgate on when he asked, "Ready?"

I nodded.

Like I was air, Mason lifted me, and the burst of renewed pain in my stomach caused me to inhale sharp and hard. My chest rose flush to his, and I froze at the feel of the hard expanse of his pectorals pressing against my breasts. Before I knew it, the ground and sky flipped, my head doing the same. My fingers dug into his shoulders, and Mason didn't let me go until he was sure I was steady on my feet.

The corners of his mouth tensed as he brushed away the pebbles and dirt from my sweatshirt, the inked 3-D butterflies moving like they were in flight when his arm flexed.

"How do you feel, Maggie?" Camden asked.

"Flatter? Is that a thing?"

Mason captured my chin and gently lifted it, eyes studying mine. Whatever he saw made his frown deepen. "I'll drive you and Jamey home, or Ben will if you're more comfortable with him."

I waved him off and stepped back, immediately missing his touch, but it had to be this way. The Scotts made me stupid, most of all, Mason. "I'm not your problem."

Mason flinched. "You're no one's *problem*. You're not a problem at all. You're—" His head arched back as he dragged down a breath like he was trying to capture the air from the top layer of the atmosphere. His head leveled back out, Adam's apple bobbing in a swallow.

Those eyes were back on mine. "Guys, could I talk to Sticks alone for a minute?"

"We're really not going to confirm if Maggie's wearing a daisy bra?" When Mason answered that with a crank of his brow, Camden trudged back toward Ben's Rover. "This sucks balls."

Following him, Ben threw an elbow into his brother's ribs. "Do you need to tell me something? You turning into a switch hitter?"

"No," Camden stated. "I used the metaphor based on the assumption that it's not a pleasant experience."

Ben smirked. "Depends on the balls."

Ignoring his cousins as they began to expand on their testicular preferences, Mason placed his attention on my platinum accessory. Who hadn't moved an inch from my side.

Crossing his arms, Jamey cocked a brow at Mason. "Until she says otherwise, I'm gonna Randy Savage it."

Randy…what?

When I looked to him for an explanation, Jamey rolled his eyes with an exasperated sigh. "I'm—"

"He's going nowhere," Mason answered flatly. "Clever."

A sly smile quirked Jamey's mouth for a millisecond. "I thought so."

My gaze bounced between the guys. "What is happening right now?"

Slanting his head at me, Mason's forehead furrowed. "Randy Savage was a famous professional wrestler during the eighties and nineties. I thought that was your era of expertise."

Jamey snorted. "There is no era of pop culture that she is an expert at."

"Fine," I yielded. "Let's all agree that pop culture references are lost on me. Jamey, it's okay."

After an agonizing minute, Jamey's glare settled on Mason. "Careful. While I'm over there, pretending not to listen, I totally will be."

Frowning, Mason watched Jamey join the guys, and then his gaze cut back to me. And…when had Charlie left? Maybe I was more out of it than I realized.

"I'm sorry about this, Maggie. All of it. If I could, I would go back to that moment in my dad's office and change everything."

"Yeah, me too. But I would have whipped out my impressive ninja moves and junk punched all three of you."

There was a tease of one dimple before he shoved a hand through his short hair, sending the dark strands in every direction. "Your father didn't say what your punishment was, but I have to admit, I'm curious."

Whoa. Back that up. "My father? When did you talk to him?"

"Saturday afternoon when he came to our house." His brows knitted together. "He didn't tell you?" I shook my head, and Mason appeared surprised by that. "Just so you know, we told him everything. He, um... Well, I wouldn't say he's a big fan of ours." He was quick to add, "Not that I blame him."

Yeah, but Mason didn't know that my father had never been a fan of the Scotts. Big or small.

"Oh. I haven't seen him since Thursday night. Been working." Not like he would tell me anyway. That would be admitting he was wrong about me. And the great Nathan Davis never admitted he was wrong.

Mason's nod was slow as he absorbed that. "Then I guess you haven't heard that Taylor's off the cheer squad for the rest of the year, and she's been required to do charity work at a homeless shelter in Pacific Cliffs."

There was a lot to say to that, but the first thing that came out was, "Do the homeless really need to be subjected to Taylor Price? Haven't they suffered enough?"

He barked a laugh, shaking his head. "I always liked your sense of humor."

"It's about all I've got left."

His lashes fanned his cheeks, chewing his lower lip like what he would say next was a struggle. "I didn't know, Maggie. Truly, I had no clue Taylor was capable of putting you through that."

"You didn't know because we live in two different worlds, Mason. You have the luxury of believing most people aren't capable of being monsters while it's rare for me to witness the good in humanity."

"I'm not...*naïve*."

"By circumstance, you are. You live where the sidewalk isn't cracked, and the streets are freshly paved with not a weed in sight. You wear clothes that are new, shoes without worn tread. You have a home that keeps you warm and dry, and there is always food in your belly. When you're not feeling well, you go to the doctor and then the pharmacy to fill your prescriptions. You have a mother and a father who love you and who are proud of you. And you can't comprehend how lacking even one of those things can change your perspective. You don't have to memorize where all the trip hazards are when you're walking home in the middle of the night from a job that doesn't pay near enough to buy used clothes and sneakers with just enough tread, so you don't slip. You never had to take a pound of ground beef and stretch it out between two people for a week. You never had to tell your pharmacist not to fill your prescription because you couldn't afford it that month. When I tell you that you're naïve, Mason, it's not an insult. I envy it."

His chin lowered, a few hairs tumbling across his brow. "Has your life been so hard that you can't believe there's good in people anymore?"

Yes. "You're going to ask me that after what I've been through over the last month? Are you really so blind, Mason? Are you deaf? Did you not see how people looked at me? What they said about me? How they treated me?"

Without waiting for his answer, I turned and reached for my Schwinn that someone had stood up for me. The helmet was dangling off the handlebar. And I was hobbling. So much for a dramatic exit.

"You know, try as I might..."

I hesitated when his gravelly voice caused my breaths to falter.

"I can't get the furniture to shine like you can. And I can't get the insert to fit inside my duvet cover. My fingers are too big or something. My room doesn't smell like lemons anymore. And my socks are dingy."

"Trade secrets. I can't share them with you."

"Come back." It was a whisper, but the pain in his words was as loud as a drumbeat. I rotated fully to see that his features were drawn, miserable really, and his head hung low. "I miss you."

"You miss your sister."

A muscle jumped in his jaw, and his eyes threatened to tear as they lifted to mine. "I do. Every second of every day, I miss her. I would have traded places with her in a heartbeat, a million times over. I would have taken all her pain, only to give her a *moment* that wasn't filled with suffering. I miss her so much that it physically hurts. But I miss you, too. In a different way, for different reasons."

The Stupid Train was pulling into the station, and I needed to leave before I handed in my ticket and hopped on. I held out the helmet. "I appreciate this. And the lights. But I can't accept any of it."

He recoiled from me as if I were holding a poisonous cobra. "Don't give that back to spite me. You need it. Didn't today prove that?"

"No. What today proved is that I need you, your family, and your girlfriend to stay away from me."

His jaw clenched, eyes turning cold. "Charlie's *not*—

"Take it, or I'll give back the money." I was playing dirty, and we both knew it.

Mason opened his mouth, ready to launch into another plea, and I held the helmet out even further to stop him.

"Take it, Mason."

Expelling a heavy sigh, he did. It took me two tries to get the bike's kickstand up. It wasn't all the rust's fault. It was mostly me and my defective kick.

I looked up to find Jamey was blocking my path, his arms back in the crossed position. His head ticked toward the Rover. "Ben's driving us home. That's it. No discussion."

I scowled. "You're not my favorite person today."

Quickly turning to avoid confrontation, Ben opened the trunk for my bike.

Jamey wasn't down to avoid anything. He popped the back door wide, giving me a glare. "Fully aware. Now get your ass inside."

Ben had my bike on the sidewalk outside of Jamey's house before I could climb down from his SUV. Holding my bag, Jamey waited for me by the curb, satisfied when I proved I could do the bare minimum and stand upright.

I gripped the handlebars as I worked the kickstand back up. "Thank you for the ride, Ben."

"I'd do more if you let me."

I didn't have anything to say to that, so I cast my attention to Jamey. His eyes darted to Ben and then back to mine. "Mags, I'll be there in a sec."

I nodded, happy to give them a moment alone. "Sure."

Leaving my bike by the front door, I went inside the house, and as I crossed the kitchen to get a glass of water, I noticed a tall pile of bills stacked on the kitchen table. My gaze trailed over to the open laptop next. I didn't mean to look, but...

Concern teemed my veins as I crept closer. That was the accounting program Jamey and Ava used for Shear Strands, and that...was a lot of red on the screen.

I knew things had been slow lately, but Jamey had never said anything. Why? Did he think my life was such a mess that he didn't feel like he could unload his burdens on me, too? He hadn't told me about the cross-country team, either.

I worried my bottom lip. It was possible Ava hadn't finished entering all the data yet, but... I peered into the salon window to see that she was pacing back and forth while speaking on the phone. By the creasing of her brow and the purse of her lips, I didn't think she was talking to a client. And she had been in a strange—okay, *stranger*—mood this morning.

Before she caught me snooping, I headed to Jamey's bedroom. One step inside, I knew there were definitely more of those blank-eyed Funko freaks in here. How did he sleep with those things?

Thankfully, Jamey didn't leave me in here too long because they were seriously freaking me out.

When Jamey joined me in his room, I swung my feet up and laid back on the bed. "How did it go?"

"Fine." Joining me on his mattress, Jamey stretched out next to me. His hand slid under mine, entwining our fingers together. "I thanked him for taking me to you."

"Yeah, I meant to ask. How did you all get there so fast?"

"Mason. He sent a text blast when Charlie called him. Ben and Cam were leaving the parking lot the same time I was, so I hopped in his SUV. And I guess Mason was already headed that way for some reason, too."

My head sunk into his pillow. "Oh."

Rolling onto his side, Jamey pressed a kiss to my temple. "How are you?"

"I'm better. My back is killing me, though. I don't think I can survive another frolf incident or a Charlie run-in or...breathing." I angled my head to see him better. "Is everything okay here? Ava still seems upset about something."

"Yeah. Everything is fine." His eyes met mine, but I...couldn't read them to know if he was lying. Jamey picked up his head to look at what was sitting on the end of the bed. "What's going on with the bag, Mags?"

I had left it here this morning but hadn't told Jamey. I figured he would find it when he got home and hide it for me. I sat up, but it took me a solid minute. From the bag, I took out the envelope and handed it to him.

"What is it?" he asked, taking it from me.

"The money Mr. Scott gave me. I haven't... Could you count it?"

Curiosity filled his eyes as Jamey flipped open the flap and peered inside. His lids sprung wide. "Holy shit." He drew out the stack of cash, and after counting the bills, Jamey breathed out, "Five thousand dollars."

"That's…" I swallowed, fingering through the pile. "That is so far beyond what he should have paid me."

"What are you gonna do with it?"

Still dumbstruck, I was tempted to count it again to make sure Jamey didn't suddenly have double vision or something. "I need you to keep it here with my emergency bag. He'll find it if I leave it at my house."

Shoulders falling, Jamey's tone went flat as he tucked the money back inside the envelope. "Sure."

I put my hands over his. "This is my way out. It could save my life, Jamey."

His gaze pierced mine. "So could telling someone."

"Who? Who would believe me against him? He's got this town and every judge in the Cove wrapped around his finger. Not to mention the freaking mayor. Everyone respects him. Everyone loves him. I'll go missing before the investigation starts, and he'll tell everyone I ran away. I was troubled, damaged, just like my mother."

He shook his head, disgusted. "Your entire back is marked up from that sick bastard. That's evidence, Mags."

"Yeah, which is why he's only ever let one doctor treat me. Yarnell. He can say whatever he wants, and there's no one to refute him or his medical records. Yarnell will say these scars are self-inflicted, and I declined all treatment. And he has no choice but to lie because if it got out that he didn't properly treat me, he risks losing his license and possibly spending the rest of his old age in jail for malpractice."

I could tell by the shock on his face that was something Jamey hadn't considered.

"No matter what move I make, my father will get his revenge one way or another, by his hand or one that he's hired. And he won't stop with me. He'll hurt everyone I care about. That is exactly the kind of monster he is. Keeping my silence has never been for me, Jamey."

chapter twenty-two

maggie

Over the next couple of weeks, I ran to school every day, went through the motions, kept my head in the down position literally and figuratively. So far, my Mason interactions had been limited to reluctant glances during class three days a week. That, and I couldn't help but notice his electric blue Raptor was in the parking lot every day. It had become a sick compulsion of mine to look for it. I could tell myself it was out of self-defense, know-where-your-enemies-are-at-all-times kind of a thing, but...I wasn't all that sure Mason was my enemy.

At least he hadn't put the lights back on my bike from when I'd returned them to Dylan. And he hadn't tried to give me that helmet again.

So...progress.

And speaking of progress, Ben was now eating with us when our schedules lined up, but that didn't mean things were back to normal. The conversation was awkward, and Jamey was the one who put the mandatory distance between them now. And if Mason was still texting Jamey every day, I wouldn't know. I didn't ask.

I couldn't say I would have been angry if Mason plopped his tray down next to me right now. That I wouldn't tell him to go to hell and shove his pizza down his throat. I couldn't say if Matt and Camden wanted to talk to me, I would turn and run the other way. I couldn't say that I would lock the door on Mr. Scott if he were to show up at the café on Saturday night. I had no idea how to navigate my feelings, and I had zero trust in myself.

So it was a good thing that they had stayed away.

Weeks ago, I had asked Frankie for the weekend off to attend the Rainbow Run. My father usually let me participate in marathons, and given that this one was for the Cove Pride Community Center and Jamey would be there, he was fine with it. Well, I assumed he was fine with it since he hadn't ripped up my note and set fire to it.

I didn't end up getting all of Friday night off because Frankie needed someone to watch the café for the dinner rush while he took care of Paula during another arthritis flareup. As I stepped into the house after work, deep chuckles and the clinks of shuffling poker chips echoed off the hollow walls, the sweet stench of Keith's cigar smacking me in the face. I'd say by the colored stacks in front of each player, the game was only at its halfway point.

Poker weaved back and forth around my legs, begging for more attention like I hadn't spent the last ten minutes with him outside. I wiggled my fingers to the group at the kitchen table. "Hey."

Lounging against the counter, my father's icy glare slid over me, most likely plotting a way to make me his bitch for the evening.

I forced the stiffness out of my voice with my initial greeting. "Sir."

"Margaret."

And that was the most we'd verbally communicated since my beating. It hadn't escaped me that he had never spoken a word of going to the Scotts'. It also hadn't escaped me how easy he had taken it on Taylor. Me, the innocent one, was beaten within an inch of my life. Taylor, the guilty one, got off with community service and had her pompoms taken away.

'Cause that was fair.

Logan's warm chestnut eyes landed on me, face brightening. "Miss Magee, what are you doing here on a Friday night?" Wearing a tight cotton T-shirt that clung to every muscle, the ink on his back, chest, and arms bled through the fabric. The dark jeans and worn boots were a nice accompaniment to the motorcycle parked out front.

In the back of my mind, I remembered that he had hugged me weeks ago. I hated that I had been too upset to appreciate that body, those arms, his scent that was a hint of soap and fabric starch. And while he and that boyish smile were a sight…a strange nothingness filled me as his eyes held mine.

I waited for the butterflies to ram into my stomach walls, that familiar flutter of my heart, hitch of breath… Nothing. And dammit, I needed there to be something. The only time I'd felt stomach flutters and hitches of breath lately had been when I was near a certain Scott. Or when I thought of a certain Scott.

Those damn winged bugs needed a good talking to.

"I didn't work a full shift because I'm running a half-marathon tomorrow." And I would have spent the night at Jamey's, but he was on a date with Ben, and I didn't want him to feel obligated to end it early to spend time with me.

"What marathon?" Gil's brows bunched as he cracked open a beer. "I didn't hear about anything local."

"The Rainbow Run. It's up in Pacific Cliffs. All the proceeds go to the Cove Pride Community Center." Back straight, I did a little shimmy. "And I'm wearing a tutu."

Without extracting the cigar from his mouth, Keith laughed deep and low. "How the hell do you run in a tutu?"

My eyes widened. "You want to see it?"

All the boys bobbed their heads, and someone said, "Hells yeah."

With a quick sprint to my room, I collected the running gear and held up the poufy skirt to my waist. Chuckles went around.

"Please tell me there is more to that thing," Gil growled, abandoning constructing a pyramid out of game chips. "I should ask the PCPD if I can staff the event. In fact…" He twisted in his chair to face my father. "Nate, both of us should be up north tomorrow."

My father snorted. "Last I checked, those knees of yours wouldn't last through a marathon detail. On foot or bicycle. And Nell will have my balls if I let you on a motor again."

Gil's head snapped back to the skirt. "Fine. I'll rent a golf cart."

"Take it easy. I'm wearing shorts under this, but…" I studied the scratchy tulle that somehow defied gravity, angling up in stiff peaks. "I have a feeling I will be the least noticed there." As Poker padded over to Logan for a rubdown, I counted heads, coming up one short. "Where's Robert? It's not like him to miss poker night."

Keith rolled the cigar between his thick fingers, leaning back in his seat. I was amazed our chairs could hold the weight of a gnat, let alone four bodies built like tanks. "He's with Ellie tonight. And I have ten bucks on him that he chokes."

Confusion wrinkled my forehead. "Chokes on what?"

Throwing a grin my way, Logan got up from the table and aimed toward the fridge that I'd stocked for tonight. "He's popping *the question*. And he's not choking."

A wicked smile curved Keith's lips as he shuffled the deck. "I don't think he shares your confidence since he was puking his guts out in the head."

Grunting, Logan gripped the fridge handle harder. "Dammit."

"I gave the guy a pep talk. He'll do fine," Gil assured Logan.

My father pushed off the counter, taking an empty spot at the table. "Was that before or after I spotted him on his knees, praying in the squad room?"

Logan cursed again as he snatched up a longneck, and my father snickered.

Maybe it was my inner girly girl, but my heart tripped over itself at the thought of Robert asking Ellie to marry him. I wondered how he would do it. If it would be a grand event or something private. Anyone could see how much he adored her. He'd taken her to the café a few times to grab lunch on his break, and I loved watching how he held the door for her, pulled her seat out, let her order first. I had wondered if I would meet a guy like that. If they still existed.

"Margaret." My father interrupted my thoughts. "Did you see the laundry bag for my uniforms? I was going to take them down tomorrow, save you the trip."

Liar. Like he would ever do that. He only wanted the boys to *think* he would. But he wasn't the only one who could play this game. If he wanted to be father of the year, then I would win daughter of the decade.

"Yes, sir, but I can take it. Jamey's going to drive by there tomorrow anyway. He wants to carbo-load on a croissant. And ten brownies. So I'll drop them off."

And take care of the basket, but I left out that part. I wouldn't welcome a conversation about it with my father. He'd never approved of that basket and equated it to me feeding mangy vermin. And now that Henry had been filling it to the brim for weeks, drawing more attention from the likes of Mayor Ryan, it was only a matter of time before someone put a stop to it.

"Alright. I appreciate it. Thank you." Frost flitted in his eyes before they smoothed into a deceptive serene blue, like a frozen lake covered with paper-thin ice, waiting for me to step on it, crack and swallow me whole. "And before you start your studies, would you mind helping me put together something for the boys to eat?"

This conversation unnerved me to my core. He was acting so…normal. Human. There was a politeness to his tone and maybe even a hint of pride if I really wanted to fool myself. It made me want to shove a screwdriver in my ear.

"Aw, that's alright, Chief." Logan took his seat. "If she's gotta study, I'll whip something up for us. I wouldn't want to be the reason our girl gets something as terrible as an A"—Logan's eyes went round, pure terror striking his features as he added—"*minus*!"

Gasping, Keith clutched his chest with both hands. "Oh, the horror!"

"Not the A-minus!" Gil cried out, pretending to faint in his seat.

"Shush it," I told them, laughing, but my father was not amused. At all. Sobering, I nodded to him. "It's not a problem, sir. I'll get right on it."

Dragging my weary butt to the kitchen in the morning, Poker padded around me as I took inventory of the aftereffects of game night. I shook my head. How in God's name were they able to function today?

I aired out the room by leaving the front and side doors open, letting the fresh morning mist weave its way into the house. While I cleaned up, Poker crunched down on his kibble. Once I had the piles of cards and chips put away, I folded the poker topper as something small and olive green fluttered to the floor. I picked it up, a smile tugging at my mouth. It was an origami elephant made from a twenty-dollar bill. Well, now I knew it wasn't Robert leaving these. Or...maybe Robert had asked the guys to plant it? Ugh. I seriously had no clue who my secret gifter was, but my prime suspect had been Gil all these months.

I peered down the hall to my father's door, snores coming strong and even. Nibbling my bottom lip, I tiptoed down the hall and eased my bedroom door shut. I put my ear to the door, listening to make sure he was still sleeping, but everything was drowned out by Poker's chomping.

Anxious knots formed low in my belly. I wished I could lock my door, but the latch had been broken long ago. I couldn't be sure if it had always been broken, had been damaged during one of his rages, or it was his reminder that he could and would enter my room whenever he wanted.

Kneeling next to my dresser, I shoved my arm behind it as far as it could go, wincing as the splintered wood cut into my shoulder. When I felt velvet, I finger crawled my way up the pouch to unhook it. As quick as I could, I added the elephant to the rest of his origami friends, rehung the pouch, and jetted out of there to finish up in the kitchen.

I inhaled a bowl of steamy oats that may have been more brown sugar than oats, donned my running gear, applied a healthy dose of sunscreen, and finished getting ready. I set out extra food and water for Poker, then spent a few more minutes with him on the carport as the sun began to peek through the dense growth overhead. We didn't have to wait long before Ava's white Focus came rolling our way with all the windows down, blasting Paramore's "Still into You."

Poker cast me a bland look, and I sighed. "I know. I'll tell him. Again."

If his volume setting wasn't bad enough, the dork yelled out of the passenger window as he rolled to a stop, "Hey, Blue Eyes. Looking *hot!*"

"Jamey!" I whisper-hissed, gesticulating frantically at the PPV. Making a face, he lowered the volume on the stereo and stepped out of the car, leaving it running. I got to my feet, too, Poker sniffing at the tutu in my hand. I held it away from him, lifting a brow. "You slobber on it, and Jamey will straight up neuter you again."

"Hell yes, I would." Jamey ruffled Poker's coat in greeting. "You ready?"

"Yeppers." I planted a kiss on Poker's nose and grabbed the bag of dirty uniforms before we headed to the car.

Jamey skipped.

"Oh, God," I groaned, staring after him as he bounced his way around the hood. "You're going to be nauseatingly happy today, aren't you? Let me warn you that I have no qualms about pushing you off a cliff."

Stopping, his mouth hung open, and it was then that I realized the tips of his bangs matched his tutu. In true Jameson Hayes style, the boy was completely coordinated.

"We're going to be surrounded by family today, Mags. Plus, I'm wearing spandex *and* a skirt. What's not to be happy about?"

Shoving the uniforms into the backseat, I blinked at him. "Family?"

Jamey released a sound of utter annoyance. "Gays! Gays in drag! Gays who are so gay they make me look *not* gay!"

A grin split my lips. "That's pretty gay."

The arms were now flailing about. "I know!"

Laughing, I got into my seat and buckled in. I looked to my side to see that the dork was now smiling. While pulling directions up on his phone.

My gaze tapered. "You sure this mood is about gay day and not last night?"

Focusing on the windshield, Jamey paid extra attention as he eased back onto the desolate dirt road like he was in rush hour traffic. "Don't know what you're talking about."

"Oh, stop." I watched the side mirror as Poker took off after what I hoped was a squirrel. "How was the date? Did you get reacquainted with Ben Scott's magic tongue?"

Jamey reached for his travel mug that read, IT'S NOT GAY UNTIL OUR BALLS TOUCH. "The date was good, but no."

I choked on my shock.

One hazel eye gave me a side glare. "I'm not a manwhore, you know."

"I'm sorry. I didn't mean it like that. I know you're not. I just…I figured— Why not?"

After a sigh, Jamey relaxed into the driver's seat, reaching over to hold my hand. "Believe me, I almost caved, but I made it clear that we were going to take this slow, and I set some ground rules."

"Which are?"

A frown framed his mouth as he pulled onto Canyon Boulevard. "That I refuse to hide who I am for him. If he's serious about us, then he needs to be willing to do the same. He has to come to terms with the fact that not everyone will accept him. That, and I require PDA." Jamey took his other hand off the wheel long enough to adjust his seatbelt. "And if we decide to become boyfriends, then he needs to introduce me like that. *Treat* me like that."

My hand tightened in his. "Those are all good rules, Jamey. How did he take it?"

A grin pulled at his mouth. "It was pretty cute, actually. He got all flustered because he didn't realize that we weren't back to boyfriend status. He just assumed we were. When I corrected him, he definitely didn't like that and explained that he was not the sharing kind of guy, which was all kinds of hot. And that was when I almost let him kiss me. So when I pressed him on the rules, he agreed to all of them, unless he thought they put us in danger."

I watched the scenery pass as we took the next turn. "How long are you gonna make Ben suffer?"

Jamey's brows edged together. "I'm not playing games with him. If we rush back into things, we won't fix the problem."

I turned to face him. "Which is?"

"Trust. If he had trusted me, listened…" Jamey glanced at me before concentrating on the road. "He's also aware that my first rule was non-negotiable, and you should know that he agreed without a second thought."

My interest was piqued, which I assumed was his goal. "And that was?"

"That you come first. You are my family, and he will never get between us. He has to protect you as he would me."

"Well…" I cleared my throat from the sudden lump that had formed. "That's…uh— Yeah."

His head bobbed. "Yeah." He copied my throat clearing. "He won't suffer much longer."

I tugged my hand out of his. "And that's where I bow out."

Hitting the marked path of bright rainbows along North Cove Beach, Jamey parked in the designated lot on the wharf. He cut the engine along with the Doja Cat jam that had been blasting out of the speakers. I opened my door and was met with a cool breeze, warm sun, and a partially cloudy sky. A perfect day for a run. Around us were bodies of every shape and size, donned in outfits covered in rhinestones and sequins, strutting in heels that seemed impossible to run in, let alone walk.

After slipping on our tutus, Jamey and I headed to the registration desk.

"Good morning, Ms. Shag Gay." Jamey sauntered up to the booth, where familiar blond curls bounced along the outside of a pair of bulging biceps.

A smile teased one side of her glossy red lips. "I hoped to see you, Jamey."

Jamey's brows perked, tone dubious. "Really?"

There was a pause before the long nails matching her lips flourished in the air. "Okay, fine. I was looking forward to those fine ass men you brought with you last time."

Jamey nodded. "That tracks."

"Sorry." I shrugged. "It's just us."

"Oh, that's okay, twinkles." A band of heavy lashes winked. "We'll take all the cute bodies we can get. Here are your numbers." She handed us the race bibs and safety pins. "Feel free to look around at the booths and shop your hearts out."

Jamey pinned the number to my back. "You sure you don't need help?"

Ms. Shag Gay waved him off and helped Jamey fasten his bib to his shirt. If I did it, I'd turn him into a human pincushion.

"You're too sweet. All the volunteers showed, so we're good." Her face lit up as she bounced on her stilettos. "I almost forgot! How did the date go?"

"Good," Jamey answered, a rare flush rising to his cheeks. "I took your advice, and...it worked."

"That's my boy." She pinched Jamey's blushing cheek. "Make him earn it."

"Apparently, he won't be *earning* it for much longer," I groused. "I would know. I was given extensive notes regardless of how much I protested."

Her shoulder rose. "Oh, baby girl. Can you blame him? Really?"

I grumbled my disagreement, and Jamey snickered as he took my hand. Once we were out of earshot, I leaned up to say, "Okay, I don't want to be disrespectful here, but I have to know... What's her real name?"

Jamey's chest shuddered with a laugh. "Joe Trazowski."

As we aimed over to the booths, the air filled with happy chatter, and instead of the usual scent of sunscreen and sweat one might expect, the bodies surrounding us were covered in artificial coconut, glitter, and oil. Cher pumped throughout the PA system with a great deal of primping happening all around us. If I didn't know better, I would think I was at one of Jamey's hair and makeup conventions.

To waste time before the race started, Jamey and I hung out at the novelty booths, reading funny T-shirts, trying on hats and headbands. Everyone began to assemble at the start, so we made our way over.

A woman appeared at the podium dressed in a yellow floor-length gown that may have fit two decades ago. With a deep, booming voice, she greeted the group and gave instructions for the event. Then it was onto our warmup, all to the tune of Madonna's "Vogue."

My mind oddly drifted back to a conversation I'd had with Mason—back when I only knew him as Pumpkin. When I'd confessed that I'd never danced with a boy. A straight boy. Still hadn't. I supposed I could have at the bowling alley after Ben's birthday party, but Mason and I were in a weird non-friend place, and he...well, he never asked to dance with me.

My attention was drawn to Jamey's head as it periscoped over the crowd, not talkative like he usually was before a run.

I nudged him. "Are you okay?"

"Huh? Yeah, I'm fine." His sunglasses were now pointed toward the parking lot, but it didn't seem like he was people watching.

"What are you looking for?" I scanned the area, assuming the answer would be obvious. But here? Nothing was obvious.

Grinning, he waggled his brows. "Prospective dates."

I would have slapped him for insinuating that he'd cheat on Ben, but I swore he'd just lied to me. I wasn't very good at reading his tells, but lying was rare for him, which was why I let it go. There were things in Jamey's past that he refused to discuss, things that I accepted were too hard for him to talk about, but those were usually BM related: Before Mags. I had a sinking feeling this was all about me.

The announcer on the podium, whose dress had to have required an entire roll of double-sided tape, belted out, "It's Raining Men" to start the race. Most runners were more interested in hitting notes rather than pavement, but Jamey and I were able to shuffle through the dense crowd, weaving between bright wigs, nearly naked men and women, and every drag costume imaginable.

Jamey was in heaven.

Guiding each other through small breaks, we pulled into a roomy opening and got cozy in our stride. I slid my earbuds in as we neared the first quarter-mile, knowing both of us would be in the zone soon and would resort to hand signals to communicate.

Out of nowhere, a body appeared in front of me, and on his bare back, I thought I had read the words COME BACK STICKS! before the man vanished into the thinning crowd.

My head spun, and so did the asphalt. My feet tripped over each other next. Somehow, and without an ounce of grace, I was able to stay upright through a vertigo spell.

"You okay?" Jamey yelled over to me.

I scanned the group of runners surrounding us, shaking my head. "Did you see that guy?"

Jamey dragged his earbud out as I did mine. "What guy? Did I miss a hottie?"

Well...huh. Even at hyper speed, Jamey would be the first to notice a shirtless man and all those muscles zooming past us. I must have been seeing things.

"No, never mind. Sorry."

Nearing the half-mile mark, another guy magicked in front of me. This time I noticed he was wearing rainbow tulle with black compression shorts underneath. It was fast, but I was sure the black lettering on his back read, WE MISS YOU STICKS! Before I could study the Celtic tattoo on his arm and shoulder, he was gone.

"What the hell?" I muttered.

"You say something?"

I flinched, covering my ears. "Tap the brakes on the volume pedal!" Geez, what was with him today?

Laughing, Jamey yanked his buds out again and used a quasi-normal voice. "You sure you're cool?"

The anxious knots sinking to the bottom of my stomach told me I wasn't. At all. One more glance to the crowd… Those men had to be part of a team, but what kind of group would have shirtless men in rainbow tutus and— Okay, considering where I was, that was a stupid question.

"Yeah," I assured him. "Cool."

He nodded but didn't appear convinced, and neither of us slipped our earbuds back in after that. Three-quarters of a mile into the race, a third shirtless guy appeared. WE NEED YOU STICKS!

Okay, seriously? Unease trickled over my skin like a cold mist.

"Jamey." My hand shot out to grip his forearm. "I keep seeing…" I checked all directions to confirm I wasn't ready for a special, snug jacket and a padded room, but the man was gone. I was sure his left arm had—

Realization dawned as to what was happening to me, and dread snaked through my chest, tightening it painfully. Oh, God. I couldn't do this. Not here. Not now. I was in the middle of a run. That had never happened before. Running helped. Running was good. I…

Jamey popped his wraparounds to the top of his head, eyes tracking me. "What's wrong, Mags?"

Breaths sliced down my throat, gripping onto Jamey's wrist. "I'm hallucinating. I keep seeing men with *Sticks* written on their backs. We have to get to the car—"

"Mags—"

"If I have a seizure here, someone will call an ambulance, and they'll take me to the hospital again—"

"Mags—"

"I need to get out of here before it's too late—"

"*Mags!*"

My head snapped back up to Jamey. "What?"

The corners of his mouth lifted. "You're not hallucinating. Look." With his other hand—the one I didn't have a death grip on—he pointed ahead.

A fourth guy was in front of us now. His back read, THE SCOTTS MISS YOU STICKS! PLEASE COME BACK! This time, he didn't disappear. He turned around, feet carrying him backward. The man was wearing a bright grin, stretched from ear to ear, cheeks dimpling. Sweat dripped from his dark, cropped hair onto his golden chest. Then it all clicked into place. The abs of a Greek god. The butterflies. The infinity symbol.

Mason.

My heart slammed against my sternum as if the mere sight of him caused the thing to defibrillate itself.

More Scotts lined up next to him: Matt, Ben, and Camden. They each had writing on their bare chests, wearing black shorts that hugged their muscular thighs beneath a matching set of rainbow tutus. Too-short rainbow tutus. As in not nearly long enough to cover what the skintight fabric barely covered.

Staring at Mason, one thought ran through my head. I'd never seen a tutu look so sexy in all my life. I couldn't tear my eyes away from the tanned skin, tattoos, or his blinding smile. My gaze slid down, past the trail of dark hair above the tulle and then lower to an unmistakable outline of a body part that I had imagined an obscene amount of times.

It just wasn't fair.

chapter twenty-three

mason

"How sure are you?" Matt demanded. "She's gonna be here, right? You're not punking me?" Angling his hips up in the seat next to mine, Matt jerked at his crotch with a grunt and bumped my arm for the fiftieth time. " 'Cause if not, we're risking the future Scott lineage for nothing."

"I'm sure," Ben assured him. "Jamey drove her, and we have our meeting place all set. She doesn't have a clue." Then Ben elbowed my ribs when he adjusted himself. Again.

"Dude!" I shifted to rub out the deep jab to my side, soon discovering that was a mistake. Nerve endings below my waist warned that vital parts of my anatomy were in danger. My other hand shot between my legs to dig out the material trying to strangle my balls.

As Dad rolled into the parking lot, he raised all the windows, cutting off the cool breeze, and though I was half-dressed, sweat broke out along my back.

Matt yanked at his shorts one last time. "Whose idea was it to pile into one vehicle?"

From the passenger seat, Mom's hand rose reluctantly.

A voice complained behind me, "And why didn't we wait to wear the gay tutus until *after* we fucking got here?"

"Camden," Mom wearily scolded for the F-bomb.

Irritated instantly, Ben's hand flew into the air, nearly smacking my nose. "Why do you have to blame everything that goes wrong in your life on gayness?" He switched his voice to a dumbed down version, which I assumed was his Cam impersonation. "The DVR skipped over *Vanderpump Rules*. That's so gay."

Cam scoffed. "It was gay because the DVR recorded your fucking *Top Chef* that was gonna repeat another sixty fucking times in the same fucking day when I had to wait a whole week for Stassi and Jax drama."

"Camden!"

Ignoring Mom, Ben kept going. "The store was out of my chocolate chunk protein bars. That's so gay."

"How hard is it to order more of the chocolate than the peanut butter? The PB tastes like shit. The chocolate…less like shit."

Ben continued, "The radio station played the Jonas Brothers twice this hour. That's so gay."

"Really? They have, like, a *thousand* songs to choose from. I'm only asking that they not replay the same one ten times by seven in the fucking morning!"

"*Camden!*"

No one was going to help Mom. This moment was priceless. It was a good thing Dad had parked already because he was bent over the wheel dying of laughter like Matt and me.

Ben didn't seem to find this as amusing. "Just because the world didn't bend to your will, doesn't make *gayness* the reason! It doesn't even make sense! The DVR is not taking it up the ass because it recorded a cooking show instead of elitist brats. The store doesn't like dick because someone beat you there first and wiped out all the better tasting shit bars. The radio station isn't a cocksucker because they are playing what's in demand for their audience. And an article of clothing, no matter how bright, uncomfortable, itchy, and deemed feminine by society is not…" As the words left Ben's mouth, we stepped out of Dad's GX, and his argument was immediately invalidated.

Rainbows abounded everywhere, along with fishnets, padded bras, over-lined lips, contoured faces, and teased wigs.

Cam cocked a brow at Ben. "You were saying."

Glaring at his brother, Ben shot back, "Fuck a bag of dicks."

Mom huffed, face going red. "*Benjamin!*"

"Fucking a bag of dicks," Cam's eyes twinkled up at his brother as he plucked up the colorful tulle between his fingers, dipping into a curtsy, "is *so* gay."

Thankfully, Dad parked next to a patch of grass, so Cam had something soft to land on when Ben tackled him to the ground. Mom looked on and shook her head in disgust.

"It was a valiant attempt, dear." Dad kissed her cheek and passed her a black marker.

She took it, using the marker to point at the grunting bodies on the ground. "You take the morons. Their mouths are your fault."

"Technically, it's a combined fault my brother's DNA, plus hearing every male Scott curse since the womb—" Pursing her lips, Mom's head tilted at him, and he held his palms up in surrender. "Of course, though, it's my fault. I take full responsibility for our nephews."

Rolling her eyes, she came at me first and carefully wrote on my chest and back. Leaning against the SUV, Dad yawned while my cousins finished up.

"My junk is barely covered by this thing," Matt grumbled when Mom started writing on him. "Couldn't we get longer ones?"

"What are you bitching about?" Cam panted from the ground, his chest and arms pinked from Ben's assault. "Every guy here will be checking you out. You eat that shit up."

"You think?" Matt's mood instantly improved.

Groaning, Ben pushed to his feet and knocked away a lump of grass stuck to his elbow. "You have to be the only human on the planet who doesn't care who or what is hitting on you."

Matt waved a hand over his bare chest. "Who am I to deny anyone this visual gift?"

"And such a fine gift it is." Mom patted his cheek, my brother grinning wide and bright. Stepping back, Mom capped her marker and gave it to Matt to write on my cousins' backs. "Okay, boys. We'll be on the sidelines, *not* running. Good luck."

"Uncle Dan, these really won't damage our balls, right?" Cam winced, digging the compression shorts out of his crack.

Dad took a little too long to answer, his head wavering with a pensive expression. "It's possible."

We all did a double take. Was he...? Shit. I— I really couldn't tell if he was joking.

Dad tossed his marker to Ben and then jogged off after Mom. For some reason, I continued to watch as he caught up with her, right up until he pinched her ass. I could have done without that today.

I waited for Matt to finish writing on Cam's chest before I punched my cousin's shoulder. "Maybe you should have put more focus into getting the right size shorts instead of hitting on the sales lady."

"I did," Cam argued. "She said these made my dick look bigger. There has to be at least one female here who likes cock, right?"

"Come on." Ignoring his brother, Ben aimed for the registration booth. "We gotta go pay and get our bibs."

We followed Ben, keeping an eye out for Maggie and Jamey. We wound up finding Ms. Shag Gay lounging behind the registration table in a legit pool lounger, sipping a drink out of a plastic coconut.

As her heeled feet swung up and then down, the straw popped out of her ruby lips. "Oh, so you did come!"

Cam coughed, and Ms. Gay winked at him. Horny minds...

"The sun has broken through the clouds and is shining upon me," she said in a faux preacher's voice as she stood.

"That's a lovely dress, Ms. Shag Gay." Leaning on the table, Matt took his time admiring her stockinged pins.

Her eyes narrowed. "Oh, you are sex on legs. Naughty, naughty boy. Don't tease me." She set her coconut down and helped us with the paperwork.

She handed over our bibs as I asked, "You see my blue-eyed friend by chance?"

"Sure did. She's wearing an outfit to match those pretty peepers. So...who's the lucky bitch, 'Sticks'?" she asked, reading our chests. "And please, God, tell me this is a reverse harem situation I'm looking at."

"The one with the pretty peepers," I explained. "And hell no."

"Oh, child." She grinned, blond curls bobbing around her impressive cleavage. "Those dimples don't do much in the way of hiding that alpha male side of yours. Get outta here before I make a fool out of myself."

Finished attaching our bibs to our shorts, we scanned the crowd again. Ben located Jamey first. As promised, he wore a sleeveless shirt with matching shorts and a tutu that might blind me if I stared at it too long. Right below his shoulders, like a tempting little pixie, I spotted a raven ponytail. My pulse revved, and my stomach tightened as anticipation buzzed through my veins.

This girl had the power to turn me into a puppy dog at the mere thought of her, and I'd do whatever she wanted if it meant she would come back, give us another chance. Hell, I'd jump through a thousand fiery hoops if she would acknowledge my existence, look my way once in class, realize I was at the picnic table behind her at lunch, ran to the café every Saturday and Sunday morning just to get a glimpse of her. If it weren't for my daily bits of intel from Ben, I would have gone out of my fucking mind by now.

Once the fat lady sang—literally—we hung toward the back of the pack, perhaps a little too close together. Pretty sure someone grabbed my ass, and I had a sneaky suspicion it was Cam.

As if this were page twenty out of Watkins' playbook, Ben rocketed ahead, tearing through the crowd and zipping right past Maggie. I watched as she ripped out her earbud to talk to Jamey. As planned, I sent Cam up a quarter-mile later. He whizzed around the crowd, planting himself in front of Maggie and Jamey long enough for her to see him this time. Though her steps faltered, she shook her head and kept going.

When it was Matt's turn, I closed in on her. My intention was to stay back for a bit longer, but when I heard Maggie say the word "seizure," guilt consumed me. I'd taken this too far.

I sprinted ahead and settled into a large pocket as the guys formed a line with me earlier than planned.

Jamey spoke loud enough for me to hear. "You're not hallucinating. Look."

I spun to face her, and all the blood cells required to perform the task of running pooled below my waist. This was the most of her body I had ever seen, including that blue dress that haunted my dreams. She was wrapped in teal blue, long legs flying beneath her without pause. Every inch of her that wasn't covered by snug fabric was toned and tight, beads of sweat glistening like diamonds on her peachy skin. Her breasts bounced under the sleeveless top, and yeah...I was staring at those pebbled tips. I blamed the fact I hadn't been laid in months that my cock shot up like the thing was spring-loaded. In the next second, my brain flipped to a fantasy montage of our sweaty bodies grinding, skin smacking, holding onto that small ponytail while I sucked on her perfect ti—

I prayed this stupid ass rainbow skirt covered me well enough. The friction of the compression shorts and the scene before me might make for my first orgasm while running. Had I been thinking clearly this morning, I would have jacked off in the shower.

My line of sight slid away from her breasts to linger on her slender waist, the sliver of creamy skin peeking out at me between her shirt and the frilly tulle. The sexiest innie teased me, and the daydream I'd had the last time I'd seen it was at the forefront again. I imagined tasting her, dipping my tongue inside that slight indent, following the curves of her body much lower to between her thighs.

That fantasy alone blew away my highlight reel with TNT, and Maggie occupied every slot. She was...*Jesus.*

Maggie's mouth was hinged open in shock, and my one thought was where I wanted that mouth, wrapped right around my hard c—

"*Whatareyoudoinghere?*" she asked.

My head rotated in every direction, but my line of sight was honed on that killer body. "Camel wrestling."

"You— What?"

A random dude called from the water table, "I'll give you a stick, baby!"

"Shit, Mase. Hurry this up." Cam coughed like he'd puffed away a humidor of cigars. "I can't keep her freakish pace."

"They're here to keep their straight team intact." Ben stumbled on absolutely nothing. "You're a hot commodity among the lesbians."

Annnd…another hit of lust slammed into me, remembering the cute brunette who had hit on Maggie the night at the bowling alley. I'd make room in my highlight reel for that, too.

"Ben's right." Matt hacked into his elbow. "No conversions on our watch!"

"Between us," I gestured to my cheeks, "I don't think even these dimples can compete with a chick who likes chicks."

"Seriously, what are you guys doing? You're crazy."

"Crazy about you. Please, give us another chance. Come back." Talking pretty much sucked at this point. "I've been training for a month…for you. And let me say that a month…isn't long enough. Pretty sure I'm gonna die today."

Pointing to herself, Maggie mouthed, *For me?*

A frizzy blonde with two melons attached to her chest swerved on her heels to avoid being flattened by Matt. Not that she looked like she would have minded.

Maggie's hands went to her flushed cheeks. "Stop running backward. It's freaking me out!"

The four of us pulled out of formation as I settled in next to Maggie. Matt took her other side; Ben and Cam sputtered somewhere behind us.

Her scratched-up, cheapo shades were pointed up at me, lips forming words without sound.

"I had a speech planned. Just know that it was the shit. But—" A hack and a few desperate pulls of air cut me off. "I have limited oxygen, forgive me. I'll skip to the end. Please come back."

She licked her lips three times. "I…"

"Give me a week. A trial," I threw that out on an exhale along with the hope that by using her logic, she'd come around.

As Maggie turned my words over, hope bloomed like the brightest rose and quickly wilted with each stride as if that very rose had been fed acid. I resisted grabbing her arm and tearing off her sunglasses, force her to stop, talk to me.

I didn't, and I really should have.

"Mason, I— I can't." Either I was slowing down, or she was speeding up.

"Don't," I begged, Nikes pounding into the pavement like I was leading a stampede. "I miss you. If Matt could talk right now, he would tell you, he misses you."

Matt grunted something indecipherable. I was sure if he could breathe, it would have been eloquent and genius.

She began pulling away, and I pushed to meet her step for step. "Mom and Dad are here, too. We all came for you. We all want you back."

As she looked away from me, I swore her bottom lip wobbled, but it was hard to focus with the running.

"Please. Stop and talk to me."

"I can't, Mason." Maggie shook her head, refusing to meet my eyes. "I don't belong. I don't belong in your home, your neighborhood, or anywhere near those gates. I don't belong in your world. If I've learned anything, it's that."

Before I could argue all the ways she was wrong, Maggie tore off in a sprint, and there was no way I'd ever catch her.

"Fuck!" Gasping for air, I stopped dead, almost getting flattened by an odd amalgam of Lucille Ball and Ariel—tail included.

Matt skidded to a halt next to me and folded in half. "Shit, this is it, Mase. Mom's gonna have to bury me in fucking spandex and a rainbow tutu!"

"Nice ass, honey," another random runner called to my brother.

"Thank...you!" he hacked back, suddenly no longer on the brink of death.

I stared ahead, refusing to pull my gaze away as the crowd swallowed Maggie.

"What happened?" As Jamey caught up to us, his head darted between Matt and me, looking for one of us to answer him. How was he not dying right now? He wasn't even breathing hard. Whatever. Didn't fucking matter.

Nothing fucking mattered.

"She's done," I rasped. "That's it." Emotion had wedged in my throat like a jagged stone, my heart aching like the thing was shrinking, struggling to function amid the pain. I thought this plan would work. Show her how much we cared. I honestly hadn't considered we'd fail.

Thighs on fire, it took an embarrassing amount of effort to kick a rock off the asphalt. I watched as it sailed over the cliffs, and a flock of sea birds squawked as they scattered into the air.

"Where the hell...are we?" Cam wondered, having caught up to us at some point. Good question.

Standing in front of me, Ben gripped my shoulder, his face red and sweaty. "We'll...catch up and...talk to her."

I stood but then had to bend in half again. I wasn't ready for the whole vertical thing yet. "And say what? What's left that hasn't been said?

Why would she come back? She has no reason to. She hates us, and rightly so."

Jamey shook his head. "Mags doesn't hate people. She's not like that."

From my position, I glared up at him. "She won't forgive me, then. Is she the forgiving type?"

Considering that, his head bobbed. "Give her time, Mason."

Time. That was the only answer anyone had for me. To wait. It had been weeks, and I'd apologized, I'd begged, I gave her space, but there was never a hint that she would forgive me.

Because you don't deserve her forgiveness.

Ben had said something to Matt before taking off, but I wasn't listening. Instead, I walked to the edge of the cliffs, and from the railing, I watched the waves batter the shoreline. I was like those rocks below, taking one hit after another, life whittling me away one heartache at a time.

I was suddenly jerked backward, the scenery spinning until my brother's image came into view. Matt studied me, his face guarded and cautious. "Mase? You with me? You good?"

It dawned on me that he probably thought I might jump over the railing just now and FaceTime with the cliffs below. "I'm good."

"Did you hear me at all?"

Uh... "No."

"We're gonna finally have that free dick party Brady wanted to throw you," he said.

Free dick...? Ah, yes. The rite of passage for every RAM who experienced a breakup. I vaguely remembered Brady announcing that after we shook hands and made nice. He'd been surprisingly quick to put the past behind us and move forward, and while I wouldn't say we were besties, Brady would use any excuse for a party.

Matt continued, "I'd say we're a couple of weeks overdue. Crystal is sending her girls, and we're getting wasted."

"Oh, hells yeah!" At the prospect of getting laid, Cam suddenly had the ability to speak and fist-pump the air.

Images of Crystal's girls dancing in my lap to pounding music while a Jack and Coke slid down my throat entered my head. There had to be something severely wrong with me because the words coming out of my mouth sounded foreign. "I don't want that, Matt."

They blinked at me.

Matt released a hard breath, gaze locking with mine. "She's not coming back, Mase. It's time you faced that. We screwed it up."

"*I* screwed it up."

Matt's eyes hardened. "No, Mase. It's on *all* of us. *We* all thought she took the earrings. *We* all refused to consider any other possibility. There's only so much we can do, so many apologies, only so many times we can try." He raked both hands through his sweat-soaked hair. "Come on." He nodded to the road where Dad's GX was idling. Damn, how long had I been wave watching? "We're going home, and we're gonna move on like we've always done."

That was just it, though. We hadn't ever done that. We'd never moved on from Faith. We kept her room the same, refused to acknowledge that nothing in it could be moved. Her chair sat at the kitchen table, and no one but a Scott could sit in it. We had stopped talking about her, stopped sharing her stories, both good and bad. Instead, we buried her memory in work, booze, women, and boxes of Kleenex. We weren't living. We were stagnant and rotting in our grief.

The one bright light who had dragged us out of the darkness and pieced us back together again was gone.

I shrugged on the T-shirt Matt was holding out for me and climbed in the back of the SUV. No one spoke on the way home because they knew what I did. It was my fault. I ignored the warnings, what was right in front of me, and because I was too late, too lost, too far gone, I'd ruined the best thing that had ever happened to us since Faith had passed.

I had taken a beautiful bird out of the sky, tore her feathers out one by one, and listened to her cries as I watched her fall.

chapter twenty-four

maggie

Words. They were just words. Good words that made me feel *wrong*. They evoked terrible things like hope, which ended with nothing but disappointment and pain. Words had only been used to cut me, bleed me of strength and dignity, and yet, for thirteen miles, I'd done nothing but replay each and every one of those words in my head.

We all came for you. We all want you back.

I shut my eyes as the emotions rushed to the surface, doing something odd to my bottom lip again. Pinching my lip between my teeth to still it, I breathed in the briny undercurrent in the air and then focused on the sea lions as they played and barked in the harbor.

Someone said my name. I think. Either that or the sea lions had learned to speak English.

I turned to find one platinum form walking toward me as the other dark-haired and equally tall body gimped beside him. Looking at the gimper and the black writing smeared on his chest, there was an awful prickling sensation in the back of my eyes, my throat growing too tight to take in air.

I looked past Ben and didn't see any other Scotts lumbering, limping, or cursing their way over. "Where are the guys?" There was an awful pressure squeezing my heart that I'd get the answer I didn't want. Or did I? Hell, I didn't know what I wanted anymore.

"They left," Ben wheezed and then sucked down the contents of a Dixie cup he'd grabbed from a water station along the way.

"Oh." The pressure squeezing my heart pinched like barbed wire now. I shouldn't have freaked out. I had run away like a deer looking at the bad end of a rifle. I should have stayed and at least listened. Wasn't I guilty of the very thing I had accused the Scotts of?

"Mason, he— We came here for you. And when…" Ben threw the cup into a nearby trashcan and kept his gaze there. "He couldn't stay."

Now the wire around my heart began to spiral through my body, the barbs rooting deeper. I hated that I felt so much *guilt*. And there was no reason I should feel that way. When had I stopped being angry? I liked that emotion better. It made sense. It was right. It was how I *should* feel. Anger made me strong, empowered me. Guilt weakened me, forced me to feel stupid things like pity, tempted me to forgive, opened me wide to heartbreak all over again.

"I don't get it." My head arched back to him. "When did I become the bad guy?"

"You're not, Mags." Mouth pulled down in the corners, Ben took my hands. "Do you remember the first day I met you?"

I nodded. I remembered that day all too well. And every day with the Scotts since. All of them except Camden had weird reactions to me, and I hadn't understood it until Mr. Scott's confession at the café.

"Faith was sick for so long, and there were so many treatments, doctors, hospitalizations. The last five years with her were a nightmare, and in the five years since, we haven't been able to fully wake up. And suddenly, there you were. At first, it was difficult to be around you, but that's changed. And I'm not asking this to make you feel guilty, but if there's a chance, even a small one that you can find it in your heart to forgive Mason…he needs it."

I scrutinized those last few words. "Why just him?"

"It's—" Drawing in a shaky breath, his lashes lowered to shield his eyes. "I can't tell you everything, but I will say this, and he'd have my balls if he knew. Mason's been a mess since you left."

Doubt colored my tone. "He looked fine to me."

"He's not. Believe me, he's far from it. He's not eating, he's lost weight, he's drinking far too much, and he hasn't slept more than an hour or two a night since you've been gone." Lifting his gaze, Ben's fingers tensed in mine. "Mason's heart was shattered when we lost Faith, and you've been the only one capable of helping him put the pieces back together again. And if I'm honest, I think he's in a worse frame of mind now than when she died. We're all worried. No one's been able to reach him."

"What makes you think I can?"

"Because you did it before." Sorrow trickled into his features with his next thought. "I can't explain it without overstepping, but… Mase used to sing to Faith. When she was sick or in pain—which was pretty much all the time—it helped soothe her. And when she passed, he stopped singing. He slowly withdrew from all of us. There was an emptiness to him as if he'd been stripped of every ounce of joy he had, and one random day after five years, he suddenly started singing again. There was a lightness about him that we hadn't seen before. Not one of us knew what to make of it. But it was you, Mags. You did that for him. Even if it was only for a little while, you brought him back to us."

Suddenly, the events from the first time I met Mason snapped together. He...he had sung that night. Twice. And the second song— Oh, God.

He'd sung "Have a Little Faith in Me." *Faith*...

"Just think on it," Ben pleaded. "And in the meantime, we could get some ice cream from that place on Laurel." Ben swung my arms back and forth, hope in his voice. "It has the best mint chocolate chip, and a big, ol' scoop helps me think better."

The swinging persisted until I agreed.

"Wow, that smells delish!" Jamey closed the car door, taking another long whiff of air as his eyes shut, chin falling back.

No traffic made quite the difference traveling on Cove Highway, and I was glad because I could eat a few gallons of ice cream right now. Directly behind us was the panoramic backdrop of Warrington U's campus of lush grounds and gray brick buildings with blinding white trim, and straight ahead, the caffeinated goodness was thick enough to taste, the sandwich shop was baking fresh bread, and then the sweet scent of waffle cones drifted over me next.

The mixture was heaven.

Looking up and down the street again, I chewed on my cheek, unease weighing on my chest. I felt like a traitor coming here since most of these shops on Laurel were Sand's direct competition, but...we didn't have an ice cream shop. So, I guess I had a pass on this one.

I shut my door, leaving our tutus in a pile in the backseat of the Focus. As I followed the boys inside the shop, Ben attempted once more to be a gentleman while adjusting his compression shorts, but there were only so many ways one could go about that task without just doing it. I shook my head. Those things looked as though they might do some damage to any procreation plans he may have.

After ordering, we settled in at a table and relished our half-marathon reward, but a few bites of my ice cream later, my eyes lifted to find that I was facing the window, in perfect view of the quad board. Papers flitted in the breeze, and it seemed like a few posts had been added since I walked past it on Friday. I pulled my focus back to the two heaping scoops in front of me. As I took another bite, creamy vanilla slid down my throat, leaving behind bits of raw cookie dough. Those damn papers moved again. It was as if they were beckoning me, waving me on to join them. I supposed there was no harm in seeing if there was another job posting. I'd had my eye on the Pizzazz Pizza Parlor down the block. Maybe I'd get lucky today.

Mind made, I shot to my feet before I lost my nerve. "I'll be right back."

Jamey's eyes flicked between my mountain of cookie dough deliciousness and me. "Where are you going?"

My chin jutted to the window. "I'll only be a sec."

Cranking his head around, his gaze tracked the grounds, shoulders dropping when he realized where I was headed. "Mags—"

I wasn't listening to yet another speech about awesome the Scotts were. Jamey may have forgotten about the beating I'd taken because of them, but I hadn't. I couldn't. After the bruises had healed, I still had a walking, talking, daily reminder of the hell I'd been put through. I had to see that baton dangling off his belt. The hand that had held it. The eyes that looked at me with such hatred, both my father's and the Scotts'. They hadn't had any compassion for me. There was no pity. No forgiveness. The Scotts had held onto their anger. I could, too.

Taking wide strides across the street and then cutting through the grass, I stopped in front of the corkboard and stood there like a dweeb for what felt like forever. Then I went to the other side and stared for the same amount of time. There weren't any job postings, and for some reason, I kept searching, reading the little strips of paper, the fine print on the posters. Interns needed. Roommates wanted.

That dude really needed to get over his lost hedgehog.

There was nothing here, so what was I looking for? A sign? Maybe a bare chest with my nickname on it? I blew out a ragged breath as the truth hit me square in the heart. That...was precisely what I wanted. I'd had four of them today, and I'd pushed each one away.

"You find what you're looking for yet?" A tiny squeak left my lips as I rounded to face Brady Hale. He was wearing a black T-shirt with gold Greek lettering. That was a frat T-shirt. Specifically, a Rho Alpha

Mu frat T-shirt. Ah, hell. Was that a sign? Sure seemed like it. "Please don't tell me you're seriously considering that used mattress for our newlywed bedroom."

I hooked a hand on my hip. "You too good for a used mattress?"

"Well…" His gaze coasted back to the listing. "It only has a *slight* urine odor. And for my new wife, I want nothing but the best. It has to have pungent urine stank or nothing."

I grinned. "We're in luck. There's a king mattress on the other side that fits the bill."

Throwing his head back, his Adam's apple bobbed. "We'll pick it up today." Those eyes did the up and down thing again. "You out for a run?"

"I just came back from the Rainbow Run in Pacific Cliffs." I twisted at the waist so he could see the number still pinned to my back.

"I was wondering what you were known for doing three hundred and thirty-one times. I thought it was a trail of broken hearts you left in your wake."

I shook my head, gaze dipping to my sneakers. "Not likely, no."

"Oh, I think it's very likely." He closed the distance between us as my eyes lifted to his. One corner of his mouth teased a smile. "Please tell me you don't have plans tonight, Maggie. You'll break my heart, and then we'll have to get you a different number."

His gaze slipped over me once more, and I…liked it. I didn't like that I liked it. I couldn't trust Brady because of his connections to the Ryans and for whatever had happened in the locker room with Jamey. But I didn't have to be a jerk, either.

"I have plans with my friends." I didn't feel it was necessary to explain that one of those friends was Ben.

Brady straightened, that curve of his lip deepening. "Guy friends or girlfriends?"

"Guy friends."

His muscular arms flung up, and that damn horned RAM logo stretched across his pecs. "Fuck. That's it. There it went." He drew the neckline of his shirt out to look at his chest. "I'm number three hundred and thirty-two." Tipping his head up, he flashed me that smile, and I laugh-snorted like a complete dork. My amusement gave him the confidence to speak again—not that he lacked a cocky swagger. "We're having a thing at the RAM house tonight. Bring your friends. You don't even have to change." His blue gaze danced in the sunlight. "Hell, you could leave with me now."

My eyes narrowed. "What is a *thing* exactly?"

He shrugged. "A party."

A fraternity party? I wasn't sure what Ben and Jamey's plans were or if I was even included in them. My father would be otherwise occupied with someone tonight. Even Ava was going out for drinks with her girlfriends after her bridal trial had canceled. It...could be fun. Or it could mean death and dismemberment if one of the boys stopped by and found me at a fraternity house.

I didn't want to be lame, so I went with, "I'll consider it."

A millisecond later, Brady was no longer in my line of sight. He was below it, on his knees again. "I'm half a man now with a broken heart, Maggie. Look what you've done to me in a matter of three minutes. I need to save the town from you. You'll go around the Cove leaving a line of men forever ruined by you."

"What is it with you and getting on your knees?"

Grin growing wide, his gaze ensnared me. "Is that a, yes? Remember, you've said yes to me once before."

"I did. But today, my answer is *I'll consider it.*"

He sighed. "Okay, but I'll be sitting on the couch like a loser, watching the front door. I won't be able to enjoy myself until you come." His lips curled on both sides like I'd missed an unspoken joke.

"I doubt that."

Brady wryly shrugged. "Guess you'll have to stop by and see." With that, he winked and turned to knee-walk away from me, flashing me one last pleading glance over his shoulder. No doubt that look had gotten him more than a few yeses. "Think hard, please."

"Okay." I shuffled backward a few feet and waited for him to look away before I turned around. Back in Cove Creamery, I slid into my seat, the vinyl fabric now cold from having been gone so long.

"Find anything?" Ben's disapproval was noted as he dumped his spoon into his bowl, refusing to meet my eyes like I had tied his bunny rabbit outside of a wolf den.

"No, and either no one's bothered to take the flyer down, or this town is still hard up for egg donors." My ice cream was now soup, my spoon kicking up all the dough chunks that had sunk to the bottom.

Something metallic *clinked* on the table and slid toward me beneath Ben's palm. "There's one job that I know of, and as a bonus, you can keep your eggs."

Ben lifted his hand to reveal a nickel-plated key that I assumed went to the Scotts' home. My stomach decided to take a trip up my esophagus. That key was different from the one I used to have, and I assumed the Scotts had rekeyed their home. Because they didn't trust me not to break in and steal some more.

278 | ashlan thomas

After a long stare at every peak and groove of the bitting, I shook my head. Ben refused to take the key back as though he didn't believe I didn't want it.

"Hey, Mags." Jamey drew my focus to him, anxiousness crowding his forehead. "Ben said there's a party at the RAM house tonight. You wanna go?"

"Mase will be there," Ben said with renewed hope in his voice.

Ah, hell. Was this another sign or a shove? And was I seriously considering this? Ugh, it didn't matter because my mind did the inevitable knee-jerk it had when Brady had invited me.

"What if my father finds out, Jamey?"

His brows pinched together. "How? You're spending the night at my place. You know what he does when you're gone."

More like who he does.

I occupied myself by playing with my soggy napkin. "I don't think Mason would want me there. Not after today."

"Mags! For the love of Madonna's cone bra!" Jamey slammed his hands on the table, and I jolted back in my seat. I think the dude behind me choked on his Oreo crumbles. "The man trained for and ran a quarter of a half-marathon just to talk to you. The same man also convinced his brother and two cousins to wear rainbow tutus with your name on their chests. *For you!* He wants you there."

Ben nodded in agreement. "It was sweet but super cheesy."

"I actually didn't think it was all that cheesy," I murmured. Squirming under their expectant stares, the same thoughts from earlier tickled the back of my brain. I'd never been to a frat party. Coincidentally, I'd always wanted to go to a frat party. Maybe Jamey was right. How would my father find out?

"Okay."

Smiling bright, Jamey hooted, earning a nasty look from a mother trying to get her baby to sleep.

I swirled my spoon in the cookie dough soup again. "I, uh, was kinda invited a few minutes ago anyway. I mean, I was invited."

"What are you talking about?" Ben's brow puckered, his head swiveling toward the window as if the answer was there. "By who?"

"Brady Hale."

The head unswiveled in a snap, and the brow went from puckered to arched just as fast. "*Brady Hale?* You...?" Ben's jaw clamped down so hard I swore the pressure he exuded on the bones forced his beard to grow. "When? How? W—what did he say?"

I shrugged, shrinking back in my seat, not having a clue what his malfunction was. "Just that there was a party, and he wanted me to come."

Looking down at the table, Ben grumbled something that sounded a lot like, "Yeah, I bet he did."

"So, it's settled," Jamey cheered. "We're—"

"She's not going." Ben busied himself with cleaning our table. Rather angrily. "No fucking way is she going, Jamey."

Jamey's happy mood deteriorated in a bat of an eye. "I think that's for her to decide, Ben."

His gaze hardened on Jamey. "You need to trust me on this one."

The heat of Jamey's eyes matched Ben's as he leaned over the table. "We're not quite at the trust stage yet. What happened in the last two seconds that made you flip your switch like that?"

Yeah, I'd like to know that, too.

Ben tipped forward to meet Jamey's glare. "Not this time, Jamey."

Okay. Now shit was getting tense, and they were either going to take a swing at each other or slam their tongues down each other's throat. Could go either way. But I didn't want the former. Not when they finally got back together.

Jamey's head tilted, not backing down in the least. "Mags deserves a little fun. She's had a pretty shitty month, don't you think?"

"You said to protect her like I would you. This is me doing just that."

I didn't like to interfere, but this would backslide into something ugly by kicking up the past. They didn't need that.

"Can we stop talking about me like I'm not sitting two feet away?"

They didn't agree to that right away, but eventually, the boys backed off, relinquishing themselves to their respective corners. I didn't get the sense this argument was over. Honestly, yes, I would much rather be at a party tonight, but the simple fact that I wouldn't be home was enough for me. I didn't need to drag Jamey and Ben down with me.

"Jamey, it's fine," I agreed reluctantly. "Ben doesn't think it's a good idea. He would know. But you two should go."

Jamey's mouth opened to protest when Ben announced, "Good. Glad that's settled." Without another word, he bolted to his feet and chucked our trash into the bin.

So...yeah. It was settled. All fine and dandy and settled.

chapter twenty-five

mason

"M*ase*!"

My head snapped over to my bedroom door that I didn't remember leaving open. Nor did I understand why Cam's brows were competing for real estate with his hairline.

Working out a crick in my neck, I positioned my pillow higher up the headboard. "What?"

He waved to the empty hall behind him, and now that I was paying more attention to the goings-on of the fraternity house, the bass of the music and laughter downstairs sounded louder than before.

Cam urged me with an impatient stare. "You coming, douche drip?"

I immediately cringed. "Jesus, Cam. That's..." I rubbed my temple, trying to rip that imagery from my brain. "That's nasty."

He blinked at me. "When did you become such a vagina? Is it because you haven't had any in a while?"

Swallowing the remnants of the amber liquid in my glass, I glared at him over the rim. "Cam, get out."

"Are you seriously not coming downstairs?" When I didn't answer, Cam's shoulders fell a fraction. "That party is for you. To get you laid and back on the Pussy Train, full speed, Coz."

A sigh that was loud enough to shake the walls left me. I set my glass on the nightstand, tapping it against the bottle that I planned on emptying. Soon. "Don't take this the wrong way, but I don't want a party, and I'm not in the mood to get laid."

Cam's mouth and eyes sprung wide to comical levels. "Even after the warning, I'm taking it the wrong way. Matt supplied the girls, Mase.

Hot, fuckable girls. *Crystal's* girls. Just like you like them. Big tits and long blonde hair who will suck or bounce any way you want."

My gaze roved to the ceiling as if it could somehow help me explain to Cam what I couldn't even explain to myself. I wasn't committed, no girlfriend—fake or real—no part to play. Pros were here, and it had been months since my dick had touched something other than my hand. Hell, the sight of Maggie had me so hard today, I couldn't see straight.

Desperation ran deep to forget this day and the complete ass I'd made out of myself by chasing after a girl. A girl, who before even knowing what she looked like, had some mysterious control over me. She had the power to make me do things I'd never do, like spend every waking and non-waking moment thinking about her, constructing elaborate plans to get her attention, and jealousy was certainly nothing that had ever afflicted me before.

That's because Maggie's not just any girl.

Circumstances took her away from me before I even got a chance to know her. Then I fucked myself over. I should be used to that feeling by now. And tonight… Tonight could help me move on. Forget. Maybe Cam was right. I needed to get laid, and I could put Charlie, Taylor, and Maggie behind me. Get back to my old self, whoever the fuck that was.

As I slid off the bed, Cam jumped and simultaneously fisted the air. "Knew it! Give the man a blonde, and his pecker perks right up." When I neared the door, Cam backed up into the hall. "Question. Crystal actually sent *two* blondes. Did you want both? Because I'm almost certain the one in green used to be a redhead. And you know I can't resist—"

I slammed the door in his face. Then locked it.

"Soooo… Is that a, no?" Cam paused. "Okay, I'm gonna take that as a no!"

Blowing out a terse breath, I resumed my spot on the bed and let my focus be nothing other than my liquor-to-soda ratio, but that changed as soon as the liquor was taken out of the equation. Dammit. With the music now pervading my walls, floor, and eardrums, along with my every thought, I was at least four drinks away from being wasted enough to sleep through the noise.

Begrudgingly, I was off my bed again to search for more—

Bang-bang-bang! "Mase!"

Grunting, I scowled at my door. "Ben, I've been through this with Cam. He can fuck both blondes. I don't care—"

"Either open the door or answer your phone! It's Charlie. She's in trouble. She went to—" The second I heard Charlie's name, I yanked the door open to see that Ben's skin tone was at least two shades too light to be considered healthy.

"What happened?" I snatched my phone off the desk, and hell, either my screen settings were off, or my eyes were malfunctioning because things were blurrier than they should be. After a long blink, I found that I'd missed calls from Taylor and— "What the…?"

Ben shut the door, closing us in my room. "I don't know the details, but Charlie took something, and it's not good. Ethan should be here—" His phone buzzed with a text. Reading the message, he said, "E's bringing her up the back stairs as we speak."

Back stairs. Otherwise known as the old servants' stairwell that had to be accessed through a hidden panel in the kitchen pantry. Story goes, this house was part of an enormous compound that belonged to a sardine tycoon back in the day and had a mansion built for each of his family members. The estate was passed down from generation to generation until someone decided it was too much upkeep and sold everything to Samuel P. Warrington III, who then turned it into a private university. That stairwell was the only thing that hadn't been touched during the renovation. I'd taken them once and vowed never again. It was pitch black with no ventilation to speak of and not built for anyone taller than four feet.

So, if Ethan was using the back stairs, whatever was going on was not good.

I shook my head, nowhere near sober enough for this. "Why is our cousin with Charlie? And why did he call me five times?"

Shoving the phone in his pocket, Ben opened the door to peer into the hallway. "That's what I don't know. His phone cut out, and Tay is her typical pain in the ass self, so now I'm reduced to communicating with Winston, and you know his stance on driving distracted."

I nodded. "Visual, manual, and cognitive. The man won't even use Bluetooth."

This was getting weirder by the second. Winston was…well, technically, he worked as a driver for my family, but he'd been with the Scotts so long, he was more like our guardian angel.

Questions whirled in my whiskey-soaked brain, but like all the times before, concern for Charlie was at the forefront. "Did Winston say what kind of shape Charlie was in?"

"Yeah— Ah, hang on." With that, Ben disappeared into the hallway for a beat, but it didn't take long to get my answer. From here, I could hear what sounded like Charlie, but the words spouting out of her mouth were ones I'd never heard her say. Or thought she'd say.

Jesus Christ.

As Ben cleared the door, Ethan followed with Charlie cradled in his arms, and the poor guy looked like he'd barely escaped the Apocalypse with the Four Horsemen nipping at his heels. Charlie…was in a far worse state. Taylor trailed behind them, her dress splattered with stains matching the ones on Ethan and Charlie's clothing, and the stench that accompanied the group was just as nasty.

Weeks ago, I would have greeted the younger Price warmly, offered my bathroom for her to wash up, given her clothes to change into. But now, when I looked at Taylor, all I could see was what she had done to Maggie, to my family, and the zero remorse she had for it.

I threw my attention back to Charlie, and yeah, *Jesus Christ* summed it up pretty well. In all the times I'd bailed her out of these situations, I'd never seen her like this. Charlie's drugs of choice were Patrón Silver and X, and both made her chill. That was why she hit them when she was stressed to the max, but I didn't know what her stress level had been recently because we weren't communicating on the regular. Not that she hadn't tried.

Maybe it had been unfair of me to place blame on Charlie for what Taylor had done. Or maybe I didn't blame her enough.

"Charlie Bear?" With her writhing and wailing in Ethan's arms, I doubted she heard me over her own howling. I guided her face around to mine and peeled one fake lash away to see her pupils better.

"They're blown, man," E shouted as Charlie added a few more entries to the Urban Dictionary. He adjusted his grip on her. "She'll be okay, but she's in for a rough night."

Rougher than this?

"Mase?" Her unfocused honey eyes found mine, body instantly transforming into a rabid squid hell-bent on ensnaring me with all four limbs. "Oh, Mase. You gotta fuck me. Fuck me hard! These assholes won't do it. My pussy neeeeeds it! *Please!*"

Eyes growing wide, I backed up into my bed. "What the fu—"

She somehow pitched her body out of Ethan's arms and cut through the air like she was part flying squirrel. It was pure luck I caught her. In my efforts to get a better hold, she nearly scraped my eyeball out with her nails. Charlie eventually got her flailing arms to coordinate enough to wrap around my neck and crush my trachea.

Ben rushed to peel off Charlie's arm from around my throat, and as soon as I could speak, I rasped, "What the hell did she take, E? And what…"

Crimson specks were splattered across the front of Ethan's white dress shirt, the knuckles on his right hand swollen and a gnarly shade of purple.

"Whose blood are you wearing?" I demanded, cringing as a tongue burrowed inside my ear.

Thrusting a sheet of dark hair off his brow with the same bruised hand, his eyes locked with mine. "The fucker who was selling Nine in my club. And he won't be making that mistake again."

Though my body was being jerked about as Charlie repositioned herself to lave my other ear, my heart...stilled.

Nine.

I'd heard of it but didn't know much about the stuff. It was a new drug that just hit the party scene, manufactured and distributed by the Sixes. Since Ethan had opened his club, E's, months ago, he had to hire extra security to keep the floor clean of dealers.

Charlie hiked her leg up onto my shoulder. "Maaaase! I need you to fuck me. *Now!*"

"For God's sake." Taylor dumped a pile of sparkly purses and heels onto my bedroom floor. Along with what looked like a mound of...brunette hair? "Can someone please fuck her already, so she'll shut up?"

Before I could respond, Ben snapped, "Tay, sit down and be quiet."

"Better yet," Ethan added, voice bereft of all patience. "Get your ass back in the car and clean up yours and your sister's mess." Face hardening into a vicious scowl, he then added, "You can stew in all night for all I care."

My brow rose. Ethan had never been a big fan of Taylor's, and I was sure the drive here hadn't helped. My gaze slipped back to Charlie and the fact that both women were wearing something best suited for a Victoria's Secret Fashion Show.

"What happened, E?" I asked, positioning my arm so it wasn't between Charlie's thighs. "And why did you bring them *here*?"

"I had no choice, because this one"—with one hand gesturing to Charlie, his other hand shoved my comforter back—"not only smuggled herself and her underage sister into my club but then swallowed Nine on the premises and then attempted to have an orgy on my fucking dance floor all while the PCPD was crawling up my ass, conducting an *impromptu* inspection of my club. So to answer your next question, hiding her in my office was problematic, my house doesn't have fucking walls yet, couldn't exactly carry her through my hotel lobby as she screamed for the bellboy to fuck her pussy, Brielle would have flipped if I took her to Richard's place, Mom and Dad are staying at the beach house this weekend because their house is being treated for termites, I don't trust anyone at the Zeta house to keep their mouths shut, and I might as well call TMZ myself if I took her to the hospital. And since Charlie turned the Maybach into a vomit receptacle, bringing her here kinda seemed like my last and only option."

"Mase. Mase, *please*. You have to fuck me!" Squirming, she somehow got one arm free, but before I could rework my hold, Charlie shifted and then so did the earth. A blast of fire exploded in and around my dick, then shot up my spine like a rocket, taking the ground out from beneath me.

"God...*dammit!*"

Halfway blind and deaf from pain, I think that was Ethan peeling five razor-sharp claws off my cock. Slowly. Far too slowly.

"Fuck! Sorry, Mase. I should have warned you." With Ben's help, Ethan detached Charlie from my torso, and together they pinned her onto my bed with her still screaming things I didn't even think an X-rated film would include. Ethan flicked his hair out of his face as he wrestled a wrist to the mattress. "Is she into kink, or is it just the Nine?"

"Gross," came from the corner.

Still somewhat bent over and gasping for air, my glare swung to Taylor. "What the fuck were you two were doing at *my* cousin's club?"

Her red lips pouted, folding her arms beneath breasts that were covered by not much more than nipple pasties and glitter. "Last I checked, it was a free country."

"Not when you're underage it's not," I ground out.

"Don't waste your breath, Mase. She's a selfish, attention-seeking child." Ethan stopped Charlie as she went for the front of his pants, snatching her other wrist out of the air. "Do me a favor, princess. Next time either of you want to work out your daddy issues, take your underage asses to Sinister, the fucking club your daddy *owns!*"

Contempt flared in Taylor's eyes. "Well, maybe you should hire a bouncer who wants his job more than he wants a blowjob."

Ethan's head whipped around, hair splaying in a wide arc. His cobalt eyes burned into her. "Do you seriously not get that I could be in the county lockup right now for drug trafficking and serving minors? Make no mistake, little girl. I didn't drag you and big sis down here for your protection. People saw you at E's, Taylor, and tonight made Charlie's London video look like a fucking Disney-Pixar collab. I don't give a fuck about yours or Charlie's reputation, but I do about mine. And my security team is getting paid exceptionally well tonight to keep my club, my name—the *Scott name*—clean of your clusterfuck."

"Why don't you send me the bill," Taylor sneered.

A laugh barked out of Ben's mouth. "*That's* what you got out of that?"

"Get her out, Ben." The words fumed past my lips as everything my cousin must have been through tonight played over in my head. "Get her out of my sight. I can't look at her."

Taylor glowered at me. "Yeah, well, you're not my favorite person—"

"Stop," I seethed, pinning her with a glare. "Fucking stop, Taylor. Ethan isn't wrong. You picked E's for your own self-serving reasons. Yours was for the attention. And Charlie..."

As she twisted and wriggled on the bed still screaming about her...needs, what little of her dress there was exposed far too much, of her body and the truth.

You didn't go to London with her, and after making the worst decision someone like her could make, she came home strung-out, planting herself in your fucking backyard so you'd have to deal with her. What better way to convince you not to bail on her again than by showing you that she can't stay sober without you?"

"Ben, take Taylor to Winston," Ethan ordered. "He's waiting in the back lot. Ask him to drive her to Stafford— No, don't get to argue. Pack up your shit and get gone."

Not without colorful commentary, Taylor gathered her clothes, shoes, and wigs. After an epic huff and a slam of what sounded suspiciously like my desk chair, plus a few more choice words, she and Ben left.

Breathing out a haggard breath, I looked down at Charlie and frowned. By the looks of those stains on her...outfit, I'd have to strip my sheets later.

"You can head out, too, E. I've got this. Been through this enough times with her."

He was already shaking his head, expression grave. "Not like this, you haven't."

"Really. It's fine. She's my mess, and I'm sure you have to get back to the club."

I sensed that Ethan wanted to continue arguing, but instead, he eyed me for a long, tense moment before nodding in acceptance. "I'm kinda itchy to wash up if you don't mind. Besides, I reached my limit with being in a confined space with Taylor. I'd rather Uber it back to the club."

"Shit. Sorry." I raked a hand over my face, guilt slicking across my skin. "Yeah, of course. Help yourself to whatever you need." My head ticked toward the dresser as I swapped places with Ethan.

Charlie had become less vocal at some point, and her writhing was down to a minimum now. I got situated while he grabbed a pair of sweats and a T-shirt.

Now that I was looking closer, there was a small tear in his dress shirt, a glob of something suspicious and yellow in his hair, and his skin was streaked with the same glitter that had been on Charlie and Taylor's skin. My heart turned over heavily. Like Maggie, Ethan hadn't deserved this. They'd been innocent casualties in a war I'd unknowingly become a casualty of myself.

"I'm sorry, E. I know it's not my fault, but you deserve to hear an apology from someone."

His eyes flew to mine, and whatever words he'd swallowed before remained unsaid. Ethan's gaze dropped to the bed before looking at the clothes in his hands. "I won't be long."

With that, Ethan headed into the bathroom and shut the door. Once the shower flipped on, Charlie stirred along with the scent of sickness. Actually...

Ah, shit. Whatever was on her was now on me, and I was suddenly desperate to join my cousin in the shower, which was not something I ever thought I would consider. I legit needed to lay off the whiskey.

Charlie was only squirming a little, so I took my hands off her and carefully removed my shirt. I crossed the room to grab a clean—

Crash!

And that would be the empty whiskey bottle meeting its end. I sighed and twisted around in time to see that Charlie was half off the bed, headed face-first into a pile of broken glass.

I was across the room in one leap, pulling her back onto the bed before she hurt herself, but just as fast, the woman morphed from a rabid squid into an anaconda on crack. Arms and legs were snaked around me, clawing at me, pushing me onto my back. Her hips writhed against me, the top of her dress falling away, lips way too close to mine.

"Thank God. You have to fuck me, Mase. I'm dying for it."

Keeping my mouth away from hers was no easy task. *And note to self:* Nine gave Charlie freakish Marvel-level Hulk strength. I did my best to push myself toward my headboard, but Charlie met me inch for inch.

I pressed a hand to her chest to hold her back. "Charlie, no."

"I need you. I need *this*." Like a whip snapping out, her hand was inside my shorts and beneath my underwear, gripping me tight, the pain from the last assault renewed. "Mase! Oh, yes!"

"Charlie, *stop!*" I felt every nail scrape and scratch my bare skin, working to arouse me. The sounds coming out of her as she ground against my thigh...

Utter shock paralyzed me. I was trapped beneath her, imprisoned as if I were helpless to stop this. I'd never felt anything like this before. So...*dirty.* Wrong.

Ashamed.

And though I knew Charlie wasn't in her right mind, possessed by the chemicals running through her veins, I couldn't help but hate her in this moment. For being so weak. For touching me this way. Making me feel this way. Her, of all people.

Charlie's demands fell out of her lips over and over until her voice transformed into grunts and moans. And that was worse. So much worse.

I could only watch her euphoria when all I felt was vile as it took everything I had not to throw her across the room. *Hurt* her. But I was a long way from sober and didn't trust myself not to.

"Well, I can't say this is completely unexpected." *That voice...*

My heart flattened and shrunk all at once. At Jamey's words, every molecule of air had been sucked out of the room, hollowing me out.

"I should be thanking you, I suppose," he said, tone edged with fury.

Struggling to look past Charlie, she was oblivious to anything and everything but using me as her hump toy. Straight ahead were hazel eyes that were hard and pissed. He looked at me with judgment and all the disgust I felt.

"Jamey. It's not—"

"No." His palm faced me and then dropped it. Slanting his head, his eyes fell to what I was sure was Charlie's entire ass and then some on display. "Do not tell me this isn't what it looks like."

"J—" Charlie's nails bit into my balls as white-hot heat raged through every nerve, rattling my brain. A noise came out of me that even I didn't recognize. I wasn't sure I'd ever been in this much pain before, and that included the times I'd broken bones.

"Fuck you, Mase," Jamey spat. "For reals."

"Jamey!" I choked out. "Goddamn it, wait!" My eyes snapped open in time to see Jamey flipping me off as he turned and disappeared down the hall. "Jamey!"

Fuck. I wasn't sure I could pry Charlie's fingers off me without causing permanent damage to myself, and my first attempt confirmed as much.

The vocal demands started up again.

"*Charlie, stop!*" It would take a miracle for her to hear me over her own noises. "No! Get the fuck off me!

God, I'd never hit a woman, never would have even considered it, but there was a legitimate concern that if I didn't knock her out, I would lose the vital body part that distinguished me as male.

As spots took over my vision, I swore I heard the bathroom door fly open, followed by a curse, but it was hard to tell with my pulse roaring like an active volcano in my ears. After more tugging and needles sawing through my skin, incapacitating me, the needles were suddenly yanked out, and Charlie's weight lifted. Pure instinct forced me to roll off the bed and onto the floor. Thankfully, on the side without broken glass. I knew breathing was rather crucial for the human condition to retain life, but the sheer amount of pain throbbing below my waist made that impossible.

"Mase? Mase, you okay?" Or...I think that was what Ethan said. It was hard to hear over Charlie's orgasmic wailing.

I wasn't sure if I was shaking my head, so I verbalized the answer between a myriad of coughs. "No. No...I am so not okay." Swallowing, I went full-on fetal position. There was no way I could deal with the repercussions of what Jamey thought he saw, so I focused on other things. It wasn't hard to do, being that *other things* were so fucking loud and obnoxious.

Working my head back, I swallowed. "This...can't be normal."

"Unfortunately, it is." He grunted while getting Charlie back onto the mattress. When her hand went between her legs to finish the job, Ethan pinned her arms to her sides and then used my comforter to...swaddle her. Like an infant.

There was no other way to describe it.

Charlie was still wriggling, sawing her legs to find release, but she wasn't vocalizing anymore, which gave us some auditory relief at least.

"Nifty trick," I said, rearranging things so my junk was in the correct anatomical position.

"More like last resort trick." Ethan frowned, tucking the end of the comforter tighter. "Restraining women isn't something I enjoy, and I really hate doing this, but yeah, it works. And please"— Ethan moved to avoid a heel to his femur—"don't ask me how I know to do this."

"Okay, then how..." I made it into a sitting position, not quite ready to stand yet. Now that I wasn't consumed with pain, I realized Ethan was only wearing a towel, water puddling on the floor beneath him. The poor guy couldn't even take a damn shower tonight. "How many times have you done this?"

"Too many, Coz. Too fucking many." His dripping wet hair dangled in front of his face as he shook his head. I had an arsenal of questions, but my cousin didn't look like he wanted to host share time right now.

"What the hell is *in* her?"

"Well," breathing out the word, Ethan readjusted his grip so he could sit on the edge of the bed. "I'm no chemist, but from what I understand, a mixture of shit for both male and female sexual dysfunction, which was then mixed with some more nasty shit. Nine is like Molly on bath salts with a Roofie chaser. Completely strips someone of their inhibitions along with their memory. And I learned this fun fact tonight. It's one helluva trigger for motion sickness."

"Did she buy from the wrong dealer, or did someone slip her the wrong drug?"

"Great questions. Had the same ones myself. So I had my security isolate the footage of the buy, and they sent me the video. I was able to watch it before my phone was impaled by Taylor's four-inch heel during tantrum number three." His gaze lifted to mine, measured and cold. "There's audio, Mase. Charlie knew what she was buying."

I looked at her again, not recognizing a trace of the woman who was my friend. *Is my friend.* Hell, I didn't know anymore.

"There's something else you need to hear." His eyes flicked to the open door and nodded to it.

Grinding my molars together, I gritted through the pain as I got off the floor and crossed the room like I was suddenly ninety years old and suffering from spinal osteoarthritis. I shut the door and then leaned against it, my head light and heavy at the same time.

"I was set up tonight," he said, and my eyes popped wide open, straightening against the door. "I've had five impromptu inspections by the PCPD in the last three months. And each of those inspections happened on nights that my security caught Nine dealers in my club."

God, I hadn't... When Ethan talked about the inspection before, I hadn't made that connection. "You think the dealers were plants."

"I do. It's the kind of shady shit Leo and Vivian Price are known for. And it's no secret they've got half the PCPD in their pocket. I expected something from them, but..." As Charlie quieted down, Ethan eased his hold on her. "Without sounding like an egotistical dick, Sinister is losing customers to my club. I understand the younger crowd and the party scene better than they do. I know what's in demand from the music to the atmosphere and even the damn liquor. And the Prices don't take losing well, so this is their way of trying to shut me down. And they'd sacrifice their own blood to do it."

I considered that for a long moment, nearly telling him how depraved the Prices really were, but even I wasn't that much of a dick. "You think Charlie and Taylor were in on it?"

"My gut tells me, no, but, Mase, this family... They're poison. All of them." His eyes held mine. "I'm sure you know that by now."

I blew out a slow exhale, head bouncing. "I do."

"I've, uh—" Clearing his throat, E glimpsed the broken glass on the opposite side of my bed. "I heard you've been having a rough time lately. I'm sorry. I should have done more than text you these last couple of weeks. I could have come down—"

"It's cool, E." I met his stare. "I know you're busy."

"That's a shit excuse. I shouldn't ever be too busy for family. My club will never be more important than you, and I'm sorry my actions make it seem otherwise." His brows furrowed. "How are you, really? 'Cause you look like you've had too many drinks and not nearly enough at the same time."

A sad laugh left me. "That's a pretty accurate description. And if things weren't bad enough, Jamey just…" Glancing away, I spotted a trail of silver sequins on my floor that must have come off whatever Taylor had dumped there.

Concern bled into his features. "Jamey just what?"

I shook Ethan off. "It's nothing."

"It's not nothing, but I'll let it go if you don't want to talk." I kept my mouth shut rather than offer a verbal answer. Standing upright, Ethan finger-combed his hair, and we both checked to see that Charlie had stopped fussing. She wasn't asleep yet, but hopefully soon. "Look, why don't you go downstairs, grab a drink, enjoy a girl. There's no reason both of our nights should be fucked. I'll stay and take care of Charlie."

I pushed off the door, the pain below my waist still clear and present, not sure I'd ever *enjoy* a girl again. "She's not your responsibility."

"And from what I understand, she's not yours either." Casting me an arched brow, he headed back into the bathroom to collect the clothes he borrowed.

"No. No, she's not." Funny how I felt not an ounce of remorse for saying that. I thought back to the night after Charlie had returned from London and how guilty I'd felt for leaving her, even if it had only been for an hour. Maybe tonight was exactly what needed to happen to finally sever that link, now that I knew what lengths Charlie would go to and who she would hurt to keep me tethered to her.

Charlie chose to go to a club that my cousin owned. She chose to take a drug, knowing how dangerous it would be. And she chose to self-destruct all to prove she wasn't as strong as I said she was, so I would rescue her.

All to manipulate me.

"Mase, it really is okay. I've handled enough Nine trips to know what to expect."

I breathed a resigned sigh. "You need anything?"

"Yeah." Coming out of the bathroom, he pulled a T-shirt over his head. "Your laptop. I need to order a new phone, and—" His cobalt gaze darkened as he scanned me. "You may want to change before you head down."

Glimpsing down, I cringed at what Charlie had left behind on my clothes.

Once I got Ethan and myself situated and cleaned up the broken glass, I headed downstairs in search of only one of the two things Ethan had advised me to get.

The moment I stepped onto the landing and into the fray of skin and sin, a dark arm landed on my shoulders. "Heads up." Dylan angled closer, so I could hear him over the pounding music. "Brady's in rare form tonight. So if you're not looking—"

"There he is! The man of the hour!"

With a curse, Dylan's arm dropped away. "Too late."

Brady proceeded to leap onto a coffee table that dozens of former presidents had used as a speaking platform before him. With a beer bottle in lieu of a microphone, he announced, "Ladies and gentlefucks! It is my distinct pleasure to announce our guest of honor, Mason Scott's free dick! After a painful bout in captivity, we're releasing it back into the wild!"

The entire house of brothers and women exploded in cheers and howls. And I think a dude just humped my leg.

Wearing a shit-eating grin, Brady continued, "Girls, stand in line. I happen to know Mase is long and hard, and he sure as fuck knows what to do with your pussy!"

"Brady, dial it down." Lounging against a pillar, Matt scowled across the room, but Brady's smirk only sharpened before taking a swig from his microphone.

Pointing to me, he said, "Mason is the one with the dimples, but hell, you really can't go wrong with any of us."

The women bounced up and down, and that right there was confirmation something was seriously wrong with me when not one fantasy entered my head. I blamed Charlie's nails that had left an impression on my broken cock. I didn't want to look too hard at what the real reason could be.

"Glad to see you finally joined us, little brother." I gathered by the ease of Matt's shoulders and the glaze in his eyes, he didn't know what had happened upstairs. He pushed off the pillar. "Come on."

My gaze followed the gesture of his head toward the hallway, his intentions clear. "I'm only here for a drink, Matt."

A grin curved one corner of his mouth. "And a drink you shall have."

Against my better judgment, I followed him to the room where everyone knew to go if you were serious about what you wanted and how much you wanted to pay for it. I figured, if nothing else, it would be quieter in here, and I could avoid any unwanted advances because, in this room, you paid for the *wanted* advances.

As Matt pushed open the door with a sign that read, THE PLEASURE PALACE, he targeted the brunette strapped inside a neon yellow dress and platform heels chillin' on the couch. The dress didn't contain her well, breasts almost too big for her body, but not obvious implants like the hack jobs some poor girls got.

"Crystal, I didn't know you were here," Matt purred, making his way over to her.

Her long pins swung around, heels meeting the floor. "Well, I've had some real assholes lately. I thought I would treat myself to another Matthew Scott experience. You never disappoint."

Matt's smile kicked up a few notches as his eyes took their sweet time taking her in. "Thank fuck for assholes." Once his back hit the couch, she climbed into his lap.

Lids laden with glitter flicked to me over the shoulder currently losing a strap that wasn't doing a damn thing to hold up her dress anyway. "Hello, Mason."

"Crystal." My greeting had no warmth to it. It wasn't that I had a problem with Crystal or what she was currently doing to my brother, but her greeting was solely spoken as a command to the two bottle blondes at the bar serving up fuck-me eyes. On cue, the one in green sashayed her way over and the other in pink wasn't far behind.

I held up my hands as if that would ward them off. "I'm not here for this."

Green Dress slid her palm down my chest, lodging my bicep between her breasts. "Baby, just tell us what you're here for, and we'll make that happen."

Yeah, I knew they would. "A drink. That's it."

"And what kind of drink would you like?" Pink Dress appeared on my other side, batting her lashes. "A slippery nipple? Sex on the beach? An *orgasm*? We're well adept with allllll of those recipes."

So much for avoiding unwanted advances.

"He wants the best orgasm you got, sweetness!" Matt crowed from the couch.

I inched back only to hit a wall with the women not giving me an inch to breathe. "Matt—"

"Just say *thank you*, Mase," he instructed, wholly focused on Crystal's lap dance.

"Is that what you need, baby?" Green Dress crooned as her hand continued its descent. "A drink? We can make it as *hard* as you want."

Yeah, that wasn't happening. And with a sly shift of her body, Pink Dress knew it.

Her glossed lips were at my ear. "It's okay, baby. We'll take good care of you. Relax and forget about everything." Something wet coursed down my neck, and my thoughts went right back to my bedroom, my bed, Charlie…

Something I couldn't identify compressed my skin, suffocating every pore, tasting rank and acrid in the back of my throat. God, all I wanted was a scalding hot shower to wash me inside and out.

Clap-clap-clap!

"And he's back in a big fucking way! Look at that!" Brady announced, his predatory glare all over the women pawing at me. "Dayum, this is almost enough to regret my plans for tonight."

Yeah, that shower was sounding real good right now.

Quiet enough for only them to hear, I said, "Ladies, please find someone else to entertain."

Without an ounce of rejection in their expressions, the women were smooth about slipping off me and crossed the room to the bar as more brothers filtered in.

Thankfully, Matt was too occupied to notice I'd denied their services.

"That would be a nice change, Brady," Matt replied dryly as his hand slid up Crystal's exposed upper thigh. "For you to feel regret."

"Well, I said *almost.*" He threw my brother a wink. "You haven't seen my plan yet. She should be here any minute."

"I'm afraid to ask," Cam grumbled and snagged a redhead with a simple nod of his head.

"And I'm so happy you did." Brady finished off his Corona and grabbed another from behind the bar. "This one is perfect. I saw her in the quad today with the tightest little ass you've ever seen, wearing shorts that should be illegal. And she had these pouty lips that— I swear just talking to her, I almost came." As his blue gaze latched with mine from across the room, an evil sneer drew up one side of his mouth. "She is…ripe for the picking."

The women at the bar flashed each other a look of disgust, and everyone else in the room was right there with them. It was no longer a secret that Brady sought out virgins. He treated them like they were no more than a prize in his sick game, luring them into bed, and once they were there, he wasn't gentle. Brady liked to fuck. Hard. And I had the unfortunate experience to see more than one of them leave his room, cheeks streaked with tears, shuffling awkwardly out the door.

He made me ill.

Matt's hands fell away from Crystal, and instinctively, she knew to incline sideways so he could talk. "Brady—"

Ignoring Matt's growl, Brady continued, "There really is nothing like being the first one to pop a cherry, knowing you've been where no man has been before. So clean and innocent." His eyes narrowed on me a fraction. "And you won't mind me soiling your little Sticks... Right, Mase?"

The world went to a tilt, and it had nothing to do with the whiskey. "What?"

In a blink, Matt was on his feet, leaving Crystal to steady herself on her stilettos. "You are not to touch her, Hale."

"Maggie? You're talking about *my Maggie*?" My brain was still trying to grip onto Brady's words like a drowning victim with a life preserver. He couldn't— She wouldn't... Hell, why wouldn't she after Jamey told her what he saw tonight? But Brady spoke to her this afternoon. After the run. After she ran away from me. Before Charlie...

"Is she yours, though?" Brady studied the label on his beer. " 'Cause she sure didn't act like she belonged to you when she told me how tight and wet she was for me."

And with that, Brady signed his death sentence.

chapter twenty-six

mason

"Mase!" Matt was holding me back. Barely. I took another swing at Brady, getting within a centimeter of doing some decent retinal damage. "Goddamn it, Cam, get a better grip on him!"

Oh, I stood corrected. Matt *and* Cam were both holding me back.

Fury rippled over my skin. "I'm going to tear out your intestines and strangle you with them, Hale."

"Gonna need a raincheck on that." Brady studied his beer label as I struggled to get at him. "An ass like Maggie's needs to have my cock in it first."

One of Matt's hands flew off me long enough to knock into Brady's chest so hard that his neck snapped backward, beer sloshing onto his polo.

"RAM to RAM, you made your point," Matt snarled. "You're still pissed about Eric. Fine. But this stops here. Maggie is *off-limits*."

Brady swiped at the stain on his shirt, molding his face into a bored expression, but his eyes couldn't lie as easily. "You're right. I didn't appreciate yours or your brother's, or hell, your entire fucking family putting their noses where they didn't belong. But Mase couldn't let it go, let things be. He needs to be taught a lesson. So I'm going to ruin something of his to make sure he learns it."

Despite being held back by two grown men, I made another lunge for Brady and got close enough that the sweet beer on his breath mingled with the whiskey on mine.

Fear, true and heady, swam in Brady's eyes, but his words hit back just as hard. "I'm imagining those big blue eyes tearing up as I drive into her, breaking through that tender pussy—"

With a surge forward, I broke free and slammed Brady into the wall.

The Jack Daniel's had definitely taken effect because any leverage I had was lost as Brady spun us, swapping places, so I was pinned to the wall. My focus cleared right as Brady's fist came at me. I somehow twisted my head in time, feeling the brush of air skating along my cheek with his missed punch.

Matt's fist sailed next and connected with Brady's eye, but my brother lost his footing and stumbled, taking Brady with him and knocking me out of the way. I got my feet under me as Brady grabbed my brother's shoulder and cranked his arm back. Next thing I knew, Matt was doubled over and coughing up his small intestine. Before I could help, I was twisted around and shoved into the hallway, my feet floundering beneath me.

As gravity took hold, the ground rushed up too fast to stop the inevitable. Thankfully, something broke my fall. Something warm and moving. And shrieking.

"Dammit, Scott."

I wasn't exactly sure who was pissed at me or if they even knew which Scott I was. The brunette I'd landed on thrust me off her and then used my stomach to push to her feet. The first thing I noticed were a pair of stilettos that would keep the practice of podiatry alive and well, a set of legs that women spent their lives in gyms for, and then two eyes imagining me skinned and quartered. Standing next to her was Pete, and that was not a happy face aimed my way.

I gathered I'd used his girlfriend as a landing pad. As the apology left my mouth, Pete's face screwed up, his arm cocked, and fire lit up my ribs.

I deserved that.

Clutching my side, I saw his fist coming at me again. Either my reaction time was a smidge delayed, or my depth perception was skewed, but I didn't move in time, and pain flashed along my cheek. Damn, I just got rid of the last bruise. Mom was going to be so disappointed.

I wasn't an I-told-you-so kinda guy, but I really wanted to shout that right now, and the dude who should hear it first just sailed past me.

A girl squealed, and Vic rolled her to safety before Cam inadvertently made her a tackling dummy.

I'd somehow ended up in the game room, Ben's chukka boots inches from my nose. It had to be a good sign that the smacks resounding above didn't result in my cousin crashing on top of me.

Everything was going a bit wonky from either the booze or a concussion, but familiar calloused hands were under my arms, hauling me to my feet.

"Get your drunk ass up, Coz." Cam shoved me through the back door where Noah just took a hit by some dude wearing a Viking helmet made from a Budweiser box. I almost didn't want to take the guy down because that was ingenious. But this was Noah, and whether or not he deserved the ass kicking, he was a brother.

Viking Dude had to go down.

I launched over the railing, Viking Dude and I crashing into a wooden bench that no doubt had suffered this fate many o' night. Picking up my head, the body beneath me was conscious, but he was out of steam. And the Viking helmet was no more.

"Damn shame." Sitting up, I licked my lip and tasted a tinge of copper. "What did that take you? Two hours?"

Leaning up on his elbows, Viking Dude stared at the pile of rubble mournfully. "Three, including the ax."

Hell, there was an ax? I would have liked to have seen that.

Noah rubbed his jaw, working it like it might be out of joint. He searched the grass for something, gaze landing on shattered glass sitting in a pool of foamy liquid. He groaned, "Dammit. That was my last fuzzy navel."

Owen clambered over, brushing a wad of mulch off his shoulder. "I gotchu, Noah. There's a six-pack in the basement fridge."

Noah threw him a sloppy grin. "I knew you loved my ass."

Owen chuckled. "Only after you wax it."

Brady's voice cut through the air behind us. "Fuck, Matt!"

We turned toward the porch as Matt's elbow pistoned back, his fist driving into Brady's face. "I hope for your sake you remember this. You see Maggie, you walk the opposite direction." He adjusted his grip on Brady's shirt, bringing their faces closer together. "And this thing with Mase dies here and now. Got it? He doesn't owe you shit."

Matt was poised for another punch when Brady held up his hands in surrender, arms shaking, eyes growing wide. "Got it!" When Matt released him with a shove backward, Brady toppled into the railing and then bent over it as he spit blood into the flowerbed below. "Alright! I won't touch her."

"See that you don't." Walking up the porch stairs, I stopped to glower at him. I waited for his nod, and with that, every fight outside and in was diffused.

Brothers assessed their wounds, icepacks were assembled, the music started up again, pros reappeared, Noah had his chick drink, and I made a new Viking friend.

All was well.

Or it was until the flashing blue and red lights spilled into the foyer like a disco ball, splashing onto anything standing within its beam. With a tilt of my head to the window, I caught sight of the black and white SUV.

Great, the last fucking thing we needed.

As people scattered, hiding liquor bottles and minors, Matt ordered, "Ben, Cam, and Mase, disappear. And make it smooth."

I briefly thought I should go to my room, check on Ethan and Charlie, but... Hell, I scratched that idea right off the list and followed my cousins up the stairs. Halfway up, I spotted Pink Dress in the foyer with her head on a swivel, eyes filled with panic.

"Hey, baby," I called down, her gaze finding mine. "Come with us."

She was quick to slap on a grin and joked as she crossed the PAM inlay on the marble floor, "All three is gonna cost extra."

"Yes!" Cam cheered at the same time Ben groaned.

We slid into Cam's room on the second floor, and as Pink Dress took a spot on the bed to check her phone, I aimed for my cousin's not-so-secret stash of JD. We could be here awhile.

"Mase..." Cam hedged, both brows winging up.

Closet door open, my hand wrapped around the bottle. "I've earned this tonight, Cam."

Shooting me a look, he freed a harsh breath. "Maybe that's the problem. You think you've earned it every night."

"He really has this time," Ben muttered as he put his ear to the crack in the door.

Down below, Matt threw out a casual greeting to our new guest. We quieted, Cam and I crowding the door with Ben.

"I received a call about the noise level. I'm going to ask nicely. Once. Keep it down."

Ah, yeah. I recognized that dickish voice. *Gorilla Arms.*

Matt said, "Of course, Officer...*Jackson.* Not a problem."

"Shit," Cam groaned with a shake of his head. "Another one who *earned* his whiskey."

I ignored Cam's dig and welcomed another burn of undiluted alcohol down my throat. "He'll keep his cool."

Cam didn't look so convinced.

LJ/Logan/Gorilla Arms/All Around Pain in My Ass continued, "Why is it that you and your family are at the center of every problem?"

Matt's chuckle wound its way up the stairs. "It's the curse of being a Scott. We attract problems."

"Yeah, and Maggie was collateral damage caused by one of those problems," Logan reminded him.

Shoulders inching higher, my molars sanded together.

The cop's belt clanged, boots scuffing the floor, probably getting real familiar with my brother's orbit. I must have unconsciously moved to go downstairs because Cam's hand landed in the middle of my chest and mouthed, *Dude, no.*

I forced the muscles in my shoulders to relax, but the effort had no effect on my tense jaw.

"She's getting her life back after your family ruined it," Logan said. "She's happier now. Leave her alone and stop coming around the café."

There was a pause, and I leaned into the door as my brother asked, "Officer, you wouldn't happen to have a special interest in the chief's daughter, would you?"

Releasing a groan, I shut my eyes. Cam might be right. Perhaps my brother wasn't the best spokesperson for the RAM house.

Logan's words came out in a growl. "I watch out for her."

"Yeah... I'm sure you do."

The seconds ticked by, and I imagined that cop's glare was drilling into my brother. "You like seeing my face?"

"I won't lie, man," my brother quipped. "I dig the ink. Muscles are damn sexy, too. But with those thick fingers of yours, we're gonna need a shit ton of lube for you to play anywhere near my ass."

Snickering, Ben relieved me of the bottle and took a drink.

"Then I suggest you shut it down," Logan ordered, "or you'll see me again tonight. At the station. Without the lube."

"You're a dirty one, Officer Jackson. I might take you up on that," Matt drawled with a smile in his voice.

Logan said something else that got my brother to laugh, and a moment later, the front door shut. We waited for the blue and red lights to disappear down the street before we exited Cam's room. Our new friend, Bernadette, joined us. I held her hand, and as we descended the stairs past the condom bowl, Cam snatched up a few.

"Really?" Ben grumbled.

Cam shrugged. "I'm done playing babysitter for the night. I might as well have some fun."

Taking the last few steps, I cast him a withering glance. "I'm overwhelmed with love."

Straightening, Cam's eyes hardened on me. "What else do you want me to do? Feed you a boner pill and prop up your dick, so Bernadette has something to sit on?"

"Believe it or not...that's happened." Bernadette pressed a kiss to my cheek and clacked her heels toward the back room.

I spun on Cam. "I didn't want Bernadette or her friend or this fucking party. But you didn't listen to me. If you had, I'd be getting shit-faced without another busted cheek."

Cam met me on the landing, chin tipping back to me. "You're right. God forbid tonight be any different from your usual routine."

I grabbed the full—okay, half-empty—bottle of JD from Ben. Shit. How long were we in Cam's room?

"What does that mean?" I challenged.

He flicked a pointed look to what was in my hand. "Like you don't know."

My lips pulled away from my teeth. "Enlighten me, oh wise one."

"I'm tired of watching you scrape bottom."

My fingers twitched on the glass. "I'm not."

Cam's eyes narrowed. "*Scraaaape.*"

Matt met us, eyes darting between Cam and me. He looked to Ben on the step above us. "Do I want to know because I'm not sober enough to dish out Scott Codes right now."

"Let's be honest, Matt." Cam's stare remained fastened to mine. "Even sober, you're fucking it up. And those moments are rare."

My brother's emerald eyes bore a hole into the side of Cam's head. "The fuck?"

"Oh-kay!" Ben shot forward, planting himself between Cam and me. "I think this chat needs to wait for sober time." A hand waved in front of my face, but my stare didn't break. "Mason."

Not backing down from Cam, I barked, "What?"

"Cam's got a point. I need you to dry up. Maggie wants to talk to you tomorrow."

At her name, I snapped out of it, focusing on Ben. "What?"

"After the marathon, I convinced her to call you."

There was a spasm in my heart as if the thing were coming back online using dial-up. "She won't want to now. Not after Jamey... He was here. He saw—"

"Saw what?" Cam chimed in, tipping his head to look at me over Ben's shoulder. "What did Jamey see?"

Ignoring his brother, Ben nodded solemnly to me. "I know. I caught him on the way out."

"It wasn't what he thought it was, Ben," I said. "You gotta believe me. I tried to stop—"

"I know." He gripped my shoulder. "I talked to Ethan—"

"What does Ethan have to do with anything?" That was Matt this time.

Ben's gaze didn't waver from mine. "Not saying it's going to be easy but let me talk to Jamey first. I'll explain everything."

I pleaded with Ben like he was my last lifeline. "Why did she want to talk to me? Is she coming back?"

"Will someone please fill the rest of the group in?" Cam complained. "Mason? Ben? *Bueller...?*"

Matt piggybacked that with, "Yeah, we're feeling left out here."

Disregarding Cam and Matt again, Ben's gaze dropped to his shoes. "Not exactly."

Not exactly was good enough. I'd worked with less.

I moved faster than any drunk man had ever moved. It really defied nature, and I deserved a pat on the back. Later.

"Mason! Goddamn it!" Ben yelled after me.

"Sorry!" I called out as I pounded back up the stairs. One of my hands was still holding the bottle of JD. The other clutched Ben's phone.

chapter twenty-seven

maggie

"Can you at least give me a clue as to why you're so upset?" I asked what had become my third attempt at posing the same question as to why Jamey had paced the length of his room for the hundredth time since returning from the party. I was surprised he hadn't worn a track through the planked flooring.

"No." One more trip around the room. One more ruffle of his chartreuse bangs.

"Did you have a fight with Ben?"

"N—not exactly."

Hmm. Okay…

Settling back onto Jamey's bed, I turned off *Love It or List It*. If those people were stupid enough to stay in their termite-ridden house with one bathroom, five bedrooms, and losing half of their wish list, I didn't want to watch anyway.

"You weren't at the party long. Did someone say something to you and Ben?"

"It wasn't—" Lady Gaga crooned from his pocket, cutting off his thought. Jamey's shoulders slumped as he swiped a stained thumb across the screen. "Ben, I told you. Whatever excuse you have for him, I don't want to hear—" His face suddenly morphed from mildly irritated to majorly pissed. "No fucking way." His free hand fisted on the pause. "You're seriously asking me that? After *tonight*?" Another pause. "I think you've had more than enough minutes. Thank God Ben convinced Mags not to come."

Now I was thoroughly confused. I mouthed, *Who are you talking to?*

I was ignored with one more full trek across the room, plus a few huffs. "If you upset her, so help me, Mason—"

I shot up to a sitting position, and my heart did a full cartwheel. *Mason?*

Jamey gritted his teeth, tacking on an eye roll. "Fine, but your leash is hella short." The white-knuckled hand holding the phone swung my way. "He wants to talk to you."

"Me?" I hesitated before accepting the device. Talking to boys on the phone wasn't exactly a regular occurrence for me. The breath I took didn't make it down to my lungs. "Hello?"

A deep sigh rattled the earpiece. "Sticks, thank God."

My heart stopped the wheeling and parked its cart. "You're drunk."

He snorted. "So I've been told."

My annoyance quickly dissipated as worry poured into my voice. "Mason, where are you?"

"Uh…Matt's room?"

Pulling the phone away, I stared at the screen a second and then returned it to my ear. "Are you asking me if you're in Matt's room?"

"I kinda was." On his end, a clinking of glass was followed by a gulp.

My eyes bulged. "Are you *still* drinking?"

At that, Jamey was right in front of me, palms in window-washer mode. "Hang up, Mags. This was a bad idea. You shouldn't be talking to him now."

"Wait, no," Mason begged. "Please. I just… I need to hear your voice. I'm guessing Jamey didn't tell you anything yet, or you wouldn't have taken my call, so this could be the last time you ever speak to me, and I— Please, Maggie."

My name coming from that mouth made me do stupid things. Stupid things like not hanging up. "Mason, are you okay?" And being concerned.

He laughed, but it sounded sad, pathetic really. "Am I okay?" Again with the questions. "No. And I can't remember the last time I was o—" A burst of giggles came over the line that were immediately dampened as if he'd covered the mouthpiece.

Mason's voice was muffled, so I couldn't hear what he said, but it wasn't hard to imagine what was happening on the other side of the line.

Mason was in that house surrounded by women pawing at him. It was no secret how attractive he was; all the women at school looked at him and whispered as he walked by. And those whispers weren't quiet. To make matters worse, by my estimation, twenty-six percent of the female students on campus knew the length and girth of his man parts.

Though I had no right whatsoever, jealousy burned like acid in my belly. "You sound busy," I snipped.

The speaker returned to his mouth. "No, I'm here. I was locking the door. And good news, I am in Matt's room. I earned a point."

"I wasn't keeping score."

"Ah, shit," he groaned. "How am I supposed to know when I win?"

"Easy. You're always winning."

"You couldn't be more wrong." What might be bedsprings creaked next, which then had me wondering what Mason's bedroom at the fraternity was like. And why he wasn't in it. "Ben said you wanted to talk to me tomorrow. It's almost tomorrow. I think. Hang on. I've gotta squint. My eyeballs are fuzzy. Why do they make numbers on watches so tiny? They're like you. Tiny. I bet you could see these tiny numbers with your tiny eyeballs." He blew out an exhale that sounded like the inside of a tornado. "You have beautiful eyes. I never told you that. I should have. Remind me to tell Sticks she has beautiful eyes."

Said *beautiful eyes* roamed up to Jamey's ceiling. "I wanted to thank you for today. No one's ever… It was sweet of you all to come for me. So, thank you."

Another pause. "Is that the only reason you wanted to talk to me?"

No. I wanted to apologize for not hearing him out earlier, but there was no point in offering an apology now. He wouldn't remember it.

"Yes."

"Well, that…sucks." Aaaand another swallow of liquid.

My lips flattened. "Can you please not drink when you talk to me?"

That earned me another stern look and the arms-crossed pose from Jamey. I held up a finger to beg for more time.

A popping sound suggested Mason gave up pouring the whiskey and started drinking it straight from the bottle. "Why did you say yes to Brady, but not me?"

Head jerking back, surprise barreled in at the detour this conversation had taken. I was trying to keep up here, but…yeah. I wasn't a miracle worker.

"What?"

"Our run by the lake that day. I invited you to the RAM house, and you made it seem like it was an insane idea. But Brady invited you, and you said yes. Why did you say yes to Brady and not me?"

How did he know about Brady, and why did he care?

"Because we're not friends, Mason." As the sharp thorn of truth drove into my chest, so did an ache I didn't want to admit was there. With one somewhat steady finger, I traced the stitching on Jamey's comforter. "Maybe that's why I didn't take your invitation seriously."

"Ouch." I flinched at that because he did sound hurt. "Alright, can I ask something of you in this one-sided friendship?"

Something that felt a lot like guilt curdled in my stomach. "What is it?"

"Stay away from Brady Hale. He's not a good guy."

My jaw hardened. "You're trying to control who I talk to now? You are in no position to do that."

A dark sound rumbled in the phone, his tone harsh. "I'd never control you, but I will watch out for you. Believe what you want, but I care what happens to *you*. I care about *you*. I miss *you*. I wanted you here tonight."

My non-cartwheeling heart got back to spinning again. "Mason, I——"

"What do you need me to do?" His voice changed to something deeper, rich and smooth like dark chocolate, the subtle sweetness spiking in my veins.

That voice reminded me of all the good moments between us, and I wanted more of that. Needed more of that Mason. I closed my eyes and imagined that voice talking to me in bed, running his fingers through my hair, along my neck, down my——

"Say the word, and it's done. I'll leave you alone. I'll disappear when you come over to the house if you don't want to see me. I'll never speak to you again if you don't want to hear my voice. I'll move out of Crescent Cove. Whatever you want, I'll do it. Just come back for my parents and Matt. Please."

I heard another clink of glass, and I shut my eyes as pain lit up my chest. This was the liquor talking. Not him. These words were as meaningless and empty as that bottle he was drinking from soon would be.

His father's words played in my head next. Those words hadn't been meaningless. They hadn't been empty. None had ever cut me so deep.

Never in my life have I been more wrong about anyone. You disgust me.

I shook my head as if Mason could see me. "I can't."

"No! Maggie, ple—" His words cut off, and I lifted my finger from the red button.

I handed the phone back to Jamey. "Thanks."

Frown pulling at his mouth, Jamey set his phone on the charger.

I watched him busy himself with organizing the papers on his dresser, shifting and tapping them into piles, avoiding my demanding gaze.

"Why are you mad at him?"

Jamey stiffened. "It really is best you don't know."

Unease expanded in my chest. I didn't need but one guess. Mason was drunk, at a party, and those giggles...

"He was with a woman, right?"

No answer. More shifting. More tapping.

"There really—" My words got caught on a lump in my throat, and I sucked in a faltering breath to clear it. "It's his life. He can do what he wants. Mason's not mine, never was, and never will be. So why does it bother you?"

It took a moment, but Jamey turned. I couldn't read the emotion behind those hazel eyes. Pity, anger, sadness? Maybe all three?

"Because they all made it seem as if he were heartbroken and puppy dog lost over you, Mags. When you left the ice cream shop today, Ben begged me to talk to Mason, help guide him on how to get you back, and like an idiot, I read too much into it, took it to mean something else. When I got to the RAM house tonight, I couldn't find Ben, and he wasn't answering his phone. Someone told me his room was on the second floor, and on the way to it, I found Mason's room first. The door was open, and I saw..." Looking away, he shook his head. "Well, he wasn't heartbroken or lost. He was fine. Like you said."

Shoulders slumped, he plopped down next to me on the mattress. "I'm angry because I helped them set up that elaborate plan today, and I was excited for you, like it was a scene out of some goddamn movie. You were supposed to happy cry, and Mason was going to proclaim his love for you and then kiss you in the middle of a gay parade."

"Half-marathon," I corrected. "And you watch way too many movies."

"I do. You're right. It didn't help that I've been going through a John Hughes phase lately." Facing me, Jamey's fingers wove through mine. "I just... I want that for you. I want you to step out of a church, wearing a frilly lavender dress—"

"I've never stepped *into* a church, much less *out* of one."

"—and see the guy with perfect hair who you've been crushing on, standing in front of a red sports car—"

"Mason drives a blue truck."

"—and he takes you to his house, and you sit on the dining room table—"

"Why are we not sitting in chairs? People eat on that table."

"—and he gets you a birthday cake, and before you blow out the candles, you stretch across the flames and have your first kiss."

"That sounds wildly dangerous. I'm wearing flammable clothing!"

"He's the kind of guy who would put the fire out with his tongue." Jamey's forehead met mine, expression earnest. "The point is, that's the fairy tale I envisioned for you. And when I saw Mason with Charlie—" He sharply drew back, and that was when the wince of all winces happened.

From both of us.

"Charlie?" Her name felt stiff on my tongue. "Charlie Price? The non-girlfriend slash lingerie model, Charlie Price?" I was gonna puke right here and now. "Forget it. Don't tell me. I don't want to know."

Holding my gaze, he threw my words back at me. "It's his life. He can do what he wants. Right?"

"Yeah," I croaked.

"You can't bullshit me, Blue Eyes. Your head may not want Mason, but your heart does." He was right. And I hated that he was right.

God... How was I this stupid? It was like Mason had me on a hamster wheel, spinning me through the emotions of lust, anger, jealousy, hurt, and 'round I went.

Truth was, it did hurt to think that Mason was with someone, but she had been nameless and faceless. Something fleeting. But Charlotte Price wasn't nameless or faceless. She was someone Mason had a history with. Nothing about her or the way he looked at her was fleeting. Mason cared about her. Loved her. He always would.

And I...I wanted that girl to be me.

"You're right," I said. "It's nowhere near my birthday, and I don't own a frilly lavender dress, but I want to be the inconsiderate asshole who sits on a dining room table and risks third-degree burns for a kiss from a boy with perfectly imperfect hair, who can't cook to save his own life, but I imagine he knows how to do a lot more than put fires out with his tongue."

Jamey cupped my face in his hands, wariness trickling into his features. "Don't kick me in the balls for this, but I think you should go back to the Scotts."

I lifted my head, surprised I could speak. "Go back? Why? They made my life miserable."

He shook his head as his hands dropped to the bed. "Let's be real, Mags. Has your life ever not been miserable? Have you ever been happy? I mean, truly?"

"I..." Oh, that answer was way too depressing.

"And that right there is why you should. Because nothing has changed. You're miserable with or without them and stuck in the exact same place you were months ago. You said it yourself. You need money to get out, and the Scotts have it to give in spades. Ask for a raise. Guilt does wonders. And when you've milked it for all it's worth, you leave."

Discomfort seeped across my shoulders. "Jamey..."

"What?" He shrugged. "I thought you were all about surviving. Seems like the perfect solution to me."

I ducked my head. "I can't do that. That's not right."

"Finally," he breathed and tipped my chin up, forcing me to look at him. "Then how about you admit the real reason you won't go back."

My lips parted. Shut. I blinked. "Which would be...?"

"You're afraid," he stated. "You want something you deserve most in this life, and you're terrified of never getting it. So you figure that if you don't take that risk, you can't get hurt again."

"What is that?"

"Love, Mags. You deserve to be loved."

chapter twenty-eight

maggie

Hours after Jamey delivered his truth bomb, I ambled through his dark kitchen toward a chair. Following right behind me with even less dexterity, Jamey released a loud yawn and blindly hit buttons on the Keurig. For whatever reason, he refused to turn the lights on in the morning. He said he needed time to decompress or decompose or…something. I'd come to learn that Jameson Hayes was not the most pleasant person when he first woke, and considering he was going on four hours of sleep, I thought it best to deal with zero light rather than irritate him further. A wise choice on my part since I'd spent those four hours of his REM cycle obsessing over Mason and Charlie. And what Jamey saw Mason doing to Charlie. Or vice versa.

Needless to say, my disposition could also be better.

"Dammit, what— Oh." After seating the K-cup into the machine on the fifth try, Jamey slammed the lever down, and things began to percolate.

He sighed in relief.

I busied myself with straightening the stack of napkins on the kitchen table, not that my tremor improved matters. "You don't have to drive me, you know. I'll walk."

"Yeah, I know," he grumbled as he leaned against the counter, arms folded. "Just like I know that after you walk home in the dark to take care of Poker and clean the house, you'll then ride your bike to the café to work the double shift that you weren't scheduled to work today. Then you're going to bust your ass alllll day long to make twenty bucks in tips, exhaust yourself, and bike back home at one in the morning. Again, in the dark. I know this because the routine hasn't changed in five years."

"See, that's where you're wrong," I objected. "It's Sunday. I'll make twenty-one dollars in tips after I bust my ass alllll day."

I couldn't see well enough to confirm, but I felt the weight of his glare settle on me. "Forgive me. How could—"

Knock-knock.

Both of our heads whipped around to look to where the knocking came from. The front door.

I licked my dry lips. "A bit early for an Amazon delivery. Is that Ben?"

"Seems a bit early for that, too. Only one way to find out." Though he tried to hide it, I heard the smile in his voice. Scampering away happily from his coffee that was still brewing, Jamey hoped it was his Scott at the door, and secretly, I wanted it to be the one with the blue truck, holding up a flammable purple dress and a birthday cake on a day that wasn't my birthday. I probably should watch whatever movie Jamey was referencing. Pretty sure no one would ever sit on a dining room table to make out.

I called bullshit.

Jamey opened the front door. "Well, you certainly know how to surprise me. I'll give you that. And I appreciate the frontal view this time."

Okay, my interest was officially piqued.

"Um, yeah. I'm really sorry about…everything." That was a female voice, not a male one. A female voice that was breathy and sexy without even trying. She'd been born to wield a voice like that.

My stomach tensed, interest instantly un-piqued.

"Can I— Is Maggie here?"

"Oh, shoot," Jamey groaned in mock regret. "You just missed—"

"I'm here," I said, reluctantly dragging my feet to the entry. I flicked on the kitchen lights as Jamey gasped.

"Mags, I thought you left!" He popped the screen door open to let Charlie inside. "Look who showed up. At four in the morning."

Charlie's face seemed to blanch a little, but it could have been the poor lighting. "Sorry, I know it's crazy early. I…can come back." Her tone and expression didn't match the sentiment. I sighed. If I sent her away, I'd have to endure another unwanted encounter later.

"Come in." I gestured to the display case on her left. "But watch the PEZ. House rule. You pick up what you knock down."

Jamey swiveled abruptly to hide his smirk. That had never been a house rule.

Gaze darting around the entry nervously, a peep toe boot met the vinyl floor as if she didn't trust it not to scuff her soles. Jamey had left enough room for her to squeeze by, and he shut the doors behind her.

I had to admit, seeing Charlotte Price, supermodel extraordinaire, in the Hayeses' modest bungalow, inspecting a display of cartoon PEZ dispensers would be laughable under any other circumstance.

"What can I do for you, Charlie?" Though I tried to fight it, my voice was tight and not at all welcoming. But, hey, I was still a little salty from when she'd snubbed me at school.

Tearing her gaze away from PEZ Garfield sporting a green visor, her lips parted. Shut. Then came the swallow. This was the first I'd seen her eyes clean of mascara and shimmery powder. Her skin was a bit pale but nearly flawless, a hint of a pimple on her chin. Her mouth wasn't pouty and glossed; instead, her lips were dry. Her hair was unusually greasy and slightly frizzed, and dark purple smudged the hollows of her eyes. Sadly, even after both Ava and Jamey used every tool in their beauty arsenal on me, I could never stand next to Charlotte Price on her worst day.

Which looked like today.

Charlie's eyes flicked to Jamey. "Is there somewhere we can talk? Just...us?"

"Ouch." Feigning hurt with a clutch of his chest, Jamey leaned down to press a kiss to my cheek. "I'll take the obvs clue and go to my room like a good little boy."

I was about to let Jamey leave when an idea struck. "Hang on." I stopped him, looking to Charlie lingering in the entry. "You may want to ask yourself how important this talk is to you because I want a favor in return."

She blinked. "Oh. Okay."

I cast a quick glance to Jamey, who appeared marginally intrigued. "Am I wrong, or did you insinuate at Ben's birthday party that you weren't happy with your hairstylist?"

She studied me a moment, perhaps looking for a sign that I was having an aneurysm. "No, you're not wrong. But my hair isn't easy to work with."

"Would you be open to someone else styling your hair?"

Brows pinching, she reflexively tugged at her limp locks. "Um, I guess?"

"Another question. I'm guessing you have some social media influence? I mean, you write something online, and people follow what you say?"

Charlie shifted, brows tugging even closer together. "Yes."

"Alright." I took a breath, never having done anything like this before and not at all comfortable with it. "If you want me to listen, then you need to stay after we're finished and let Jamey's mom do your hair. Cut, color, style, I don't care. And then explode that online. Ever since the shops by the marina opened, her business has been slow, and Ava's a damn good stylist. She could use the exposure that a name like yours could bring."

The wariness in Charlie's features softened, and she almost looked relieved. "That's it? Yeah, totally. I can do that."

I nodded, shocked she agreed so fast. "Okay, uh— Is the kitchen private enough?"

Charlie peered into the next room, which looked like a diner straight from the fifties. With a nod, she went in. The second she was out of view, Jamey curled a hand around my wrist, lips pressing to my temple. "Thank you."

And in those two strangled words, I heard it. All the worry and weight he hadn't wanted to burden me with. It made me question how much he'd been hiding from me, all the secrets he had kept buried.

Pulling away, Jamey's eyes met mine, his shining with tears. "I guess I better go wake up the Avanator. Hopefully, she didn't get into the appletinis last night."

"Hope hard, my friend."

Snorting, Jamey padded down the hall to Ava's room as I drifted into the kitchen. Charlie lingered near the Keurig, giving the abandoned coffee a longing stare.

"Would you like anything to drink? Coffee? Jamey just brewed some."

"I'll take tequila if you got it," she volleyed back, glancing over to me with a grin.

Stopping mid-way to the kitchen table, both of my brows shot to the ceiling.

The little color that remained in her face drained to match her white chiffon blouse that no doubt was purchased in a fancy boutique. "That was a poor joke. Sorry. A glass of water would be perfect, please. I'm pretty sure I'm dehydrated to a point I might need medical attention soon."

I waved toward the table. "Have a seat."

While I poured her non-alcoholic beverage, she took a chair, crossing long jeaned legs, sitting straight and prim as if prepared to balance a book on her head.

"Thank you." Charlie reached to take the glass from me, but I set it on the table in front of her instead. Though I'd only filled the glass three-quarters of the way, water had slopped over the brim, spilling onto the table's white top and my hand. I snatched a stray napkin out of the holder and sopped up the mess. Any benefit yesterday's marathon would have had on my tremor had vanished overnight.

Tearing her gaze away from my hands, Charlie offered me an awkward smile and then drew a tentative sip from the glass as if to test the lead levels in the water. Her fingers were clenched white. "I…ah. About last night—"

"No offense, Charlie, but I know where this is going, and I really don't want to hear about you and your boyfriend." I cut her off as I took my seat. "It's none of my business."

"Mason was never my boyfriend."

My eyes met hers. Jesus, even without a trace of makeup on, it was as if every insecurity I'd ever had was embodied in this woman. "So I keep hearing, but I was at the rally. I saw the way you were together."

She tucked her hair back with both hands. Ugh, even her ears were perfect. "You saw an act. The same one we've been playing for years. I mean, we did hook up and tried the relationship thing, but it was short-lived and forever ago. There's nothing between us but friendship. Mason makes appearances at parties, he puts on a show, lets me post pictures of us as if we were madly in love. It's all lies. For me. All to help me with my image."

"How so?"

"Our relationship draws public interest, which in turn gains me followers and improves my standing on social media. The more I'm in demand, the more designers desire me because I will draw a bigger audience to their show along with bigger names and bigger checkbooks, as well as a bigger contract for myself. My relationship with Mason also appeases my parents. Love doesn't matter to them. Never did. They want me with…well, someone of wealth and a pleasing appearance. Someone who will help keep me relevant, and by extension, keep them relevant. I didn't want to be in a relationship and neither did Mason. He was happy to fill the role, get my parents to back off. But it wasn't until today that I realized how selfish I'd been to ask him in the first place. How unworthy I was of Mason's friendship. How much he'd sacrificed for his loyalty to me."

I loosed a strained breath. I might have been a little hasty making this deal with Charlie. I wasn't sure I could keep up my end of this bargain for Ava. Before I realized what I was doing, I pushed my chair back to stand. "Look, I fail to see what this has to do with me—"

"*Iwasraped.*"

I froze halfway off my seat. Her words were choked and rushed, but I swore she said—

"I. Was. *Raped*." Not looking at me, Charlie repeated the words as if she didn't believe them either. I sat back down as a laugh absent of any humor bubbled past her lips. "God, five years and I still can't say it like a normal person. Do you think that I will? Do you think it gets easier to explain the moment the last piece of your innocence was ripped away from you violently and without your consent?"

I swallowed. I knew what it was to be assaulted, to be restrained and helpless while unspeakable things were done to you against your will, but not to the extreme she had.

My chest ached for her. "I think this is normal, Charlie. Whatever you're feeling is normal. Angry, sad, broken, weak, afraid, singularly or all at once… There's no *correct* way to feel or any timeline to feel it."

She stared at me a long moment. "I completely hate that answer." She sniffed, plucking a napkin from the holder in the middle of the table and dabbed her nose with it. I was sure Ava had tissues somewhere in her salon, but it didn't seem like an appropriate time to leave Charlie here by herself.

"Have you ever spoken to a counselor about this?" I asked.

Her head was already shaking. "I can barely think the words. I can't imagine what it would be like to dedicate an entire hour speaking them. Especially not with a stranger. They could sell my story, and there would be legal ramifications if that happened. I can't take that risk."

"But you're telling me now. I'm a virtual stranger. You barely know me."

She blew her nose into the napkin this time. "I'm only telling you because of Mason. Believe me, if it weren't for my epic stupidity, I wouldn't be. Outside of my…family, he's the only one who knows. So I'm taking a huge leap of trust here that you won't ever share my secret."

"I won't." I held her gaze, trying to assure her of that. "So, you were…fifteen at the time? Who was he?"

"He was— Correction. He *is* a famous designer." I waited while she took another sip of water, and I wasn't the only one having issues keeping the liquid contents inside the glass.

After a thick swallow, she set down her water. "You're right. I was fifteen. I hadn't broken through internationally yet or had any editorial work. My mother was convinced that if it didn't happen soon, it wouldn't. Back then, I wanted nothing more than to be a model. To have a career like my mother's. I would have done anything to earn her approval."

Pinching her eyes shut a moment, Charlie inhaled deeply. "Everyone in the industry knows that one good show from the right designer can launch your career overnight. Vinsant *is* that designer. He and my mother are old friends, and she asked him if he would do her a favor, let me walk in his next show. He said he'd have to meet me first and wanted me to come to his home rather than his studio. He wanted to give me his undivided attention."

Choking on a shattered laugh, Charlie balled the napkin in her hand like she wanted to strangle the thing. "And I agreed because I had no reason to question him. But Mason... He told me not to go. Begged me. He wanted me to wait to meet Vinsant until he could come with me. I thought he was being overprotective like usual. I mean, my mother was coming with me, so I ignored Mason and went. And everything was going fine until— Until she suddenly announced she was leaving to give us a better chance to get acquainted. I didn't know any better. I just figured that was the process. And I suppose it was because she...didn't come back until he was done."

As her meaning sunk in, it felt as if all the air had been stripped from the entire bungalow. "Are you saying that she *knew* what he would do to you?"

Nodding, Charlie's gaze dropped to the table. "Yes. I'll spare you the details, but yes. And when she came to...*collect* me, they signed the contracts. Right there in front of me."

My God. My eyes burned at the mere horror of it all. "What happened next?"

One shoulder rose and fell. "I walked for Vinsant, my career took off, and I never forgave my mother. She said it was a small price to pay for a lifetime of fame."

Jesus. "Did you ever work for him again?"

She slowly shook her head. "No, but we both got what we wanted, I guess." Lifting her gaze to mine, a sad smile pulled at her mouth, her eyes glistening with something far more profound than pain.

God...the betrayal she must have felt, and still felt.

"Charlie, I'm so sorry. Did Taylor ever...?" At her sister's name, her face paled further, and an old conversation tickled my memory.

In short, she pissed off the wrong designer, which ended her editorial and runway career.

"Oh, no," I whispered, settling back in the vinyl chair. "Your rapist was the designer she pissed off?"

"Yes." She took another drink of water, letting it linger in her mouth before swallowing. "I tried to protect Taylor, but you have to understand my mother. She's deceptive, manipulative. She's the kind of woman who dotes on her daughters in public, but in private, she pits us against each other. She would say it was all in the name of healthy competition, but there's nothing healthy and loving about how she treats us. It took me a long time to see that. She tore Taylor and me apart. My sister had never been as involved as me in modeling and high fashion. That upset my mother. She used my success to make Tay jealous and hate me, to motivate Taylor to want a modeling career. It worked. And when I heard Tay had a meeting set for Vinsant, I broke my NDA—which I paid for—and warned her. She didn't believe me, but when she was told that Vinsant wanted to meet at his estate, Taylor realized I might be telling the truth.

"The moment my mother suggested she should leave so they could get acquainted like I said she would, Taylor freaked and ran out the front door. And while I'm so grateful she listened to her instincts, there are consequences for rejecting someone as powerful as Vinsant. Taylor essentially killed any chance she had in high fashion, regardless if she wanted it or not. My mother was irate that I'd interfered, told Taylor that I'd sabotaged her career because I was the jealous one. To punish me, my parents placed me under their conservatorship, which basically means they are holding the money I've earned and my trust fund hostage. I'm forced to keep modeling, socializing, showing up to their clubs, charity events, build my social media platform… And every time I don't, they extend the terms of the conservatorship. They'll never let me out of it. They can't. They know that once I have my money, I'm done with modeling and with them."

"Does your father know what your mother did?"

"He knows she left me to run errands." Charlie watched her manicured fingers dance across the glitter-speckled tabletop. "He's under the impression that I seduced Vinsant. He's just a man after all, and it wasn't his fault he fell to temptation. I got what I wanted and shouldn't throw a tantrum because I wasn't prepared to deal with the consequences. The consequences being, of course, that I should have known what it would be like to bed a mature man. Because that's what my mother told him, and he trusts whatever she says. It's why I can't stand to go home. I can't bear to be around my parents, and Taylor…she's hated me for so long and has been so horrible towards me, it's hard to remember why I should love her. But I do know that I hate being a Price. I'm nothing like any of them. Or…at least, I didn't think I was." Uncrossing her legs, her gaze lifted to mine. "Mason was my only true friend, Maggie. And last night, I lost him. And me being here now… He'd be furious if he found out."

"I'm sure whatever happened, he'll forgive you."

"No. I really messed up this time. He's uh…" Her lips trembled as her throat worked. "Ben and Ethan told me it would be best to stay out of Mason's life until he wanted me back in it."

My forehead gathered. "Ethan?"

"Oh, sorry. Ethan is Mason's older cousin. He owns E's up in Pacific Cliffs."

Yeah, none of that helped. "E's…? Is that a store?"

"Nightclub. And Sinister's direct competition. It's also the last place I should have been last night." With both elbows on the table, she wrapped her hands around her water glass. "For weeks, my manager, agent, publicist have all been pressuring me to walk for Vinsant again. To walk for my rapist. To let him touch me, fit me in his clothes. To suffer his taunts… I've refused. But yesterday morning, I discovered my parents were the ones behind it all. They demanded I walk for Vinsant, and I told them no. Then they hung my conservatorship over my head like they always do, and I… I just lost it. Completely. I needed to talk to Mason because he's been the only one I could talk to about this, but things haven't been the same between us for a while. Lately, the only one who's been semi-decent to me was Tay. Go figure, huh?"

Shaking her head, Charlie nibbled her bottom lip. "Anyway, I was angry and frustrated and desperate. So, I did what I do best. Fuck up my life in the most epic way possible. I took Taylor to E's last night. We danced, drank, and then I took a drug that…left about five hours of my life blank."

My eyes popped open. "You…took a drug? On purpose?" I realized how awful I sounded far too late. "Sorry. I didn't mean it to come out like that."

"Yes, you did," she said quietly. "It was an honest reaction. I know it's shocking. And even more shocking, I like it, which I shouldn't because that was the very excuse my parents used against me in court. That I was a drug addict and couldn't be trusted to make financial decisions. But I'm not an addict. I— I just need to get lost sometimes. That's all I wanted last night. To not remember how awful my parents are, the things Tay has said to me, and…*him*. And I got my wish. I don't remember anything that happened after I took that pill." As a fresh sheen glazed her eyes, she squeezed her lids tight and bowed her head. "Unfortunately, I have about fifteen different angles on surveillance video to show me."

I took a breath. "What happened?"

"I went there to buy X, but the dealer in the club didn't have it. He was only selling Nine. I'd heard of it, and— Well, he made it sound amazing, and I needed something, or I was going to go out of my mind, so…I took it."

I wasn't so out of it that I didn't know what Ecstasy was, but… "What is Nine?"

"It's—" An inhale shuddered in her chest. "At first, it felt a lot like X. I was relaxed and smooth and drifting. But then I couldn't control myself. My urges. The things I did. Said. It stripped me of who I was. I was completely uninhibited, nothing more than an animal." Biting her bottom lip, she couldn't stop it from wobbling, her voice thick with tears. "Do you have any idea what it's like watching yourself groping and getting groped by people you don't know or remember? And you look as though you love every second of it?"

My insides curdled at the thought. "Oh, Charlie."

"That's not even the worst of it." As her lashes fluttered, a single tear streamed down her cheek. "My *sister* was with me, Maggie. I know our relationship is far from great, but she watched me hump and grind everyone and everything. Ethan's security stepped in before I was taken to the bathroom. By three men. If that had happened in any other club, even the ones owned by my parents—" Shivering, she wrapped her arms around herself. "Ethan… I don't know how he did it. There's not one picture of me, one video, or post on social media. He got Tay and me out of the club, but he didn't have anywhere safe to take us while I came down."

"That's why he took you to the RAM house."

Her throat dipped as she swiped the tears away from both cheeks. "He did. Carried me right to Mason's room, both of us covered in my vomit and who knows what else. Ben walked Taylor downstairs to their driver to take her back to school, and Ethan went into the bathroom to wash up from the mess I'd made. That's when I… I attacked Mason. There's no other way to put it. And that was when Jamey walked in. When I was on top of Mason with my hands—" Gasping, she covered her mouth as she tried to hold down a sob.

I wrapped my hand around hers that was still on the table, and her cry broke free, shattering the quiet.

Shaking her head, Charlie's words were rushed and warbled, but I understood them. "I made Ethan tell me what happened, and it's so awful, Maggie. Mason told me no. He told me to stop. And I didn't. I'm so ashamed of myself. I disgust myself. I know what that's like to be touched, *forced* to do things you don't want to do or have done to you. And I did that to my friend. My *best* friend. Even if he forgave me for that, I could never forgive myself."

I held her hand tighter. "It was the drugs, not you, Charlie. Mason will forgive you."

Charlie swallowed thickly, head swaying. "Maybe, but what he can't forgive me for are the things I did completely sober. The things I did before last night."

Releasing her hand, I sat back in my chair. "I don't understand."

Grabbing another napkin, she asked, "Do you remember that Taylor and I left Ben's birthday for my parents' dinner party?" She peeked up at me long enough to see me nod. "Vinsant was supposed to be at that party. In *my home*. My mother expected me to eat dinner across from my rapist. With a fucking smile." Rage shuttled through her as her mouth curled.

"Rather than refusing to attend or make up an excuse, which was what I should have done, I asked Mason to go with me and be my shield. I knew what I was really asking, and I knew he'd be upset. I just didn't realize how upset he would be, and I should have. I didn't have a chance to tell him that Vinsant would be coming because once I asked him to leave Ben's party for me, I knew... He'd had enough.

"After years of pretending, lying, being maligned by the media, this was the one thing he wouldn't do. Family means the world to Mason, and I was asking him to put them aside for me all because I'm too afraid to confront my parents and stand up for myself. Right then and there, he asked me to break off our fake relationship. Publicly. He couldn't stomach lying anymore, for y—" Her gaze flickered to my face before returning to the table. "For people to think less of him. For being with me."

"I don't think he thought of it that way."

"He should because I told him I would do what he'd asked of me, which was the only thing he'd ever asked of me, and...I didn't. I'd hoped—*selfishly* hoped—he'd change his mind. But the longer I put it off, the more upset Mason was with me, the more betrayed he felt. If I'd only done what he'd asked, *when* he asked, Taylor never would have stolen those earrings."

"You don't know that."

"No, but I did know what would happen when I went to E's last night." Dragging down a shaky breath, she folded her hands in front of her. "Like I said, our friendship had been strained, and I knew if I got wasted, Ethan would call Mason. And like all the times before, Mason would swoop in and save me. Feel sorry for me. Forgive me. And everything would be okay. He would go back to pretending, and everything would be as it used to be."

Her features twisted in disgust. "I actually didn't realize that's what I had been doing for years. I really didn't see it. I was using him, manipulating him. But I see it now. And last night, I was so caught up in my own selfishness, I not only put myself at risk, but Taylor, Ethan, his club, and the Scott name, too. Ethan could have lost everything because of me. Hell, he could be in jail right now because of me. And Mason did lose you because of me. I took advantage of Mason. Time and again. I exploited the guilt he felt for not being there to protect me from Vinsant. And do you want to know why he couldn't go with me that day? Because he was home, taking care of his dying sister, Maggie. That's the kind of person I am. A Price, down to the bone."

Lifting her gaze to mine, two more tears slid down her cheeks. "I just…I needed you to know that he is a *good* man. Everything Mason does is out of loyalty and love. Mason will do anything for his family. And if I'm being honest, I think the only reason Mason kept saving me all these years was that he couldn't bear to lose anyone else. The best thing I can do right now is walk away from him, and I'm begging you not to do the same. Mason deserves someone good and kind and selfless in his life. He deserves you, Maggie. He deserves to be happy."

He deserves to be happy.

I replayed those words on the drive home. Along with what Jamey had said last night. He'd been right. Fear was what had kept me away from the Scotts. Fear of being rejected again, hurt.

I had thought of Mr. Scott as a father figure, one who was decent and kind, nothing I'd ever known before. Mrs. Scott was a mother figure, one that I was desperate for. Matt offered me the warmth and security of a family. And Mason…a home for my lonely heart. And if that heart never felt love, then it wouldn't break when it was taken from me.

Love had never been a constant in my life. I'd only had fear as a companion.

Jamey stopped the car far enough down the road so as not to wake my father but close enough that I could see the strange Elantra in the drive. How many different cars had been parked in my driveway this year? Five? I seriously could not fathom how women didn't run screaming from this place once they realized their "date" was taking them to a shack in the woods.

As I popped the passenger door open, a brisk breeze infiltrated the heated air in the cab. I placed one foot in the dirt when Jamey's voice stopped me. "I put the key in your backpack. In case you change your mind." I twisted back around, mouth open and ready to protest. "Just hold onto it. You never know."

I didn't bother to argue again. He knew where I stood and why. As I knew he was a hopeless romantic who watched way too many movies and still believed in happily ever afters.

Walking through the dark woods, the fog misted my skin, the scent of ozone and earth dense, stinging the back of my throat. It reminded me of the night I met Mason, the sweet boy who was determined to be my hero. My knight in black armor.

I didn't need a knight.

I needed armor of my own. A sword to wield. A win in the battle to give me spark of hope that I wouldn't lose this war.

As the headlights from Ava's Focus swung around, the mist snaked along the forest floor, swirling in the beam. The clang of Poker's tags sounded louder as he neared, and a smile tugged at my mouth. I knelt and waited for his front paws to land on my thighs and then for him to lick every inch of my face.

"Yeah, I missed you, too. But I better not have mud all over my clothes, buddy." Knowing Poker and his love for digging holes, he had to be covered in the stuff. "Did you finish both bowls of food right away, or did you ration them out like I told you to?"

He chuffed in answer, and as he pushed off, a damp tail whacked me in the eye, spinning away to show me that he'd licked them clean.

I grunted to my feet, following Poker to his bowls. Not only was his food gone, but he was almost out of water, too.

Though Jamey had brought me here after we'd dropped Ben off at the RAM house, I should have just stayed. I wasn't selfless like Charlie said I was. I took every opportunity to stay away from this hovel, which kept me from being home with Poker. He was my responsibility, my family, and I'd left him here alone last night not because I was working to earn money to get us out of here but because I wanted to have fun. Turned out, last night wasn't remotely fun.

Once I had Poker de-mudded and fed, I assessed the kitchen damage. From the mess, I gathered Elantra Chick liked Thai. Or did Date Dad like Asian food? I grimaced.

I didn't want to know or imagine Date Dad.

Done cleaning, I left my father a note that I was going exactly where Jamey predicted I would. The café.

One bike ride across town later, my foot slapped at my kickstand to get it down. Turning into the headwind, I cinched my hoodie a bit tighter. The ride here had nearly frozen my ears off, and my fingers had gone numb. Any hopes at warming up inside the market were dashed away when I noticed Henry had all the doors open. But the man was nowhere to be found.

I blew on my cupped hands to warm them. "Henry?"

His voice carried from the back. "Hey, Mags! Just finishing up with Billy!"

Working the top off my ChapStick, I tipped up onto my toes to find the men were unloading a crate of ice and what looked to be yellowtail. "Hi, Billy! How's Trisha feeling? She get over that bronchitis?"

They set the crate down, and Billy repositioned his ballcap that had lost its company logo to fish guts and sweat long ago. Two aquamarine eyes met mine beneath the brim, and the tan lines on his face disappeared with his smile. Looking at the man's upper half, no one would guess that beneath his yellow bib were legs whiter than that ice in the crate.

"Better. She's almost finished with her antibiotics. I'll tell her you were asking about her, Mags. Trish'll appreciate that." How he could speak so clearly with that wad of tobacco in his cheek, I'd never know.

"Mags, I have a bag right there by the register for you." Henry pointed as if I couldn't see the green tote on the counter. "Help yourself if you're in a hurry!"

Finished with my lip balm, I snapped the cap tight. "Thanks."

As Henry and Billy fell into a discussion about their other love, football, I meandered toward the register. Peering past the fabric handles, the bag was filled with a mixed bag of items Henry had been donating over the past month. Next to that bag was a ledger with…receipts stapled to it. Strange. Henry used the same accounting program as Ava and scanned his receipts because he didn't like paper cluttering his store. I usually wouldn't be so nosy, but even upside down, I swore I read…

What in the hell?

With another check to the back, Henry was now demonstrating either a ritualistic monkey dance or a touchdown. I slid around the counter to take a closer look at the ledger. My stomach was suddenly filled to the brim with lead.

Right there on the header was the name MASON SCOTT and next to that was a positive balance of…two hundred dollars. My throat practically convulsed as I swallowed. Each day of the week was listed below, along with numbers totaling anywhere from twenty-six to thirty-one dollars for each day. Sunday was empty, but that was today's date on the header. Next to the ledger was what I would guess was today's receipt for thirty dollars and some change for oranges, apples, canned soup, rice… Everything that was in today's bag.

I flipped the page back to see last week was completed, the receipts corresponding to each day to total two hundred dollars. I flipped the page again. And again. All the same. All with Mason's name written on the header. *What is this?*

"Ah…you weren't supposed to see that."

"Henry?" I croaked, too confused to feel ashamed for poking around in his books. "Why is Mason's name written on these pages?"

"It's…" His cheeks went scarlet. Looking away from me, he slid his hands into his stained white apron. "It's what it looks like. Mason's been donating money every week for your basket. He asked me not to tell you."

"He—" I blinked. "*Mason's* been donating to my basket? How long?"

One cheek puckered as he slid a look my way. "Started the day of that birthday party you went to. Mason's been coming down here every few days to make sure I have enough to fill your basket."

My throat thickened and seemed to only get tighter the longer I stared at that ledger.

I just…I needed you to know that he is a good man. Everything Mason does is out of loyalty and love.

My movements were jerky as I flipped the book back to today's page. "Henry, I have to go. Can you…?"

Chuckling, his hand wrapped around my shoulder. "Yeah, Mags. I'll put it out for you. Go on. And if you could, ask Mason what you give to a sick lemon."

"A sick lemon?" I cocked my head at Henry. "I don't get it. Why give it anything? Wouldn't you just throw it away?"

Henry laughed harder, shaking his head. "Oh, Mags, no. You give it lemon-aid."

chapter twenty-nine

maggie

As soon as I pulled up on my Schwinn, the door to Crescent Lake Estate's guardhouse opened to a man with eyes that measured me much like the first time I had come here. I instantly cursed myself for not having brought him a bribe in the form of chocolate and sugar.

"Good morning, Bernard. The Scotts aren't...expecting me. If you wouldn't mind calling—"

Movement out of the corner of my eye tempted my gaze to shift to the gates. I sat dumbly as they swayed open, my heart thumping. Either the man had orders to let me in should I return, or he was using me for target practice.

I was leaning toward the latter.

I placed my foot on the pedal as I said, "Thank you, Bernard."

It wasn't until I made it past the gates did I realize what I hadn't heard and what hadn't happened. He'd never slammed the door in my face. Never leered at me. Not once. I risked a glance behind me to see that Bernard was still standing there, watching me. Huh.

Pedaling along the paved road, whatever bit of sun had risen over the horizon was now hidden behind the building clouds. I rolled up the Scotts' driveway to find it was empty, and my stomach toppled over at what that meant. Mason wasn't here. I guess it was silly to expect that I'd see that blue truck, especially since he lived at the RAM house, and when we spoke on the phone last night...it didn't sound like he'd be without company.

Telling myself not to get upset was an epic fail. Disappointment rode me hard, along with a lot of other emotions I would prefer to ignore.

But I wasn't here for something unattainable, a fantasy. I was here for a job. For the Scotts. However faulted and broken, these people were good and decent. People who cared about me and this town. I saw that now.

I unzipped the front pouch of my bag, withdrawing the new housekey and the slip of paper with Ben's handwriting scrawled across in a sequence of four numbers. A new alarm code. Hurt and a wave of irrational anger rolled through me. But what did I expect?

Once I slipped inside, I took note of the updated keypad, but it was disengaged, which was odd. The Scotts always had it set. Maybe Mr. and Mrs. Scott were home. In hindsight, I probably should have rung the doorbell. A bit late for that.

Standing in the foyer, I took in the living room and clutched the shoulder strap of my bag until my fingers ached. As the *tick-tick-tick* of the grandfather clock mocked me, my gaze fell to the couches... Just like that, the memories slammed into me, knocking the air out of my lungs.

You. Disgust. Me.

Okay, I needed a moment to ease into this. Like a wuss, I thoroughly assessed the basement and main floor before going up to the second level. Recalling the last time I'd been on these steps, my clammy palm slicked along the handrail.

From the hall window, the dim morning light spilled across the landing with the crystalline blue surface of Crescent Lake glittering in the backdrop, and beyond that, the lush redwoods and firs lined the walking trails I was painfully familiar with.

Matt's bedroom was closed to signal that he was home, which would explain the alarm being disengaged. Mason's door was wide open. I stood in his doorway and blinked. Twice. I must be imagining things. His carpet was visible, and if that wasn't shocking enough, his duvet wasn't in a lump on the floor. The bed wasn't technically made, but there was a noticeable effort.

I was ready to head back downstairs and grab the cleaning supplies when a noise stopped me. It had come from the room I wasn't allowed to go in. The room with the door that was always shut. Faith's room.

I tipped my head to the side. Something large was on the floor, blocking the light. It seemed odd to place anything that big near the door, but perhaps someone had fallen...? I had promised Mrs. Scott that I would never enter this room, but since I was all about crossing ethical lines today, I might as add one more.

I turned the knob and peered inside.

What I saw behind that door shattered my heart.

Any wisps of lingering anger and resentment vanished. The walls that I'd been building, desperately holding up, crashed. All it took was this one moment, and everything hard and hateful that I had turned into was no longer.

Mason was laying on a shaggy blue rug, gripping a plush butterfly pillow to his bare chest like it was the only thing keeping him on this side of sane. Across his back were remnants of black marker, my nickname on his skin. Next to him was an empty bottle of JD on its side, but it was capped as if he were afraid to taint the room with its poisonous scent.

My gaze swept from one wall to the next, absorbing the space that was full of color and life. This was what I imagined a little girl's room should look like. Crayon drawings were tacked to a corkboard, the dustless shelves were filled with completed Lego sets, the ceiling was painted to look like the night sky, and every wall held a scene, the same images on Matt's canvases. Mermaids in the ocean depths leapt onto a shore where unicorns raced through the woods and chased radiant butterflies above a clearing of vibrant flower beds...

This was a room of fantasy, to take Faith away from the reality of her illness, to comfort whatever fears she may have had, to ease the pain she had to endure.

Mason pushed himself to a sitting position and wiped his face on his shoulder, keeping his back to me. "Sorry, Mom. I thought you and Dad left. I didn't mean to—" When his head moved to the side, he inhaled sharply, quickly tossing a purple blanket over the JD bottle. "I'll clean up, I promise. Could I have a minute?"

His voice was hoarse and thick as if the mere effort of forming words was too much for him. With a rough sniff, he swiped more tears from his face using the back of his arm this time.

His skin was paler than I remembered, hair dull and longer than he usually kept it. Mason's spine was more pronounced, but weirdly, his muscles were bulkier. At nearly twice my size, his stature was slumped, head hanging low. This wasn't the confident, strong man I had known Mason to be.

This was a boy, broken and lost.

He's not eating, he's lost weight, he's drinking far too much, and he hasn't slept more than an hour or two a night since you've been gone.

I hadn't seen what was happening to him. I'd been too caught up in my anger.

He was in so much pain, exposed and vulnerable. I couldn't help but reach out to him.

As I knelt next to Mason, his eyes squeezed shut, the hollows sallow and marked by dark smudges. Though he tried to turn away from me as if ashamed, he couldn't hide the tear tracks staining his cheeks, nor the ones crawling to the surface in heavy swells.

He was so much like his father in this moment.

With a hesitant hand, I cupped his jaw, the thickened stubble rough as it poked my palm. The left side of his upper lip was freshly scabbed from a cut, the flesh swollen and red. His cheek was also recently bruised, the scent of whiskey lingering around him like an impenetrable haze.

I gently caressed his cheek, but my fingers were unsteady, so it was a struggle not to stab him in the eyeball. With one stroke of my thumb, his eyes flew open.

Lips gaping, he blinked several times. "Sticks?" His glazed eyes began to clear, studying my features as though he didn't trust his own vision. "Are you... Are you really here?"

"Yeah. I'm really here." I thumbed his face dry, careful of his wounds. He didn't speak, but as his lips closed, they trembled like he was trying to hold back a tidal wave of sorrow, but it was overtaking him, pulling him under before he could take his last breath. I imagined being in this room, surrounded by his sister's memories, looking directly at her doppelganger would put even the hardest of men in a freefall.

In a moment of compassion mixed with bravery and a dash of stupidity, I looped my arms around his neck to catch him, ground him here to the present. He may shove me off, yell at me, tell me to go to hell. I didn't care. I couldn't walk away when he was hurting this much.

Just as things got super awkward, Mason's arms swept around me, hauling me into his lap. He crushed me to him without a centimeter of space between us, his hand cradling the back of my head. A choppy exhale escaped him as though my touch had broken through an invisible dam blocking his air.

It was inappropriate and wrong, and yet, I couldn't help from threading my fingers through his hair, the thick strands softer than I remembered. As Mason nuzzled his scratchy jaw against my neck, his lips grazed my pulse point, shallow breaths dancing across my skin.

Suddenly, Mason's entire frame began to shudder as if every beat of his heart brought him closer to splintering apart.

I held him tighter. "Mason? Are you okay?"

"No." His head shook against my shoulder. "I miss her." Mason's voice was strangled and filled with so much anguish, my heart clenched for him. "It hurts to be in this room, but I keep coming back in here. It hurts to stay in this house, but I can't seem to leave it. It hurts to close my eyes and see... Everywhere I look is a reminder that she's gone."

He drew back enough for his forehead to rest against mine, and I stared at his long lashes that shielded his eyes as more tears crawled to the surface.

"I'm sorry I forced myself into your life," I said. "No wonder you hated the sight of me."

His lashes swept open, peridot gaze colliding with mine. "Oh, Sticks, no. That— I meant what I said. I never hated you. *Never.*" A deep crease furrowed his brow, his eyes filling with regret. "God, the things I've said and done to make you think that. I was such an ass. But I wasn't trying to hurt you. Not really. I just needed to push you away. To protect my family and me. I'm sorry. I'm—"

"It's okay."

"No." His head shook. "It's not okay."

Mason took his hand from my lower back, and I watched as the tip of his finger skimmed my brow, down my nose, cheekbones, then traced my lips as though he was proving a point to us both. That the same pattern had been drawn on another girl, another time, and the outlines matched.

His hand curved to fit my cheek, molding to me. "I met this amazing girl who was funny and quirky and so different. Who made me want to be different. And in an instant, I realized I couldn't have you in my life in any capacity. Letting you in, knowing you would have hurt more because you would eventually leave us, and I would be empty all over again. I've lost too much already. I—" His voice broke as the next words came. "I had to protect my heart because there's nothing left of it, just muscle and tissue, a shell of a beating organ. I gave her the most important part of me until we were together again."

There were….no words. The more I learned about Faith, the more I understood the chasm of emptiness she left behind. They were all suffering, and I couldn't imagine what hell they had gone through and were still going through.

"At some point, I realized it was too late. I let you in, began to care about you more than I wanted to. I needed your friendship more than I could admit. But please know that it's you I miss. It's you, I see. No one else." Mason rested his head back on my shoulder, wrapping himself around me, drawing us together like he couldn't tolerate a hair's distance. "Maggie… I'm a bastard for asking, and I don't deserve it, but I'm begging you. Please don't hate me anymore. You don't have to be my friend or be in my life. Just please don't hate me."

I squeezed my eyes at his plea. I knew how that felt. To be hated and abhorred when all you needed was a scrap of compassion and kindness. There was a time that I would have given anything to have my father love me. For him to hold me, offer a moment of affection, speak one word to let me know he cared. Just once. And, if I were being honest, there was a small part of me that still held out hope for that day. I knew all too well that denying yourself to feel empathy could destroy your soul.

The reality of what I'd done slammed into me with an indescribable weight. I had turned into the one thing that I had promised myself that I'd never become.

"I don't hate you, Mason."

A heavy breath rattled his chest, gaze lifting to mine. "God, how... How are you here right now? After last night—" He flinched as if the memory stung him all over again.

He didn't know that Charlie had visited me, and he seemed too raw to discuss it now.

"I'm here because I found out today that someone very kind and generous has been donating food to my basket. And I thought he should know how grateful I am to him."

Groaning, Mason's head swung side to side. "You weren't supposed to know. It was nothing. It—"

"It wasn't nothing. It was everything. To the people who need it. To me. Even when you thought I stole from your family, you still donated that money. You have no idea what that meant to this community."

He cringed away from me. "I don't think I can stand you praising me after what I've done to you."

"Then how about you accept my gratitude. I can never thank you enough."

He didn't seem on board with that either, but he didn't argue.

Tearing my gaze away from him, I looked to the room again. It was impossible to dismiss that it looked like it had been preserved, as though Faith had never left. What it must have been like for them to have me here, a ghost of a beloved memory.

I held his face, fingers caressing the prickly hair on his jaw as he kept his head lowered. "Would you share her with me?" I asked. "I want to know her. What was Faith like?"

His head shot up, blinking unclear eyes, and I instantly regretted asking. I'd stepped over a boundary that I was not welcome in. Mason tipped his chin back to the ceiling, his throat bobbing with a thick swallow, confirmation that I'd asked the one question everyone knew never to ask. Everyone but me.

I was ready to apologize, take it back, tell him to forget I asked, when he said, "You would have liked her. Faith's heart was a lot like yours. Kind. Full of empathy." His thumbs drew some sort of design on my back, but I couldn't decipher what. "She was so sweet. We would sometimes watch *America's Funniest Home Videos* as a family, but most of them were of people getting hurt, and she would get angry with us for laughing." A smile teased the corner of his lips. "She'd get off the couch and stomp her feet and everything. And when she realized where meat came from, she declared she was a vegetarian, and we all should be, too. You can imagine in this house she had her work cut out for her."

Bringing his head back down, his line of sight locked onto something behind me. "She was imaginative, too. Faith would make up stories to convince me to take her to my room because she didn't want to be alone. I would never tell her no, but sometimes I fought her just to see how creative she could get. She would say silly things like the unicorns were filing their hooves on her bedpost. Or that the mermaids were keeping her up by throwing starfish at her head."

His tired eyes drifted back to mine, and it seemed as if his pain had eased slightly. "She loved music. All kinds. She liked to sing with me. Her voice was…"

With that faraway look, I could have finished his thought. "Beautiful?"

"God, no. It was awful." Oh. "The girl's tone could shatter glass. That didn't stop her, though." Mason drew me closer, relaxing into me as if he was prepared to talk about his sister all day. I would listen. "She loved dancing, too. Matt would pick her up, and they'd twirl…" His eyes clouded over again. "She had the best laugh, one of those that were so infectious, before you knew it, you were laughing along with her." His dark lashes rested on his cheeks as his voice dropped to a whisper. "Her laugh was a lot like yours, too. Though you…you don't laugh very much."

Hesitantly as if he was worried about smearing the ink, Mason dragged his fingers across the infinity tattoo on the left side of his chest. "This is for her, 'cause she'll be etched here on my heart—" He didn't look at me as he struggled with his next words. "Until the…" Shaking the rest of the thought away, he traced the bright teal and purple wings of the last butterfly, the one that touched the infinity symbol. "You know that each of us has this tattoo. But this…this is her butterfly. Matt used to tell her stories about being flown away from all of it. On the back of a giant butterfly. That was her one wish. This room is full of the bedtime stories he'd tell her at the hospital. When it was too much, and she was scared, she—"

Those deep peridot eyes pooled with more tears. And it was if I could see them, the silenced memories that were too painful to speak of. There were no words I could offer him, no platitudes to ease his hurt.

He had to feel it to let it go, but I wasn't sure if that day would ever come for him.

I didn't know why I did it, and before I could stop myself, I dipped low and pressed my lips to her butterfly. His chest shuddered.

"Sticks?" My name grated out of his throat, and I froze, lips hovering over his smooth skin. I pinched my face, having realized I was not respecting any boundaries today.

Mason cleared his throat roughly. "With the risk of scaring you off...could I ask you to do something for me? It's okay if you say no. In fact, I expect you to."

I tipped my chin up to meet his eyes, our faces mere millimeters apart. "What is it?"

As his brows furrowed, his head lowered, gaze anchored somewhere between us. "Would you...come to bed with me? I just... I don't want to be alone right now."

I think my heart hit my sternum.

"Shit. I— I didn't mean it like that. Sorry, I haven't...had much sleep. I'm not going to try anything. I swear."

"O—okay." Probably should have dedicated a second and a few brain cells to that answer before giving it.

His body wilted, all the tension bleeding out of him. Mason threaded his fingers with mine and stood, guiding me to my feet. I was glad he was holding my hand because my vertigo decided to make an appearance.

As I dipped to one side, Mason caught me, his reflexes uncanny even when he was this hungover. He tugged me closer as his gaze found mine. "You okay?"

"Yeah, sorry." I shut my eyes until the world righted again. "Just needed a second there."

"Take all the time you need."

My heart skipped an entire beat. Mason...he was patient with me, never rushed me to go faster than I was able to, and he never made me feel weak or less than.

Faith...had been lucky to have him as a big brother.

Opening my eyes to him, I inhaled a shaky breath. "I'm good."

He didn't look convinced, and he kept a hold on my hand as we walked out of Faith's room and into his. This entire morning was surreal, and all I could concentrate on was how large his hand felt in mine, how thick his calluses were against my palm, his grip firm but gentle, and that somehow, fingers twice the size of mine fit perfectly in my hand. His body exuded power and strength, and though he towered over me with the top of my head barely coming to his broad shoulders, I didn't feel threatened next to him. I felt strangely...safe. Protected.

It wasn't something I was used to.

Mason had two sides, a duality at complete odds. One was adept at hurting, could cut me in two with his words. But the other Mason was kind, full of love, stumbling through a world that was darker than I realized, and like me, he was clawing his way out to find the light. This sweet Mason was the one I was desperate to win control. But if I knew anything about men, it was that they would succumb to the darkness within.

Though I'd been in his room countless times, this was different somehow. Still holding my hand, he tucked the covers and sheets to the side with care, as though he wanted to prove that his intentions were pure. Releasing my hand, he stepped back and waited for me to climb in first. Mason's eyes were wary, like he expected me to knee him in the crotch and make a run for it.

I wouldn't.

I toed off my sneakers, clambered into his high bed, the mattress caving under his weight as Mason followed me. My belly dipped. Oh, God. I knew there wasn't a shred of impropriety on Mason's end, but...was this really happening?

Mason pulled the covers over us before settling in. I'd left at least a foot of space between us, but his arm wound around my waist and drew our chests together like this was so normal. When the planes of our bodies met, shock paralyzed me. Mason tucked my head beneath his chin as his legs rested against mine. A pleasant shiver trilled through me, heart sputtering and stammering as his hand skimmed up my spine, finally stopping to curl his palm around the back of my neck.

I was tucked inside his cage as if I were the most precious thing in the world to him. My eyes slid closed, blocking out the little sunlight that leaked through his heavy curtains, desperate to cherish this and the way his chest rose against my cheek, heart thumped in my ear, arms of steel wrapped around me. His fingers combed through my hair as though he could feel how tense I was, encouraging me to relax. I couldn't. No one...no one had ever held me like this. Jamey, I guess, had come close, but this was not the same.

A sliver of fear sliced into me that this was all a dream, and I forced my eyes back open to hold onto this moment. My gaze landed on the black link of the infinity tattoo, his sister's name in elegant script. I wasn't sure why I was so drawn to it, but it seemed just as exposed and vulnerable as Mason. As if he needed help protecting her now.

I placed my palm over the pain embedded in that ink, and there was no mistaking the tremor that wracked his body at my touch. The hand combing through my hair abruptly lifted and tore off me. I tilted my head to see his forearm was covering his eyes, bottom lip warbling a little.

"Mason?"

"Sorry." His throat worked as if he'd swallowed rocks. "I didn't realize how hard this would be."

"I'll go." As I began to pull away, his other arm held us together.

"No. Don't," he begged. "Stay. Please. I need to do this."

Not sure what that meant or what to do or how to help him, I shifted so I was higher than he was on the pillow and drew him against me this time. The arm slung across his eyes lowered to drape around me again, and I thought I did a decent job of ignoring the fact his face was all up in my boobs.

Mason held me closer, almost too tight to breathe, his shakes worsening to the point that the bed quaked. When I was locked in my body during a seizure, I was usually alone and terrified that I may not wake up. But I remembered the moments Jamey was there, the way he would talk to me, comfort me, let me know that I was safe and wasn't alone.

I had no clue why I said the following four words, but they came to me then. "I've got you, Mason."

And that was all he needed. The sound that broke free... I prayed I never heard it ever again.

Struggling to comfort his pain in some way, I ran my fingers through his hair, across his broad back, down his tattooed shoulder and arm. The grief ripped out of him without mercy. I wasn't sure what he was seeing, where his head was right now, but if I didn't know any better, it seemed as though he was just coming to terms with Faith's loss, and five years of denial and sorrow had come crashing down all around him.

I didn't know how long it took before his shakes eased, until his ragged breaths came even and slow. As his body relaxed into a deep sleep, his weight grew heavier. I didn't dare move.

Bound in his arms, being here for him... As wrong as it was to feel this way, this was perhaps the best moment of my life. I knew it didn't mean the same to him. He didn't want to be alone, and I happened to be here. But for me, it was everything, and that was what scared me so much.

The other side of Mason would break me over and over again, and if only to catch of glimpse of this sweet boy, I would let him destroy me until there was nothing left.

I'd somehow fallen asleep. Checking the clock, it had only been an hour. Mason was using me as a teddy bear, and damn, he was heavy. Like he was made of cement. How was I even breathing? The head smooshing my breasts prevented my lungs from fully expanding, his hips pinned me into the mattress—which meant his man parts were on my thigh, but I would have to process that and the boob thing another time—and a leg covered in wiry hair immobilized both of mine. One of my arms was trapped between us, so that left me with one free limb.

Clutching the side of the mattress, I fisted the sheet and pulled with all my might. All my might got me one centimeter and beads of sweat on my upper lip. It was so freaking hot in here. I really needed to crack a window next time I agreed to this. I internally scoffed at that. Like there would be a next time.

Back to the task at hand. *Let's see here.* If I… Yep, that could work.

I twisted my hips into the bed to create an inch of space between us. By jacking my left knee up, I was able to slide my right leg out and hooked it on the side of the mattress, shifting me lower on the bed. Assessing my new position…

Oh, dear.

Those full, pink lips were now a breath from mine. Thick lashes dusted his high cheekbones, hair mussed in that artfully disheveled way, features devastatingly striking. Each muscle was cut and molded flawlessly as if he'd been sculpted by artists. Damn, he was ten kinds of wow.

Okay. Creepy ogling time needed to stop.

By some magic I didn't know I possessed, I was able to slink and slide the rest of the way out from under him, and how he didn't wake up, I'd never know.

Grabbing my sneakers, I crept across the carpet and shut Mason's door behind me. I ducked inside Faith's room, placed the pillow and blanket back on the bed where I assumed they came from, and then grabbed the empty whiskey bottle. With another door soundlessly shut, I went downstairs to evaluate the damage.

Damage was an understatement.

The fridge situation was worse than I feared. Styrofoam filled the shelves, everything in the freezer required ninety seconds in the microwave, and there was a glaring absence of fresh fruit and vegetables. The pantry was shockingly messy for being so bare, and there were a lot of bags with large plastic clips holding them shut.

My bike could never handle the load necessary to replenish half of what they needed. A vehicle would be best. Using the house phone, I called Jamey, and luckily, Ben had just picked him up. As an added bonus, Camden was already planning to drive BB over since it was still at the RAM house.

In the meantime, I started defunking the kitchen. I got rid of all the Styrofoam containers and wiped down the fridge. There was nothing but condiments left when I was done. After a good scrub to the counters and sink, I threw out the trash.

As I began to attack the pantry, I heard the lock turn on the front door, male voices filtering through the house. I drifted into the living room, greeting Ben and Jamey as they entered the foyer.

Camden was last to file in as he looked over to say, "It's good to see you back here, Maggie."

"It's good to be…" As my words trailed off, my hands flew to my mouth on a gasp. Ben had a black eye and Camden's lip was busted. "What happened to all of you? Mason's face took a beating, too."

Camden's sleeves stretched as he folded his arms across his chest. A cocky grin graced his mouth. "Just another night at the Ram House. The party doesn't start until a fight breaks out."

Ben's brow climbed up his forehead, flinching when he realized that was a bad idea. "Guess I've been doing parties all wrong."

"Personally, I think it sucks that they can all pull off black and blues and still look sexy," Jamey grumbled. His black eye had finally healed, and while he could totally rock a runway next to the Scotts, his face didn't handle bruises as well.

"Hey, Maggie?" Sliding around the couch, Camden stuffed his hands into his pockets, unease tightening his features as his gaze met mine. "I— If you think you can stomach it, I would like to apologize. I wasn't sure when the right time would be, but I can't keep standing here, pretending all that shit hadn't gone down. I hope that you can forgive me. If not today, someday."

"I already have. It's okay, really."

He cringed, stocky frame tensing. "It's not okay, Maggie. I should have given you a chance to defend yourself and not jump on the wagon with the rest of the band. Taylor can be immature, yeah, but none of us thought she..." After a hard expel of air, his eyes filled with genuine remorse. "I'm sorry."

"Why are you Scotts so good at apologizing?"

"Lots of practice. We fuck up a lot," Ben stated. "It's what we're known for."

I lifted a brow. "It's not the hot bodies, good looks, charming personalities, or the fact you curse every other word?"

Camden's grin was pure sin. "I knew you thought I was hot."

Ignoring that, I said, "I need to go to the store unless they plan to live on mustard and Italian dressing. Who's gonna come?"

Camden cleared his throat, sliding me another smirk.

I stared at him. "Seriously? What is that?"

Eyes twinkling, he laughed.

chapter thirty

mason

Without any concept of how many minutes or hours had passed, I woke to find the little body that had been curled up next to me was missing. The sheets were cold, and I felt a pang of something dark and bitter shoot through me that had nothing to do with the pounding behind my eyes. Although, that wasn't helping. With remnants of Jack on my breath and in my blood, I had overdone it by at least half a bottle.

I'm tired of watching you scrape bottom.

Cam hadn't been wrong. There had been way too many mornings like this. I needed to get my shit together before my parents hosted an actual come-to-Jesus meeting.

I dangled my head over the side of the bed, finding those raggedy white-ish kicks were gone. Stupid of me, yeah, but I had expected to wake up with Maggie next to me. I guess the drunk-off-my-ass-crying jag wasn't a turn on.

I want to know her. What was Faith like?

No one… No one had ever asked me about Faith before. Not like that. It was always: *How did she die? Did you try any clinical trials? She had how many rounds of chemo?* Maggie had wanted to know her, the beauty and light my sister had brought to this world, rather than the darkness she had left in her absence. And no one had ever touched me like Maggie had, either. As though she understood the devastation and heartache that these tattoos represented. In the moment, she didn't seem to care how weak I was, how raw my emotions were, and once I let them out, there had been no stopping them.

Or maybe she did care because she ran. Again.

This was why I drowned myself in whiskey, women, and bad decisions. It was easier and far less humiliating.

Every moment with you is precious to me, even the sad ones.

The words I had once said to Faith played through my head. I had refused my sister when she'd asked me to only remember her as she was before she was sick. I had lied to her. Unintentionally.

I'd been so naïve to what pain the future would bring, and I'd give anything to have the last night with Faith out of my head. I never spoke of it, I never acknowledged it, but my memories were rooted too deep, and they were far too dark to ever see the light. If I couldn't forget what was inside of me, I'd do everything I could to hide it.

Just laying here in bed, every ounce of sweat, grime, and whiskey itched my skin. I dragged my ass into the shower, hoping I could wash it all away along with the shame that the water and soap couldn't. Not bothering to wait for the water to warm, I scrubbed the fragmented letters off my chest and back still on my skin from yesterday. The shower floor blurred in my vision as my stomach roiled, and my throat felt like it was coated with sand. I tilted my head back, heavy and loose, drinking down gulps of the hot spray, but it didn't quench my thirst. Once dried and dressed, I popped back a few aspirin and headed downstairs.

Disappointment demolished any hope of eating when I found the fridge was empty of to-go boxes, eggs, lunch meat... Christ. Starved and craving any kind of juiced fruit, I knew I would have to leave the house. If I found my balls, I could go to the café and order from Maggie. Maybe she and her cop boyfriend wouldn't throw me out on my—

Ah, shit. My truck was at the RAM house.

Matt slunk down the stairs, hair damp, eyes half-lidded. His chin sported mottled purples, bottom lip swollen. Though he'd taken a shower, he hadn't scrubbed his nail beds very well because they were still marked with coal or lead or whatever he used to sketch with.

Taking a moment to study my wounds, he said, "How's your face?"

"Had worse. Yours?"

"Still pretty enough to get laid." He opened the pantry, shoulders dropping at the empty shelves. "Is there anything outside of cereal?"

"Nope, and you'll have to squirrel it. We don't have any milk or wheels."

Flinging his head back, Matt groaned. "Perfect." He took his phone out and opened an app. "Guaranteed this time of day will take an hour to get an Uber."

"Maggie was here," I threw out as I grabbed a stool at the island.

He straightened and shut off his phone, leaving the pantry door open as he wandered over. "She was? What did she say?"

"Not much." I ducked my head as heat crept up my neck. "I was…in Faith's room when she arrived."

I snuck a long enough glance to watch him register that news. Everyone knew what I did in there, but no one spoke of it. Just like the drinking and the women. Like Faith's untouched room and the fifth chair we kept at the table. All the skeletons we had tried to hide were really on display for the world.

"I did something stupid." Focused on the granite counter, I swallowed before lifting my head. "I asked Maggie to go to bed with me."

His lids flew wide, and so did his mouth.

"Not sex," I amended. "Just…to lay down with me. And she did. But when I woke up, she was gone."

His next words were hesitant. "Why do you think she was here?"

I pinned my eyes shut, not wanting to say it, but I knew the answer. Maggie…she would need that final goodbye. Closure. "The basket. She found out I'd been donating to it and wanted to thank me."

Considering that, his mouth opened again. Shut. Brow furrowed, Matt nodded—

Thump. Thump.

The sound of car doors outside forced us to go still. We heard several baritone voices before the lock on the front door turned, and something deep inside me sang in relief. My gut possibly. One problem was fixed. I'd have a way of getting food into my stomach before the aspirin gave me an ulcer.

Ben, Cam, and Jamey appeared with fabric bags from Henry's Market that my mind wanted to believe were full of something edible and nutritious, but with these guys, anything was possible. My cousins were also rocking new bruises from the fight last night.

My lips parted to ask how they were—

"That girl can slay time at a store. Is it ingrained in them to do that?" Cam complained, hauling bags toward the island.

Girl? My heart knocked into my sternum so hard, it had to be bruised.

Ben heaved his load onto the counter. "One thing's for sure. Shopping's not a gay thing."

"Depends on the type of shopping," Jamey argued.

Ejecting a lollipop out of his mouth, Cam used the candy end to point to Jamey. "You're right. If we had gone to a sex shop, I would have picked up the double-sided dildo and said—"

"That's so gay," Ben and Jamey finished for him and not without glaring.

"It wouldn't have taken so long if you nimrods didn't keep filling the cart with nothing but empty calories." The sweet rasp of Maggie's voice trailed in, and my heart stopped.

Screeching. Fucking. Halt.

Either I was in a state of disbelief or afraid of scaring her off, but I didn't move. I didn't so much as breathe. Like an opossum playing dead.

Matt took a different approach and tore off toward her. Not caring that she was holding eggs and bread and what looked to be a dry cleaning bag, he flung his arms around Maggie, lifting her off the ground. "I'm sorry. God, I'm so fucking sorry."

Head angled down, Maggie's hair's curtained to hide her face from me, so I couldn't read her expression. Was she smiling, crying, were the blue flames alight, ready to knee my brother? Or were those eyes dulled and empty, masking her emotions?

"I don't know how you Scotts look the way you do and eat nothing but junk," she said.

"We're fucking amazing. That's all there is to it." Grinning wide, Matt set her down and relieved her of the groceries.

With her chin tipped up now to Matt, I still... I couldn't read her. "Well, I was morally offended by the contents of your fridge. I couldn't have that atrocity on my conscience."

And there it was. I was right about why she'd come back. Maggie was a caretaker at heart. With a *thank you* and a final meal, she was done with us.

You don't have to be my friend or be in my life.

I just had to add that in there, didn't I? I was such an asshole.

I hadn't taken a breath yet because I was sure she'd jet before my blood required oxygen.

Weighed down by her backpack, Maggie hung the garment bag inside the hall closet, meticulously getting out every wrinkle in the plastic before shutting the door. Then I watched her dig out the receipt and change from her pocket beneath the faded gray T-shirt that hung loose around her shoulders, the hem brushing the tops of her thighs. The change went in the jar and the receipt on the counter.

Okay, this was taking too long. I needed air. I let myself take one lungful.

My disbelief that she was finally here began to wear off, but I was petrified to speak, say the wrong thing. Instead, I watched her, hung onto her every word, tried to decipher all her movements and the inflection of her voice.

Rifling through a bag to fill the fruit bowl with natural goodness, she asked, "So, what was this fight about?"

My brother shot me a look, clearing his throat before throwing on a cocky grin. "I've been waiting for an opportunity to try out my new MMA moves."

Her lips pursed as if she were holding back all the ways she wanted to call out his bullshit. Maggie finally slipped off her backpack, and it hit the floor with a *whump*.

As the guys unloaded the groceries, they helped themselves to the Doritos and Oreos that had gotten past Maggie. She fished inside her backpack for something, extracted a small tube, and crossed the room to me. I sucked down some oh-twos and held them.

With every step, those inky locks swayed around her jaw, so soft and inviting. My hands itched to run through her hair like they had hours ago. My skin craved her touch. My arms yearned to hold her close. Since she'd walked in, it was like the air cracked with electricity, yearning for us to connect like we had our own gravitational force.

Her lips wore a fresh coat of ChapStick that no doubt was her tenth application today, and there was one more freckle smattering her button nose. Everything about Maggie was beauty personified, but her eyes captivated me the most. They were a bright topaz, such an extraordinary fusion of blues, and they bore right through mine. She'd seen all sides of me now with those eyes. The villain and the hero. The child and the man. The wrecked and the utterly broken.

Her petite frame settled between my legs, smooth calves tickling the rough hair on mine as she squirted a strip of ointment onto her shaky finger. I could make more room for her, but I needed to feel her against me. Every cell that touched her came alive, and I was desperate for more of her warmth to chase away the cold that had hardened my edges.

As Maggie dabbed my split lip with the tip of her finger, I could tell it was a struggle for her to keep steady, not to split the wound open again. She could have poked my eye out with that finger for all I cared because every touch became a spark beneath my skin that turned to hot need coursing down my spine, settling in my groin.

Having her this close was nearly too much, and I fisted my hands around the stool.

Tilting her head to the side, she studied my mouth as her lips separated slightly, and I imagined how she would taste. Sweet. Like her scent. Her hair fell away from her jaw, gleaming like raven feathers in the sun, and her sugary cinnamon fragrance drifted in the air all around me. The thick fringe of lashes framing those intense eyes lifted, gaze lingering over my jaw, cheeks, and the slight crook in my nose until finally colliding with my eyes. An array of blues from the colors of a summer sky to the deepest midnight ensnared me.

I was not worthy to be in the presence of someone this beautiful.

My throat was thick, causing my voice to sound gruff. "Are you back, or are you just here?"

Bags ceased to ruffle, crunching chips stopped, and the happy chatter died as the entire room froze, waiting for Maggie to speak.

Capping the cream, those eyes lifted to mine. Suddenly, those little arms wove around my neck, her chest meeting mine, lips teasing my ear. The world came to a standstill.

"I'm back."

"Thank God," I breathed. Winding my arms around her waist, I held her to me. Tiny and perfect. Strong yet delicate. I burrowed my face into the crook of her neck to hide the block in my throat that I'd tried to swallow. Having her this close eased the vise around my heart so it could beat without hurting so damn much.

"Can I make you something to eat?" She slanted her head back to look at me.

I just want to hold you for a while longer. All day if I could.

"Please. I'm starving, Sticks."

Her brows drew together. "Why didn't you call me that for my legs? That would have been way cooler."

I glimpsed down to her creamy pins that had the fascinating ability to never tan. "Sorry. When it was time to designate a nickname, I only had your nut-cracking knee and the two ChapSticks to go by."

And staring at those glossed lips temptingly close mine, the need to have her slammed into me. But honestly, after literally just getting her back, I didn't want to push my luck. I'd vacillated between my heart and brain too many times. I'd broken all the trust I had with her.

I was in unchartered territory. I'd never had this type of friendship with a girl—*woman*—before. Not like this. Actually, though much of last night was fuzzy, I distinctly remembered Maggie's pronouncement that we were never friends. I also remembered the sharp pain that tore through my gut when she'd said it. And though I wanted a hell of a lot more than friendship, I knew to get to the next phase, I had to not only earn her trust but learn all there was to her.

I wasn't sure how much I could give her yet or how much she was willing to give me. There was only one speed that I could take this.

Slow.

One side of my mouth quirked. "I could call you Nutcracker if you prefer that to Sticks."

Her face screwed up adorably. "Let me feed you before you come up with any worse names."

Since it was past lunchtime, Maggie made everyone sandwiches. Without reminding her, she made one for herself and ate with us in the dining room, but during the meal, I noticed things about her that I hadn't before. She'd set the table, the utensils spaced perfectly on top of folded napkins, plates and drinking glasses the same distance apart all around like she had taken a class in the Art of Table Settings.

Maggie had filled her glass of water no more than halfway, and she only sipped from it when she thought no one was paying attention. Her tremors made the simple act of drinking from a glass…difficult. I also noticed that she only drank over her plate to catch what spilled.

Eating wasn't any easier. She used one hand only, and as soon as she took a microscopic bite, the hand disappeared with the other beneath the table. And her chewing was controlled. Almost as if she were struggling to eat as quietly as possible. Thinking back to the few lunches we'd had together, she had done the same then, too.

It didn't occur to me until now how much she had tried to hide in plain sight. Like when she combed through her hair to make sure her left temple was covered, concealing that scar. I wondered what other symptoms were connected to that trauma. Her unsteady balance could be an indication of damage to her cerebellum. And it was possible that her obsessive lip licking was a neurological issue since she did it more when she was stressed and tired, along with the seizures.

She has PTE…

Post Traumatic Epilepsy. I'd been somewhat fixated with digging up every article and blog related to PTE, only to find that Dad had been right. The disorder was unpredictable and challenging to treat. People went years before they found a drug or a combination of therapies that improved their quality of life, and the path to get there hadn't been easy or cheap. The difference was that those people seemed to want to keep trying, whereas Maggie had given up and accepted her fate. Which confused me because *giving up* didn't seem like something she knew how to do. Maggie was a fighter. She hadn't let her disabilities stop her from doing a damn thing.

However, she was too proud to ask for help, and that might be the very thing that would be her downfall.

After lunch, in a rare moment of Scott domestication that only Maggie had the power to wield, the guys pitched in and cleaned the house. Or tried to. Honestly, I swore the girl was going to break out in hives anytime the word *help* was spoken. Unfortunately, we weren't much help. At all. We sucked so hard at cleaning that Maggie had to reclean everything anyway. But it gave me an excuse to be around her all day.

Evening came far too fast, and I hated that I'd wasted so much of today sleeping and hadn't stayed awake while I held her. *In my bed.* Maggie had no clue that equated to me leaping over the Pacific Ocean in one bound. She was the first woman I'd ever wanted in my bed. Truthfully, I never thought it would happen, that it was possible, to allow anyone into a space I'd held sacred to my sister. With Maggie, there hadn't been a moment of hesitation, as if being with her was…meant to be.

Okay, I really needed to pump the brakes.

Lingering near Maggie in the kitchen, I had stolen three meatballs from her pot, and she glared at me as the fourth one disappeared behind my lips with a groan. The groan was entirely necessary because it was that fucking good. Everything was good.

Better.

Right.

Still chewing while trying to steal meatball number five, the vibration of the garage door hummed through the walls. All at once, the side door opened, Mom streaked across the kitchen in a blur, and a black purse flew in my general direction. If the woman had any aim whatsoever, I would have caught it.

"Maggie!" By the time I scooped up Mom's bag from the kitchen floor, Maggie was sandwiched between my parents. I shook my head as if I should be surprised at their reaction.

"Sweetie, we are so sorry," Mom went on. "So sorry you were put through all of that. Thank you for coming back. This house hasn't been the same."

She meant *we* hadn't been the same.

As my parents gave her an inch of breathing room, there was an odd look splashed across Maggie's features. It read like something between shock and pained longing.

"Can you stay for dinner? Eat with us?" Dad lovingly tucked a lock of hair behind her left ear, and Maggie flinched slightly as she ducked her chin.

"Thank you, Mr. Scott." She reached up to fix her hair. "That's very generous, but I'm expected home."

"We'll call your father. I'm sure—"

"Eve," Dad interrupted, voice smooth and low, eyes apologetic. "You're doing it."

I was sure that exchange alluded to my parents having a preemptive discussion to not scare off Maggie if a miracle happened and she returned.

"Sorry. You're right." Mom squeezed Maggie once more. "Of course, your father expects you."

Maggie glanced to my parents, uncertainty lingering in her gaze. "I did want to thank you for keeping the position open for me."

Dad smiled. "We wouldn't have been happy with anyone else. You spoiled us."

Maggie didn't look convinced by that as she looked away from him, but Dad hadn't been lying. "Ah, well, goodnight." Head down, she grabbed the garment bag and backpack from the hall closet.

And hell if I'd let her go that easily.

My keys were already in my pocket when I called out, "Don't let anyone poach my meatballs. I'll be right back!"

In two strides, I caught up to Maggie and lifted the backpack off her shoul—

"No!" She whirled on her heel, grasping for the bag and losing her balance for the second time today. Maggie swiftly caught herself, and a bright red stain splashed across her cheeks when she realized she'd screamed like I was about to hack her to pieces with a machete.

My brows popped high, her bag dangling from my grip. I swore the girl put actual bricks inside it this time.

Maggie's head slanted all the way back, gaze bouncing between me and her bag. She gulped. "I—I meant no, thank you. I'll get home fine."

Dad made a point to look out the window. "There's a storm rolling in, and it's getting dark, Maggie. I'd feel better if Mason drove you."

Discomfort ruffled her pretty features. "I've been doing this a long time, Mr. Scott." I made a grunting noise at that, which she ignored. "It's fine. Really. I'll be back tomorrow." She tugged on her bag, but I didn't let go.

Chin to my chest, I stared at her, utterly affected and overwhelmed by her. "I'm driving you."

"Mason, I can—" She lurched, flicking a glare to Jamey as his elbow drew back, a look of innocence on his face. Interesting.

If I was reading that right, Jamey was shipping us. After last night I should be the last person on earth he should want his best friend to be with, but that train of thought crashed as I wondered what our super-couple name would be.

Magson? Maygie? Those were dumb. Whatever. Didn't matter.

Maggie cast her gaze across the room as if mentally tallying all the people ready to argue with her. Her frame tensed with something. Anxiety maybe. Over what, I couldn't be sure.

After a torturous moment, she said, "Thank you, Mason."

With a shaky hand, Maggie readjusted the garment bag of...uniforms. Her father's uniforms. Huh.

My gaze tracked over to my platinum helper. "Need a ride?"

Jamey's mouth parted to answer, but Ben beat him with a, "Nope."

I noticed Jamey didn't argue.

After saying goodnight to everyone again, Maggie trailed behind me to the truck. I opened the passenger door for her.

"I knew you'd see it my way."

Foot rising, she grumbled, "It's impossible not to when you're five feet taller than me and take up my field of vision."

My grin kicked up one corner of my mouth. "I'm only four feet taller than you, but I like that you're an overestimator."

Maggie mumbled something else under her breath, and I watched her ass as she scaled the footboard. Then took another generous look when she reached into the back to hang the dry cleaning.

"Oh, my bike!" She was already scrambling back out of the cab, and I held up my hand to stop her.

"On it." Before she could argue, I plopped her backpack on the floorboard and shut the door.

With a quick jaunt to retrieve her bike from the side of the house, I placed it in the truck bed, somehow avoiding a puncture wound that would require a tetanus shot. The thing really did belong at the bottom of a landfill.

Smirking to myself, I wiped away a smudge on the handlebar light that Matt had screwed on for me when he was supposed to be emptying the vacuum cleaner in a—and this was a direct Maggie quote, "Well ventilated area to reduce the reestablishment of dust particles."

I snickered. So damn cute.

I hopped in the cab and closed the door as Maggie said, "Thank you again. This isn't necessary, but BB should know that I'd much rather ride in her than PM."

At those words, my body locked into place. I was only able to move from the neck up. My head went on a swivel, eyes and mouth popping wide. "Cam told you his Tundra's nickname?" Wow, I didn't know my voice went that high.

"Yeah. There's something not quite right with him. He doesn't talk about anything but girls and girl parts. *Pussy Magnet*? Seriously?"

Motherfucking Cam. "I'm sorry. There's no way to explain my cousin to anyone. We have to love him. It's an obligation." I pressed the start button, engine roaring to life. "Okay, so what tunes does Sticks like?" I sat back, waiting. This was going to be easy. Phase one of my Getting to Know Everything About Maggie Davis Plan.

"Folk music."

Shit. She wasn't going to make this easy. Not one bit. Maggie was going to bust my balls at every turn.

And actually…that could be fun.

My lips teased a grin. "You going to dazzle me with your accordion skills?"

"Yep. Gonna strap it to my chest and everything."

Like a horny ten-year-old with zero life experience, my eyes went right to her breasts at the mention of her chest, and then I diverted my gaze to the windshield, but it was too late. The image of those peaked tips wrapped in running gear was at the forefront of my brain. All it took was one glimpse of her, and I was done.

And very uncomfortable.

I should slam my head against the dash. I honestly wasn't sure at this point that would even get my dick to calm down.

"Oh!" Maggie exclaimed. "Maybe I should get Bob Dylan tattooed on my back instead of AC/DC."

Hmm. That wasn't the first time she'd mentioned getting ink on her back. Poring over the radio stations, I asked, "What's with the tattoo obsession?"

She shrugged. "I don't know. It's better than—" Looking to her lap, Maggie licked her lips. I had no idea how that sentence was supposed to end, and I wouldn't know because she flipped the conversation. Peeking up at me, she asked, "You don't like tattoos on women?"

"Oh, it's not that. I do, in fact, but—" I thought over how to word this. "There's a lot of reasons people get ink. Be it for fashion, attention, rebelling, choosing a prison gang… For me, tattooing your body should be about self-expression, and the art you choose should be meaningful. That's what I find sexy versus the art itself. Believing in something so much that it becomes a physical extension of your soul, whether or not you choose to make it visible to yourself or others."

Those lush lips parted, a blush stealing across her cheeks.

I wound up picking a country station to find Eric Church was getting his wrecking ball on. Nice. A song about wild sex was not a bad tune to drive to. At. All.

"So, where to, milady?"

"Um…" I waited to leave the driveway as it took her three attempts to click in her seatbelt and then she focused on fixing the straps that didn't need fixing. "Uh, stop where Canyon meets Verde Way, and I'll tell you from there."

I tumbled over her directions as I got the truck moving. "*Verde Way?* That's… That's outside of town."

Occupying herself, she tucked her backpack to the side. "No, it's not."

I took the turn off my street, glancing over to see that she was now busy pulling at her sock. "Sticks, that's the forest. Please do not tell me you ride that rickety heap all the way into the forest in the dark." No answer. "Preictal?" Nothing. "Without a helmet?" I pressed.

She didn't speak, but as she sat up, her fingers disappeared beneath her thighs, and her tongue stroked over her lips five more times. The longer I stared at her, the more she shrunk into herself.

Back off, Mason. The goal wasn't to piss her off. Time to switch topics.

"You know, no self-respecting eighteen-year-old doesn't drive. We need to get you a license."

No response.

"Seriously. I can give you lessons. I'll even let you drive BB. She's partial to me, but I think she'll do right by you."

Maggie's chest lifted and fell heavily as she rested her head on the window, staring out at the passing neighborhood. "I told you, Mason. I can't."

Hell, I was fucking this up a lot faster than I thought I could. I had said something stupid but had no clue what, and I could usually figure it out as soon as the words left my mouth. Not with Maggie, though.

I pulled up to the gate and waited for it to open, all while praying Bernard stayed in his little house. "Why? In return for lessons, you can run with me. You're getting the better end of that deal. There's no way you can drive worse than I run."

Her words were so quiet that I almost didn't hear them. "So I can have a seizure and kill us along with everyone else on the road? I *can't* drive, Mason."

Shame slipped over my skin like thick oil, something that couldn't be washed away with an apology, and yet... "I didn't put that together before. I'm sorry."

I had a feeling most of our time together would be spent apologizing to her.

"I know you didn't. It's okay." Maggie dragged in a slow breath. "The state might have given me a license if my seizures were controlled, but they're not. So...yeah."

As I advanced onto the main road, I turned the volume down on the radio to hear Maggie better. "I know I asked before, but what's it like? When you have a seizure?"

I peered over to see that her gaze was now locked onto her feet. She took so long to answer that I'd given up hope that she would. And then she surprised me.

"Helpless," she answered, and in my periphery, I caught the roll of her throat. "I don't always have a warning when they come, but when I do, I hear things, see things…hallucinations. Sometimes I don't remember what happens, and sometimes, I remember too much. I have no control over my body, the things I say and do. If I'm conscious, I want to move, but I can't. My mind is locked inside, screaming in silence. Alone. Helpless." Maggie folded her arms, hugging herself. "I wake up with bruises I don't have a clue how I got, swollen lips from almost biting through them, scratch marks on my skin, and I'll spare you the details of what a seizure does for bladder control."

God. Was that why it was so hard for her to accept help? Because she couldn't stand feeling helpless?

"How long have you had them?" I asked.

"As long as I can remember."

"I'm sorry." There was another apology.

Sorry, you have epilepsy, Maggie.

Sorry, your life is so hard, Maggie.

Sorry, I made your life worse, Maggie.

Looking out her window again, she said, "I think the worst part is how people treat me when they know. Or when they see my tremor. I'm either pathetic or a freak. A spaz. *Mags the Spaz.*"

That wasn't the first time she'd said that about herself and Eric…had said that to me before. My hands clenched the wheel. "The kids at school called you that?"

The red-orange rays from the setting sun warmed her skin, highlighting the flick of her lashes, blinking fast as if to keep her eyes dry.

"It was the one that stuck. One of many."

Nodding, I chewed on my lower lip, vaguely remembering that Maggie's bottom lip had been swollen last month. She'd made a joke about a chicken wing, and I wondered if she'd had a seizure then, but now didn't seem like the right time to ask.

"Faith had nicknames, too. Sickie Scottie. Faith the Wraith. People are assholes."

"Yeah." That one word held far too much weight. "Can I be honest with you about something?" she asked. "It's kinda personal, and you might get upset."

"With you? I won't. Promise."

"Not with me. I don't think." Twisting toward me, Maggie tucked her knees beneath her, so her feet dangled off the seat. "Charlie came to Jamey's house this morning. She apologized and explained what had happened last night. Among other things."

Well, that answered why Jamey didn't try to wax my head today. But Charlie… The mere mention of her name caused a sudden heaviness in my chest as if the atomic mass of oxygen weighed more in my lungs. Ever since the earrings, I had distanced myself from her. We all had. Even my mom had stepped down from planning the hospital gala because she associated it with the Price sisters. It had all become too much for her.

"I didn't know Charlie had done that. I'm sorry if she upset you."

"She didn't. I'm glad she explained her relationship with Taylor and her parents. It cleared up a lot." Maggie paused to lick her lips. "It's just that you took Charlie's pictures down in your room. I thought you should know that she wants to apologize to you, too. She didn't think you were ready to listen."

"She's right. She should apologize, and I'm not ready to listen." Bouncing along the empty stretch of road, I shrugged. "But I didn't take her pictures down because I'm petty. I— I cared for her. For a long time. I still do. I don't think Charlie's a bad person, just the opposite. But I don't think she's the right person to have in my life. Not right now. Charlie doesn't bring out the better parts of me. Does that make sense?"

"It does." Repositioning herself again, her brow bunched. "I guess— I wanted to make sure that it wasn't about me. Not that I presumed it was. You can be friends with whomever you want. Date or be with whomever you want. I would never ask you to edit your life for me."

I wasn't really loving the direction this conversation was taking. "I know you wouldn't."

Her tongue took another swipe. "How do you know that?"

"Because you're the *right* person to have in my life. You bring out the better parts of me."

"Oh." Gaze back on the window, Maggie's feet met the floorboard, far too quiet again. And somehow, it didn't seem as if those words reached her. If anything, she drew further into herself.

Rolling up to the intersection of Verde and Canyon, I slowed the truck for more instructions. Not quite at a complete stop yet, I heard the seal of the passenger door break. What the…?

"Where are you go—"

And then she was out, the door shutting in my face. By the time I threw the gear in Park and bolted out of the truck, she already had the backpack on her shoulders, and the back door was open to get her dry cleaning—her *father's* dry cleaning.

"Listen, we need to have a chat about this obsession you have with jumping out of moving vehicles."

"Huh?" Her head popped up on the other side of the bed.

"You jumping out of my truck while it's still moving?" I prompted, and she blinked at me. "No more of that. It's not safe."

"Oh, sorry. I'm just trying to efficiently use my time."

Efficiently use her time? She seriously couldn't wait five seconds?

Before I knew it, she'd slung the dry cleaning bag over the side of my truck, and with a quick scale of the tire, Maggie tried to lift her bike out of the bed. Why she was still disillusioned that she had muscles, I'd never know.

"What are you doing?" I asked, rounding the bed of my Raptor.

"Yak racing." Gritting her teeth, she dragged the bike closer to the wheel well. "What does it look like? I'm getting my bike. I'm gonna take it from here."

My head spun in every direction. "Take it from *here* to *where?*" She didn't answer me, wholly intent on her task, grunting with her next attempt. I put a hand on the frame, keeping the bike in the bed. I really only needed a pinky to complete the job. "Sticks, I'm not dumping you in the middle of the woods for Christ's sake."

One arm gesticulated to the woods behind us. "My house is right there."

I squinted in the general direction of her flailing motion. The only thing out there were trees. "Is there a cave I'm not seeing? A tree house? A magic cloaking forcefield?"

Using all her might, the bike moved an inch. "I'll be fine."

My jaw hardened as she continued to fight with the bike. "I know you'll be fine. Evidently, you do this all the time in the motherfucking dark. Why can't you accept that I want to take you home?"

Tilting her head, she stared at me as if this concept truly confused her. "I'll accept it when you accept that I don't want these lights on my bike. Seriously, when did you have time to put these on? I was watching you all day."

"My blood is made of fairy dust and magic." I waited while she lost the inch, cursing the likes of Aristotle, Galileo, and Newton. "Sticks..."

Determination settled in her shoulders as she struggled to lift the thing again. "What is wrong with— Oh! You're holding it down! That's not fair."

"I don't play fair. And I'm driving you home."

Flattening me with a look, her forehead smoothed, mouth turning down in the corners. "No, you're not."

I adopted the same stern look, too. "Yes. I. Am."

"No, Mason. You're not."

"Tell me why and I'll back off." Had I known this drive would result in her glaring at me like she wanted to use my balls as a speed bag, I would have packed my cup. "Maggie, why dammit."

After a long stare down, the fight seeped out of her, and just as I was about to declare my win, Maggie's chin lowered, formulating her concession speech. But what she actually said next was not that.

"Because I don't want you to see where I live. I don't...live like you, Mason. There's nothing about my life that's like yours."

Shit. "Sticks..."

She climbed down from the side of the truck, meeting me on the ground, chin still attached to her chest. Dark lashes fanned her cheeks in rapid succession, and it could be she was fighting back tears again or that she had a gnat in her eye. I honestly couldn't tell with this girl. But the longer we stood there, the more I picked apart her words and the deep shame that was etched into them.

"You asked me last night why I said yes to Brady." Without looking at me, she shook her head. "I didn't say yes. I told him that I would consider his invitation because it was nice to be... I don't know."

"You do know. Please, I want to hear it."

Plugging her hands into her back pockets, Maggie's throat worked. "He saw...*me*. In the light of day, he saw who I was. Not my dumpy clothes, my shitty bike, my tremor, or this hideous scar on my head. That had never happened before, and I— I liked it. I wanted more of that." Her voice dropped to a whisper. "To be noticed."

This girl... Damn, this girl was infiltrating every dark corner in my heart.

I should tell her that the guy who made her feel so good was a sexual predator, hellbent on ripping her virginity away from her, but...I couldn't. I wanted her to feel good. Something told me those moments were too rare to steal from her.

I set the bike on the ground and dipped my head to chase her gaze. She avoided me. "Maggie, I don't like you talking about yourself like that."

Her face screwed up in a cringe. "I know what people see when they look at me."

"That's just it. I don't think you do at all."

Shaking me off, she wrapped her fingers around the handlebars and tugged, but I refused to let go, still gripping the frame. "Please."

It was her *please* that made my hand curl tighter around the Schwinn's frame. God help me, I should have listened to every instinct roaring inside me to pull her close, hold her to me, comfort her. My brain, though, was screaming for me to make things right between us.

There were too many cracks, too many weaknesses in the foundation. I had to fix them, so we had something firm to stand on.

"On one condition," I offered.

She squeezed her eyes shut. "What is it?"

I thought about that. "I lied. I actually have two conditions. One, I never want to hear the word *spaz* out of your mouth ever again. Can you do that?"

There was a meek nod and a murmur that sounded a lot like, "Okay."

"Two…" I gnashed my molars together. This was gonna suck. "I would like you to make me a replacement watermelon medal."

Her head slowly angled back, the pain in her eyes gutting me. Right down to the bone. I deserved it.

"It was childish of me, but I threw the first one away, and I hate that I did that. I'm sorry. We were friends or…I considered us friends, and when I thought— Anyway, I was hurt and angry, and that's what I did."

She dropped her head again. "It was a stupid joke. Just a yogurt lid and yarn."

"It was. It was completely stupid. Your seeds were sloppy, the yarn was too short, and I could break that thing by breathing on it too hard." With two fingers, I tipped her chin up so that she could see how serious I was. "And it was the best gift anyone has ever given me."

"You could make—"

"I could." I cut her off. "I could make another one, and it would be the shit, way better than yours. But it wouldn't be from *you.* That's why I want you to make it. That's why it was special."

There was a long pause before she repeated her answer from before, but this time, I heard her. "Okay."

"Thank you." My hand returned to my side, missing the silk of her skin. "That was a little easier than I thought it would be."

Her gaze shifted to focus somewhere behind me. "Well, I kinda, maybe, said some things last night on the phone that I didn't mean."

My heart thumped inside my chest so loud, she had to have heard it.

"I thought— I hoped we were friends. At least…that day."

Another thump. "We were. We still are."

Her lashes swept up, gaze locking with mine. "I…uh— I was going to apologize—"

"Whoa. No." I put my palms up, and she blinked at me. "I can't stomach an apology from you. You did nothing wrong."

"I did. You all came out yesterday, and I could have stood still for a minute and listened."

"I deserved it, Maggie."

She shook her head. "I'm not that way. I don't like to be spiteful, and I don't like the thoughts I've been having lately. It's not me."

"I know."

"No, you don't know." Maggie let go of the bike, quietly groaning as she hid her face in her hands. "I refused to listen to Charlie until she agreed to tell all her Instabook followers about Ava's salon."

I chuckled at both her shocking lack of social media knowledge and her embarrassment. "Good."

"Good?" Hands falling to her side, Maggie gaped at me. "I extorted a person!"

"More like negotiated, but I bet Charlie didn't care. Did she?"

"Well…no."

"Allow me to break down the why of that." I reached over and grabbed the uniforms, setting them across the basket. "One, you *negotiated* not for your benefit but for someone else's. You got nothing out of that exchange except the joy of helping Ava's business. It was a selfless act. And two, part of the celebrity game is being the first to discover the undiscovered. Be it music, clothing, makeup… Followers don't want an idol who is late to the trend. They want to follow an idol who *is* the trend. Charlie wasn't doing you or Ava a favor. You did her a favor."

Maggie stared at me. "Really?"

I nodded. "Pretty messed up, right? It's one of the many reasons I stay away from social media."

Looking up at me, she licked her lips three times, and I waited for the next words to spill. Instead, she mounted the bike.

I watched her foot meet the pedal, and as I waited for her to ride away, she spoke my name, voice soft and melodic. "Mason?"

"Yeah?"

Over her shoulder, those bright azure eyes met mine, and with everything in me, I wished she would give me some hint that she wanted more than friendship, wanted me to be her first kiss. We were secluded out here, and this moment was kinda perfect—

"I unintentionally lied earlier when I said I would never ask you to edit your life for me. There is something I would like to ask of you."

"It's done. Just say the word."

After a long pause, her eyes dropped to the ground. "If you drink, don't do it around me. It doesn't bring out the better parts of me."

If that wasn't a kick to the balls, nothing was. I eased a knot down my throat, getting stuck midway. "Okay. I can do that." As she turned away, my hand lifted to stop her but then let it drop. I was afraid to push her and make this worse. "Night, Maggie."

"Night."

She disappeared down the dirt road, and I let the tall trees and thick brush swallow her and everything I wished our last moment could have been.

chapter thirty-one

maggie

Each turn of the bike pedal away from Mason was another rip, another shred of my heart, but it was the right thing to do. If I'd let him take me all the way to my house and my father was there… It wouldn't be good.

Once the bend in the road straightened, the empty driveway came into view, and I freed a lungful of strained air. With it just being Poker and me here, I could relax and get my chores done without fear of upsetting him by cleaning too loud, cooking too long, breathing too often.

That last one wasn't an exaggeration.

Dinner was ready when he stepped through the door, and I began to plate his meal with the intent to disappear like he preferred me to. I soon learned he had other plans this evening.

"Where the fuck have you been?" he demanded, slamming the front door so hard the dishes in the cabinets rattled.

I swallowed, forcing my hand to unclench the serving spoon, leaving it in the pot of mashed potatoes. His boots thumped across the living room, and as I turned, my spinal column tensed like the thing was trying to become a living fossil inside of me.

The moment he realized Poker was right beside me, he stopped at the edge of the kitchen, but even from a distance, his presence rippled through the room like cold waves.

"So? Do you have an answer for me? 'Cause if I read your shit handwriting right, you were supposed to pull a double at the café. You can imagine my surprise when I went to the café to find that Frankie never saw you. But Henry did. Twice. The first time you were by yourself. The second time you weren't."

I cleared my throat, reluctantly meeting his eyes. Frost lined the edges of his pupils, chilling the house by at least twenty degrees. I dampened my lips. "Sir, I'm sorry. I—"

"Who were they?" The words were damn near pulverized on their way out of his clenched jaw. "Who was with you?"

Poker's low growl vibrated against my thigh, but it was too quiet to hear across the room. "Jamey, plus Ben and Camden Scott—"

"*Scott?*" Their name was spoken with a blend of disbelief and revulsion. "What the fuck were you doing with the Scotts?"

"Grocery shopping, sir. I…" The revulsion in his voice had bled into his features, pulling back is upper lip, and my stomach shrank painfully. "I went back to work for them today—"

"Went back?" he snarled, coming closer. "Tell me, how did that come about?"

"Um…" My knees quivered as Poker rose to all fours. "Sir, they asked me—"

"*Asked you?*" His eyes rounded but were quick to narrow into arctic shards. "After I specifically told them not to, they still asked you? Those rich fucks not only embarrassed me but then went behind my back and defied *me*? And I suppose it didn't take much for you, did it? For you to scurry back with your tail between your legs."

I gulped, but a hard lump of *oh shit* got stuck in my throat. "Sir, I didn't know you would be upset—"

"Just how fucking damaged is that brain of yours that you would think I'd have any other reaction? After what they did to my name?"

I didn't answer. I assumed that was a rhetorical question. "Sir, I'm sorry. And I wrote you that letter before I made the decision. I forgot—"

"Forgot? You forgot what you wrote this morning? Are you really that stupid, or do you think I am?"

Poker's growl was audible now, and I bumped him with my leg to hush. "No, sir. It was a mistake. I didn't sleep well, and I did forget. I'm sorry. It wasn't my intention to lie to you." And I left it at that.

There was no *I'll get it right next time.*

There was no offer to quit to appease his ego.

If that was what he wanted, he was going to have to demand it.

Disgusted, he stalked toward the kitchen table like he was trying to intimidate it, and I took that as my cue to plate his dinner.

"I don't know why I'm shocked that you went right back to the people who bought you like a cheap whore." He yanked the chair out and sat. I placed his meal in front of him as he speared me with a glare. "You think you won this one, huh?"

That right there was the essence of Nathan Davis. Every interaction with him revolved around one thing: control and who had it. The control over me had been taken from him, or so his twisted mind believed. He could command that I no longer work for the Scotts, but it would make him look vindictive and irrational. I was an adult, free to make my own decisions. I made money with the Scotts, whereas at the café, I didn't. And if he took that away from me, he would no longer be the hero this town once believed him to be. I would win the public's affection.

It was all too fucked up, but truthfully, I had expected this to an extent. My father didn't want me working for richies, and he certainly didn't want me around doctors of any kind. Daniel and Eve Scott checked both boxes. But I didn't know he had told them not to ask me to come back.

The Scotts had won in his sick mind, and Nathan Davis wouldn't take that well. He didn't know how to lose.

I said nothing and grabbed the whiskey from the fridge. Hands trembling, I poured him a double and set the glass and bottle by his plate, hoping to distract him or have it act as my silent plea not to bruise me today.

"So did they?" He stabbed the fork into his steak, his knife throwing off a dull glint from the florescent lighting.

"Sir?"

"Pay you like a cheap whore." There was no question in his tone.

I would be better equipped to answer that question if I knew the going rate of sex workers. Nevertheless… "No, sir."

The knife and fork were set down so he could pick up his glass. He guzzled the whiskey and pulled the rim from his lips, lids sinking into a squint. "I warned you, Margaret. You are not to discuss our business with them, and you stay away from that fucking boy."

He didn't have to add the "or else." The warning was clear. *I'll fucking kill you. I'll fucking kill him. I'll fucking kill his brother, his parents, his cousins. I'll burn your fucking world to ash.*

Icy terror pooled in my stomach at the thought of my father putting his hands on any of the Scotts. "Yes, sir."

He poured himself another double, setting the bottle down as he studied me, assessing me as if he'd hadn't seen me almost every day for eighteen years. Then he grunted as though what he saw had confirmed the sick thought running through his brain.

"I think the boys were right." The next bite of steak was thoroughly masticated, and he washed it down with another sip. "You're too fucking ugly for anyone to want. The only dick you'll fuck is the one you pay for."

I didn't think the boys would say something so awful, and I stood there, taking it without a flinch, but damn, that one hurt. On so many levels. "Yes, sir."

Eyes locked with mine, the knife drove down again, and the shrill scrape of metal against the plate was its own unspoken threat. "You better hope the Scotts don't embarrass me again. I will hold you responsible."

I swallowed, knowing that was a real possibility. "Yes, sir."

So…walking in the mud sucked. As did walking in the rain. It had started to storm not long after I'd cleaned the dinner dishes last night and hadn't stopped. Mother Nature had ensured my trek to school would be a challenge. I could push my bike through the mud until I got to the asphalt, but there wasn't a covered rack at school, and my poor Schwinn didn't need any more rust. So, walking in the mud and rain was my best option.

I reached the end of Verde Way, blowing into my cupped hands as I lifted my gaze. Something electric blue and truck-like idled up ahead. My heart flipped in a full three-sixty spin, and the fact that I was water-logged top to bottom and partially frozen was a distant memory. I made an ass out of myself to get to Mason as fast as I could, slip-sliding across the mud and soggy foliage.

The window lowered to reveal twinkling peridot eyes and a smile that could cut through the gloomy clouds above. "Morning!"

Reaching the passenger's side, my head tipped all the way back, and a big, old raindrop smacked me in the eyeball. Grimacing, I swiped at my face. "What are you doing here?"

"Joggling. Get in." Leaning over, he shoved open the door. Warm air drifted out along with a yummy scent, something with a hint of Mason but richer. I'd take it over the stench of damp wood and rotting earth any day.

My right foot began to sink into the mud, and I gripped the door handle to keep from sinking further. "I can't. I'm headed to Henry's. Someone donates a lot of money to make sure I show up there every day."

"Then it's a good thing I already planned on taking you."

Oh… I shot a glance to my sneakers. "Yeah, but I'm filthy."

"And a hose works wonders on rubber floor mats. Come on, my tires are gonna sink, and then we'll be stuck out here, which…" His grin kicked up into something positively wicked. "Never mind. Take your time."

Raising my chin, my brows inched together. "Don't you want to go to school today?"

Okay, asking a frat boy if he wanted to go to school was next-level stupid.

He turned that over a moment. "The alternative seemed more fun."

Alternative? Getting stuck in the mud? He was so weird.

"Fine, but you've been warned." I flung my rain spotted backpack onto the floorboard, noticing a plush bath towel was spread across the passenger seat. That towel hadn't come from the Scotts' house. Had Mason planned on picking me up before he left the fraternity, or was this a last-minute decision and he happened to keep a spare towel in his truck? It was too early and too cold for so many questions. I climbed into the toasty cab, shut the door, and the chocolaty scent within intensified.

"Shit, you're soaked." After turning the heater up, Mason reached over and pointed the vents toward me. All of them.

I fought a shiver as my sweater and jeans molded to my skin like shrink wrap. "It's not that bad."

Dismissing my comment with a lift of his brow, Mason motioned to my sweater. "Take that thing off."

"Uh…okay." Probably should have asked at least one question before agreeing.

As I worked the fabric over my head, a gust of heated air tickled my bare stomach, my damp T-shirt having stuck to the hoodie and going up with it. Holding my shirt down, I separated the two, pulling off the sweater. I made sure my hair was combed back into my ponytail before looking to my side. Mason's gaze was glued to the roof.

"All done." I wasn't sure why I needed to say that, but it seemed like he was waiting for the go-ahead to bring his eyes back to a normal position.

Once he looked my way, his gaze shot right back down to his lap, a muscle flexing in his jaw. Before I could ask what was wrong, Mason reached back between his shoulder blades to grip the material of his Warrington sweater and then yanked the blue and gray fabric over his head. Like my shirt had, his black Henley rode up, exposing the valley of taut golden skin above his jeans, those tantalizing grooves of his Adonis belt, along with that damned trail of hair starting at his navel and going way low. My eye line refused to travel anywhere near the roof.

My God…

"Here." My eyes widened as Mason leaned over the console and slid *his* sweater over *my* head.

"Whad—" I got a mouthful of cotton and his delectable scent. My head appeared like a prairie dog peeking out of its hole as he tugged the sweater down, being careful not to disturb my ponytail. "—are you doing?"

"Saving your life depending on which of my family members you ask," he said, arranging his sweater on my shoulders. "My nana would say that you'll catch your death of cold, and my parents would argue statistically speaking for someone of your age and health that it's highly improbable. But I'm a good, little boy and I never argue with my nana. She'd be terribly upset to see you in this state, and it's possible back in her day, people really did die of the common cold. So here we are. You're welcome."

I wasn't sure I was tracking this conversation because Mason was close enough that I could make out the individual hairs on his jaw. And he'd literally given me the clothes off his back. Again. May not seem like a big deal to some, but for me, someone who had grown up with a father who couldn't care less if I died in my sleep any given night…this meant everything.

The beginning of a knot began to form in my throat, touched at his thoughtfulness. "Thank you."

Those long, dark lashes lifted as his eyes took their sweet time lingering over my features, gaze darkening with every blink. I suddenly felt a little too warm.

"You should…uh…take off your T-shirt. It's soaked. You'll never get warm like that." His voice sounded deeper, rougher if that were possible.

"Oh, yeah. Good idea." Using his sweater as a cover, I shimmied out of my shirt and pushed my arms back through the sleeves. The material was warm and soft against my skin, the next best thing to having his arms wrapped around me. Looking at the T-shirt in my hands, I fought the urge to smack my forehead. It was white. And see-through now that it was wet. I seriously doubted Mason had looked long enough to see there were stars printed on my bra, but still.

Mason was now concentrating on a spot in the woods. Risking a peek over at me, he cleared his throat. "Better?"

"Thank you, yes. And I'm sure if I had a nana, she'd thank you, too." My eyes lowered to the butterflies inked on his left arm, exposed and bare now that he'd given me his sweater. "Wait. Now you're going to catch your highly improbable death of cold, and both our nanas—real and hypothetical—are going to be angry at me."

He stilled, staring at me for what seemed like hours. In reality, seconds. One dimple finally appeared, shaking his head.

"What?"

The smile dropped as he looked to his dashboard. "It's nothing."

Okay, if it was nothing, then why the weird reaction? I squirmed in my seat. "Are you sure?"

"Yes. Besides, I came prepared." That was followed by a wink and a cocky grin right before he twisted over the console and reached into the back.

I hadn't a clue what he was searching for because the skin above his jeans had made a reappearance. Along with the last two ridges of his eight pack. And dear heavens, the boy was so ripped, even his veins were jacked as they swelled beneath the thinly, stretched skin and trailed below the metal button of his jeans that I was secretly praying would spontaneously pop open.

Damn, he was lickable. I wondered how far down that V of muscles went, what that bulge straining against his zipper looked—

Black leather broke my stare, and Mason was back in his seat, placing his leather jacket on the console between us.

"Now, give me these." He scooped up one of my hands and began to roll up the sleeve. His deft fingers gestured for the other arm and ended up skimming my skin a total of seven times. Totally wasn't counting.

Sitting back, Mason gave me another once over before nodding. "You'll do."

I looked to my lap, at the rolled sleeves that he'd cuffed perfectly for me. What had taken him ten seconds would have taken me ten minutes. "Thank you."

My eyes lifted to his to see his pupils were dilated, the peridot hue deeper than a moment ago. His head bobbed once, turning his head to stare at the woods. "My pleasure."

His tone sounded odd again, and that strange tension returned. This was his idea to come out all this way for me, right? Or had his parents asked him to pick me up, and this hadn't been his idea at all? I frowned at the latter, but I shouldn't have. It was nice, and I should be grateful they had cared. And I was grateful.

"Here. I got you a hot cocoa," he said as I shoved my wet clothes into my bag. Mason handed me one of the two paper cups in the console.

As our fingers met, I could have sworn he inhaled a sharp breath. Or maybe that was me. "I wasn't sure if you drank coffee."

"Thank you, I don't. Caffeine makes my tremor worse. Not that anyone can tell." I eyed him speculatively. A question snuck out of my mouth before my brain could reel it back in. "Why are you being so nice?"

"I'm not. I'm ensuring my running partner isn't twisting an ankle or contracting Nana's highly improbable death-inducing pneumonia on the way to school." Flashing me his pearly whites and two dimples, Mason shifted gears and pulled the truck onto the asphalt.

I studied him over the top of my cup—the cup from the coffee shop on Laurel, down the street from the RAM house. "What time did you wake up today?"

He shrugged, reaching for his cup. "I'm still in football mode. If I start sleeping in, then I'll never get back into the schedule. Then I'll miss team meetings, and Watkins will make me do the Wolverine Special Drill."

"What's that?"

He drank a sip of cocoa. "All I know is men can't walk for two days after. It's a documented fact with the University Clinic. So I plan on never finding out."

"Oh!" For whatever reason, that was the moment I remembered what I'd done last night before bed. I set my cup in the holder next to his and dug inside my bag. This was so stupid, and I couldn't believe I had made two of these in my lifetime. I couldn't believe Mason *wanted* another one.

From my bag, I carefully removed the yarn necklace attached to a pink foil Yoplait lid. "Your medal, sir."

Mason tore his gaze off the road, eyes rounding. "Holy shit!" His smile was heart-melting and pointed right at me. "I didn't expect it so fast. I gotta pull over. This moment requires my complete attention."

He pulled the truck over to the side of the road and turned off the country station that was playing. When he settled in to face me, I held the medal up for him again. "Sorry, it's not red. I only had pink ones in my fridge because it's close to Breast Cancer Awareness Month."

"Hell, that's even better." As he grasped the thing like it was a delicate artifact, the side colored with my pathetic sharpie seeds and green rim faced me. Mason barked a laugh when he read the back. "For taking twenty-nine minutes to choose a watermelon. The longest ever in history."

At first, I was surprised he could read my chicken scratch, but then my smile took a nosedive.

He let go of the Yoplait medal. "What's wrong?"

I forced a smile, but it felt crooked and off. "Nothing."

Frowning, Mason slumped in his seat. "I saw that, Sticks. You're hiding it, but I know I did something. What is it?"

"Nothing, really." His brows crept up to his hairline expectantly. I should have tried to get out of the ride to school a bit harder. "It's just— I wrote the exact same thing on the first one." Dipping my chin, I mumbled, "Obviously, you didn't read it."

Eyes closed, his fists went white on his thighs. "Maggie—"

"You apologized. I'm not gonna beat you up over it. I'm sorry, I girled-out or something."

Those lashes were flush to his cheeks, and he still wouldn't look at me. "Please stop saying you're sorry," he said, voice gruff with remorse.

"But I am. I didn't intend to make you feel bad. Really. Let's… Can we start over? Fresh? Like none of this ever happened? Maybe pretend this is the first time we met or something? It would make a better story, and you'd never have to tell people you got your junk kneed by a grown-ass petite woman."

"No," the answer came swift and hard. Mason's gaze lifted, locking with mine. "By wiping away the bad moments between us, you're asking me to forget the good ones, too. I refuse to do that. I'd take a million memories of your tears for just one of your smiles."

I couldn't help it. A silly grin pulled at my lips.

"See." His hand slid around my neck as his thumb swept across my cheek in a warm caress. "That right there. Your smile is like the sun, Sticks."

My throat felt odd, thicker than it should. "You're so weird."

He tweaked my nose. "I'm awesome."

"And humble." That earned me a smirk. I was still holding the medal for him like a doofus, the watermelon twirling in front of the air vent. I wiggled it in front of him. "You gonna take this sometime today?"

His gaze flicked to the medal and then back to me. "You have to put it on me."

"What?" I laughed.

"That's how the ceremony works. I earn the medal, and you place it on me." Mason's head lowered, leaning over the console.

"This is so dumb." I slipped the yarn over his head and fixed the string, so the tie was in the back. Suddenly, he straightened with both of my hands wrapped around him, taking me up with him, bringing me halfway over the console.

The breath I took went nowhere. He was so very close. His mouth even closer. His eyes were open, but his lashes shielded his gaze from mine, and I wasn't certain, but I thought he was staring at me. One part of me, to be exact.

There was a good chance I was wrong but sitting on the side of a darkened and desolate road, with rain pinging off every inch of this truck and my hands wrapped around a boy whose lips were a mere centimeter from mine, was kinda screaming *FIRST KISS*!

Mason's throat bobbed in a swallow, the timbre of his voice rich and husky as it vibrated on my palms. "All good?"

I wet my lips, and there was no mistaking it that time. He tracked the movement. Oh. Dear. Lord. "Uh-huh."

He blew out a controlled breath that was a heady combination of mint and chocolate, and it danced over my moistened lips, tasting him on the tip of my tongue. My throat went dry, and there was no way he couldn't hear my heart thumping against my sternum.

Mason's gaze lifted to mine, not moving or blinking for an excruciating moment. Before I knew what was happening, he sat back in his seat, breaking my hold on his neck, leaving me pressed against the console with my arms in the air like I was hugging an invisible body. I sunk back, and though the heaters were going full blast, a chill of disappointment snaked down my spine.

Wow, I couldn't have read that moment any worse.

Chin to his chest, Mason admired his foil watermelon. "I didn't know you were into *The Office*."

"Huh?" Still reeling from the moment that never was, I grabbed my cocoa from the console in hopes it could distract me.

"The show, *The Office*," he prompted. "Jim and Pam hosted the Office Olympics…" Eyeing me, his words died off. "Michael *Scott?*" He paused, waiting for me to do anything but blink. "You don't know what I'm talking about, do you?"

My head went back and forth. "Not in the least."

I was awarded two dimples again. "That makes it even more special." Suddenly, his warm lips were on my cheek in the bestest, briefest kiss to my cheek there ever was. I gripped my cocoa tighter. "Thanks, Sticks."

I may not wash my face for a year.

Though he was back behind the wheel, I could still feel the softness of his lips, the rasp of scruff on my cheek, the tingles along my skin making their way down to my toes. I was breathless. "No prob." And that was about all I could manage.

Mason got us back onto the road, glimpsing over to me. "Now, admit it. Isn't this better than walking?"

"It is." I held up my cup. "And thank you for this."

"You're welcome, but don't get used to it. I think I used up all my chivalrous gestures for the year in one morning."

I laced my fingers around the warm cocoa, the disbelief that he'd come all this way for me beginning to wear off. He was right. What he'd said was a reminder that today was singular and precious.

I forced a smile, trying to assure him. "That's okay. I don't have any expectations."

That tension swept into the cab again, a vein jumping in his temple as he kept his focus on the windshield. "It bodes well for me that you are easily impressed and have low standards. You're gonna think I'm freaking amazing."

"I already do." *Shit.* Did I totally just say that aloud?

By the brilliant grin he was sporting, I'd go with a yes.

Mason had made me promise to meet him by the *big ass oak tree* in the quad after school, so on the way from my locker, I spotted him under said tree with the phone to his ear, and it looked like he might crack that thing in two if he applied any more pressure.

The grass squished beneath my feet as I approached, close enough to hear him snarl, "Why are you calling me?"

Whoa. I stopped and glanced around. Mason's back faced me and didn't seem to know that I was behind him. I knew it was wrong to eavesdrop, and yet...

He turned enough that I could see the corner of his mouth had pulled up, but this was the furthest thing from a smile I'd ever seen. "And when did I give you the impression that I gave a fuck?"

Whatever was said caused his nostrils to flare. The person on the other end of that call should be thanking their lucky stars that a cell tower separated them.

"That's enough," Mason growled, his shoulders bunched tight, mouth tense. "I—no, you listen. Maggie's my friend and nothing more. So leave it the fuck alone."

Ouch. Yeah, if *friend* wasn't a kick to the gut, the *nothing more* sure as hell was.

"Don't call me again with this shit. In fact, don't call me again." He stabbed the screen with his thumb and jammed his phone back into his pocket. I watched him pace under the tree once and then twice. A hand was shoved into his hair, sending dark strands in all directions but never managing to lose its styled appearance.

I didn't sense he would calm down anytime soon, but I couldn't stand here all day. Cue the casual walk out to him.

He turned on his last march toward the tree, head snapping over as if he'd sensed me. Like a switch flipped, he went from scowling to smiling, just like that. Pushing off his boots, he closed distance between us. That was when a glint of metallic pink on his chest caught my eye. Suddenly, that ache in my stomach from a moment ago vanished.

He's still wearing my medal. Had he worn it all day? Because of our schedules, we didn't have lunch together today, so I didn't know.

"Hey, you." His gaze swept from the top of my head down to my feet, then back up to my eyes. "How was your day?"

"Okay. Yours?"

His smile broadened, stopping in front of me. "A hell of a lot better now." My heart did a happy jig to that. "Did you do your homework?" he asked, lifting one brow.

"Ugh, Mason," I whined, my arms flapping up and then down. "I told you. I suck at that stuff."

"I'm aware. Henry got the best of you this morning with that celery joke. That's not going to happen again. Not on my watch. Seriously. Five-year old's have better game than you. One joke. Just one. That was all I asked for you to come up with."

"Fine. But let me preface this by stating that not only is this joke stupid, but it makes no sense. And you can blame Dylan because he told it to me."

"I live for stupid and things that make no sense." Crossing his arms, he dug his heels in the wet grass, grinning down at me. "Hit me."

I puffed out my cheeks, letting them deflate. "What do chickens grow on?"

"Eggplants."

"Oh, come on! How did you know that? How would anyone know that? Chickens don't grow on plants! They don't grow on anything. They grow *in*side eggs. Because they're *birds*."

Laughing, Mason uncrossed his arms, shoulders shaking. "Goddamn, you really don't like jokes, do—" In an instant, his smile collapsed, frame stilling with his gaze locked behind me. I looked over my shoulder.

Charlie was standing on the edge of the grass as if she were about to cross the lawn toward us but had thought better of it. Her hair was two inches shorter, the color still blonde but the shade a tad cooler to compliment her skin tone. Her curls even had more shine and bounce if that were possible. Ava had done well. So well that Jamey had said that Shear Strands was booked solid for the rest of the month.

I opened my mouth to tell her, thank her, but her focus was nowhere near mine. It was on Mason.

"You ready, Sticks?" Mason was already walking toward the parking lot.

Frowning, I watched Mason leave without looking back. I shot another glimpse to Charlie. Pressure clamped down on my chest at the hurt etched into her features.

I mouthed, *I'm sorry* to her before I chased after him.

My steps met up with his much larger ones as I angled my head back to his stony expression. "Are you really not going to talk to Charlie?"

"Trust me when I say you don't want me striking up a convo with her right now. I'm not in a good place."

I sighed, knowing I shouldn't push it. He was right, I guess. Mason knew how to strike where it hurt. "Okay, but you don't have to drive me to your house."

He looked at me like I had dropped more than a few IQ points. "Right, I should let you walk there. That should only take you five times as long as driving. I have to keep up with my workouts, and I have a perfectly good gym at home, which is also your place of employment. We are going to the exact same location at the same time. It makes no sense not to drive you."

I shrugged. "Fine."

Mason lifted my bag off my shoulder, placing it on his. "Don't sound so excited about it."

"Well, I'm not excited about you carrying my bag again."

I tried to take it back, but Mason just switched shoulders, so it was out of my reach. While we wove past a group who I swore were chanting in a circle around a golden statue of a squirrel, my eyes meandered to his chest, to the shiny foil between the opening in his fitted leather jacket. Dorky Yoplait medal aside, the boy looked like he was ready to hop on the back of a motorcycle or rock a fashion shoot.

"So, how many people made fun of you today for wearing that thing?"

Glancing over to me, his chest seemed to grow at that. "I'll have you know, all the guys want to earn one of these."

I gave him a look. "Right."

"I'm dead serious. Dylan and Adam are already planning to commission your medals for the Greek Games in April." By the time we reached his truck, a light drizzle had started up again. He popped the handle for me.

"Thank you," I said as I climbed into the seat. Mason set my bag at my feet, and I looked at him with my brows raised. "Greek Games? That's a thing?"

"A *thing*?" Offended, Mason hung onto the door frame, leaning in. "I'll have you know, the Greek Games are bigger than the Super Bowl. We're gonna have the three-legged jockstrap race, beer pong tournament, Solo cup pyramid contest, keg throw, condom toss...the usual." Sliding closer, the wall of his hard abdominals pressed against my thigh as his lips quirked up on one side. "But this year, instead of beer can trophies, we'll have Maggie Medals."

My head hit the seat. "Oh, my God. You named them? You guys need hobbies."

"In the worst way." His eyes were hooded, spiced scent warming me in the ozone-tinged air.

"Okay, I have to know." I swung my head to face him, and his hands flexed on the frame. "How do you toss condoms?"

The other side of his mouth got in on the mix, and his wicked grin was all for my viewing pleasure. "I guess you'll have to join us to find out." Biting his lower hip, his gaze dragged down over me and appeared to linger on my breasts for a beat too long, but I couldn't be sure. The possibility, though, sent a flash of crazy heat to whip through me. "I'll give you a hint..." His eyes lifted to mine. "White T-shirts are mandatory."

"Good grief." I shoved his face out of the door, and he chuckled loudly.

Once at the Scotts', Mason stayed in the basement to work out while I cleaned the house and made dinner. I hadn't a clue how he knew when I'd finished, but within moments of putting my cleaning supplies away, the rock music humming beneath my feet shut off. He jogged up to the main floor with his wallet and keys in hand. I knew I wouldn't win the argument not to drive me home even though it was entirely out of his way, so I conceded and let him. We listened to a country station again, and thinking back, I couldn't remember when he listened to this genre when he wasn't driving.

When we were close to the intersection near my house, I said, "You can stop here on the asphalt."

After a grunt, the truck proceeded onto the muddy trail of Verde Way, risking stuck tires.

"Are you always so stubborn?" I asked.

He scoffed, and because once wasn't enough for him, he threw out another one. "Me? Sticks, you've got me beat on the stubborn front."

"I'm not stubborn. I'm very bendy." Mason's eyes flared with shock, and I corrected myself. "I...I mean affable."

A grin notched the corner of his mouth. "I prefer bendy." When I groaned, he laughed a deep, rumbly sound that made my lady parts happy.

The rain had stopped, the rays of bright oranges and reds splintering between the storm clouds. Turning the wheel, the truck advanced, so we faced west, and I briefly wondered if he did that so we could watch the sunset.

"Hot cocoa again? Whipped cream?"

I tore my eyes off the horizon to find Mason staring at me. "What?"

"Tomorrow morning when I pick you up. We got to school pretty early. How about we hit Henry's first and then go to the coffee shop on Laurel. We can sit for a while and talk."

He... I thought today was a one-time thing. Wasn't that what he meant this morning when he'd said not to get used to this?

I shook my head. "You don't have to do that. My house is out of your way."

He waved to the road. "It's gonna be muddy again and impossible to ride your bike." He wasn't wrong.

"I'll be fine. I can handle a bit of mud."

"Okay," he sighed. "You're a capable, independent, affable woman, and you're always fine. I *want* to pick you up."

Wanted to or felt indebted to? And did he call me a woman?

"You don't owe me anything," I assured him. "You don't have to drive me anywhere or buy me hot cocoa. You don't have to make anything up to me."

Mason's head went back and forth, lips pressed together. "That's not what I'm doing. I'm trying to as—"

Blip! Blip!

At the electronic sound blaring behind us, every organ in my body came to an utter and complete stop. I didn't even move on a cellular level.

Oh, God. The timing couldn't have been worse.

I was so dead. So very dead.

Though I knew what I would see in the rearview mirror, I looked anyway. And gulped.

It was a black and white Tahoe.

It was my father.

chapter thirty-two

maggie

Mason had said something, but things were a little hard to hear with my pulse booming like a storm siren in my ears. As I watched the patrol vehicle pull to a stop on the main road, nausea washed over me.

There was no way out of this. For either of us. And being that we were at the crossroads of Nowhere and No Witnesses, chances of our mutilated bodies being found were…not great.

The second the patrol door opened, I tasted bile and debated if I could roll down the window fast enough to stick my head out of it and throw up. As my reluctant gaze went to the mirror again, I saw a ray of hope that Mason and I would survive one more day.

It was Logan who exited the PPV, rounding the bumper like… Like we'd stolen all the kale in the Cove. I may have been too hasty to assume we had one more day on this Earth.

"Oh…shit," I whispered, watching Logan's brows slam down above his dark wraparounds as he jogged toward us.

Mason shot me a reassuring smile. "I'll handle him."

Handle? Logan? The jacked dude with a gun and who *volunteered* to be the target for taser practice? "No, Mason, I don't think—"

"It's fine, Sticks." Mason lowered his window, the dank air wafting in to mingle with the warmth of the heater. Words died on my tongue as Logan appeared in the window. Mason greeted him with a flat, "Officer."

Logan ignored Mason, pointing that stern look at me. "Does your father know you're with this boy, Magazine?"

"*Magazine?*" Mason repeated under his breath.

I angled over the console so he could hear me better. "He drove me home today because it was raining."

"You didn't answer my question." His jaw was stiff and fixed, reminding me how much of a *cop* Logan was.

I deflated in my seat, hoping I could melt onto the floorboard and drip out the door. "No. I work for his parents, and they asked him to take me home." They hadn't today, they were at work, but I thought it was a good cover, and Mason didn't so much as flinch at my white lie.

"I know who *he* is, and this isn't your home," Logan retorted. "It's the side of the road. Things can happen out here to girls like you."

Ah, shucks. In less than a minute, I'd been downgraded from a woman to a girl. It was nice while it lasted.

Mason was all out glaring now, but Logan made a point to look at the woods before returning the glare. "What do you think you're doing out here with her, kid?"

"Birding. What do you think? I drove her home." I put my hand on Mason's arm in warning. His tone was too sharp, and Logan's chest looked like it was ready to bust a button that could shoot through the glass and take out an eye.

"Logan, really," I interjected. "Mason only did what I asked. This is where I told him to stop. He's not doing anything wrong. I'm getting out right now to walk the rest of the way."

Logan studied Mason with a cold, measuring glower behind his sunglasses. "I'm not letting the chief's daughter walk home in the mud," he said as if he were condemning Mason, all while throwing out a reminder that my father was even scarier than Logan.

Mason's bicep flexed under my hand, and I was pretty sure that was a growl working in his throat.

Logan's chin jutted behind him to the main road. "Hop in the rig. I'll drive you." Without waiting for my response, he left us and walked back to his vehicle.

Body far too tense, Mason's lids tapered into mere slits, watching Logan in the side mirror.

"Mason, thank you for today. It meant more than you know."

His head cranked back to face me, brow relaxed now. "Bring your appetite tomorrow morning. The coffee shop has some decent chocolate croissants, and I can slay half a dozen. I might let you have one."

Dread clamped around my throat, words like acid on my tongue. "Please, don't come tomorrow. Okay?"

The brow was no longer relaxed. "Why?"

I glanced to the red and blue flashing light bar in the back window. "Logan's right. I don't have permission to be in your truck."

"What is this elementary school?" he laughed the words, and I winced. "Jesus, it's not like I'm driving around in my raper van, promising you puppies and candy."

I worked my throat, but it felt too dry, my voice rasping as I said, "I know."

Mason stared at me, and in those seconds, the air became thin and brittle in my chest. He snatched up his phone from the console, thumb bringing it to life. "There's an easy fix. I'll call your father and get his permission."

I threw my hand over his before he could ask what numbers to press. "Please, Mason. I'm not being stubborn. I'm asking you to respect my wishes and not come tomorrow."

Dropping the phone in his lap, he shook his head. His aggravation with me soured my stomach, causing it to cramp. "Fine. If that's what you want."

I shouldn't have said it, but before I could stop, the words slipped out. "It's not." I twisted to the door, ready to hurl my mortification out into the mud.

Something *clicked*, and after two tries, I caught on that the door wasn't opening. I turned back to see there was hurt, true and deep, in his eyes. "Can you give me ten more seconds so I can pull to the road?"

Oh... "I— Yes, of course. Thank you."

Grumbling something unintelligible about gorillas, Mason spun the wheel, and the truck advanced out of the mud and onto Canyon Boulevard. He stopped, put the gear in Park, and released the locks.

"See you at school." His tone had a hard edge to it, and my throat felt as if it were trying to seal itself shut.

There was no mistaking that he was upset with me. Swallowing, I gripped the handle with my slick hand. "Bye, Mason. And thank you again."

I jumped down with my bag, looking up at him one last time, expecting Mason to ignore me like he had Charlie, but...he didn't. His gaze was locked with mine until I closed the door, and even through the tinted window, I could feel those eyes on me.

I trudged back toward Logan as he opened the passenger door. I gave my shoes a good stomp to knock off anything on them before I slipped inside. Logan shut me in and strode over to his side of the Tahoe.

After he had settled behind the wheel, Logan's sunglasses aimed my way. "What are you doing out here with that kid?"

"I told you." That was the harshest I'd ever spoken to Logan, and I didn't feel an ounce of regret for it. "We weren't doing anything wrong.

I just don't want him to see how crappy my house is, so I asked him to drop me off right here. He was being nice."

Logan tore his sunglasses off, chestnut eyes narrowing at me. "No, Maggie. I meant, what are you doing with the boy who framed you for stealing?"

"It wasn't him. It was his ex's sister. Mason didn't know."

The Raptor hadn't moved yet, and from behind the wheel, Logan studied the tailgate, either memorizing the license plate or hoping to melt it with his glower alone. "You like him?"

"He's my friend." And that was all. Nothing more.

Logan finally released his death glare off the truck. "That wasn't an answer." His words were clipped, and heat infused my chest, rising up to my cheeks. He'd never been upset with me, never used that tone with me before, and my frustration burned brighter.

Mason hadn't been wrong to get angry. It was polite of him to offer me a ride home. It wasn't his fault that my father was a psychopath and would prefer I suffer than be shown any kindness. And for his kindness, Mason had been branded the villain.

It was all too fucked up.

"It doesn't matter what I think of him. It will never matter. We're from different worlds. I work for his family in a house that's in between the ocean and a manmade lake with yachts lining the dock. There are flat-screen televisions in every room of his home. I clean their knickknacks that cost more than everything I own, wash their designer clothes in machines that have touchscreens, and cook meals for them with food that I can't afford to eat myself. And after I do all that, I come home to this." I waved to the dark woods. "I'm not under any delusions here. I'm a have-not, and I don't belong."

Though Logan's frame was still taut as a bowstring, his voice softened. "Then maybe you should focus your time on where you feel like you do belong."

Slumping, I cast my eyes down to my knotted fingers. The flare of irritation had been smothered, only to be replaced by defeat. "I don't know where that is."

His large hand slid over both of mine and stayed there. "It's closer than you think, Magi."

I lifted my gaze to find his expression was filled with warmth and maybe a dash of pity. My lips parted, ready to ask him to elaborate, but Logan dragged his hand away before I could. He shifted the engine into Drive and advanced down Verde Way. My gaze drifted to my side mirror, and when we turned the corner, Mason's truck was still there.

Logan pulled up to my house, behind my father's PPV that was sitting in the carport. As per usual, because the patrol vehicle's technical gear sucked down the battery, Logan didn't turn the engine off when he exited.

The front door opened to my father as Poker whipped around from the back of the house and sprinted right for us, wagging his tail like a happiness propeller. Logan gave Poker his requested rubdown, not caring that his coat was damp and muddy.

"What's going on, Jackson?" My father never called Logan *LJ* like everyone else did, and I wasn't sure if that was at Logan's request or my father's need to control everything, even down to someone's name. His icy glare slid between us, and by his prolonged blink, I'd guessed he'd had two doubles so far.

"Just gave Maggie a lift is all. I was making my rounds when I spotted her."

Uh, okay. I honestly hadn't expected Logan to lie for me.

My father's gaze narrowed on Logan, voice dropping to a low growl as an eerie chill trickled across my skin. "It stopped raining a few minutes ago. If that were true, she should be wet. What's the truth?"

Ah...shit.

Logan started, "Chief—"

"Mason Scott drove me to Verde Way," I interrupted, "and that's where Logan found us."

All his attention turned toward me, and my chest suddenly felt like it was caving in on itself as if my sternum were trying to escape through my spinal column. "You were parked with that boy? Alone?"

"Yes, sir. And I was just thanking him for the ride when Lo—"

"*Jackson.*" Glare focused on me, he asked, "What were they doing?"

Logan didn't answer right away, but by that uncomfortable shift in his boots, I'd say he was regretting his life choices today. "Chief, they were sitting in the cab, talking. Nothing else."

My father's frame was far too stiff, but one finger lifted to punctuate his words. "Jackson, when I ask you a question, I expect a direct and truthful answer."

"Of course, Chief. I pulled up to the idle truck, and I was concerned, but it did seem as though the boy only drove her to where she directed him."

After a long glare, he gave Logan a curt nod. "Continue your patrol."

"Yes, Chief." Logan turned, and when only I could see, he mouthed, *I'm sorry.* With my father's eyes on me, I couldn't react. Logan had tried to help me, and I appreciated it, but he should have let me walk home.

Once Logan's PPV drove away, my father returned to the house, the front door slamming shut behind him. Whatever awaited me tonight was going to suck.

Setting my bag by the back door, I slipped off my muddy shoes and damp socks. I grabbed the dog bowls, and Poker followed me, taking the lead inside. I groaned, having forgotten to wipe down his feet as the muddy paw prints on the linoleum reminded me.

"Po—" My voice cut off when my head snapped backward, pain searing throughout my scalp as each hair was wrenched at the root by his hand. The shock to my vertigo had me reeling, Poker's bowls dropping from my hands. The dishes clanged off the floor, spilling what was left of his water and food crumbs.

Panic inundated me down to the bone, raw instinct flooding my muscles. I twisted my shoulders, knocking away his too-large grip from my too-short ponytail, but I slipped on the floor and went into a freefall. Before I hit the ground, he caught me around the throat, crushing my windpipe. Air was locked in my lungs as I was lifted up, the back of my head and shoulders slamming against the wall. My gaze was pinned to the ceiling, fighting against him as I gasped for air.

Barks and snarls filled my ears. As the roar of my pulse dampened the noise, I felt my father lurch to the side, Poker yelping sharply.

Rank horror filled me, knowing he must have kicked him. "Poker!" His hand tightened around my throat, mere wisps of air able to pass through my windpipe.

I clawed at his fingers, choking out, "No! I'll p—put him outside. Pl...ease."

He let me go, gravity welcoming me as my knees cracked off the floor. Between heaving coughs, I dragged in precious gulps of air, the room swirling in my vision. Over by the coffee table, I spotted a lump of tan and black fur. On my hands and knees, I crawled to Poker, and he met me with laps of his tongue, bathing my face. He seemed okay, maybe a bit stunned, but I didn't have time to fully assess him. The monster was ready to rage, and I had to get Poker out of the house before things got worse.

I somehow found my legs as my fingers wrapped around his collar, and I tugged him to the laundry room. I prayed he didn't have a broken bone because I wasn't gentle with him.

As I pushed the door open, the damp air swathed my heated skin. My arms shook from a toxic concoction of adrenaline and fear, and I needed all my strength to wrestle Poker outside. As soon as I got his tail past the door, he whipped around, hard muzzle thrusting against me to get back inside.

"No, boy. You gotta stay out," I pleaded.

Out. Free. Safe.

I lifted my gaze to the darkening woods, desperate for the same. To get out. To be free. To feel safe.

Poker's back straightened as if sensing my thoughts, those brown eyes meeting mine, urging me on. Poker could run. His foot was healed. My backpack was outside, too, but the weight of it would slow me down. Jamey had my emergency bag at his house. I'd have to run there or find a phone to call him for help.

I didn't need to decide which now. All I had to do was run.

I flung the door back open and squeezed past the bumper of the Tahoe, scraping my hip in the process. He shouted my name like it was a curse, and I pumped my legs as fast as they would go, welcoming the fire as it tore down my thighs. Leaving the carport, the wind stung my eyes, icy air lacing my throat, seizing inside my chest as if it were trying to slow me down for him. My bare feet slicked across the cold mud as I tried like hell to get traction.

Huff, puff. Huff, puff.

His breaths were getting closer, and I pushed faster, dug my toes in firmer, swung my arms harder. I could beat him at long-distance. I only had to get a good enough sprint in. The tree line was just feet away, Poker leading me to freedom.

Huff, puff. Huff—

In the space of one heartbeat, the bones in my wrist were crushed, my entire body jolting backward. As my feet were taken out from under me, my startled cry fractured the silence. Birds were flushed from the trees as the Earth spun, my tailbone colliding with the ground so hard, my brain rattled, scrambling my thoughts. Before I could catch my breath, a bolt of heat tore through my shoulder, ripping down to my fingertips.

The ground began to move beneath me, my legs tumbling across the muck and grass like useless sandbags. I tipped my head back to see that he had me hooked by the wrist, hanging by the fragile bones as if I were a fish on a line.

Poker barked and snapped, lunging around me to get at his target. The woods were getting further away, shrinking in my distorted vision. With a savage growl, Poker lunged again, and this time, he accidentally gouged my ribs with his nails. With a roar, my father hauled me to my feet, but they faltered, slipping and sinking wherever I planted them. The more I stumbled, the harder he crushed my wrist. Unable to keep his pace, I was more or less dragged back to the house, my heels scraping across the concrete of the carport.

He shoved the front door open so hard it cracked against the wall. As he lumbered through the doorway with me dangling from his grip, I inadvertently blocked Poker from getting inside. He pounced once more, and I had to twist sharply to the side before he mauled me with his ferocious canines. As his nails scraped down my jean covered thigh, ready to leap and attack again, I was heaved over the threshold and spun, knocking Poker to the ground. My father's foot kicked out, and the door slammed shut, locking Poker outside. He released my wrist, the walls blurring together as I flailed. Landing on the carpet, my cheek took the brunt of the fall, the taste of earth and copper stretching across my tongue.

I flipped over to see his hand working at his waist, shoulders bunched forward. "You've got some nerve running from me."

Poker's barks leached through the walls, and I heard him run to the laundry room door, ramming into it, searching for any way inside to get to me.

My chest heaved as I fought to control my voice. "I'm sorry. You scared me when you kicked Poker. I panicked. It won't happen again."

His lids drew down, sharpening his pale eyes as he stalked toward me. "*I'm sorry?* One of my officers brought you home after finding you parked with a boy. That *Scott* boy. The very one I told you to stay the fuck away from. Did you really think I wouldn't punish you after that?"

Did he not realize I was alone with Mason *in his house* five days a week? Some things were best left unsaid.

"No, sir. I know I deserve it. You took me by surprise. I reacted."

"And now you've got my men lying for you?" He worked his belt free and let it fall straight down by his leg. My eyes glanced to it, then back up to his tempered fury that was sure to break free at any moment.

"Yes, sir. I asked Logan to lie because I knew how mad you would be. It's all my fault. But it was only a ride home. Nothing happened."

He loomed over me, fury seething in that frosty glare. "You didn't have my permission or let me know you were getting a ride home."

"No, sir." My voice shook, and I tried swallowing, but it didn't help. "Mason was being nice. He offered since the roads were muddy, and I accepted. I didn't want to be late because I know how you hate it when I'm late. I'm sorry."

Leaning over me, he closed the distance and wagged the leather in my face. "I am to know where your ass is and who you are with. I know the Scotts have a telephone. I saw it in their motherfucking house."

With everything in me, I resisted the urge to crawl away, scream, scratch out his eyes. "Yes, sir. You're right. Of course, I should have called."

The belt slid along one hand until it reached the end, and then he folded it in half. "You need a reminder of my rules."

I dug my hands into the carpet, shrinking before him, making his target smaller. "Please, sir. It was a mistake. I made a poor judgment call. I'll do better next time."

He gripped the belt tighter, the leather keening as if pleading for a taste of my skin. The corner of his mouth lifted in a smirk as if both of them were about to enjoy every second of what they were going to do to me. Stark terror seized me.

"Looks like your day was full of mistakes and poor judgment calls, Margaret. I guess I'll have to give you a lesson about accepting a ride home without permission. And for wearing a sweater that isn't fucking yours."

Oh…fuck.

chapter thirty-three

mason

I should have said to hell with what Maggie wanted and drove to her house this morning. I didn't doubt that damn cop was armed and waiting for me. Probably stayed there all night, eagerly awaiting to put me in a rear naked choke hold or whip out a machine gun and quote *Scarface* at me.

So instead of waking my ass up at the crack of dawn to sit on the side of the road for a half-hour, wearing a smile the entire time like an ass, I slept in and sulked in the parking lot while Ben and Jamey discussed...something. I was too busy stewing in my own *coulda-woulda-shouldas* to listen.

This blows.

No football. No cocoa. No chocolate croissants. No little raven beauty.

Bam! I startled as the vibration along BB's frame shook my back, and within a cluster of bleary-eyed Wolverines, Cam sauntered toward me. Because that was what Cam did. *Saunter.* And throw me a shit-eating grin because I was scowling at him for pounding on my tailgate.

"Good morning, loser and dick lovers. Were you waiting for us?"

I pushed off my Raptor, leveling my cousin with a glare. "If you mean, were we waiting for the biggest twatwaffle on campus? Then, yes."

Cam snorted. "Please. If we weren't related, you'd do me."

"I wholeheartedly disagree. I'd bang Adam or Noah long before you."

"The fuck?" Cam blinked at me in utter shock and then looked down at himself. "You would rather Fabio or the dude who drinks wine coolers over *me?*"

Adam adjusted his ballcap, tucking his blond locks back as he groused, "I'm not even Italian, by the way."

"And there's nothing wrong with wine coolers, asshole." Noah shouldered his bag. "Technically, it's a malt beverage, in the same category as beer."

Cam swung his head toward Noah. "Are you really gonna defend your fuzzy navels to me?"

"You weren't complaining Saturday night." Noah winked and blew Cam a kiss. "You know it makes my cum sweet."

Taking a step back, Dylan held his palms high. "Okay. For reals. I so *don't* want to know if that's a true fact."

Cam made a noise of dismissal in the back of his throat, whiskey eyes trained on me. "Anyway. Back to the real issue here. There is no way you wouldn't want to fuck me. We'd be so hot together."

Assessing us, Pete nodded thoughtfully. "You do have an appealing height ratio."

"Pete would know." Mike popped open a family-sized bag of chips. "He's the king of porn."

A single brow arched as Pete stole a BBQ Ruffle from Mike. "I prefer *connoisseur of porn.*"

Ben coughed, water spewing from his lips, and Jamey smacked him on the back until he could talk. Ben choked out, "Are you legit discussing gay incest right now?"

Cam's head spun back to his brother. "You bet your shaved balls we are." His attention zeroed in on me again. "Let's get one thing straight, Coz—"

"It wouldn't be this convo, that's for sure," Jamey muttered, and the rest of the guys chuckled.

"—I'd be the best fuck you ever had," Cam rolled on. "I'd suck you off balls deep, and then I'd fuck that sweet ass of yours until the morning. I'd have you begging for my cock. Nothing would be off-limits. Dick, balls, taint…" Words trailing off, Cam's gaze crawled to my side, eyes widening to the point that would fascinate anyone with an ophthalmology degree. "H—hey, Maggie."

Oh. Sweet. Moses.

I pinched my lids shut until my eyes threatened to retreat into my skull. "Please, don't tell me that Sticks is standing right behind me and she heard any of that."

"Okay," Owen drawled. "We won't tell you that Sticks is literally one inch behind you, and the chances she heard all of that are pretty damn good."

God, I sensed her. The skin on the back of my neck warmed, my blood pumping faster, muscles tightening, body coming alive at her very presence.

Her sweet voice asked, "Do men really shave their balls? Aren't they...wrinkly? Isn't that dangerous?"

Swiveling, I pounded my forehead on the truck door. "Motherfucker. How did not one of you see her there?"

"We can't help it!" Jordon cried out. "The chick moves up on you like a Prius."

"Is it true about the fuzzy navels?" she asked.

My head flew to the side so fast, I gave myself whiplash. "Don't you dare answer that shit, Noah."

"That's not fair," she protested, and I imagined those topaz eyes of hers were burning holes into the back of my head. "Why can't I be included?"

I turned to face her. "Because, Sticks, you are— Why do you look like Hell chewed you up and spit you out?"

Not only did the slumped posture and purple smudges under her eyes make her look like she hadn't slept in five weeks, but mud was splattered all over the bottom cuffs of her jeans, and her not-so-white Chucks were now dirt brown. Because she rode her bike in the mud. Because she refused a ride from me today. Damn stubborn girl.

"I'm fine." She set her bag down without any finesse, and my thoughts about how she probably got her tires stuck fifty times this morning died.

Her hands were usually pretty steady by the middle of the week. These were Sunday tremors. Either she hadn't slept, or she was stressed about something. Maybe a combo.

"You are not fine," I argued. "Were you tossing and turning all night because you realized you wouldn't see me first thing this morning?"

She gave me a weak laugh and knelt to unzip her bag. "Hardly."

Ouch.

While I nursed my invisible wounds, my sweatshirt made an appearance as Maggie stood. "Thanks for letting me borrow that."

I swore my heart was shrinking the longer I refused to grab the perfectly folded blue and gray sweater. I shook my head. "You can keep it. You know I've got more at home."

The sweater was now being shoved against my stomach. "It's ridiculously huge on me, Mason."

Still declining to take it, my brows flew up. "Which is different from the rest of your clothes, how?"

Her lips pressed together, giving me a look. "Funny. Now take it. I can't wear it." She pretty much thrust the thing into my face, and the scent of laundry detergent hit me. Right in the gut. Hell, she couldn't even leave her cinnamony goodness on it for me?

Since I didn't want to have an argument about something so absurd, I took the sweatshirt and chucked it inside the backseat of my truck. As soon as I shut the door, Maggie blew out a sigh, relieved maybe, and yeah, that hurt more than the *hardly* she threw at me. I liked her wearing my clothes. I liked seeing her in them yesterday, pretending this was more than friendship. I also liked that other men on campus had noticed that she was wearing something of mine. As if she were mine.

She wasn't, and this morning drove that home.

"So, really. Why did you stop talking when I walked up?" She looked to me expectantly and then to the group of morons surrounding us.

"Because you're...Maggie," D explained.

"And?" she pressed. "What am I, like, your mom?"

"No." Vic rubbed the back of his neck, casting me an uncomfortable glance. "It's just that this...uh—"

"It's locker room talk, Sticks. We're busting each other's balls. It's not appropriate in front of a lady."

"I can handle it." Maggie stood straighter, and there was something in her stance, a determination in her eyes that launched me back to moments like this with Faith. She'd catch Matt and me throwing out curse words like candy. We'd stop talking, and she would wear that same look, wanting in, desperate to be one of us. We wouldn't give in, of course, because she was our baby sister, and our job was to protect her, shield her from hearing about cocks, pussy, pros, and booze.

I felt that same desire now to shield Maggie but in a different way. More like...*I* wanted to be the one who brought her to the dark side, make her ears burn, talk dirty to her with my tongue between her thighs, whispering all the things I wanted to do to her as she begged for more.

"I know you can handle it." I shifted the bag on my shoulder. "I'm not excluding you, but this was going too far, even for us. Believe me, I need another shower after that."

She crumpled her lips, looking away from me. "Fine."

It was as if I could feel the energy drain right out of me with that resignation in her tone. This morning wasn't going at all how I hoped. Being with Maggie was like climbing Everest, and every time I made it past base camp, I slipped and fell right back down the mountain.

I went for the only opening there was and nudged her arm. "I know it's not Sunday, but you up for a run after school? You can make it hard and get me all sweaty."

Cam cleared his throat. Annoyingly.

When I slid him a sideways glare, his eyes gleamed with mischief. Then the idiot crew laughed along.

Picking up on that, Maggie rotated toward Cam. "Okay, why do you do that? I know I'm missing something."

I flashed him a look that promised testicular pain. "Sticks, ignore him. Cam's a Richard."

"A…what?" She tilted her head at me. "What does that mean?"

Damn, she was too innocent to be around us.

"A dick, Mags. Richard is code for *dick*." Laughing, Ben slid an arm over her shoulders, and I could have sworn she winced.

Before I could ask if she'd hurt herself again, Maggie shifted those blue eyes to Cam. "That coughing thing…you're making fun of me, aren't you?"

"No, he's not," I said, trying to reassure her.

Not convinced, she flattened her lips. "I'm gonna figure it out, Camden."

Smirking, he rocked on his heels. "I hope you do, Maggie."

I needed a change of topic.

"So, guys!" I clapped once to divert the discussion. "Three-day weekend coming up. Where's the party gonna be?"

Pete nabbed another chip from Mike's bag and crunched down. "Brady's having something already."

Owen snorted. "When is Brady not having something?"

"Frat's getting a little done. I could use a different venue," Jordon piped in, and I completely agreed. "The beach?"

Noah stretched his arms, almost knocking off Adam's ballcap. "D won't be able to discover the aftereffects of my fuzzy navels if we go to a public beach."

"True, and we had the last party," Ben replied, looking at me pointedly.

I didn't like having parties at my home, but chances were looking nil that I would ever get Maggie to the RAM house. She'd been to Ben's house, and my place wasn't off-limits. Maybe it could work. Maybe this weekend we could take the next step.

"The 'rents are going out of town. Saturday okay?" Everyone nodded. Everyone *but* Maggie, the one person I really wanted there. In fact, she was the only reason I wanted to have a damn party. Canting my head, I playfully flicked her paintbrush ponytail. "Well?"

"I have to work," she told her shoes.

I chased her gaze but couldn't get that low. "Ask for the day off."

She nibbled her bottom lip, at the last bit of ChapStick left. "It's not that easy."

Jamey slid his fingers between hers. "I'm sure Frankie—"

"Fine." She cut him off, shaking out of his hold. "I've gotta go to my locker." And that was that. Maggie was out.

Did something happen this morning? Was she really that upset about us not including her?

"See you guys later," I tossed out over my shoulder as I took off to follow her. Taking three strides, I caught up. "Hey, what's the hurry?" I tugged on her hand, and I caught her wincing that time. Drawing her hand away to tuck inside her pocket, Maggie's eyes remained firmly planted on her feet as we stopped. "Are you okay? What's wrong?"

Her chest fell with a breath. "What's wrong is I can't go to a party, Mason. You put me on the spot. I don't know why you bother asking me."

"Bother asking…?" I tore off my sunglasses. "I asked because I want you to come. I like hanging out with you. That's what friends do, you know. Hang out." My shoulders dropped a few notches. "I thought you felt the same way."

"I do," she amended, arching her head back to face me. "I just…I don't fit in. Isn't that obvious?"

My eyes shot skyward, trying to figure out what the hell she was talking about. All the guys worshiped her. And yesterday, I wasn't exaggerating about the Maggie Medals. The brothers had seriously rocked green when I strolled across campus with that.

I brought my head back down. "No. It's not obvious at all."

Releasing another tense breath, her gaze dipped somewhere around my chest. "I'll try. That's the best I can give you. Okay?"

"That's all I asked." Without thinking, I tucked a few loose hairs behind her left ear, but Maggie lurched away from my touch as if I'd burned her.

My stomach hollowed as my hand remained in a holding pattern mid-air. "Sorry, I— Sorry." I was sorry but hurt, too. I thought she had trusted me enough to see her scar now.

"No. It's—" Sighing, she patted the hair down on her temple, voice hesitant, eyes refusing to meet mine when she asked, "Do I need a mirror?"

"A mirror?" I dumbly repeated. "Why?"

"To hide the dent in my skull, Mason." Those eyes flashed a deep azure as she waved an irritated hand to her temple. "Is it showing? I haven't checked it yet after riding my bike."

Oh. While I didn't love her terminology, I took the request seriously. Thinking about it now, she usually did take a trip to the bathroom in the morning before class. Totally dumb of me, but I never realized she was checking to see if her scar was hidden.

I examined the area, finding nothing. "No, but so what if it was?"

The look she gave told me that was the wrong thing to say.

"I meant that it's not a big deal. To anyone else." And it wasn't. Not to me anyway.

Frowning, Maggie tightened her ponytail. "We'll have to agree to disagree on that one."

My sour expression mirrored hers. I hated when she debased herself like this. "Okay. I'll concede to disagree, but if I think you'd want me to tell you to fix your hair, I'll tell you. How does that sound?"

"Perfect." Still frowning, she aimed toward her locker, and I chased her. Because that was what I did now. I was a six-foot-three, 215-pound puppy dog, panting after her and ready to heel at her command. "So when is your suspension over?" she asked.

I followed Maggie into a tunnel that I had discovered by accident last year, and at first, I thought the lockers had to be either a joke or a relic like one of the fifty statues of the founders on campus. Imagine my shock when I learned that they actually had a purpose and worked. Kinda.

I leaned against the locker next to hers and watched her wrestle with the combo lock. It took her four tries and three huffs to get the thing open. I knew better by now not to offer the dreaded H-word. I'd considered buying her a biometric padlock, but she would never accept it from me. Besides, the extra time with her gave me a chance to think up some fresh fantasy material.

"Next Friday. It's our first game. It wasn't much of a punishment, but Evans had to do something with me, and I'm hoping Watkins won't live up to his threat of having me dig the grass out of the team's cleats with my teeth."

Gasping, her lids flared, mouth gaping as she stared at me. "That's disgusting. Can he really do that?"

I chuckled. "Nah. Or…" My smile faltered when I thought back to the gleam in his beady eyes. "Anyway, I've been keeping up with my workouts, but I missed out on the team practices and meetings, which sucked. I'd like you to come—"

"*Mason.*"

Rotating my head to the lilting voice, I jutted out my chin in greeting. "Hey, Rebecca."

My physics partner clipped her way toward us, a finger curling around a straight bundle of blonde hair right at the popped buttons of her top, and by the fuck-me eyes she was sporting, Rebecca was ready to pop the rest and show me the very little I couldn't see of her black bra.

"Catch ya at lunch," was mumbled below me, and I turned around to see Maggie walk—correction—*run* off. The hell? "Sticks? Where—" And she was out.

"So, Mase…" Rebecca swung into my line of sight, taking the very spot Maggie had been occupying, and blocked my view of her leaving. "I hate to ask, but can I borrow your notes again?"

"Yeah, no prob. I'll snap pics and send them by next period. Is that cool?"

Catching her bottom lip between her teeth, she nodded. And then the batting of the lashes began. "So, Vic said there's a party at your house Saturday?"

Her tone was both questioning and suggestive. I gathered she wanted an invite, which wasn't necessary. Parties were kind of a come-one-come-all thing.

"News traveled rather quickly this morning," I muttered dryly.

Her lips formed a cute pout. "That it did. I only ask because I didn't get a chance to show you my bikini at Ben's party. You were a little busy with a certain ex. It would be a shame if you missed it again."

I was ready to shut that down when Rebecca stood even closer, close enough for her chest to brush against mine, her flowery perfume itching the back of my throat. The valley she thrust in front of me begged my attention, and, well, I was a guy. Without making the conscious decision, I took the invitation.

Something must have short-circuited in my brain because words began to tumble out, unbidden. "If you're there, I'll be sure to check out your bikini."

What the fuck was I saying?

Batting her eyes, Rebecca whispered huskily, "How about if you check out what's *under* the bikini?" She covered her hand with her body and grabbed my cock over my shorts. The shudder that tore up my spine was purely physical, and her glossed lips formed a satisfied grin, knowing she had the response she was looking for. She just didn't know that she wasn't the one who elicited that response. *Maggie had.*

"I'll see you both this weekend." Before I could reply, she spun on a heel and clipped away with her plaid skirt kicking up to reveal a matching black thong that hugged a perfect ass.

All I could do was stand there in the middle of the underpass, hard as ever as my stomach twisted around what felt like shards of glass. I really needed that shower now. My skin tightened like it wanted to swap places with my bones. Even my chest felt weird and…empty.

What was this? *Guilt?* Guilt for what exactly? Being a dude? Getting hard—well, *harder*—because a woman threw herself at me? Wasn't that a normal response? A healthy response? Didn't men take little blue pills to have that very normal and healthy response?

So why did I feel like such a shit? Why did I feel like I was…*cheating* on Maggie? Stupid question. Because Maggie was who I wanted and had that same, very normal and healthy response to on what seemed like an hourly—okay, twenty-minute basis—and she was who I wanted to see in a bikini.

I grimaced as my shorts rubbed against me all wrong during my walk to class, and my situation was getting worse, balls getting bluer. Fuck, I hated that I had this thing between my thighs, that someone who wasn't Maggie had touched me. Again.

I should have told Rebecca no, made it clear where my head was at. The head on *top* of my body. Maybe I needed to add a mandatory jerk-off session to my morning routine.

I flipped through a scene from *Gone Girl*—the one where the poor schmuck got his throat slashed by the psycho chick. That did the trick pretty damn quick.

Half the day down, it was Maggie time, and I grinned when she appeared on the lawn with her ratty blue lunch bag. Jamey and Ben were already on the grass with me, settled with their trays of food. Speaking of…

"Why are you late?" I asked her. "Your locker giving you trouble again?"

Picking a spot next to me, Maggie was occupied with her backpack, probably looking for her ChapStick. There wasn't a snarky response thrown my way, so I figured she hadn't heard me since we had a bird chorus above us in the oak tree, and I overheard the group on the lawn next to us arguing about where to host the next zombie attack.

I tried again. "How were your morning classes?"

Crickets. Huh.

"Sticks?"

Her head stayed down, quivering fingers rifling through more pockets.

Okay, I knew Maggie's mood was off this morning, but I didn't take her for a girl who would give me the silent treatment. "Maggie?"

Hearing the concern in my tone, Jamey snapped his attention away from Ben. "*Mags?*"

Her head shot up as an immediate nauseated look came over her. Grunting, Maggie squeezed her eyes shut until the vertigo passed. "What?"

His brows pinched together. "Are you feeling okay?"

Her lashes stayed pinned to her cheekbones, forehead bunched tight. "Yeah. I...was just thinking."

"Were you thinking about the first time you saw a unicorn?" I was referring to our speech due in Allen's class tomorrow.

Lifting her gaze, Maggie's stare drifted to...well, nowhere.

Concern stamped into Jamey's features as he cupped her face. "Mags!"

Blinking, she shook her head, focusing on her friend. "Sorry. What?"

"Where are you right now?"

"Here." Maggie tugged his hands off her. "I'm here."

Yeah...no one believed that.

Leaning in, I brushed the back of my knuckles along her cheek. Her breath caught, but she didn't swat me away this time. "Do you need to go home and rest? I'll drive you."

"I'm okay, really. I was spacing for a minute. I'm good. I promise." Maggie's focus was back on her bag, and it was then I realized she hadn't looked directly at me. Not once. "How did it go with Rebecca?" Her tone came out so casual, like D would ask me, and I so didn't want to discuss Rebecca or any other girl with her.

"Fine. She needed to borrow my notes. I was going to introduce you, but you left." *Ran* to be more specific.

Nodding, she finally withdrew the tube of ChapStick from her bag, checking that it had a broken seal instead of the new one that was in her back pocket. "Oh. She seemed nice. Pretty, too."

Uh...

Nice? Pretty? Was I crazy, or was Maggie pushing Rebecca into my lap? I kinda thought Maggie and I were on the same page here. Friends first. Then friends who flirted. Then friends who were a hell of a lot more than friends.

Right?

My lips thinned. "Yeah, she's pretty. And hot." I waited for a response. A flinch. A hitch of breath. A scowl.

Nothing. *There really was nothing.*

Was Maggie saving face, or was this really it between us? Motherfucking friends?

I hadn't a clue where Maggie's head was at the rest of the day because it wasn't with me. I think the most I'd gotten out of her was a nod, maybe a headshake. Bernard communicated more than this.

After taking her home, we sat quietly in my drive, and Maggie had made no effort to unbuckle her belt, which was unusual as hell for her.

"Sticks?"

Her head drifted over to me, eyes the color of tropical waters under black clouds.

I waved to my house. "We're here."

She turned to look out the window, blinking. "Oh."

Before her fingers wrapped around the buckle, I noticed her shakes had worsened since lunch. And her gait had been hella unsteady when we'd walked to my tru—

Shit. Oh, shit.

My hand shot out to cup her jaw, bringing her head up to study her glazed stare. "You've been out of it all day. I can't believe I didn't think of it. You could be having complex partial seizures. I should call Dad."

Shrugging me off, Maggie unclipped herself and grabbed her backpack. "I'm not, Mason. I just have a lot on my mind.

Frowning, I hoped that was it. "You didn't have a chance to answer me this morning. Do you want to run with me? You can borrow Mom's gear again." Maybe I could get her to relax and open up a little. And I had been jonesing to run with her, as odd as that sounded coming from my brain.

I prepared myself for the inevitable argument that it really was okay to spend part of her shift running with me, and that Mom wouldn't care if she borrow—

"Sure. Sounds good."

That...was too easy. Maybe we'd finally turned a corner.

She hopped down from the truck and headed toward the front door. Maggie waited for me to unlock it, not bothering to get her key. With her tremor being so bad right now, we both knew she'd only get frustrated if she couldn't get the door open on the first try.

She followed me inside and keyed off the alarm like this was our old routine.

We both changed and grabbed a water from the fridge, at some point deciding we'd try for five miles today. We headed outside and began our warmup with a light jog. The trail around the lake had firmed since the rain, and the sun glinted against the water, necessitating shades. It didn't take long for me to catch on that something was definitely wrong when there was an absence of burn in every muscle, and I could breathe without losing a lung. I knew she was a little off today, but we were going slow. Too slow.

"What's going on? I'm only ten steps behind you, and I can actually talk."

"Just a little sore, that's all." She wasn't even breathing hard.

"Sore from what?"

She swiped a dismissive hand through the air. "I pulled the fridge out to sweep behind it and yanked my back again."

"Are you *fucking* kidding me?" Maggie came to a startled stop at my louder than necessary decibel level that flushed three ducks out of the water. "Why the hell didn't you say something when I asked if you were okay this morning? I never would have dragged you out here if I knew you were hurt."

She gave me a lopsided shrug. "If I took it easy every time I wasn't feeling good, I'd never get off the couch."

My mouth folded down in the corners. "If you hurt your back, the last thing you should be doing is running five miles. You haven't been yourself all day. What is going on with you?"

She shifted under my stare. "Nothing."

I mashed my lips together. "*Maggie...*"

"Okay," she conceded. "I might have a little too much going on this week. One test I need to study for, plus I have two papers due. The fictional story for Allen isn't even halfway done. And are we really supposed to give a speech about freaking unicorns? It's kinda stupid."

It wasn't kinda stupid. It was completely stupid. "Why didn't you tell me?"

"I didn't want to say anything because..." As her gaze skipped over to the lake, I could see all the scratches lining her cheap lenses. I didn't have a clue how she could see out of them. "It doesn't matter."

I stepped closer, and she visibly stiffened. "It matters. Why, Maggie?"

I couldn't see, of course, but by the tightening of her mouth, I imagined she was pinching her eyes, too. "It may be presumptuous of me, but I don't want you to feel pity or guilt about me working and running with you."

"It's not presumptuous. You're exactly right. You should be studying—"

Her head flew back, but she kept her feet planted this time. Funny how the littlest of exercise could help ease her symptoms, which frustrated me to no end that I couldn't do more for her.

"I knew what I was signing up for when I took two jobs, Mason. And I was handling it fine until I hurt my stupid back again, and it... I didn't need *one* more thing. You know?"

Okay, I could buy that. "So, let's go back."

She flinched like I'd slapped her. "I don't want to go back. I want to finish. I want to run with you. This is the only time that I get...to enjoy something." It was so quick, but I was pretty sure her lip trembled before her tongue darted out and started licking manically.

I got that, too. I understood what she was saying, but her damn stubbornness was only going to cause her more pain and delay her healing.

With a gentle hand, I held her sweaty cheek. "I'm not going to put your health at risk. You're hurt. So, we'll walk back unless you want to be affable and let me carry you."

Just like earlier, I had expected more arguing, a snarky comeback at least, but that wasn't what I got. The flames inside her died then and there without so much as a whiff of smoke. She withdrew into herself, going somewhere that I couldn't reach her. She quietly slipped away and walked back to my house without a word.

Well, hell.

chapter thirty-four

mason

Maggie's demeanor hadn't changed all week. And worse, we'd hardly spoken in days, and I didn't know why I felt responsible for that. Honestly, I hadn't done anything wrong that I could think of, and I'd done nothing *but* think about it. Obsess would be a better term for what I was doing. I also didn't know if Maggie was coming to the party since she was noncommittal every time I asked her.

When I woke up Saturday, my thoughts went right to Maggie, which was no different from any other morning. I knew she would be working now, and this was around the time that cop would be there. Matt and I needed to make a run to the liquor store in Pacific Cliffs, but he was still sleeping, and I didn't think he'd willingly step inside the restaurant again anyway. I decided to swing by the café alone, but the second my tires hit Sands Drive, my chest began to feel as if a giant were using it for a stress ball.

Maybe this was a bad idea. The closer I got to the café, the less confident I felt that I could actually do this. There was only one reason I didn't turn this truck right back around.

That raven beauty.

Maybe I could find my balls and order breakfast, draw this out. Try a little flirting today, get Maggie to blush in that cute way of hers. With a bit of luck and a few answered prayers, I'd convince her to come to the party later. At the very least, I would show her that Gorilla Arms had competition.

But when I rolled up to the lot, those plans went to shit. Lined out front was a fleet of patrol vehicles, and my stomach began to kink in that familiar anxious knot. I exited the Raptor, and feet from the café's door, the scene on the other side of that window came clear.

My steps froze.

The navy-blue uniforms were at their table. So was Maggie. She was bent over, laughing, touching *his* arm. The sight of her small hand on his skin sent an eruption of something bitter and hot to course through me, and my fingers curled around my keys so hard, pain flickered along my palm.

She's flirting.

Maggie never flirted with me. Never hung onto my arm like that. Never laughed like that with me. *Never.* Not once.

I have to work.

Like a blow to the knees, it hit me. It wasn't work she didn't want to miss. It was the cop. And his kale jokes, the stupid ass nicknames, the opportunity to feel up his tatted arms.

Yeah, it was pretty fucking obvious this was where she wanted to be today. With him. *Just like she'd wanted him to drive her home instead of me.*

She said she hadn't ever been kissed, so why was she on birth control? To regulate? Just in case? Because of this guy? Clearly, it wasn't for me. No, for me, she barely had anything to say outside of a *yes* or *no* for four days straight. Because of her back pain, I had refused to run with her all week, and then she stopped popping into the gym when she brought down my ice water. She had left it sweating on the bar for me to find. She didn't even say goodbye when her shift was over.

A seed of anger took root in my chest, spreading through me with poison-tipped barbs. How had I read her so wrong? I had been convinced there was a connection, physical at the very least. Maggie...well, I thought she was attracted to me. An insidious voice in my head wondered if her reactions all stemmed from being inexperienced and had nothing to do with *me*. That voice needed to be tied to a cinder block and drop-kicked into the Pacific depths.

In a blink, I went from angry to pissed. Irrationally and utterly pissed.

And I did stupid shit when I was pissed.

Stupid shit like turning around, driving back to the RAM house, waking up Matt and convincing him that we needed a second case of JD at the liquor store.

While Matt set up the basement bar, I took care of the kitchen, rigging it to act as the main bar. Since we'd all be drinking at this party, I put Faith's chair in her room to keep it safe and locked her door. Not long after, my cousins and Jamey arrived.

Cam sidled up to the island and flung back a few pretzels, chomping down obnoxiously. "So…I heard Rebecca is coming?"

My hand stilled on the cooler stacked with Coronas. Hell, I'd forgotten all about her and her proclamation, *I'll see you both this weekend*.

I dismissively shrugged. "I guess."

"*I guess?*" His hand landed with a smack on the granite, shaking his head in disgust as he muttered, "Stupid motherfucker."

I straightened. "Excuse me?"

That whiskey gaze speared into mine. "You invited Rebecca *and* Maggie?" he asked as if I'd forgotten in the last one point three seconds.

My forehead creased. "Your point?"

Shaking his head again, he snatched up a potato chip and crunched down. "Aye shhoodn't eed doo shell id oud fah oo."

I shut the cooler. Cam seemed intent on being dramatic today, and the ice could melt by the time he was finished. "Why don't you impart your infantile genius upon me anyway."

He swallowed, reaching for a Dorito this time as if he needed to sample every snack for quality assurance. He didn't shove it in his mouth yet, so this must be important.

"For a while, I thought it was the resemblance thing, like you couldn't stand to see Maggie with anyone, and that's why she was off-limits, but then I realized that wasn't the case. You started acting like she was yours. Still are. So, I and every other dick on campus have been waiting for you to make it official. And then you pull this shit. Were you trying to make Maggie jealous, or is this her punishment for not spreading wide for you like Rebecca will?"

A general sense of unease pricked my skin, not helping my overall shitty mood. If I admitted my feelings for Maggie, Cam would never leave this alone. And it would all be for not anyway since the girl didn't want me.

Concentrating, I forced my shoulders to relax as I stated, "One, I'm not trying to make Maggie jealous because I don't want her like that."

He stared at me. "Riiiiight."

So much for all that hard work. My shoulders went right back up. "Two, you seem to be forgetting that I didn't invite Rebecca directly. It's a party. People just show up. And I never said that I wanted her to spread anything for me."

He wagged his uneaten chip at me. "But did you tell her you *didn't* want her to?"

Stunned at his question, I drew back. "I… No."

He gave me a look. "Like I said. You're a stupid motherfucker." Cam pushed off the stool and popped back the Dorito.

"Just because I didn't clarify the sitch, doesn't mean that's the go-ahead to fuck. I'm not a slut."

He choked on the remnants of the chip, grabbing another. "Of course, you are. You're a male Scott. We're all sluts."

This was the exact point that Ben walked up with Jamey, both of their brows raised. Ben's gaze bounced between Cam and me. "Do I want to know?"

Organizing liquor bottles, I grunted, "No."

Thankfully, the front door opened, and people began to file into the house, so I didn't have to continue that conversation. Friends filtered in. Then friends of friends. I didn't know everyone, which was fine because there was only one girl I wanted to see come through that door.

Before long, there was a house full of half-dressed and horny college students. We had two designated drivers for later and plenty of booze. Turned out, irrational and utterly pissed, plus stupid, did not mix well with booze.

I finished three Jack and Cokes by early afternoon. Wasn't the wisest choice in retrospect, but I hadn't been able to do much outside of obsessing over that scene at the café this morning.

Sipping my fourth drink at the island, Jamey's voice rang out behind me. "Mags!"

Instantly, as though I hadn't been brewing in some serious anger issues all day, I was ready to start handing out warm hugs and Olaf the shit out of this place.

I spun on my stool to watch her come in like the freaking sun. Even her T-shirt was yellow. Those jean shorts were hella short, and she had on her ratty Chucks that were stained gray after she'd tried to bleach them, and it looked as if they'd shrunk a size in the wash. That meant she rode her bike. When she ran, she wore her knock-off runners. Had I one iota she was coming, I wouldn't have even looked at the JD. I would have been there to pick her up, drive her here.

Whatever. She was here now.

In five paces, I had that little feather in my arms, grinning up at her. Goddamn. How was it possible to miss someone's face this much?

I loved how she felt against my bare skin. Everywhere we touched, a bolt of heat zinged through me and shot straight to my groin, coiling low and tight.

"You made it."

Angling her head down, a curtain of inky hair hid her smile from everyone but me. And I liked that. A lot. Like that smile was my secret to keep, but her smile slowly faded. "Sorta. I have to be back in a couple of hours. Frankie could only give me a long lunch."

Okay...I could work with that. If I stopped drinking now, I'd be sober enough to drive her back, stretch out our time. We'd be alone in the truck. Maybe this time, I wouldn't puss out and kiss her like I'd wanted to on Monday. She was always in work-mode when she was here, and I didn't sense that she was now. *I* had her attention.

"I'll take it," I rumbled.

Sliding down my body, she gripped my biceps, and my muscles flexed under her shaky hands as shocks of electricity hummed between us. I didn't miss the way her breasts felt against my stomach nor the blush staining her cheeks as she dragged her hands down my skin, curling her fingers around my forearms. When she looked up at me with those big blue eyes, our gazes locked. She inhaled shallow and fast, and those plush lips fell open as if she could feel the lust as it slammed into my veins. The mere possibility that she might have this reaction with another man was totally fucking with my head.

Up against me, I couldn't help but feel that she was soft in all the places I was hard. And a second later, I was *hard*. Damn, she looked good. If she were in a bikini...even better.

I took a healthy step back before this got awkward. "That is the worst swimsuit attire I've ever seen. Where is your bathing suit?"

"I'm not wearing one."

I blinked down at her. "Clearly. Really, Sticks, there was one requirement for today, and you failed."

Sighing, she tucked her hair behind her right ear, but the raven locks fell forward again as she glanced to her feet. "I don't have a suit."

"Why didn't you say so? I lost fifteen seconds of my life on this conversation. Come on."

Scooping her hand into mine, anxiety clenched my chest. All week long, her tremors had been bad like this, gait unsteady. The vertigo got her every time she stood or moved her head too fast. I wasn't sure if it was due to her back pain that—ah, I probably shouldn't have picked her up like I had. She had said she was feeling better yesterday, but who the fuck knew with her. Maggie could have a steel beam running through her chest, and she would say she was peachy.

I guided her into the guestroom and opened the bottom dresser drawer. I dove in. "How is your day so far? Better now that you're with me?"

I grinned up at her, and okay, that was a pathetic plea for attention even by my standards.

"Um…" Her gaze tracked the scraps of red material I flung onto the bed with all the affection she would bestow a cockroach. Yeah, it wasn't my first choice either. I kept digging. "It was mostly normal, I guess."

"Did you get good tips, at least?" Ooh, this one had potential. Now, what size— No, Sticks definitely wasn't a medium. Even a small might be loose on her.

"Not the kind of tips I wanted," she murmured, a sourness framing her tone.

My hand curled around a little black number as my gaze sought hers. "Did someone stiff you?"

"No, it wasn't anything like that." Emotion shadowed her face, but I couldn't read what was bothering her. "Mason, I need to tell you…" I waited for her to finish, but instead, Maggie shook her head and looked away with her brow tensing. "I have to leave soon. I'm not going to have time to swim."

I found another two-piece and tossed it onto the bed as I stood. "You'll have time if I drive you back." Her lips opened to deliver at least five different arguments, and I placed a single finger over her mouth to silence them. "Pick one and come out."

Brushing past Maggie, I closed the door behind me and waited for her in the hall. I felt like a fucking twelve-year-old ready to palm his first boob. I honestly didn't care if I looked like a tool, grinning and rocking on my bare heels. She was worth it.

After a few minutes, the door opened and so did my mouth. And not in a good way. "You're not wearing a suit."

She swallowed, those eyes inching up to mine. "Nothing fit."

"Nothing?" Scooting around her, I saw that not one suit had been left on the bed. I yanked the drawer back open— I blinked.

Not only had she *not* tried on the bikinis I'd picked out, but she'd folded them plus all the other bathing suits in the drawer and had them sitting in neat little rows. Something wasn't right about this.

"What are you talking about?" I plucked up a wad of white string, and the scant material it was attached to that might be a little see-through when wet. "I know this will fit you because I happen to be well versed in bikini sizes."

There was a grumble meant for the floor that sounded like, "Yeah, I'm sure you are." I didn't bother disputing it, she was right, but that didn't mean the dig didn't sting. Slowly, her eyes lifted. "They don't fit. I tried."

"Bullshit, you tried. What's going on?" I slung the white scraps onto the bed and crossed my arms, waiting for an answer.

Looking everywhere but my demanding gaze, she struggled for an explanation. "I don't want to go swimming."

"Why?"

Maggie's hands flew up into the air. "I just...don't, Mason. I have to go back to work later, and I don't want to smell like chlorine and have wet hair."

I dragged down a cleansing breath. "Fine, don't swim. How about you put on a suit, relax by the pool, and get some sun with the rest of us?" I waved to my bare chest, hoping to at least get checked out by her. Nothing. Absolutely fucking nothing.

She squinted at me. "What's the point of putting on a bathing suit if I'm not going to swim?"

This girl was going to drive *both* of my heads completely crazy. I knew that now. I had been fantasizing about Maggie in every state of dress and undress for months. Shit, I was impossibly hard just thinking about her prancing around my pool with that tight ass and toned pins.

Closing the distance, I leaned over her, forcing her head back. "Why are you so goddamned difficult? Put a suit on!"

Azure flames flashed in her eyes. Maggie stood on her tiptoes and met my scowl. "Why? So I can listen to every guy here compare me to all the D-cups and get laughed at? Was your party not entertaining enough?"

Anger engulfed every cell, and my body fed off it, heating my skin. Did she really think so little of me? That I would *compare* her? Use her in such an abhorrent way? That I would be friends with anyone who would treat her like that? And that I would tolerate that shit?

What. The. Fuck.

I was somewhere between taking over the few centimeters between our mouths and shutting her up with my lips or going downstairs and taking my aggression out on the punching bag. "I wouldn't make fun of you, and neither would my friends. I know you believe I'm a Neanderthal who only thinks with his dick, so it shouldn't surprise you when I say that, yes, I would like to see you in a bikini, and believe me when I tell you, there is no comparison to those girls." I thrust a finger in the general direction of the pool.

She fell back on her heels, and there went the fire. Completely snuffed. "I know there's not."

The way I was gritting my teeth, I was going to need a dentist by the end of today. "We are not on the same page here, Sticks. I doubt even the same fucking book. Put a suit on."

I stepped out, and she closed the door in what I assumed was her consent to have fun. I really should know better by now. Five seconds. Five seconds later, she peeled the door open, still dressed.

I made no effort to hide how irritated I was and walked to the backyard before saying anything else. This party was for her. Today was for her. My raging hard-on that wasn't catching on to my current state of anger was for her. Every moment since I'd met that girl had been for her. All I was asking was for her to disengage work-mode for two hours.

"What's eating you?" Ben called over from the lounge chair.

I waved to the blond next to him. "His friend is being difficult."

Wiping sweat from his brow, Jamey laughed. "Oh, you really have no idea how bad she can get. What did she do?"

"For starters, she won't put on a bathing suit."

Sitting up, Jamey's grin crashed onto the decking, his tone brimming with caution. "Let it go, Mase."

He had my full attention. "Why?"

Lips flattening, he shook his head. "You're gonna have to trust me. Don't push her. Not on this."

"I—" Suddenly, that conversation Maggie and Jamey had behind the hospital curtain came to the forefront.

No one saw, right?

Saw...what? Her body? It made the most sense. Her shirts were typically three sizes too big, and she tugged at them often, making sure they were in place and the hem was never above her ass. Was there something she was hiding? Thinking back, she'd refused to wear a suit at Ben's party, too. I had assumed...

Shit.

Once again, Maggie had the power to remind me how much of a dick I was. I didn't know why I kept forgetting.

I ducked back inside to apologize, and...she was nowhere in sight. She couldn't have left. She wouldn't. I darted out front to the driveway to find that her bike was gone.

Son of a bitch. She really left. I was in no state to drive after her, and walking was ill-advised, considering I had no idea where she'd gone to. She didn't have a phone, so there wasn't even the possibility of a lame apology via cell. She ran again, and I had no choice but to let her.

I didn't get it. Was it that hard to confide in me? Rather than give me ten lame excuses, all she had to say was that she wasn't comfortable in a bathing suit. I'd understand something like that, but this girl didn't even trust me enough to tell me what goddamned music she liked.

Back in the kitchen, I downed another drink before finding Matt alone in the basement. While I nursed another drink, we played a game of pool.

About six—no, seven—drinks in, hell, I wasn't really sure, I was firmly stuck in a JD haze. Somehow, I'd made it back outside. Still no Maggie.

Relaxing in a lounge chair, I thought it best not to swim, given my current state of intoxication. That was perhaps the only wise decision I'd made all day. In the middle of catching my rays, Rebecca appeared, wearing enough fabric to constitute a bikini but not enough for my imagination to play with. I watched as her head rotated, stopping when she found me. Sporting a demure smile, she walked, her hips swaying like she was in a slow-mo porn, giving me plenty of time to appreciate those curves.

"Hey, Mase." She did a little twirl, and the damn bikini was pretty much ass floss. Hardened nipples had pebbled against the lavender material, and my eyes rested on that V-shaped stretch of fabric between her thighs. "What do you think?"

"I like it," I stated.

She played with one shoulder strap to pull my attention back to her tits. Canting her head so her blonde hair would spill across her tanned skin, she bit her bottom lip. She even had the slightly angled leg pose down so her thighs would part just so. "Do you think you'd like it on the floor, too?"

I did a mental count of the tally marks scratched into my skull. *Eleven weeks.* Eleven long, painful weeks. Maybe it was the Jack, maybe it was the fact I'd been rejected by the one woman I wanted, or maybe I knew Maggie could do better than me because I was nothing but a slut. She hadn't cared that Rebecca would be here. She even thought Rebecca was *nice* and *pretty* and didn't flinch when I said she was *hot*. Because Maggie was already with someone else.

So there was no reason, nothing to stop me from saying, "Yes."

After a long lick of her lips, Rebecca asked, "Can we go somewhere for that to happen?"

This was the point I should have remembered how much I did not want to fuck this girl.

I totally blamed the Jack.

"Yes." I stood, and she followed me to the guestroom. Once inside, I heard the lock click behind me, and eyes of bright topaz flashed in my mind.

Maggie.

She had been standing right here hours ago. I shut my eyes, and I could still smell her sugary, cinnamon scent, see the glisten of ChapStick on her lips, feel her silky skin on mine, the heat of her body imprinted into me.

I opened my eyes, and it wasn't raven hair and blue eyes that I saw. Rebecca was in front of me, and I recoiled, barely holding myself upright so my ass didn't hit the floor.

A blink later, her mouth was on mine. Lips sticky with gloss coated my mouth, and her perfume was so thick, I could taste it in the back of my throat. I wasn't even kissing her back, and I didn't think she noticed as her tongue thrust past my lips and floundered in my mouth. My hands were like dead weights at my sides, refusing to touch this girl. I had kept my eyes open, which I never did, and had nothing else to look at except the false lashes, glittery eye shadow, thick liner, filled brows. *A bit much for a pool party.* And her hair was curled. Rebecca didn't have curly hair.

There was a hand on me, the waistband of my shorts slipping down my hips, and…that was when I knew.

This moment was like all the others. Using Rebecca as nothing more than a Band-Aid for a cracked soul. She wouldn't care about my past, the hurt left behind from Faith. She wouldn't understand the tattoos she barely eyed before examining my tonsils with her tongue. She wouldn't ask to know my baby sister and try to ease my pain. She wouldn't take the time to know my family, worry about them when they were hurting. She wouldn't go out of her way to make sure that everyone's needs—strangers even—were met before her own. None of them would ever be Maggie. None of them would have my heart like Maggie did.

Maggie was right earlier. I *was* comparing every girl to her. And they were all left wanting.

I wrapped my hand around her wrist, pulled her away, and jerked my shorts back into place. "I'm sorry, Rebecca. I can't."

"What?" she asked, blinking, brows arched.

I backed away from her in disbelief at what I was about to say. "You're a beautiful girl, and please believe me when I say it's not you. I just can't."

Eyes narrowed, her forehead wrinkled, and the overhead lights shone on the lip gloss that had smudged around her mouth and chin. "What the hell, Mason? It's called a hookup. I'm not looking for a diamond ring. Just a good fuck."

"I'm sorry. This was a mistake. My mistake."

Her lips fell open, and without another word, I walked out of the room and went straight to the empty basement. Straight to the Jack. I put my head down on the bar, so fucking confused.

My tongue smacked against the roof of my mouth, the lingering taste of florals and wax nauseating me. I tore a paper towel off the roll and wiped it over my lips. It came back with a coral sheen. The same one that had been on Rebecca's mouth.

In the next second, I was on the other side of the counter with the water running scalding hot. I scrubbed my face with dish soap, letting the suds into my mouth, finger scouring my teeth, washing away the evidence.

I was so far from the man I wanted to be for Maggie. No wonder she wanted Gorilla Arms and not me. She saw me for what I was. A fucked-up mess.

I smacked off the faucet, and with my face dripping wet, I downed another drink over my numb teeth, willing the numbness to reach a different ache in my heart, obliterate the guilt of what I'd done.

Then another, then another.

chapter thirty-five

maggie

"Shit." I watched helplessly as tiny sugar grains sprinkled the café's counter, sparkling like diamonds beneath the pendant lights. I set the bag of sugar next to the dispenser and rubbed my eyes, but it did nothing to remove the image that had occupied my brain all week. The image of Mason's face when Pretty and Hot Rebecca walked up to him, along with the way his breath paused, lips parted, eyes locking onto an exposed and ample bosom...

I could have been engulfed in flames, and he wouldn't have noticed me. The world could have collapsed, meteors could be hurtling toward Earth, the tectonic plates could have broken apart right under his feet, and the boy could only see the black bra veiled by a transparent white shirt.

As I wiped the concrete counter clean, everything blurred, and my lips were doing things that weren't natural. My legs were wobblier than they should be, and there was something not quite right with my throat because swallowing became difficult.

Rebecca would be at the party today. Mason would get all up in her *closeness*. In his room. In his bed.

A bed I had to make tomorrow.

There was a used condom in my future.

I might throw up.

Knowing my father would never give me permission to go to Mason's party, I had asked Frankie for a couple of hours off today, so I could prepare for an upcoming marathon. This way, if my father stopped by the café or Candi blabbed, I had an excuse at the ready. And because

Frankie couldn't promise me a time that I could leave, I couldn't tell Mason I was coming.

Like everything in my life, the situation was precarious and out of my control.

I gave up on refilling the sugar dispenser as the old bell clanged, the door opening and stirring up dust motes to dance in the morning light. Deep laughter boomed throughout the dining room as the boys filed in, seemingly rowdier today.

I blinked my eyes dry and met them at their table with a strong pot of brew, creamer, and sugar loaded on my tray. "Hey, boys!"

"Magnitude!" Logan's grin was extra charming and bright, and I didn't have the energy to feign irritation over the nickname.

Using the next table over, I poured the first cup of coffee. "Don't tell me. My father lost the deed to the house during last night's poker game, and I'm sleeping in the forest tonight?"

"Nope!" Gil chuckled, swapping mugs with me. "We did break up a wedding, though."

"I think, technically, it was the honeymoon," Robert amended.

"What? I thought your shifts didn't start for another hour."

"This call was worth answering," Keith explained, dark eyes twinkling. "You see... Old Man Lyle had a bit too much to drink last night."

"Or this morning," Logan clarified. "We couldn't tell."

Gil took the last of the mugs I had filled. "He decided to get hitched in the middle of Reems Road."

I mentally logged the available women in town, coming up short. "To whom?"

"To *what*?" Logan corrected me, and my eyes widened. This could go so many different ways. Logan's mouth curled with a cheeky grin. "He married the Clarks' tractor."

"*Norma-Jean!*" the boys sang.

"Good God," I breathed out.

Robert shook his head, fighting a smile. "There's more."

"He was wearing a bowtie..." Gil offered, and when I failed to react to that, he grinned. "That was it. *Just* a bowtie."

"Oh." I swore my entire body cringed. "That had to have been a sight to burn retinas."

"That's not the worst of it." Logan's broad shoulders shook, gripping the side of the table as he tried to sober himself. "The fuel cap was off."

That took a few seconds to hit home, and once that tidbit settled into my gray matter, I folded over into a fit of giggles. "Oh. My. God!"

Swiping an imaginary tear from his eye, Keith poured sugar into his brew. "That poor tractor. A virgin no more."

"*Norma-Jean!*" they sang out again.

"That's it! That's enough." I could hardly speak, and I had to use Logan's arm to get me back upright. "You're gonna eat whatever I bring you!" As I shot to the back, the boys laughed louder.

"Alright, Mags," Frankie called from the open walk-in. "It's deader out there than this chicken salad."

Clunk-clunk-clunk! I flinched as he knocked at least three pounds of chicken slathered mayonnaise into the garbage. Such a waste, but I couldn't risk putting that out in the basket for fear it could give someone food poisoning. If we only had an outdoor fridge...

Frankie gave the Tupperware one more knock. "Why don't you head on out for a bit."

"Really? I was about to get around to the basebo—" What was I saying? "Okay!" As I scrambled out of my apron, failing to get my fingers to work the knot, Frankie chuckled at me.

Shaking his head, he set the dirty bin in the sink. "How anyone is so eager to *run* all the time is beyond me."

There was no way I wasn't going to Hell for all the lies I'd told. "Yeah, well, I—" I finally undid the knot and slipped off my apron. "I guess I feel the same way about running as you do about the shooting range."

Frankie grunted at that. "Two completely different things, Mags."

I slung my backpack onto my shoulder, but I somehow forgot about the welts on my back until the weight of the bag slammed against the tender skin. At least they'd scabbed over now.

Once the pain subsided, I twisted to face Frankie. "I shouldn't be more than a couple of hours if that's okay? I'll be back before the late afternoon rush."

"If there is a rush," he grumbled, heading back into the walk-in.

Yeah, the café was...slow, which said a lot because it was already slow. I'd made twenty-five bucks in tips so far, and twenty of that was in the form of an origami owl the boys had left me.

I left through the back alley and set my bag in the basket before mounting my bike.

It didn't take but five turns of the pedals before I had to slam on the brakes, and it was far too late to backpedal and go the opposite way.

Motherfu—

"Miss Davis! What a pleasant surprise!" Mayor Ryan announced with a clasp of his hands. His head canted with an unnerving gleam in his brown eyes. "And where are you off to this Saturday afternoon?"

I eyed the two people with him who were no longer studying what looked to be blueprints of some kind as they zeroed in on little ol' me. The woman appeared especially displeased. Though, to be fair, I didn't think all the Botox and fillers lent for a wide range of facial expressions.

I shifted my focus back to Marcus. "I'm going to the bluffs for a run."

"And it's such a wonderful day for it." Tucking one hand inside his suit pocket, Marcus gestured to his groupies with the other. Or perhaps he was the groupie. "Have you met Vivian and Leo Price?"

Not bothering to dismount the bike, I shook my head. "No." And they didn't appear eager for a meet and greet either.

"Well, allow me to formally introduce—"

"That won't be necessary, Marcus," Vivian purred, one suede pump bringing her closer to me. Her dark lashes fanned against a set of sharp cheekbones as her honey brown eyes measured me. Judged me. And found me wanting by quite a lot. My chin angled back to meet her stare. "You're Maggie Davis. I've heard your name pricking my ears often these last few months."

Funny how so much contempt could drip from her tongue, yet her face remained smooth as glass. Disturbing and impressive at the same time.

I didn't bother replying.

"I hear you work here at the café and for Evelyn Scott." Striding closer, Vivian's white jeans squeezed her legs like they were trying to become one with her skin, and it seemed the affinity for going braless was not limited to the Price daughters. "You're the one Mason is fixated on for some...ungodly reason. You're the one responsible for my daughters' recent humiliations. And you're the one we have you to thank for our current— What did you call it, Leo darling?" The brim of her white panama hat exaggerated the movement of her head as she aimed a wrinkleless scowl at her husband.

"Pest infestation," he supplied, focused on his phone now.

I trembled so hard with rage that I didn't think I could get a syllable out, let alone whole words.

"Yes, that's it." The intricate blonde twist at the base of her neck disappeared from view as her head snapped back my way. Her plump lips twisted as she repeated, "Pest infestation."

"Those are people you're referring to." My fingers clenched around my handlebars to stop them from shaking. "*Human beings.*"

"Hmm…" Her eyes narrowed, the skin barely giving way to the effort. "Use whatever term helps you sleep at night, dear. It really doesn't matter because very soon, the ground that you're standing on will be the grand atrium of Exalted Resort and Spa of Crescent Cove, and there won't be anywhere left for your *people* to infest."

My lips parted as I rasped, "What?"

"Oh, you haven't heard!" she exclaimed with unbridled glee. "With Marcus' help, the procurement of your street came at a bargain. One we couldn't pass up. Now that there are no longer any emotional ties between your employer's son and my daughter, demolishing the café won't have any unwanted ramifications. And while the plans and permits are finalized, it'll give us a chance to increase the rent on these properties. Again."

My legs went leaden as a sharp barb of hopelessness penetrated my stomach. I suspected this had been Marcus' plan all along, but to hear it laid out so clearly, that he'd schemed to have everything I loved about Crescent Cove to be bought, destroyed, and rebuilt with some gaudy monstrosity…gutted me.

Frankie and Paula, Chuck and Darlene, Henry, Trudy, Rick, Etana, Ronnie…everything they had was here on Sands.

And the Scotts. *Oh, God.*

"How can you do this? Of all the available shoreline in Crescent Cove, why here? The Scotts are your friends. Your children grew up together. This café holds the last good memories they have of their daughter. This will *kill* them."

Vivian's lashes tapered until her eyes were nothing but too small points of disdain. "Young lady, I didn't get where I am by being a sentimental fool. You'd be wise to remember that. And this…" Distaste pursed her mouth as she cast a glance to the street and waved it off like a gnat buzzing around her head. "This simply cannot stay. It's unsightly. I can't have this anywhere near my properties, so it must go. No one wants to vacation next to a slum. And I'll earn my money back tenfold when developers buy my land to put up homes that are not…unsightly."

Jesus. I could see that any argument based on morality and ethics was a waste of time with this one. Not that my next target would be any better.

"You don't have enough?" I spat at Marcus. "You're rich. You're powerful. What more could you possibly want?"

"Oh, Miss Davis." Marcus' head swayed as he made a clucking noise with his tongue. "Your lack of vision disappoints me. Can't you see it? Guests climbing out of their luxurious king beds in the morning, sipping coffee on the veranda with an unimpeded view of the ocean? Enjoying a massage with the soothing sound of waves in their ears? Golfing along the hilly terrain of one of the world's most elite courses on what used to be homely subdivisions? Do you have any idea what the tourism alone would do for Crescent Cove? The housing market will triple. All the jobs this hotel would provide to a certain standard of people. And speaking of jobs…"

One corner of his mouth twitched, and the barb in my stomach twisted. "Perhaps that position on my staff wouldn't be the right fit after all, but I'm sure the new general manager of this resort would have a place for you." He paused for dramatic effect, and I really should have used that time to launch my foot between his legs. "Thoughts, Eric?"

"It's a large resort. We'll need *servants*, I suppose." I didn't know how I didn't see him until now. It could be because he had just walked out of the café with…four cups of coffee and a to-go bag of pastries. His face had healed of bruises only to be replaced by his sneer.

I was so very tempted to take those cups of scalding liquid he was holding and do something awful to each of their faces. They were seriously planning to tear down all these businesses and homes, too?

Where would the people of Crescent Cove go? They wouldn't be able to sustain a life here, and I didn't get the feeling that many who lived in this town would fulfill Vivian's *standards* for employment.

I exhaled a ragged breath, aiming my glare at father and son. "Do the world a favor and hold your breath for the day I demean myself to work for filth like you."

Eric's nostrils flared. "Here's a tip, Spaz. You may want to watch that bitchy little mouth of yours. In case you haven't figured it out yet, your days as a townie in Crescent Cove are numbered." A disturbing smile pulled at Eric's face, and I noticed the left side didn't move in sync with the right as if the nerves hadn't been connected right.

As he handed out the coffees, it hit me that this was not the first time this group had met here. He had come to the café months ago and ordered four coffees. I hadn't considered then that this was the group he had run the errand for.

I wasn't a religious person, but I had heard of the Four Horsemen of the Apocalypse. The *Bible* got it wrong on one count, though. Their names weren't Pestilence, War, Famine, and Death. They were Marcus, Eric, Leo, and Vivian.

And Nathan Davis played the role of my own personal Hades.

I had to tell Mason. Warn him. And I walked into the Scotts' house with the intent to have that very conversation.

Unfortunately, that plan veered off course rather quickly.

My attention was diverted from all the oiled skin scarcely covered by bathing suits sitting on the cream sofas, the red cups not resting on coasters, all the chips destined to be ground into the grout lines, to the fact that Mason was drunk...ish.

I'd asked him not to drink around me. That had been a week ago. I had to be fair, though. I didn't tell him I was coming to his party or that I'd even try to come. He'd given me plenty of opportunities.

But I was here now, and he was drunk, which meant telling him about the café would have to wait. And in hindsight, I could have handled the bikini thing better.

Standing there, alone in that guestroom with a pile of fabric and string, there was not a doubt in my mind that I could ever show Mason my back. I knew what it looked like, and there wasn't a feasible lie on this planet to rationalize what was on my skin. And there were fresh marks just from Monday. Because I accepted a ride and wore Mason's sweater. Because I didn't pick up a phone to explain that I wanted a ride instead of trudging home in the mud. Because I had lied, and I'd been caught.

Clearly, I hadn't learned my lesson since being here today could earn me more of the same.

And for all that risk, my reward was pushing Mason further away. So while he was at the pool admiring a plethora of thongs, I was sitting by the lake...birding. Literally this time.

With a glance at the sun, I knew I'd been out here too long and needed to head back to the café soon. I could bike from here... Or I could put my big girl panties on, stop sulking, and go talk to the man.

I may never be Mason's, but I did have something none of those girls had. His friendship. I had a place in his life, and however insignificant that was to him, it was the world to me.

Mind made, I decided I'd say goodbye to Mason and promise to see him tomorrow when I showed up for work. If he wasn't too hungover, we could go for a run in the morning, and then I'd find some way to tell him about the café.

A short bike ride later, I was back inside the house. I slapped my blinders on to the spilled beer by the grandfather clock, a suspicious green smudge on the rug, and the failed Dorito tower on the coffee table, zeroing in on Matt behind the kitchen island.

I gripped the counter, my words hurried and breathless. I'd be embarrassed about that later. "Have you seen Mason?"

Matt lifted his chin with a slow blink, emerald eyes losing a bit of their glaze. My focus dropped to the paper towel in front of him, and on it was a penned drawing of a T-Rex being ridden by a busty woman. A busty woman not wearing the top half of a bikini. Although weird and slightly pervy, it was drawn well and oddly...realistic.

"Mason?" His blue pen tapped against the granite as his head rotated. "He's been missing for a while."

The floor dropped out from under me. The words *missing* and *Mason* used in the same sentence couldn't mean anything good. This house had a lot of rooms and beds and—

"Mags, try the basement!" Camden called to me from the living room.

"Thanks." I wasn't sure if Camden heard me since I was already yanking open the hall door and sprinting down the stairs. I shouldn't be this eager to be in a basement alone with Mason again during a party because the last experience hadn't gone well.

Once I reached the last of the steps, I released a relieved breath. Mason's back was to me as he tipped a glass to his lips. He was alone. Thank God.

"H—hey," I squeaked, clutching the railing.

Mason whipped around in the stool, throwing out a foot to stop himself from toppling over. The citrine in his irises glimmered within a pool of peridot, eyes like unpolished opals. He bent forward, squinting as though that would help him see through the JD swimming in his eyeballs.

Once the image of me registered, he spun around, squeezing his lids tight. "What are you doing here?"

I flinched at his harsh tone, swallowing past the tightness in my throat. "Limbo skating." His response to that was sucking down the rest of what was in his glass. "I can go if you don't want me here."

Please don't send me away.

His head swung up and down and then side to side as though the alcohol had disintegrated his spine. "I invited you to the party, remember? I wanted you here. You were the one who left." At least, that was what I deciphered through the string of slurred words coming out of his mouth.

As I drifted closer, I tangled my fingers together. "I went for a bike ride to clear my head, but I...I have to leave soon."

There was a grunt, possibly an acknowledgment that his hearing still worked. "You want a drink? I need a drink." Turning, he snatched up the Jack from the other side of the bar. How his reflexes rivaled Superman's, but it took him a solid minute to unscrew a cap, I'd never know.

"No one needs alcohol, Mason." I dumbly watched him reach over the counter for something else.

"Drunks do, or they get the shakes." Ice plinked into his glass one by one, and then amber liquid splashed down until it pooled to the rim. "Oops. That looks like a lot, doesn't it? It's probably just the ice."

"I think drunks use that excuse."

Intently staring at his glass, Mason gripped the bar and folded over to get level with it. Exasperated, his bulky arms swung above his head. "Dammit, there's not enough room for the Coke!" He dipped forward, slurped down a mouthful, and smacked his lips. "Ah...that's better." Then he topped it off with a drop of soda.

I inched toward him. "How much have you had to drink, Mason?"

"Not enough! I'm still awake. Still got shit to forget!" He held up his glass as if to toast me, wobbling on his feet.

"Sit down before you fall and hit your head." I rushed forward, pressing my palms against his chest. Both of our equilibriums must be off. His butt hit the stool faster than I expected, and I slipped forward, face smashing into a hard pectoral. I quickly detached my face, gripping his biceps to keep my balance. Blowing a wad of hair out of my eyes, I held his face, tipping his gaze to meet mine. "Mason, you're drinking too much. Please, stop."

Leaning into me, his eyes tapered low. "You're gonna fuck that cop."

Hands falling away, I recoiled, not expecting him to say that. In no known universe did I expect him to say that. "What cop?"

"Lionel!" He bolted back up, and since there was little room between him and the stool behind me, we nearly bumped heads. "I watched you. I drove by this morning and saw you flirting with him. Touching him."

Most probably would have been creeped out by that stalker alert, and I should have been, but my heart was a little busy doing backflips that he had come by this morning, had thought of me.

"*Logan's* my friend, and I wasn't flirting. Ironically, he was telling me a funny story about the town drunk."

His head swiped back and forth again. "You laugh with him and smile at everything he says. You let him drive you. I couldn't get you to even talk to me this week."

That's because I couldn't speak to you without begging you not to sleep with Pretty and Hot Rebecca.

Mason ate up the scant inches remaining between us. The whiskey's cloyingly sweet scent turned my stomach. I hated that he smelled like that shit, erasing that spicy musk that was his alone.

"Luke wants in your pants, Sticks. They all fucking do. Believe me, it's *exhausting*."

Wow. Okay…

I shook off his crazy rant. "Logan's nice to me. He's one of the few who have always been nice to me."

"Bullshit." Somehow, Mason maneuvered us, so my back was against the bar, his hard chest pressing into mine, and I couldn't shut off how good that felt even with the whiskey overpowering my senses. "Why else would you be on birth control? You wanna fuck someone. You wanna fuck Linus."

"Logan," I corrected, anger nipping at my patience. I could go into an extensive list of reasons why women took the Pill, but I'd have to table that for another time. "And how do you know I'm on birth control?"

His eyes flashed down at me. "I know a lot of shit. What I don't know is why you never flirt with me."

Uh… "I— I have no idea how to flirt." Not like I would if I did, but that comment died on my tongue as I watched Mason slam back the rest of his drink.

With most of our bodies still attached in all the interesting places, he was able to lean over me to get *more* JD. "You know how to flirt. You do fine with Gorilla Arms."

I shot him a steady glare. "He doesn't have gorilla arms." Folding myself around his bare torso, I gave a good attempt to guide him back to the stool, which was useless. He wouldn't budge. Oddly, neither would my arms. "Mason, please stop. Don't do this."

"Why did you come back?" He poured another drink.

"Because I wanted…" I considered lying, but to be honest, I was morbidly curious to know what he'd say. I blew an unsteady breath onto his bare chest. "I wanted to see you."

Holding the glass, his dark brows shot up, pointing to himself. "Me? Mason Scott? Why?"

"I wanted to stop you."

"From drinking?" Cue another tip of the glass to empty down his gullet. How much could one man drink before getting alcohol poisoning? "You're doing a terrible job, by the way." Dimples flashing, he grinned a crooked smile that any other time I would have melted to.

I spoke around the knot in my throat. "From Rebecca."

Every hard plane of his body met mine, including a part of him that felt…very hard. I swore my lungs stalled out.

"Too late, Sticks! Been there. Done that."

My heart imploded. It really was possible. All the blood drained toward my feet, lungs collapsing, ribs crumbling into piles of dust. "You did? You…were with her?"

"Oh, I didn't fuck her. I thought about it, 'cause, well, I'm a dude. Came close. She had a firm grip of my cock." For demonstration purposes—as though I needed it—his hand rose to my eye level and curled into a fist. Yeah, I could have done without the visual aid.

"W—why didn't you?"

Exhaling harshly, his hand fell. "Because she wasn't you." Mason's forehead thumped against mine, lashes brushing his cheekbones. "She's nothing like my sweet little Sticks."

Man, he was super wasted.

"Speaking of sticks." His eyes opened but barely, and I swore… I swore he was staring right at my mouth. My belly dipped and warmed unexpectedly. "My lips are dry, and you have soft pink lips. I need some of your ChapStick."

I drew my face away from his, but our bodies were still plastered together. "No. I don't know where your mouth has been."

"Nowhere I wanted until you."

Sweet baby Jesus.

No question, he was definitely staring right at my mouth, and I was also confident I heard a deep growl in the back of his throat. That was my only warning. I was suddenly hauled over Mason's knee so that I was straddling his thigh, the thick padding of muscle pressing the material of my shorts directly against my center. White-hot need blazed from that one point of contact and flared throughout my veins. All the air in my lungs left me in a rush.

Before my mind could catch up, Mason's chest was flush to mine again, and I fought to silence my moan when his heat bled past the layers of clothing separating us.

I swallowed. Hard. "W—what are you doing?"

"I think that's pretty obvious." His breaths fanned my lips so close that if I stretched another millimeter, our mouths would touch. "Does it not feel obvious to you?"

"I—" Mason rocked forward, triggering a shockwave of mind-bending sensations to tear up my spine that had me seeing stars. My hands flew to his biceps to grip tight as a pleasant tug pulled low in my pelvis. My non-existent nails dug into his skin, the urge to move against him crazy intense. His gaze prowled over my features, connecting with my eyes, and there was no mistaking what I saw there.

Mason looked...*hungry*.

My mouth went dry.

Holding my gaze, Mason's voice spun around me like smoke, smooth and dark. "Why haven't you been kissed yet?" Ten fingers, then two palms slid up my waist and settled at my ribs, thumbs resting on the underside of my breasts that felt heavier, fuller somehow.

It was humiliating how out of breath I was. "I told you. No one wanted to."

"Nothing could be further from the truth. I've wanted to kiss you."

I squeezed my eyes at the welling ache those words caused. That was the very thing I had wanted to hear from him for months, but not when his thoughts were tainted with alcohol.

"In fact..." His breaths stirred the hair at my ruined temple, lips lingering there. "I want to kiss you now, Maggie. Every. Sweet. Inch."

My heart must not have imploded earlier because I could feel it beating in my throat.

I opened my eyes, disbelief flaring them wider as his head dropped low. Then *lower*. His soft hair tickled my jaw as he licked his way across my collarbone. My thighs clenched around his, and the tips of my breasts tingled as a heady feeling intoxicated me, drugging my thoughts. Mason dragged his tongue along my skin, alternating licks and sweet kisses up my neck to behind my ear. My toes curled.

It was pure bliss.

My head fell back, arching into him. "*OhmyGod.*"

His growl of approval reverberated through me as he nipped my jaw on his way to the other side. "Fuck, you taste sweet. Like..." Another flick of his tongue. "Apple pie."

A different sound vibrated in the back of his throat that time, something preternatural and instinctual. As if he were...purring.

"And, Maggie? You should know…I fucking love apple pie."

His thumbs began to move, sweeping in a soft caress over the sensitive tips of my breasts. Once. Twice. Pleasure jolted through me, settling into a pulsing ache between my thighs. This time, there was no stopping the moan he wrung out of me.

Lifting his heated gaze to mine, a sinful smile curved the corner of his mouth, revealing one lickable dimple. "I wonder if I can get you even louder."

I bet he could. "Doubtful."

Mason liked challenges. I knew that much about him.

The fingers wrapped around my ribcage tightened, and I watched the brilliant array of green and yellow in his eyes darken a mere moment before his gaze dropped to my lips. As he brought his mouth to mine, I was still trying to convince myself that this was actually happening. This was wrong. He was drunk and had no clue what he was doing, but I was too weak to stop him.

Couldn't. Wouldn't. Didn't.

His smooth lips swept over mine the same way his thumbs had my breasts. Once. Then twice.

"Maggie?"

I gulped loudly, and all I could get out was, "Uh-huh."

"I'm going to be your first," he said against my mouth. "Do you know why that's important?"

The last working synapse in my gray matter fired. He didn't say your first kiss…just *first*.

Oh, God. "Nuh-uh."

"Because you never forget your first."

An unwelcome stab of sorrow pierced into me at that. I wasn't Mason's first. She had a name and a place in his mind, as she should. They all, however fleeting to him, deserved a place where they were remembered. But none of them would be as special as her, whoever she was.

And I didn't feel special, either. But I never had, anyway, so why did this bother me so much? Or at all? I knew his history, his experience. This wasn't news. We had led vastly different lives. Mason was the prince and I the frog, never to be changed with the magic of a kiss.

I supposed under the effects of a large bottle of whiskey, a frog could be kissed, even if the prince would never remember it.

That stab of sorrow ebbed as one of his hands briefly palmed the space between my breasts and then skimmed up my throat, curling around the back of my neck. It was so slow and methodical that I didn't realize he positioned me right where he wanted.

Those tantalizing eyes latched onto mine. "Maggie, no matter what happens, you'll always remember I kissed you first. I touched you first. You'll always remember it was me, and *no one* can take that away from us." Tenderly tugging my hair, he tilted my head back until I had completely submitted to him. "This moment is mine. *You're* mine."

I gasped at his claim over me, and Mason didn't hesitate to take what he wanted. His mouth covered mine, and everything and every thought faded away with that one point of contact of his lips on mine. Warmth tingled over my skin, down my neck, sinking into my chest, and quickened the beats of my heart.

His mouth moved over mine, but I didn't know what to do or how until I felt his tongue trace the seal of my lips, begging me to part for him. I did. I let him inside me, knowing how foolish that was, how much he would break me. He'd done it before, many times. This would end no differently.

What happened in the basement shouldn't have. I'm sorry that it happened, that I let it get that far. I know this is the last thing you want to hear right now, but I need to say it. I wasn't thinking about the consequences.

He wasn't in his right mind to think about those consequences now either, but I was too needy to stop him. I was that desperate for affection, craving it as I did air. I'd take scraps, the leftovers. I'd scrounge for whatever beauty there was in this world, even if it was merely concealing the ugliness within. I'd trade a world of pain for a second without it.

Without any wings to stop me, I sliced through the air and fell without care of the impact.

This kiss was sweet devastation, soaring and falling all at once. His tongue was velvety and hot, exploring me in long, languid licks as though he had to learn, map, and memorize my mouth. I still didn't have a clue as to what I was doing, so I did my best to mimic his movements, our tongues meeting in their own unchoreographed dance. He made that noise in the back of his throat again, so I figured I wasn't doing half bad.

Mason's beard was dense and coarse, each score to my skin marking me as his, the softness of his lips soothing the burn and hurt. His hands were rough but not cruel, and the taste of bitter whiskey was sharp on my tongue and oddly sweet.

I should be shoving him away and rinsing my mouth out with a gallon of bleach, but I couldn't. Because that tongue? That tongue was the most pretty fucking accurate tongue ever in the history of tongues. It should be in the tongue hall of fame, winning every tongue award there was.

Wasted or not, the damage had been done. *He* kissed *me*. Fuck what was right. Fuck what I should have done, which was stop him, back away, leave, go home. Fuck all of that. As much as I was his in this moment, he was mine.

I looped my arms around his neck, tangling my fingers in his hair, eliciting another deep groan from him that I felt *everywhere*. Mason's body shifted so that he set me on my feet. Before I could question what he was doing, his knee knocked my thighs open, spreading me wide.

Crouching down, Mason's hands were on the move, too fast for me to track. His kiss stopped long enough to say, "Hang onto me."

I was mentally five steps behind when he grasped the back of my thighs with both hands and lifted me so that he fit nice and snug against me. I inhaled sharply as my core pressed against the hard ridge in his board shorts, the heat of him going even further. I had no choice but to twist my legs around his waist, the increase in pressure creating intense shivers to ripple up my spine and settle in the tips of my breasts. When his eyes flashed up to mine, I had no doubt that he knew exactly what he was doing to me.

As he leaned over me, sinking into another kiss, a stark chill bled into my tailbone from the cold stone of the bar top. My shirt had gotten untucked at some point, and I should fix it before his hand roamed back there, but my thoughts were silenced when Mason rolled his hips, grinding into me. There was no other way to define it. A gasp lodged in my throat as every delicious inch of him slid over the tender bundle of nerves. And there were…a lot of inches.

The rumors, feminine whispers I'd heard about Mason these last few months were most definitely accurate.

"Holy fuck," I whispered against his kiss, and he answered me with another glide of his hips.

"Holy fuck is right."

I knew it was the booze that elicited his response, but the building friction coiled into a desperate ache and scrambled my thoughts. My hips made restless circles to feel more of him, chasing this feeling to find some relief. It did just the opposite. The need only intensified.

Mason broke the kiss again, breaths mingling as we struggled to slow our panting. "Do you feel that, Sticks? That electricity between us? Like sparks?"

Sparks? No. It was lightning. "Mason, you're really drunk."

"No. I've always felt it. From the first time we touched, I knew. We're connected, Maggie. Whatever this is, there's no denying it." His tongue made another decadently torturous lick into my mouth. "Tell me it's not just me." Slanting his head, he ran kisses down my neck. His lips were like the sweetest sin, and his touch was going to send me to Hell. Every move he made further twisted the muscles deep in my core until I was strung so taut, I'd thought I'd snap. "I don't believe you can't feel this between us."

He was right. This connection was…undeniable. As if all the dark fractures in my soul were suffused in his light, warming a cavernous depth of pain that had never seen the sun.

As his tongue scorched a path behind my ear, my toes curled again, head lolling back. "I feel it. It's not just you."

"Thank fuck." His mouth slammed back onto mine.

His hands were everywhere, moving too fast, lingering too long. My ass, hips, waist, then finally, on my breasts again. I hadn't realized how hard my nipples were, how sensitive they had become. Lust arrowed through me, my body seemingly knowing what to do even though my mind felt like a bumbling idiot. His fingers did something positively wicked to my nipples next, and I let out a moan the dead could hear.

"That's it, Maggie. Let me hear you." His mouth returned to mine in a kiss that was demanding, consuming, the entire world disappearing until we were all that existed. His arms held me to him as his hips thrust into me. Mason found a rhythm that we were both moving in tandem to. Moans, groans, and whispered pleas came from both of us. The simmering heat in my blood became an inferno, and I welcomed the flames.

I'd let Mason burn me until I was nothing but ashes.

I clung to his heavy shoulders, my calves pressing against his ass that flexed with each movement. "Mason, we shouldn't…" I wasn't sure what part of my brain allowed my mouth to say such stupid things, but it really needed to stop.

His forehead pressed to mine, hips working even faster. His lashes lifted just enough, focusing on where our bodies met. Pleasure thundered through me and then concentrated onto that very spot.

"We should. We should have been doing this the entire time." As his gaze lifted to mine, Mason stilled between my legs, and I bit back a plea for him to keep going. "But you control what happens here, Maggie. Only you. Tell me to stop, and I will."

This was so fucked up. He'd said these words to me before. When he was much more sober than this. When he'd regretted almost kissing me. If the roles were reversed— It didn't matter. What I was letting happen was wrong, but I was too damn selfish, craved him too much.

"Don't stop."

Mason's fingers dug into me so hard I might bruise. He groaned, and another tremor of need shot through me. "Maggie, I'm gonna take all your firsts and blow them to fucking hell. Tell me you want me as much as I want you."

I was as drunk on him as he was on the whiskey. "More. I want you more."

His hands gripped my ass, holding me up as he pushed off the bar. Keeping my legs folded around his waist, our mouths never broke contact. I wasn't sure where we were going, but I didn't care. I felt drugged and yet awake, memorizing everything I felt in this moment. The heat of his skin, slip of his tongue, silk of his hair...

Somehow, we ended up in the guestroom. Where there was a bed. My stomach fluttered with both hope and panic as he kicked the door shut, and his hand left me long enough to engage the lock.

Mason sat on the edge of the bed, guiding my legs so that I'd straddle him. I wasn't sure what to do in this position because he transferred the power to me, but my goodness, it kept getting better. I felt him beneath me, thick, long, and impossibly hard. Were they all that big, or was it just him?

"Mason," I pleaded against his mouth. Honestly, I didn't know what I was begging for at this point.

His answering growl gave me the courage to move my hips, dipping low and then sliding up his erection without his guidance. This...was different. I didn't know how, but it was, and the sound he wrung out of me was foreign even to my own ears.

Mason's hands had a firm hold of my hips, encouraging me to keep going. My body took over for my hormone-addled brain. Pure instinct drove me to move faster, harder. He let me use him for my pleasure, meeting me thrust for thrust. Mouths locked, our breaths came ragged and harsh, our hearts drumming to the same frantic beat. Mason's chest met mine, my breasts rasping against his solid frame. The maddening friction scattered my brain cells.

My hands couldn't decide what part of him to touch. His hair, neck, chest, shoulders, biceps, abs... I wanted all of it, and he didn't seem to care where I touched him, just that I was. Every cell in my body demanded to strip us bare, to feel him everywhere and all at once. It was as though something so much stronger than either one of us had taken control.

"Are you wet, Maggie?" His gaze was hooded, lingering somewhere around my breasts. I didn't doubt he could see the peaked tips being this bra's fabric was so thin. "Are you wet for me?"

Now, his hands were on my upper thighs, and I guess I didn't need his help moving anymore. I was doing alright on my own. The knowledge that I was riding Mason Scott was a thrill, unlike anything I'd known. I took no shame writhing against him, and with the next press of our bodies where he was hardest and I was softest, I drew a sound from him that was all man.

"Fuck," he grunted, every muscle strained, gripping me harder, and all the parts in me that were woman *loved* doing that to him. I was giving him the same pleasure. My body that I'd found lacking did that. "What I wouldn't do to spread those pretty thighs wide and taste you." Honestly, I wasn't entirely certain what that meant, but it all sounded good to me.

His hands slipped up the backs of my thighs, edging beneath my shorts that seemed a lot shorter than a moment ago. A shard of fear spiked through my chest when his fingertips skimmed the skin there. He was close. He would feel them. The scars. He would ask, demand to see them.

"Mason, maybe this is too fast." My head was screaming to stop this, but my hands were all over him, clawing at him, my legs cinching around him, hips grinding, mouth drinking from his lips. I was wanton and wild. I was spiraling off an edge I couldn't see. *What is he doing to me?*

"It's just the right speed. Everything about this is right because it's you and me. The way it should be."

Those words... My heart skipped a whole beat and pushed the rising fear away. That maybe...*maybe* this wasn't all the whiskey talking.

He kissed me like I was the very thing that made his heart beat, infused his lungs with breath, and brought life to his soul. His hips rolled into mine like an ocean during a storm, unrelenting and hypnotic.

I didn't realize his hands had gone beneath my shirt until I heard the quiet snick of my bra. The snug material around my chest loosened, my T-shirt tickling the tips of my breasts, which seemed to make them...ache. For him.

Oh... *Oh, Lord.*

In one swift move, Mason laid back and lifted me higher, throwing me off balance, so my hands were planted on the mattress above his head. Then something utterly heart-stopping happened to my breast that I felt in every part of me. Through the fabric of my shirt, warmth blossomed over the puckered nipple, his mouth drawing me in, tongue flicking, teeth just grazing the sensitive tip. My teeth drove right into my tongue to keep from crying out as a bolt of pleasure made me ache and throb. He worked me with his mouth, his fingers, his erection...all of him.

"I've got to be inside you, Sticks. And I don't want to leave. I've never wanted anyone like I want you."

Okay, I knew what that meant. I squeezed my eyes shut. I had to stop this and soon.

Just...just a little more.

His mouth abandoned my breast, and I let out a pathetic whimper. I heard him smile, his words sleepy and sluggish. "I'll come back to those. Don't you worry."

Mason tugged me down with him, resting his head on the bed. I sealed my lips to his, and his tongue danced in slow, seductive movements as if he realized he didn't want to rush this so he could thoroughly explore me.

And he did.

The rough pads of his fingers trailed down my stomach, leaving a blazing path in their wake. I felt the button on my shorts release and the fabric give way. Heat pulsed not far from where his fingers were and washed over me.

I was such a liar. I wasn't stopping him. No way would I stop him.

Getting the hang of this kissing thing, I took control, holding myself up over him, spreading my thighs wide so he could touch whatever the hell he wanted to. His fingers slid under my panties, the tips hot and teasing the delicate skin beneath my navel, and I braced myself for what would come next as if I could.

But those magic fingers went no farther. In fact, they kinda...stopped.

And there was a significant lack of movement in and around my mouth, too.

Like none.

Like none at all.

"Mason?" My lids flipped open to see his chest was rising in even, deep breaths. "Mason?"

His eyes were closed, lips parted, body slack.

He...he passed out? Was I that bad that I put him to sleep?

My forehead thumped on his chest, staring right at the dark swirls of ink on his golden skin. Wow, that was not how I saw that going at all.

Disappointment crested, cutting through me in chopping waves until the swell overtook me, my chest crumpling under the weight. Knowing I'd never get this chance again, I pressed one last sweet kiss to the infinity symbol on his chest, tugged his hands out of my shorts, and with a heavy heart, I slunk off the mattress.

Once I fixed my clothes, I ran my hands over my hair to smooth it down and didn't look back as I shut the door behind me. Leaning against the wall in the darkened hallway, bad thoughts kicked through my skull and ended up somewhere around my eyes. I needed to leave before any of it escaped. This was my fault, and I had no right to shed a tear.

I slipped out the front door, but not before Jamey spotted me. And chased me outside.

"Hey, Blue Eyes. Did you find Mason?" I kept my back to him, nodding. Nonverbal responses weren't good enough for him, evidently. Jerk. He spun me around to face him, and his eyes went from concerned to angry in all of one second. "What did he do?"

"He kissed me." To this day, I didn't know how Jamey understood that. Or how he never asked about the suspicious wet spot shaped like a mouth on my boob.

Jamey's hands cradled my face. "Did he hurt you?"

"No." I wasn't sure if I shook my head because I was trying to figure out why my vision was blurry. "He was so wasted, Jamey. I came here so he wouldn't hook up with Rebecca, but he did—or kinda did. I don't know. I mean, he told me she touched his… She touched him. And he probably kissed her. Actually, knowing him…"

I grimaced at the mental image of Mason and Rebecca. "I took advantage of him. I let him kiss me while he could barely see straight. I let him touch me right after he'd been with someone else. He… He didn't know what he was doing. He didn't know what he was saying. And…oh, God— What I did was no better than what Charlie did to him."

The consequence of what I'd done hit me like a battering ram right into the gut. Pain cleaved my heart, knowing it was very possible that our friendship would be over after this.

"Why did I do that?" I croaked. "I knew it was wrong, and I wanted him anyway."

His hazel eyes filled with pity for me. "We're teenagers. It's our rite of passage to do stupid shit that make no sense."

"It hurts, Jamey." I curled over and held my stomach. "None of it was real, and it *hurts*."

He gathered me into his arms and held me tight. "You know what that sounds like to me?"

I begged against his chest, "Don't say that fucking word. I'll tear out every hair on your head if you do."

"Noted."

chapter thirty-six

mason

Somewhere nearby, there was a chick screaming, voice slicing through my gray matter like a serrated knife. She sounded like she was getting hacked to pieces by an ax murderer, so I should get my ass up—

Okay, now she was...squealing? No, that was giggling. Alright, Screaming Chick was good, and my home wasn't turning into a *Saw* movie.

Daylight streamed through the window, cutting across my face, yet my body was in a completely different time zone. Like, well beyond daylight hours. I made a decent attempt to lift my head, but after three point five seconds, I'd hit my limit. My cheek landed back onto what I hoped was a pillow, and either my mouth was shrinking, or my tongue was swelling. Where the hell was I? I cracked a lid. Guestroom? How did I...

Rebecca.

The simple task of flipping onto my back could have gone smoother. Limbs flailed in an uncoordinated effort, taking three times longer than it should. At some point, I discovered that I wasn't wearing a shirt, but I was still in my board shorts. Exhaustion laced with relief ran deep as I slumped onto the mattress, blowing out a ragged breath. Chances were good that if I was this drunk and had sex, I wouldn't have put my shorts back on. Also, I didn't *feel* like I'd had sex. I had told Rebecca no...right?

Shit, I— I couldn't remember. It was as if my brain was covered in a layer of fuzz.

The walls began to shift, and if I didn't empty my bladder soon, this would get embarrassing. Using the moving walls for guidance, I made my way to the toilet. Two minutes later, one need was taken care of, and I washed my hands, but the mirror wound up seeing more soap than my skin. I'd Windex that later.

I made it into the hallway, and it looked as though there were more people in my house than before. *This may be getting out of hand.* I was somewhere between too drunk and too hungover to care.

On my couch was a head of blonde curls, and those three scraps of imported lavender polyester fabric were now in Vic's lap. I assumed that I was right, and I did tell Rebecca no. Good on Vic.

"You look rough." An arm I was genetically linked to wrapped around my shoulders, Ben guiding me to a kitchen stool. Once I was settled, he slid a glass of water in front of me.

I pushed the tumbler away. "I want a real drink."

"After the water, Coz." Ben thrust it back under my nose.

Staring at the water swishing against the rim, I rubbed my temples and struggled to remember *something*, but there was a big, fat nothingness in my skull. "What happened to me?"

Sucking a breath between his teeth, Ben added a hissing effect. I glanced up. This was gonna be bad. "Uh, Mags came back," he said.

Though my face was numb, I felt my eyes pop wide. "Did she see me like this?"

"Oh, yeah. She found you downstairs. I don't know what happened beyond that, but she left— Actually, she more like ran out of here."

I drew a sip off the rim, and my gut churned. The water was too pure, too clean. My cousin was mean. Great, now I was Dr. Seussing shit.

Wait.

Ben's words finally landed on solid ground. My lids squeezed together until the blurry halo around him cleared. "*Ran?* Explain that. Did someone fuck with her?"

His brows lifted. "Pretty sure that someone was you. Jamey was outside with her for a while."

"*Shutthefuckup.*" I threw my hands over my face, dragging them down as if they could wipe away the remnants of whiskey in my brain. "I gotta find Maggie, figure out whatever I did and make it right." Stepping down from the stool, the floor slanted under me. Whoa. "Why the hell is my home all of a sudden in funhouse-carney mode?"

Ben forced my ass back down, and I was too weak to fight him. He lowered himself, brown gaze burning through mine. "She went to work, and you are in no shape to speak to her. Your liver needs a legit break, Coz."

The doorbell rang, and I assumed those were strippers by the way the men were hollering, but with my whiskey vision, I wouldn't even be able to find the big E on an eye chart from two feet away. The music was loud but not loud enough to piss off the neighbors. The house…could be worse.

I cracked my neck. "Where's Matt?"

Ben answered with a tip of his head. "Upstairs. Comatose, I think."

"Well, if you won't let me leave to find Maggie, then that's what I need to be. Upstairs and comatose." Finishing the water only to satisfy Ben, I then poured and swallowed a gulp of whiskey. Ben's words had been as bitter and sharp as the liquor.

Maggie had run. *From me*. God, what had I said to her? I wished I could punt kick myself in the head. Either of them.

My chest ached, and I rubbed my palm over the infinity tattoo. I swore I could feel Maggie's fingers there as if she'd branded my skin.

"Mase, take—" Ben's gaze shifted, narrowing on something over my shoulder. "Now's *really* not a good time."

Okay, albeit wasted, my interest was mildly piqued. Ben didn't deploy his dick tone often. "Who are you…?" With a half turn on the stool, I had my answer. I gritted my teeth and spun to face the kitchen again. "Ben's right, Charlie. You should not be here."

"Mase, we need to talk." Charlie touched my bicep, and I lurched away, twisting to glare at her, but my frame warbled, feet stumbling on nothing. Someone kicked the stool out from under me. I was sure of it. Once my feet steadied, her gaze dropped to the stool laying on the floor and then back to me. She gulped so loud I could hear it. "You won't speak to me or return my texts. There's something you need—"

"The only thing I needed from you was loyalty."

"I know. I know you did." She reached for me again, but when I drew back, she let her hand fall. "This isn't about—"

"I don't give a fuck what this about. I asked for one thing. Space. And after all I've given you, gladly and willingly for *years*, you can't even give me that much. All you know how to do is take, Charlie."

"Mase, please," she pleaded, stepping around the stool to get closer to me. "I'm sorry I hurt you. I'm sorry for not doing what you asked. I'm sorry about what Tay did—"

"What Tay did?" My lips pulled back from my teeth. "What Tay did was ruin Maggie's life. What Tay did was take something of my sister's and then used that to hurt everyone I care about!"

She flinched and cowered before me.

"And you… You did so much more than that, Charlie. You *lied* to me. Over and over again. You never intended on letting me out of our arrangement, did you? And when you saw that you were on the losing end of that battle, you got desperate to hold onto me. Manipulate me.

You betrayed my family and my trust. You put my cousin's business, reputation, and life at risk. You threw away all the love I had for you because you cared more about your Instagram followers than a twenty-year friendship. I hope it was worth it."

Her eyes glistened as she reached for me. "Mase—"

"Don't," I warned. I pointed to the door, giving zero fucks who could hear. "Get out."

Not bothering to wait for her to leave, I snagged the bottle of Jack off the island and stormed upstairs. I unintentionally slammed my door when I kicked it closed, but I intentionally put my music on loud enough to drown out the sounds coming from downstairs. Then I planned to drink myself well beyond physical and mental numbness.

As I collapsed onto my bed, I uncapped the bottle, and a flash of metallic pink caught my attention. My watermelon medal was proudly on display among a myriad of trophies. Maggie couldn't know that stupid sixty-cent yogurt lid was my favorite thing in this room. I remembered every detail of the moment she had slipped it over my neck, the way her fingers felt on my skin, the flush of her cheeks, her cinnamon scent...

Hell, my chest *hurt*.

As my lids shut, Caribbean blue eyes were the only thing I could see, and somehow, the fissure widening my chest broke through the whiskey haze. Tipping the bottle to my mouth again, everything I knew about her came to the forefront.

Maggie was wicked smart and had a quirky sense of humor, but I didn't have a clue what she thought about when she went quiet and hid inside her own head. She liked to run, but I didn't know where her favorite trail was. She enjoyed music, but I didn't know what genre. She had mad skills in the kitchen, could cook a five-course meal out of a can of beans, a chicken wing, and a wilted carrot, but I had no clue what her favorite meal was. She had a Schwinn that was held together by rust and prayers, and I didn't know where she parked it at night.

She was kind, generous, and her heart was out for the world to see, but her emotions, her thoughts, her dreams were closely guarded and locked away. One tear from her could slice me open. One of her smiles could chase the darkness from my soul. She was beautiful. So *goddamned* beautiful, and selfless, and...full of secrets.

Secrets I wasn't worthy of. Never would be.

The amber bottle tipped back to my lips, one final thought searing into my skull. The one that hurt the most.

Maggie didn't want me.

chapter thirty-seven

maggie

Rolling up to the entrance of Crescent Lake Estates Sunday morning, I blinked. Then I blinked again. There, stepping out of the guardhouse was something I'd never seen before. Teeth were gleaming. Cheeks were protruding. Eyes were dancing. And a hand was…waving. Too bad none of those body parts belonged to a man named Bernard. Unless I was hallucinating right now. I'd had a headache since last night, so it was possible.

I set both feet on the ground, balancing the bike between my legs. "Where's B?"

The scrawny arm attached to the waving hand went down to the stranger's side. The eyes were no longer dancing. Cheeks no longer protruding. Teeth now hidden by a frown. Ah, crap. I'd ruined it.

"I'm sorry. That was rude. Good morning. I'm Maggie Davis, and I work for the Scotts, and—" I blinked. "It's just— Well, Bernard is never *not* here."

As his head bobbed, a set of thick glasses slid down to the tip of his nose. He shoved the square frames back up, so his blue eyes were magnified to twice their size again. "I know who you are. I'm the overnight watch, George."

I blinked again. "Oh. I don't mean to sound obtuse, but I didn't know anyone else worked here. I honestly thought…"

Bernard was an alien or a robot or a witchpire—whatever the hell Jamey said that was. Didn't matter.

"Is Bernard okay?"

A shoulder swimming beneath a black windbreaker rose. "Don't know. He called last night and asked me to cover his shift."

A single brow rose. "He asked?"

The corner of his mouth slid into an easy grin. "Well, I was *voluntold* to cover his shift."

Nodding, I chewed on the inside of my cheek. "That sounds about right. Well, this is yours today, then." I held up a goodie bag from the café that had been tucked inside my basket. "I've been working on a new menu item. Brownie lasagna. Not as gross as it sounds. It's six thin layers of brownie and vanilla cream."

Groaning painfully, George reluctantly took the bag. Oh-kay. Not the response I was expecting.

He studied the bag mournfully. "That sounds amazing, but I have strict orders that anything you bring me will *under no circumstances be consumed by anyone other than Bernard.* And please don't insist or argue with me. The orders were...strict." Planting his head straight, his eyes deliberately flicked to the camera over his head and mouthed, *He could be watching.*

Seriously? That was...creepy.

"Will you be here tomorrow?" I asked. "I'll bring two treats. One for you and one for B."

George squirmed in his sneakers before leaning in to whisper, "Well, I uh—" The phone rang, cutting him off, and the guy moved faster than I thought any human was capable of. "Good morning, Crescent— Ah yes, sir. No, I— Yes, I did... Yes, of course, sir." George appeared in the doorway, phone in one hand, the café bag clutched in the other. I only needed one guess as to why the guy's already pasty complexion was now pastier.

"Do not tell me that is Bernard on the phone." Eyes now triple their size, he nodded to me, and I huffed. "What did he say?"

His fingers tightened on the phone. "The rule goes for tomorrow, too. No treats for George. Those were his exact words, and he wanted me to tell you that."

"His exact... That's—" Scowling, I faced the camera. "That's mean, B, don't you think?"

Movement in my periphery forced my head to rotate. The gates were opening. George hadn't moved a muscle. And that was even creepier.

I pointed at the camera. "If you're not here to get your treats, then too bad. That brownie is for George today, and I'm bringing two tomorrow, and one is for George, too. If you can't learn to share, I won't bring you sweets anymore."

George gasped, his grip crinkling the bag.

"Dammit, George. Woman up! If you don't, Bernard will just bully you and keep taking your snacks." I balanced the bike on both wheels and readied to push off when I paused to whisper, "But don't do anything to get yourself dead. Okay?" I pedaled away before Bernard shut the gates on me.

Man, who knew there was so much guardhouse drama? Bravo was missing out, wasting so much of their time on all these spoiled housewives.

Pedaling up the Scotts' driveway, I noted that the front yard didn't show major signs of destruction, but the same cars that were here yesterday still lined the streets. I knew exactly what that meant. The people who drove them here had never left.

A few beer bottles and red cups littered the lawn, and I was hopeful that the inside would bear the same minimal damage. As the front door opened, my hope disintegrated.

As if the Solo cups and longnecks—still without coasters—weren't bad enough, there was a whole lotta skin strewn all over the floor. And dining room table. And…my God, that spatula was going right into the trash.

An acrid odor brought me to a pile of puke down the hall, and whom I assumed was the naked puker was not too far from the mess. He earned a sympathy point for making it within three feet of the bathroom.

Concern for Mason teemed through my veins as I vaulted over Puke Dude and raced toward the guestroom. I shoved the door open, my jaw unhinging as my lids peeled wide enough for my eyes to flop on out of my skull. Holding my breath, I shut the door without a noise.

I guess Ben and Jamey had solidified their boyfriend status. I'd be happy for them later, right about the time I discussed the importance of door locks with them at length.

After a quick check of the basement and finding it blessedly clean, I stepped around and between bodies and landmines, making my way upstairs. Pulse erratic, my hand shook as the breath wheezed out of me when I lowered the handle of Mason's bedroom door. Slowly this time, I edged the door open and peered inside.

In a blink of an eye, I realized yesterday's broken heart over the drunken make out session could be considered heartburn compared to what I was feeling now. Someone just tore into my chest cavity, strangled that small, beating organ and then ripped it clean from my body. There was no other way to describe this pain.

In his bed, beneath a pile of naked blondes—I didn't bother counting how many there were—was Mason.

I didn't know how long I stood there, but I gave myself a pat on the back for keeping my shit together as I backed out and shut the door. I stumbled down the hall, winding up in…the laundry room. Good enough. I closed myself in and clapped my hands over my mouth, slinking into a corner and letting my knees give out.

Either Mason didn't remember what had happened in the basement—and then in the guestroom—or everything we'd done had meant nothing to him. I wasn't sure which of those hurt more.

If Mason didn't remember our kiss, then what he'd done wasn't a betrayal in his eyes, and we'd still be friends. Nothing would change between us, and he could keep fucking and drinking his way through life. But if Mason *did* remember… He knew I'd be here today. He knew I'd see him with those women.

You're too fucking ugly for anyone to want.

On that, my father had been right.

As every bone in my chest splintered and pierced my heart, I had a pretty good idea where I stood with Mason. If in a single day, he could jump from Rebecca's mouth to mine and then beneath an orgy, then a moment that had meant everything to me, meant absolutely nothing to him.

At some point, I remembered that I had a job and might lose it if I didn't get my ass going. Since the café could close any day now, I couldn't afford not to work.

Matt was out cold in his bed, clutching an empty JD bottle to his chest like he was snuggling with the thing. Surrounding him were balled up papers, his hands smudged black. I hadn't a clue if charcoal washed out of sheets, but I supposed I'd find out later.

Slipping into Mr. and Mrs. Scott's room next, rank anger infused me. A nudist colony had set up camp on their white bed, carpet, sofas—both bedroom and balcony—and the jetted tub. This so wasn't helping my headache. My eye twitched as I logged all the surfaces that would need to be disinfected.

I did my best to avoid touching skin as I shook them awake. Reactions of embarrassment and horror made me feel somewhat better as I waited for everyone to complete their walk of shame. And, okay, the dude wearing a coconut bra and a skirt made from bananas was clever. I just wished the bananas had been a bit thicker. And longer. And included the backside. Yeesh.

With the first load of laundry going, I headed to the main floor. Relieved to see the rest of the partygoers had evacuated, I glanced through the back doors, and my momentary relief went *poof!* The toilet paper wadded up on top of the pool skimmer better not have been used.

And what the hell did they need a bajillion rubber ducks for? At least the T-Rex drawing Matt had penned yesterday made a bit more sense now.

I stuck to the inside of the house, focusing on the messes that had left stains while keeping up with the laundry. Hours had passed, and it was nowhere near enough time to get the main floor presentable.

The longer I was here, the hotter the anger stirred beneath my skin, along with an unwelcome tinge of panic. Mr. and Mrs. Scott were coming home tomorrow afternoon from their trip up north, and with one more glance to the living room…

I was so fucked.

I jarred as the sound of knuckles knocking against the front door echoed through the house. I figured someone had either returned for their phone or their pride. I left my supplies where they were and went to answer the door. Since I needed a stepladder to reach the peephole, there was no way for me to see who was on the other side. The guardhouse was supposed to announce visitors, so I assumed someone had the gate code. Or…shit. A neighbor. If I had to go next door to pick up after these assholes…

As I opened things up, the oxygen outside inexplicably dissipated, being sucked from my chest like a vacuum.

On the opposite side of the threshold, mere inches away, was a gleaming bald head and a body bedecked in leather and tattoos. And if I thought I didn't belong behind the gates of Crescent Lake Estates, this dude certainly didn't.

Unease churned restlessly in my stomach, reaching up and gripping my vocal cords. "Can I help you?"

He had one shoulder perched against the house, dark eyes glinting at me over a pair of black wraparounds. "Yeah, girly. I'm here for my whores and money."

The ground left me as I sputtered, "I— I'm sorry?"

Inked fingers—that I believed spelled DEAD on first glance—pushed the sunglasses back up his hooked nose. "You will be if you don't supply me with what I came here for."

My fingers tensed around the door handle. He must have known what I'd do next because right as I tried to slam the door shut, his boot shot out to act as a wedge. His jacket gaped open to reveal the holster on his waist, and my eyes widened as horror squeezed my throat.

The man tsked with a slow shake of his head. "Now that wasn't very hospitable. Want to try that again?"

I mentally played out a few scenarios, finding that none of them ended up with me living. What I was about to do was monumentally stupid, but I'd have to draw on my years of experience at handling an armed psychopath to get through this.

I stepped back, pulling the door away from his foot that hadn't budged from the threshold. I tried swallowing, but it felt as if the cartilage had fused together in a tight knot.

I cleared my throat roughly before I gestured for him to come in. "Please."

Brushing past me, he was quick to duck inside and waited in the foyer while I shut the door. I didn't tear my gaze away from him or the hand that was on his hip. He stood close enough to grab me if the need should arise.

Since I wasn't getting out of this and didn't have any whores or money… "Sir, I'm not sure how I can help you just yet, but may I get you something to drink first?"

Waxy skin stretched tight over his hollowed cheeks as his mouth drew into a sneer. He lifted the shades, so they sat on top of his bare head, revealing who and what he was. Tiny goosebumps appeared on my arms as icy fear tiptoed down my spine.

The skin beneath his left eye was skewed, but I could make out the faded ink that had been tattooed there. I knew what he'd done to earn that mark.

"Yes, you may. Coffee, please. Black." His mocking tone came out haughty and weirdly English as his hand flourished in the air.

Dread dug its acid-tipped talons into my flesh. My smile was weak and dissolved quickly as I rasped, "Of course."

Step for step, he followed me within arm's distance, the scent of leather and stale cigarettes not far behind. His boots thudded on the tiles as we wove through the living room, past my red bucket of supplies and the ten messes I had left to clean. I stepped toward the kitchen counter, and the man settled on a stool at the island. His eyes shifted from one surface to the next, constantly assessing. His pupils appeared to be a normal size, reacting to the light as they should. I wasn't a doctor, but from what I could tell, he wasn't completely insane or high.

He was controlled and careful. Smart.

Deadly.

Popping a mug under the Keurig, I said, "I'm Maggie."

"Trey." He watched me intently as I placed a new K-cup in the machine.

As I pushed the button to start his brew, I realized the man's stare hadn't wavered. Not even long enough to blink. Fear and dread had now melded as one, crawling and pressing along every nerve. If it could, my skin would peel itself off my body and run for its life. I wouldn't stop it.

His eyelids tapered as he said, "I know you."

My palms felt clammy and cold. "I don't believe so. I would remember you." That was the truth. I didn't know this man. Had never seen him before. But I didn't think he'd said that to get a rise out of me. No, I could guess the reason he thought he knew me.

Trey snorted, the anatomy in his nose not sounding quite right. "I suppose you would. I'm not an easy image to forget, am I?" His patchy brows wagged at me, and the tiny hairs along the back of my neck rose.

The coffee had finished brewing, and I set it on the island so he would have to reach for it. Those beady eyes held mine as his fingers wrapped around the handle.

"Good choice not throwing that hot coffee in my face, girly. That would have been most upsetting." I didn't move as he took a sip from the steamy mug, moaning his approval. That noise made my veins shrivel. "Now, how about you be a bit more hospitable and tell me where my whores and money are. Camden owes me."

Christ on a crutch.

"My apologies, Trey. I only work here, and when I arrived this morning, I didn't see Camden. This isn't his house, but I'm sure I can find his number and call him for you."

His gaze narrowed, head tipping to the side to look past the island to assess me. Those eyes raked over me from my worn sneakers, shabby clothes, to my simple ponytail. Being from similar economic classes, he recognized my appearance as a clear sign of my status in Crescent Cove, and more importantly, that I wasn't lying.

"Hmm...I like you."

"Thank you?" The words scraped out of my throat.

The corner of his mouth twitched like he was jumpstarting the muscles before cracking a smile, which, no doubt, would look creepy as fuck on his gaunt face. "You're not exactly what I come across on the daily. How old are you?"

"Eighteen, sir."

Two palms smacked the counter as his eyes rounded. "Fuck me. You could pass for fourteen. Maybe twelve. You have any clue what a hot commodity your pussy is? Please tell me you still have your V-card."

I so was not interested in continuing this conversation. And yet, I was asking, "What is a V-card?"

Oh... Oh, dear God. He really should *not* smile. It was so much worse than I imagined.

"I'll take that as a yes," he cooed, lips stretching wider.

A tense moment later, the pipes whined in the walls from the shower upstairs.

"Ah, it looks like we will have some company shortly, Maggie. I'm intrigued to see what will come down those stairs." He patted the stool next to him, and I obeyed his silent order, tamping down every instinct I had to sprint out the door.

My limbs felt rubbery and disjointed as I took the seat. "Have you been in this line of work a long time, Trey?" I asked, hoping to keep him distracted and happy, so the gun stayed where it was.

He laughed, the sound as comforting as a creaky door opening in a haunted mansion. "Twenty years. I quite enjoy it."

I wetted my lips. "How wonderful for you."

His own lips cracked with another smile, hints of metal shining in the late morning sun. My insides became pure liquid.

A door opened upstairs, and like he was a member of the SWAT team, a flash of black and silver whipped out to my side, and the barrel of a gun was trained on me. That creeper ass grin of his grew.

Yep. I was so very fucked.

chapter thirty-eight

mason

At some point during the night, I'd crawled under a shit ton of sandbags. They were lumpy and hard, and I swore they had tentacles. Weird. Cracking open a heavy lid, a tuft of tangled blonde hair hijacked my vision.

The fuck?

Not one but two blonde heads plus a hell of a lot of skin were draped all over me. What in the...?

Who are these people?

More importantly, what did I do with them? Peering under the sheet, I saw that I was wearing my board shorts, the tie intact and double knotted.

Thank the sweet Lord.

Snoring sounds rose from the floor, and this sitch just got all kinds of disturbing because that was definitely a male throat sawing the air. Looking over Bottle Blonde Number One drooling on my arm, I faced a familiar ass, and I only recognized it because it had been flashed at me during my entire twenty-plus years on this planet. I also shared DNA with the fucker.

A whole other set of questions sent my stomach into the Hurl Zone.

"Cam."

"What?" His irritated voice was muffled by a pillow. *My* pillow.

"Are these yours?" I hissed at him.

Picking up his head from my duvet—that now needed a good and proper Viking burial with flaming arrows and shit—his dark hair was bent to one side, and lines from the bedding had imprinted on his cheek. With one eye, he examined the women on top of me.

"Yeah," he answered as if I had asked the stupidest question ever.

I shut my eyes, praying for the power not to kill my cousin. Aunt Ash might get upset. Well, maybe— No, I was pretty sure she would get upset. "Please tell me I did not participate in this."

Now both of his eyes were open. "Fuck no. I know I joke, but I'm really not gaycestual."

I was going to research every god that had ever been prayed to and thank them, but first, I needed to ask, "Then what the fuck are they on top of me for?"

Cam blinked at me. "All the beds were taken."

I breathed through my nose as if that would help temper my rising anger. "Again, I ask… What the fuck are they on top of *me* for?"

He moved to sit up, finally turning his ass away from me, but the new view was even worse. "They had to sleep somewhere. How insensitive do you think I am?"

I shook my head because there was really nothing else to say after that. That was when I saw the time, and my insides instantly froze with panic. "Get them the fuck off me, Cam! Sticks is here. She can't see me like this."

"Why do you care if Maggie—" As if someone had just plugged in his brain, Cam's eyes and mouth opened wide. "I knew it! I was right! You do want to bang her!" Cam shot to his feet, much closer to me now, closer than any naked, straight men should be, related or not.

"I don't want to— *Cam*! Get your dick out of my face and take your fuck buddies off me!"

Ignoring me, he kept going. "You have feelings for her! You like Maggie!"

I lay prisoner in my own bed, staring at my naked cousin, who chose now to have his aha moment.

The remnants of sleep in his whiskey eyes cleared. "No! It's more than that. You're *in love* with Maggie. That's why you haven't fucked her yet. That's why you've been such an asshole and turned every pussy— Holy shit!" Cam grabbed his hair in both hands. "It's the death of Mason Scott's dick! We need to have a funeral!"

"Oh, we're gonna have a fucking funeral, alright." A molar cracked in my skull. "Cam, I need you to get your focus hat on. For the love of God, cover that dick, take these girls off me, and get them out of my house."

How these women hadn't woken up yet was beyond me, but I wasn't waiting for Cam's help. Screw it. I shimmied out from under them, touching as little as possible, and then scrubbed my body under the shower as scalding hot as I could tolerate. Twice. Then I applied the same dedication to the rotten death emanating from my mouth. I was out of the bathroom minutes later with raw as hell skin and a few aspirin brewing in my sour stomach.

With Cam finally rocking pants, he had the girls sitting up, but they didn't look like they were in the present or on this planet.

There was only one explanation as to why they were that shade of green and weaving. "What are you girls on?" I asked.

"M—molly," one blonde said, rubbing her eyes. Then kept rubbing as though her synapses were stuck on a loop.

I was going to have to apologize to my aunt.

"Cam." I drew in a steady breath. "Where did you get them from?"

He grimaced, and I knew the answer before he said it. "Brady."

I pinched my eyes, counting down from ten. I should have started at one hundred, but there wasn't time for that. My cousin, who was the same age as me and knew the Scott Codes just as well, was going to get the schooling of his life today. "Did you take any X, Cam?"

"Fuck no."

I searched the room for wrappers, not spotting any on first glance. "Did you wear a condom?"

His head tilted to the side, the planes of his face hardening. "I'm a dumbass, I know. But I'm not that dumb."

Gripping the doorknob, I eyed the pros on my bed. "I have two reasons why I'd debate that. I'll deal with you later. Get them up, feed them something, and call them an Uber." Nearly breaking my neck running downstairs, I called out, "Sticks! Sticks!"

She didn't answer. Maybe she hadn't come today. I didn't think I was that lucky, but if so, she'd never know about this mess and—

Oh. Holy. Jesus.

The scene in the kitchen was like slamming into the ground after my skydiving parachute didn't open. Every molecule of air was sucked out of the room as fear seized me down to my cellular structure.

Maggie was sitting at the island, hands trembling, licking the hell out of her lips, which was nothing new. Lack of sleep and stress caused her nervous system to whack out, making her more prone to a seizure. So while her current neurological state was enough of a warning, it wasn't what set off DEFCON 1. It was the silver barrel and black grip that my eyes were locked onto, along with the tatted hand holding the gun right at her.

"Ah, so is this the famous Camden?" Looking to me, his thin brows shot up, and whatever ink was scrawled beneath his eye became distorted. The letter V maybe. His tongue clucked against the roof of his mouth. "Looks like you lied to me, Peach. And we were getting along so well."

"I'm not Camden." An expression of what I would guess was disappointment flitted across his face. My gaze shifted back to those azure eyes that were fully dilated and unblinking. "Are you okay?" God help me, if this bastard touched her, I'd gut him with my bare hands.

Prison Tat Dude didn't let Maggie speak. "I want my girls, and I want my money, Not Camden. This sweet little thing didn't know where he was. But I bet you do."

My line of sight stayed on the hand holding a gun. At Maggie. "Sticks, answer me. Are you okay?"

"I've been better." I had expected her voice to sound as shaky as her hands, but instead, she was uncannily calm. How long had he been here? Didn't matter. This piece of shit had to go.

"Look, uh—" My brow rose at the man to prompt him.

"Trey," he offered coolly.

I gave him a curt nod. "Trey, your girls are upstairs. How much?"

"Five."

"*Five?*" I repeated, knowing we didn't have that kind of cash at home.

"My girls brought X, Nine, and their wet pussies. Your guests indulged in all three. It's five," he stated as though he were ticking off a grocery list.

Nine...

That wasn't a V under his eye. It was a VI. A Roman numeral six. And if the rumors were true, for him to earn that tattoo, he'd had to...have taken a life.

I had a legit member of the Sunset Bay Sixes in my fucking kitchen.

"I don't have that kind of cash lying around. I can get you half the green right now and jewelry to cover the rest."

Trey relaxed against the counter, his empty hand wrapping around the back of Maggie's stool. Dread coiled around the top of my spine. "Let me tell you how this works, pretty boy, because you seem to be mistaken that I'm running a pawn shop or some shit. I'm the motherfucking pimp. You call me, and I supply the pussy and the drugs. You then pay my whores and send them back to me. But you failed to do your part, so I had to haul my ass up here to collect. And if you can't pay, this sweet peach is gonna work off the interest until you can."

"Fuck you," I seethed, vibrating with rage that was rife and foul. Maggie's eyes flared wide with a warning to keep my shit together.

"Fuck *me?* Fuck the guy holding the gun? You may want to rethink how you speak to me. You know…" He sucked on his front teeth, gold glinting in his mouth. "You richies are all the same, no respect until it's demanded. You could learn from Maggie here. She welcomed me in, offered me a beverage, called me *sir*, and she's entertained me with a lovely chat while we've been waiting for you."

Goddamn it.

A ragged breath hacked through my lungs, and I swallowed the rage that would get everyone dead. "My apologies, Trey. Your girls are right upstairs, along with half of your money. It's Sunday, so I have to hit a few ATMs for the rest."

"You've got thirty minutes."

I recoiled. "Shit, man. Come on! This town only has two banks. It'll take me thirty minutes just to get on the highway."

An evil grin warped one side of his mouth. "That's why I picked thirty."

Instinct flared to life and blasted through me as I made a lunge for Maggie, but it was the metal *snick* of the gun's safety that broke through to the rational part of my brain and stopped me from grabbing her. Her eyes slowly shut, a thick swallow rolling along her throat before she eased a stuttered breath out of her nose.

"CAMDEN!" I yelled.

A dark chuckle slithered out of his thin lips. "See, Peach? Just takes the right motivation to get what you want in life. We'll let that be your second lesson."

She opened her eyes to look at the barrel and then Trey. "I'm almost afraid to ask what the first lesson was."

A noise of approval hummed in his throat that had my firsts curling in, fury fogging my thoughts. "Never open the door for strangers."

The more this guy talked, the more I knew I would do something to earn a hole in a vital organ. "*CAMDEN!*"

"Fuck, Mase. I'm coming. You have no idea what it took for them just to get their clothes on." He appeared at the banister, holding the women's hands, and I suspected without his help, these chicks would tumble down the stairs face first. They really needed to lay off the drugs.

Matt trailed behind them, rubbing his eyes as he stumbled into Bottle Blonde Number Two. His brows furrowed, gaze tracking over until landing on Maggie. My brother's face paled as he breathed, "Holy fuck."

"Look, Matt, I know. I'm taking care of..." Cam's gaze then drifted to where Maggie was and froze mid-step. "Who the fuck is that?"

"Their pimp," I answered, my words strangled by a tight jaw. "And he wants five."

"Fuck that! It was three," he argued.

"We're paying whatever he wants, Cam," I growled.

"It was three. Before the X and Nine," Trey explained, and Matt cursed under his breath, now mostly caught up on this clusterfuck.

Cam looked to Maggie again, face screwing up tight. "I don't have five."

Trey jutted his pointy chin toward me. "Not Camden and I already discussed the ramifications of *not* paying me in cash. Do we really want to waste more time? I'll gladly go over them again."

Somehow, I kept my tone at a normal decibel level over the roar of my pulse. "No. We're good, Trey."

Maggie said, "Guys, go wake up Jamey, please. He's in the guestroom."

How Jamey would help matters right now, I hadn't a clue, but I'd jump off whatever cliff Maggie asked of me, wearing ten-inch heels and a thong. I shot down the hall and threw open the door. "Jamey!" A silver platinum head bolted up behind Ben's. "Get to the kitchen. *Now.*"

Jamey and Ben were out in record time, neither one wearing shirts or sparing the extra seconds to don underwear beneath their jeans. All the color in Jamey's skin leached out when his eyes found the mess at the island.

Jamey was about to speak when Maggie held up her hand. "There's no time. Jamey, get my bag from your house. We need it for this man. Okay?"

"All of it?" he wheezed, eyes bulging.

"Please, hurry."

Trey shook his head, the gleam from the pendant light reflecting off his scalp. "They all go. It's only gonna be me and the Peach."

"Fuck that!" I barked, my pulse revving up a few more notches. "I'm not leaving her with you."

Eyes as warm as blackholes shifted to me. "Oh, you will, and if you're not back in twenty-eight minutes, I'm popping this cherry. And that's not all I'm gonna be doing to her."

I couldn't move. I swore I tried, but just thinking about this fucker's dirty fingers on *my Maggie* stopped all other thought.

"Guys, go. *Please*," Maggie implored.

Her voice broke me out of a scene of *Matrixing* over the counter and kicking Trey's hooked nose through the back of his head. I flew up the stairs to grab my keys and shoes. Back down in the kitchen, having not breathed yet, I left my sweet little Sticks there with a pimp and his drugged-up girls.

Without questioning why we needed to go to Jamey's house, Matt, Cam, and I piled into the Raptor, tires rolling before the doors were shut. Ben and Jamey were already ahead of us in the Land Rover.

With Matt behind the wheel, he tore out of the driveway, barreling toward the gates. As I tied my right sneaker, I glimpsed the side mirror before we turned the corner, a matte blacked-out Mercedes in the reflection. I made a mental note to run if I ever saw that car again.

"How did he get in here? In our neighborhood?" Matt gritted out, waiting for the gate to open.

Movement from inside the guardhouse caught our attention. George sent us a wave on the tail end of a goofy grin. I hoped he kept that chipper attitude. He'd need it to write a resume after today.

Matt punched the gas as soon as the Rover cleared the way. "Cam, who the fuck was that guy?"

On a pause from Cam, Matt shot a glare to the rearview. Our cousin finally answered with, "Brady's guy."

"You fuckass!" Matt took a sharp turn toward the back road to Jamey's, leaving the asphalt for dirt. That was best. We'd miss the lights and avoid traffic. "Why didn't you use Crystal? Those girls were drugged to the max and probably riddled with diseases."

BB bounced over every damn rock and hole out here, the scenery swirling around me. I shut my eyes as an image of Maggie and that fucker drove through my throbbing brain like a hot poker. I bowed my head between my knees, ready to vomit the acid eating up my stomach.

"It was short notice, and Crystal didn't have any girls left on her party list."

"Oh! So you thought dirty pros and their meth-head, gun-wielding, gangster pimp who wants to rape our little Maggie, whom we had to leave as insurance, was okay? You're fucking adopted! You have to be. No one related to me could possibly be this fucking stupid! How many times? How many fucking times do I have to tell you, Cam?" A charcoal-stained hand pounded on the dash to punctuate each point. "Clean girls! No drugs! Wear protection! There's only three things you have to remember. Please, please tell me you wore a condom."

"I wore one," Cam snarled back.

My brother's head snapped over his shoulder long enough to shoot daggers out of his emerald eyes. "Don't. Don't you dare, Camden. You fucked up! This is the fuckup of epic proportions!"

"I get it! I'm a fuckup," Cam yelled back. "You don't think I know that? You don't think I'm shitting my pants right now and want nothing more than to tear that fucker's limbs off his body?"

Shifting my gaze, I looked to the dash clock, struggling to read the numbers. When the digits swam together, the dread coiled at the top of my spine unfurled and whipped down into my tailbone, paralyzing me.

"Matt, we gotta go faster."

"I know. But we're pushing speed as it is. Five-O patrols the back roads, too. We're all still hungover enough to qualify as drunk, and for sure that sick bastard is going to—"

There must have been something in my face that killed the end of that sentence, but we both knew what he was going to say.

Matt focused back on the road. "We gotta stay cool. We're okay on time." He probably meant to reassure me, but his freaked-out tone kinda ruined it.

I rocked in my seat as another wave of sickness crested. "No. No, we're not. There's no way we'll make it back before—"

With another roil of my stomach, my hand shot to the window control. I almost didn't thrust my head out fast enough. The sharp burn of sickness stretched from the pit in my stomach all the way to my teeth, gut spasming, but nothing came.

I watched the dirt and wildflowers fly past as my tires ate up the road, following the tracks left by the Rover, pebbles plinking beneath the frame. The cool breeze stung my skin at these high speeds, but no matter how clean and briny the air was, each inhale felt like there was grime coating my insides.

Maggie.

Abruptly, the brakes were deployed, and I was hurled forward. The seatbelt cut into my neck as the tires skidded to a stop on the asphalt. We'd hit the suburbs on the southern end of Meadowbrook outside of Jamey's house. Next thing I knew, a blond blur sprinted out of the front door with a black duffel, aiming right for me.

Jamey shoved the bag through my window, scraping it on the frame. "Go."

Matt didn't need to discuss it. He jerked the wheel around and completed a one-eighty right back to our house. The bumpy road wasn't helping the situation in my gut, so I concentrated on the duffel in my lap. It was full and decently weighted, which surprised me.

I didn't know how much time had passed before I finally unzipped the bag, and…blinked. On top were crisp, folded clothes, still with tags on them. They were Maggie's size and in far better shape than anything she owned. I rifled past a few basic outfits, underwear, bras, newish sneaks, and at the very bottom was the envelope of cash. The one my dad had given her.

Matt's eyes bounced between the road and me as I passed the envelope of cash to Cam to count out what we needed. "What is all that?"

"I don't know," I muttered, sifting through the bag. "Toiletries, duplicate IDs, water...protein bars? Why would she have this at Jamey's house?"

Matt shrugged, pounding on the gate remote above our heads. "Beats me."

"It looks like she's ready to skip out," Cam observed over my shoulder.

My gut knotted. He was right. It did.

"For what reason?" Matt asked, taking the first turn.

That I didn't know, but in that instant, I did know that Maggie Davis had become an even bigger question mark.

With my hand on the door handle, Matt had the speedometer tipping to sixty as Cam counted out two grand and kept the rest in the truck with Maggie's bag. There were forty-two seconds to spare, and as the Raptor pulled into the drive, I didn't bother to wait for the truck to stop before I pulled a Maggie and flew out the door.

chapter thirty-nine

maggie

Once the Scotts got their heads out of their asses and left, I was alone with Pimp Dude and two sex workers who were using each other to prop themselves up on the sofa. I prayed if they had to puke, they would aim for the tile. That fabric was a bitch to clean.

"Finally, we're alone. Me and the three amigas." Trey's words came out on an exhale as he stepped back from the front window and examined his *employees* with a shifty eye. He wagged the muzzle of the gun between them. "How much X did you pop last night?" The more time that stretched in which they didn't answer him, the more his shoulders hunched forward, eyes narrowed, and veins in his temples bulged.

His rage was growing, and either they were too high to realize they might trip his trigger finger, or they were beyond caring.

"Three," one blonde answered.

"Bitch." The back of his free hand swung as a *smack* resounded through the room.

Huddled on the same cushion as her partner, she covered her cheek with both hands. Maybe it was morbid curiosity, but I found myself drifting closer, searching for her reaction to find there wasn't one. No gasp, cry, or a slew of expletives. She didn't even glare at him.

She had accepted this. The abuse. Emotional, mental, and physical. Had she been like me? Had she endured men like this her entire life? Had she given up on fighting for better and resigned herself to surviving the only way she knew how?

Is this what I could turn into?

With a bit more swagger in his step, Trey sauntered my way, stopping inches in front of me, but the stench clinging to him did not.

The back of my throat itched as he said, "Your body doesn't hide fear as well as your face does, Peach. You look like you're going through withdrawals."

I figured hiding my hands wasn't the wisest move considering he was holding a semi-automatic pistol. "I have a neurological disorder. I'm stressed, not scared. A little slap across the face doesn't bother me."

I had his complete attention now. The taut skin around his eyes crinkled, skewing the VI tattoo on his face. "What does?"

"Batons," I answered. "That shit hurts."

Throwing his head back, his Adam's apple jutted sharply against his skin with a cackle. "Yeah, I've had a few of those." That creepy gaze snaked over me top to bottom. "You know, Peach, I could use a levelheaded pussy like you on my crew. These bitches are always dippin' into my stash and don't know which end is up half the time."

"No offense, but that is an unappealing offer, which I would never consider. Do not mistake my composure for anything but a need to keep those bullets in your gun."

His shoulder poked up in a lazy shrug. "Fair enough." Sliding past me, he returned to his stool and emptied his coffee mug.

Despair settled over my skin, boring its way into my bones. I had no option here but to ride this out.

Following him back to the kitchen, I offered, "Let me make you all something to eat." My head slanted to the slouched bodies in the next room. "They could use a meal."

He saluted me with his mug in appreciation.

I scanned the fridge, those dark marbles tracking my every move. Breakfast would be easiest, and I could drag out the minutes by cooking an entire package of bacon. I gathered what I needed and set everything on the island.

"So, what did a sweet thing like you do to earn the stick?" Trey asked.

I slid a pan over a burner. "Believe it or not? Nothing."

Trey made that crackly, snorting noise again. "Oh, I believe it. No one's more corrupt than cops."

That comment made me pause. He was either slapping his gums or speaking from experience. Honestly, that answer required too many brain cells, ones I didn't have to spare. This headache was getting worse and creeping into migraine territory, and as I opened the package of bacon, the scent of meat hit me, nausea rolling through my stomach. I breathed through it.

Feeling sweat bead on my upper lip, I said, "Not all cops are bad, Trey."

"Oh, they are. You can't hold that much power and not get drunk off it. And you can imagine in my line of work, I've known some real psychopaths. Present company included." He traced a swirl on the granite countertop with a dirty, chipped fingernail. "But the worst...? Yeah, the worst of humanity stands on the other side of the law. Hiding in plain sight. In this town." Those eyes met mine. "The head of the blue snake."

Dread blossomed in the pit of my belly and rose up my throat, acidic and bitter on my tongue. He was referring to one person, Police Chief Nathan Davis. When and under what circumstances had a Sixes gang member gotten involved with my father? The only connection I was aware of had to do with my mother and...me.

"I swear I've seen you before, Peach."

My hand trembled a bit more as I lined the meat inside the cool pan. I had seen a picture of my mother once, and we bore a close resemblance. I suspected that resemblance was one of the reasons my father beat me, to indirectly punish her for running away and leaving him with a damaged baby. And the man responsible for my damaged brain could very well be sitting feet away from me. Wearing a boot similar to the one that put this dent in my skull.

"I, uh—" My voice wavered. I inhaled a few shaky breaths as I lit the pilot light and then slid a mesh cover over the pan. "I don't know why. I don't make it down to Sunset Bay often."

"And I don't make it this far north in the Cove often either. Kinda breaking the rules today, which has me a bit on edge." He set the SIG Sauer 9mm in front of him on the island, barrel facing me. "Sorry, not sorry."

I started cracking eggs into a bowl, forcing my tone to stay even, bored. "What do you mean, breaking the rules?"

He studied me for an uncomfortable moment, and each of those seconds ate into what was left of the twenty-three minutes and fifteen seconds I had left.

"Ah, what the hell. We're bonding and shit, right?" Trey planted his elbows on the counter, and he sucked on his front teeth, staring right at me with those dead eyes. "You ever wonder why you don't see more people like me in your town? You think there's some magical forcefield made of unicorns and rainbows keeping the Sixes out of your backyard? Because I'll let you in on a secret." A bony hand flicked toward the woman who hadn't moved in a good five minutes. "The reason clearly has nothing to do with lack of demand for whores and drugs."

"I'll be honest," I rasped. "It was something I didn't want to think about."

"You and everyone else, Peach. But if you did think about it, what might the motivation for someone of little to no moral character be to stick to my side of that imaginary line? And who would have the power and means to encourage me to keep to that line?"

I think my stomach and all that was connected to it dropped to the floor.

His eyes danced with pure glee as his palm landed on the counter with another jarring *smack*! "I can see it! Damn, you're quicker than I thought. Come on, Peach. Say it. You know you want to."

The name scraped out of my throat. "Marcus Ryan."

"*Ding-ding-ding!*" Trey cupped his mouth with both hands to create a bullhorn. "Get this lady a gold watch, Bob!"

I could seriously puke right now. "You're saying that Marcus Ryan pays the Sixes to stay out of Crescent Cove? Why? To attract investors? To get a hotel built?"

His palms returned to the island, fingers framing his gun. "Oh, you're very warm, but not hot. Still, I'm impressed." The lights gleaned along his head as it swiveled side to side. "You gotta think bigger. How else do you think he keeps those hands of his so pretty? Man's not digging his own graves, Peach. Dead men tell no tales and all. By the way, same goes for women and children."

Contrary to what you believe, I do know all the dirt. Specifically, the piles of it covering the buried bodies. And I know how they got there. So don't make the wrong choice here, Spaz. Nothing good happens to those who do.

I'd had more than a few unnerving conversations with Eric, and I wholeheartedly believed Marcus had something to do with Jenna's death to cover up what his son had done to her. If Marcus was willing to kill a sixteen-year-old girl…what else had he done?

And to whom?

"Have you…dug a lot of graves for him?"

Those eyes lifted to mine, one side of his mouth twisting. "Him and for those who benefit him."

I wasn't sure the last time I took a breath, but my lungs sent up a reminder that it had been a while. "And who benefits Marcus Ryan?"

Leaning toward me, his leather jacket complained with the movement. The corners of his eyes wrinkled. "Pay closer attention. I already told you."

Oh, God.

The head of the blue snake.

"Think it's time to flip that bacon, Peach. Tick-tock."

Giving him a rickety nod, I focused on the food because...the alternative might be too damn much.

With three plates of scrambled eggs, toast, and bacon done, I freshened Trey's coffee and poured juice for the women—the sugar and vitamin C couldn't hurt. With my last glimpse at the clock, my pulse was all I could hear.

There was one minute left.

Sixty seconds were the only thing standing between me and certain rape. Possibly death. Trey expected Mason to fail, and that was why he told me his secrets. Because they wouldn't leave this house.

My heart pounded painfully against my ribs. These women would help me, right? There were three of us and one of him. Okay, they each counted as a half since they were still on their way down from their respective highs.

One more glance to them and the effort it took just to lift their forks, I wasn't convinced they would do a damn thing to stop Trey.

With his mug near emptied again, Trey slurped down a sip, his eyes connecting with mine over the rim. They were dark, soulless pits.

Hitting women, abusing them, treating them like slaves was no different than breathing to a monster like this. At least he was honest about what he was. He didn't hide behind a mask, a badge. No, he wore the beast with pride.

And I had every intention of going down fighting. I would lose. There was no question about that. But that didn't mean I wouldn't do some damage in the process.

Setting down the mug, the corner of his mouth drew up, one side of his face warping with what looked like a smile. Fear embedded into my skin and quickly rooted its way down to the bone.

The knife block was right behind me. As he rose from the stool, I took a step backward—

The front door flew open with a *bang*! "STICKS!"

At Mason's voice, shock and relief inundated me with such force that I nearly crumbled where I stood.

Mason tore through the house, coming at me eyes wild and chest heaving. I didn't have time to react before his arms were around me, crushing me to him. "Did he touch you?"

Camden—I think—charged past us, tearing up the stairs in a whir. I totally got why the Scotts were on Warrington's football team now.

"I'm alright, Mason." That part was muffled because my mouth was now jammed into a pectoral muscle, and the arms wrapped around me weren't big on letting me breathe. I shifted enough to speak. "Just pay the man so he can go."

the silent fall of a magpie | 451

With one arm still squeezing me to him, Mason slammed a pile of cash onto the counter and spun us as if to shield me with his body. The heartbeat in my ear was going scary fast, and I could barely hear Camden as he stormed down the stairs with the remainder of the money.

Sporting a frowny face that only made him look even more like the sociopath he was, Trey tucked all the bills into a neat pile and tapped them against the granite as though the cash had suddenly morphed him into a prim bank teller. Then he proceeded to lick his thumb before counting every dollar.

Those eyes flicked over to me as he counted the last bill. "I must say, I'm disappointed you arrived on time. I was looking forward to that little cherry."

I would never eat peaches or cherries again.

Mason's arms tightened around me, and I was certain that was a growl working in his throat.

"We're square now." Matt stepped over to block Mason and me from Trey, and then the rest of the guys finished the wall, but I could still see that man through the cracks.

"That we are." Trey slipped the money into an interior pocket of his jacket and set something on the counter in its place. "If you change your mind, Peach." The last D finger of DEAD tapped what looked to be a business card.

Staring at the thing as if the card would sprout legs and attach itself to my face, tingles raced down my spine. Everything about Trey's business card looked familiar, from the glossy white card stock to the simple block lettering in raised black font, but this was the first time I'd seen it.

I heard myself say, "No, thank you, Trey."

Possessively tucking me closer, Mason forced me to face the other way, so I was looking at the lake, but my gaze slid down to the butterflies on his bicep that weren't covered by his sleeve. As I studied their blue hues, the black and gray scrolled along the corded muscle, there was a noise, a low hum or ring that I couldn't identify. Coming from...somewhere. Feet shuffled behind me, words were said, and the front door chimed and then shut. As though I were listening with buzzing pillows over my ears, I heard the front lock engage, and the house alarm was turned on.

Mason's deep voice rumbled against my forehead, one hand pressing us together, the other on the back of my head, fingers threaded into my hair. "Thank God. Thank God you're okay."

Was I? Because I didn't feel okay.

I should because that was Mason's hard body against mine, his strong arms holding me, his chocolaty scent infusing me, his large hands pressing into my skin. As if he really cared. This was everything I should want. And rather than process everything that had happened in the last few hours, I couldn't. I'd blocked it out or something. Instead, I was deep in memories that I couldn't shut off.

Images replayed in my mind that forced every wretched emotion a human could feel to reach up from within me and take me by the throat. Mason covered in naked women. In his bed. Rebecca and the look on his face at school. The girls on the phone. Mason's mouth on Charlie's…

Maggie's my friend and nothing more.

Mason wasn't mine and never would be. He gave himself to women who *looked* like women. They wore designer everything and didn't have nails cut down to the quick and had hair with highlights or lowlights or whatever the fuck lights and clothes that weren't threadbare and shoes that weren't split on the sides and a smidge too tight after washing them.

Mason didn't care about me, not the way I cared about him. He was using me to play the role of my hero to atone for his sister. I'd somehow forgotten that, romanticized this as something more when I should have been remembering that I was *nothing more.*

I shoved him away, stumbling over my feet as I floundered backward, but I caught myself before falling. Embarrassment seared my cheeks with heat as I refused to look at everyone pitying the broken girl about to break once more.

I didn't want their fucking pity.

Mason reached for me. "Sticks, I'm sorry. I'm so sorry."

A sharp sting lanced the back of my eyes, taking me up the stairs because my walls were ready to shatter, and he would see how much he'd hurt me. There would be no hiding it. I needed to keep busy until I could.

Admittedly, a poor decision on my part, I started cleaning Mason's room. The first thing I found was the empty bottle of Jack on his nightstand. Did they all drink from it, sharing sips off the rim between kisses and lap dances?

I dragged my focus to the duvet that was in a pile on the floor as if it didn't want to be any closer to that bed than I did. The sheets were wrinkled, pulled back from the corners of his mattress. The pillows were dented and covered in blonde hairs.

Did he bother to consider that I would make his bed? The bed he just had sex in with two women whom he didn't seem to know the names of? Did he touch them like he had me, kiss them with all the desire that he had kissed me? Did he let their touch linger on Faith's tattoo? Did he tell them about his sister? Did he use her memory to get them into bed?

I'd probably taken that a step too far, but the thought ripped through my gut with near crippling pain, nonetheless.

Before I landed myself inside a padded room, thinking about the logistics of having sex with two women at once, my fingers curled around the sheet. My gaze dropped to my hand that was shaking, worsening by the hour since I'd woken up today. It wasn't the only symptom that had gotten worse.

The dim ringing sound in my ears was still there, growing louder. The headache, nausea, tremor, aura…

It was coming, and I needed to get help.

And yet, I did nothing.

I hadn't heard anything over the ringing, but the hairs on the back of my neck began to rise, sensing Mason somewhere behind me. Here I was acting the maid for him, picking up his room after he fucked those women, and he was just standing there, watching me. Maybe he wanted to remind me to scrub down his desk again.

My body felt heavy, my skin too tight, and the walls were closing in as if the atmosphere was about to collapse on top of me.

"Sticks, stop. I'll clean up. It's my mess."

I wheeled on him, catching my footing as the ground shifted, head going light. Someday I would learn my lesson and not move so damn fast, but that day wasn't today.

His dark, cropped hair was in disarray as though he'd been running his fingers through it—or four female hands had been. His almond-shaped eyes were like bright peridot gems banded with citrine that had been appreciating other women for assets for which I didn't and would never possess. His mouth was parted with lips that had been kissed by many who weren't me. His immense frame towered over me, a body that had been worshiped by countless others, women who would never see him like I did.

I've never wanted anyone like I want you.

How many women had he said that to?

"Damn right, it's your mess," I snipped. "But your parents are coming back tomorrow. The house looks like the RAMs had a rager here. I can't even guess what the fuck went on in the backyard. And every room needs to be scrubbed with an ungodly amount of disinfectant. So now it's *my* mess. If I wanna keep my job, I've gotta clean up after you Scott fuckups."

He blinked down at me. "The house isn't that bad."

He did not just say that to me. My foot's sole purpose was to change his testicles into ovaries. I wasn't sure if that was possible, but I wouldn't mind trying.

"You know, Mason, you may want to consider setting your bar of life a little higher. Like an inch off the ground would be nice." As I bent to grab the duvet off the floor, my hand touched something rubbery, sticky, and oh so familiar. Screaming out, I threw the duvet down and launched myself back five feet. "Goddamn it! Do you seriously not know how to throw that shit away? Do you do this on purpose?"

Confusion wrinkled his forehead until those eyes I was so keen on earlier centered on what had started this newest tirade of mine. His lids expanded wide. Then the mouth followed. "It's not mine! And neither was the last one!"

"Whose are they, Mason?"

"Cam's! They're Cam's, Maggie."

"Really?" I seethed, storming past him and into the bathroom. I flipped the hot water on and then pumped out every drop of soap from the dispenser.

"Sticks—"

"You're foul. You know that? All of you assholes are foul!"

He risked a step inside the bathroom with me, standing way too close to the sharp angle of my elbow. "I get you're upset, and you have every right to be, but you seem...volatile. Have I done something?"

Meeting his bewildered reflection in the mirror, I shook my head in amazement. "Have you *done something*? Like, other than not throwing your semen-filled condom away? Again? Or finding you buried under the two body cavities that condom had been inside?"

He flinched and took a step back, finally clued in as to how pissed I was. "Maggie, I didn't touch those women. I never saw them before this morning."

"Wow. Just...wow." Over my shoulder, my eyes narrowed. "You must really think I'm a special kind of stupid."

His gaze shifted from the mirror to look directly at me. "I know those aren't my condoms for one reason. They're made of latex, and Matt's highly allergic to latex. I only use his brand, which is made of polyurethane, as an extra precaution to keep him safe."

"And you can tell the difference when you're wasted? Because I saw you wasted yesterday, Mason. I wasn't impressed."

Mason paled, the hard planes of his face softening. "Maggie, please. Camden was with those girls, not me. He'll tell you."

A lump formed in my throat, burning and thickening. What was this? How much shit would I take from him? At what point would I stand up for myself? If I had been at OHU, I would be the girl—no, the woman—I wanted to be. Not this. I didn't want to be this anymore. I didn't want to end up like those two women, working for a pimp who pistol-whipped me when I took drugs to numb out because all the abuse, the sex, the what-I-could-have-dones were too loud to shut off.

It had to stop. I had to end the pattern now. I had no power against my father, against Marcus and the Prices, but I didn't have to be this for everyone.

"I'm done, Mason." Drying my hands on the bathroom towel, my bottom lip trembled, and the damn lump in my throat made it hard to breathe. As much as I didn't want to let the Scotts go, as much as it killed me to no longer be in Mason's life, I had to leave. It was a mistake to come back, and the worst part was, I'd known it all along. From the first time I pulled up to those gates months ago. I never belonged here. "I shouldn't have come back."

"No, don't do this." His hands clamped around my shoulders, drawing me back toward him.

Grimacing, I wrenched away, refusing to look at him.

"Maggie, please," he pleaded. "I swear I'm telling the truth."

I kept my eyes locked on the raw skin of my hands. "Please, tell your parents that I'm sorry. This isn't going to work."

"No. No, I'm not going to tell them that, dammit."

I shut my eyes when my hands blurred together. "Mason, I'm done."

"The fuck, you're done. *Camden!*"

Mason charged out of the room, the floor vibrating as his weight pounded down the stairs. I bit my tongue, diverting the pain away from my heart. I wouldn't cry. It was a waste of time. I needed to leave, move on. That had to be my focus. My heart lurched at the promise I'd broken to Poker. Without this job, I was never going to get us out of here.

As I stepped out of the bathroom, I heard Camden shout, "You're gonna punch a hole in my spleen, Mase!"

Oh, hell.

I shot to the railing to find Camden pinned to the kitchen floor. Above him, Mason's elbow drew back, then his fist pistoned a sickening *thud* into Camden's stomach.

"Jesus," I muttered.

Camden's eyes flared with panic when Mason's fist cocked back for another blow. "Come on, Coz!"

Matt sipped his coffee at the island, looking on with little interest. "Personally, I would leave him with two black eyes."

"Then I'd have to explain this fucked up day to Aunt Ash. I don't want to break her heart when she realizes how much of a fuckstick her son really is." Mason's fist drove down again, and Camden flipped to his side, holding himself with a pained groan.

Matt nodded. "Ah. Good thinking, little brother."

These men were all kinds of whacked-out crazy.

"Tell her!" Mason demanded. "You're gonna go up there and tell her the truth about those women! And you're gonna tell her those were your fucking condoms she found in my room. Both times! Make it right, Cam! I'm not losing her because you're a fuckup!"

Coughing up what could be vital organs, Camden waved his arms in surrender. "Get off me, and I will."

Mason sat back on his heels, chest rising and falling in fast succession, death glare affixed on his cousin.

Still holding himself, Camden rolled over, head lolling back as his brown eyes lifted to collide with mine. He was a concerning shade of green as he rasped, "Maggie, he's right."

Mason and Matt's heads whipped around to find me coming down the stairs.

After a grunt and a swallow, Camden continued, "The condoms were mine. I can't stand the non-latex shit. My guy needs a bit more stretch and—"

Camden's words were cut off when Mason cocked his arm.

Eyes rounding, Camden's hand lifted to stave off the hit. "Right, that was too much. Sorry. Ah, anyway, there was a party here a few weeks before classes started. I had sex in Mason's bed and forgot to throw away the rubber. Full disclosure, she had this tongue that... Is your eye okay, Maggie, because that twitch doesn't look—"

"Cam," Mason growled, rolling his shoulders. "Get to the point."

"Yeah, okay. So I was distracted. And those women last night...*I* hired them. Mason didn't know they were here. He was wasted when they arrived, and right after, he took a bottle of Jack to his room. By the time we were...well, every room was taken, and Mase was comatose. Clearly, not my best decision, and I own that. But *I* had sex with those women. Not Mason. I was drunk, and I might have suggested they crawl into his bed. Honest, Maggie, Mason was passed out, and he never knew."

Slowly, I made it down to the landing. "I don't even know what to say anymore. You Scotts are an avalanche, and you keep taking me down with you."

Mason stood and closed the distance between us, so we were eye to eye. But we weren't equals. Never would be.

"Sticks, don't leave. The guys and I will clean, order a pizza, maybe watch a movie. It will be fine. Just stay."

Was he for real? Did he seriously not see what they were doing? How messed up this was?

"*Fine?*" A rod shot into my spine, taking the last few steps as my head angled back to face him. "There's nothing fine about any of this, Mason. This is fucked up beyond all conceivable fuckedupdom. What aren't you getting? I don't want to eat fucking pizza! I don't want to watch a fucking movie! I don't want to fucking be here! I don't want to see, hear, or be around you or any other fucking Scott! I came here yesterday to tell you something important, something I thought you'd give a shit about, but I'm coming to the painful realization that you don't give a shit about anything *but* Mason Scott."

Mason reached for me, slipping his hand through mine. "Mag—"

"DON'T!" I ripped my hand away from him. "Don't you fucking touch me ever again!"

I didn't remember walking away from him. I didn't remember grabbing the handle. But I did remember the slam of the door behind me.

chapter forty

mason

The guestroom door blew up, and if it were possible to feel any shittier, I couldn't imagine it. She stayed, though. She didn't run this time. That was something. For Maggie, that was huge.

"Jesus. This is…" Matt sighed, looking to the hall. "I don't have words."

Cam struggled to his feet, holding his ribs like they'd been rearranged and put back wrong. "Mase, I'm sorry. I—"

My head sharply rotated his way, cutting him off. "What for exactly?"

"Everything, man." As Cam's shoulders dropped, so did his chin. "I'll talk to her. I promise—"

"Do me a favor and don't," I said. "Don't do anything else. Don't fuck this up more than you already have."

Wincing, Cam conceded.

When I took a step toward the hallway, my brother's hand landed on my shoulder, stopping me. "Give her a minute, Mase. If you try to talk to her right now when she's this pissed, she won't hear anything you say, and you'll get rattled and say the wrong thing. Then she'll really leave." My body tensed, ready to spring out of Matt's grip. His hand tightened. "She needs a little breathing room. This was a lot, and who knows what happened to her while we were gone. She was alone with that piece of shit—" Matt's free hand fisted like he wanted to do some rib rearranging, too. His eyes met mine. "Let me talk to her first, okay? Make sure he didn't touch her."

I took a breath, the air burning like acid eating through my lungs. I had asked Maggie if that bastard had touched her, and she hadn't answered me. Not really. My gaze went to the bedroom door. Maybe Maggie would open up to Matt, feel more comfortable admitting to him that something had happened.

And it was true that I'd seen Maggie irritated. Frustrated. Angry. But this was next level. A door slamming like that necessitated a cooling-off period. The Scotts just so happened to be experts on the cooling-off period. After she spoke to Matt, we'd talk. I'd see where her head was at. Make sure she believed me about those women. This was a hiccup. Okay, my second in two days. Alright, it had been a week of hiccups.

Since I wouldn't be fixing anything right now, I might as well make myself useful. Ben and Jamey were outside cleaning, so that was as good a start as any. I stepped through the French doors, passing five full trash bags lined up on the patio, maybe another two to go. The couch cushions were stain-free, and the water in the pool was still blue.

Overall, not that bad.

I hauled three bags to the trashcans while my brother lingered just inside the back door, demanding to know if Ben got all the ducks, then proceeded to list every location around the yard. I shook my head. Matt may never get in the pool again. When I threw the bags inside the can, an orchestra of *quacks* broke out. Something told me Pete and Vic had been behind #duckgate.

I came back to the patio to see Matt hadn't budged, craning his head to look behind a nearby hedge.

"Matt." The back of my neck warmed as the words surfaced. "I...don't remember a whole lot."

He crouched to peek under the lawn chairs. "That's 'cause you were into the JD most of the day."

Ben dragged the net through the water to fish out two thongs and pink toddler floaties from the pool. "You don't remember anything with Mags?"

"I remember trying to get her to put on a bathing suit before she left."

Cam popped the stopper of the inflatable T-Rex and sat on it. "What about Rebecca?"

I raked my fingers through my hair as if that would help drag a memory out of my gray matter. "Ah...I think I turned her down." Tongue in mouth. Hand on cock. Complete and total lack of hard-on. Telling her—

"You did," Matt confirmed, and a wave of relief swept through me. "She came down to the basement *pissed* and offered to suck me off. I sent her to Vic. He obliged."

I processed that. "So, Maggie didn't come back until this morning?"

"Noooo." Ben drew the word out hesitantly, setting the net back on its hooks. "She went for a bike ride to cool off and then came back. She found you, and less than thirty minutes later..." As his words trailed off, he looked to Jamey to finish for him.

"Whatever happened between you wasn't good." Jamey refused to meet my eyes, and my gut clenched.

Ben supplied, "You came out of your first blackout, I told you all of this, and you started drinking again. And right before your second coma, Charlie stopped by."

Charlie...? Goddamn it. She'd been blowing up my phone all week. I assumed she wanted to apologize, and I hadn't been ready to hear it.

"Where—" Jamey cringed when he opened the skimmer, then dry heaved. After a cough and a cleansing breath, he asked, "Where is Mags anyway?"

"Oh, uh... She had a little blowup. And now we're letting her chill," I explained, feeling proud of my growth and ability to give her space.

"What does that mean?" Body tensing, his hazel eyes flicked to the house and back to me. "*WhereissheMason?*"

Jamey's tone was a bit too freaked out for my liking. "Guestroom, but you don't want to go in there. There was screaming and slamming doors, and I strongly advise against touching her."

In a breath, his eyes widened and he threw down the skimmer lid. "Shit!" Jamey was a blur, tearing into the house, pushing past Matt. "Mags! *Mags!*"

The hell?

I wasn't far behind Jamey as he barreled into the guestroom. Not a foot past the threshold, the pungent stench of vomit slammed into me. I tore my gaze off the mess on the floor and looked to the bed. Cold fisted my heart and then began to crush my spine.

She was too still, too limp, too pale. The bed hadn't been made yet, and why that was something I noticed, I didn't have a clue. Maggie was facedown on the mattress, raven hairs splayed out around her. As Jamey flipped Maggie, her limbs flopped over as if the bones had been removed from her skeleton. It was then that I saw her jean shorts were darker between her thighs, and the faint scent of ammonia hit me next.

Oh, God.

"Is she breathing?" Matt asked, brushing past me.

Jamey blew out a sigh of relief as he lifted his ear away from her mouth. "Yeah, I think she's okay." Looking to the mess smeared on her face and hair, his head shook, aggravated. "I should have been watching you. I knew it was coming. I'm so sorry." His gaze shifted to her stained shorts, grimacing. "Mason, do you have her bag? I need to clean her up."

Dread frayed my voice. "We need to get her to the hospital, Jamey."

His eyes lifted to mine, filled with pleading and guilt. "Don't do that to her. It's not what she wants. Mags needs time to wake up. That's it. Let me take care of her, Mason."

Blowing out a controlled breath, I considered that and looked to Matt for guidance. I should have known he wouldn't have any because he was just like Faith. They both had detested hospitals. She cried every time we had to take her and would only go if Matt went with her. Matt had held her hand through the worst of it. I imagined Maggie had her fill of doctors, needles, and tests. Matt was the last person on Earth who would force that on her.

"Thirty minutes, Jamey. If she's not coming around by then, I'm taking her." He opened his mouth to argue, and I cut him off. "That's my deal. I'll get her bag."

By the time I returned from my truck and placed the black duffel inside the bathroom, Matt had taken off her shoes and socks, Cam had cleaned up the mess on the floor, and Ben started the bath.

"I'll get the rest, guys." Jamey tucked a possessive arm around her. "She wouldn't want you to see her."

Respecting her privacy, we filed out of the room, giving Jamey the time he needed. Once I heard the bathroom door shut, I peeked inside. He'd left her dirty clothes on the bed, and I tugged off the comforter, sheets, and mattress pad. I shoved as much as I could into the washer and added various blue liquids to the interior cups. By the time I made it back down, Matt was pulling new sheets on the mattress.

After three attempts to get the corner of the fitted sheet to stay, Matt's voice broke the silence. "I was wrong." His words were hoarse, and with that, his movements were jerky, body taut, eyes far too focused on getting all the wrinkles out of the sheets. "I should have let you go to her."

Eyeing him carefully, I slipped the clean case on the pillow. "You couldn't kn—"

"I. Was. Wrong." Matt swallowed thickly, fingers strangling the thread count. "She was here, under *my* watch, and she…" A muscle thrummed in his jaw. "Maggie could have been molested or raped, and I still don't fucking know." His words cracked at the end, and when I moved forward, his palm shot out to stop me. "She was here with a gun to her head, and I was right upstairs. Fucking sleeping. Then I left her with him." A ragged breath rolled through his chest. "Maggie's right. She shouldn't be anywhere near us. We've done nothing right by her. *I've* done nothing right by her."

"Matt—"

"I was just down the fucking hall, Mason!" Gaze lifting mine, tears welled in his eyes. "She was in here having a seizure, helpless, suffering all alone! She could have suffocated, choked on her vomit, hit her head—"

"We didn't know, Matt."

"But I should have! Of anyone, *I* should have known."

"What...? What does that mean?"

"Mase, I wasn't..." Matt's hand shot to the left side of his chest and gripped the skin roughly as the color drained out of him. Taking an unsteady step backward toward the hall, his eyes were fixed on his feet. "I wasn't here. I left y—"

Brows pulling together, I inched closer. "Matt...?"

"I'm sorry I left," he rasped, and I couldn't be sure who he was apologizing to because it didn't seem like he was speaking to me any longer. "I'm, uh—" Matt was suddenly bent in half, holding his stomach like the contents were about to spill out. "I can't fucking breathe."

I rushed across the room, shock barreling through me when I felt his entire frame shake. His skin was far too cold though sweat had beaded on his brow. His balance was precarious at best, and I grabbed his arm to keep him upright. I had no clue where he checked out to, but he wasn't here with me.

"Ben! Cam!" I called.

Two sets of feet thundered down the hall. The second my cousins rounded the corner, both their eyes widened to find Matt losing it. Matt never lost it. Matt was the rock, the voice of reason, the cool head. I kinda understood now why he shut down when emotions played into the mix. He couldn't handle them. He really couldn't.

If I had to guess, he was on the verge of a full-blown panic attack.

"Get him some fresh air," I instructed. "Stay with him. Both of you."

Cam hadn't moved yet. Or blinked.

Ben was a little quicker on the uptake. He wrapped an arm around my brother, guiding him along. "Come on, Coz. Let's get out of the house for a while. We can go for a drive along the bluffs or something."

"I left." Matt sniffed, looking back to me. "I'm so fucking sorry I left, Mase."

While Matt's record kept skipping, Cam hooked an arm around him. "Let's get you outside, Coz. You'll feel better."

It took a minute, but they finally ushered Matt outside, and then the rumble of Ben's Rover disappeared down the street. I freed a tense breath as worry gnawed at me. I couldn't focus on him right now. My brother was in good hands with Ben and Cam. Jamey and I would take care of Maggie.

I got the room situated as Jamey opened the bathroom door. From the bedside, I could see that Jamey was shirtless, and his cargo shorts were soaked. Muffled groans carried me closer to find Maggie on the floor, dressed in nothing more than a shirt that reached the top of her thighs. Thank God she was coming around. A weight, albeit all of one ounce, lifted from my chest.

"Whoops." Jamey knelt at Maggie's side as I stepped into the doorway. "Let's keep the clothes on, Mags."

Jamey's position blocked me from going much further, but I could see that Maggie was pulling at her shirt. Her eyes had rolled back, body moving without purpose or reason.

Jamey pried her fingers off the hem of the thin cotton, and as the fabric snapped up, a peek of blue flashed before he tugged the shirt back into place. I forced my gaze to the cabinets.

"Boy, you're really pulling a *Magic Mike* routine this time," he joked. An arm flailed, smacking the wall. I winced, praying her hand was okay. "I know," Jamey continued. "Don't worry, I'll be happy to watch that movie with you. Anything to look at Channing Tatum's ass."

"Is that…?" Trusting she was covered up, I risked a glance. Her leg swung out toward Jamey, and he caught her knee before she did some damage to his shin. "Why does she do that? Pull at her clothes?"

Jamey shook his head as he pushed her leg down. "Her mind is in an altered state, disoriented while trying to recover from the seizure. It's common for epileptics." Maggie made another move to pull at her shirt, and he was quick to catch her. "I wasn't asking you to prove my point, Mags."

Her head lolled, rolling on the tile, hair pooling in wet clumps. The floor was splattered with soapy water, multiple towels balled up in the corner. Unease crawled across my skin at the sight of her down there.

"We need to get her off the floor," I urged.

"Yeah." Jamey shifted to rest back on his haunches, blowing out an exhausted breath. Jamey wasn't a weak guy by any means, but I imagined bathing an unconscious person wasn't an easy task, even one as tiny as Maggie.

"Let me help, Jamey. Please."

"Uh…" Frown lines bracketed his mouth. I geared up for another battle with him when he said, "Yeah, okay. Thanks."

Jamey positioned himself closer to the shower to make room for me, and I knelt, sliding my arms underneath Maggie to cradle her. Jamey helped stabilize her head and neck while I stood with her. A quiet moan snuck past her lips as her wet hair dampened my T-shirt. I tucked her closer to my chest, my movements agitating her as she both pulled me closer and pushed me away. Her face was pressed against my chest one second, and the next, she was trying to writhe out of my arms. If I didn't keep a tight grip, I'd drop her.

"God, she's really wig—"

"Mason."

I glimpsed up to Jamey, surprised to find his expression stony, brows low. "Huh?"

"She's here," he said. "Don't treat her like she's not. Talk *to* her."

Shame weighed heavily in my gut. Jamey was right. I had been talking about her, treating her like she couldn't hear me as if she were an object and not *Maggie*. I curled her close as the scent of sandalwood and golden amber from our bath soap intensified. It was off, wrong. She should smell like a roaring fire and a warm apple pie on a cold fall day.

"Sorry, Sticks."

I placed Maggie on the bed, and Jamey was quick to cover her with a blanket. I settled down next to her, tucking back the raven strands that had stuck to her pale cheeks.

"You're okay. You're safe at my house. I've got you."

Without warning, she spun toward me, her skull nearly cracking against mine. Then there was a hand on my ass and a mouth on my neck.

I couldn't help it. Chuckling, I grinned. "I knew you couldn't resist my body."

Jamey snorted.

Peeling Maggie off me, a regrettable decision, I gently held her down. My gaze slipped lower along with any lingering humor this moment held. Her bottom lip was swollen, and...teeth marks had gouged her skin.

Regret poured down my throat, roughening my voice. "Jamey, how did you know? That she was in trouble?"

He delivered a long stare before slipping off the bed and ducking into the bathroom. "You said that she didn't want you to touch her." Fabric shuffled in the other room, and he returned with a towel wrapped strangely high around his waist. "When a seizure is coming, Mags goes into a heightened flight mode. She can't stand to be touched, tries to escape, sees and hears things that aren't there, and does things she wouldn't normally do."

I swallowed, but that lump in my throat was growing. "Like scream and slam doors?"

He nodded solemnly. "It's important to remember that in those moments, she doesn't know what she's doing or saying. Your only job is to protect her from hurting herself the best way you can without getting hurt in the process. Her tremor and balance are good indicators a seizure is coming, but an aura is a definite sign."

"What's an aura?" Maggie's hand came a little too close to grabbing my junk, and not in a fun way. I swerved and pinned her arm to the mattress.

"It's a hallucination a lot like déjà vu. She gets a feeling that she's been somewhere before or sees something familiar when she hasn't. Do you remember her staring at Trey's business card?"

I thought back to that blank stare of hers. "Yeah. It was odd, but I figured she was in shock."

"No. It was a symptom that I—" He scrubbed his face hard, looking to his friend. "It's a preictal sign that it's coming in a matter of minutes, hours, days. There's no way to know for sure. Regardless, I saw it, and I shouldn't have left her side."

She rolled again, so her back faced me, wet hair parting at her temple, and for the first time since the emergency room, I had a clear view of the scar on her scalp. The damaged skin was pale and thick, following the path of the depression in her skull. Whatever had happened to her…it had been ugly and brutal.

I tenderly traced the rutted bone. "What happened to her? What did this?"

Glimpsing the scar, Jamey's mouth thinned. "It's not up to me—"

"Please," I implored. "This is what caused her PTE, right? The tremor, vertigo, headaches? You were at the hospital. You heard my dad. I want to understand. What did this to her?"

With a sigh, Jamey pinched the bridge of his nose, taking a spot on the other side of the bed. He fixed his towel, adjusted his legs, sighed again. "Not a what," he finally said. "A who."

My heart thumped so hard, I questioned if a valve had malfunctioned. "Okay. Who?"

Jamey concentrated on the blanket covering Maggie, a pucker appearing between his brows. "Her mother was an addict. An addict so desperate for her next hit that she took her baby to her dealer's house, a member of the Sixes, someone she'd racked up a considerable debt with. She didn't remember how much she owed him, or…didn't care. Either way, she couldn't pay him. And he punished her for it." His Adam's apple bobbed roughly. "By kicking Mags in the head."

I couldn't feel if my heart was still beating, but the pulsing sound in my ears was proof positive that the organ was still working overtime.

"He…*kicked* her?"

Jamey nodded. "Mags' mother took her to the hospital but couldn't face Nate and what she'd done. She left town before Nate got there."

"Sweet Jesus," I breathed.

What kind of sick fuck would kick a baby? *In the head?* Scratch that. I already knew.

"The Sixes? You mean that psychotic fuck that was in my home could have been the one who—" My stomach roiled as the rest of that question went unspoken.

"It's possible."

Working my throat, I looked back to Maggie. No matter how many times I repeated it in my head, I couldn't comprehend what Maggie had been through, how every aspect of her life been changed forever because of that one moment. Something that had been done to her when she was innocent and defenseless.

"Is that what her back injury is from?" I asked.

He paused, considering his answer for an uncomfortable moment. "No. That was from…something else." Jamey's tone suggested that he wouldn't elaborate.

I turned my attention back to Maggie, not having realized she wasn't stirring as much, possibly slipping into sleep. There was a peace to her, the hard edge that I'd caused fading. A strong urge pounded through me to slide under that blanket, snuggle up with her, and watch over her. Jamey might yank my eyebrows out if I pulled that move in front of him.

Since he seemed somewhat open to Q & A time, I fired another. "Did she ever come back? Her mother?"

Jamey fixed his gaze on the window. "No."

"Do you know if Nate ever tried to find her?"

Slowly, he shook his head. "He wrote her off a long time ago, Mason."

"Damn. I can't— I can't imagine my mom leaving me. To choose a life without her family, her children. She could never walk away from us like that."

"Yeah, well…" An emotion I couldn't quite identify caused his frame to stiffen. "Sometimes it's better that way."

Another thought occurred to me, and maybe it was nothing, but I had to ask. "Before… Maggie said she came here yesterday to tell me something important. Do you have any idea what that was?"

Gaze drawing back to mine, he said, "Yes."

"What was it?"

That stiffness in his frame began to harden his features. "Mags found out yesterday that with Marcus Ryan's help, the Prices bought out every building on Sands Drive. The café included. They're planning to tear down everything plus the nearby subdivisions to erect a beachside resort and a golf course. And when she biked ten miles across town to tell you, you gave her shit for not wearing a fucking bathing suit."

My stomach suddenly filled with sharp gravel.

The café. The last good memories of Faith were there. My dad. Matt...

"I didn't know," I muttered. Was that why Charlie had come yesterday? To warn me? Maggie was going to lose her job. They were all going to lose...everything. "The Ryans and Prices really are shit people."

"True. But I can't hate on Charlie, and you shouldn't either. If it hadn't been for her, my mom would be filing bankruptcy right now instead of stinking up the house with apple cider vinegar baths to soak her feet after standing all day. Mason, one IG post from Charlotte Price saved my mom's business and likely our home, too. So, maybe take it easy on her." Frown drawing down the corners of his mouth, he stood and tucked his towel higher up. "If you don't mind watching Mags for me, I'd like to go home and change. I won't be long."

"Yeah, sure." I grabbed the keys out of my pocket. "Ben, Cam, and Matt took the Rover. You can take my truck, but you're more than welcome to grab some clothes from my room."

"Thanks, but I should go home. Kinda freaked Ava out earlier when I Tasmanian deviled through the house." He took the keys from me. "Where'd they go anyway?"

"Not sure. Matt needed some air. I don't know when they'll be back."

He nodded and aimed for the door. "Okay. I have my phone if you need me. Mags should be fine, though. It looks like she's asleep now."

He was almost out of the room when I stopped him. "Did I make her cry? I know I fucked up yesterday with her, but I... I don't remember what happened."

Jamey's gaze reluctantly met mine. "She'd punch my junk if she knew I told you, but yeah, you did."

My throat rolled thickly. "What did I do?"

Discharging a long breath, Jamey smoothed down his hair. "It's not my place to share that, but I will tell you this. She needs to be shown love, Mason. She's desperate for it, and she deserves it. Her life has been harder than you can possibly imagine, and you're making it harder. If you can't love her, I'm begging you to walk away because she won't. She doesn't know how."

And with that, he left.

Love. There was that word again. I didn't know if I had that kind of love to give her. If my heart could be resurrected after being dead for five years, imprisoned behind this infinity link on my chest.

The door chime broke me out of the deepest and most restful sleep I'd ever had. I blinked, listening to the sounds of three sets of feet scatter throughout the house. At my side, Maggie hadn't moved, and I glanced to my watch to see that I'd only been out for fifteen minutes. Huh. So, power naps really were a thing. I had drifted off watching her, thinking about her, wondering if this would all be over between us once she woke up. The debilitating ache in my chest told me exactly how I felt about that.

Matt popped his head into the room. "Hey."

I rubbed my eyes with a stretch of my legs, doing my best not to disturb Maggie. "How're you doing?"

He stepped inside and took a spot on the bed next to Maggie. Matt's hand slid under hers, and though our hands matched in size, it struck me how tiny Maggie's looked in his. "How is she? Did she wake up? You doing alright? You need— Hell, did she do that to her lip?"

I leaned on my elbow. "Her lip will be fine. Maggie's okay, and I'm okay. I asked how you were."

Matt's jaw worked as his chest expanded with a deep breath, keeping his focus on Maggie's hand in his. "The waves were wicked, man. Wish I had my board. We hit the taco truck and brought back a haul. You should eat."

Damn him. "Matt—"

"I gotta get some grub before I pass out." Cutting me off, he leaned forward and pressed a kiss to Maggie's head before shooting to his feet. "Don't take too long, 'kay, Mase?"

I watched him hit the exit. Matt was the master of the shutdown and deflection. He might be better at it than Maggie was.

When Ben and Cam waltzed in next, I threw a what-the-fuck gesture to Matt's general direction.

Ben kept his voice low. "He shut down as soon as we hit fresh air."

"All the dude could talk about were tacos." Cam shrugged, casting a long look to Maggie. "So we bought a shit ton of tacos."

My mind should be on Matt right now, but he was right. We'd skipped breakfast, and my stomach was working on digesting itself, especially after the surge of adrenaline from dealing with a gang member pointing a gun at the very girl lying next to me.

"Did you get the battered fish with white sauce?" I asked.

Ben's head jerked back. "Please. Have you met me?" Turning to leave, Ben said over his shoulder, "Cam failed to mention that we also have a shit ton of chipotle salsa and chips."

My stomach grumbled. "Sweet."

Head hanging, Cam followed his brother out, but I was faster. I vaulted off the bed, my hand clamping down on his shoulder. Cam stopped but didn't face me.

"I'm not going to apologize for what I said because you deserved it. But we're cool. Okay?"

Camden stiffened under my grip, and he was quiet for a long while. "You know, for a minute, I wasn't the fuckup. I wasn't the Scott joke. I actually thought that idiot was you, and it makes me a complete ass, but I liked that. I should have known it wouldn't take me long to dethrone you."

"Cam—"

"No, it's true. I'm not gonna Marsha Brady you, Mase. It's my fault. I never think, I only act. I knew I was drunk last night, but I wasn't *that* drunk when I called for those women. I knew better. It's like I can't stop myself from being a total jackhole. Usually, I just embarrass myself and maybe the fam a little, but I'll never… I'll never forgive myself for putting Maggie at risk like that."

"Hey." I tugged him close, wrapping my arms around his shoulders. "I know I give you a hard time, but I've never been embarrassed of you, Cam. No one has." Now I understood how my dad felt when he spoke to me about this very thing. "You made a mistake, and all you can do is try to make things right. I know you will. And as much as you fuck up, I'll always love you. Even though you're a total jackhole."

He didn't laugh, and I knew what I'd said to him today had done some damage, or what he'd seen with Maggie had affected him far more than I realized. Like Matt, Cam wasn't an emotional guy, but unlike my brother, Cam was open about what was on his mind.

He smacked me on the back. "Let's eat."

Once our bellies were full and we'd polished off all but a few tacos, the five of us got to work. Leaving the bedroom door open, we checked on Maggie in ten-minute intervals as each of us took one section of the house to clean. Hours had passed, and there wasn't a sign that she was going to wake up soon. Jamey didn't seem concerned, but that didn't keep me from asking if we should take her to the hospital a million times, and after a lengthy phone call with my parents, I felt a little better.

It was nearing the time that Maggie usually left, but she was still sleeping. With this being a three-day weekend and no class tomorrow, I didn't see the point in taking her home. At least, that was how I reasoned it in my head. Truthfully, I was terrified of what would happen once she walked out the door.

"What should we do with Maggie?" I asked the group over pizza, already knowing what I wanted the answer to be.

Jamey glanced to the hallway. "Honestly? I think she should stay. She's out longer than I expected, and the longer she's out, the more disoriented she is when she wakes. She'll need someone to take care of her, and her father…" Jamey fixated his attention on a napkin that didn't look like it could absorb another micron of grease. "Her father's a hard sleeper. He may not hear her if she needs help. I'll call and let him know what happened and that we'll take her home tomorrow."

Jamey was a mind reader.

But his sales tactics could use some work.

By the sound of his end of the conversation, it didn't go well. Matt had to speak with the man, and then Jamey had to promise to spend the night. Maybe a smidge overprotective, but I couldn't fault him for that. Maggie was his daughter. His *only* daughter. I couldn't say I would be okay if Faith had ever been in this situation, either.

Ben and Cam decided to stay, too, and I told them I'd move Maggie to my bedroom to keep an eye on her. This way, Ben and Jamey could sleep in the guestroom again, and Cam would take the basement sofa.

When I lifted Maggie, she didn't stir, utterly lax in my arms. With her face resting against my chest, black lashes fanned across her cheeks, I studied the light freckles on her button nose. Even though her lips were bruised and swollen, they were pink and inviting, lips I'd wanted to kiss a thousand times, a thousand different ways.

My gaze crawled to the other end of her body. Earlier today, I didn't allow myself to look, and I shouldn't now, but my eyes weren't listening. Her little toes were plain, legs creamy and incredibly long for someone so petite, muscles strong and lean from a lifetime of running.

The hem of her white T-shirt flirted at the top of her thighs. However wrong, I couldn't help but notice how very thin the shirt was. The outline of her blue panties was visible along with her flat belly, dip of her navel, and… *Oh, fuck me.* Her pink nipples peaked the fabric, and that was where my eyes lingered. *No bra.* The only thing between us was one layer of cotton and a set of morals that seemed to be weakening by the second.

It took all of one of those seconds for lust to slam into me and for my body to respond.

I forced myself to look away and shook my head as if that would purge the image. Didn't work. I set her on my bed, taking a moment too long to tug the shirt down over the enticing hip it was exposing. Snapping up the sheets and blankets, I tucked her in tight.

After a quick change of clothes, I shut the lights and settled down on the carpet with a pillow and an extra blanket from the hall closet, wishing I could curl around her like I had earlier. There had been a rightness in holding her, a warmth that filled my chest that dissipated with our distance now.

Love.

Camden said I was in love with her. I had to admit, it was possible. I didn't know what that kind of love felt like, but I... I was emptier when she wasn't near me. My heart pounded like crazy when I thought of her, my breaths stalled when she looked at me, and at her touch, the world stopped. And still, after all these months, I really didn't know her. Maggie was guarded, and deep inside me was a hope that I would tear all those bricks down by hand. For her.

Maybe that was love.

chapter forty-one

mason

Stretching out, my calf swept over warm, itchy fibers instead of cool, smooth Egyptian cotton. An ache rippled up my spine and settled deep in my muscles as if I'd slept on a concrete slab all night. Wait. Had I?

Where the hell…?

Oh, right. The floor. I'd slept on my floor. Which wasn't much softer than sleeping on a concrete slab. I would know. I began to work out a kink in my neck when I stilled.

Something was off about the room. Wrong.

I shot up to a sitting position, blinking until my eyes could focus on my rumpled bed. "Maggie?" Silence.

My gut hollowed out, and I jumped onto the mattress, yanking everything back, finding nothing. Nothing but warm sheets. Where did she…? My head swung around to the bathroom. Then to every corner of my room. There was enough moonlight to see that I was alone, and the bedroom door was cracked open.

Beep… Beep. Beep… Beep.

The alarm code was being entered from somewhere in the house. A moment later, three more beeps followed to indicate a point of entry was being opened. Chances were slim that Maggie had woken up to open a window in the middle of the night, which meant she was leaving.

I flew off the bed, and then everything went south. Literally.

Whomp! My face met the carpet first while the rest of my body was still north, somehow tangled up in the bedding. Blood rushed to my head as I jerked my torso around and then thrashed—

Whomp number two. Now free of the sheets, I scrambled to my feet like my knees were missing some vital cartilage, hip-checking the corner of my desk. If I made it out of my room without breaking a bone, it would be a freaking miracle.

I spared enough time to shove my feet into the first set of shoes I found, and as I rubbed out the sharp pain in my side, I yanked open my door and bolted down the stairs. Soles slipping on the tile, I nearly biffed it when I landed on the main floor with a *boom*! I charged through the living room and out the front door, the chilled fog misting my bare chest and legs. Lungs heaving, I scanned the yard, and in the buttery glow of the house lights, I spotted a tiny shadow darting across the lawn. Next to her was a piece of junk on two wheels.

"Sticks?"

Coming to a halt, Maggie turned to face me, and before my brain launched the order, my legs were closing the distance between us as blades of wet grass slicked beneath my soles.

"What are you doing?"

Gaze wild, her pupils had taken over her irises, only a sliver of blue reflecting in the faint light. "Going home."

"Going home?" The wind, cold and harsh, burned my skin, and I folded my arms over my bare chest to keep my core warm. She had to be freezing, considering she was wearing as much clothing as me. "Sticks, it's the middle of the night."

"Yeah, and you didn't wake me." The air curled in clouds around her mouth, teeth chattering together.

"I didn't wake you because you had a seizure." Maggie dismissed me as she pressed toward the road, but my hand snapped out and curled around her wrist to stop her. Hell, she wasn't much warmer than the icy handlebars. "There's no reason for you to go home. Your father knows you're here. Jamey and Matt talked to him. I'll take you home in the morning. When there is daylight. Right now, you should stay and rest."

She looked at me as though I had proposed to run an alligator farm out of Crescent Lake. "I can't wait until the morning. I have to go home. Now!"

Maggie darted ahead, but I was faster. I skidded to a stop, and so did Maggie and her bike.

"Maggie." I cupped her trembling jaw, chasing her focused gaze, which was the road and not me. "You're not thinking clearly. You're not even wearing pants. It's pitch black out here. How are you going to see your way home?"

She used the bike to shove me aside. "I'm fine."

"The man jackhammering your teeth would disagree." Enough of this. I yanked the bike out of her grip and perched it on my shoulder.

Chin kicked back, she delivered a ball-shriveling glare.

"Scowl at me all you want. You're not riding your bike home at one in the morning, half-naked for fuck's sake."

I should have seen it coming. Totally didn't, though. She zipped around me and sprinted toward the road.

"Son. Of. A. Bitch." I set the bike on the lawn. If I didn't haul ass, I'd never catch up to her, and running in slides on wet grass was a hell of a lot harder than it sounded. Busting out some Wolverine drill moves, I flew past her and landed in her path. Maggie slammed into me with a grunt, and I had to be quick to grasp her shoulders as she struggled to find her balance.

If she wasn't having a seizure or a neurological event, then this had to do with our fight earlier. "Cam was telling the truth. I didn't know. I was wasted, *alone* in my room—"

She somehow slid out of my hold and raced toward the exit.

"Dammit, Maggie!" It took me five leaps before I was close enough to loop an arm around her waist, and I lifted her off her feet that were still pedaling in the air. "Please," I breathed into her hair as I carried her back to the house. "Please, listen to me. Don't run—"

"I know this is a huge hit to your monster ego, but this has nothing to do with you! Let me go!" She writhed and struggled, and I had to change my grip, so I didn't drop her.

"I'll let go if you tell me the reason you want to leave."

Eons of heartbeats passed, and with every one, her pulse ramped up, but by the time I hit the walkway, she stopped fighting.

"Please, Mason. Let me go or…help me."

I drew up short. That was something she never asked of me. In fact, Maggie would sooner chop her own arm off before saying the H-word.

I set her bare feet on the frozen pavers and leaned down, so our faces were level. "The only way I'm letting you go home is if I drive you there." I closed the millimeters between our noses. "All the way."

Her breath caught, but after considering my stipulation, she nodded. Alarms went off in my head. That was way too easy. She was either planning to bolt the second I turned my back, or her state of mind was worse than I thought.

Taking her hand, I guided her back to the bike I had discarded in the grass, never breaking my grip with hers. I picked up the Schwinn, and after propping it against the house, I released her hand and met her wide stare.

"Stay. I need to get my keys, and I'll be right back."

By some miracle, Maggie didn't bolt in the time it took me to make it back outside, and less than a minute later, we were inside the truck. The chilled leather seat against my skin combined with the subzero cab was brutal. I turned the engine over and cranked up the heater. The only sounds in the cab were the *whir* of icy air pushing out the vents and the *squeak-squeak* of the wipers to clear the windshield of condensation.

Along with the frantic metal versus metal noise next to me.

Cringing, I glanced over to find Maggie fighting with the seatbelt, missing the buckle over and over. I wasn't sure if her nerves or the cold were to blame but lining those two up was so not gonna happen. Last time I had witnessed this had been after our first shopping trip to Henry's. It hadn't been pretty. Maggie flat out refused my help and wound up sitting on the belt instead. I wouldn't allow that again.

"Mag—"

"Here." She shoved the latch into my hand and then proceeded to unwind every inch of the belt from the spool until there was enough to secure ten of her. "Just do it so we can go."

Yeah, this...wasn't good. I did what she asked and tried my best to prevent the belt from retracting too fast and tearing her skin. I put the gear in Drive and pulled out of the driveway.

Once I was past the gate, I hit Canyon. I tried to speed up since Maggie was checking my speedometer every zero point six seconds, but with the roads this dark and the fog this thick, I had to ease up on the accelerator.

"Mason, go faster." Rife panic laced her voice, and in the cast of the blue dash lights, her hands were balled in her lap, frame as slack as a steel beam.

My eyes bounced between her and the misty scene ahead. "Sticks, talk to me. What's going on?"

"I told you. I have...to get home."

"No, you don't. Jamey is sleeping in the guestroom. Matt is in his room, too. Your father knows all of this."

"And I was sleeping in *your* bed with you on the floor only wearing shorts, and me"—she glanced down and grimaced—"only wearing *this*. Did my father know that?"

I shifted in my seat, swinging my focus back to the road. "We may have omitted that part."

"Just...go faster, Mason."

My jaw clamped shut, knuckles strangling the wheel. She was right.

I should have asked Jamey to dress you in a shirt I couldn't see through, Maggie. I shouldn't have hesitated to pull that very same see-through shirt down, Maggie. I shouldn't have been thinking about the five hundred different ways I wanted to wake you up, Maggie.

I pulled onto Verde Way, to the spot I was never allowed to go beyond, slowing down on the dirt road.

"Keep going for another half-mile, and then the road bends."

The woods. I was driving a half-naked girl into the blackened, foggy woods. Where was Logan now? I was sure he would love to beat my ass. Fuck Gorilla Arms. Her father would take one look at my shirtless state and load his gun.

I was driving to the site of my own murder.

Maneuvering deeper into the forest, the dense haze swallowed my headlights, pebbles kicking up beneath my truck in tinny *thwacks*. The turn appeared, and I took it, looking to Maggie for further instructions.

"In another half-mile on this road, there will be houses on the right. When I tell you to, turn off your lights and stop, but keep the engine going. Okay?"

"Y—yeah." Concern along with a healthy dose of confusion bunched my brow tight. This was not normal. People lived out here? Crescent Cove's Chief of Police lived out *here*? At the scene where horror films took place? I swore if I saw someone wearing a mask, I'd mow them over on principal alone.

Taking the road slowly, I stopped and flicked the headlights off when she told me to, but not before I spotted a familiar car in the distance.

I opened my mouth to ask who that belonged to when Maggie said, "I'll be right back."

I shut my mouth. Deep in the land of Whatthefuck, I kept the engine going and stayed put as Maggie hopped into the dirt, closing the door like it was ticking down numbers and strapped to a stick of dynamite. She sped off into the tree line, feet weaving, balance unsteady.

The fuck I'd just sit here.

Stepping out of the truck as soundlessly as Maggie had, the scent of damp earth was thick in my throat, dry pine needles and leaves snapping under my weight, pebbles feeling like boulders as they dug into the thin sole of my shoes.

Unease tingled along my nape as the chilled night air settled over my skin, goosebumps lining every inch of me. The moonlight cut between the branches but not enough to see more than two feet in front of me.

To my right, I heard Maggie whisper-hiss, "Poker! Poker, come on!" A smacking sound came next as if she were slapping her thigh.

Hold up. Did she just say...?

"Sticks?" I whispered, nearing her, but she moved, darting away from me.

"*Poker!*"

Yup. I heard her right. She was hallucinating, of that, I had no doubt. I finally reached her again and loosely laced my hand around her arm, fingertips touching on the other side. "Sticks, you're not okay. You need to come back with me." She needed a hospital, but I could deal with that later. I just had to get her to my truck—

Breaking my grip, Maggie shoved me away with a surprising amount of strength and dashed deeper into the woods. "Poker, *please!*"

Exhaling a harsh breath along with a ripe curse, I whipped out my phone and aimed the light at her feet. I followed her to a large boulder; a hole had been dug at the base as if an animal had burrowed there. An animal that might be fairly substantial in size.

It dawned on me that we were in the middle of the woods. The middle of the motherfucking *woods.* The last thing I should be worried about were masked ax-murderers.

Bears were out here. Wolves. Bobcats.

Oh, my fuck.

Thoughts of becoming something's fourth meal were silenced when I heard a distinct sniffling sound from Maggie. It wasn't the kind of sound someone made to clear their sinuses. Her shoulders were shaking as she hugged herself, looking so much smaller suddenly.

"Maggie." I held her face, skin alarmingly cold in my palms, shivering to a degree that suggested her fingers and lips were blue. "What are you looking for?"

"P— Poker." Hot and wet drops met my palms. Tears. More spilled over the back of my hands, ripping my heart wide open. I didn't know how to break it to her that not finding a poker game in the middle of the woods in the middle of the night was not a bad thing.

Without warning, her knees gave out, slamming into the ground. Then her mouth opened and out of it came silent cries, ones that were too painful, too heartbreaking to be heard.

Maggie gripped handfuls of the rich soil as though it could stop her from shattering, keeping her cries from fully breaking free.

Kneeling with her, I gathered her in my arms and tucked her tight to my chest. Her entire body shuddered so hard, I questioned if she was having a seizure. "Maggie, please let me take you back." Her tears continued to splash onto my chest, nearing the point of hiccupping sobs, and I…I truly didn't know what to do for her. Only one other time in my life had I felt this helpless. "Maggie, let me carry you home, and we'll get your father."

Her head snapped up, and true, bone-chilling fear reflected back at me. "No. No, please. Don't—"

Shuffling in the thicket brought our attention to somewhere deep in the forest. Oh. Sweet. Mother. Everyone knew bad shit happened in the forest. Look at *Harry Potter*. Unicorn bloodsuckers, werewolves, Grawp the Giant, Fluffy the Three-Headed Dog, and no one could forget Aragog the Acromantula from everyone's nightmares. See? All bad.

I prayed that whatever was out there was bigger than me and was sporting a shit load of teeth that could finish me off in one gulp. I wasn't that lucky. It would be slow, agonizing, *The Revenant* type shit with my back clawed to hell, legs paralyzed, crawling my way out of here.

"Fuck." I shot up with Maggie in my arms, head angling back to the truck to assess how fast I could get us there.

Something shadowed and low to the ground wove out of the underbrush. I moved, and the faster my feet propelled backward, the faster it came after us. Whatever it was looked like it would be classified as a predator. The lethal and carnivorous kind.

Maggie squirmed in my arms, reaching for it as it charged. "Poker!"

Dear God, she thinks it's her friend.

"Maggie, stop!"

Trying to keep her in my arms, she writhed until I couldn't hold her anymore. Maggie landed on her feet, and the two headed toward each other.

One for a snack and the other to *become* the snack.

"Maggie, no!" Terror fisted my gut as I scrambled after her, and I was close but not close enough. She collapsed on the ground, throwing her arms around...

A dog?

"I'm sorry." She planted kisses on every inch of his furry head. "I'm so sorry. I didn't forget you, I promise. I didn't mean to leave you. Are you hurt?" She ran her hands over him compulsively, searching for wounds, blood, a missing limb. "You're okay?"

Poker—the dog—answered her with a tongue bath.

I could only stand there, watching the two exchange kisses, completely dumbstruck. "*Poker's a dog*? It's a goddamned dog? You have a dog?" I didn't care if I sounded like Captain Fucking Obvious. "Shit, I thought... I thought you'd cracked." I knelt as a laugh full of wracked nerves departed from my throat, Poker rolling over to get a belly rub. I obliged.

I shook my head. "He's a fucking dog."

Eyes the color of the ocean during a midnight storm met mine over the German shepherd's prone body. "Thank you. I'm sorry for all of this. I didn't come home, and he could have—" Her whispered voice caught, throat working before she spoke again. "Thank you for bringing me to him."

Finally, she had taken one of her bricks down, just enough for me to glimpse behind the wall. And what I found there was a girl with her heart wide open, willing to go to Hell and back for the ones she loved. Emotion constricted my chest, making it hard to breathe. Maggie was exactly like me.

"You're welcome."

I turned my focus toward the shacks. These couldn't be functioning homes with electricity and water. There had to be generators and wells for houses like these. The chief of the CCPD could afford better. Why out here? Why not in Jamey's neighborhood on Meadowbrook? Even the apartments on Midland were better than this.

Maggie dragged herself to her feet, fixed on Poker as he twirled around her mud-caked legs. "Thank you again. I know this must seem like a ridiculous waste of your time, but I... I needed to know he was okay. I'll, uh, see you tomorrow."

"Ridiculous waste of my time?" The words tumbled out past my lips, not entirely sinking in. A snapping twig brought me back as Maggie and Poker slogged away toward the three shacks—houses—no, they were shacks.

If she expected me to just stand here and watch her walk away, this would get loud and ugly. I refused to let her push me away, hide behind that wall again. I fell into step with Maggie, reaching out to lock my fingers between hers.

Gasping in surprise at my touch, she stilled. I lowered my head to her ear to whisper, "Maggie, come home with me. Poker can come, too." When she didn't respond, I stood between her and that shack as if blocking her path would work this time. "He knows you're staying the night. What's a few more hours? You have to come all the way back to work tomorrow, and your bike is already there anyway." I may have sounded a tiny bit desperate. I was. So very desperate.

Her blank stare drifted away from me, and I'd give anything to know what she was thinking. What excuse would she give me this time?

Sorry, Mason. I have to perform the Dance of the Druids by the light of the moon, buck ass naked. Maybe next time.

Her throat rolled, voice strangled and quiet. "I need...Poker's food. He hasn't eaten since this morning. Or yesterday morning, I guess."

Holy shit. Seriously? I did it?

"Okay." Wow, even I was impressed that I was able to keep the shock out of my voice.

Walking toward the houses with her hand wrapped in mine, the leaves in the canopy above made a tinkling noise as they swayed in the wind, almost like warning me to not come any closer. An eerie chill unraveled what few nerves had remained calm.

Poker and I followed Maggie to the pale light haloing the carport when noises from within the house forced us to a dead stop.

Those were moans. Groans. And then two distinct names. One belonged to our Almighty. The other...*Nate.*

Honestly, by gauging Maggie's expression, I didn't think she understood what those noises meant. I half-expected her to show concern in the next second like she thought someone was hurt and praying for help. I didn't want to be the one to break it to her that her *father* was fucking a woman's brains out. Or it could be a dude with a high-pitched voice. Didn't want to assume anything.

Releasing my hand, Maggie whispered, "Go to the truck. I'll be right there."

I dumbly nodded.

As I stepped away, I glanced over my shoulder to see Poker was waiting by the door Maggie had slipped inside. And, well, since it was my mantra...*fuck it.* I lingered, listening as the grunts grew louder, the pleas for him to fuck her harder, faster. If Maggie hadn't figured it out, that was the clincher right there.

My gaze drifted back to the blue Versa. I knew I'd seen it before—The café. I saw it at the café. It belonged to the other waitress Maggie worked with. Camille... Constance... *Candi.*

So, *not* a dude with a high-pitched voice.

Right as the crescendo hit, Maggie slipped out the door, holding a bag of food that was more than half her size. Doing her best to keep her balance, she bent to grab two silver bowls off the concrete that were empty and dry. Poor dog hadn't had any access to water. This was weird. Too weird. Why didn't her father take care of the dog and bring him inside?

When I walked out of the shadows to meet Maggie, she jerked to a stop, flared eyes meeting mine. I saw the exact moment that she realized I'd been privy to all the *Oh, Gods!*

I took the bag from her and held her hand in mine. Without discussion, we crossed the woods back to my idling truck. I placed the food in the back, and Poker jumped into the front as though it was a known fact that he only rode shotgun. As I settled into the warm cab, I could see him better in the overhead lights. There was a little gray on his muzzle, and though there was a slight haze to his brown eyes, they were sharp and keen. I couldn't help but give the little guy a rough scratch to the back of the ear, which he leaned into. Shockingly, after being outside in the woods, his fur had a sheen, the undercoat absent of dirt and grease. His nails had been freshly clipped, and only a hint of his natural scent lingered beneath a fragrance of...crisp apples.

Once Maggie was buckled and had Poker settled, I advanced the truck with the doors shut but not closed all the way. It wasn't until I took the turn on Verde Way that I took Maggie's cue and shut my door. It dawned on me that maybe Maggie had expected her father to be...occupied, which was why we were in *Call of Duty* mode.

The entire drive home, Maggie's arms were wrapped around Poker, face buried in his coat. Maybe she was cold, but something told me it was more. That she was struggling to keep it together. I wanted to hold her, pull off to the side of the road and be the one she clung to, sought comfort from. But more than that, I wanted to get them home where it was warm, quiet, and safe. I didn't know why, but I had a feeling that above all else, that was what Maggie was most desperate for.

To feel safe.

As I pulled into my driveway, Maggie still hadn't said a word, but she and Poker jumped out when I turned off the engine. I grabbed the food bag, and as I headed to the house, I observed how Poker interacted with Maggie. He didn't take a step until she did, the two moving in sync together. He watched her, looking up at her adoringly, protectively. Over half Maggie's weight, Poker could easily knock her over by bumping into her too hard. Instead, he was patient and gentle, waiting for his cues.

But as sweet as that dog looked, I sensed one wrong move would earn me an open carotid.

I got us inside, reset the alarm, and padded to the kitchen where Maggie was already filling a glass with water. I figured she was getting herself a drink since she had to be dehydrated. While she was busy, I dumped kibble into one of the two bowls. As soon as the last brown ball fell on top of the pile, Poker dove in and began chowing down. Poor guy.

Maggie stepped over to us with her glass filled only halfway, but with her tremor, the water sloshed so hard it kissed the rim. She didn't drink it. Instead, she dumped the water into the other bowl and then went back to the sink for a refill. A sudden ache fisted my chest. God, is this what she had to do when her tremors were this bad? If this was how she would fill his water bowl, it would be daylight before she finished.

"Hey." I stopped Maggie halfway to the sink, taking the glass from her. "Let me get that."

Without argument, Maggie dropped down to kneel on the tile next to Poker. While I filled his water bowl, Maggie lifted Poker's paws, examining them as he munched away. He let her do whatever she wanted, never pulling away from her or showing an ounce of impatience. She ran her fingers through his coat, a few sticks and leaves falling to the floor. She didn't care that her own feet were scratched and raw. She didn't care that she was covered in mud and dirt. She didn't care about her soiled shirt or that she was shivering with cold. She didn't give a damn about anything but that dog.

As Maggie sat there, a renewed shimmer welled in her eyes. *Guilt.* She felt so much guilt for leaving him. For not returning when he expected. For letting him go hungry and thirsty. For disappointing him.

Guilt was a bone-deep, crippling emotion that I knew all too well.

Maggie's head bowed as she squeezed her lids tight, but not one tear fell. I didn't want her to do that. This night was fucked up. Yesterday was even more fucked up. She needed to cry. She had to let it out, or it would come in another form.

Stooping next to them, I folded my hands around Maggie's shoulders. "He's okay, Sticks."

A tremble worked down her frame, her head swiping back and forth.

"You got him, and he's okay now." I pulled her to a standing position, and she let me. All at once, she looked so damn weary, so tired of being strong. "Come on. You need to rest."

It took a moment, but Maggie gave me a hesitant nod and then swerved toward the couch. My hand caught hers, stopping her. "You're going to make everything difficult tonight, aren't you?"

She blinked up at me. "Huh?" This was progress. That was the first word I'd gotten out of her since we left the woods.

"You're not sleeping on a couch," I said this as though it were the equivalent to bedding down in a compost heap.

She still seemed out of it and wobbly, so I guided Maggie upstairs, keeping a firm hold on her hand. I left my bedroom door open a crack and released her hand, so I could cross the room to flick on my lamp. I grabbed a T-shirt from my closet, turning to see Maggie assessing herself.

"I'm sorry. I'm a mess."

Frown pulling at my mouth, my hands went to her tangled hair and smoothed it down. "Please stop saying that you're sorry. You have nothing to be sorry for. You were worried about Poker. That's love, Maggie. Love isn't something you apologize for. Ever."

Her blue eyes lifted to mine, and I felt it then. It was the way she looked at me, kind of like that first night we met each other in Jamey's living room. The way her eyes held mine spoke to something deeper between us. I wanted nothing more than to kiss her right now, explore what that look meant, and I think she would have let me, but her head wasn't in the right place. And that bruise on her bottom lip was a huge reminder that I had a lot to fix before I was worthy of her kiss.

"Are you—" I cleared my throat from whatever had clogged it. "Are you hungry? I can make you something to eat."

Dropping her gaze, Maggie's chest inflated and fell. "No. I— I think I just want to get cleaned up if that's okay."

"Yeah, that's more than okay." I didn't like that she had gone so long without food and water. Dehydration would make her vertigo worse, but I could understand that she wanted to wash up. I hoped that she'd change her mind after a shower.

I steered her to the bathroom, and now that she was under brighter lights, a heavy ache centered in my chest. There were deep scratches on her ankles, blood mixing with mud on her feet. In retrospect, I should have given her my slides before she ran into the woods or any moment after that, but I hadn't thought of it. Gaze trailing over her porcelain skin for more wounds, my eyes got caught up on parts of her that were far too visible, and my cock kicked up in a plea to keep looking.

I was a dick.

With an abrupt turn, I grabbed a plush towel and washcloth from the cabinet and flipped the hot water on in the shower. I looked to her once more, those blue eyes following my every move.

"I'll get those scratches fixed up when you're done. Alright?"

I waited for her nod before leaving and shut the door behind me. A moment later, I heard the shower door open and shut, ignoring the fact that she was naked on the other side of that door. Okay...I tried to ignore it. Parts of me were not on board with that plan.

I went back downstairs and grabbed a bottled water from the fridge as Poker licked his muzzle clean. He sat there on his hindquarters, intense gaze tracking my every move, but it was very different than how Maggie had looked at me. Especially with that long tongue stroking those big ass canines over and over again. Like he was playing the part of the dad cleaning his gun as the date arrived to pick up his little girl.

I paused before him, and his head cocked to the side, ears perked. "If that was your warning not to fuck around with her, message received."

The damn dog chuffed as if he were answering me.

I narrowed my eyes at him, cracking open the bottle, so Maggie didn't have to fight with it. "I do like her, though. A lot. And I fully intend on being in her life for a long while, so I'd like us to be friends." One brow lifted at that as if he wasn't on board with that plan.

Jesus Christ. Was I legit having a conversation with a dog right now? I so was.

"Okay, I get it. She's your person, and you'd do bad and terrible things for her. As would I. So how about this? The bare minimum I'm asking for here is that my junk is off-limits. You need to bite me, go for anything but that. Agreed?"

He sniffed once and then plodded off toward the stairs, taking them two at a time. I had no confidence in that deal. None whatsoever.

I trailed Poker into the bedroom to find that he was staring at the bathroom door like he was mad at the thing for blocking him from Maggie. He glanced back at me as if to demand I open it for him. It occurred to me then that those two brown eyes had seen all of her, and while it was crazy to be jealous of that, I was.

"She gets privacy, man. Sorry. I'm not opening that door." I fixed the sheets and patted the bed. "Cop a squat and wait like the rest of us poor bastards."

And he did. This was getting a bit unnerving.

Minutes later, the bathroom opened, the scent of my body wash and shampoo drifting through the room. My heart started doing pushups in my throat. The sight of Maggie in my T-shirt, smelling like me…maybe it was a bit caveman of me, but an unexpected seed of possession took root in my gut. I knew then and there that if I ever saw her in another man's clothes, I'd bust the shit out of the world.

Standing before me, she looked every bit of the angel she was. Strands of shiny raven hair hung wet and heavy around her chin. My gaze dipped, and I couldn't help but notice those two soft swells covered by a thin layer of cotton because this shirt wasn't any less transparent. The material ended at the tops of her thighs, and damn if those legs of hers didn't stretch from Earth to Heaven. But those eyes…they were shockingly empty as if the shower had finished stripping her of all emotion.

A jingle of tags forced Maggie's head to rotate toward the bed, to the body occupying the end of it. She gasped. "Poker! You… I'm sorry, Mason. He's used to sleeping with me."

Lucky dog.

"What?" she asked, steps halting midway toward the bed.

Oops. I must have verbalized that one. "He's fine. I invited him up here. Sit down, and I'll take care of those cuts. I grabbed a water for you." Ticking my head toward the bottle on my nightstand, I stood and did my best at keeping the situation in my shorts covered as I retrieved the first aid kit from under my bathroom sink.

When I returned to the bedroom, Maggie was sitting on my mattress, feet dangling over the side. Poker had shifted, so he was right up against her, gaze stalking me as I neared. Maggie hadn't touched her water, and while dehydration was a top concern of mine, I knew she'd heard me. She didn't need me to nag her.

My knees hit the carpet and popped open the kit. Exhaling a deep breath, I struggled to focus, but there was a lot of Maggie in front of me, and that was…hella distracting.

After her shower, these cuts on her ankles weren't as bad as I first thought, but they had been covered in God only knew what and should be treated.

I ripped open the antiseptic wipe and perched one of her feet on my knee. Holding the little square, I glanced up to find her watching me again. "This might sting."

She nodded for me to go ahead, and if it hurt, Maggie didn't show it. She didn't so much as move while I carefully cleaned the abrasions on the outside of her right ankle, over the delicate bones, and then along the top of her foot. She had cute feet, though a little big for her size. Her toes were unpainted and looked as if she cut her nails with clippers. I doubted she had ever seen the inside of a nail salon because Maggie wasn't the type to spend a penny on herself if she didn't have to.

I switched over to her left ankle where there was a deeper gash, and Maggie startled a little when I swiped it with a fresh antiseptic wipe. I cringed. "Sorry. I think this is the worst one."

She didn't respond, so I peeked up at her beneath my lashes. I couldn't read her expression. Never could be certain of what was going on behind those eyes. Her gaze was firmly planted on her fingers in her lap, refusing to look at me now. Wherever her thoughts had taken her, I wanted to draw her away, bring her back here with me.

"I always wanted a dog. Guess most kids do, right?" I opened the ointment and smeared it on the cuts using gauze. "We never got one, probably because Matt and I were never home. But I bet if Mom agreed to it, she would have only let us get one of those yippy things that can fit inside a purse. I'd want a *dog*. One like Poker. Something big that I could roughhouse with."

While I worked, her thick swallow hit my ears. "He…doesn't roughhouse, but he likes to run with me."

Okay, so it seemed like Poker was open for discussion. He was my in.

"Yeah? We should bring him next time. Then I'll have two Davises to kick my ass." I tore open the Band-Aids.

"I haven't been able to take him in a while." Her voice was hoarse with something I couldn't identify. More guilt, maybe. "But I don't think he'd beat you…by much."

I loved that she never shied away from taking a shot at my ego. I chuckled at her dig as I placed the first bandage on her right ankle. "Well, it makes sense you haven't been able to take him. You've been busy, and you hurt your back."

"It's not just that. He…" Her shaky hand reached out to sweep back the hair between his ears. Poker closed his lids as if that felt like nirvana. "He stepped on a fishing hook almost two months ago and had to have surgery to remove it. Took a long while for his paw to heal."

"Ouch." As I stuck the next Band-Aid on, her words caught up to me. "Fishing…? You run him on Cove Beach?"

"Yeah, that's my second favorite place."

Wow, I was getting all kinds of insight tonight. "Where's the first?"

"The bluffs. It's perfect for a long run when I have the time. I like how the trail isn't easy to get to by vehicle, so it's quiet, remote. The scenery is beautiful with the private beach below and the homes overlooking the ocean…"

As her words came to a trickle, I looked up to see her face was drawn with sadness. She didn't have to say what she was thinking. I could see it. She'd resigned herself to this life. To be a have-not, stumbling along the pothole-ridden streets only to catch a glimpse of where the sidewalks weren't cracked. She thought she was destined for a life of wanting, struggling to make ends meet. And that trip to the vet was a reminder of that. It had to have wiped out her bank account.

"Treating Poker…that had to cost a pretty penny."

She shrugged, shoulders returning to a lower position. Yeah, I was right. It had been a hard hit. I could see it now: Maggie with tears in her eyes, pacing the vet's office, waiting for Poker like a newborn mother. She'd be licking her lips, wringing her fingers, handing over stacks of green like it was nothing because if it was for Poker, it was nothing to her.

This girl… She had me. She so fucking had me.

I closed the kit, collected all the trash and threw it away in the bathroom. Standing over the bed again, I looked down at the top of Maggie's head. She hadn't moved yet.

"So, you're getting the bed. That's non-negotiable. And I'll take the floor again." *Please, don't make me take the floor again.* "Or I could crash in my parents' room if you're not comfortable with me sleeping in here."

I waited for a response. But there was…nothing. Shit.

Suddenly, those big blue eyes lifted to meet mine, and yeah, not a clue what was going on behind them.

"Or I can find a fiery cavern in Hell if you prefer."

She blinked once. "I'm okay with you in here. In the bed, I mean."

The lump in my throat was immediate. I gulped it down. "Are you sure?"

Hell, was *I* sure? I should put on more clothes. And cast-iron underwear because I could already feel my core warming, the need for her rising all over again.

"It's okay. Really, Mason. I was just upset about Poker earlier and took it out on you. I didn't mean to make you feel bad. That wasn't right or fair. I'm sorry."

With that, she turned and crawled to the other side of the bed. Air punched out of my lungs so hard, my head went light. Desire slipped under my skin and burned through my veins. I was all-out staring and not doing a damn thing to stop myself. That shirt wasn't nearly long enough, and the bottom curve of her ass was close to being the last straw of my self-control.

Tonight was going to test every ounce of my willpower. We'd slept together before, of course, but the first time, I was an emotional wreck, teetering around rock bottom. And earlier today, Maggie had been unconscious. So, technically, this would be the first time we were both fully aware we were *sleeping* together.

A rush of heat in my groin had risen up and wrapped around my vocal cords. "Okay."

Before she noticed the tent in my shorts, I clicked off the lamp and climbed onto the sheets. My eyes hadn't adjusted to the dark yet, so I didn't realize how close we were until my knee pretty much went between hers. Maggie's breath caught, and I winced. This was probably a pretty big deal for her, and she didn't know how to define it.

I didn't either.

I positioned my hips away from hers, working on cooling things off down south, but even with Poker delivering an unyielding death stare from the end of the bed, I didn't see that happening anytime soon.

"Come here, Sticks." My hand found hers, and I tugged her toward me. She didn't hesitate. That little body snuggled against mine, and then it was my turn for my breaths to stall out. I swore something happened to the universe on a molecular level when we touched.

I held out hope that this was the beginning of us finally shedding the ruse that friendship would be enough for either of us.

I drew the sheet and blanket up, but she still wasn't close enough. Wrapping my arm around her waist, I tucked her tighter to me, her cool skin meeting mine at every point of contact. And there was a lot of contact.

As she rested her cheek on my chest, I combed through her damp hair, finding that depression at her temple. I traced every dip and rise of jagged bone. My heart clenched for her, remembering what Jamey had said earlier today and what had happened to her. My other hand rested on her waist, drawing a design on her hip with idle swipes of my thumb.

"Forewarning." The gruff edge to my voice had only gotten worse. "Since you interrupted my beauty sleep, I need to start the eight-hour cycle over again, so don't even think about getting up before ten."

I felt her nod as she whispered, " 'Kay."

Lifting her hand, her fingers danced along my skin, knocking the air out of my chest all over again. Maggie rested those delicate fingers over Faith as if she wanted to keep my sister safe for me. My chest felt tight, like my heart had Grinched-out, growing a few sizes.

"Thank you, Mason. Thank you for helping us."

I pressed a kiss to her forehead, letting my lips linger there. "You only need to ask. No matter what. I'll be there."

I felt her tense, keeping her chin tucked, but there was no hiding the hot droplet that splashed onto my chest. I held her tighter. I didn't ask what she was thinking. I didn't tell her everything would be okay. I didn't tell her not to cry. When I was falling apart, she let me *feel*. She held me, gave me that time selflessly. I would do the same for her, and I repeated the words she had spoken to me then.

"I've got you, Maggie."

Ten tiny fingers sunk into me, and her body began to tremble, but that was all. There weren't any more tears, silent cries, sobs that I had expected. She kept it in, locked it down, and refused to let it out. Maybe she didn't trust me with her pain, or maybe she didn't know how to let go of something that had been imprisoned inside her for so long, but more of Jamey's words tumbled over in my head.

She needs to be shown love, Mason. She's desperate for it, and she deserves it. Her life has been harder than you can possibly imagine, and you're making it harder. If you can't love her, I'm begging you to walk away because she won't. She doesn't know how.

There wasn't a shred of doubt left. I wouldn't be walking away from this girl. I'd have to be dragged away by my cold, stiff corpse. Maggie had taken the most broken parts of me and pieced them back together. She breathed life into my soul, started the beat of my heart, and gave me a reason to smile again.

I'd fallen for this girl. Hard.

chapter forty-two

maggie

There was a thick thigh lodged between my legs, and…I was totally okay with that. There was also a large hand on my hip, and I mean *on* my hip, skin to skin with little to no barrier. A long thumb was stretched out across my belly, nearly touching my navel. The rest of the fingers were curled around my backside, and…I was okay with that, too.

Somehow, my borrowed shirt had ridden up during the night, perhaps around the same time I decided to ride Mason's thigh. That thing was really jammed all up in there.

As I lifted my head to scan the room, Poker shifted around my feet, his jaw unhinging with a yawn and then snapped shut. His head rested back on the mattress, and it didn't seem like he was going anywhere for a long while. I couldn't argue with him. This was the softest bed we'd ever slept in. I would be a complete moron not to enjoy every second of this, too.

Carefully, so I didn't wake him, I relaxed onto Mason's bicep that was currently doubling as my pillow. My gaze drifted down, catching on the five 3-D butterflies linked by black and gray swirls that started at his wrist, wove around his golden arm, up his broad shoulder, licking at his neck as it swooped down and stopped over his heart. Each butterfly was tattooed in a different spectrum of blue, his sister's in bright teals and purples, the end of one wing kissing the top of the infinity symbol with her name etched in the bottom right link.

His scent was all around me of warm chocolate and dark spice. As I stared at him, he looked so peaceful. A boyishness had begun to soften his hard features as though he hadn't suffered with a ghost for the last five years. The pain was still there, locked inside his heart, and I didn't think he'd ever be free of it. But perhaps it didn't have as much weight on his soul that it used to.

My gaze explored his square jaw covered in dark stubble, the slight hollows of his dimples teasing me. There used to be an emptiness to his smile like he was mimicking the facial movement. Now? Just a hint of that smile could devastate me.

A sliver of daylight had peeked through an opening of the gray curtains and danced along his long lashes that skimmed his high cheekbones. An otherwise perfect and refined nose was slightly offset at the bridge from an old break. His hair so dark it almost looked black, a little longer than when I'd first met him, but cropped short on the sides. Since his eyes were closed, my gaze dipped to my second favorite facial feature and stayed there.

A shallow breath lifted my chest. My goodness, his lips were full and expressive and so very kissable. We were close enough that if I stretched another inch, I could press our mouths together.

I didn't.

Laying with him this way, I couldn't help but remember every detail of our kiss. My first kiss. How his lips molded to mine, how his touch had scorched my skin, the way his hips rocked into mine, and how he had felt between my thighs…

All at once, a heavy weight pulled low in my pelvis, nipples tingling with need, the desire for him threading through every cell.

Mason's breaths were heavy and even, his stomach meeting mine with each inhale. The coarse hairs that trailed down his navel tickled my belly, and as the memory of our kiss replayed, my breasts seemed fuller and more sensitive. A fantasy played of him waking up right now, drawing me close, lining our bodies up in all the right places, willingly being pinned beneath him as he shoved my legs open, kissed me, ripped off my clothes…

Okay, that fantasy would never happen, but I couldn't douse the blaze as it burned bright in my center, heat churning between my thighs. My panties felt damp suddenly, the urge to move against his thigh growing, desperate to relieve the ache there. But if I moved, I'd wake him, and instead of being turned on like the hero in a bodice ripper novel, Mason would be horrified.

And he would be more horrified to hear what I'd done, what I'd allowed him to do.

Everything about this is right because it's you and me. The way it should be.

I pinched my eyes shut as disappointment swelled in my chest. It wasn't fair that he'd said those words, and they hadn't been real, and the pain of that speared through me, deep and sharp.

This moment is mine. You're *mine.*

They were meaningless, drunk ramblings. *Nothing more.*

I knew I had to confess, but I didn't know how to broach the subject, let alone tell him how far we'd gone, how long I'd touched him, where I'd let him touch me. The truth could ruin our friendship; if that was what we were. The definition of our relationship had been murky, along with a lot of other things.

When I'd woken up in the middle of the night, I didn't understand why I was in Mason's bed or why he was asleep on the floor. Why he'd helped me or insisted on driving me. But last night, I didn't have time to question it. Getting to Poker was all that had mattered.

Mason could have walked away and left me in the woods, but he'd…asked me to come back with him. He'd taken care of Poker and me. He'd cared for my wounds tenderly, almost lovingly. He held me while I fought back every tear except that one. The one I hadn't been able to stop.

Those fingers on my hip had combed through my hair, touched that rutted bone on my skull, rubbed my back as if he knew where every lash of the belt had scarred me, and he was simply *there* for me. And I hadn't understood one second of it.

But I did understand one thing with stark clarity.

Mason Scott was a heartbreaker of the worst kind. He was the air, and without him, I'd suffocate. With one word, one look, he could make me fly or send me crashing to the earth. He'd shown me both sides of him, the serrated edge and the silk, and there was a large part of me that didn't care if he wrapped me in his warmth or cut me in two.

For now, I was safe here, lying between my two protectors against the evils of the world. For a few fleeting moments, I could just be. No one would hurt me. No one would strike me, make me bruise, bleed, cry, or scream. I was safe, if only for a moment, and that was more than I'd ever had.

I continued to stare at Mason like a creeper until my bladder disagreed with my decision to ignore it. I attempted to extract myself from beneath a dude that weighed five of me—or so it seemed—because seriously, how were limp bodies this heavy?

Seven minutes and a lot of grimacing later, I had detached our upper bodies. Now for the lower half… His leaden thighs had trapped one of mine, and it was nothing short of a miracle that I was able to extract myself without doing serious damage to his man parts that seemed oddly…hard. I really couldn't think about that now.

As my foot slipped out from between his legs, I swore I heard a low grunt deep in his throat, and I froze. I still had my toes between his thighs, and all doubt gone, he was *hard*.

I swallowed.

Did that happen when guys were asleep? I seriously needed better access to Google.

Mason's deep breathing resumed, and I shimmied the rest of the way out of the bed, landing palm-first onto the floor, face following a second later.

With a cringe, I shot to my feet, the room going on a swivel for a moment. As I regained my balance, I heard another snap of yawning jowls from the bed. I shot Poker a thanks-for-all-the-help glance. He was never going to want to sleep in my bed again.

When I glimpsed down at myself, my eyes bulged out. Mason's white T-shirt was gathered up around my hips and was so not covering my underwear. I yanked the hem down to the tops of my thighs, my blood going cold as the last flash of color left my vision. Last night, I'd been in a daze, but I felt clearheaded now. I peeked beneath the neckline to verify what I'd seen.

Yup.

Light blue cotton panties. Those had been in my emergency bag, which meant someone had changed me, and there was only one reason someone would have done that.

Oh, God. I was going to be sick. I—

"A pair of perfect breasts should be stared at—"

Yelping, I flipped around and clutched my chest.

"—but not usually by the one who owns them." A pirate smile was stretched across those lips I'd been gawking at minutes ago. In the morning light, eyes the color of summer maple leaves gleamed, and Mason looked awake. Like…wide awake.

A pit opened in my stomach as it occurred to me that Mason may have been watching me. He could have seen the back of my thighs. Those scars weren't as visible as the ones on my back, but I couldn't be sure if he had seen them. Considering that his smile was growing, I'd say he hadn't.

Whatever my next thought was died a sweet death when Mason shifted up in bed.

Dear Lord.

Propped up on one elbow, the sheet slipped indecently low on his waist, so every muscle in his torso was on full display for me. Even down to those V-shaped cuts on either side of his hips where the skin was taut and thin, veins bulging and running parallel to the dusting of hair that disappeared beneath the sheet. I was suddenly desperate for a glass of water.

Ripping my stare away, I stammered, "I...uh— Someone changed my clothes?"

His palms lifted to face me. "Jamey. It was all Jamey."

That should have eased me some, but the lingering panic clouded my thoughts. "Was it...bad?"

Like I did something that starts with P and ends in ooped.

His eyes drifted up to mine and then back down to the sheet, which wasn't helping to temper all the bad thoughts kicking around in my head. "Nah. You just threw up, but it was messy. The best thing to do was give you a bath. But again...all Jamey." While my shoulders sagged in relief, those eyes locked with mine, humor dancing in the peridot depths. "I offered to help, but he wasn't having it. No offense, but your friend is a bit selfish."

I snorted. "He was probably doing you a kindness. I'm sure it couldn't have been an attractive sight."

A chuckle rumbled through him that sounded throaty and rich, and that yummy eight-pack rippled. "You'd be surprised."

I hadn't a clue what he meant by that, but my brain kicked off as Mason's arms went over his head in a stretch. Diverting my stare from his chiseled, well, everything turned into an epic fail.

He folded over and buried his head in Poker's coat, rubbing his furry belly. Poker flipped onto his back, and one leg kicked out, pedaling the air as Mason found the sweet spot right under his ribs.

"You must be starving." He peered up at me, concerned. "When's the last time you ate?"

"Uh... Breakfast yesterday."

Frowning, he sat up and with a shake of his head. "I need to feed you."

That was a weird way to put it. I nibbled my bottom lip and hissed as pain sparked.

"Yeah, you did a number on that."

I gingerly touched my lip and pulled my finger back, expecting it to be covered in blood. It wasn't. "I know this will probably sound funny, but I prefer to put my clothes on, or at the very least, find a bra before I eat."

"Why is that funny?"

"In case you haven't noticed, I'm not as well-endowed as the type of women you're attracted to, but I'd feel more comfortable wearing a bra. It's a bit breezy under here."

Those eyes darkened as they dropped to my bare feet and tracked all the way up my frame. Slowly. My body reacted as though every part of me that his gaze lingered on was a physical touch. My heart pounded, breaths coming fast and short, the tips of my breasts furled tighter as warmth blossomed low in my belly. I squeezed my thighs together to ease the building pressure, but it only intensified.

He did all that with a simple look.

"Now that you mention it, I did notice," he said. "Don't think of me as a perv. It's just a guy thing. Kinda like looking up at the sky to see what the weather is like every two seconds."

Two seconds? That couldn't be right.

I waved over myself as if he needed reminding. "So you know, it was by choice. I went with the small, almost non-existent models. I've heard large breasts can knock you out while running. I figured I had enough problems."

His hooded gaze flared wide. "That does sound dangerous. Wise decision." A grin played in the corner of his mouth, dimple on display, voice thick as smoke. "Do you mind if I do a bit of comparing? I've never held the small, almost non-existent models before."

"Sure. I'll slot you in right after Hell freezes over and just before breakfast."

Laughing, he climbed out of bed, and his nylon shorts had slipped below that V of muscles like an arrow pointing to what lay on the other side of the waistband. Before I could ogle him properly, Mason turned so his back was to me, which was…well, this view was nice, too. Then he did something I never thought he'd do, and if I hadn't seen it in person, I wouldn't have believed it. He pulled the sheets up, fixed the corners, folded the creases. The blanket followed. Tucking was involved.

Wait. That bedding was from the hall closet. Where was his duvet? Time for that later. A moment such as this needed to be celebrated.

"Holy shit," I muttered.

"What?" Mason stilled, holding the pillow against his waist.

"It happened. Hell just froze over. You made your bed." I leaned to one side to observe his work. "Really well, too."

His eyes swung to the clock. "And it's breakfast time." Jumping on the mattress, he sat up straight, eyes bright with mischief, the pillow still in his lap. "I'm ready to compare." His arms went up and made grabby hands for my chest.

"Funny." I shoved him, but he didn't have the courtesy of falling backward. He only laughed louder. Damn him.

Still laughing, Mason strolled out of the bedroom. Sighing, something pink—the only pink thing in here—forced my gaze up. My heart rate jacked like a kitten tweaking out on catnip. My watermelon medal was tacked to the wall, the other trophies on the shelf sloppily pushed aside, so it was in plain view. It was the stupidest thing ever, and I loved that he kept it. I loved that he put it on display like he was proud of the thing.

My moment of giddiness vanished when Mason reappeared with my black bag. Correction, my black bag with my white cotton bra lounging on top. Heat licked up my neck and settled in my cheeks.

There was no way the A-cup label evaded him.

He plucked up the strap and let it dangle in the air an inch from my eye. "I wanted to make sure you found it. Damn thing is so tiny, it almost got lost in the dryer."

"Ass." I swiped my bra and bag from him, and he chuckled again.

I shut the bathroom door with more *oomph* than I intended and frowned at my reflection in the mirror. My hair was tangled like I'd been in a windstorm, scar on full display, my lip swollen to three times its size and the color of something that looked diseased.

Gaze trailing down… I might have to apologize to Ben and Ava for murdering Jamey. It didn't take much, but with a little tug on the fabric, my nipples were pretty much saying, *howdy!* How could Jamey not put a bra on me? And how was I so out of it that I didn't notice how thin this shirt was?

As I placed my bag on the counter, I studied my hands. My tremor wasn't nearly as bad as yesterday, but it could be better. Sometimes it could take a day or two for my body to recover after a seizure, though…it seemed like it had been taking longer lately.

I unzipped the bag, and from inside, I pulled out a pair of jeans and a blue T-shirt. As if my luck wasn't bad enough, I started my period and…yep, one tampon. One. For the entire day.

Way to prepare, Maggie.

I peered inside the bag again and tucked to the side was the envelope that felt fuller than it should be after paying Trey. I thumbed through the stack to find the Scotts had returned the money at some point yesterday. I wasn't sure how I felt about that. I had never wanted the envelope to begin with, and it seemed like having the Scotts' money, honestly earned or not, had been a curse more than a gift.

Shoving my thoughts aside, I opened the new toothbrush package, scrubbed my teeth with minty paste, and then brushed my hair out with the travel brush that still had a sticker on it. I'd have to replenish the items I used when I could.

I opened the bathroom door to find Mason stepping into his jeans, only wearing the Calvin Klein boxer briefs that I had imagined him in every time I folded them. My imagination was grossly inadequate. Seeing that thick bulge…all my girly parts lit up like the freaking Fourth of July.

Completely unaffected that I was in his room, Mason took his sweet time tugging his jeans up the rest of the way and zipped the tines closed. I was sure he was used to dressing out in front of the team, but the last thing I wanted to be thought of was one of the guys.

I had meant to say something… Oh, right. "You didn't have to return the—"

"I did." He cut me off, working the button on his waistband. "It's done. You should never have been put in a position that we needed your money. I'm sorry."

I shrugged. "It's over. There's no use rehashing it. But about yesterday, I have to tell you—"

"Maggie." Gaze latched with mine, Mason sunk onto the mattress, still shirtless. I was starting to think the boy had a shirt allergy. "Indulge me a moment because I need to rehash it."

He patted the bed and waited for me to sit next to him. As I took my spot, I was also beginning to wonder if Poker would leave this bed today.

With our thighs pressed together, Mason leaned even closer, so our arms touched, awareness tingling along every inch of my skin from that one point of contact.

"First," he said, "I need you to know that nothing happened with Rebecca or anyone else."

My breaths hitched, getting caught in my throat, and I couldn't stop the little flips my heart was making. I played it cool, though, because those little flips made me do dumb things. Dumb things like making out with a drunk man and having him completely forget about it the next day.

"It's none of my business what you do."

His eyes turned hard, flashing an emotion that looked a lot like anger. "It is absolutely your business because this"—he waved to the room—"would have been pretty fucked up if I *had* been with someone and brought you into my bed after. I wanted you…" His lashes swept down for a moment before opening them again, meeting my eyes. "No, I *need* you to know what kind of man I am, or the man I'm trying to be."

I was doing my best to stay on track here, I really was, but this shirtless thing and all those inked muscles made that so very hard. "Okay."

"The reason isn't important right now, but my head was in a bad space Saturday. I started drinking and almost made a huge mistake. It didn't go very far before I stopped it, before I realized what I was doing."

His gaze lowered as his hand slid over mine, fingers threading with my own. The connection was like a tantalizing bolt of lightning up my arm.

"Maggie, I don't want to be this man anymore, but it's what I've known for so long, and it's the only way I know how to deal. That's all it ever is to me, though. I use alcohol and…women to numb out. It's a temporary fix, to forget for one *fucking* minute, but it's all still there when I wake up. I have to live with shit no one should have to live with. Shit that's stuck in my head and won't leave, but I come out the other side feeling worse. I'm not proud of the things I've done, and however ashamed I am to admit any of this, you deserve the truth."

He wasn't proud of women…things…*plural*. Was he including me in that? Had I been a mistake, too?

"I want to be a man who's deserving of your friendship. I don't like the man I am, but I like the man you make me want to be." His lashes lifted, those eyes filled with so much pain that it almost hurt to look at him.

"Seeing you yesterday with that gun pointed at your head… I thought that piece of shit was going to ra—" Brow furrowed, his fist clenched on his thigh as he took a hard swallow. "If I'd only done what you'd asked, I wouldn't have been drunk, and none of that would have happened, but I…" Gaze falling to our hands again, his thumb swept across my knuckles. "There will never be enough apologies for what you went through, but for what it's worth, I'm sorry."

And there it was. The reason for all of it. *Guilt*. That was why he helped me last night. The heart flipping came to a screeching halt.

"Mason, I…" My confession stalled out somewhere around my vocal cords. I was a coward. I had so little in this world, and Mason took up a big part of what I did have. And Mason…he could be kind and empathetic as easily as he could be cold and cruel. It was the cold and cruel part of him that scared me into keeping quiet now.

"Mason, I know it's not my place, and I'm sorry for butting in, but I can't help but point out that you asked forgiveness for the very thing you're angry at Charlie for." His entire demeanor changed, ramping up for an argument when I stopped him. "Wait and hear me out a second. I'm not excusing anything she did, but there's something you don't know."

The citrine bands in his eyes hardened. "That with Marcus' help, her family is tearing down half the town to build another fucking hotel? That you're going to be out of a job? That everyone you care about is losing their homes and livelihoods? Jamey filled me in."

My mouth parted. Shut. "I'm sorry I didn't tell you yesterday. I wanted to, but—"

"But I was drinking, and you had to wait. You had to wait because I was an asshole. Maybe not as much as the Prices, but still an asshole."

I frowned. "Mason, none of this is Charlie's fault. She doesn't have any control over what her parents—and I use that term loosely—do. She feels terrible about going to the E's, and she wants to make things right with you. She needs a friend now more than ever, and I think you need her, too."

A muscle in Mason's jaw thrummed. "No, I—"

"Vinsant was supposed to be at that dinner. The night of Ben's birthday party."

His head cranked over to face me. "What?"

"He was supposed to be there. That's why Charlie invited you."

Mason's throat worked. "She...never said anything."

"Charlie knew she crossed a line when she asked you to leave the party, and she knew she should have told her parents no. But she didn't. I don't know if Vinsant ended up going or not, but, Mason, she made a mistake. Several. And she knows it. And like you"—I curled my fingers tighter around his—"she's trying to deal with her past the best way she knows how. To forget what he did to her. I think she deserves another chance."

Slanting his head to the side, dark hairs fell across his forehead, eyes tracing my features for a long while. "How are you this good?"

"I'm not. I'm selfish. Because if you can't forgive Charlie when she messes up, you won't forgive me when I inevitably do it."

Or have done it.

A smile tugged at his mouth. "Sticks, I could never not forgive you."

My eyes squeezed tight at that. "You...don't know that." I opened my eyes to his again. "Please, Mason. For me?"

He sighed. "Okay. For you, yes." Before I knew what he was doing, Mason pressed a kiss to my left temple, and I...didn't pull away. His lips lingered there as he released another sigh, but this one was different somehow. Like he was relieved.

"Thank you," he breathed against my skin. I wasn't sure what he was thanking me for, but he was already dropping our linked hands and crossing the room to his dresser. "Whatcha want to do today?" He pulled a plain white T-shirt out of his drawer and tugged it over my last indecent glimpse of skin.

"I have to work."

He headed into the bathroom. "Wrong. You have the day off. With pay. You're not working."

Since I had the view, I stared at what I imagined was a perfect backside since everything on the boy's body was perfect. "Don't do that."

"It's done." He put a strip of paste on his toothbrush. "We're gonna do something fun. Beach, movies, pool. Name it."

I narrowed my gaze at his reflection. "Two out of three of those require a swimsuit."

His fingers rubbed his chin to make a *scritching* sound to suggest how rough those hairs on his jaw were, which brought to mind a few more fantasies that I hadn't considered yet.

"You noticed that, huh? I thought I slipped that past you."

"Uh-huh," I grumbled, and he laughed at me as he stuck his toothbrush in his mouth. I looked to the furry lump on the bed. "I know you're not sleeping." One brown eye opened, followed by the second. I ticked my head to the hall. "Come on."

I left the room with Poker trailing me. Once I let him out to the backyard, I heard feet padding down the stairs. Leaving the door open, I peered over to see Matt step into the kitchen, scrubbing a hand through his wet locks. I imagined that was how the Scott men styled their hair. Except for Ben, the gel fanatic.

"Maggie." Matt stood feet away as though there was an imaginary sinkhole around me. "How— Are you feeling okay?"

"Yeah, thanks."

Matt shifted from one bare foot to the next. He crossed his arms, the Scotts' matching butterfly tattoo twitching along his bicep. Weird. He was nervous, and I didn't understand why he would be.

"I don't know if Mason spoke to you about this, and I'm not sure you'll be comfortable talking to me…" As his words drifted off, so did his emerald gaze.

"What is it?"

A painful look strained his features. "I need to know, Maggie. Did that man touch you? In any way? Did he—"

"No. He didn't." Those striking eyes returned to mine and held my gaze as if waiting for me to break down and admit to something that didn't happen. "I promise, Matt. He didn't."

"Thank God." Then I was in a Matthew Scott burrito, his cologne filling my senses, spicy with a hint of something else that was pleasantly sweet. One of us was shaking, and it wasn't me this time.

I spoke into his chest. "Matt, are you okay?"

He released a choked laugh, void of all humor. "With all you went through, you're asking me if *I'm* okay?" Yeah, I guess that was stupid.

Pulling away just enough, he tucked a lock of hair behind my ear. It was such a brotherly act, so normal for him. "I failed you yesterday."

I opened my mouth to protest, but a finger landed on my lips to silence me.

"I did. And I'm not going to say I'm sorry for the mere fact that I don't deserve your forgiveness, Maggie. That bastard was in my home, and I didn't know. He had a gun to your head, and I was fucking asleep. I left you with him, which was the worst thing I could have done. Instead of making sure that you were okay, I told Mase to give you space, and you ended up having a seizure. You could have died when I was five feet away from you. *Nothing* about that is okay. *Nothing.*" His lips went to my forehead and stayed there. "All I can do is tell you that I promise to do my best to never fail you again."

Geez... "I must have really let some curse words fly for you to feel this bad."

He barked a real laugh that time, gathering me into his arms for another hug.

Tucked against him, I shut my eyes and cherished this moment. It was simply *wonderful* to be held by him. It wasn't a feeling I would ever take for granted.

I looked out to the living room that was... "Did you guys clean?"

"We did. I was shocked we were capable, as well."

Wow, even the baseboards were dust free. "I'm impressed."

"What else would you be in the presence of Scotts?" That voice had us turning toward Mason as he stepped onto the landing, sliding his phone into his pocket.

Mason shot Matt an odd look that must have come with a telepathic question because Matt answered with a shake of his head. Mason released another puzzling sigh.

Satisfied with whatever that was, Mason clapped his hands. "Come here, boy!"

Matt pinched his brows in confusion and jolted when Poker appeared in the doorway, tags jingling, trotting his way into the house like he owned the place.

Matt knelt to ruffle the dog's coat. "Who's this?"

"Poker," Mason answered, shutting the back door.

Matt blinked at Mason and then me, a slow grin splitting his lips. "Holy shit. A *dog*? Poker's a *dog*? Maggie, we thought you were a card shark!"

I wrinkled my nose. That was a weird assumption.

Mason propped his arm on my shoulders. "Maggie and I rescued him from bears last night."

Uh…was that what he thought we were doing, because the whole time, I thought my father had done something to Poker to punish me, like break his leg, kick his ribs in, shoot him between the eyes.

"Bears?" Matt questioned, now getting a tongue in his ear.

"She woke up in the middle of the night to get him. Poor guy was starving outside of their house on Verde Way."

Gaze flicking to mine, Matt's mouth formed around the street name, realization setting in. *Yes, I live in the woods.* With a shake of his head, he said, "Maggie, you really are an angel."

Angel? I was so far from anything with wings and a halo.

Mason tugged me closer, drawing my gaze to his. "Too bad your father didn't let him inside. Could have saved you the trouble of worrying." His eyes had taken on a hardened edge again, as did his voice. "Guess he was preoccupied."

"Yeah." I needed to change the subject and find a Brillo Pad to scrub the late-night noises from my brain. I could usually distract the Scotts with food. "How about some breakfast?"

"Yes, please." Matt fished the egg carton out of the fridge, Poker following as if this human breakfast included him, as well. "Mase, I've got a study session today. Do you mind running me to the RAM's after?"

Mason's arm hadn't budged from my shoulders, and I wasn't doing anything to change that. "Sure, we were probably going into town anyway and see a movie."

My brow arched. "We were?"

The corner of Mason's mouth lifted, eyes sparkling with mischief. "Unless you changed your mind about the bikini."

"Nope."

The grin deepened, revealing a dimple. "Movie it is."

Bodies shuffling down the hall forced us to twist around, Mason's arm falling away.

"Morning," Ben yawned. Shirtless and with his shorts low, his hand dragged through his hair that was sticking up in opposing directions. His long arms folded around me. The faint scent of his cologne had mingled with something sweet, which no doubt had come from Jamey. "How are you feeling, Mags?"

"Fine, thanks."

"Man, I'm starv…" As Jamey trailed in, his words died off. "Fuck," he rasped, gaze shooting to mine. "Mags, I— I'm sorry."

Everyone went quiet. Ben glimpsed down at me and then Jamey. "Why are you sorry? What happened?"

"I'm so sorry," Jamey repeated. "I didn't—"

I cut him off before he said something he shouldn't. "It's okay. Really, Jamey."

"What—" Poker poked his head around the island, and Ben stepped back from me. "Hey, whose dog?"

Matt fired up the Keurig to brew his coffee. "Ben, meet Poker. Maggie's Poker."

Ben was already on the floor, giving Poker a rubdown. "I didn't know you had a dog, Mags."

"No one knew she had a dog," Mason threw back with a sour tone.

"I did." Jamey covered his mouth, hand muffling his words. "I didn't even think about him. I should have picked him up, fed him for you, brought him to my house—"

I shot him a look to shut up. "It's fine, Jamey. Really."

He swallowed and mouthed, *I'm so sorry.*

Grabbing the butter from the fridge, I mouthed, *Stop.*

Thankfully, Camden stepped inside the kitchen next, yawning with his arms above his head in a stretch. Poker made his way over and—

Oh, dear.

I didn't think I'd ever see Camden's eyes bulge this wide ever again. "I'm not dreaming, right?" he asked, voice cracking with fear. "Will someone please confirm there is a big ass German shepherd with his nose in my junk?"

"Po—" Mason's hand clamped over my mouth, his other arm snaking around my waist to stop me. God, Poker never did this. He was really digging in, too.

Every inch of Mason was pressed against my back, lips teasing my ear. I would enjoy the moment if I wasn't so appalled.

"Even if Cam didn't deserve this, it's too good to stop. Let it play out." Holding me closer, he called over, "Yeah, Coz. I wouldn't move if I were you."

"Oh, for the love of all *The Real Housewives.*" Camden's arms were still in the air, whiskey eyes filled with pure terror. "Please tell me he's almost done."

Matt blew on the rim of his steaming mug. "Sorry, Cam. He's a search and rescue dog. His specialty is balls. This is gonna take a while."

An hour later, the guys' stomachs were filled with eggs, sausages, and more pancakes than any one human should consume, and I'd called the café to find that Henry and Frankie had taken care of the basket for me. Camden, Ben, and Jamey were joining us on our movie excursion with a plan to stop by the pharmacy near the university first. Thankfully, no one asked me why such a stop was necessary.

While Matt and Mason took the truck to the RAM house, Ben drove the rest of us in his Rover.

Inside the pharmacy, we all split with a silent understanding we'd meet up when we were done. Or so I thought. Camden went for the magazines up front. I aimed right with two sets of feet behind me.

I turned to see Jamey and Ben were right on top of me and stopped them in their tracks with a palm face out. "What are you doing? I don't need a chaperone."

Ben's cheeks went red, his gaze quickly shifting to the razor display. "I think we're going to the same place."

"For?" I glanced up at the sign to find what else was in this aisle. Damn boys and their penises. The corners of my mouth drew down. "I have to get...things."

"Well, we have to get...*things*," Jamey parroted.

My eyes narrowed. "You can't have the same code word as me, Jamey."

His hazel eyes rolled. "They are related products. Hence the same aisle. We are in college, right? You can say tampons and pads, and I can say condoms and lubricant."

One brow inched up my forehead. "Do you want to watch me pick out tampons and pads? Discuss applicators and the pros and cons of wings?"

Jamey's face screwed up. "No."

"And I don't want to see what brands of condoms and lubricants you buy."

"Okay," Ben whispered even though we were the only ones in the joint. "Let's all agree that this is embarrassing and just get it over with."

"Fine," I huffed. "I won't look at you, and you two won't look at me. I'm paying first."

Jamey's long arms folded over his chest, biceps popping against his sleeves. "Perfect. My boyfriend and best friend are both raging prudes."

That got Ben's attention. "Really? Because I seem to remember—"

"There's a no TMI rule around me." I skedaddled to the end of the aisle.

Armed with my choices in record time, I went to the counter, and Camden was notably absent. That was never a good sign.

Scanning the first item, the cashier moved like she was stuck in an invisible tar pit. Flashing me smiles, her hot pink lipstick bled into her wrinkle lines, and she had to lick her fingers three times to separate the bag.

My head rotated to see Jamey and Ben were in deep discussion over two small boxes. Was it really that hard to decide? How many options could there be? I wasn't sure I wanted to know. Okay, I totally wanted to know, and I knew Jamey would draw me a diagram if I asked.

I made a mental note to ask.

"That time of the month, huh?" Camden's breath tickled my ear, and I shot back, wheeling around. His massive arm thumped onto the counter between the cashier and me, smirking that Scott smirk. With his free hand, he snatched up the box, studied it, and then brought it to his nose to breathe it in. "That is a refreshingly fresh scent. Who knew?"

Oh, dear God.

"They just came out with it," the voice behind the counter croaked. "Back in my day, they didn't have all these fancy designs or scents. And it felt like you were wearing a diaper. Young women are so lucky now."

Camden gave her an emphatic nod. "You are so right. Women shouldn't bear the sole burden and inconvenience of reproduction. Should they, Maggie?"

I steepled my hands beneath my chin. "Please, don't say anything to Mason. I had no choice but to do this right now."

I reached for the blue box to get things moving, but it was above my head before I could nab it. "Toxic shock syndrome?" Camden read aloud.

I groaned.

"My cousin wound up in the hospital from that," the cashier added. "Almost died."

Camden tilted his head at her. "Really?" Brown eyes refocused on me, wide with concern. "You are changing every four to eight hours, right, Maggie? It says so on the box."

I gulped. Hard. "I'm well versed in the usage of tampons. Can I pay, please?"

Camden returned the box to the counter, gaze scrolling over me much too slow. "Doesn't bother me. Just so you know."

Staring on, I shook my head at him. "What is wrong with you?"

"All the right things." His club of an arm slung over my shoulder and smooshed me against his side. "I'm only saying, in case you were wondering. Some guys it does, freaks 'em out. To me, it lets me know your woman parts are in working order. It's healthy. It's natural."

Hazed over peepers shone behind a set of thick glasses that made her eyes look five sizes too big. "That is an excellent attitude, young man. If only all men were as open and wise."

Camden threw her a wink. "I try."

Mother Time and I finally exchanged the money, and in one move, I snatched up my bag and wriggled out of Camden's fifty-pound limb. He chuckled as I ducked inside the pharmacy bathroom, admittedly taking longer than I needed with my freshly scented feminine hygiene products that he was so fond of.

I emerged from the bathroom, not having taken long enough because Camden was now harassing Ben and Jamey.

"Ultra-thin. Nice! You should really feel it up the ass with these. Oh! You should have picked up another tube of lube. They have a sale going."

The cashier nodded to her new bestie. "Good eye, young man. A dollar off the second purchase of lubricant."

Ben glared at his brother. "Don't you have a magazine to go jerk off to?"

"Oh, we don't encourage that in the store," the cashier advised. "But he can purchase one and take it to the restroom."

What. The. Hell.

Jamey spotted me lingering near the doorway and chucked Ben's keys at me. I missed but was quick to recover and shot out before Camden could offer me tips on tampon insertion. I tucked my bag under the passenger seat of the Land Rover, slumping against the closed door.

I should have anticipated how much of a bad idea shopping with Camden would be. He had no impulse control to speak of.

When the boys finally joined me outside, Ben was looking at his phone. He clicked it off and disappeared it inside his pocket. "Mase should be here in a minute."

Camden waltzed over, planting his hand next to my head, leaning against the SUV with his sunglasses pointed down at me.

Ignoring Camden completely, I glanced over just as Jamey's mouth flopped open. "What's with the face?" I asked.

Without tearing his eyes away from whatever hijacked his attention, he slid his hand over my mouth. "Shush it, Mags. You're gonna ruin this for me."

"Whad ah oo dooin?" I mumbled under his palm. As I angled to look in the same direction, Jamey's hand melted away and then so did the cartilage in my knees.

Coming down the street on the back of a black and yellow Harley, clad in a leather jacket, boots, and a shiny black helmet was perhaps the sexiest thing I'd ever seen in my life.

I pursed my lips together to stop the drool from trickling out. Good heavens, this was so unfair.

Jamey released a strained breath. "I think I'm having my once in a lifetime *Top Gun* moment."

"What is that?" I breathed out, hoping I was having it, too.

Camden snorted, sidling up next to me as he crossed his arms. "Maggie, you lead a sad life."

No shit.

Mason pulled into an empty spot, cut the Harley's engine, and dragged off his helmet. Shaking out his perfectly imperfect tousled strands, he slipped on his aviator sunglasses.

Mason canted his head at us and then glimpsed behind him. Then back to us. "What are we gawking at?"

You. But since I wouldn't be admitting that, I went with, "What's a *Top Gun*?"

It took what felt like an entire minute of Mason staring at me before the boy burst into hysterics. I think there was an actual knee slap in there somewhere.

Shaking his head, Mason swung one leg over the bike to dismount it. "Another pop culture reference that I'm sure went right over your pretty head."

The words *pretty* and *your* just flew out of Mason's mouth. I was sure he didn't mean it the way I wanted to take it, but there was time to analyze that later because something else needed to be addressed.

I faced Ben. "You're okay with Jamey openly checking out another guy?"

"Hell yeah, he is," Jamey declared, and Mason's dimples were out to play as he walked over to stand beside me.

I shook my head. "I don't get it. You guys are monogamous, right?"

"Hell yes, we are," Ben assured me and anyone within a ten-mile radius who also might question their relationship status. He gave a half-hearted shrug. "But he can look, as long as it ends there."

"So, if I had a boyfriend, I can still check out other guys, and that's cool?"

Mason's head jerked back as if I'd delivered a throat punch. "Fuck no! Those are Ben and Jamey's fucked up gay rules."

The boys shot him a bland look.

I absorbed this, truly not having a clue how relationships worked and what was acceptable. "What about a girl? Can I check out another girl?"

Now I had Camden's complete attention.

Mason's head swung up and down like the thing was hinged onto his spine all wrong. "You could check out any hot chick you wanted. In fact, I would encourage it."

I tilted my head at him. "Do all guys think like this?"

Mason was still nodding. "The sane or straight ones do."

"Ass." Ben snickered and delivered a middle finger to his cousin. "You taking Mags?"

"Yep. Come on, Sticks." Mason held his hand out to me, and I stared at it. Why was I staring at it? And where was he taking me?

"Where are you taking me?"

His answer included two dimples and a blindingly beautiful smile.

chapter forty-three

mason

"It'll be fun, Sticks." I waved to the Harley Sportster as if she weren't already intently staring at it.

Crickets.

This wasn't going as well as I'd hoped. If I were being honest, I wasn't even offended when Matt threw the keys at me and told me I needed to up my game because I was a disgrace to all male Scotts. I wasn't offended because I was too busy conjuring up a dozen fantasies about the little raven beauty on the back of a fucking Harley. She had been naked in each one.

Not breaking that stare from the Sportster, the manic lip licking started. "Uh…"

"I have an extra helmet." Like a dumbass, I procured said helmet from the saddlebag, and why Matt owned a woman's helmet embossed with delicate yellow swirls, I had no clue because he never let anyone but me ride his bike. Ever. In fact, he had acted kinda weird when he handed the helmet to me and had confirmed three times that *only* Maggie would be wearing it.

Dipping her head to the side as if the view of the Harley would change, a thick draping of hair fell away from her jaw. "Where's BB?"

"Matt needed her today, so we swapped." Lies.

She blinked up at me all blue eyes and parted lips. "You don't have to lug me around. I could ride in Ben's Rover."

Did she really just say that? Did she not know how much I was dying to get that body wrapped around me? Maybe… Hell, maybe it was only me. Honestly, I thought I had cleared that up in bed this morning. I'd been watching her for over an hour when I felt her heart rate double and pound against my chest. Then she stirred awake, her warm breaths drifting along my skin as she watched *me* for the next hour.

It had taken every ounce of restraint I had to keep pretending to sleep while she squirmed out of my arms, legs, bed... She had no clue what she was doing to me. Or what I wanted to do to her.

My brows pulled together over my sunglasses. "*Lug you?* I want you to come with me. We're taking Cove Highway up to Pacific Cliffs. You're gonna have a blast, I swear."

"That's a long way. And I've never"—she examined the two-up seat again—"ridden before."

My grin kicked up on one side. "Even better. I get to be your first." My smile wasn't going anywhere because I knew what "firsts" I wanted mine to be, but if I didn't rein in that thought, I'd end up with a hard-on. For the tenth time this morning.

The fidgeting started up again, and I sensed refusal on the horizon. Dammit, I'd lost my powers of persuasion over her.

"What do I hold onto?"

Did she...? Holy shit, it worked? It took me an entire five seconds to get over the shock. If she wasn't standing right in front of me, I'd fist-pump the air like a dweeb. Instead, I waved over myself. "Me."

"Oh." Her chest rose and fell faster, tongue darting over what I was sure to be the seventh application of ChapStick today. Her widened eyes gave the bike another once over. A small, worn purse that may have been beige at one time was slung across her chest. It was a good thing I had my sunglasses on because my eyes had locked onto those small models that were anything but non-existent. They sure as hell existed to me.

I observed, "I've never seen you with a purse."

Head arched all the way back to me, she froze. "Um..."

"It's rag time, Coz!" Cam called out.

Shutting her eyes, Maggie muttered, "Seriously?" A pretty pink blush blazed across her cheeks, and I couldn't help but laugh.

"She's lucky," Cam continued. "She must not be one of those heavy flow girls. She bought the regular size tampons."

"Oh. My. God." Maggie face-planted into her hands. "He literally keeps getting worse."

"I made her aware it didn't bother me!"

"I'm sure little does, Cam." I grabbed Maggie's trembling hands off her face and set them to her sides. "Here, let's take this off." As I lifted the strap off her chest, the back of my knuckles innocently grazed the tip of her breast, and she sucked in a sharp gasp. I stilled, and though I tried my best not to let such a slight touch affect me...no such luck.

"Sorry." I cleared my throat, but my voice still sounded rough. "I'll put this in the back. I don't want you worrying about anything but the ride." Once her purse was tucked away into the saddlebag, I brushed off the awkward moment with, "Come on. Let's pretend you're eighteen and have some fun today." I slid the extra helmet over her head, both of us noticing it was too big like everything else the girl wore. "Hmm. You'll do for now." I'd have to get her a smaller helmet if we rode again. Speaking of…

I shrugged off my jacket and slipped the sleeves up her arms.

"I'm not cold."

Shaking my head, I worked the zipper on the jacket. "It's to protect you from road rash in case we get into an accident."

That and I love how you look in my clothes.

I'd been dying to see her in this, but I wanted to get it dry-cleaned before I let that happen. Though it had been months since Charlie last wore this, I could still scent her perfume in the lining.

"But what if you get road rash?" She moved to take off my jacket, but I stopped her by putting her hands back down to her sides again. I would have snagged Matt's jacket had I been thinking straight, but it all had happened too fast.

"I'm more concerned about you getting hurt. I'll drive better knowing you're safe." I slipped the visor down over those panicked topaz eyes. "I'll let you know when to mount after I start the engine and then climb on from the left like me, okay?"

She nodded, the movement exaggerated by her helmet.

"If you need anything, tap my chest, and I'll find a spot to pull over. Don't worry about distracting me or bothering me 'cause you're not. During the ride, move your body with mine and keep to my right. Questions?"

The helmet wavered from side to side.

I settled on the bike and started the engine, keeping the frame stable for Maggie. With the loud putter of the exhaust going, I motioned her to mount. Maggie used my shoulders to keep her balance as I guided her, showing her where to put each foot on the pegs.

"Hold on tight, Sticks!"

Her hands rested on my sides.

"Tighter," I yelled again. Taking Maggie's hands, I hauled her chest to my back, feeling her press against me, hands low on my stomach. An inch lower, and Maggie would know more about me than she did a moment ago. "A little tighter!"

Her hips tipped up, thighs hugging mine. My dick thickened to an uncomfortable degree, and I had to shift to accommodate, but there was no way I'd stop this.

"Come on, Maggie. You're gonna fall off like that," I urged her.

Her hand left my stomach to flip up the shield to get a better look. "Okay, how can I possibly get closer without defying physics? There isn't—" She finally caught on as to why I was now laughing, and she smacked my arm when she realized I'd been teasing her. "You're such an ass."

"I never contested that fact." I slipped my helmet on and knocked both of our visors down.

When I eased off the clutch, the bike rolled forward, and her arms snapped around me in full anaconda mode. Once the throttle was engaged, I had a slight fear that she might bruise a rib. The world whizzed past us, and that free, flying feeling buzzed through my veins like a fine whiskey. I hoped Maggie could get out of her head long enough to enjoy this today. She deserved some fun.

Reaching the highway, the salty air whipped through the fabric of my T-shirt, wind lashing my skin so hard that it burned. I looked out to the Pacific as a wave crested against the cliffs, spraying the rock and sand. The sky fused with the water, blanketing the Earth in blue, waves glimmering under the sun as they stretched into oblivion. She was a pretty sight, but the blues of the deepest sea to the highest point in the atmosphere could never compare to the eyes of the beauty holding me.

I took the turns with ease, our bodies like one with the bike, and it seemed as if Maggie's hands had dropped lower through the ride. Having her fingers so close to my cock and the vibrating beast between my legs was not helping my focus. My mind wandered into a fantasy of pulling over, lifting off her helmet, her straddling me while I kissed the hell out of those lips. The shirt she was wearing wouldn't take much muscle to rip away, pop the button on her jeans, get beneath those panties and see if she was wet—

Slow.

I had to take this slow. Letting my dick navigate this was a bad idea. Especially with Maggie.

The changing scenery broke through my thoughts, and I took the exit to Pacific Cliffs. I cut through downtown, past the contemporary architecture of the looming skyscrapers that merged with the timeless structures of the older cityscape. The traffic thinned as we hit the edge of the city.

Passing the shops, galleries, and then finally the boutiques of the Promenade, I noticed Maggie's helmet was pointed right at a dress shop while we waited for the light to turn. Right there in the window was a little black lacy number that I'd kill to see her in. What I wouldn't give to take her to dinner, walk on the beach with her as the sun set. What I wouldn't give to have a couple hours alone with her.

Along with a million other things, Maggie deserved a dress like that. Not that she didn't look stunning in Ava's hand-me-down blue dress, but it was just that. Someone else's dress that belonged to someone else's night. Not her own.

Once I pulled into the movie theater parking lot, I cut the engine and helped Maggie off the bike. As we removed our helmets, she awarded me with a smile brighter than the sun. That right there...? This girl lit up my world.

"Holy wow, that was fun!"

"See?" I crossed my arms. "And you wanted to clean the house today."

"Feel free to stop any lame thought I may have from now on."

I grinned. "Done."

Taking in that smile, her beauty damn near paralyzed me, and she didn't even know it. And the fact she had no idea that her inner beauty was just as incredible only made her more gorgeous.

I hated to think it, but I suddenly regretted this outing. My cousins and Jamey would be pulling up any second now, but I wished it would have been just the two of us. If I'd only had the balls to tell her what I wanted...

"Hey, Maggie. I—" The Land Rover drove into the lot, the words dying then and there.

Staring at me, those eyes rounded. "Yeah?"

As I watched Ben pull into the space next to me, the last thing I wanted was to have this conversation with an audience. And there was the possibility she'd reject me, which would be hella awkward.

I occupied myself with locking our helmets to the bike. "Don't forget your purse."

"Oh, right. Thanks. I totally would have." Maggie grabbed her things from the saddlebag as the guys hopped out of the dark gray SUV.

Stretching my back, I asked, "So? What movie does Sticks want to see? Rom-com? Thriller? Action? Sci-fi?"

Stilling, her gaze bounced between all of us as we waited for her answer. "I..." A somewhat pained expression took up res on her features. She shrugged. "Whatever you guys want."

"She's open!" Cam cheered and sped off to the theater.

I shook my head in disgust. "You really should have picked. We might end up seeing a porno."

"Couldn't hurt," Maggie shot back. "Maybe I'd learn something."

My heart came to a skidding halt. Just stopped beating then and there. She did not say that. Did she...? Hell, if that was what she wanted to do, I would buy the movie theater and show her every damn porno on the planet.

Jamey scoffed. "Learn what? How to fake an orgasm?"

Her nose scrunched. "How do guys fake orgasms?"

"He's not referring to the guys, Mags." Ben threw her a wry grin.

"I think that depends on if the director wants the big action shot," Jamey argued.

"So those women aren't actually..." Her lashes swept up to me before her eyes darted right back to her shoes. Cue the crimson stain blossoming across her cheeks in three, two— Freaking adorable.

Suppressing a snicker, Ben said, "I'm sure some of them are, but I've seen my fair share of porn. There are telltale signs to know if they're faking or not. And the vast majority I've seen aren't real."

"Sadly, he's right," I agreed. "Damn shame, really."

"How can you—" She stopped herself, growing even redder. "Maybe we should catch up to Camden."

"You were going to ask how you can tell if they're faking it?" Maggie meekly nodded to Ben. He slid me a look. "I'll let you explain that one."

Her gaze strayed to me, eyes nowhere near their normal size.

Ben sniggered.

I ignored the asshat, and in all seriousness, I said, "There's a certain flush of the skin when a woman orgasms. That's not something you can fake or hide. If a man knows what he's doing and focuses on your pleasure rather than his own, you wouldn't ever have to fake anything."

I wasn't sure how much pinker those cheeks could get, but damn, I was imagining that exact shade chasing across her body as I made her come.

Maggie audibly swallowed. "Oh. So, you, ah— That's...good to know."

About a hundred different comments—all inappropriate— shriveled on my tongue. Also, I was glad she didn't ask how I knew that. Wasn't something I really wanted her thinking about.

I took Maggie's dainty hand in mine, lacing our fingers together. An entire minute of walking passed before I realized we were holding hands for no apparent reason. It felt as natural as could be.

And right then and there, I knew down to my marrow that being with her would feel the same. Natural and right.

Holding hands had to constitute as a first step, didn't it? I wouldn't know. My first step always started with getting enough clothes off to insert peg A into slot B.

As we made our way to the theater, I observed that she was on the wrong side of me. I dropped her right hand and switched sides, picking up her left hand so that I was closer to the street.

"Sorry," she muttered.

I glimpsed down at her. "For what?"

She scrubbed her right hand down her jeans. "My palm's all sweaty and gross."

Sweaty and...? Oh, hell. She didn't get it. Of course, she didn't. A man had never held her hand before, let alone taken the more dangerous side of the sidewalk for her. That was the kind of thing Dad would kick our asses over. I was both sad and happy for Maggie at the same time. This was another first. Maybe one day I'd tell her that it was the gentlemanly thing to do, to stand on the side of the sidewalk nearest traffic, but I wanted her to figure it out on her own because when she did, when she learned the reason for all my little gestures...they wouldn't be little to her.

"Sticks, your hands aren't sweaty, and they sure as hell aren't gross." I gave her my best panty-dropper smile. "But the left should have equal hold time to the right. I don't need jealous hands."

She squinted up at me. "You are so weird."

"You mispronounced awesome and thank you." It was then that I saw her scar was showing a little, and though it didn't bother me, I knew it bothered her. I wasn't sure if she'd let me touch her temple again like I had this morning, but I lifted my fingers and combed through the strands. She stiffened but didn't jerk away or slap me. But she also wasn't looking at me. "There."

Ducking her chin, she muttered, "Thank you."

I pulled us to a stop, letting the guys go on ahead. Once they were out of earshot, I placed my fingers beneath her chin, encouraging her to look at me. She allowed her head to tilt back, but her eyes didn't follow.

"Please don't thank me for that," I said. "I should be thanking you for allowing me that privilege. I know it's not easy."

"No. It's not easy. And I..." Maggie sighed, withdrawing from me and lowering her head back down. Her eyes squeezed shut. "I would change me if I could, Mason. I would take this hideous scar away, and I would have hands that don't freakishly shake, and a dumb brain that doesn't short out every other time I move too fast, and a memory that actually remembered things I needed it to. But thank you for making me feel like I don't *have to* change."

Huh. *I would change me if I could…* That didn't sound like someone who had accepted her fate, who didn't want to improve her quality of life. That didn't add up with what her father had said at the hospital. I could push it, but…I wasn't sure I'd word it the right way.

"The reason I don't make you feel like you have to change isn't because I'm a swell guy. It's because there isn't a damn thing about you that I would change. Not your scar or your hands or your brain, and nothing about you is hideous or freakish or dumb, so stop saying that shit."

Those deep blue eyes lifted to meet mine, so much doubt swimming in them. She was so self-conscious about what she would view as her shortcomings. I saw it at breakfast this morning. It was in the way she cautiously carried the plates to the table as if she expected an earthquake any moment, refused to fill our glasses unless they were set down and out of spilling range, cut her pancake into uneven micro-sized pieces, sipped her juice over her plate, and the scowl she gave her eggs every time they had slipped off her fork. There were ways I could help her with all of that. Make her life better. If she would let me, I would.

My thumb traced a design on the back of her hand. "Maggie, you're be—"

"Are we watching a movie today or what?" Cam called down to us.

Impeccable timing as always.

Tearing my gaze away from hers, I stared at my idiot cousin. A grunt rolled down my throat as I tugged Maggie along.

I was happy to see that Ben and Jamey were also getting in on this hand-holding phenomenon. Ben was finally breaking through the cracks in his shell, and Jamey was using a sledgehammer to help him along. It was good. Exactly what Ben needed.

"Oh, do you want your jacket back?" Maggie asked.

She was swimming in that thing, and it was sort of ridiculous on her. I loved it. "Nah. The theater is usually cold. You should keep it."

She gifted me another smile. "Thank you."

Cam had a handful of tickets by the time we reached the window. He doled them out, two for me, and I advanced to the doors, but there was a pull on my hand to stop me from going in.

"He paid for me?" Her accusatory gaze pointed to my cousin.

"Yep," I answered.

Rising on her tiptoes, she damn near climbed up my arm to whisper, "I don't want him to. I can pay."

Cam spun and walked backward. "Too bad. It's done. Suck it up, Short Stack."

I pinned my cousin with a cold glare, and he grinned back. Giving her a nickname was not cool, and he knew I'd have a problem with it. Nicknames in the Scott world... It was like our way of staking claim, marking someone as ours. Stupid and Neanderthalish? Absolutely. So did Cam mean it as a direct challenge, or was he being an ass?

I'd say by the way he chased a set of blonde twins into the theater like a dog in heat, it was the latter. I hoped.

Taking her ticket from me, Maggie grumbled something that didn't sound complimentary.

I opened the door for Maggie and, as always, never failed to thank me. As we were hit by the scent of buttery popcorn and musty carpet, we handed over our ticket stubs to the usher. Short lines of people stood at the concession stand with little kids running around the arcade area, squealing. Cam was now getting not one but two phone numbers.

"What kind of snacks do you like?" I peered down to Maggie, tugging on her hand to draw her attention away from the trailer playing overhead. "Are you a choco-fiend or a gummy worm kinda snacker?"

Maggie's eyes flicked to the menu board before she forced her gaze to a movie poster. "Nothing, thanks. I'm still full from breakfast."

Was everything going to be a battle with her? Based on the last eight-ish weeks, I'd go with a yes.

"I've gotta hit the bathroom," I said, dropping her hand. "You guys go on ahead and grab our seats."

"We're gonna hit the head, too." Ben nodded to Jamey.

Cam returned in time to sling an arm around Maggie's shoulders. "Sweet. I get Maggie all to myself in a dark theater." A second ago, that thought would have bothered me, but now it oddly reassured me.

"Ah hell." Maggie pouted, and even her pout was damn cute.

Cam threw me a wink. "Knew she'd be excited."

chapter forty-four

maggie

"So, you're not seeing anyone, huh?" Camden plopped his jacket onto the last seat to reserve our row and took the aisle seat next to me.

Since it was warm enough, I shrugged off Mason's jacket and hung it over my seat, careful not to ruin the leather. I rested my head against the lining that was infused with Mason's scent as I sunk into the soft cushion. Wow, these seats were comfortable. And they— Whoa. They reclined.

"No, I'm not seeing anyone," I muttered, working the controls, so my feet went up. Then back down. Okay, once more.

"Are you into chicks, because I can work with that, too."

I rolled my neck to face him, and there was something in his eyes that was too endearing to ever be irritated by. Camden was too damn cute. And like all Scotts, he knew it.

"No. I'm not into chicks."

"You don't like blonds, do you? Is that why you've never hit on me? Because I could dye my hair. I totally would for you. Jamey would jump that shit in a heartbeat."

I wasn't sure I'd ever entertained the notion of having a type, but thinking back, I'd say I was into tall, dark, and Mason Scott. "Don't dye your hair. You're perfect the way you are."

"Fuck yes!" He fist-pumped the air. "There's a chance."

I giggled. "Why do you do that?"

"Do what?" Arm still hovering above him, his warm whiskey eyes glimmered in the light of the SILENCE YOUR PHONE ad.

I shrugged. "Pretend that you could ever want someone like me?"

He sobered, sitting up as though the seat had shot him in the ass. "Do you seriously think I don't?"

"Come on. You're just being...Camden."

His eyes lost their twinkle, brows drawing tight. "What does that mean?"

Mouth working soundlessly, unease crept down my spine. "I'm sorry. I don't mean that in a bad way. Just that you're a natural flirt, and you're being nice to the poor townie girl, taking pity on me. I get it. You dragged me along because you guys felt bad about what happened yesterday."

He blinked at me. "Maggie, I don't even know what to say to that. I mean, yeah, I feel like an asshole, more so than most days, but that's not why you are here with us. This may shock you, but the only reason I haven't seriously made a play for—"

"Hey, good seats!" Jamey squeezed past us, followed by Ben.

"Oh, hell no." Mason kicked Camden's boot with his own. "I'm not sitting next to Ben. He's gonna be sucking face the whole time, and neither of you respect armrest boundaries. Get up."

Camden ground his jaws together as he leaned in to say, "You couldn't be more wrong, Maggie." Keeping his gaze locked with mine, Camden sat on my other side.

"Wrong about what?" An ICEE tanker appeared in my cup holder. What the...? Mason's arms were full of little boxes and a bag of fluffy popcorn.

Reaching for the Junior Mints and popcorn, Camden answered, "Maggie has some ideas that need to be dispelled. I was telling her that she's with us today because we think she's a kick-ass chick and not our charity case."

Mason's gaze cut to me. "Did she hear you, or do I need to reiterate that?"

"I'm good." *Thump. Thump.* Two boxes of candy landed in my lap. My gaze crawled back up to Mason as he handed out the rest. "Did you rob the display?" I balked.

One brow angled high as he blindly chucked the Milk Duds to Jamey with eerie precision. "This is what happens when you don't tell me what snacks you like. Next time, give me an answer, or I'll buy one of each again."

My mouth hinged open.

Pleased with himself, Mason settled into the seat next to me and opened a pack of gummy bears—a pack of gummy bears that were priced at four times what they were at Henry's.

"I don't want you to pay for me," I whisper-hissed.

Those moss-rimmed eyes seemed to glow brighter as the overhead lights dimmed, and then he dipped close, so close that his lips brushed the shell of my ear. Suddenly, there was a knot in my throat, and I couldn't swallow.

"And I don't want you to pay, period. It's gonna be fun seeing who wins that war." A bag appeared under my nose. "Have a bear. Rip his head off. You'll feel better."

Squinting at him, I grabbed three.

Okay, I knew two things.

One, I loved the movies. We could have watched a French film without subtitles, and I would have enjoyed it as much as aliens taking over the Earth. Honestly, I didn't care.

Two, Mason required an ungodly amount of room to sprawl out. The dude's knees must have knocked against mine every minute, shoved candy in my face every two minutes, and he wasn't the only one who didn't respect armrest boundaries.

Before I realized it, the movie was over, the house lights were on, and a large hand was wrapped around mine again. I wasn't sure if this hand-holding thing meant something, or Mason was concerned that I couldn't get down the stairs without guidance. Probably the latter. And it was either the diabetes-inducing amount of sugar I had consumed or the fact Mason was holding my hand, but I was jacked.

"That was awesome!" I crowed. "The alien's head blew up all over the place! It literally stuck to the ceiling. And did you see how the pilot got that trick shot with the switch? Man, and the bomb they planted in the ship? Genius."

"Jesus, Sticks." Mason chuckled, pulling me outside as the crisp ocean breeze lifted my hair. "You act like you've never been to the movies before."

"I haven't."

Everyone stopped dead then and there and turned to stare at me. Mason dropped my hand, mouth agape.

"What?"

"Holy shit." Camden grabbed his hair in both hands, short brown strands sticking up between his fingers. "No fucking way. You've never been to the movies?"

"No…"

Ben's head tilted, brows inching together. "How is that possible?"

"I don't know. I just— Stop looking at me like that. It's not that weird."

Squaring off with me, Mason folded his arms. "Oh, it's weird. You've never been to a birthday party, never bowled, never been to the movies, and your knowledge of pop culture is appalling. Are you from Earth?"

Jamey snorted.

Okay, he made good points, and with everyone staring at me like I was a chemistry project gone awry, I wasn't exactly feeling normal here. I may as well roll with it.

"Well, you found out my secret, boys. I'm really an extraterrestrial sent here to examine the finest human male specimen, but you guys were the best I could find. My overlords are extremely disappointed and want me to return to the mothership tomorrow."

Camden shoved his way closer to me. "You tell your overlords you haven't seen our dicks yet, and you need more time for a proper evaluation. We'll be happy to show you."

Mason threw his palm onto Camden's chest to stop him. "Dude, I'm all in for show and tell, but I'm not down with probing."

Camden immediately sobered. "Good point."

Laughing, Mason grabbed my right hand this time and pulled me along to the parking lot. "Come on. Let's get home. I'm starving."

"How is that possible? You just ate a convenience store."

Once we were back on the highway, I noticed the Land Rover was absent, and we were taking the roads slower this time. I wasn't complaining. I rested against Mason's back and soaked up every second we had together.

I turned to look at the Pacific and its gleaming waves as they licked the horizon. It was rare for me to leave Crescent Cove, and it made me wonder if OHU hadn't been damaged by that mudslide, would I have done things like this? Ride on the back of a motorcycle, take a day off work, go to the movies? Or would I have been the paranoid, workaholic I was now? Still stuck in survival mode?

Pressed against Mason, his back to my chest with my legs wrapped around his thick thighs, my hands were outstretched along that rippled eight pack. This had been the perfect afternoon. I wanted more of this, more of these stolen moments with him. Like this morning when we were tangled together in bed. I was inexperienced, yes, but it didn't seem innocent. And neither did this ride on Matt's Harley since the ache I'd felt hours ago was back with a vengeance.

As the scenery changed and the bluffs along Hacienda Trail whizzed by, disappointment began to gnaw at me, and that feeling only worsened as we passed the beach houses on the cliffs. They had the best view in Crescent Cove, and I'd wondered what owning a home there would be like, waking up to the ocean waves, having my own private stretch of sand below that Poker and I could run along every day...

Well, I didn't have to wonder. It would be hella awesome.

The bike stopped at the light on Midland Lane, ending my fantasy. Taking a second to stretch my back, I spotted something black and white in the left mirror, in the lane next to ours. Dread drove a hard spike into my stomach as fear caused my heart to ricochet between my spine and sternum. *Oh, God.* Pinching my eyes shut, I spun my helmeted head the other way and plastered myself against Mason like a remora fish to a shark.

I hadn't had a chance to read the number on the front bumper of the PPV, so I didn't know who was behind the wheel. No doubt, if it was my father, the siren would be blaring in my ear right now. And lucky me, we happened to be sitting at the longest light in town.

Mason's feet finally shifted, and the bike righted. I risked another peek to the mirror. My heart was thumping so hard, I was sure Mason could feel it. The Tahoe pulled up behind us.

Nearing Crescent Lake Estates, the PPV stayed on top of us, never relenting in distance. Mason pulled into his neighborhood, and the Tahoe went straight, but it wasn't until we were in Mason's driveway that I could take a normal breath.

Hopping off the bike, I removed my helmet. My words were jumbled and rushed as they fell out of my mouth. "Who was it, Mason?"

Still seated, he rubbed his side, somewhat oblivious that I could be facing certain death today. "I think you bruised my kidney."

"Seriously. Who?"

"The cop?" I nodded frantically, and he shrugged all casual like as if my life wasn't hanging in the balance. He withdrew my purse out of the saddlebag. "Not sure. The older guy?"

"Oh." My hand wrapped around the strap of my purse. I assumed the "older guy" meant Gil, and he might say something to my father. Gil had kids and—

"It's kind of impossible to tell who you are with the jacket and helmet, but... Does it matter?" Mason asked, locking our helmets away.

"I... I'm supposed to tell my father where I am and who I'm with. I'm not allowed to be out with you, and I definitely shouldn't be anywhere near a motorcycle."

His brows flew high, voice full of indignation. "Hold up. You're not *allowed* to be out with *me*?"

I cringed. Wow, I was sucking in communications today. "I didn't mean it like that." My gaze tipped down, unsure of what to say to make this right. "My father's...not a fan of anyone but Jamey, for obvious reasons. He's overprotective."

Mason gave an aggravated shake of his head. "I apologize for putting you in such a terrible position where fun was involved." His leg swung over the bike, faster and wider than necessary, forcing me to move out of his way. "Forgive me. I won't do anything like that again."

I curled my hand around his arm to stop him, desperate for him to understand, but there was no way to explain it. "Mason, I would do today all over again in a heartbeat. It's— He's strict and..." I lowered my chin as a rush of unexpected shame clogged my throat. "I don't have fun. I go to school. I go to work. I go home. I have one friend. If anything deviates from that, it has to be preplanned. Discussed at length. It's exhausting."

His bicep turned rigid beneath my hand. "Weird, because this whole time I thought you had more than one friend."

His harsh tone forced me to look into those sharp citrine and peridot hues as they bored right through me.

"I'm sorry. You're right." I muttered, "See? I'm a spaz."

"I really hate that *fucking* word," he ground out, and then he was in my face before I could blink. My breath caught, getting stuck in my already tight throat. "And I really hate that you call yourself that. We had a deal that I'd *never* hear you say it again. I never saw you that way, Maggie."

I released his arm as I shrunk into his leather jacket, drawing it tighter around me. "How do you see me?"

At my question, Mason's entire demeanor relaxed, inching closer, so the tips of his boots met my sneakers, his heat radiating all around me. "I think you're loyal and kind. You're innocent and sweet. Maggie, you're more be—"

Before the next syllable could fall, Ben's Rover pulled up, and Mason's lips compressed into a thin line.

Seriously? He was going to stop and leave it there? As if to answer me, he turned and occupied himself with the Harley.

Son of a bitch.

Loyal and kind. Innocent and sweet. Those were qualities that could be attributed to a puppy.

I followed the guys inside the house, and the second we were through the door, Poker sped across the living room and received a greeting from everyone. As I straightened the couch pillows that I suspected had been moved by my four-legged friend, a ferocious growl trickled into the air, and my heart stuttered. I whipped around as Poker rose onto his hind paws, the front two slamming into Mason's chest. Mason went down.

Panic shuttled down my spine as I raced across the room. "Oh, God! Poker! No! Get…" My words came to a stop when I realized he wasn't making an afternoon snack out of Mason. Poker was…pouncing. Like a deranged bunny rabbit. I'd never seen him move that way before. He sprung backward when Mason reached for him, and then he pounced forward where he was just outside of Mason's reach. His tail was loose and wagging, eyes keen and body fluid but ready for his next move.

Poker was…playing.

As he jumped onto Mason's stomach, Mason flipped him onto the floor. Poker was quick to get out of the hold and then pinned Mason. This happened another half-dozen times.

They both looked so young, so carefree…

It was completely dumb and girly, but the back of my eyes pricked with heat. How could I not see what Poker had been missing? Someone to play with. Someone that he didn't have to protect, be careful with, be on guard for twenty-four/seven. He needed a buddy.

On the floor, both boys were sprawled out and breathing hard. Mason's gaze found mine. "Sticks, since I gave you the day off, I'm making lunch. Peanut butter and jelly?"

I did my best to shut my emotions down as I forced a smile. "Don't hurt yourself."

Grinning wide, Mason popped to his feet and swiped a hand over his scruff to remove the dog hair. Poker stood, too, and followed Mason, not leaving more than a foot between them.

I swore those were hearts in his eyes.

Mason eyed me as he situated himself at the kitchen sink. "Sit your ass down. You're about to have the worst PB and J ever in the history of PB and Js. I need another medal." He ran his face and hands through a quick wash.

As the guys drifted into the kitchen, I took a stool. "Shouldn't it be the best PB and J ever?"

Scoffing, Mason dried his face and hands on a paper towel. "I'm pretty amazing, Sticks, but I know my limitations. Cooking is one of them."

"There's actually no *cooking* required. Assembly only. How have you been making them this entire time?"

"Smartass." Grinning, Mason threw the paper towel in the trash. "You're trying to get out of making me another Maggie Medal. It won't work 'cause I'm gonna guilt you into it."

"No doubt."

He disappeared into the pantry and returned with two containers. "Creamy or chunky?"

I screwed up my face. "Creamy. I don't like nuts."

"Fuck! It's over!" Camden planted his forehead on the island. "Just when I thought she was perfect for me, that we were meant to be... I can't be with a girl who doesn't like nuts."

I rubbed his back, and Camden smirked at me.

After we ate, Jamey thought it would be a good idea for us to watch *Top Gun*, and that was when I learned it was a movie. I was going to watch two movies in one day. *Two.*

Ben and Jamey snuggled up on the loveseat, and Camden hogged one half of the couch, leaving Mason and me to fight over the other half. While Mason was busy in the kitchen, I considered his refusal to sit next to Camden in the theater. I took the small slice of real estate next to his cousin, sitting in the middle again as the buffer.

It didn't take long before Poker was done getting a lap of ice water and padded his way over. I held my hand out to pet him, but his nose went right to Camden's crotch.

"Oh, my God. Poker, stop!" I dragged him away, cringing. "I'm sorry, Camden. He's usually well behaved."

Camden chuckled, scrubbing Poker's head. "You can't blame the little guy for checking out the only true male in the room."

Ben snorted. "Please."

Camden ignored his brother. "Besides, you gotta admire him for using second base in lieu of a greeting." He winked at me. "He's got moxie. I like that. You could learn something from Poker, Maggie."

"That shit ain't gonna happen," Mason said, carrying two glasses of bubbly soda. One was a Coke, and he held out the other to me that I would guess was Sprite from the bar downstairs. My glass was filled two-thirds of the way and had a straw. Mason's glass was full to the brim and didn't have a straw.

The Scott's didn't own straws. I would know being that I'd organized and cleaned every drawer and shelf of their home.

My gaze tracked back to my soda, to the bobbing red plastic that…looked like the one from the theater. Mason had brought that here. For me. He probably didn't want me to spill my drink, which I had with my juice this morning, but still. How could such an insignificant gesture make me feel so special? And he remembered what I had told him about caffeine making my tremor worse…

My chest felt uncomfortably tight as I accepted the chilled glass. "Thank you."

"My pleasure."

The couch hog balked, "Where's mine?"

A dark brow lifted at Camden as Mason took the glass from me after I pulled a sip off the straw. It was Sprite.

"In the fridge, lazy ass," Mason answered. "Thanks for leaving such a generous amount of room on the sofa, by the way."

"My pleasure," Camden threw back.

Grumbling, Mason settled on my other side, but his weight dipped the cushion, and I went nose-first into his shoulder. "Oof."

His body vibrated with a chuckle. "You okay?"

I pushed myself to a sitting position by planting one hand on a rippled stomach and the other on a thigh as thick as a tree trunk. "Peachy."

Still laughing, his arm went up and rested on the back of the couch, creating more room for me. "Here, we'll share since Cam's in selfish mode right now."

"I always sit like this on the couch," Camden commented.

"He does." Ben added, "But I'll caution you, Mags. There's one less layer of clothing between you and Cam than you might assume."

My brows rose in question, and Mason cursed under his breath.

"There's nothing wrong with going commando," Camden argued. "My boys need to breathe."

The meaning finally landed. I was much too close to Camden's boys than I ever wanted to be.

I burrowed into Mason, and he stiffened. Before mortification set in at having done that, his arm lowered, tucking me possessively to his side. Mason's hand curled around my thigh. I might have been a wee bit grateful for Camden's boys now.

Mason growled over my head, "If I see one digit near your groin to scratch or adjust, I'll break it off. You'll scar her for life."

Camden's gaze bounced between himself and Mason. "She's closer to your balls than she is mine."

That I was, but it didn't stop me from planting my head on a very yummy chest. "Can we stop talking about balls," I begged.

"You wanna talk about dicks? Vaginas? Asses? I'm an equal-opportunity conversationalist."

I picked up my head to be met by Camden's eyes, alight with amusement. "I'm really good with not talking," I said dryly.

He shrugged a broad shoulder. "Your loss."

Mason grabbed the remote. "She'll get over it." A few menus and remote clicks later, the movie started. The hand on my thigh hadn't moved yet.

At first, I thought *Top Gun* was just an action movie about naval pilots, but then Maverick was losing his loving feeling to Charlie, which clued me in to this movie being about something more. However, I needed a moment to get over the fact that Movie Charlie was both blonde and Mason's sorta-kinda ex's name. And yeah, when the love scene started, I felt all kinds of awkward. Seemingly, I was the only one who was uncomfortable, and I struggled to appear chill as if I had watched movies like this lots of times.

I totally hadn't.

Snuggled up against Mason, I worked to control my breaths while I watched a half-naked man—who bore strikingly similar characteristics Mason—tongue and writhe against Movie Charlie, who thankfully, didn't look anything like Lingerie Model Charlie.

I weirdly began to wonder how Mason had sex and what I would prefer.

The hard and fast kind that made girls pray out loud, or sweet and gentle to the tunes of Berlin, backlit in blue with drapes billowing in the breeze.

I think I would like both, but the latter…the latter looked nice.

The hand on my thigh had, in fact, moved several times throughout the movie, making its way higher. There had been the post-stretch hip rest, the casual drumming on my stomach during the volleyball scene, and lastly, the after-Coke readjustment. Currently, his thumb was drawing a design high on my ribcage with my heart rate well into the "Danger Zone."

I risked peeking up at him beneath my lashes, and Mason appeared relaxed, but the longer I watched him, I realized his jaw was locked, gaze far too intense, and his hand—the one that wasn't drawing little swirls on me—was wrapped around a now empty soda glass, knuckles white.

Maybe he was stiff and achy, and that was why he looked like he was about to break the glass. Did he want me to move and was too nice to say it? That wasn't likely. No, Mason would pick my ass up and—

A figure eight. His thumb was drawing a figure eight or…*an infinity sign*. This…this was what he was always drawing on me? How did I not notice it until now?

His thumb made wider strides over my shirt, the strap of my bra, the very edge of my breast. *Holy Moses.*

The hum of the garage door opening blended with the jet noises from the movie's dog fight, and Mason didn't make any move to get off the couch or stop his thumb. Ben hit the pause button as Mr. and Mrs. Scott wheeled their luggage inside.

Camden vaulted up to help Mrs. Scott with the one bag that Mr. Scott wasn't carrying.

"Oh, thank you, Cam," she said, scanning the room. "Hey, everyone."

I stilled as if that would make me invisible. Without Camden sprawled out next to me, taking up half the couch, there was no feasible reason as to why I was all but sitting in Mason's lap. And there was no way to explain why I hadn't done my job but had time to watch two movies while having infinity signs drawn a centimeter from my boob with their son's thumb.

Wow, that sounded horribly bad.

And as a black and tan body trotted past the couch with tags jingling away, the situation got worse. I hadn't once considered what Mr. and Mrs. Scott would think of me bringing my dog here.

I fought to get up, stop Poker from sniffing Mr. Scott's crotch, but *someone* had me pinned to the freaking couch.

"Mason," I whisper-hissed my plea, but it went ignored.

"Hey, who is this furry guy?" Mr. Scott knelt to pet my dog.

"I'm so sorry, Mr.—"

"He's the infamous Poker." Mason cut off my apology, yanking me back down after I successfully gained an entire inch away from him.

"Wait." Mr. Scott straightened, head periscoping toward me. "*This* is Poker?" I meekly nodded. His head shook and then repeated it to himself in statement form. "Why did you need so much money for him…that day?"

When we referred to Earring-gate, it was always *that* day.

"For his food. He's on a hypoallergenic diet that I have to special order, and it's expensive."

Mr. and Mrs. Scott stared at each other for a long moment before Mrs. Scott burst into laughter, garnering Poker's attention. "We thought you were involved in some illegal gambling ring."

Okay, still a strange assumption to make. "I'm sorry I brought him here. I—"

"You have nothing to be sorry for, sweetie," Mrs. Scott assured me, wiping a tear from her eye. "But the more we learn about you, the more we realize how little we know about you."

Believe me, that's for the best.

I waved to the lack of food on the counter. "I didn't make dinner or—"

"Good," Mr. Scott broke in. "You should be resting after a grand mal."

Wait. He knew?

"How much did she argue?" Mrs. Scott asked.

"Wasn't too bad. Either I'm wearing her down, or I caught her on an off day." Mason stretched, and the arm trapping me lifted to the back of the couch.

An array of emerald, sapphire, and citrine met mine, a mixture of his sons' eyes as if the colors had been divvied up between Matt and Mason. "How are you feeling?"

My cheeks burned hot as the attention returned to me. "Uh...okay." Now free, I tried to shift away from Mason, but the cushion had sucked me in. "Thank you for asking."

Mrs. Scott mindlessly ruffled Poker's coat. I could only cringe as I watched a million dog hairs sprinkle the floor. "So you're having seizures about once a month?"

"No—"

"Try once a week," Jamey answered from the loveseat.

I shot him a look to shut his yapper, and he gave me one that promised he would do no such thing. "He's exaggerating, but lately, I've had more than usual."

Mr. Scott's brows knitted with concern. "I'm grateful you were on the bed when it happened. A hit on the head would be extremely dangerous for anyone, but you..."

The bed...? Gasping, I looked to Mason, remembering that Jamey had to bathe me. I must have soiled the bedding, too. "I'm sorry."

That earned me a don't-be-dumb look. "Yes, you should apologize for having an uncontrollable disorder that gives you sporadic seizures."

Well...some people did expect me to apologize.

Mason twisted in the sofa, his knee skimming up the length of my thigh. "Dad, did you have a chance to talk to Uncle Will?"

"I did." Mr. Scott shot me an uncomfortable glance. "I'll tell you about it tonight."

That was weird. Or maybe it wasn't. I wasn't entitled to anything personal that pertained to the Scotts, and whatever Mr. Scott had spoken to his brother about was certainly none of my business.

"How was the trip?" Ben asked, changing the subject.

"Ah…" Mr. Scott and his wife shared an anxious look. "Hell, you'll hear soon enough."

Mr. Scott plunked onto the couch next to me and patted the cushion for Poker to join him. Poker sprang at the invite, and I sighed. Man, it was going to take an entire lint roller to remove his hair from this fabric.

"Richard got engaged," Mr. Scott said. "The wedding will be in Grove Point, the week before Christmas, and he wants you guys to be in the wedding."

While everyone reacted to that news with little to no enthusiasm, Mason leaned down to whisper, "Rich is my oldest cousin."

I wasn't sure why that affected me so much, but I loved that Mason took a moment to ensure I was included, especially after feeling excluded a minute prior.

"They want *all* of the cousins in the wedding?" Ben asked.

Mrs. Scott nodded. "She has a lot of bridesmaids."

Camden's question chased a yawn. "What's Brielle's parents do again? They're into booze of some sort, right?"

"Wine," Mason offered. "They own the Young Winery vineyard in Grove Point. The estate is pretty nice for events, too. They having the wedding there?"

His parents confirmed.

Ben ran a hand through his hair. "They just got engaged. Isn't it a bit sudden for a wedding? That's only two months from now."

Mr. and Mrs. Scott traded another look. Mrs. Scott smiled, but it didn't reach her eyes. "I guess she has a thing for winter weddings and didn't want to wait until next year." Her head snapped over to the guys, panic sinking into her voice. "When is Mutton Chop Month again?"

"November, we're good," Mason reassured her.

"What is Mutton Chop Month?" Jamey and I asked in unison.

"The entire football team grows mutton chops for a month," Camden explained. "It's our take on No Shave November."

I couldn't hide my horror at imagining Mason's handsome face covered by badger strips. "Why mutton chops?"

"Wolverines," Camden clarified.

"Yeah…?" I prompted because in no way did Camden clarify anything with that.

Mason chuckled. "I need to make a freaking pop culture reference guide for you. The comic character Wolverine has mutton chops, so we grow them, too."

Camden rocked back on his heels. "Don't worry, Maggie. I assure you that my sex appeal will not be affected by facial hair."

"That's such a relief."

He winked at me and tacked on what I was sure he believed was a sexy grin. Okay, it was sexy, but he was wasting it on me.

"Aaaand that needs to stop." Mason all-out glared at his cousin. Camden's smirk grew.

What was that about?

"Dad, do you mind if I take the Lexus? Matt still has my truck, and I've gotta get Sticks and Poker home." "You don't have—"

I swiveled to Mason. "You don't have—"

Keys were already being handed over, and Mason shot to his feet, bringing me with him like I was a sack of cotton balls. "It's happening. Get your stuff."

"He's right, Maggie," Mr. Scott concurred. "I don't want you going home alone after an event like that."

I opened my mouth, then shut it. There was no point in arguing. I'd never win. Mason collected Poker's bowls and food while I grabbed my bags from upstairs.

With a goodnight to everyone, Mason and I piled inside Mr. Scott's SUV, and Poker hung out in the back, head out the window. Shockingly, Mason didn't put any music on, and he hadn't during the drive last night either. His music choice varied depending on his mood.

No music? No clue.

Once I waved goodnight to Bernard and received a scowl in return, Mason finally spoke.

"I know it's none of my business, but why isn't that cash in a bank?" His chin jutted to the back where my duffel was. Dammit. I knew I should have left it behind so Jamey could take it home with him. I hadn't because I figured that would raise questions with Ben, and it wasn't right to put Jamey in a position that he'd have to lie to his boyfriend.

I squirmed in the passenger seat while searching for an answer. "You never know when the Great Depression could hit again. I might try stuffing it inside my walls."

"Or you could stuff your Beanie Boos instead."

I blinked up at him. "You remember that?"

"I remember everything."

No, you don't.

Not about to let it go, he urged, "So…?"

My head hit the seat while I drummed up my next lie. "The bank is on Midland. Not exactly a quick trip if I'm in a pinch for cash. Besides, there's no place safer than a cop's house."

He eyed me sideways. "Yeah, but it was at Jamey's house."

Shitballs. I'd slipped. Epically so.

My voice was surprisingly steady, but inside, I was struggling to stay afloat among a sea of lies. "Well, it was at my house. That's my overnight bag that I like to keep at Jamey's, and I accidentally left the envelope in the bag when I packed. I keep forgetting to take it home."

His jaw tensed as if he were holding back words he was desperate to say. "Okay, so let's talk about the other stuff in there because we both know there's a hell of a lot more than money and overnight shit in that bag. Why do you need all of that?"

The lie tasted like ash in the back of my throat. "You're not the only one preparing for the zombie apocalypse."

His jaw clamped down again, the tendons in his neck straining. "You should probably pack a knife then."

Guilt tugged at my chest. "Great idea."

So, no music meant a Maggie inquisition. Good to know.

"Sticks, why haven't you ever been to the movie theater? I mean, that's completely weird."

My gaze stayed glued to the passing landscape, my skin growing uncomfortably tight and itchy. "I'm sure my father took me when I was younger, but I don't remember it. Memory loss, if you haven't caught on, is another side effect of brain trauma." Not a total lie.

My next thought hit me like a bullet and had me bolting up in my seat. "I forgot my bike."

Mason threw out a careless shrug. "Gives me an excuse to bring it by tonight."

That was so not happening, and we'd gone too far on Canyon to suggest he swing around and go back. "No. I'll get it tomorrow but thank you."

"I could pick you up in the morning," he offered cheerfully.

"Mason…" I chided.

Hands clenching the wheel, he grumbled, "It was just an idea."

"And I appreciate it. I do, but—" Mason had reached Verde Way, and he wasn't stopping. Holy fuck, he really wasn't stopping. "Mason, pull over here."

"No," he growled and released a slow breath as if to calm himself, but his shoulders remained up by his ears. "I'm taking you home."

Unease bubbled in my gut, quickly turning to roiling panic. "No. Mason, pull over."

He sped up. "Sure. As soon as you tell me exactly how you are going to carry fifty pounds of dog food and your *overnight bag* home."

With an audible huff, I folded my arms.

"That's what I thought."

My lips pinched together. "Is there ever going to be an argument that you will let me win?"

There wasn't a response until he took the bend. "I'll make you a deal. You tell me something *real* about Maggie Davis, and I promise that I will let you win the next argument."

I gaped at him. "I tell you real stuff all the time."

His shoulder lifted unapologetically. "Then this shouldn't be hard for you."

Mulling that over, I nibbled my lower lip and then stopped once the pain reminded me it was still swollen and tender. "I prefer cake to pie."

"Ah, see?" He grinned that annoyingly boyish smile at me. "That was painless."

The woods opened before us, the two abandoned homes up ahead, plus the one in the middle that was not so obviously occupied aside from the black and white Tahoe. I didn't have the cover of night, so it was all out in the open for his viewing displeasure.

Humiliation gripped me, and I refused to look anywhere but my lap. The SUV stopped on the gravel, and since I didn't hear gunshots yet, I figured Mason would get out of here alive. Me? Not sure.

Mason hopped out of the cab to gather my bags, dog bowls, and food from the back before I could. Poker jumped down and waited for me on the edge of the carport.

Mason headed right for the house, and I sprinted in front of him to block him before he did something completely idiotic, like go inside.

"Please," I begged. "Please, don't make me ask you."

I couldn't look him in the eye, but I imagined Mason was staring over my head, to my house. The longer he stood there not speaking, the more my chest filled with shame until I was choking on it.

This was nothing like where he came from. This was another planet. He had wrought iron gates that didn't so much as squeak. I had a redwood forest filled with creepy crawlies, and all they did was make noise. He had streets lined with pavers. I had a dirt road. He had a two-story home with gorgeous landscaping, flowerbeds, and a lakeshore view. I had a shack with mud and patches of crabgrass where the sky was rarely seen.

He set my things at my feet.

Locking my stare onto his boots, I said, "Mason, I know how sad this will sound, but this was the best day of my life. Thank you."

"Sticks." He made a noise that suggested his hand was running over his thick scruff. "Please, look at me."

I couldn't, but I caught the deep rise of his chest before he blew out a sigh that stirred the hair at my ruined temple. It was taking all I had not to wrap myself around him, hold onto him, keep him with me.

"Maggie, what you don't possess, where you live, the struggles you've endured has given you an empathy few have. Life has uniquely shaped you to become someone who has more heart and goodness than anyone I know. That is never something you should feel ashamed of. I admire you. I'm proud to call you my friend. You make me want to be a better man. There is no greater compliment I could give you."

With that, his boots disappeared, and the engine turned over. I stood, unmoved for an entire minute feeling Mason's heavy gaze lingering before the tires began to spin away. Without picking up my eyes, I hauled everything into my arms and lugged the load toward the side door.

I didn't know what to expect from him this time. I had left a note for my father when I'd snuck in last night, but there was the glaring fact I hadn't *stayed* home. Not only that, Mason drove me. Twice. He'd beaten me for that last week.

But the worst…? Yeah, the worst of humanity stands on the other side of the law. Hiding in plain sight. In this town. The head of the blue snake.

My legs wobbled as I turned the knob.

One step inside the laundry room, I stopped dead in my tracks. Hanging there, plain as day so I wouldn't miss it was the dry cleaning bag. His uniforms.

When I went downtown yesterday morning, I'd been so distracted over the kiss and that stupid brownie lasagna that it hadn't occurred to me what day it was. It had been Sunday. Uniform Day. And this morning, when I'd called Frankie about the basket before we left for the pharmacy, I hadn't thought about them then either.

I'd forgotten. And he made sure I knew I'd forgotten.

"Good evening, sir," I greeted him as I approached the recliner, his gaze tracking me. "I'm sorry about not picking up your uniforms. With everything going on, I did forget, and I apologize. I'll do better next time."

He didn't speak, but his icy glare felt like stingers on my skin, the poison coiling low in my gut.

"I'll get your dinner going, sir."

I set my bags inside my room and returned to fill Poker's food and water. Expecting the worst, I set the bowls outside to keep him safe.

While making dinner, I washed the cookware and utensils I used along the way, never leaving more of a mess than necessary, and then cleaned up from the night before. I served his plate and put foil over mine.

Getting his uniform ready for tomorrow, I heard the fork hit the ceramic in a final *plink*, and the recliner cranked up. The clinking sound of a whiskey bottle versus glass was the fourth count since I'd been home.

I returned to the kitchen, and as I picked away the foil from my dinner to microwave it, he called over from the next room in a slurred voice, "Did you have a pleasant sleepover at the richies?"

A breath rattled through my chest as I re-covered my plate.

"No, sir." I rooted my feet at the edge of the linoleum, unwilling to go any further. "I had a seizure yesterday afternoon, and I didn't wake up until the middle of the night—"

Something in the way he gripped the whiskey glass cut me off, the room inexplicably dropping in temperature. He drew a sip. "So you had that boy drive you here to get the fucking dog, and then you went right back?"

"Yes, sir. I saw that you had company and—"

"Bullshit." He slammed the glass onto the side table, ice clacking together as the amber liquid spilled over the rim. "Do you think I'm fucking stupid? Do you think I don't know what you were doing over there?"

A cold sweat broke out at the nape of my neck. I opened my mouth and then closed it. I didn't ask what he thought I'd been doing. He would tell me.

The recliner lowered, frosty irises imprisoning mine. "You stayed the night to fuck him. Him or the brother. Maybe both."

Terror knotted my throat, my palms growing clammy. "I didn't."

His upper lip pulled back from his teeth. "Get over here and stop cowering in the kitchen."

My heartbeat was the only thing I could hear as I stepped toward him. My gaze swung to the new bottle that was half-filled. His eyes were glassed over, lids lowering in a squint. He poured another double, the precise amount without looking.

Lifting the tumbler to his lips, he downed the contents, never tearing his eyes away from me. "Take off your shirt."

I couldn't have heard that right. He had to have said something else. "Sir?"

"I spoke in plain. Fucking. English. Remove your shirt."

My stomach clenched and collapsed into itself. My pulse roared like the tides in my ears, breaths slicing through my lungs. He'd never asked me to do this before.

Legs tensing, my foot drew back, voice trembling. "No. I won't."

"TAKE IT OFF!" Spit dotted his lips, his chest rising and falling heavily, ready to attack.

My emergency bag and all the money I had was in my room. I'd never make it down the hall and back in time.

Poker's already outside. That was all that mattered.

In that moment, my mind went blank, and instinct took hold. Feet spinning, my legs carried me to the front door, an easier exit than through the laundry room. As I reached for the handle, he caught my arm. The room whirled, feet disappearing from beneath me. I landed in a heap, my back crashing into the coffee table. Twisting on the coarse carpet, I scrabbled to my feet and lunged for the laundry room with Poker's barks bleeding through the thin walls, nails scraping down the door as if he could dig through it.

Heavy steps and labored breathing closed in on me. Before I could grip the knob, five fingers bit into my forearm, wrenching me around to face him. He slammed my back against the door, the blinds bending so the sharp edges of aluminum sliced into my head and neck.

His nose smashed mine, whiskey breath like gasoline fumes in my nostrils. "You are going to regret that."

I struggled against his iron grip and tried to leverage enough space to knee him in the groin like the boys had taught me, but he hauled me back to the living room like I was nothing more than a squirming rodent that needed to be exterminated.

He whipped me around again, pulling me against him, forcing me to face him. "Keep fighting, and you're gonna get the lesson of your life!"

I stopped cold at that threat. There it was. I could see the triumph in his eyes. He knew he had me.

"Take. Off. Your. Shirt."

He released my arm and stood watching, waiting, his promise clear. I'd never survive another baton beating. I couldn't...I *couldn't* do it again.

I didn't think I could hate him more than I did right now. He probably knew that, too.

Gritting my teeth, I tore off my T-shirt and balled the material in my hand. I held my head high, glaring at him, doing nothing to hide my loathing for what he was. My mortal enemy.

Standing in front of him, so exposed, I tried to tell myself that my bra was no different than a bikini top. Thing was...I had never worn a bikini or had so little clothing on in front of anyone. This wasn't about humiliating me or controlling me. He was searching for something. Proof that I'd lied, given my body to someone. Maybe a stamp that read, MASON SCOTT WAS HERE.

It didn't make any sense to me why he was so intent on keeping me away from Mason. Even though he said I was too ugly for anyone to want, his paranoia ran deep. My body was the only evidence as to what his true beast looked like. And the only way he could get rid of the evidence was to get rid of me.

Except for his heaving chest, he didn't move for what seemed like an eternity. Then he spoke two words. Two words broke through the wall of rage I'd built, and they blasted it to dust. Only he had that power.

"The pants."

Tears speared the back of my eyes, fear seizing my lungs. Bile crawled up my throat, and before I could stop, the word tumbled out. "No."

He spun me with incredible speed, my brain swirling, feet stumbling beneath me. The impact of his palm on my backside jarred my spine, skin stinging with an incomprehensible mixture of fire and ice.

He knew not to hit my face, not even wasted. He knew never to leave a mark that couldn't be covered.

His grip on my arm released, looming over me, breaths hot on my bared skin. Panic poured over me, sinking deep into every muscle, immobilizing my mind. Dear God, this couldn't be happening. This couldn't be my life.

My hands wouldn't work, and he just stood there, unyielding and cold. I couldn't be sure how much time had passed before my trembling fingers managed to flick the button open and then slipped my jeans down much slower than with my shirt. A fresh chill swept over my exposed skin, and my fingers screwed into the thin fabric of the shirt balled in my hand as if it could somehow keep me safe.

It couldn't.

Nothing would.

I hadn't lifted my head since he spanked me, and the tears were now streaming in rivulets off my nose, splashing onto my sneakers. I shook violently as he circled me, his rank breath harsh on my collarbone, shoulders, and then neck. I was vulnerable, so pathetic. He could do whatever he wanted to me. We both knew it.

"Bend over the recliner."

My mouth went dry as my insides turned to liquid. Movements far too stiff, a whimper caught in my throat. I shuffled to the chair and leaned over the arm, fabric scratching and poking into my flesh. I was facing his open whiskey bottle; the little alcohol that had spilled earlier had made wet rings on the wood. I wasn't sure why I noticed that, probably because I'd be expected to clean those later.

I didn't know how far he would take this. I shouldn't have left my pants around my ankles. I had trussed my own legs up for him. My arms were wrenched backward, eliciting a surprised gasp as he pinned them behind me. Dread skewered right through me, forcing a scream to build in my throat.

"You want to act like a whore?" he hissed. "Like your mother? Maybe I should start treating you like one."

My thighs snapped together and clasped tight. Eyes like new blades of grass came to my mind, long fingers threading through mine, Mason's arms holding—

The *smack* of his hand sounded before the pain registered. I let out a grunt from the sting zipping across my skin.

"You leave me no choice but to beat her out of you!"

I struggled to focus on Mason's chiseled features, the dark hair flopping over his brow, the dimples on either of his cheeks, the blue butterflies inked on his skin—

He struck again, harder, the flash of heat sinking deep. I bit into the fabric of the recliner to stop myself from crying out.

Angling over me, his weight pressed me into the chair. My shoulders howled in agony as he stretched me further. His shirt was touching my back, his jeans on the back of my thighs, the rough calluses of his hand causing my stomach to pitch.

"She whored herself for drugs. Pumped her body full of the shit. And then she left me with the house, the bills, and a damaged kid. And what does that kid do in return? Defies me at every turn."

I endured thirteen more. Each assault of his tongue was followed by a strike of his hand. It became harder to hold onto Mason's features like they were being erased with each hit. By the time he was done, I'd felt as if I'd been pulverized, mind and body, and I slumped into the chair. My arms went slack, vaguely aware my shoulders were on fire, my fingers having fallen asleep.

Without warning, my head was jerked back, each hair follicle straining against my scalp, and my legs wobbled as he dragged me to a standing position. I refused to look at him.

"You will remember my rules. You will stop testing me. In case you haven't figured it out, know this. You're never going to leave. *Never.*" He continued to stare at me, eyes scalding my skin that was on display for him. He released me, and I wouldn't doubt he had had a fistful of my hair in his hand. "Put your fucking clothes back on, whore."

I staggered and hobbled out of the room, not bothering to pull up my pants until I reached the hall. I went to my bathroom, shut the door, and locked it. As another wave of tears threatened to come, I climbed into the tub, still wearing my underwear and jeans, not bothering to remove my pad that I knew he'd seen. I was still holding my shirt as I turned the water all the way to H.

Water sputtered and choked out of the showerhead. I didn't care that it was ice cold and wouldn't warm for another few minutes. I wanted to wash him away, but no matter how much soap I used or how hot the water got, I could feel his stare clinging to me, the foulness embedded in my blood. I scoured my skin with the coarse pouf until it hurt, until I was raw. My ass was on fire, and I didn't care. I scrubbed harder and faster, hoping to see a river of blood at the bottom of the tub.

Thankfully, I had clean clothes beneath my sink and quickly put them on before dashing across the hall to get to my room. Once I shut the door, I crawled into bed, desperate to get Poker, but I was too scared to leave my room, too scared to move, too scared to make a sound. Shutting my eyes, I took my pillow from beneath my head and held it to my chest, imagining it was Mason, back in his bed, wrapped in his safety, his scent all around me.

It didn't work. I was here. In purgatory. And each repeated tinkle of the ice, the glass of the bottle against the tumbler, reminded me of that fact. Not long after he'd finished his whiskey, he shuffled down the hall, casting shadows beneath my door. I tensed, ready to slip out of bed, knowing there was nowhere to hide. The shadow slithered past, and then I heard the click of his door.

As my muscles began to relax into my mattress, my ears picked up a sound that was low and guttural as it seeped between our joined wall. Once it registered what it was, stark terror paralyzed me again. I was too scared to cover my ears, so I used my hands to stifle a cry. I didn't know how long I laid there, enduring those sounds, my eyes fixed on the door, on the lock that didn't work.

chapter forty-five

maggie

Waking before my alarm, my stomach growled, feeling no bigger than a desiccated pea inside my belly. I dragged myself into the kitchen, skin stinging and muscles aching with each step. I let Poker inside, and after he inspected every inch of me, he covered me in kisses as if he were apologizing for not protecting me last night.

I didn't want his apology, but I did soak up every kiss and snuggle he had for me. As I sat with him on the linoleum, I kept my back to the other room. To the recliner. To where *it* happened. I didn't want to see that room in the light of day. The only light it belonged in was one from a blazing fire.

After I got Poker settled, I threw away my dinner of pork chop and yams from last night that had sat on the counter. Next to it was an empty JD bottle, my not-so-subtle reminder to get another for him today. I wished I could hide a few bottles out in the woods for times like this to make it easier on myself, but that would mean I'd have to ask Henry, and he was already leery of selling me liquor.

By the time I'd walked to town to take care of the basket, my backside hurt worse than last night, the friction of my clothes chafing the tender welts. I had wanted to bring my emergency bag with me so Jamey could take it back to his house, but I couldn't manage the extra weight. That and Mason would notice. He would ask questions, and I would have no choice but to lie.

My best option was to bring the bag to the café at some point this weekend and ask Jamey to swing by and pick it up for me. In the meantime, I'd hidden the envelope of money behind my dresser with a slim hope that it would stay untouched.

As I stepped onto the university lot, I spotted Jamey huddled with the Scotts next to BB. An unexpected surge of an emotion I couldn't put a name to swelled in my lungs and threatened to suffocate me. I tried to focus, take deep and even breaths, but the sensation only worsened, slowly strangling me from the inside. I pushed my sunglasses up and fought like hell to keep it together.

But then it happened.

It took one smile from Mason to make my walls crumble. Every second of last night was on replay. There was only that recliner, the slapping, the breath on my skin, the moans...

I was so dirty. So tainted. So worthless.

"Sticks is here!"

I couldn't even muster a response. Shame. That was the emotion I couldn't put a name to. I felt so much shame that it had taken me by the throat. An ungodly amount of pressure inundated me, pain spearing into the back of my eyes.

Mason rocked back on his heels, two dimples on full display. "I slept like shit last night, and Dylan informed me over breakfast that I was a Cranky McCranky Pants. He thinks you should move into the RAM house, into my room. Make it easier on everyone."

Though I tried, words wouldn't form. There was no room, only that crippling shame. I swallowed, but it didn't work.

I didn't think there was a cool way to pull off running away from your group of friends, but I gave it my best shot.

"Mags?" Jamey called, voice chasing me. "Hey, wait up. You okay?"

I kept on, feet carrying me faster as I choked out, "Go away, Jamey. Please. I can't—"

His hand wrapped around my wrist and tugged me to an abrupt stop. Heat zinged along my shoulder that I couldn't help but flinch to.

Trying to pull out of his hold, I felt his stare all over me. "What did he do?"

"S—stop. Please. I'll lose it, and Mason will see." Everything and everyone blurred behind my sunglasses. I think my lips were wobbling, but I couldn't tell.

"So lose it," he urged. "Let him see already!"

I shoved Jamey off me. Hard. And the hurt on his face was too much. The shame had begun to eat away at my insides. The only time I was physically hostile was when I was preictal. We both knew I wasn't now, and it sickened me to think that I'd allowed an ounce of my father inside of me just then.

"I'm sorry," I rasped. "I didn't mean... When are you going to get it?" My voice cracked with my next words. "I have no power here, and my silence is the only thing keeping you safe. *All of you.*"

Heavier footsteps were nearing, and I knew who they belonged to. I had that pattern and sound engrained in my head and heart. My lungs were burning, the pressure demanding a release. I moved before my brain could give the command to my muscles, finding myself inside the bathroom as Mason's voice carried inside the closing door.

"Jamey, what happened? Is she okay? Sticks?"

"Mason, give her a—"

The door shut, and though the bathroom was empty, I locked myself in a stall. A breath lined with razor blades finally tore out of my throat. I wasn't sure how long I'd stayed, but it was enough time to exhaust an entire roll of toilet paper. After only the cardboard tube was left, I checked the time on my iPod and cursed. I had to get to class. I gave one last swipe to dry my face and thanked the bathroom gods for stocking the good TP.

I eyed the mirror as I washed up at the sink. I was a splotchy, swollen mess, and with my bruised lip, I looked like I'd run face-first into a wall. I slid my sunglasses back on to hide the worst of it. The guys had to be gone by now, so I opened the bathroom door and walked into the breezeway—

I slammed into something that resembled a wall. Stumbling backward, my ass hit the doorframe, and a new wave of pain sparked across the raw skin.

I hissed, "Shit.

Mason's lids popped wide, his palms flying up to face me. "Sorry. I guess I was hovering in your airspace there."

"A smidge." I shouldered my bag, eyeing the matching concerned looks from Jamey and Ben.

"It's just that—" Cringing, Mason ruffled his hair. "You were crying in there."

I went for the all convincing, "No, I wasn't."

Mason's brows popped high to call out my bullshit, and then he said it. "Bullshit."

I bit my tongue and looked down because I was floundering. I needed him to not be here. I needed him to not care. I needed him to not stare at me with those eyes, waiting for me to explain why I'd spent the last five minutes in the bathroom testing if Charmin really was two times more absorbent than other brands. Each second that ticked by, the closer I was to really losing my shit. Because apparently, I hadn't already.

"I am. I'm okay." Yeah, the snot building up in my nostrils made that super convincing.

I watched Mason's boots slide up to mine, and my gaze didn't rise any higher than his jeans. They were distressed and worn, and I knew he'd paid a premium price for them. It never made much sense to me. To *pay* someone to make your clothes look like you bought them off a poor townie. Like me.

The weight of my bag lifted from my shoulder, and Mason set it on the concrete. A large hand molded to my cheek, fingers threading through my hair and then around my neck. I squeezed my sore eyelids together and pinched my lips to keep them from trembling.

Sliding closer, Mason's other hand went to my lower back, cocooning me in his arms. Misery knifed into my chest, twisting the serrated edges until I felt utterly shredded. I should shove him away, run. But I didn't. I was so damn desperate for a speck of affection and safety.

Mason's mouth dipped to my ear, breaths warming my skin. "Let me take you out of here. We'll get some hot cocoa, drive to the bluffs and just sit." His voice was thick with concern, and a rush of tears stung the corners of my eyes. "I won't ask you a damn thing. You don't even have to talk. Just nod and let me do this for you."

With everything in me, I wanted to say yes. I needed him to hold me, make me forget, take all my dirty secrets and drown them, so I'd never have to think of them again. I leaned into him, soaking up his scent as if it would strip the memory from me. The words were right there, ready to spill from my mouth.

My father made me take off my clothes.

My father looked at me, too much of me.

My father touched himself after he touched me.

My teeth drove down into my tongue until I tasted a tinge of coppery metal. Mason's thumb stroked my cheek as his other hand made gentle circles along my back. My heart wrenched painfully, another emotional avalanche ready to drop. I drew away from him and kept my covered eyes down.

His chest lifted and fell, hands fisting at his sides. "Maggie, please. I want to help. Let me do something."

"Okay. I lied." *I'm going to lie to you now, and I hate it.* "I hurt my back again, and on top of that, I have horrible cramps, and everything from this weekend is catching up to me. It was too much all at once, but I'm better now. I promise."

Time seemed to stretch, and no one spoke or moved. The three of them weren't doing anything but staring at the top of my head.

Finally, Mason asked, "Fridge?"

There was an opportunity here, and I took it with both hands. I forced my chin up, evening my voice. "I slipped in the shower and hit my tailbone on the side of the tub."

"Sticks, I might have to come over and help you bathe from now on." A grin lifted one corner of his mouth, the bands of citrine in his eyes sparkling. "I'll do whatever is necessary for my running partner. How am I supposed to get ready for the next marathon I don't run?"

Ease filtered through me that this was going to be over, and I cocked my head at him. "You have a treadmill."

The grin promptly dropped. "It's not nearly the same and about as fun as watching two dudes make out."

Ben snickered, "I told you to stop watching. Perv."

Mason chuckled at his cousin, bestowing me with a full smile. "Besides, I like it when you kick my ass and emasculate me. It's good for my character."

I pushed his chest, feeling the contrast of the rigid muscles underneath the soft cotton of his Henley. "Go to class."

"Yes, ma'am." He gave me a salute and ran from me. Backward.

"Freak."

Laying on my stomach under the shade of the oak tree, the boys surrounded me as we dug into our lunch. I ignored that Jamey's pepperoni pizza was making my tummy all rumbly and fought against stealing a meaty circle as he made googly eyes at Ben. But I didn't ignore that he was wearing brand new Vans, and his wardrobe was beginning to match Ben's, or that his Ray-Bans were no longer knock-offs.

I was a horrible friend.

My yogurt container was suddenly snatched from my hand, hovering an inch away from my eyeballs.

"Make you a deal." Mason inched closer. The fabric of his jeans tickled my leg, and thoughts of waking up in his arms were at the forefront of my brain. "How about I save you from this evil and naughty Yoplait container, and in return, you do me a favor."

"Like what?"

His eyes were covered up by those damn sunglasses, but his voice was full of hope. "Go to my first game Friday."

My shoulders fell, disappointment gouging right through me. I would love nothing more than to sit in the bleachers and cheer for Mason, watching all the Scotts play football alongside him. I'd sit with Jamey, listening to what was sure to be inappropriate commentary about jockstraps and bulges for hours.

But that wasn't my reality.

My reality consisted of a father who exerted control over every aspect of my life and punished me when I tried to enjoy it. After what that man had done to me last night, I couldn't even look at him, let alone ask permission to go to a football game.

"I have to work Fridays."

"I know." Mason settled against me, shoulder bumping mine, his chocolaty scent competing with the freshly mowed lawn. "I thought maybe you could get the night off. The team kinda started to think of you as our unofficial lucky charm and wanted to see if having you there would help."

I lifted a brow. "I thought I was the water girl."

That earned me one dimple. "That, too."

"I can try," I lied somewhat convincingly. "That's all I can give you."

"I'll take it." Pleased with his efforts, Mason tapped the circumference of the yogurt lid and then once in the middle. He pried up the tab and then peeled the foil away with a careful tug. As the seal broke, a pale purple glob spit out onto his long finger. "Dammit," he complained, ripping the lid away. "I thought I had it that time."

"Yeah, I…"

My words died a sweet death as Mason brought his thumb to his mouth. A pink tongue darted out, licking the yogurt away. A breath hitched in my chest at the memory of where that tongue had been and how silky it felt when he tasted my neck like I was a dessert he couldn't get enough of. Those heated feelings I'd been holding back blasted through me, inundating my veins, warmth settling low in my belly.

I worked my throat, words coming out broken and croaky. "Yeah, that technique has a failure rate of ninety-two percent."

"Hmm. Well, knowing your love of yogurt, I'll have another chance." Mason handed the container back to me, completely unaware of what the simple act of opening a yogurt container could possibly do.

After school, Mason drove me to his house, and he went downstairs to work out. He said it was easier at home than at the fraternity since he wasn't allowed to exercise with the team, and most of the RAMs were on the team.

I wasn't complaining. Especially since Mason didn't wear shirts when he exercised.

I headed downstairs with a water pitcher and a glass of ice. Though the filter had been fixed a few weeks ago, I hadn't stopped bringing him water. Mason hadn't pointed out that it wasn't necessary, either.

"Thanks, Sticks." I hadn't announced myself because I hated disturbing him, but he must have heard me over the Pearl Jam streaming out of the speakers. Actually, ever since I came back to work for the Scotts, he didn't play it as loud as before. He stopped his leg presses and loped out of the gym. Chest heaving, beads of sweat dripped off his hair and slipped onto his broad shoulders, pectorals, abs, lower…

He downed the glass and then hit my earbud that bounced across my boob, bringing my attention back up to him. "Okay, what is it? I've gotta know what you're listening to."

"Rap," I quipped.

Dark brows hiked toward the ceiling, forcing more sweat to trickle down, getting caught in his scruff. "So you like the rhymes, huh?"

Shaking my head, I refilled his glass. "Not really. I can't keep up with the lyrics. My mouth doesn't move that fast. But I noticed a lot of nineties rappers wore baggy clothes, and, well, I thought that could be a style option I'd fit into. However, I don't own any big, heavy jewelry, and I'm pretty sure corn rolls are cultural appropriation, so I should probably just rethink this one."

A laugh burst out of him that sent all his abdominals rolling, and my hands itched touch every ridge and valley. "It's cornrows." With a shake of his head, his voice came deep and husky. "I'm glad you're my friend, Sticks. No one makes me laugh like you."

My smile was a bit tricky to muster. These days, *friend* sounded like another F-word to me.

With a wink, he drank down his second glass and returned to his machine, leaving me to watch every delectable muscle along his back flex.

Damn, that boy was fine.

Dinner was finished when Mrs. Scott arrived. She gave me a side hug as she complimented the chicken casserole, and we bid each other goodnight. Mason had turned on Aerosmith, which meant he was deep into his cardio, so I slipped out the front door.

Turned out it was a good thing I'd left my bike here the other night because I had to stop by Henry's anyway. Riding it would suck, but if I didn't, I might be late getting home. As I began rolling the bike down the driveway, I heard the front door slam shut.

"Hey!" Panting and still shirtless, Mason aimed right for me. "You didn't say goodbye." As he jogged over, I swore that was hurt drawn across his face.

I shrugged. "You and Steven Tyler sounded busy. I didn't want to interrupt."

He reached me in a few more strides. "I would never consider you an interruption. I want you to let me know when you're leaving." I couldn't help the whirl my heart did to those words. His hand landed on mine on the handlebar. "Come on. I'll take you home in the truck."

I tried to tug the bike out of his grip, but it was futile. "It's okay. I've got it."

He gave me a look. "You've been hobbling around all day, trying to make it seem like you aren't, and I lost count as to how many times you cringed after fifty-six. Your balance is for shit, and so is your tremor. Let me help."

It was impossible to hide my disappointment because I wanted nothing more than to spend a few more minutes with Mason. But I couldn't tell him that. "I've got an errand to run before I get home."

He inched closer, forcing my head to arch all the way back, that determined look in his eyes settling in. "Even more reason I should take you."

Sweat prickled along my upper lip as the lies formed on my tongue. "Not this time, Mason. I appreciate it, I do, but it's personal."

He still hadn't let go of my hand as he gave me a half-hearted smile. "How personal? I know when you get your period, and I've washed your bra. I've jumped those two embarrassing hurdles with ease. I can take another. What is it? Illegal Beanie Boo sale?"

That horrible pressure was back in my throat as my stomach churned with nerves. "You promised that you would let me have the next one. That was our deal."

In no time at all, the small quirk in his mouth fell, a stony gleam filling his eyes. "Jesus, Sticks. I mean…Christ." His hand whipped off mine, stepping back an entire two feet.

"What?" I asked. Because I was stupid like that.

"*Cake*? Really? You think that tells me what I want to know about you? Open up a little, for fuck's sake. Even after that night with Poker, after sleeping in my bed, you're still shutting me out. You never answer my questions, not really. Let me in, dammit."

"I… I thought I was."

"No, Maggie. You haven't." An irritated hand raked through his hair, and his gaze went over my head as if he couldn't stand to look at me. "Why were you crying today?"

"I told you why."

His eyes jumped back to mine as his arms folded over his chest. "And I think there's more. Something else happened. What was it?"

I hated the look in his eyes, knowing I put it there. I wanted to let him in, but the closer he was to me, the closer he was to my secrets.

I forced my gaze toward the lake, the impossibly pure water scorning me along with all the filth in my blood. "It's getting late. I have to go."

"Then go." He stood, jaw hard, eyes hard, body hard, and waited for me to walk away from him.

And I did.

I arrived home later than usual, and I was met by the expected frigid glare over the tip of a beer bottle from the recliner.

Lowering the footrest, my father bit out, "Where have you been?"

I drew the amber bottle out of my backpack for him to see. "Sir, I saw you were out. I stopped by Henry's."

He grunted as his gaze drifted back to the television, bottle returning to his lips. "It's nice to see you're not always so fucking stupid."

"Yes, sir."

chapter forty-six

mason

Matt slapped my pads as he passed me on the way to his locker. "So, did you impress Maggie with your studly moves on the field? Hate to say it, but if tonight didn't turn her head, you're screwed, Bro."

"She had to work," I grumbled, waiting for Dylan to finish his play-by-play with Mike so I could get to my locker.

Just thinking about the raven beauty, bitterness streaked the back of my tongue. I wanted her here tonight. I wanted to look up in the stands and see her clapping for our team, dancing along with the band, laughing, chucking popcorn at Jamey's head when he inevitably said something inappropriate. I would have thrown her a smile and a wave from the sidelines, washed up, met her in the parking lot after. Maybe do one of those innocent-but-not-so-innocent twirl hugs, pressing her body to mine. Then I would have tried to convince her to come to the RAM house for the afterparty.

And yet...none of that happened. She had to work. Thing was, she always had to work, get home early, write a paper, study for a test, cook dinner for her father, the laundry was piling up, or she had to run some secret errand.

I don't have fun. I go to school. I go to work. I go home. I have one friend. If anything deviates from that, it has to be preplanned. Discussed at length. It's exhausting.

She had fun with me. One day. One afternoon. I gave her that. She had let me take her to the movies, ride on Matt's Harley, and we had, well, snuggled. I'd been so fucking nervous sitting next to her on the couch as if she were the first girl I'd ever sat that close to. But those nerves quickly dissipated into something else when I realized how perfectly she fit against me, the way her body molded to mine, our hearts pounding in a synchronized, frantic rhythm.

God, I could still *feel* her breaths hitch when I not so innocently touched her. She had to know that I wanted more. I mean…she'd *slept* with me. In my bed. If she had asked me to sleep anywhere else, she knew I would have. She didn't. She came right to me, wrapped her arms around me, undid me every time her hand went to Faith.

That weekend had to mean something to her, right? Hell, if I knew. She'd been so distant lately, and whatever had her crying in the bathroom stall on Tuesday hadn't gotten any better. She had put the wall back up, dug a moat, and filled it with crocodiles to keep me out.

"Cam, you were a beast out there!" Hollers echoed off the tiled room, snapping me back to the present.

Noah and Adam squeezed past, and I was hit with an interesting mixture of sweat, dirt, and…wow. Whoever invented that body spray should be shot.

"It was all for my coz." Cam snagged a few items out of his shower bag. "I can't let Matt's pretty face get dinged up."

Matt dipped his head once. "And my dick extends many thanks, Cam."

"It should," Vic chimed in. "That sad excuse needs all the help it can get."

Brow arched, Matt cupped his junk and grabbed tight. "Your ass wasn't complaining last night."

Vic shot him an unimpressed look. "Exactly. It's called girth, man. Get some."

Chuckling, Matt tore off his gear, and I got busy with my own. "Hey, uh, Mase?"

"Yeah?" I turned to watch my brother pick a wad of grass out of his mask with too much focus.

"We, uh— I was thinking that instead of pizza tonight, we could…go see Maggie. If you want." He sucked in a breath before lifting his eyes, a hint of uncertainty in them. "I mean, she should hear about that beautiful pass I made to Brady. Don't you think? How long was it again, Ben? Sixty-five yards?"

My cousin slung an arm over my shoulders. "Sixty-eight, but I'm sure she'd be more interested to hear that your brother tackled a— What was it, Mase? A pickle?"

Ignoring the snickers, I shoved Ben off. "How many times do I have to say it? Pickles don't have arms. It was a fucking cactus. And their mascot was on the field, so the jackhole deserved to get his spines bashed in."

I was seriously never going to hear the end of that one.

Owen adjusted the icepack on his elbow. "Where does she work again?"

"The Crest Cent Café on Sands," I answered, attempting to read Matt's expression, but he was wholly occupied with his cleats now.

Pete used a towel to mop up the gallon of sweat his chest hair was hosting. "I'm in. I could slay a cow right now."

Honestly, stepping into that café again was going to suck, but the more I thought about seeing Maggie, the more I knew the pain would be so worth it.

I nodded. "Let's do it."

Turned out, half the team plus a handful of cheerleaders were ready to get their burger on. Ben already had plans with Jamey, but Matt and Cam were coming. At some point along the drive, the reality of being inside the café again began to sink in, and I was somewhere between throwing up and devising a plan to do terrible and wicked things to Maggie in the walk-in cooler that were more than likely frowned upon by the Health Department.

I was a loser.

As I pulled into the last parking spot, it occurred to me that the quaint restaurant may not hold everyone in this caravan. "Shit, maybe this wasn't the best idea."

"We didn't think this one through," Matt muttered as he watched thirty hulks step out of their rides. "Hey, where are you at with Uncle Will? He find out anything?"

"More than I cared to learn." I put the gear into Park. "Back when I'd asked Will to investigate those permits for Maggie's community fridge, he learned the Prices had been buying up buildings here on Sands. Not only that, but they've been using their close associates to be the faces of their shell companies to build and own every new business by the marina."

His eyes narrowed. "You mean, the marina that Marcus Ryan lobbied his ass off for?"

"The very one. Turns out, the fabulous threesome treated Crescent Cove like their own personal Monopoly board. Their first move was to have Marcus pull funding from community and beautification programs and then siphon that money into the marina. Problem is, the programs that were cut were all for the south side of town."

"Which would drop the market values here and raise it in the affluent areas of Crescent Cove," he cut in.

"Exactly," I said. "Together, they've systematically built up one part of town while suffocating the other. When new construction started on their storefronts and apartments by the marina, the Prices slowly increased the rents in these walkup apartments and then the buildings. As home equities plummeted, Vivian and Leo started scooping up land and foreclosures, pushing out townies a little at a time, and no one's been the wiser. And they're getting it all at bargain basement prices. They're betting the resort will attract home developers that will buy their land at an inflated price and basically create a new Crescent Cove with their name all over everything."

"Greedy fucks. Without any competition, the Prices are free to jack up the market whenever they want." A low whistle passed Matt's lips. "Dayum. I'm a bit green on this subject, but it sounds like someone's been naughty with federal and state antitrust laws. And knowing both the Ryans and the Prices, I'd bet good money they've got a judge or two in their pocket. Is Will going to pursue a class action lawsuit?"

"Well, he—" My gaze shot to the side mirrors as headlights swung around in my rearview. "He's concerned litigation will take too long. These poor souls are months, if not weeks, away from bankruptcy. And you know the Prices will drag this out for years, and there's still no guarantee there will be a settlement. So, he's got a different plan to stop them, but Maggie can't know that we're helping yet."

Matt sighed. Heavily. "Mase, if you just tell her, she'll—"

"No. I'm not going to use this to earn favor with her, Matt. It's why I didn't tell her about the basket. I don't want her to feel obligated to be with me. I want that decision to be hers without any influence. Besides, if— If it doesn't work out, I can't break another promise to her. I've already broken too many."

"Yeah, I get that. I do." He nodded, chewing his bottom lip. "Okay."

"Thank you." I exhaled a harsh breath, looking to the café. "You're really cool with this?"

After staring at me for a long beat, he shoved his phone in his pocket and cleared his throat. "Yup." And then he was out.

Yet another person in my life who couldn't give me the truth.

Stepping out of BB, my gaze landed on the café—specifically, the window of the café—and everything came to a halt.

Motherfucker.

Gorilla Arms was here. Here sipping coffee and watching Maggie's ass sway in those baggy shorts as she wiped down a table across from him.

I didn't know he came Friday nights, too. Was he the reason she'd been acting weird lately? Did she feel like she'd been…what? Unfaithful to Logan by hanging out with me?

"You want us to deliver your chow in the fucking parking lot or what?" Matt barked at me.

I blinked only to discover I was still standing by my truck like a tool. "Shit." Cutting across the lot, I passed the blue Versa that had been parked outside of Maggie's house on Sunday night.

I'd be lying if I said I had never heard a snippet of Matt or my cousins having sex before, but that night in the woods? Her father was all-out fucking the woman she had to work with. Like the two were starring in an eighty's porno. I didn't know how Maggie could stomach facing her on the daily.

Passing the group, I approached Jordon waiting in front of the door with his arms crossed like I had to guess the magic word to pass. "We decided we'd let you go in first, Mase."

"Thanks?"

"Fair warning," Adam tacked on behind me, "we also decided that if you strike out, we're done watching you tank."

I spun on him so fast, he jolted back but then was quick to meet my stare. "What does that mean?" I asked.

He shrugged. "We're gonna take our shot. So…don't strike out."

I couldn't tell if he was serious or trying to get me to up my game. My game sucked ass—we all knew that much. A slight curve teased the corner of Adam's mouth. It was the latter.

"Fucker."

He snickered, and I ignored that along with the digs working through all the assholes surrounding me. With Jordon out of the way, I drew the door open, and we filed into the café like good little boys and girls.

The moment that spiced, sugary scent hit me, I swore my skin tightened in anticipation. That was Maggie's scent. It wrapped around me like the warmth of a fire on a cold fall day. Another three steps in, I was awarded with her brighter-than-the-sun smile, and then my heart seemed to malfunction next because that rapid heart rate wasn't normal for me.

Crossing the room, my gaze flicked over long enough to catch Logan's scowl. His dark ink bled through his white cotton T-shirt, both arms covered in half sleeves, and his back was fully tatted, grabbing the attention of every female in the building.

Women and ink were like peas and carrots.

Filing into the dining room, the entire team announced, "Sticks!"

On the turn, Maggie's eyes rounded as her hands clasped beneath her chin in that adorable way. "What are you doing here?"

I smirked. "Spelunking."

"Did you win the game?" she asked, hope filling her big blue eyes.

Matt propped his chin on my shoulder. "Destroyed them. Fifty-two to twelve."

As her feet left the ground in a jump, she let out a small squeak. "That's amazing!"

"What's really amazing is that you're here to save us." Owen slid by to grab a chair. "Your man's been in a shit mood. I haven't seen him crack a grin all week."

I threw the dick a glare. While the commentary was unnecessary, he wasn't wrong. I was in a shit mood. Ever since I confronted Maggie the other day, things had been strained between us, and on Wednesday, Watkins had rescinded my suspension. Because of my morning meetings and after-school practice, I'd only seen her in class and at lunch.

"Really?" she asked, that hopeful gleam was now fringed with concern as her eyes met mine.

I gave her a lazy one shoulder lift. "There may be some truth to that." Dylan smacked me on the back of the head, and a chuckle rolled through me. "Okay, yes."

Without another thought, I went for what I wanted. What I was dying for. Honestly, I couldn't *not* touch this girl for another second. My arms encircled her, crushing her to my chest, her feet dangling a good two feet off the floor. I buried my face in Maggie's neck, holding on tight and breathing her in. What I wouldn't do to have Owen's declaration be my reality. *Your man...*

Without missing a beat, she looped her arms around my shoulders, fingers threading through my hair like this was so normal for us.

I tipped my head back, my lips teasing the shell of her ear as I whispered, "Damn, I missed you." The shiver that ricocheted down her spine didn't escape me. She felt amazing. And...*right*. She had to be feeling this, too.

In my periphery, I saw that Logan's jaw was ready to crack, lids narrowed as though he was working out the best way to swap my neck with my ankles. This guy may or may not be competition, but whatever upper hand he thought he had, I just blew it away by walking in the fucking door.

She angled her head down, positioning our mouths a mere breath apart, and an essential part of my anatomy took notice. "Are you hungry? You want dinner?"

Oh, I'm hungry, but not for dinner. Since I wouldn't be saying that, I set Maggie down, my hands lingering on her waist. I kept my gaze on her while I asked, "Burgers and fries all around, guys?"

Having taken their seats, large hands pounded the tables in response.

"Okay." Maggie's eyes hadn't strayed from mine, and when she nodded, wisps of raven hairs that had escaped her ponytail danced around her chin. "Candi and I will get everyone's order."

Ah…shit. This was a bad idea. I'd never get a chance to sit and talk with her if she was busting her ass all night.

"Thanks." My hands skated down the gentle flare of her hips, perhaps a bit too friendly, and pink stained her cheeks before she whirled away.

I took a spot in the middle of the dining room, one that would give me the best view of Maggie. She rose to her tiptoes, calves popping with muscle to speak with the inquisitive gray head on the other side of the kitchen window, then she bustled into the dining room. It didn't take as long as I thought it would for the ladies to take everyone's orders. While Candi filled soda glasses and flashed her assets at every guy here—Logan included—Maggie went to the back and helped Frankie cook.

We were a few seats shy, but some of the guys had no problem letting the cheerleaders use their laps. Cam had a redhead tucked against him, a hand a bit high on her thigh. She didn't seem to mind.

As plates were ready, I watched in awe as Maggie effortlessly moved around the room. A tray precariously stacked with plates sat on her shoulder, and until that moment, I didn't think the girl had the muscles or balance to pull that off. She threw out smiles like it was breathing, and I would be jealous that they weren't aimed at me, but I was too enthralled by her to drum it up.

As the surrounding tables were tended to, I quickly realized that mine would be served last. My pulse doubled at the thought that she may have planned it that way. She could stick around, chat with me while Frankie and Candi took care of things like soda refills and delivering extra napkins.

As she set a plate in front of me, Noah's eyes twinkled at Maggie. "We sure missed our lucky charm tonight."

A delicate brow rose to call out his bullshit. "You won the game without me."

"Yeah, but we definitely could have scored more if you'd been there." Matt grinned at Maggie. For the first time since the word *café* had been uttered, he seemed relaxed. That was all her doing.

Winding my arm around Maggie's waist, I pulled her close, my lips an inch away from her breast. Wasn't planned, but I didn't change our positions either. Maggie smiled down at me, once again blowing me away with her beauty.

"Our next is an away game," I said. "We're gonna have to do without her again."

A cacophony of groans erupted at my table and the few surrounding it.

"Sorry, boys." Leaning against me, Maggie curled a hand around the back of my neck, fingers branding my skin, and if she wanted to touch me, I sure as shit wasn't gonna stop her.

The old bell over the door rang behind me. Before the second chime sang in my ears, Maggie's complexion went waxy, frame turning into stone. In less than a beat, she propelled away from me like I'd just given her third-degree burns.

"What the...?" I examined the new space between us.

"Hey, sugar!" Candi exclaimed, swaying toward the chief in what she qualified as a skirt.

The chief's eyes raked over Candi, his lips quirking when she placed a hand on his chest to use as leverage to whisper in his ear.

I glanced to my side to find Maggie was gone. Like behind the counter gone. She had already poured a steamy mug of coffee and set it on an empty spot at the counter next to Logan. Once Candi was done greeting the chief, his heavy boots and clangs of his belt reverberated in the now quiet dining room as he cut between the tables.

"Sir." Logan nodded with his greeting.

A sardonic grin pulled at the chief's lips. "Jackson, no amount of caffeine is going to help you win at cards tonight."

Riiiiight. That was why Maggie had refilled his mug twice since I'd been here. He needed caffeine.

Two near inflexible arms flung into the air, pulling the cuffs of his shirt taut to reveal more ink. "Chief, I had to try a different tactic. I'm tired of losing my savings to Robert and his Camaro fund."

My gaze traveled over to Maggie, who had transformed into someone else within the last twenty seconds. Cold splintered my chest. Her head was down, shoulders up, eyes dull. So odd. She was happy and playful a moment ago.

It was as if she were trying to be...invisible.

"Sir, would you like a plate?" she asked once there was a break in the cops' conversation. There was no hint of a smile on her lips, no inflection in her voice, no warmth to her. At all.

"Please, Margaret," he answered, unrolling his linen napkin to set out the utensils. "I'm starving."

Without another word, Maggie scrambled to the back.

Conversations in the dining room had resumed, but I refrained from joining as I watched Candi giggle when the chief's mouth disappeared under a screen of her caramel curls. A moment later, the waitress clipped off to the side hall where the restrooms were.

While I enjoyed my second perfect medium-rare burger and popped back fries with just the right amount of crisp and salt, Maggie served his plate of steak, potatoes, and green beans. Candi returned to the dining room, freshly primped without her apron. She settled next to the chief at the counter, a clear sign that she'd be leaving Maggie and Frankie to finish the night themselves.

The hell.

Sodas in the dining room needed topping off, and Maggie brought out a couple of pitchers. I noticed both were only filled halfway, the liquid sloshing and kissing the rim. I swore her tremor was more obvious than it was earlier, but her hands weren't what had gotten my attention all night, so I couldn't be sure.

Frankie wove between the tables, ensuring everyone had what they needed. Right as Maggie had made her way toward my table and our gazes locked, Logan's deep voice called over to her. She stopped a mere foot away from me.

"Maggie Blue Eyes, could I get a to-go cup?"

I made no secret of the glower meant for him, as he made no secret that he enjoyed snagging her away from me. The asshole even popped a brow when I continued glaring.

Maggie darted back to the coffee pot and handed Logan a paper cup, ending our staring contest. "Five cups?" she said. "I don't know if it'll help you."

"One can only hope. Keith has the best poker face, and the aces love Gil. Maybe we should take you home since the kids here seem to think you bring some luck."

Kids. Such a dick.

"Sorry, Logan." She patted him on the arm with the same hand that had been around *me.* The burgers and fries soured in my stomach. "Someone has to close, and someone has to lose." Then she smiled at him.

Fuck. *Seriously?* A heated flare tore through me as ugly thoughts stirred in my skull.

The chief's voice boomed off the café's tin ceiling, quieting the low chatter and clinking plates. "You Warrington boys win tonight?" Though speaking to all of us, his eyes were squared with mine.

With an air of pride, I said, "Slaughtered them, sir."

"Good to hear." Grinning, he added, "Make sure you don't celebrate too late, stay safe on the way home."

"Yes, sir." Matt brought the Coke to his mouth, whispering behind the glass, "You have some shit on your nose, Bro."

"Shut it," I muttered just loud enough.

With those eyes still planted on me, the chief wiped his face with his napkin. "Margaret, I'd like to speak with you a moment."

Balancing a full tray of dirty plates, her gaze darted to his. "Of course." Like it was nothing, she made her way to the kitchen, and he followed her through the double doors. Not long after, I heard the clunk of the back door shut. The dining room carried on, and I finished my plate along with everyone else.

A few minutes went by before the chief returned with a tip of his head to all of us. "Have a pleasant evening."

"Goodnight" was given back in varied lilts of cheerleaders and baritone mutters from the guys. Candi and Logan followed the chief outside, the latter trying to intimidate me one last time.

Trying being the operative word.

The back door swung open, and I craned my head, expecting Maggie to return to the dining room. When she didn't, I assumed she was in the kitchen cleaning, which had to be an extensive mess considering all the mouths that had been fed.

I took a sec to scan the room. The tables were full, and the guys had ordered enough to generously boost the café's bank deposit tonight. In fact, if we hadn't come, there probably wouldn't have been a need for the café to remain open at all. And with that twinkle in Frankie's eye as he relived his days playing high school ball, a thought occurred to me. It was a dirty tactic, one that I'd very recently refused to exploit, but the circumstances were a tad different. At least, that was what I told myself.

"Hey, Frankie?"

With his big mitt still on Noah's shoulder, the older man whipped around to me. "You need something? Another burger?"

"No, two were enough, thank you." I laughed. "I was wondering what the chances were that Maggie could knock off early tonight?"

I felt my brother shift in interest next to me. I ignored it.

"Oh." Frankie's brown eyes widened. "Yeah, we could arrange that."

I hooked a thumb toward the kitchen. "You mind if I scoot to the back and tell her?"

A grin pulled at his mouth. "Be my guest."

And with that, I was shoving through the double doors, following the sound of running water like a bloodhound on the scent. I passed rows of neatly arranged pots and pans, not a speck of dirt or grease in sight, every surface gleaming. I found Maggie facing the sink filled with dirty dishes, perfectly stacked. I waited for her to acknowledge my existence. She didn't.

"Hey."

Her head remained down while she continued with the scrub and scrape routine. "Hey."

Settling against the side of the sink that I guessed was used for rinsing, I canted my head, brows squeezing together. "You okay?"

"Sure. Why do you ask?"

"Um…" I took a moment to assess the way her shoulders were positioned near her ears, frame far too stiff, and focus going nowhere other than the sink. "Because it seems like you're not okay?"

"I'm fine. Just need to clean this up so Frankie can head out."

"Well, about that…" I waited for her to look up at me, but all she did was piston that elbow even faster. "The guys and I were headed to the RAM house for an afterparty and—"

"You don't need to ask my permission, Mason. Go to the party. Have fun."

A sense of foreboding chafed my skin. This wasn't going as well as I'd hoped.

"Right, yeah. But I'm not asking permission." I tugged her chin up to look at me. "I thought maybe you'd like to join us."

She pulled her chin away, and the elbow went to work again. "I can't. I'm closing tonight."

"Okay, but what would you say if *Frankie* was closing tonight? I asked him for you, and he agreed to cover the shift."

The elbow stopped, but her gaze didn't move from the sudsy water. "You asked Frankie before asking me if I was cool with not getting paid for the rest of my shift?"

My lips spread apart. Shut again. "Ah, well—"

With a shake of her head, the scrubbing resumed once more. "Wow, that was so thoughtful of you, Mason."

My hand dropped, the growing tension becoming a rigid weight in my chest. "I thought it was actually because I figured someone who claims to never have any fun would rather go to a party than bust their ass for the non-existent tips from the non-existent customers you're so upset about. Since Frankie *doesn't* pay you and all."

A smile I *really* didn't like pulled at her lips as her head shook again. "And did you consider that I needed to use Frankie's computer during that downtime to finish my paper for Dabney's class? Because a friend would."

There was probably something I could say here to diffuse the situation. Like, anything. But, again, diffusing wasn't my strong suit. Nor was ignoring the term she'd used for me.

"Friend." That word was like sandpaper on my tongue. "Is that all we are? *Friends?*"

"What else would we be? Buddies? Pals? Fine." She shrugged. "Use whatever term you want. Go and do whatever you want."

"*Do whatever I want.*" I was sure my guts were unspooling onto the floor, and all this girl cared about was getting her fucking Dawn bubbles on. "Does that include getting wasted? That wouldn't bother you because we're just *pals?*"

It was then I got my first real look from her, and it came in the form of blue flames flashing at me. "What is it that you want me to say? What reaction are you looking for here? Surprise? How could I be surprised? This is what you do. You told me that. You drink and fuck women. *Plural.* I'm not your mother. I'm not your keeper. It's your life, Mason. If your biggest concerns tonight are how fast you can drink the JD and picking the right legs you can get between, have at it. I have more pressing matters to tend to."

I think my heart just cracked open. "This is turning out to be a pretty shitty friendship."

"Your idea of friendship, Mason, is to bully me into doing what you want."

Bully her? Anger burned through me from the top of my head to my feet. "Maybe if I knew one goddamned thing about you, I'd know what you want, and we'd do that."

She stood a millimeter taller. "Here's a hint. I have no interest in watching you get wasted and finding you under a pile of legit sex workers. Again."

I knew I'd already gone far beyond the point I ever wanted to with Maggie, and I was going to really hate myself in about ten seconds. And God help me, I was my own worst enemy, knowing how much this would hurt both of us. I couldn't stop, though. I never could.

"I wasn't gonna ask you to watch, sweetheart, but if you change your mind, I'll be at the RAM house. Second floor, third door on the left. It'll be the one with all the moaning."

Her lids narrowed until all that was left was a sliver of topaz. "Fuck you, Mason Scott."

I winked, and her nose flared. "Oh, I plan on getting good and fucked, Maggie Davis."

I stormed away and stepped into the much too quiet dining room. Throwing a wad of cash onto the table, my hand trembled almost as much as Maggie's tremor.

I looked to the owner, catching his attention. "No worries, Frankie. Go on home. Maggie's gonna close." My voice sounded like it had barbed wire attached to it, and I compensated by putting my dick tone into play as I addressed the room. "Who's ready?"

As mutters bounced all around, chairs scraped the wood flooring, and I watched to make sure there was not only enough coin for Frankie but that they left hefty tips for Maggie. More than satisfied with the piles of green, I was dimly aware that Matt had followed me outside and climbed into the passenger seat of the truck.

After I'd pulled out of the parking spot, Matt peered over at me. "Dare I ask?"

"Nope." I spun the wheel a little too hard, tires squealing on the damp asphalt.

Sighing, he depressed his window control and let the briny air into the cab. "You want a girl?"

"Yeah, I want a girl. Too bad it's the one who'd rather scrub a sink of dishes than spare five seconds to talk to me." My hands wrung the wheel as I pressed on the accelerator. "Do me a favor, would you? Feed me enough whiskey so I can forget all the shit I said to her tonight and keep everyone else away from me."

His hand landed on my shoulder and gripped tight. "Proud of you, Mason."

Taking my eyes off the road, I asked, "For what?"

His emerald eyes locked with mine. "For not being a shit and doing something that will completely destroy Maggie."

I let out a hoarse laugh void of all humor. "That's just it, Matt. It wouldn't destroy her. Not in the least."

I was a good three drinks in when Cam arrived at the RAM house with the redhead from the café. Eyeing me, he whispered in her ear, and then took the spot next to me at the bar. Brow low and getting all up in my personal space, he growled, "How drunk are you? Because I really want to kick your ass, and I need you to remember it."

I recoiled in my seat. "Why?"

"Why?" His eyes practically bulged out at me. "How could you say that shit to Maggie? How could you leave her like that?"

I blinked at him. "Like what?"

Cam leaned even closer, jaw locked tight. "She was crying so hard, she could barely talk!"

The JD magically disappeared from my bloodstream, and my head cleared. "She was crying?"

Now I had Matt all up in my face. "What exactly did you say to her, Mason?"

My mouth opened, but Cam cut me off. "Let me tell you what she thinks your little brother said. She thinks Mason's fucking an entire brothel and invited her to watch."

I slumped in my stool, shame riding me hard. "I…may have given her that impression."

"Why did you do that?" Matt demanded.

"I don't know," I balked. "It kind of came out when she called me her *friend.*"

Two different hands from two different people I was related to smacked my head.

"You're a dumb fuck." I shot Cam a look that guaranteed he'd be leaving on crutches. "Did you not see that smile on her face when you walked in tonight? That smile sure as hell wasn't for anyone but you, Mase. You don't see how she looks at you? Christ, man… If she didn't give a shit, she wouldn't have been crying her eyes out."

"Well, I don't get emotionally available Maggie, Cam. I get stone-faced Maggie, who shuts down the moment I try to get close to her." I swirled my drink, clinking the ice together.

Matt's brow angled high. "And you're one to talk about emotional availability?"

My lids flipped up to glare at my brother. "Don't."

"Okay, then," he shot back. "Do you think pulling this shit is going to earn her trust? Do you think by hurting her, she's going to open up to you?"

I shrugged. "Maybe. Nothing I've tried so far has worked."

Cam got up to grab a beer from the other side of the bar. "Mase, I've had a few conversations with her, and for whatever reason, maybe oh, I don't know, being bullied and called fucked up names all her life, she has the shittiest self-esteem that I've ever seen. It's almost like her brain can't process a compliment. It bounces right off her head and into the atmosphere. She doesn't think she's worthy of your friendship, and she sure as hell doesn't think she's worthy of anything more than friendship."

Running my finger along the rim of my glass, I grumbled, "She doesn't want anything more than friendship."

"If that's true, then I don't blame her."

The drink suddenly left my hand, and Cam dumped it into the sink. All I could do was blink at my cousin. He shook the empty glass at me, spraying the bar top with droplets of whiskey. Whiskey that had gone to waste.

"You're gonna stop drinking and go see Maggie in the morning to apologize. You're also gonna stop being such a dick to her and give her a reason to want more than friendship."

I swallowed. "Okay."

"Holy fuck." Matt's hand slapped the counter, startling everyone. He threw his arms up and announced to the house, "It happened! Cam's balls just dropped. He's a real boy!"

Among the hoots and cheers for Cam and him flashing two middle fingers to my brother, I heard a familiar voice behind me. "Mase?"

I watched my brother and Cam shift their gazes over my head, their arms crashing almost as fast as their smiles.

Swiveling on my stool, my mouth parted on an inhale. "Hey. I'm glad you're here. We…should talk."

chapter forty-seven

maggie

"Margaret, I'd like to speak with you a moment."

At my father's words, my stomach rolled somewhere under the fryers to cower in a dark corner.

"Of course," I croaked around the knot of fear in my throat that had appeared the moment he walked into the café.

As I pushed through the double doors, I felt him tracking my every movement, the hairs on the back of my neck bristling. His boots thudded on the tile, closing in on me, and with a shaky hand, I set my tray by the sink. Goosebumps raced down my arms as I faced him.

There was no question what this was about. Mason. The only thing I didn't know was how long he'd been watching me from the parking lot before he decided to come inside the café and announce his presence.

I waited, thinking the cleaning station would be private enough for him. As usual, I was wrong. He opened the door and held it, his icy glare a silent command for me to exit. My gaze flicked to the empty alley, and my throat went bone dry. We'd be alone. In the dark. He could do anything he wanted to me out there.

His brow lifted to convey I'd used up his patience, and I scampered past him, the chilled air cooling the beads of sweat on my forehead. Once the metal latch clicked shut behind me, I gulped.

Exhaling a fragile breath, I turned and lifted my gaze as his mask fell away. "You really do think you're a sly one, don't you?"

Panic fastened around my throat. "Sir?"

Lips pulling back from his teeth, his meaty finger jabbed at the door. "How many times do I need to tell that damaged brain of yours to stay away from that boy?"

"Sir, I didn't invite him. The team came to celebrate their win."

My father leaned in, pinning me against the damp brick wall, his presence pervading what little space there was between us. The salty night air mixed with his aftershave, a rare scent of clean to cover our filthy secrets. The aroma of whiskey was more honest.

"And did you also *not* invite him to put his fucking hands on you? Did you also not turn right around and flirt with Jackson?"

Flirt? "Sir, no. I—"

Suddenly, there was a blurred image in my face burned into the screen of his phone. I blinked once. Twice. Oh... *Oh, God no.* Dread trickled down my spine and pooled in my limbs, hollowing them out.

That was a picture of Mason and me inside BB last week, at the worst moment possible. I had been taking off my hoodie, my damp and near transparent shirt riding up to expose my stomach, the very edge of my bra visible, and Mason— Mason wasn't looking away. No, he...was staring right at me.

Without any context, this picture made it look like I was stripping for Mason.

Who had taken this? Who had sent him this? With a flick of his thumb, the image changed to another. One I had seen before.

Lover's Inlet isn't very original for a midnight rendezvous, but neither of you seemed to mind.

Marcus.

Horror rooted me to my spot. Why would he do this? I'd done everything he asked of me, followed his rules, and—

A romantic relationship between you and Mason Scott is less than ideal. I want to keep that leash short and his hands off those pink cheeks. As soon as this business between us is finished, you will distance yourself from him.

Okay, I hadn't kept the latter part of the deal because I thought the deal was dead when Eric had been expelled from school. That hadn't been my fault; it had been Eric's. So why was I expected to stay away from the Mason *after* the fact? Why would Marcus do this now? To prove he could fuck me over anytime he wanted? Or was this his retribution?

"Go ahead," my father seethed. "Tell me some more lies."

I didn't. I didn't say a word. He wouldn't believe me anyway.

The tip of his finger was now centimeters from my eye. "You work for his parents, Margaret, and that's where this ends. If I see or hear that it's anything more than that, you're going to wish for a beating. And if you're so eager to open your legs to anyone and everyone..." He drew back to stand at his full height so that I'd feel smaller, weaker. It worked. "Maybe I should teach you a special lesson about that, too."

Holy God. He couldn't have said that. I had to have heard that wrong, misinterpreted it.

As the words replayed in my head, picking each one apart, my eyes widened, and all my blood drained to my feet. The fact he could threaten something so abhorrent while he was sober meant it wasn't a threat. It was a promise.

I forged every ounce of courage I had, voice shaking as much as my legs. "No."

In an instant, his lips were at my ear, breath scalding my neck with snarled words. "Act like a whore, and that's what you'll get. Keep your pussy closed and away from that boy."

Leaving me reeling, he opened the back door, the kitchen lights and the sweet scent of false safety spilling over me. As the door shut, darkness and loneliness swallowed me again. I slumped against the side of the café, my knees barely able to keep me upright. Minutes or hours passed, I couldn't be sure, but I heard the rumble of Logan's Indian start and drive away.

I couldn't stay out here much longer, so I forced my stumbling feet back into the kitchen. Tears scorched the back of my eyes. I wanted to scream, rage and fight, but my body was beaten and worn, mind weary, heart…much too small. I needed something to occupy my thoughts, keep those words out of my head. Looking over, the tray I'd abandoned was there, the sink piled with dirty dishes. As far as distractions went, it was good enough.

Over the sound of running water and my scrubbing, I heard the double doors swish open, followed by footsteps that should have calmed me. Instead, I felt as though I'd fissure apart the closer he came. I felt him. Behind me. Inside me. I was hyperaware of Mason, every nerve firing, sending waves of electricity along my skin.

"Hey," he said.

Fear had entrenched my veins, and I had to shut it down, slam the barrier up before Mason saw any of it. Heard it in my voice. "Hey."

He sidled up closer, leaning his hip against the sink. "You okay?"

No. No, I was so very far from okay, but since I couldn't say that, I went with, "Sure. Why do you ask?"

"Um… Because it seems like you're not okay?"

He was waiting for me to look at him, but I couldn't. There was no way I could hide the fact that I wanted to run into his arms and never leave.

"I'm fine. Just need to clean this up so Frankie can head out."

"Well, about that…" Mason paused, again waiting for my eyes to meet his. Without a doubt, the second that happened, I would crumble right here on the floor. "The guys and I were headed to the RAM house for an afterparty and—"

"You don't need to ask my permission, Mason. Go to the party. Have fun." And he could. He should. He shouldn't be here. He shouldn't be anywhere near me. But I didn't know how to push him away, save him from me.

"Right, yeah. But I'm not asking permission." His tone sounded sour, but I was more concerned that my vision had gone blurry. A large hand curled around my jaw and forced me away from my Dawn bubbles. His skin was warm and soothing to my aching soul, eyes filled with hope along with something else. Something I couldn't identify. "I thought maybe you'd like to join us."

My throat was instantly clogged with a riot of emotions, burning my tongue with every truth it wanted to spill. I did want to go with him. I would go anywhere with him. And I both loved and hated that he was asking me to leave with him right now.

I tore my chin away and began cleaning a— Well, it resembled a dish. I think. "I can't. I'm closing tonight."

"Okay, but what would you say if *Frankie* was closing tonight? I asked him for you, and he agreed to cover the shift."

I was struck with a stark clarity then, the trail of poison my next words would shape, the destruction they would bring.

This is it, and you know it. It's the only way to save Mason from you.

He had a temper and a willingness to sever ties, and I knew the buttons to push. If I cared about him—*really cared*—I'd push as hard as I could. It would make things easier, right? For Mason to no longer be in my life? At the very least, my father wouldn't threaten to… *Jesus.*

There was a phrase in life: This is going to hurt me more than you. I never believed that because I was always the one left bruised and bleeding. I got it now. Completely understood it. What I was about to do would utterly shatter me in a way that wouldn't leave a physical wound and couldn't be healed by balms or bandages. This was the kind of pain that made you wish for death because that was the only way you'd ever escape it.

I stilled, gathering a fictitious sense of anger. "You asked Frankie before asking me if I was cool with not getting paid for the rest of my shift?"

"Ah, well—"

I shook my head in disgust, forcing the emotion to bleed into my voice as I continued working. "Wow, that was so thoughtful of you, Mason."

He shifted, but I couldn't see much outside my periphery. "I thought it was actually because I figured someone who claims to never have any fun would rather go to a party than bust their ass for the non-existent tips from the non-existent customers you're so upset about. Since Frankie *doesn't* pay you and all."

Mason knew how to push my buttons just as well. I was counting on that.

I turned slowly, my lips pulling into a smile that held nothing but cold despair. "And did you consider that I needed to use Frankie's computer during that downtime to finish my paper for Dabney's class? Because a friend would."

"Friend." He said the word as if it were rancid meat. "Is that all we are? *Friends*?"

The truth was, I didn't know what we were. "What else would we be? Buddies? Pals? Fine." I shrugged as if my heart wasn't fracturing right in two. "Use whatever term you want. Go and do whatever you want."

"Do whatever I want," he repeated before his demeanor changed and that rageful spark took hold. "Does that include getting wasted? That wouldn't bother you because we're just *pals*?"

I tapered my eyes at him. "What is it that you want me to say? What reaction are you looking for here? Surprise? How could I be surprised? This is what you do. You told me that. You drink and fuck women. *Plural*. I'm not your mother. I'm not your keeper. It's your life, Mason. If your biggest concerns tonight are how fast you can drink the JD and picking the right legs you can get between, have at it. I have more pressing matters to tend to."

His eyes turned cold and dark as the forest on a winter night. "This is turning out to be a pretty shitty friendship."

"Your idea of friendship, Mason, is to bully me into doing what you want."

His face hardened to match his eyes as he leaned over me. "Maybe if I knew one goddamned thing about you, I'd know what you want, and we'd do that."

I straightened, meeting his glare. "Here's a hint. I have no interest in watching you get wasted and finding you under a pile of legit sex workers. Again."

That did it. I could see it in his eyes. I'd hit him where it hurt.

I'm sorry.

I could have sworn he paled, but then he hit me right back. Took my legs out from under me and watched me writhe on the ground. "I wasn't gonna ask you to watch, sweetheart, but if you change your mind,

I'll be at the RAM house. Second floor, third door on the left. It'll be the one with all the moaning."

I was gonna throw up, and this side of the sink didn't have the disposal. That would really suck. Wow, he was so much better at this than me.

Doing a shit job of controlling my voice, I said, "Fuck you, Mason Scott."

He winked. "Oh, I plan on getting good and fucked, Maggie Davis."

He stomped out the doors, swinging wide behind him as I caught the surprised glances of onlookers in the dining room. As the doors shut, an empty pit opened where my stomach used to be, and by the way my heart hurt, it must have been turned inside out and hooked back up all wrong.

What had I done? *Oh, God.* What had I done?

The ache in my chest grew with each clang of the bell until it poured out of my eyes. Little drops fell onto the bubbles in the sink, and I felt so small. So very small. I was nothing more than a piece of ripped paper, crumpled in a thousand different ways, discarded and forgotten.

"Hey, Maggie."

I startled to Camden's voice, and chastised myself for being so careless and weak, crying at work when anyone could have seen me. I'd been so caught up in my emotions, I hadn't heard him come through the kitchen.

"We're gonna go," he said.

Nodding, I choked out, "Okay, thanks for stopping in. Have a good night." That seemed pretty convincing.

Warm whiskey eyes appeared around my hair that had loosened enough to curtain between us. His mouth went flat, brows drawing low. "What did Mason say to you?"

Guess not. "Nothing."

He scoffed and tucked a lock of hair behind my ear, hand winding around my neck. "I know my cousin well. He left here pissed, and you're in tears. How bad do I need to fuck him up?"

"Don't," I pleaded, the words scraping out of my throat. "He's just—"

Camden's other hand settled between my shoulder blades, and I pinched my eyes to stop the sob from escaping. He made large, soothing circles along my back, voice tender. "Just what, Maggie?"

"Going to get wasted and then have an orgy with a bunch of sex workers." I wasn't sure how much of that was coherent English.

He shifted closer. "Yeah, you seem pretty cool with that."

"Sure." I dragged in a shuddering breath, keeping my line of sight no higher than his chest. "Sounds fun."

Gently, he tilted my face up with his thumb, and I blinked, feeling hot streams run down my cheeks. "Then you must be crying because you're cleaning. That always reduces me to tears."

"You know, they put this Dawn shit on baby ducks, but it's not so great for your eyeballs."

His gaze softened. "Right. Yeah, I thought maybe it had to do with the fact that you were in love with Mason and too scared to tell him because you think you'd never have a chance with him."

"Wow, you are so far off there, buddy." I couldn't stop my lips from wobbling. "Because he invited me along, to go watch. He even gave me directions. Second floor, third door on the left with all the m—moaning."

Camden's mouth became a white slash as he turned the water off, and then smooshed my face into his chest. It was surprising how comforting he felt. His cotton T-shirt smelled like laundry detergent and clean soap from a recent shower. He felt so much like Mason in that moment, and my father's warning played over in my head as I gripped onto Camden, pretty much using him as a human Kleenex.

"This is a new one for me." One hand smoothed my hair down as the other held me tighter. "Girls are usually crying out in my arms, not literally crying *in* them."

I sniffed. "Well… You're doing pretty good."

"That's 'cause I'm thinking perverted thoughts of you in your daisy bra."

"It's striped with bows."

"Ooh, even better."

I laughed through my tears.

Camden pressed a kiss to my ruined temple and drew away to look down at me. "That's better. For a second, I considered dragging you over to Nana's. That shit was funny."

Sobering, I angled my head back to face him. "Do I really look that much like Faith?"

Frowning, he thumbed my tears away. "Yeah, you do. My nimrod cousins and brother were already giving you a hard time about it, so I pretended not to notice. No one sees you that way anymore, though." Sighing, his palms slid down my arms. "Maggie, it's not my place to tell you, but you should know that Mason's…experienced things that he may never recover from. I know I never could. I'm not excusing him or his behavior, but it changed him. And, honestly, I can't blame him for that or how he copes with the things that keep him up at night. But I truly don't think he means to take it out on you."

I blinked away the next rush of tears. "I completely disagree. All I do is piss him off. I never say or do the right thing with him."

"I think you do. More than you realize." I wasn't convinced, and Camden's mouth pulled into a sad smile. "Let me put it this way. I've never seen him as happy as he is when he's with you or as miserable when he's not. That has to mean something, doesn't it?"

I shrugged. "I wouldn't know."

He gave me a look. "It means something, Maggie." His head dropped down to meet my eyes. "You know, I thought it was worthwhile mentioning... It's Friday."

My brow perked. "Yeah...?"

"You said that Friday and Saturday are topless days. And I can't help but notice that you are not adhering to your days very well." When the grin appeared, I hit him upside the head, and he left after he kissed me on the cheek.

chapter forty-eight

maggie

Between the poker game that went on past two a.m., Candi's revelations that she had found Jesus plus all his disciples, then obsessing about Mason covered in a harem of women, I had no sleep. None.

The only thing that had brought my spirits up a smidge was that when the boys left the café this morning, an origami bunny waited for me on Gil's chair. I tucked it into my apron to have him hide out with the rest at home.

Cleaning up the dining room, my head swung over to see a head of silver platinum hair with violet tips following the ring of the bell.

"Morning, you," I said.

Jamey crossed the dining room and gave me a hug, one that was longer and tighter than usual, but I wasn't complaining. He pulled back, leveling me with a stare. "You look like hell, Blue Eyes."

"You say the nicest things."

I observed Jamey's board shorts and felt a surge of shame for being jealous. Jamey worked, but not like I had to. Jamey had gone to the football game last night, and I was here at the café. Jamey had a boyfriend, and I didn't. Jamey had a mother who adored him, and I would never know what it was like to be adored by a parent. Jamey had a mother who didn't beat him, and I would get the belt for allowing the oven timer to go off for more than ten seconds. Jamey had a mother…

"Are you going swimming?" I asked.

His tank read, THE FEW, THE PROUD, THE GAY, and he struck a pose, popping out his hip. "It's a beach of a day. Or, more accurate, a heated pool kind of a morning. Then we have plans later this afternoon to go up north."

I nodded slowly like I understood. I assumed the plans fell under our TMI agreement, and that was why he'd been vague. "How are things going with Ben?"

He glanced out the window to said boyfriend, waiting in the Rover for some reason. "He certainly knows how to put a smile on this handsome face." Jamey threw a grin my way. "We partied at the RAM's last night, and I may have had a few or ten shots."

And Jamey went to frat parties where he drank and had fun.

The weak threads keeping my heart together began to snap and fray. "That's great, Jamey."

"Right. You look thrilled for me," he said dryly as his gaze went over my head. "Frankie, I'm stealing your girl for a minute!"

"Make sure you hold her hand if you need to cross the street. Drivers have to look twice to see you once, kid."

Laughing, he tugged the door open for me to walk through first. When I refused, I'd earned a cocked brow.

"So it's gonna be like that?" Before I could reply, Jamey yanked me outside, and I had no choice but to let him. I wiggled my fingers to Ben on the way to the bench that would soon become my confessional.

Settling beside me, the brow still hadn't relaxed. "You're gonna stop pretending that life isn't shitty and talk to me. What's going on with you?"

I sagged against the splintered slats, letting the metal rivets burn my exposed skin. "I can't do this here, Jamey."

"You can't do it at school, you can't do it at work, and you can't do it at home. You're bottling it up, and then you're gonna have a seizure. Tell me."

After a long pause, the hard edge to his face softened. A blue-stained thumb brushed along my cheek, and in an instant, my eyes watered. He was right. It was too much, more than I'd ever had to deal with before, and I couldn't hold it in.

Before I knew it, I was hauled up against his frame, nose smooshed into his chest. "Mags. Please, talk to me."

Fingers curling into his shirt, I heaved in a ragged breath, and it all tumbled out. "When I came home on Monday, he accused me of getting with Mason and Matt. He made me undress in front of him to prove I hadn't. I had to stand there in my underwear and bra... Then he made me bend over the recliner, and he— He spanked me until I was r—raw. That's not even the worst of it." Pinching my eyes, my voice dropped to a whisper. "I heard him in his room after. He...got off."

At some point, Jamey had gone rock still. Without looking at me, he stood. He paced a few steps, holding his gelled hair, and why it was styled when he was going swimming later, I'd never know. When his hazel eyes met mine, they were the darkest I'd ever seen them. "*Mags—*"

"Jamey?" Ben called from the window of the SUV. "Is everything okay?" Those chocolate eyes were locked on me, and I turned away so he wouldn't see me.

"Jamey, please," I begged, fighting back the tears. "He can't know. No one can."

Jamey sighed heavily. "Just…a few minutes, Ben." He sat back down, taking my hands in his. "Why didn't you come to my house?"

I worked my throat, but it was like the thing was collapsing in on itself. "I tried," I rasped. "He caught me, and then he said he would beat me with the baton again. I can't…I'd never survive another beating like that. I had no choice but to take it." I sniffed, but I seriously needed a tissue. Or a roll of toilet paper. "There is nowhere for me to go. No one can help me."

His fingers tightened around mine. "That's not true. The Scotts can help you."

My head swung back and forth. "No. Not after last night."

Jamey drew closer. "What happened last night? And don't say *nothing* because Cam asked us to come here and check on you."

"He did?" I blinked back another stinging rush of tears as Jamey nodded. I swiped my cheeks onto my shoulders, leaving my shirt damp. I couldn't believe I had allowed myself to lose it in public like I had. Twice. If any of this got back to my father…

"Mags," Jamey urged. "What happened?"

I released a low breath, dropping my gaze from his. "Last night, my father came here and saw Mason's arm around me. He took me outside and— He had pictures. The ones from Marcus at Lover's Inlet and…newer ones. Marcus is still following me. I don't know the reason exactly, but it's clear that Marcus and my father don't want me to get close to Mason. And both Marcus and Eric acted like they were scared of the Scotts. My father— He was so angry that I went back to work for them, and he was furious with the Scotts because he *told* them I wasn't allowed to work for them again, but they asked me back anyway. And last night, my father said that if I didn't keep my distance from Mason, he would…"

"What?"

The hopelessness was like a thick cloud all around me. "Don't make me say it. Please. It's so horrible."

Pulling me to his chest, Jamey's lips were at my temple. "You're gonna have to. I need to hear it."

I squeezed my eyes so hard I saw spots. "If I act like a whore, then he would teach me a special lesson about that." Try as I might, I couldn't stop the tear from slipping out. I was so tired of this weakness, so tired of being scared. So tired of this never-ending nightmare. "I hurt Mason last night, to push him away. All Mason did was ask Frankie to close so he could take me to a RAM party, and I was so awful to him. I hate myself for it. I hate what I said to him. And now he hates me."

"Mags, you've gotta tell someone. You have to get away from him."

"He'll never let me leave," I sniffed. "He'll never let me go. No one leaves him."

"Your mom left," he pointed out.

Dead men tell no tales and all. By the way, same goes for women and children.

The words grated out of me because this had been a fear of mine for so long, but I never let it see the light of day until now. "What if she didn't?"

Jamey sucked in a sharp breath. "What...? What are you saying?"

"She cared about me enough to take me to a hospital. What if...what if she didn't leave like he said she did? What if he did something to her? That Trey guy said some things— Terrible things about Marcus. He pays them, Jamey. Marcus pays the Sixes to do his dirty work. And Trey knew my father, too. I've always thought my father and Marcus' relationship was weird. They don't seem to like each other, and yet they shield each other."

I took another moment to gather my thoughts. "Trey said that he digs graves for Marcus and those who benefit him, and maybe he was being metaphorical, but I don't think so. He specifically mentioned women *and* children. And Eric said something similar. That he knew where the bodies were buried. I suspected for a while now that the Ryans had done something to Jenna, but they would have needed my father to cover up the investigation. A suicide after a public breakup would be a perfect cover story. But why would my father help Marcus unless Marcus had something on him first?"

Jamey's Adam's apple bobbed. "Your mother?"

My head jerked in a nod. "I think my father...needed Marcus' connections to the Sixes to hide what he had done to her. That's the only logical explanation I can think of."

Jamey visibly paled before me. "Mags..." Two arms enveloped me again, and I buried my face in his hard chest. I knew he'd been working out, but he seemed...bigger today.

"Is this Mason's doing, Jamey?" Ben's voice was a foot away on the sidewalk, sneakers lining up in my periphery.

"Only partly," Jamey answered, smoothing down my hair.

Ben's keys jingled as he held them up. "I'll leave the Rover here with you, so you can spend the day with Mags. Cam will pick me up, and we can do that thing another time."

Shaking my head, I quickly swiped at my eyes. "No. I'm okay. You guys go and enjoy your day. Really."

Jamey and Ben exchanged worried looks in lieu of a conversation.

"Oh, geez. Seriously, go. I'm a teenage girl. I'm dramatic, and life always sucks."

Ben's jaw hardened as he folded over to hold my chin in one hand. "If you were any other teenage girl saying that, I would agree. Anyone with two brain cells can see that you're not okay, Mags, and I know you don't have a dramatic bone in that scrawny body."

"Okay. Then, eventually, I'll be fine. I'd much rather work than wallow." I pressed a kiss to Jamey's cheek. "Have fun." Not giving them a chance to argue, I dashed back inside.

Not twenty minutes went by when the door chimed, but I was in the back, deep in pie dough and misery.

Without a word, Frankie shimmied to the front for me. I was fairly certain he thought I was having my "woman time."

There was some whispered discussion up front, and Frankie shuffled back to the prep table. "He wants a slice of apple pie, a scoop of vanilla ice cream, hot chocolate with whipped cream, and five minutes with you. I'll give you ten. According to Candi, he's one of the yummy ones."

My belly dipped.

"Dimples?" I brightened, forgetting all the reasons I shouldn't be over the moon excited that Mason was here.

His eyes crinkled. "Two of them."

As though I had downed ten shots of espresso, I ran to the sink to wash my hands as Frankie laughed at the water splashing all over my apron and floor.

I flew out the double doors to find Mason leaning against a booth. My heart did a big, old whomp against my ribs when those green eyes met mine.

"Hey, Sticks."

I should tell him to leave, run. Get the hell out of my life. I should tell him I no longer wanted to be friends and to go back to his orgy or brothel or whatever.

But what came out of my mouth instead was a, "Hey."

His gaze roamed over me, stopping somewhere around my hands. His jaw clenched. "Did you get any sleep last night?"

"No."

576 | ashlan thomas

He seemed shocked that I answered him. Hell, I was shocked that I answered him. "Is that because of me?"

"No. Because of me. Because of the things I said to you."

With a roll of this throat, he closed the distance, boots echoing off the wood floors. "I'm sorry. I was a real ass."

"I wholeheartedly agree, but I think I was the ass first."

Ducking his head, a single dimple teased an appearance. "I..." He scrubbed his fingers through his damp hair that looked near black. His scent drifted over stronger than expected. He must have just taken a shower. "I wanted you to know that I didn't do anything, and I honestly had no intention of doing anything when I left here. I drove to the RAM house and got drunk with Matt. That was it."

I chewed my lower lip and shrugged. "It's none of my business."

"So you keep saying." His tone had that hint of sourness again as he looked away from me. His hand fell to his side.

"I just meant that if you want to drink or party or be with...someone, that I don't have the right to tell you not to. I should accept you the way you are and all that jazz."

His head snapped over to look at me. "I don't want you to accept me the way I am. I want you to expect the best of me because that's what you deserve. I want you to be honest with me and get angry with me and call me on my shit. That's what friends do, Sticks. But what friends don't do is take it too far and say what we don't mean, which was what we both did last night. I hope, anyway."

Every ounce of despair I'd felt since that awful moment last night melted away. The crack in my heart had sealed. With only a few words. I marveled at his power to bring a thunderstorm or the sun. I had given Mason my heart without expecting to, and I knew there would never be another to hold it.

A large hand lifted to frame my cheek, thumb gently skimming under my eye like he was tracing something. Lips tipped down in the corners, the fingers of his other hand eased between mine, and my breaths hitched at the tantalizing warmth of electricity at his touch.

"I care about you a hell of a lot, Maggie, and I always will. Nothing will change that. Okay?"

I should back away and tell him not to touch me, but how could I when one gentle touch from him erased eighteen years of painful ones.

I licked my lips and nodded. "Okay."

Both hands were on my face, fingers weaving into my hair, and I swore that was relief in his features. "I should have told you the truth last night, but instead, I lied. I'm sorry. And I'm so damn sorry that I made you cry. I wouldn't have left if I had known you were upset. I thought you didn't give a shit." Locking his gaze with mine, Mason's brow puckered. "And this isn't an excuse, but most of the time, I don't have a clue what you're thinking. The only emotion I can read on you is when you want to throw a dick punch."

I released an unsteady stream of air that I hadn't realized I was holding. "You hurt me."

"I'm sorry."

Tears tinged the back of my throat. "I'm sorry, too. I said things to hurt you first. And I think for the first time I'm happy to hear you got drunk."

His arms were around me in the next heartbeat. I relaxed into him, fisting his shirt to keep him closer. As close as I could.

His words chased a sigh. "I'm good at it."

"Well, since you want me to be honest, then I wish you would stop."

"I can do that," he said without hesitation. Keeping the lines of our body together, he drew back to look down at me. "This may shock you, but I don't particularly enjoy waking up under two naked strippers that my cousin slept with and their pimp pointing a gun at you."

"I don't blame you. I've only touched Camden's used rubbers. They gave me nightmares."

A deep laugh rolled through him and into me, and it was everything I needed. With him holding me, the world was better, safer, and I felt whole again. I didn't know what this meant or how I would handle my father and Marcus but letting Mason go wasn't something I could do.

I knew that now. I wasn't strong enough.

Mason's gaze traced my features again. "I thought you'd like to know that Charlie and I made up last night, too."

"Really?" I felt my eyes grow wide. "That's great, Mason."

"Yeah. It is. We have a lot of trust to repair, but it's because of you that I was open to that. So, thank you." He found a loose hair and tucked it behind my ear. A pleasant shudder fluttered down my spine. His touch lingered, and for once, I wasn't focused on that he was touching my scar but just that he was touching *me*. "So, I was thinking you still owe me for saving you from the evil yogurt since you couldn't come to the game."

My brows knitted. "What did you have in mind?"

Bottom lip pinched between his teeth, a look of pure sin settled into his eyes as he shook his head in slow swipes. "It's too good. You have to wait until tomorrow."

I tried for what I hoped was a look that would convince him, pouty lip and all. "Please. My day has completely sucked."

His lids tapered. "Begging doesn't work on me. You'll only embarrass yourself. Besides, my day's gonna suck way worse. I have to go to Pacific Cliffs for a suit fitting."

"Suit?" My girly parts really liked that image. A lot.

His gaze went over my head before returning to mine. "Yeah, there's not a lot of time left before my cousin's wedding, and the bride is just now figuring that out. Literally, like, today. We're all taking pity on Richard and heading up there this afternoon."

Ah, so that was what Ben and Jamey were doing today. Why couldn't they tell me that?

"That sounds fun."

Mason's expression didn't convey his agreement.

"Please, tell me what the surprise is. Pretty please." I clasped my hands under my chin, but then Frankie appeared with Mason's pie and cocoa. I didn't stand a chance next to that pie.

Mason held onto me until Frankie disappeared behind the swinging doors again, and then his head lowered. Soft lips teased the shell of my ear, warm breaths tickling my skin. My pulse jumped in my throat.

"I'm not going to tell you to stop begging again because it's pretty fucking adorable, but you still have to wait until tomorrow morning. And right now? I'm going to eat the best slice of pie ever made and make you watch me enjoy it."

I nearly took out an innocent calla lily plant with my bike when I flung it into the side of the Scotts' house. It was a good thing I missed because not only was it pretty, but it did a decent job at camouflaging my transportation. I'd had two nights without sleep, but last night was for a good reason. Mason's surprise. And the very person with my surprise was here.

I skipped past the Raptor and up the stairs, digging out my bottle of Excedrin. Turned out, no amount of giddiness could distract me from the pounding ache in my temple. Once I swallowed two pills and chased them with a gulp of water, I opened the door. And stopped. The sound of running water perked my ears. And…scrubbing? Weird. I was usually here at least an hour before anyone woke for the day.

Curiosity rose as I snuck through the living room, stopping on the edge of the kitchen. Mason was at the sink, washing his bowl. I must have gone into a state of shock that he was cleaning *and* awake this early because I didn't realize he was looking over his shoulder, right at me.

His smile was big and bright. "Morning, Sticks. You ready for your surprise?"

"Right now?" My gaze traveled to the upstairs landing. "I should—"

"No, you shouldn't." He turned off the water and set his bowl on the drying rack. Crossing his arms, he leaned against the counter. "So this is how today is gonna go. After my surprise, you're gonna take me on a run, and then with whatever is left of the day, you can do what you do around here so well."

A surprise *and* a run? I'd never have time to do half of what I needed to do today. And Mr. and Mrs. Scotts' bedroom chandelier needed another dusting that I'd been putting off because the last time I cleaned it, I almost broke my neck a half dozen times.

My mouth parted to object.

"My way or no surprise. You can call my tactics bullish, but I like to think of myself as an opportunistic persuasion expert."

Pursing my lips, I squinted at him. That sexy grin of his appeared. One that said he knew he was going to win.

A minute. I made him stand there for an entire minute before I said, "Fine."

"Good." Mason disappeared upstairs and returned, still wearing a smile that was seemingly permanent today. Somehow, that smile of his only made the excitement dissipate in my chest.

I dumbly followed him outside to BB, and it was then that it occurred to me that this surprise meant we would be in public together. This whole staying away from Mason thing wasn't going so well.

He held the truck door open for me while I thanked him and stepped up the footboard, appreciating the leather scent of the interior. The chrome accents gleamed in the morning California sun, not a fingerprint in sight. I resisted the urge to wiggle in my seat. I loved this truck. I wasn't sure if it was a reminder of the night he'd asked me out or those little smiles he threw me from the driver's seat or that his eyes always met mine before he slid his sunglasses over them…like now.

I noticed he didn't ask what music I would like today. Instead, he flipped through the stations until the first notes of an electric guitar stopped him, seemingly knowing what song was about to play.

Head bopping and hands slapping the wheel, Mason got the truck moving as he sang along with Tyler Rich's "The Difference."

And the boy could definitely sing.

On the high note, Mason's voice caught, and he rubbed his Adam's apple. "I think I pulled something."

"I don't think singing is your thing."

"Poppycock! Of course, it is." He shot me a sly grin. Geez, he was in a good mood today. His voice dropped to a rough timbre, dipping low to look at me over his shades. "I'm good at everything related to my mouth, Sticks."

I wouldn't debate that.

I arched a brow. "Poppycock?"

That awarded me two dimples. "Yup. It has my favorite word in it. Cock."

"I thought *fuck* was your favorite word."

The truck suddenly swerved, and I slid, my shoulder slamming into the door. "Shit." Mason laughed and righted the wheel. "Sorry. You okay?"

I rubbed out my arm. "I'm fine. More importantly, are you okay?"

Mason shifted and cleared his throat, focusing on the road. "Yeah, I…" Another shift. Another throat clearing. "It's not much further now."

The truck rumbled down Canyon, past Midland and Laurel. The slamming waves along the cliffs appeared on the left as we zoomed by the bluffs. Then we traveled inland, past Reems Road.

Where was he taking me?

Mason finally pulled the truck onto a dirt road that I doubted was on any map, and we wound up in a desolate field of tall grass and sparse trees.

Coming to a stop, Mason shut off the truck with a pair of aviator shades and a Crest 3-D smile pointed my way. Before I could ask what the hell was going on, he hopped out, and I tracked him as he coasted around the bumper all the way to my window.

My door opened, and Mason waved for me to get down. "Come on."

Confusion steeped beneath my skin as I unbuckled and fed the belt into the spool. "Are we looking for buried treasure? If so, I forgot my metal detector."

"Better." He took my hand, and I leaped down. "I'm gonna teach you to drive."

Oh…fuck.

chapter forty-nine

mason

"Do you have a death wish?" Maggie cried.

I made a point to look at the empty fields surrounding us and the fact that there wasn't another human being or large structure within ten miles of this place. "It's perfectly safe out here, Sticks."

Shaking her head, Maggie's feet carried her backward until her shoulders hit the truck, and she squeaked. Like a terrified mouse. "It's perfectly dangerous. I don't know what I'm doing. I know there is a wheel and two pedals and a stick thingy. That's it. And I closed two nights in a row. Look at my hands!" Two tiny vibrators were then shoved into my line of sight within a centimeter of my eyeballs. "*We're gonna die!*"

Of course, I'd seen her hands, like I had every Sunday because that was when they were at their worst. Along with her shit balance. And I bet good money that she had a headache right now. This was what happened when she was overworked and needed sleep. And if she weren't so freaking stubborn, I'd give her money, so she'd never have to work again, but I couldn't even buy the girl a pack of gummy bears without an argument.

Those trembling digits were still shoved in my face, and I bit off a laugh as the next idea flew into my head. And it was my best idea. Ever.

I took her hands in mine, weaving our fingers together and returned them to her sides before they went blue from lack of blood. "We're not gonna die. I'll be with you the entire time."

The manic tongue started, swiping the last of the ChapStick off her lips. "What if I have a seizure, and my foot goes rigid on the gas pedal, I swerve into a ditch and roll us? We'll both be incapacitated, and no one will know because we are in the middle of nowhere!"

I fought a grin. "Not likely, but I appreciate this extreme death scenario you've conjured up." I pulled her to the other side of the truck, her sneakers sliding backward, kicking up clouds of dirt.

"It's not extreme." She let out a growl like a baby tiger when she lost the tug of war with me and then tore off her sunglasses to give me a glare just as vicious. "It's all very likely. That's why the state refuses to give me a license."

It took a minute, but I got her to the driver's side and popped the door. I slid behind the wheel and moved the seat back as far as it would go, discovering it already was.

I patted the space between my thighs. "Come on. We'll do it together."

Her gaze drifted to the desolate field before locking onto the seat. Or my crotch. It was hard to tell her where her exact focus was since her long lashes shielded her eyes from me. "That's— Uh…"

I was sure I was sporting a cat ate a cage full of canaries grin. "You can say it. Mason is fun. Mason is amazing. Mason has the best ideas."

Tilting her head at me, a single brow arched. "Your ego doesn't need any more stroking. I'm shocked there is room left in the cab for your big head."

A wicked thought crept into my mind and then across my lips. "Oh, Sticks. My ego always needs…stroking." My vocal cords also liked the idea of her stroking more than my ego.

Her arms folded under her breasts, pulling the fabric of her ginormous shirt taut so that it looked like it was only three sizes too big. "Do you seriously think that you are the best person to teach me to drive?"

My head dipped to one side as my voice adopted a robotic Dustin Hoffman impersonation. "I'm an excellent driver."

She blinked and then did it again. "W—what are you doing? What is that?"

My head returned to a vertical position. "*Rain Man.*"

That earned me a nose scrunch, so her freckles wrinkled together. "*Rain*…huh?"

"*Rain Man.* Tom Cruise and Dustin Hoffman are brothers, and they travel cross-country. Raymond is autistic, and he says it like a bajillion times…? He counts cards in Vegas…? 'Ten minutes to Wapner'?"

I was staring at a blank face. Albeit a gorgeous, blank face.

I shook my head, dumbstruck. "Okay. That's it. I'm ordering a mandatory Cruiseathon for you. All of the *Mission Impossibles, Cocktail, Days of Thunder, A Few Good Men, Jerry Maguire*—"

"I've heard of that one!"

My eyes narrowed. "*Heard of* is simply not good enough. We are planting our asses on the couch, consuming unhealthy amounts of junk food, and rotting our brains until we are so sick of Tom Cruise, we can't even stand to hear his name."

She scrunched her nose again. "That seems like a weird plan."

I threw back, "It's the second-best idea I've ever had. First being this." I patted the seat between my legs again. "Hop up, Sticks."

Biting her cheek, she gave the field another wary once-over. What the hell was she looking for? Magical sprites crawling out of the trees?

Eyes returning to mine, she proposed, "Maybe Matt would be better suited for this task."

I loved my brother. Trusted him more than anyone on this planet. He'd never do me wrong, never would think of making a pass at Maggie. And yet...

"He's recently become morally opposed to driving anything but Harleys. Now get your little ass up here." Reaching down, I clamped a hand around her wrist to haul her up. With my other hand, I palmed her hip and guided her between my thighs.

And, yeah... Best. Idea. Ever.

As Maggie settled in, her feet were a mile from the pedals, which meant I'd have to bring the seat closer. A lot closer.

I grumbled as I guessed how my knees were going to fare during this endeavor. "Shit, why are you so short?"

"It was a package deal with the small, almost non-existent models. Sorry." Ah, hell. I had been thinking about her ass from the moment she climbed into the truck, but now it was all about those small models that I was dying to get my hands and mouth on. If she had any idea how many times I'd jerked off to that fantasy...

I moved the seat closer, which forced Maggie directly into my crotch.

Fuck. Me.

Being a realistic guy, I figured there would come a time in the very distant future that I would wish for moments such as these. That all it would take was one touch, look, thought...

Today? Today I was cursing how embarrassingly little it took to get hard. Mere minutes ago, I'd gotten the last erection to deflate after Maggie had thrown out an F-bomb from that sweet mouth. Almost flipped the damn truck because she had no clue how much of a turn on that was.

Her sugary scent floated throughout the cab, and my mouth watered. It was all I had not to dip my head and taste her right where her raven hairs tickled her jaw. To flatten my tongue and run it down the column of her throat. I imagined her arching her back for me, thrusting her tits out for my greedy hands, whimpering as I teased those furled tips—

She wriggled in my lap, and a jolt of heat shot up my spine, cutting into the Maggie porno reel rolling in my head. My balls drew tight, the tip of my cock tingling with release, and I couldn't help from spreading my thighs a little wider. If she didn't know I was rocking a steel rod, it meant that delectable ass of hers was numb.

"Okay. Uh…" I tried clearing my throat for the third time this morning, but it still felt rough, as if I'd gargled gravel. "Let's get the most important thing out of the way, first. Driving music. What tunes would you like today?" I perched my chin onto her shoulder, all the right places lining up.

Maggie turned her head to face me, her hair snagging my scruff, so it acted like webbing between us. My gaze dropped to her enticingly close lips, then back up to her eyes. In the morning light, each band of sapphire, topaz, aquamarine, and cobalt shimmered like the Caribbean waters.

So very slowly, a smile tipped her lips, and I held my breath, anticipation humming along my skin. "Bluegrass."

It should bother me—and there may be a niggle in the back of my head screaming—*How fucking hard is it to tell me what music you like?*—but a laugh erupted instead because it was dumb of me to expect anything other than a smartass remark out of her.

"I thought I could sell banjos for a living, but I don't play, so that could be a problem."

"Nah, you could sell ice in the Antarctic, but I do suggest you purchase overalls and boots to complete the look."

I reached for the radio and realized my damn hand was shaking. I prayed she didn't see it. I started up the country station we'd been listening to on the way over. Thomas Rhett was singing "Crash and Burn." Perhaps not the best jam for a first-time driver, but whatever. The dude had pipes.

I turned the volume down, so Maggie could hear my instructions. "Next, seatbelt."

I yanked the belt out to cover both of us, forcing her back against my chest. But because she was so small and my hand was so big and I clearly had boundary issues, I pretty much palmed her entire right breast. I'd slammed into second base without even trying.

For the second time in a week.

Maggie drew in a sharp breath, stiffening against me, and I immediately jerked my hand away as my gut fisted sharply. "Sorry. That, uh— That wasn't intentional."

She swallowed and expelled an unsteady stream of air. Her words warbled as she said, "I know it wasn't. It's okay."

Dammit. No, it wasn't. Maggie obviously wasn't used to this, and I was okay with that. More than okay with that. Cam hadn't been wrong the other night. I hadn't given her a reason to want more with me.

I was going to change that today.

Being more careful this time, I clicked us in. "Okay, let's adjust the mirrors so you can see."

I showed her how to move the mirrors, chuckling when she almost yanked the rearview mirror from the socket. "Oops."

"It's all good." Reaching above to the sunglass holder, I withdrew a pair of Ray-Bans that I bought her yesterday after the suit fitting. "Next, you gotta look the part."

She stared at the mirrored blue lenses that not so coincidentally matched her eyes. And were clearly too small for me. "Whose are those?"

I wagged them in front of her face. "Yours. Let's see how they fit."

She pitched herself to the side as if they were carrying the Black Death. Then gaped at me. "You bought me sunglasses?"

"Yup." I lifted the plastic frames off the top of her head. "How you can see through these scratched up things is beyond my comprehension. You're saving me valuable brain cells."

She blinked at the aviators. Then me. "Mason—"

"Take them before I chuck the old ones out the window and then buy you another pair to run in, and I can guaran-damn-tee that they won't be five dollars from the general store."

That earned me a hard stare before she grumbled something under her breath that I had come to learn as acceptance. Taking the frames from me, she slipped them on. That was way too easy. More than likely, she'd already hatched a plan to hide them somewhere in my room by the end of the day.

I set her old sunglasses in the console and angled over, using two fingers to tip her chin toward me. I swore her hotness level had tripled. "You'll do."

My widening grin only made her lips pinch tighter, and they parted long enough to say, "Thank you, Mason." Her voice had a sharp edge to it, but she was wearing the shades.

Little by little, I would whittle down her defenses. Too bad she was making me use Andy Dufresne's rock hammer from *The Shawshank Redemption*. Maybe in twenty years, I'd learn her middle name.

I turned off the engine to show her how to start the truck. "Alright, put your hands on the wheel at nine and three."

Unstable hands listened to my instructions, knuckles turning white and threatening to leave impressions on the wheel. I covered her hands with mine and slid my foot on the brake.

I said, "Rest your sneaker on top of mine so you can feel how much pressure to apply."

She shifted her ass farther up with another accidental rub straight up the shaft of my cock. A heated shock tore through me, and I bit off the tail end of a groan.

She gasped, stilling against me. "Did I hurt you? Are you okay?"

I couldn't speak until I gulped, and the damn birds in the trees had to have heard me. "I'm good," I wheezed out, and in no way was that convincing anyone. "Okay, so the gear is in Park, we need to get it to Drive. Pull down on the gearshift, otherwise known as the stick thingy."

It took more than a few seconds plus two squeaks, but she did it and returned her hand beneath mine on the wheel. Feet moving as one to the accelerator, I eased the truck onto the field, and she yelped this time that had me snickering. Then Maggie threw all her concentration into the windshield as we aimed straight into the nothingness.

After a few minutes, I lifted my fingers from hers.

"*Whatareyoudoing?*"

Oof. That one hurt the eardrums, but another idea hit me just as fast. I braced my hands around her ribcage, the tips of my fingers just on the underside of her breasts, teasing the band of her bra. Her body was as soft as one of the petrified logs out here.

Lowering my mouth to her ear, I said, "You're doing great, and it's only us. You can make all the mistakes you want. I'm right here if you get in trouble." I grazed her ear with my lips, and whether or not it was intentional, she leaned into me as a shiver rocked her frame. I didn't hide the amusement in my tone. "Cold?"

Her fingers tightened on the wheel. "Huh?"

My hands left her torso and rubbed the goosebumps on her arms. "Are you cold?" I asked, hiding my grin.

Glancing to her arm where my hand lingered, she swallowed. "N— No."

" 'Cause I can turn off the air."

"I'm good," she insisted.

Deciding to give her a reprieve from my teasing, we worked on wide turns and then braking. Next, I set the gear into Park and shifted my foot away, leaving hers on the brake.

"Now, it's all you. Put the gear in Drive and press on the gas."

She ate up an entire minute staring at the dash, possibly thinking about how to launch herself out of the window. Maggie's hand finally drifted to the gearshift, moving it smoother and faster this time, and then her foot lifted from the brake. When she depressed the accelerator, we shot backward at warp speed, my head hitting the headrest, the back of her head slamming into my collarbone. Collectively, we lurched forward to a dead stop.

Both of her feet were on the brake.

"Shit! I'm sorry!" she blurted, staring at the instrumentation as if to make sure the speedometer was firm on zero. "Why is it so much better when you do it?" She cursed again, and though it was damn cute, disappointment was thick in her voice, causing me to frown.

"Because I've been driving since I was twelve and had older cousins and uncles who let me do very bad and illegal things. I've had a different life than you, but there's nothing to this that you can't learn. Don't be so hard on yourself." I didn't realize until now that I had her cocooned in my arms like I was on a self-appointed mission to become her body bubble. I let her go and rested my chin back on her shoulder. "Try making a fist with your toes."

"Fist with my toes?" she parroted.

My hands returned to her ribcage in hopes I could ease her nerves and turn her focus to where my hands were. "It's an old trick. That's how I learned." I adopted a New York accent. "*It's better than a shower and a hot cup of coffee.*"

Her head spun around. "What?"

My eyes rolled to the roof. I was such a jackass. "Let's put *Die Hard* one through twenty on that movie list. Scratch that. After Cruise, we're doing a Bruceathon."

"Bruceathon?"

"Really?" My shoulders dropped low as our gazes met. "Bruce Willis?"

She pinched her brows and shrugged. If I wasn't so appalled, I'd be dumbstruck by her cuteness.

"He's one of many action heroes that we need to get you acquainted with. Stallone, Snipes, Schwarzenegger, Chan, Van Damme…there's simply too many of them and too many decades of kick-ass movies to add up at the moment." I jutted my chin back to her feet. "Try again."

Releasing a breath, she turned forward and moved her right foot to the gas. I applied gentle pressure to her sides as my thumbs swept up, just shy of breaching a line. The truck advanced in a smooth motion. I grinned. It worked, but the damn needle didn't go above five.

"Sticks, you can go faster."

Cringing, her shoulders rose to her ears. "Mason, I— I'm scared."

My lips returned to her ear. "Nothing will happen. We're on a flat part of the field, and no one is around. Gun it already." I swore the needle hit twelve. "Jesus, do you do everything slow?"

Taking at least fifty feet to hit the brakes, she spun back around and snapped, "You have a hot date or something?"

She had no idea how much I wanted to devour that smart mouth of hers, but considering we just had a fight, and my balls were in a vulnerable position, it wasn't the best time.

I quipped, "She waited for me so long that she's stone-cold and six feet under."

Her elbow jerked back into my stomach, and I laughed. Groaning, she rubbed out her sore joint. "I swear you have granite in there."

"It's my Thor-like strength."

Her hands went back on the wheel. "What's a Thor?"

I shook my head. "I need to rethink my pop culture references. You can't appreciate any of them."

"So I've been told," she grumbled.

Maggie finally braved higher speeds, and the needle was close to thirty-five at one point. I had her practice braking and parking between shrubs. She did surprisingly well at reversing. Then I coached her to try driving at fifty miles per hour, but she maxed out at forty-one.

At some point during a parallel park between a boulder and a tree out of a Dr. Seuss book, a burnt orange blur came up behind the Raptor and flew past us, horn blaring, kicking up a cloud of dirt to obscure the windshield as it pulled to a skidding halt feet ahead, blocking our path.

"Holy Snickers shits!" In an instant, Maggie's body coiled, eating up the non-existent space between us. Her little hands became vise grips on my thighs, nails biting into my skin.

On instinct, my foot flew to the brake, and I grabbed the wheel. Once the truck was secure and stopped, I folded my arms around Maggie. A slight tremble worked through her frame as her breasts heaved against my forearms, and I did my best to fight the inevitable reaction already happening down south. Here she was in the middle of an anxiety attack, and all I could think about was anything but calming her down.

"I'm sorry, I wasn't paying attention." I sloped my head around to see her pupils had eaten up all the blue in her eyes, heart running sprints in her chest. I didn't know how much more stress she could take before her neurological system tripped. "Are you okay?"

I waited for her nod and then lowered the window, sticking my head out. "You jackwad! I'm teaching Sticks to drive!"

From behind the wheel, Cam grimaced. "Sorry, Maggie! I saw BB and couldn't help myself." He pounded the side of his Tundra. "Come on, Mase, stop pussyfooting around, and show her what trucks are for."

Well...we'd been at this an hour, and my intention had been to teach her to drive and get her to relax. I conceded and brought my focus back to Maggie as I lifted one brow. "What do you think? Wanna have some fun?"

Her head periscoped, scanning the desolate land for a solid minute. Then a grin that was an odd mixture of sin and innocence reflected back at me. A wicked gleam in her eyes had my heart doubling its beats. "Yeah."

Fun it is, then. "Alright, Sticks, I'm taking over."

Maggie reached for the buckle as her hips rose off the seat. I gripped her waist and pulled her back down, giving me another unintentional dick rub. Fuck. That...that felt good.

"Nope, you're staying right there," I said, and with a push of a button, I cranked up the music, and Maggie kept her feet tucked away, grip easing. My lips returned to her ear. "You may want to keep hanging onto me."

"Huh?" That was when she glanced down and gasped, drawing her hands back into her lap. "I'm sorry."

My eyes tracked to where she had dug in, little crescents embedded into my thighs.

I grinned. "Nail marks never bothered me." Then I topped that off with a wink.

She groaned, and I laughed. Without warning, I gunned the truck, forcing her to slide back into me.

Cam was a genius.

"Now, tell me the truth. Was that fun?" I put the Raptor in Park and gave one final wave to Cam as the Tundra sped off. We'd been at this an hour, taking each hill, bump, muddy track, and water trap that I'd been avoiding when Maggie had the wheel. My blue truck was now brown. My time with Maggie had been worth every drop of dirt.

"Fun?" Maggie twisted toward me. "That was awesome!" Her smile was possibly the best thing I would ever see, and I'd never heard her laugh so much, squeal so loud, or throw together such interesting curses before. "Thank you!" Her hands balled into fists, arms stiffening like she was getting ready to throw a hug my way, but then she thought better of it.

"My pleasure." I thought I hid my disappointment pretty well. "Why don't you take us home."

Her smile died a quick death, the head shaking already happening. "No, I—"

"Too late." I threw the truck into Drive, pitched my arms away, and my foot punched the gas.

"Mason!" Her hands flew to the wheel to control the truck.

I chuckled as I watched her struggle to get the Raptor lined up. "Keep it straight and then turn left once you hit asphalt. You're doing great."

Taking over the accelerator, Maggie maneuvered BB perfectly, easing up to the main road. "We really need to work on this compromise problem you have."

I leaned back into my seat and admired the view. "It's working in my favor so far. I have a gorgeous girl in my lap doing all the work."

Ball's in your court, Maggie. Come on, you heard me.

"Then we'll take you to an optometrist next," she groused.

Son of a bitch. Cam was right again. The compliments bounced off her head.

Sitting forward, I growled, "I know you didn't just—" My gaze dropped to the dashboard. "Shit. Pull over."

Her shoulders tensed, foot easing off the accelerator. "What did I do wrong?"

I tapped the dash where the indicator light was. "That's the tire-pressure warning. We probably picked up something in the field."

Once Maggie pulled to the side of the road, she put the gear in Park, and I popped the door handle. She climbed down, the absence of her warmth instantaneous.

I dropped down next, and we inspected all the tires, stopping at my back left. "There. A nail." I pointed to the shiny metal fixed in black rubber. It was only fifteen miles to town. I was confident we'd make it without the hassle of changing the tire, and I knew Maggie would drive us there fine, but she didn't need the extra stress. "Hop in the passenger side. I'll take us back."

"Okay," she rushed to agree and scampered off.

We climbed inside, and while Maggie worked on buckling in, I opened the browser on my phone, finding the local shop by the marina was open. For safety and convenience sake, I'd have to overlook the fact that the tire shop was more than likely owned by the Prices.

Out of the corner of my eye, a pink tongue began the wash cycle over those lush lips. Then the swallowing and fidgeting began. Now that I had a better understanding of how Maggie's mind worked, I knew what thoughts were running through her head, and, well, I couldn't help myself. I shouldn't have, but...

My jaw went taut, and I didn't speak, eyes centered on the road while I drove toward town.

Maggie wrung her fingers like she was trying to knit the damn things together. "I'm really sorry, Mason. I'll pay for a new tire."

I shot her a quick glance. "Do you even know how much they cost?"

Angling toward me in her seat, she tore off her sunglasses, eyes flared wide. "No. A lot?"

"Easily six hundred."

"S—six?" she gasped. "Okay. Um...I don't carry that kind of cash on me."

I grunted as I checked my mirrors. "It's fine. You can pay me back later."

"Thank you. I... I'm so sorry."

"Me, too. I can't believe..." I shook my head in mock irritation. "I can't believe...you're this gullible!"

Staring at me, her mouth hit the floorboard.

I laughed, glimpsing over to her. "It's a fucking nail. It was in no way your fault. They'll take it out and patch it. I probably won't even have to pay. Besides, I would never ask for your money." I grimaced at the thought. "Unless Cam invites another member of the Sixes into our lives. I'm really hoping that was an isolated event."

"You gave me a heart attack!"

I chuckled. "Then don't be so easy to fuck with!"

We stopped at the tire shop and were told it would be at least a fifteen-minute wait. It struck me that I'd already spent two hours alone with this girl, and it only felt like two minutes. While I was sure we could get into some shenanigans here at the shop, and Maggie would be up for it because she always was, I looked out the window and had another idea.

I lowered my head, eyes catching hers that regarded me speculatively. "I know you and I should be morally opposed to this, but what do you think about getting a hot cocoa across the street?"

Her gaze drifted to the window where Sugar Buns was in view, a place definitely owned by the Prices and the café's direct competition. But not for too much longer if my family had anything to do with it.

After studying more of the marina end to end, those eyes returned to me. "As long as you tell me how much it *isn't* as good as the Crest Cent Café, I'll go along with it."

"Done."

Though I had this idea weeks ago, and it didn't go over well then, I felt like I'd ridden a thirty-foot wave on a foam kickboard when we stepped into the coffee shop.

"Well, hey there," a sultry voice announced from behind the counter. A sultry voice attached to a woman with a rose and skull tat on her thigh and more piercings than I remembered. "Long time no see, stranger."

Ah...shit. Apparently, I wasn't the only one with a good memory.

Suddenly, I was hyperaware of a pair of azure eyes latched onto me. Okay, this was turning out to be not such a great idea.

"Hey..." *Oh, hell.* What was her name? I should know. I'd flirted with her on countless occasions. And she had offered up an MFM threesome with Matt. That I never took her up on.

"Chrisee," she happily supplied. "One S, two Es." And punctuated that with two fingers in a peace sign by her left breast, her shirt doing nothing to hide her pierced nipple.

"Right, Chrisee. Sorry. This is my friend, Maggie."

With a tilt of her neck, she revealed one side of her blonde head that was shaved. Chrisee's heavily lined eyes surfed up and down Maggie's body before nodding in approval. "Very nice."

Uh, I was pretty sure Chrisee would be cool with an FMF threesome, too.

I had Maggie order first, and I added my cocoa plus two chocolate croissants. As I reached for my wallet, a green bill appeared at my side. I snatched it out of Maggie's hand. "No."

I was mid-reach for my wallet again when another bill popped up, and Chrisee stretched for it.

"No again."

Maggie's jaw clenched, and then so did my thighs because I knew that look all too well. Maggie waited for me to turn my attention away, and a third bill appeared in the corner of my eye.

I shook my head. "Just know it's your fault. You make me do these things."

"Wha— Mason!" I went into UFC mode, locking Maggie's arms down in a bear hug, and hauled her off her feet with one arm. "Ugh!" Her forehead thumped onto my shoulder, warm breaths dancing along my chest. I threw a grin to Chrisee while I handed over *my* twenty.

"I knew you were into kink." The barista winked.

Maggie grumbled something I was sure was well deserved.

Once the change was handled, I dumped it all into the tip jar. I grabbed Maggie's money and my wallet and walked to the end of the counter.

"I'm putting you down," I said.

She grunted into the crook of my neck. "Watch your crotch, Scott."

"I always do around you, Sticks."

As I set her on her feet, Maggie huffed, tugging her parachute shirt into place with more tug than necessary. My gut wrenched at the glare she sent my way.

"Come on," I pleaded. "Don't be mad."

She crossed her arms and mashed her lips, having no issue relaying how much she wanted to hurt me right now.

"I'm sorry?"

With Chrisee bustling behind the counter, Maggie's hands flew up as she whisper-hissed, "Why couldn't I pay?"

Frowning, I handed over her money. "Why is it a big deal?"

She took the three bills, and I waited. It was quite the process to tuck up the shirt, locate the desired pocket, and readjust everything back into place. She let out a shaky breath, not looking at me. *Here it comes in three, two…*

"My point exactly," she stated.

Chrisee had our order ready, throwing out another suggestive wink and sultry farewell. I plucked the cups off the counter, and Maggie grabbed the to-go bag.

Her shoulders were drooped, but she lifted her chin to me. "Thank you."

It still surprised me to hear those two words. Normally, in my circle of friends and family, we just did things like that. Picked up the tab, no big, no thanks necessary because they would probably get the next one. But Maggie… Maggie hadn't known that kind of life, and honestly, it made me want to keep spoiling her.

Without discussion, Maggie headed toward the back patio, and I hopped ahead to open the door for her with another soft "thank you" hitting my ears.

And there it was again. Maggie made each gesture into *something*. Even though it was no problem for me to drop a few bills, open a door, or carry our cocoa, she noticed. And I *liked* that she noticed.

"It is a big deal to me, you know." While Maggie talked, I followed her to the table she picked that happened to have the best view of the marina. And if she were paying any attention to the situation, she would realize that I just delivered close to all her wishes for a first date.

I guess I'd like to go somewhere remote, quiet, where he and I could talk, get to know each other. And I'm sure we'd get hungry. A picnic?

But Maggie didn't think like that because she was still doing things like...

"The bike lights, basket money, bowling, movies, the candy, the ICEE tanker, and I—" I pulled a chair out for her, and she stared at my hand like it was an elephant riding a tricycle. After a shake of her head, she finally sat, and I scooted her in. "Thank you. And I admit, the tire thing freaked me out, but I would have paid it, Mason."

I took the seat across the table from her. My mouth opened, and she cut me off.

"I'm not only getting out of my responsibilities at work, what I'm getting *paid* to do, but you're spending money on me with the gas, the sunglasses, and our second breakfast." She waved to the table that she had begun to set up with napkins as our placemats. "Big gestures like a six-hundred-dollar tire are hard for me, but this is something I *can* do and *want* to do. I wanted to show you my appreciation for today. We're entirely imbalanced in every way, and I needed to do that."

I took a sip from my cup, letting the rich chocolate coat my tongue. "Can I address those issues now, or were you not finished?"

She sucked in a breath as if she were preparing an hour-long lecture, and I would have been more than happy to hear her talk all day. "I was finished."

I was never going to read her signals right.

"Good. Take a drink, and you are welcome for your cocoa and croissant, pulling out your chair, and opening the door." I waited for her to pick up the cup. It took a minute. And a sigh on her part. "I know you can pay, and I never once thought we were imbalanced. Believe it or not, I enjoy spending money on you, almost as much as I enjoy spending time with you. One thing that has been drilled into me since I was a kid was that, yes, my family is wealthy, but it means nothing, *absolutely nothing* if we don't do something good with it, something that enriches our lives. You do that for me, Maggie. You make me see what I should be seeing, the life that's going on around me, and that's the balance. It may sound silly to you, but nothing about this morning was insignificant to me. This morning is one that I will remember."

She gasped at that little ditty, and I kept rolling. "I have an entire childhood tainted by bad memories, and there was a time that I really didn't think I'd have any more good ones. *This* is a good one. And if it only cost me a tank of gas and a second breakfast to feel this good? The happiest I've felt in a long fucking time? I'd say I made out pretty damn great, and I'd pay a million dollars to have a morning like this. You did that for me. So this is me showing my appreciation to you."

Maggie's delicate throat rolled. The ocean breeze kicked up her raven hairs, so they smacked her across the face, getting snagged in her ChapStick. "Oh. Well, this was…" Brushing her hair back, Maggie tucked her chin tight to her chest. "This was a good memory for me, too."

"Alright then. Would you like to do this again next weekend? Make some more good memories together? Have fun…*together*?"

She picked up her head, looked to the coffee shop, studied the boats lined up at the dock. "I… I have to wo—"

"You're overthinking it. Just answer. Yes or no? Would you like me to teach you to drive?"

Another lick of her lips. Another glance to the water. "Can I pay for the gas?"

"Yes or no?"

"Are we still running after?"

I leaned over the table. "Maggie… Yes or no?"

Whatever she was about to say must equate to ripping spikes out of her throat. "Yes."

I tugged a good hunk off my croissant and settled back in the metal chair, shaking my head. "You… I swear you could give Watkins a run for his money." I popped back the pastry and grunted. "Okay, the cocoa's not half bad, but this…? Compared to yours, it's shit."

Her brows furrowed as she put her new sunglasses back on. "I— I'm sorry. I know I'm difficult."

I snorted and tore off another chunk of the pastry. "Honestly, Sticks? I wasn't complaining. Spending time with you, whether we're arguing or laughing, is not time wasted to me."

Her fingers stilled on the cup, the gears cranking in her head, picking that apart, working out a way to make that negative. I needed to figure out a way to shut off that brain of hers.

"So, this will be our thing," I said. "Sunday mornings, I'll teach you to drive, you kick my ass around the lake, and then you finish whatever is left of the day at the house, and there will be no gas money and no change in your pay. Glad we could work that out."

Her pouty lips dropped open into a perfect O. "*We* didn't work anything out. You just decided."

The corners of my mouth pulled down. "Is my idea really so terrible?"

Brows tugging together, she picked at the chocolate swirls on her croissant. "No. But I'm taking advantage of your parents and you."

I shook my head. "You're the only one who sees it that way. All you need to do is say yes, which you have, and I'll take care of the rest."

A look of doubt pinched her pretty features, but she lifted her cup and drank, looking out to the water. I followed her gaze.

The seabirds were like vultures, diving down and plucking up whatever their beaks could along the pier. As the boats rocked with the waves, I shut my eyes and thought about spending a day like this at the beach with Maggie, watching her splash around in the water in a teeny bikini. I bet she would try surfing with me, throw a Frisbee to Poker, and not sit on her ass working on a tan. No, that wasn't Maggie.

"We should get going." My eyes opened as she began bagging what was left of her croissant that had all of one bite taken out of it. "The truck's probably done."

Translation: *I have to work, and I'm freaking out that I'm not working.*

My hand swung out to stop her, wrapping around her wrist. "The truck will wait for us to finish. It's not going anywhere." Her pulse kicked up against my fingers, and I waited for it to chill before I dragged my hand away.

While we finished our croissants and cocoa, it looked like she wanted to say something but opted for silence instead. That usually wasn't a good thing.

"What are you thinking about?" I asked.

Shrugging, Maggie's nose wrinkled. "Nothing."

I groaned, "Sticks…"

"Okay. Obviously, Chrisee with one S and two Es is hot. You noticed. And to be fair, I noticed, too. I was just wondering if maybe one day a guy would notice me like that."

Talk about an unexpected subject change.

I wasn't going to deny that I had noticed how attractive Chrisee was because that would have been a lie. One Maggie would see right through. And I wasn't an asshole who would disparage one woman's appearance to build another woman's confidence. But what I should have explained was that the attraction ended there on the surface. It was Maggie who made me want to dive deep and keep sinking until I hit bottom.

"I think it's entirely possible. I actually believe that it's already happened." Like with me every single time I was around her.

"Right." Disbelief framed her voice as her focus returned to the cocoa again. "Could you tell me if it does? I'd really like to know."

Jesus. How did anyone this beautiful have a self-esteem this shitty?

I lied, "Sure, Sticks. No prob."

chapter fifty

mason

Twenty-three horny assholes huffed around me, sucking down the brisk November air, my eyes set on the cute ass in front of me because that was the only incentive I had to risking a collapsed lung. These running sessions weren't standard because the Athletic Complex was now fixed and mold-free, and Watkins usually had us leaving our souls either on the gym floor or the field. But on a blessed day such as this, a rare day, we took our workout to the lake trails while I competed for Maggie's attention against twenty-three horny assholes.

I was number twenty-four.

I couldn't remember when these group sessions started or who suggested them, but I did know they did nothing to improve our team. While Warrington wasn't the best in our division, we weren't the worst, either. And with some luck and a few answered prayers, we'd make it to the playoffs. Friday night was known as not only game night but now café night, and my Maggie greeted me with the best smiles and hugs, even with the burgeoning Wolverine mutton chops.

My Maggie.

Shit, I really had just thought that. She wasn't mine. Not in the slightest.

Three months had passed, and I wasn't any closer to knowing Maggie outside of the fact the girl was a walking accident. She would come to school hobbling from time to time from pulled muscles, a fall, or straining her back.

And unless it was Sunday, I couldn't get the girl within ten feet of my truck. There were no rides home, nothing to deviate outside of going to the store, taking care of the basket, or driving lessons. I swore Maggie had a list of ready-made excuses as soon as I offered. And when she was in my truck, she rocked some deep paranoia as if petrified of being seen with me.

My patience was thinning by the day, and I had no clue how to get over that wall she put up around her. It also didn't help that it had been roughly fourteen weeks since I'd been with anyone.

Fourteen.

That was depressing. And sure, I could remedy that problem anytime I wanted. A call to Crystal, Rebecca might still be game, flirt up a cheerleader… Hell, I had my pick of about ten cats and fifteen angels at the RAM's Halloween party last weekend to end my dry spell. I'd even left Rich's bachelor party early because there was no way Ethan would let me go through the night without putting a girl in my lap. Things were far too delicate between Maggie and me, and I didn't want to give her a reason not to trust me. My one focus was on that raven beauty ten yards ahead and nowhere else.

I was whipped. I was a goner. I was fucked.

I was in love with my best friend.

There was no question about that.

I woke up thinking about Maggie, continued thinking about her all damn day, dreamt about her, jerked off daily—okay more like three times a day—to the thousand and one fantasies I had, and the moment I did see her, I was cursing the clock at how little time it would give me with her. But there was never a right moment to make this something more. There was always someone around, somewhere to go, something to do, and when there was a blessed second that we were alone, a moment that the door might be unlocked for me to nudge open, she shut down.

Every. Fucking. Time.

I was stuck in the godforsaken friend zone.

I had sworn to take this slow, but I couldn't get any slower than this. I was at a standstill. Dead slugs moved faster.

Stopping for a water break and letting the laggers catch up, the tiny brunette opened her water bottle and tipped her head back. *I love when she does that.* The position elongated her neck, pushed her breasts out, and she stood with her toned thighs parted.

Fantasies ran rampant during water breaks.

Beads of sweat dripped off my scalp and slipped down my jaw, collecting in the hair. It ruined the moment. My skin felt like it had been pulled too tight over my skull and scored by a million miniature razors, and one drop of sweat made me want to take a rake to my face. Finding a shady spot under the nearest tree, my hands shot to my jaw and dug in. There was no way it was sixty degrees out.

"Fuck!" I swore if I didn't have a layer of hair as a protectant, I'd hit bone. "I fucking hate November. I hate Mutton Chop Month. Whose stupid ass idea was this anyway?"

Forty-six other hands were scratching their faces now, too. This itching shit was like yawning; one person started, and soon the entire group was going at it.

Maggie joined me beneath the maple tree and hip-checked me. "You're in a mood this week."

She was right. I was in a mood. A rank mood because I had a porcupine on my face and balls that were purple and retreating inside my body cavity. And her standing in front of me in her ballcap, paintbrush ponytail, chest heaving with her perky nipples was not helping. If she ever knew how often and how long I stared at her...

I was a perv.

Straight up.

Joining us, Cam swallowed a drag of water. "You don't shave every day anyway."

"I know, but I try to a couple times a week. This is cruel!"

"I wish I could only shave a couple times a week." Maggie stuck a leg out and glanced at it, and then so did every other dude. As her thigh and calf muscles popped beneath the expanse of smooth peaches and cream skin, I imagined what they would look like wrapped around my waist. Better yet, perched on my shoulders with my face—

"Oh, yeah?" Cam raised a brow, deploying his hookup voice which wasn't helping my level of irritation. "What do you shave, Maggie."

A sly grin slid over those plump lips as Maggie reached to put her hands on my cousin's shoulders. He leaned down so she could whisper in his ear. Cam knew the rule. She was off-limits, but that didn't stop the flare of jealousy in my chest when her lips were a mere breath away from his skin, their bodies inches apart, and I knew exactly where his mind was right now. My hands curled into fists.

The urge to drag them apart and catapult my cousin into the lake stalled out when whatever Maggie had said made Cam's smirk crash, and his eyes damn near launched out of his skull.

"Fuck," he exhaled.

Clapping once, she was back on the trail. "Time's up, boys. Let's go! Second place gets a Maggie Medal for losing to me!"

I wasn't proud of it, but I'd push a brother down to get another medal. I had six so far.

Cam hadn't moved yet, mouth gaped open like he was on a mission to control the lake's bug population.

I smacked his arm. "What did she say?"

He didn't answer. He hadn't so much as blinked.

"Camden!" I implored.

"*Everything*," he whispered. "She shaves *everything*."

Shutting my eyes, I swallowed. Hard. "Sweet Jesus."

Maggie said something to us, but I couldn't identify the words due to the relocation of blood from the head on the top of my body to the one below my waist.

"Mase..." Cam gulped, staring at Maggie while she dragged Noah back onto the trail. "I hate you."

"I know."

Those brown eyes met mine with all seriousness. "No. I mean, I really hate you."

I knew what he meant by that. I'd hate his ass, too, if the roles were reversed. I kinda hated myself for getting stuck, scared of moving forward with her, not risking what we had for more.

"Yeah," I sighed.

Cam shot a look down to the tent in his shorts. "How the fuck am I gonna run with this monster, now?"

He had a good point. I wasn't gonna win my seventh Maggie Medal today.

I shouted, "Go ahead, Sticks. Cam and I are gonna take another...minute."

chapter fifty-one

maggie

"What are you doing for Thanksgiving, Maggie?" Having just come home from work and not yet changed out of her lavender suit, Mrs. Scott placed a wine bottle in the fridge after pouring herself a glass.

Thanksgiving… That was two days away, which meant nothing to me. Jamey and Ava usually went to Arizona for the holidays to visit family, but since Jamey had a boyfriend now and Ava's salon was booked solid for the next two months, they were spending it here with the Scotts. I was disturbed by how much that bothered me.

I wished Frankie and Paula would keep the café open, so I had an excuse not to be home. When I asked them, though, they thought I was crazy. Even when I argued that business had picked up recently, which was true. Though it wasn't nearly what it used to be, the RAMs were coming every Friday night, and with their social media influence, more attention had been drawn to Sands Drive. The café had already outsold last year's Thanksgiving pie sales by five percent. Wasn't much, but it was something.

Working on my answer, I closed the oven door and reset the timer for the roast. "Oh, uh, my father and I don't really celebrate it."

The glass of wine was now hovering near her lips, questions filling her crystal blue eyes. "You don't have family over?"

"No, it's just us. And since it's a lot of work for only two people, I get turkey slices from the deli, and he's fine with that," I lied. Because that was what I did now. All the time.

Mrs. Scott set her glass on the island, gaze lingering on the pale gold contents. "Why don't you spend Thanksgiving Day with us?" Her eyes flicked up to mine, eager and bright. "You can kick back and relax for the day. Maybe have a little fun?"

I wasn't sure how long I had stared at her, but it had to be much longer than deemed socially acceptable. "Oh, Mrs. Scott. Thank you, but I couldn't."

She straightened as concern ruffled her brow. "Maggie, do you not feel welcome unless you're here to work?"

Well, it was more of a case that my father would never agree to anything that could be described with the words *kick back, relax,* or *fun.* Particularly if the Scotts were involved. But sure, we could go with her line of thinking.

"No, I feel welcome. But I…" I squirmed, grasping for a way to explain this without being insulting. "The times that I've been here without actually working, I've felt a little uncomfortable. I'm your employee, and it doesn't seem right to be here otherwise."

That was clearly not the correct response because I could practically see her mind racing as her short nails drummed on the glass. "Okay, so what if you worked Thanksgiving? If that would ease your discomfort in some way, we could do that. I'd pay you double, of course. And from here on out, I promise that any fun or enjoyment you may have that is not work-related, incidental or otherwise, won't count against you on major holidays."

She was much too eager about this, and while the entire idea of being here on a holiday made me squirm even more, double pay was too hard to pass up.

I wrung my hands together. "Thanksgiving is a family day, Mrs. Scott. But I'd be happy to cook the meal and leave. Or after serving and cleaning—"

"Maggie," she rushed to cut me off. "Though I love your cooking, and I know you would create a wonderful meal, it's your company that I'm really after. I'm just grasping at whatever angle I can to convince you to spend the day with us. Besides, you're practically family, and it would be nice to get to know your dad better."

My stomach lurched as my blood ran cold. "My…father? Y—you want my father to come?"

"Yes." She drew out the word as if she were trying to remember its meaning, and then her eyes grew wide. "Oh, did I not say that earlier? I meant to. Of course, he can come. Especially if it's only the two of you. I wouldn't want him to be alone on Thanksgiving."

Good God.

My father? *Here?* I didn't want him to step one foot inside the Scotts' home, let alone eat a meal with them. My father only had contempt for the Scotts. And any sane and rational person who didn't care for the host of a party would turn the invitation down, but I didn't know what he would do because my father wasn't rational.

Or sane.

I smiled, but it dimmed quickly. "Maybe. I can talk to him about it. But if we come, I can't accept payment. It wouldn't be right."

Laughing, she stood and swung her arm around me to give me a half-hug. "Nonsense. I've tried my hand at Thanksgiving dinner, and I know how much work is involved. The guest list is now up to twelve mouths to feed. You will absolutely be accepting pay for that."

With that, she and her glass of chardonnay disappeared upstairs. I glanced over through the butler's pantry to the dining room as unease slithered across my skin, trying to picture my father there.

As good as their intentions were, the Scotts really did have the worst ideas.

My shift was over, and Mrs. Scott's meal was plated. Mason hadn't stopped over after practice, and I was secretly glad because that meant I didn't have to see the look on his face when I declined a ride home. I needed to make an excuse journal for all the lies I'd told. Between the after-work ride offers, Friday night game invites, and explaining why I was intermittently handicapped, I was beginning to forget which reasons I'd exhausted already.

Arriving an hour before my father was due home, I pulled my bike into the carport and got to work with Poker making loops around me, itching for a long run.

Cue another stab of guilt.

I prepared dinner and had the chores finished as the Tahoe crunched over the sticks and leaves outside. My pulse kicked up, palms immediately clammy. Poker plodded his way over and sat next to me, facing the front door while I put away the cookware. Unfortunately, Poker's close proximity did nothing to calm my nerves.

As the door opened, I pulled a beer from the fridge and set it on the counter. He made quick work of plugging his phone into the charger as I plated his meal, keeping to the other side of the kitchen. He swiped the beer bottle into his thick paw as he went down the hall to change his clothes, returning with the beer emptied.

All without exchanging one word.

Because that was how we both preferred our relationship. Wordless. But that didn't work when I had to use words to invite him to the Scotts' for Thanksgiving.

He took his spot at the table, picking up his fork and poking at the mound of spaghetti as if searching for its weak point first. I imagined that was how he approached everything and everyone in his life.

I swiped my damp hands on my jeans as I swallowed. "S—sir, may I speak with you?"

If I struggled to remember the last time we spoke, I think it had been six days ago. When I was belted five times for not putting enough ice in his whiskey glass. He'd been sober then. He never used to punish me for such trivial things, but it had been like this ever since Marcus had sent my father those photographs. He used any excuse he could.

Sliding me a sideways glare, he reluctantly set his fork on the plate. Then spoke with even more reluctance. Or maybe that was abhorrence.

"What is it?"

I stayed rooted to my spot by the counter as I said, "The Scotts have invited us over for Thanksgiving. Mrs. Scott asked me to cook for her family, and she thought it would be nice for us to spend the day and get to know you better."

His dark brows climbed toward the ceiling, tone sardonic as he repeated my words. "Nice to get to know me?"

Right. I had to speak in terms he'd understand because any human emotion that wasn't fueled by hate confused him. "She offered to pay me double. I would like to work if you don't want to go."

Either considering the offer or disregarding it completely, he took a long swig from the fresh longneck I'd left by his plate. He pierced me with a wintry stare. "So if you go, I won't have dinner Thursday. Is that what you are telling me?"

It would take decades of the world's leading forensic psychiatrists to diagnose everything that was wrong with this man.

Maybe...I could appeal to his sense of nostalgia. Surely, at some point in his life, he had celebrated Thanksgiving. "Sir, it's just that— We've never had a Thanksgiving dinner. I thought it would be nice." Yeah, nice was the word of the day apparently because *good* or *fun* couldn't be substituted in there.

A grunt worked in this throat. His focus went to twirling the spaghetti strands again, marinara splattering the rim of the plate like a murder victim bleeding out.

"Tell them I'll try to make it."

I was somewhere between wanting to jump for joy because I'd have my first real Thanksgiving and desperate to bash my head against a rock because I'd have to spend my first real Thanksgiving with my father.

"Yes, sir."

A red stick of licorice appeared in front of my face, the limp candy slowly bending to its own weight. I blinked at it and the fingers holding it.

"When did you buy...? Never mind." I plucked the Red Vine out of Mason's hand and took a bite. Oh, that was good. I think I moaned. "Ava really doesn't know what she's missing with the magic of corn syrup and red dye number forty."

Mason chuckled as his left hand controlled BB and his right switched the radio from Brothers Osborne to Florida Georgia Line. This morning's football practice had been canceled, and Mason had taken me to Pacific Cliffs because I needed to buy an obscene amount of food for tomorrow. Sadly, being that tomorrow was Thanksgiving and everyone had done their shopping already, Henry's didn't have everything I needed.

During an extensive shopping trip, even by my standards, Mason hadn't batted an eye at the list, which may have been the length of his arm. He didn't laugh during my ten-minute external debate on cooking one giant turkey versus two smaller ones. He didn't hesitate to ask the butcher if they had defrosted turkeys the second I freaked out after we learned how long it would take to defrost the sizes I needed. He didn't balk at the total that popped up on the register after I insisted he sign up for one of those shopper loyalty cards. And he didn't drive us straight home after we packed up the truck. He took that hundred-dollar savings to Target and had me pick out socks, scarves, jackets, and blankets for the homeless.

He then walked out of Target with five hundred dollars worth of merchandise and my entire heart. And now we were headed back to town to hand out our goodies like Santa's elves. In November.

I was sure he'd rather be doing anything else today, but he didn't act like it. He actually seemed to enjoy spending time with me doing the most mundane tasks. And before I asked him why and made a complete ass of myself, I focused on something else.

I wagged my licorice at the radio. "Why do you only listen to country in your truck?"

Mason glanced over at me, eyes shielded by his Ray-Bans as he paused his singalong to "Sittin' Pretty." One dimple popped. "Why do you think I only listen to country in my truck?"

"Because you don't listen to it any other time," I stated. "Heavy metal is for when you work out—hard rock specifically for cardio, though. Alternative rock is reserved for when you're broody. Pop music when you're feeling chipper, and country…" I thought that over, coming up blank. "Well, I haven't pinned that down yet. It's similar to your pop mood, but there's a subtle difference."

Now his brows were reaching for the atmosphere. "I get broody?"

"Oh, yes." I nodded. Emphatically. "Very."

He seemed to be fighting it, but the other dimple appeared when he looked toward the windshield. "And you noticed all that?"

"What can I say?" I grinned while I nibbled at my stick. "The stimulation in here was lacking."

Head tipped back, he barked a laugh. "I'm impressed. Truly. No girl has ever noticed that about me before. Hell, I didn't even notice that about me."

The thought of Mason with other girls knocked the giddiness right out of me. Girls…they noticed Mason. Maybe not his musical preference, but everything else was well noticed. Wherever he went, there was a constant flirt fest, from striking up a casual conversation to all-out touching him with zero regard that I was there or not. And why should they care?

Mason and I were *nothing more*.

And I knew those girls interacted with Mason when I wasn't around, too. They were in every class, all over campus, at the games, and at the RAM house. If he'd been with any of them, I didn't want to know.

I think there was something wrong with the candy. Like it had gone bad or something because my stomach wasn't feeling so great anymore.

Mason shrugged. "I guess when I listen to country, you could say that I feel…relaxed. At ease."

Oh. Yeah, I could see that. But apparently, I didn't see that I'd finished my Red Vine because Mason was already offering up another. I took it.

"Thanks. Hey, did you get around to asking Charlie what she was doing tomorrow?"

While things weren't exactly back to normal between Mason and Charlie, I was happy they were friends again. She'd joined us on the lawn for lunch a few times—or her version of lunch, which consisted of a lot of salad that she picked through rather than eat while she handled her social media. It wasn't my place to invite her to the Scotts' home, but I didn't want her to be alone on Thanksgiving. Nor did I want her to have to spend it with her awful parents.

Mason slowed the truck at the yellow light and stopped. He could have made it if he'd punched the accelerator. "Oh, I thought she told you. Charlie was offered a last-minute spot for the spring *Vogue* shoot. Model got sick or something. She left for New York this morning."

"Oh. No, I hadn't heard. Good for her."

"Yeah." From somewhere on the side of his door, plastic crinkled, and another Red Vine appeared. And I took that one, too. "Sticks, I had an idea."

The candy paused outside of my lips. "Is it better than shoving a Cornish hen inside of the turkey and convincing Camden that the turkey was pregnant?"

Mouth wide, his palm smacked the steering wheel. "You laughed, but he would so fall for that!"

I giggled because Camden so would have. From the corner of my eye, I realized Mason was watching me. I must have made a fine sight, grinning like a goober with licorice smashed between my lips. Pulling it out, I gestured to him. "Let's hear it."

He cleared his throat, taking the turn once the light was green. "I'd like to pick you and Poker up early tomorrow. He could stay at the house for the day, so he doesn't have to be alone on Thanksgiving, and before you start working your food magic, the three of us could go on a run around the lake. I think Poker would like that."

My heart pranced around in my chest like a happy deer. "That's…" *Sweet. Thoughtful. The best idea he'd ever had.* "That's okay. But thank you."

His free hand gripped the wheel, the muscles in his forearm bunched into tight cords. He'd been acting this way a lot lately. I could bring on instant irritation with one look. The candy in my stomach soured again, expecting the inevitable blowup. It took three seconds. Last week, it was eight.

"Why do I get the feeling it's wrong for us to hang out?" he asked.

Because it is. Because I can't be caught within ten feet of you or my father will… God, I still couldn't think those words.

I turned a little too fast in my seat, and the belt locked up, sending me backward. I tried it again…success. "My father has rules, Mason. I'm following them. Don't forget, he has eyes everywhere."

More specifically, Marcus has eyes everywhere.

Only one side of his face was visible, but I imagined both corners of his mouth were folded down. "I can't forget because you're constantly scanning the roads for black and whites like we're pedaling meth instead of driving to the fucking grocery store."

He was right. Guilt festered like a cancer in my chest, spreading with every tense moment between us. I shrunk in my seat. "I'm sorry. I don't mean to make you feel that way."

Eleven seconds later, his voice lost the sharp edge, but his body language didn't. "Help me understand. What's the rule exactly? Is it me? Because of what Taylor did?"

Well, that certainly didn't help.

I lied...kinda. "I'm his only daughter, Mason. He's overprotective."

The skin around his mouth whitened. "You're eighteen. What's he gonna do? Take your mascara away?"

I shot him a dry look. "No, but that's a good one. I'll put it in the suggestion box for next time."

He blew out a deep, practiced sigh. "You drive me insane, just like these fucking things on my face."

"Yeah, you need to boycott Mutton Chop Month next year. Stupidest tradition ever."

He grunted and ripped off a bite of his Red Vine. "Tell you what, I—"

BB came to an abrupt stop in the middle of Sands Drive, the seatbelt thankfully preventing my face from becoming one with the dashboard. As I dug the belt out of my throat, Mason had taken his sunglass off, gaze latched onto something in the distance.

"What's wrong? Why did you..." I followed his line of sight to the street across from the café, and the three strips of candy I'd eaten threatened a reprise. "Oh, no." Almost a month since Trudy had closed her doors, Rick had put up a sign in the barbershop window. In fact, I think it was the same one.

GOING OUT OF BUSINESS.

My gaze trailed over to the alley between Rick's and what had been Trudy's storefront. There was...nothing there. My eyes snapped over to the basket outside of the café. The brownies I'd put out this morning were still on top. Those should definitely be gone by now. A shiver of dread raced across my flesh, leaving goosebumps in its wake.

I couldn't remember if I said anything to Mason before unclicking my belt and flying out of the cab. The brisk ocean wind ripped right through my jeans and hoodie as I sprinted across the street and toward the alley.

"Ronnie? *Ronnie!*"

The closer I got, the more I could see the alley and what wasn't there. I stopped dead right in the opening, breaths sawing out of my chest. There wasn't a ratty brown blanket, cardboard box, pile of newspapers, orange peels… There was no Ronnie. There wasn't even a trace that anyone had been here.

"Mags?"

I flipped around to Henry crossing the street, wringing a rag between his hands. My mouth opened. Shut. There were so many questions I wanted to ask, but fear kept the words from escaping.

"Mags, I'm sorry," Henry began. "The boys came right after you did this morning. But they…they were real good about it."

"Real good about what, Henry?" Mason growled, coming to stand next to me. With a quick check, Mason hadn't bothered to put his sweater on before coming over here. In fact, he hadn't even turned off his truck. It was still idling in the middle of the street with both doors winged out. "What were the boys real good about?"

Henry's eyes bounced between Mason and me, and then his chin met his chest, no longer able to look at either of us.

"The vagrant laws," I choked out, eyes pricking with heat. "Right? Marcus made the boys enforce the vagrant laws. They took them away."

Mason gaped at me and then Henry. "No. No, we— We bought clothes and deodorant and pretzels and…" Mason stomped over to the other side of the barbershop before coming back. His chest heaved, hands curled into fists at his sides. "Where? Where did they take them?"

Henry was now strangling his rag. "Pacific Cliffs. I overheard LJ say he found a shelter up there that could take them. It's not a bad thing, Mags. It's getting colder out, and you know Ronnie's had a bad cough lately. And that new guy with the limp—"

"Ed," Mason cut in. "His name is Ed. He's a vet and has severe PTSD, but the VA kept shuffling him around and ignoring him, not giving a damn when he lost family and then his house. I suppose Mick is gone, too, along with Tessa and Bo?"

I was in too much shock to be impressed that Mason had not only learned but remembered all their names. I shouldn't be shocked because he'd spent as much time with them as I did lately.

Paling, Henry looked away from Mason, his throat working. "Yeah," he said roughly. "But I meant it. The boys did right by them. Marcus, he… He wanted to throw them in jail, but the boys—They came down on their day off and got them out of here first, so Marcus wouldn't know."

Mason grumbled something, but his jaw was so tight, I couldn't understand what. It wasn't fair for Mason to take his anger out on Henry, but this was a lot to take all at once. He'd…he'd gotten close to all of them. Gave them silly nicknames, and he truly cared about their welfare. That was why he'd spent all that money shopping for them today. He even thought to get feminine hygiene supplies, too.

I nodded, feeling a knot in my throat expand. "I know they did, Henry, but they wouldn't have had to if we had the means to help. *Really* help. Marcus didn't have to cut taxes for himself and his wealthy donors. He could have used that money to build shelters, provide medical and psychiatric care. They needed a break, not to keep getting broken by a broken system. And it's only a matter of time before you and—" My shoulders fell along with what was left of my spirit. There was no use. I was fighting a battle I didn't know I'd lost more than a year ago. "Thanks, Henry. Thanks for telling me. Have…have a good Thanksgiving."

I trudged back over to BB, climbed up, and buckled in. My palm was sticky, and I looked down to find it was covered in the remnants of corn syrup and red dye number forty. I must have dropped my Red Vine somewhere outside.

Mason climbed into the cab a minute later and slammed his door. I flinched. He didn't have to say why he was so pissed. I knew the only thing running through his mind wasn't the five hundred dollars he'd spent for people who had just been carted away. It was that this was a reminder that very soon, none of this would be here. The café…wouldn't be here. Along with the remnants of the good memories he had left of Faith.

I blinked my tears back. "I'm sorry. I'm so sorry, Mason."

He fully turned to me, his gaze colliding with mine. In those peridot eyes, rage brewed, so turbulent and deadly, it knocked the air out of my chest. The lines of his face sharpened, a shadow of fury darkening his features. Both of his hands reached out and gently cupped my cheeks, a stark contrast to the anger inundating his veins.

"There is not one goddamned thing you should apologize for. They're the ones who are going to be sorry, Sticks. The ones responsible for this. I'll fucking make sure of it."

chapter fifty-two

maggie

Thanksgiving morning, I arrived at the Scotts' before the crack of dawn. I knew I'd need extra time to prep today, and since I hadn't been able to sleep anyway, I came early and used the quiet time to knock out most of my knife work. My tremor didn't make that task easy or pretty. Thankfully, no one was around to see it.

With the first batch of bacon cooked, Mason and Matt roused. I smiled to myself when I heard them on the stairs. Food was like a siren's call to those men.

Stepping into the kitchen first, Matt hugged me good morning and kissed my forehead before grabbing the steaming cup of coffee I had brewed and ready for him on the Keurig. Muttering his greeting as he slid past me to the plate of bacon, Mason was unusually quiet and had been since we'd left Sands Drive yesterday. I hadn't helped matters when I turned down *another* ride home at the end of my shift. Each lie, excuse, and denial of him burned a little deeper than the last, and it was unfair of me to hope that he'd never stop trying.

By late morning, Jamey arrived with Ben's family. The guys went down to the lakeshore to play football, and Jamey went to watch Ben take off his shirt. I wouldn't have minded joining the view—Mason's shirtless body, of course—but there was too much left to do.

"You should come, Maggie!" Ashley declared, snapping me out of the fantasy of a sweaty, shirtless Mason covered in dirt.

"Oh! That's a great idea, Ash!" Mrs. Scott set her wine glass on the island and gripped her sister-in-law's arm with both hands. "Mason would love to have you there, Maggie."

"Love to…? I'm sorry." I shook my head, lowering the oven door. "Have me where?"

Ashley refilled her glass with the bottle of chardonnay the women had been sharing. "Our nephew's wedding, silly. It's in three weeks."

I stood with the baster in my hand, shocked stupid. Me? Go to a wedding? All the way out in Grove Point?

"I…my father wouldn't be comfortable with that." At all. For a million punishable reasons.

Mrs. Scott wiggled in her stool, an eager grin playing on her lips. "We could ask him tonight."

I shut the oven door before I fell into it and we ended up with Maggie-flavored turkeys. "No, please, Mrs. Scott. I'll ask him another time. Really." That must have flown out a little fast since both women drew away with matching winces.

Awesome. I'd offended three Scotts in two days.

Ashley plastered on a forced smile. "It was just an idea."

"And it's very generous. It is. But I don't ha— Thank you." I cut my thoughts short because they didn't need to know that even if I could go, I didn't have extra money for random overnight getaways to wine country. Not to mention the clothes I would need for a shindig like that. Grove Point wasn't likely to host a wedding where thrift store duds and used Chucks were acceptable attire.

Mrs. Scott's eyes widened as if she'd read my mind. "Oh, Maggie. Is that the reason? I didn't expect you… Sweetie, we would take care of everything. I wouldn't dream of inviting you otherwise."

A drop of sweat slipped between my shoulder blades, and in an odd contrast, my throat dried. "Mrs. Scott, that's too much."

Glass back in hand, she waved me off like I was crazy. "It's not, Maggie. It's not too much at all."

I assumed they had already made up their minds by their renewed cheeriness, so I preoccupied myself with dinner, but I couldn't help overhearing the wedding plans this time since I was no longer fantasizing about Mason.

Apparently, the bride's family owned a vineyard and had booked a nearby hotel for the weekend. Something told me it would be one of those that put chocolates on pillows and offered fancy things like turndown service. There was a rehearsal dinner on Friday night, a family breakfast Saturday morning, and then the wedding in the late afternoon. Plus, a brunch Sunday morning before the couple left for their honeymoon in Bora Bora.

It sounded perfect. Well, perfect except for the outdoor winter wedding part.

For a split second, I let my mind wander as I tended the cranberry sauce. That weekend, my father and the boys were going to Vegas for Robert's bachelor party, and I had planned to ask Frankie for the time off so I could enjoy a few days of freedom. I let myself imagine what dancing with Mason would be like. Him in a suit. Me in a dress. Mason *not* wearing a suit and me *not* wearing a dress—

That fantasy would never happen, and that...something bitter and caustic rose up the back of my throat. The likely outcome was that Mason would be at that wedding, and he'd wear a suit. He would look striking and handsome, and then he'd drink. There would be beautiful women there, wearing beautiful dresses and beautiful heels also drinking. Those women would notice Mason, and he would give them that dimpled smile and take them to his hotel room, and then her beautiful dress would be in a pile on the floor next to his suit.

I was gonna lose my oatmeal.

"Maggie, are you alright?"

As Mrs. Scott's voice cut through my thoughts, the wooden spoon flew out of my hand and hit a cabinet.

"Huh?" I tracked the trail of bright cranberry sauce that made the kitchen look as if a crime scene had occurred here. "Oh, shoot. I'm sorry."

Mrs. Scott stood from her stool and met me on the other side of the island, gripping onto me. "The mess can wait. What happened? You zoned out."

"Yes, Mrs. Scott. That was all it was. I was just in my head. I thought I added too much sugar and ruined the sauce."

And that would count as lie number 5,301.

Hours had flown by, and I had most of the food ready. Ashley and Mrs. Scott did their best to help, but their skills were limited, and the wine hadn't improved matters. Mrs. Scott was usually a hugger, but somewhere around the sweet potato casserole, she started to throw kisses in, making my heart squeeze with longing every time.

"We kicked your ass, and you know it!" Mason's deep voice carried through the French doors, and yep, he was shirtless *and* sweaty *and* dirty. His voice alone caused a maelstrom of nerve endings low in my core to ignite, but that body plus his voice? Mutton chops be damned, my ovaries just exploded. It was obscene how sexy Mason Scott was.

Fingers digging into the sides of his face like his bones itched, Mason crossed the kitchen, and I turned my focus to the tray in front of me, but my knees were getting wobbly the closer he came.

Snagging a cheese cube, Ben argued, "I had the interception. If Cam hadn't tripped—"

"Whoa, whoa, whoa!" The crackers in Camden's hand were at risk of crumbling in his grip. "I have never fucking tripped!"

"Oh, bull-fucking-shit," Matt jeered.

"Fuck you very much," Camden fired back, grabbing a hand full of pretzels. "I run like a fucking gazelle."

Mason snorted. "A gazelle on crack, maybe. You're so fucking—"

"Boys!" Ashley yelled, and all the guys stopped dead, eyes wide, heads snapping to her direction. Her face was red, possibly on the verge of taking someone across her knee. "*Enough* with the F-bombs."

"Sorry, Mom," mixed in with, "Sorry, Aunt Ash," and she nodded, satisfied and relaxed now.

The guys relocated their attention back to the food, and I was swarmed with bare torsos. Okay, so…Thanksgiving might be my favorite holiday.

"Ew! Dan!" Cringing, Mrs. Scott pushed against his slick chest to keep him from hugging her. "You're all sweaty and dirty. You all better take showers before dinner. I will not have you smell up my house."

He chuckled, attempting to wrap his arms around her again. "I remember a time that you didn't mind that I was sweaty or dirty."

She scooted around the island. "You're delusional. There was never a time that I didn't mind it."

He stilled, amusement lighting his eyes. "Really. Because I seem to remember just last night—"

"Finish that sentence, and we're going to have more than turkey innards rotting in our trashcan."

Conceding, Mr. Scott laughed.

Ashley's fine brow arched at her advancing husband, onyx eyes full of warning. "She was talking to you too, Will. Hit the showers."

Under the ends of my hair, the nape of my neck tingled while I refilled the cashew bowl. A familiar tattooed arm swung in front of me and stole a handful.

I frowned at the bowl and then him. "You didn't wash your hands."

Ignoring my complaint, Mason grabbed more nuts with his other hand, effectively trapping me between his body and the counter. While everyone was bickering about showering and football fumbles, I felt

Mason slowly press against my back, his chest spanning my shoulder blades as his knee brushed the outside of mine, arms caging me. He was so casual about it, but it was taking everything I had to keep still. Mason's warmth bled past my clothes, breaths softly floating along on my neck, my heart pounding within my ribcage as if to test the structural integrity of the cartilage keeping the bones together.

I tipped my chin up and to the side, and as soon as our gazes collided, the muscles in my belly tightened, breaths coming to a halt.

Oh, goodness. His dimples—both of them—were out to play, and in the next strained heartbeat, the array of citrine and peridot in his eyes darkened. I had thought at one time this was a hungry stare of lust and want. I'd come to learn that it was simply the way Mason looked at me now.

Nothing he desired.

Nothing special.

Nothing more.

Dipping low, his smooth lips teased the shell of my ear, and I was legitimately questioning if there was something medically wrong with my lungs now. I couldn't seem to get any air.

"You don't know what you're missing, Sticks," he rumbled just loud enough for me to hear, the dark vibration of his voice going where it had no business going, and I swore my panties felt damper than a moment ago. "Nuts are pretty damn delicious. Even the dirty ones." A wink followed that gem right before he shoved off and headed up to take a shower.

Yeah…I got the meaning.

Along with a short fuse, Mason had been channeling his inner Camden lately, too. He wasn't shy about the innuendos or dirty jokes, and Mason no longer threatened Camden when they flew out of his mouth either. I had accepted that to mean Mason thought of me as one of the guys.

Freaking perfect.

As the men herded toward their respective showers, I assessed the damage. What in the…? Herded was the perfect descriptor. It looked as if a pack of wild buffalo had trampled through the kitchen and all over my appetizers. I sighed.

Jamey helped me replenish the snack trays as the doorbell rang in its elaborate melody. Mrs. Scott leapt up from her stool. I figured it was Ava. She'd taken a last-minute client this morning, and word was that client was über famous. Her third über famous client this week.

"Coming! I swear I'll get there!" Mrs. Scott clopped across the living room in her heels, the alarm chirping as she opened the front door. "Oh, you made it! Wonderful. Maggie, your dad's here," she called with drunk enthusiasm.

Swallowing was suddenly impossible. And the situation only got worse when I heard Candi's voice.

Jamey clutched my hand, whispering, "Holy Winchester brothers."

I didn't know why Jamey was referencing a rifle manufacturer, but there wasn't time to find out. What was Candi doing here?

I mouthed to Jamey, *What the hell?*

"Thank you for the invitation, Dr. Scott," my father said. "This is Candi, my girlfriend."

Girlfriend? My face immediately soured, and Jamey muttered, "Well, he can't exactly say 'fuck buddy,' can he?"

Squeezing my eyes shut, I whimpered, "So gross."

"Call me Eve. Pleased to meet you, Candi. Come in, come in." Mrs. Scott was too happy, tipsy, and clueless that she had welcomed a dragon into her house and was leading it right to his prey. "This is my sister-in-law, Ashley."

Ashley greeted them with an elegant handshake and didn't seem to notice or care that Candi's dress was a size too small, and her heels were best fit for a stage and bills raining over her.

Jamey's hand curled around my hip, sensing I needed the support because my blood pressure had just plummeted.

My father trailed the Scotts into the kitchen, those eyes of ice finding me. They were bright and clear for a change. His chiseled features were clean-shaven and undeniably handsome. He was wearing the Dad Face today. It was like a Halloween mask, and underneath was a monster so ferocious and ugly that I was the only one to see it.

Taking in the spread on the island and the food ready to be served behind me, he said, "Eve, you've put my daughter's excellent skills to work. It's been a long time since we've had a Thanksgiving dinner. I can't wait."

Long time as in…*never?*

His gaze rested on me, heavy and suffocating. And even in this home of sanctuary and everyone in it who cared for me, I cowered like I always did in his presence.

chapter fifty-three

mason

Buttoning my jeans, my stomach growled at the scent of all the savory turkey goodness melding with sweet butter and pie crust. I groaned, throwing my head back and all. If I wasn't careful, someone would get the wrong idea as to what I was doing in here.

From the closet, I yanked out the first shirt I saw, far too excited to get down those stairs. I'd been looking forward to this dinner ever since Mom told me she'd asked Maggie to come, but it wasn't just the food I was jonesing for. Today would give me a chance to get to know Maggie's father better. Maybe try to change his opinion of my family. That and he struck me as the ask-my-permission-first kinda guy.

Pulling on my boots, I heard the chief's voice downstairs. A grin tugged at my mouth. This was it. Today, I would start Operation End the Friend Zone.

I was gonna blow that fucker to smithereens.

Running a hand through my wet hair, I stepped down the stairs to find Dad shaking the chief's hand.

"Nathan, so glad you could make it."

I didn't know why, but I had expected the chief to be wearing a uniform. Maybe because that was the only thing I'd ever seen him wear. Today, though, he was sporting dark jeans and a black polo with sleek black shoes. While not bedecked in designer labels, it was far nicer than the rags that Maggie usually wore, and it took me a second to realize he had brought Candi with him.

The chief withdrew his hand, placing it around the woman's waist at his side. "It's Nate, please."

Dad looked to the chief's plus one with a warm smile. "Candi, it's wonderful to see you again."

"Thank you for having us." She swayed her hips in a way that I honestly couldn't tell if she was trying to flirt or that was her state of being.

Either way, the act was lost on Dad. Candi could strip down to a thong and tassels in front of him, and the man's only frame of mind would be to ask when the last time was that she had her moles checked.

"And you've both met my other son, Matt." Dad directed the focus to my brother.

Matt reached over with his hand out. "Good to see you again, Chief."

"You, as well." Shaking hands with Matt, the chief asked, "Hey, what position do you play? I never asked Margaret."

"Quarterback," he answered, and as I settled on the landing, Matt threw an arm around my shoulders. "Mason's my RB and drooling for my spot on the team."

Ignoring my brother, I greeted the couple. "Mr. Davis, Candi. Thank you for joining us today."

"Thank you for the invitation. It was very generous of your family to include us." The chief's brow suddenly creased, gaze bouncing between us as he switched back to the previous topic. "Playoffs are coming up, right?"

"They are. The schedule's been an absolute mess because of the storms," Cam answered from the other side of the kitchen. The side where Maggie was. I watched as he nabbed a deviled egg from the tray in front of her, and then…lingered in her airspace.

My eye twitched.

"Hell, I haven't even caught a game yet," the chief mused, bringing my attention back to him. When our eyes met, my breath got hung up somewhere around my diaphragm. It was apparent he'd been watching me, just wasn't sure if he knew who I'd been focused on.

"Welp," Cam threw back the egg and spoke out the side of his mouth, "I don't expect we'll make the playoffs, but there are a few games left still. If you can only make it to one, I suggest our game against Pacific Ridge."

The chief's gaze skipped back to my cousin. "If history is any indication, that might be an interesting night for us at the station."

As Maggie stepped past the island, Dad folded his arm around her, and she glimpsed up at him in shock as though he hadn't done that a hundred times before. Usually, a bright smile would reflect back to him along with flushed cheeks and a look of pure adoration, but not this time.

She had…pretty much turned gray.

"I'm glad you could spare your daughter today, Nate. I don't know what I would have done without Maggie's cooking. Or her pies."

She gave Dad a brittle smile. "I wouldn't have made you suffer, Mr. Scott." Maggie slipped out of his arm and aimed toward the stove, leaving Dad with a puzzled expression. Okay, so it wasn't only me who thought something was off here.

Mr. Davis grinned. "The Crest Cent Café's pies do seem to be something of a legend around the Cove."

"Yeah, and lately, not only have the preorders been insane, but we can't even keep them on the shelves for walk-ins," Candi chimed in.

"Is that because Dad keeps buying them all every day?" Matt snickered, leaning against the wall.

Dad scoffed. "I'm not that bad. Am I, Maggie?"

"It really is best I don't answer that, Mr. Scott." She finished stirring up little cabbage heads in a skillet before lifting her head. "Dinner will be ready in about thirty minutes. Sir, Candi, would you like something to drink?"

It struck me that she never called him anything but *sir*. It was a little weird and…formal. But Maggie had refused to use my parents' first names, as well.

"Oh, a glass of white wine for me, please." Candi nodded appreciatively.

Mr. Davis answered, "Beer, please, Margaret."

Maggie swiftly moved to the fridge and drew out a Corona.

"*Margaret?*" Mom wondered, pouring Candi a glass of chardonnay. "Is that your given name?"

Maggie's lashes drifted down to shield her eyes, grip going white on the neck of the bottle. "Yes, it is." She popped the cap off as easily as any bartender could.

I hung back to watch as Maggie asked everyone else what they would care to drink, and as she moved, a cold sensation drifted through my chest. It wasn't my imagination. She was different, stiffer. It wasn't because of her balance, which was crap at best today. More like the transparent walls she put up had become solid before my eyes. During our shopping trip, she'd said she was nervous about cooking a holiday meal since she'd never done it before. Maybe that was all it was.

The doorbell rang again, and I left the room to answer it. On the porch, I was met by a head of blonde curls, warm hazel eyes, and a megawatt smile. "Ava, happy Thanksgiving." I drew her in for a hug since her arms were already splayed wide. "You're looking younger every time I see you."

Gasping, she drew back and clutched my forearms. "Be sure to tell my son that. I've been trying out this new face mask with bee venom and manuka honey—"

"God, Mom. Stop," Jamey complained behind me. "Mason doesn't care."

Still gripping onto me, she glared at him over my shoulder. "If it's good enough for the Duchess of Cambridge, it's good enough to discuss at a dinner party. So there." She stuck her tongue out at him.

I didn't doubt she received one in return.

I grinned as I swept aside for her, and with the grace of a duchess, she clipped in, wearing a dress that belonged to the Woodstock era, but she could pull it off. "Benny! Oh, you look so handsome!"

Benny? I mouthed, holding back a laugh, looking to my cousin. Never in my life had I heard anyone call him that. And never in my life would I have thought he'd allow that travesty to happen.

Throwing me an evil eye, a middle finger came my way that thankfully neither of our mothers saw. And if Ava noticed, I wouldn't know because she was busy squishing Ben's cheeks together.

My chest warmed at how loving she was toward my cousin, like she considered him as much a son as Jamey was. I wondered what that would be like with Mr. Davis. Would he put his arm around me, welcome me into his home? Would he be proud to think of me as a son?

I was probably getting ahead of myself.

Once Ava made the rounds with Ash and Will, Jamey introduced her to my parents, and while it didn't surprise me that Ava knew the chief, it was odd for me to witness their banter since their personalities were complete opposites.

"Nate, your daughter gets more gorgeous by the day. Soon, you're going to have college boys at your door." She threw a secretive wink my way that made my gut tense.

Looking to Ava, the chief wore a glint in his eye. "I don't know about college boys. I think I agreed to let her date when she's thirty."

"Thirty!" Candi exclaimed. "My God, just put her in a convent, then."

"The closest one is right outside of San José," he volleyed back, a smirk tugging at the corner of his mouth. "Or I could build one of those Rapunzel towers. Keith scouted the perfect spot. Gil's already agreed to help with the masonry work. Robert can design—"

"Nate," Candi chided.

He feigned innocence. "What?"

"You're so bad." Candi smacked his arm playfully, and he chuckled warmly at her.

Mom had everyone meander toward the living room with their drinks, laughter filling the house. I, of course, went right to the kitchen to help or ruin whatever Maggie was working on.

"Well, *Margaret*, are the turkeys ready to move?" I grinned, waiting for her to come at me with a smartass comment, but what I got made my balls run for cover.

With her head down, Maggie's frame went stiff, knuckles blanched on a serving spoon she was holding. "Don't call me that."

I blinked down at her, confusion swamping me. "I'm sorry. I was just—"

Whipping her head up to face me, Maggie's feet swerved a little, but she was quick to catch herself. The haze in her eyes vanished a moment later, and in came the fire, blazing right at me. "I know what you were *just*. Don't call me that. I hate that name."

My shoulders fell as my stomach bottomed out. "Maggie, I'm sorry. I didn't know."

Everything about her hardened when she spat, "Now you do."

I could only stand there, feeling about as tall as an ant as she shifted away from me, busying herself so she wouldn't have to look at me, talk to me. I meant nothing by it. I called her by her given name, for fuck's sake.

Her reaction was so visceral that panic slammed into me. I could almost see the waters raging between us, the waves too high, threatening to crash down, the current forcing us to separate shores.

Yesterday had been a wake-up call to both of us. The barbershop was closing. The huddled bodies along the walks and alleys were missing. Cardboard boxes and ratty blankets were cleaned out. Maggie hadn't wanted to talk about it, and I didn't blame her. Everything and everyone that she'd been fighting for was on the losing end of the war. However, she wasn't giving up. That wasn't Maggie. But her condition didn't allow her to handle stress well, and yesterday was a lot for anyone to take. Today…may have been too much for her. I'd seen these little vertigo spells kick in at least four times already, her tremor wasn't great, and she began rubbing her left temple ten minutes ago.

None of those were good signs.

I lowered my mouth to her ear, resting my palm flat between her shoulder blades. At my touch, she drew in a sharp gasp, going still.

"Maggie, I'm sorry. I really had no idea it bothered you."

She slowly released an unsteady breath. "I know you didn't." Maggie set down the spoon and rubbed her eyes with both hands. "I'm sorry I got all snippy. I haven't slept after everything that happened yesterday, and I'm pretty sure I screwed up your family's Thanksgiving dinner about fifty different ways." Before I could reassure her, her hands dropped, and those blue eyes lifted to mine. "I don't think of that as my name. I like being called Maggie. I like it when you call me Sticks. Mags, too. Just…any name but that one."

My hand skated down her spine, curling around her hip. Maggie's eyes slid shut as she leaned against me, resting her cheek where my heart was, and that damn organ beat faster me. I didn't realize how tense she was until that moment. Had I any clue how much stress she was carrying, I would have put a stop to today. She was so damn good at hiding her emotions that they didn't reveal themselves until she'd reached a breaking point.

Or her body did.

"I'll never say it again. Promise." Keeping my arm around her, I waved to all the serving dishes. "Can I get these for you now? I won't even make you say the H-word."

Oh, so slowly, her chin tipped up, eyes locking with mine. I was rewarded with a tease of her lips, not really a smile, but I'd take it. "Please."

"I'll carry. You tell me where to put them."

It was brief, but I caught it, and so did one vital part of me. Her lashes lowered to my mouth, lips parting on an inhale. With our bodies lined up, our mouths weren't but a few inches apart. It would only take a tip of her toes for her to close the distance if she wanted to. I wouldn't do a damn thing to stop her.

After a roll of her throat, her gaze rose to mine. "Okay."

She really couldn't know the strength it took to let her go just then.

Being the good boy I was, I carried everything to where she directed me, and I had to say, I never would have guessed this was Maggie's first time preparing a holiday dinner. The spread looked good enough for a MasterClass in Holiday Hosting. As everyone filed into the dining room, they were as astounded as I was. We'd never had a meal like this made from scratch in our home.

From one end of the table to the other sat sparkling crystal, my great grandmother's china, elegant silverware, and our fine linens. The table was decorated with three floral arrangements from Trudy's personal garden that I generously compensated her for. Unfortunately, she hadn't been the Prices' first victim, but I vowed she'd be the first to get her life back.

Among the flowers were baskets of warm rolls, two turkeys, mashed potatoes, sweet potatoes, green beans with almonds, cornbread dressing, Brussels sprouts with bacon, gravy, and cranberry sauce. Not the canned jellied stuff. Real fucking cranberries.

This was a Thanksgiving Day miracle.

Dad stood at the end of the table, admiring it all. "Our Thanksgiving didn't come in a box this year, guys!" He laughed and looked to the raven beauty next to me. "Maggie, thank you. And, Nate, I have to say, you certainly raised a lovely young woman. Maggie's earned a special spot in our hearts. Eve and I think the world of her."

"Us, too!" Matt said affronted, pointing between himself and me.

"And us." Ben waved to himself and Cam.

"And your brother and sister-in-law," Will added. "We're still hatching a plan to steal her from you."

Between Matt and me, Maggie's gaze had lowered, locking onto the floor. I couldn't be sure if she heard any of those compliments.

Mr. Davis looked across the table with an earnest smile. "My daughter had to grow out of her childhood faster than most. She's always been a hard worker."

I held up my soda. "To Sticks! Thank you for an awesome Thanksgiving."

"To Sticks!" Everyone but the chief repeated, clinking glasses.

"What is that nickname for, Mason?" he asked, helping Candi in her seat.

I waited for Maggie to slide into her seat before taking mine. I grinned wide and bright. "Well, the first time I met your daughter, I learned she keeps two ChapSticks on her at all times. The name kinda stuck."

He snickered at that. "You should have seen her in junior high. It used to be four. One in every pocket. Remember that, Jamey?"

Laughing, Jamey nodded. "And only the black or blue ChapStick."

"No cherry!" they said in unison.

Chuckling, the chief shook his head, wrapping a hand around his beer. "You know, it took me three years to realize that she hated the cherry flavor."

Mom gestured to Matt to pass the wine bottle. "How did you figure it out?"

Mr. Davis grinned at his daughter. "They were the only ChapSticks to meet their demise in the wash."

Giggling, Candi nudged him with her elbow. "Three years to figure that out? Some cop you are."

His laugh was deep and low, and then he whispered something to her that I couldn't hear.

Uncle Will and Dad began slicing the turkeys at each end of the table—or hacked into them would be a better description.

I leaned toward Maggie. "So… How many innocent cherry ChapSticks have died by Tide because of you?"

"Not enough." Maggie's voice sounded a bit strangled as she picked up her glass of water that Cam had filled for everyone earlier.

"I didn't know you were so coldhearted." My arm looped around her shoulders, and Maggie startled, splashing water in her lap.

I cringed for her, looking down to see the obvious wet spot spreading between her legs. Damn. I wish I thought to get her a straw. Or at least remind Cam not to fill her glass to the top.

"You know…" Mr. Davis watched Maggie furiously mop up her lap with a linen napkin. "From what I understand, Margaret has quite a few nicknames from my officers."

Candi giggled behind her napkin. "Yeah, they have a game they play every Saturday with her."

I felt my good mood evaporate, the jealousy creeping in like the fog, thickening, choking me by the second.

Matt shot me a knowing look. He knew which of his *officers* made my blood boil.

"Oh?" Mom said, looking to Maggie. "Do tell! Or, what is it you kids say these days? Spill the…something?"

"Tea," Ava offered, chin perched in her palm, looking to Maggie with the same eager expression. "It's spill the tea."

"God," Jamey grumbled.

Maggie's eyes darted between Mom and Ava before focusing on the mess in her lap. "It's silly. Besides, they don't know I know."

"Don't leave us in suspense. What's the game?" Dad asked, examining the turkey as though it were a patient, and wow…he killed that damn bird twice.

Discomfort tensed Maggie's features as she glimpsed back to Mom. "They…use part of my name to make up ridiculous nicknames for me like Magazinist or Maguey with the sole purpose to annoy me. And whoever guesses the right amount of times I roll my eyes or huff in irritation doesn't pay for breakfast. It's something they do to pass the time. Like I said. It's silly."

"Logan usually wins," Candi added, twirling a loose curl around her finger. "He hasn't paid for breakfast in months."

My molars ground together. Of course, Logan usually won. Gorilla Arms probably thought of nothing outside of Maggie and how much weight to stack on the barbell. He probably fantasized about using Maggie as a barbell.

"Jackson, huh?" Mr. Davis lifted a single brow, his jaw growing as tight as mine. "Sounds like he has too much time on his hands."

Huh. Who knew Nathan Davis and I were kindred spirits? I almost asked if he could give Logan traffic duty the next time a sewer pipe burst.

Candi shouldered him. "LJ's only having fun." The woman's hand slid under the table and into his lap. She was so sly, I think I was the only one to catch it. I could imagine she might have been a pro at some point.

The dishes were passed along, and once the plates were full, we began eating since we weren't the praying kinda fam.

During the meal, Maggie kept her eyes anchored to her plate like she wanted the chair legs to come alive and run her out of here. While I was more occupied with Maggie and her strange mood, I dimly heard Matt tease Cam about the three passes he missed because he heard Addison hadn't worn her panties to cheer one night.

Ashley held her glass of wine out for Will to refill as she asked, "Ben, did you show Jamey the house listings yet?"

I swore Maggie stiffened at that, and I glanced over to see she wasn't the only one. Jamey had stopped mid-chew of his turkey, hazel eyes locked with hers.

"Yeah," Ben answered, "but we also discussed moving into the RAM house next year. Not sure what we want to do yet."

"What?" That word was a little more than a whisper, but everyone heard Maggie say it.

Jamey's face was almost as pale as his hair, eyes still latched onto Maggie. "We were just talking about it. That's all, Mags."

"But we were—" Her gaze skipped to her father before crashing in her lap. "Sorry. It's none of my business."

"Mags, it is your business. If I don't stay at Warrington…" Jamey's words trailed off at the look of shock on both Ben and Ava's faces. He pressed on, "I'm sure we can find another place like before."

Maggie's shaky grip tightened on her fork. "Doesn't really seem like there's much of an *if* for you, Jamey."

Ben set his utensils down. "I'm sorry, Mags. I didn't mean to upset you. I didn't know—"

"It's my fault," Jamey offered. "I—"

"It's fine. Really," she cut him off, and the sprout she was trying to impale with her fork flew off the plate. Since it was closest to me, I nabbed it off the tablecloth and popped it into my mouth as if nothing happened. Except that it left a decent grease stain that I was sure Maggie noticed and was now internally freaking out over.

Jamey deflated in his seat. "Mags…"

"Look, we'll sit down and talk it over. All three of us. Right, Jamey?" Ben's gaze bounced between Jamey and Maggie.

After a thorough swallow, Jamey nodded to Ben.

A few beats of awkward silence passed, and Chief Davis excused himself to the bathroom. Silverware resumed scraping plates, and with Maggie focused on whatever plan Jamey had shit all over, Matt stole her buttered roll. Matt was a genius. Hopefully, that would get her mind off whatever was bothering her.

Maggie scanned the floor for her missing bread as I scooped the cranberries off her plate. When she popped back up, she studied her meal like it was a biology assignment. Busy piling on more cranberry sauce, she didn't notice Matt had pulled the napkin off her lap, so I could take her turkey.

Maggie righted herself, placing her napkin back in place, and her head sprung back and forth between Matt and me, both in deep conversation, ignoring her.

She collected another slice of turkey, and while Mom asked her about finals, Matt swiped up her sweet potatoes. Maggie turned back to the plate and gasped.

Shooting out of her seat, nearly knocking her chair over, Maggie's voice trembled. "Mr. Scott, can I see you outside, please?" She hadn't finished speaking when she bolted out of the dining room, disappeared around the corner, and then escaped out the back door.

Dad was already standing as he threw his napkin next to his plate. "I've got her. You guys stay." He sprinted after her, and regardless of whatever he said, I was on his heels. We found Maggie outside by the patio furniture, licking her lips manically, hugging herself in the chilled air.

Dad's hands went to her cheeks, stilling her movements. "Maggie? My God, you're pale. Sit." He helped her settle down on the cushion while I tried like hell not to freak out. I wasn't doing a very good job. Dad knelt next to her, and as he studied her eyes, his fingers went to her pulse point. "Take some deep breaths for me, okay."

She did, but the oxygen particles seemed laced with acid the way her chest rose raggedly. "I— I'm so sorry, Mr. Scott."

"None of that now. Tell me what's going on."

Her throat rolled thickly, looking to him. "I…I think a seizure's coming. I thought— I'm hallucinating, but it's never happened quite like that before."

"What did you see?" he asked, concerned.

Her pupils were huge, picking up the dwindling red rays of the sunset glimmering off the lake. My thighs tensed, ready to charge upstairs to get Dad's medical bag.

"I thought I had food on my plate, but then it was gone. Maybe I never put it on there. I've been a little stressed, but I—"

Oh, shit. This was my fault?

"Sticks, I'm sorry." I knelt next to Dad. "That was Matt and me. We were stealing your food."

She blinked at me. "What?"

"Sorry," I repeated, wincing. "We were just having fun."

"Poor thing." Laughing, Dad drew her in for a hug. "Give it some time, and you'll get used to the Scott pranks."

"Pranks?" she repeated, drawing away, and I nodded. She sagged into the cushion, head in her hands. "I really thought I was going crazy. I'm so sorry I dragged you out here."

"Stop apologizing. There's a reason their nana calls them pests." Dad lovingly brushed a few stray hairs behind her ear. "Are you ready to go back inside?"

Another shaky breath knocked around in her chest as she grimaced. "I actually would love a minute."

"I'll stay with her, Dad."

Patting me on the back, he nodded to me, and I waited for him to close the door. Inching closer, my hands went around her, sneaking beneath her oversized purple sweater and rested on her narrow jean clad hips. I couldn't help but notice the shudder that swept through her at my touch.

It was taking everything in me not to satisfy the need for more of her. To reach up just another inch and feel the silk of her skin. But I had to be patient, talk to her father, ask her out on a proper date.

"I'm sorry," I said, chasing her gaze. "I never would have done that had I known you thought you were having an aura."

She waved me off. "It's fine. I just...never know. I would hate to ruin your dinner."

Ruin our dinner? Did she really say that?

"Yes, while you had a seizure at the table, we would have been cursing at you because you ruined our meal." I shook my head, but Maggie avoided my gaze by staring at the lake over my shoulder. Since I had a private moment... "What was that about between you and Jamey?"

Her shoulders plummeted as if I'd punched her in the gut all over again with that reminder. "Nothing, apparently."

An unexpected spark of irritation ignited down my spine as my brows slammed down. "Dammit, Maggie." She startled at my tone, and I softened my voice. "Sorry. It's... Will you please talk to me? Jamey upset you. Why?"

Maggie's dark lashes lowered to dust her cheeks, licking her lips twice before answering. "Jamey and I were going to move together to Ocean Hills. We had an apartment, jobs, and scholarships ready for us before the storm ruined everything. Until tonight, I didn't know that plan had been completely derailed. I didn't know he wanted to stay at Warrington next year, let alone move in with Ben or join the fraternity. He never told me. I assumed— I thought we'd still do what we had planned, just a year later. That we'd be going to OHU and we'd get the apartment again and the jobs, and that was…stupid, I guess."

Now it was me who had been punched in the gut. She didn't have a clue she'd yanked the earth out from under me. "You— Wow, okay. I need a second with this." I took ten of them, and it wasn't enough, but I couldn't keep staring at her and not say anything. "You're not going to Warrington next year?"

Her eyes met mine, the sun discovering every spectrum of blue in her irises. "No, Mason. I'm going to OHU. The storm repairs should be done soon, and I'll need to get everything set up again."

Was that why she had been keeping me at arm's length because she was never going to stay? Didn't think I could be loyal enough to do this with her long-distance or willing to follow her?

"Are you okay?" Her cool hand came to my scruffy cheek, and I wished I could have shaved so I didn't have that thick barrier between us. It hit me like a battering ram that I didn't have that much longer with Maggie.

She was leaving.

I fought to speak around the lump in my throat. "Okay? No. No, I'm not okay. My best fri—"

"Margaret?"

With a squeak, Maggie jumped to her feet, and I somehow landed flat on my ass. "What the…?"

"Sir?" Maggie's shifted nervously, placing her hands behind her.

The chief's eyes yo-yoed between his daughter and me—the one still on the ground. "Dan said you were feeling ill. Do you need to go home?"

Her head was already shaking. "No, sir. I only needed some air. I'm much better now. Thank you."

Flicking another glance down to me, he nodded stiffly. "Okay, but fair warning, I think Jamey might sweat off his highlights if you take much longer."

"Yes, sir. I'll be right there."

Wearing a soft smile, he closed the door, and I waited for him to retreat to the dining room before I got to my knees again. I groaned as my tailbone cried in relief. "I think you broke my ass."

Maggie's hands flew over her mouth. "Sorry."

I pushed to my feet, brushing off my jeans. "Listen, about OHU—"

"I need to get back inside, Mason." Maggie was already aiming for the door.

"Maggie, wait." It took one leap to reach her, linking my fingers with Maggie's, but she jerked away from me. I examined my hand and the distance she put between us. "What the hell is going on with you?"

Her lids flared, eyes filling with regret. "I..." She shot a glance to the door. "My father's here. I'm sorry."

Realization crashed into me like an anvil dropping off a ten-story building. She had pushed me away when I was kneeling in front of her. And she had spilled her water because I had put my arm around her.

Something bitter and viscous teemed in my veins, leaching into my voice. "My deepest apologies. How stupid of me. I can't touch you, talk to you, look at you. God forbid I breathe the same air as you. I'm the asshole here. Got it."

"Mason," she pleaded.

I yanked the handle down and held the door open, glaring at her. "Before you run back inside, let me know where I can eat. Is out here far enough for you?"

Her lids narrowed at me. "Don't be mean."

One shoulder tightly shrugged. "I am what I am."

Stepping up into me, those eyes of hers bore right through me. "No. This is you taking it too far. My father has rules, and I'm trying to respect them. You're punishing me for it."

She was right. I was punishing her for that and for keeping the truth from me about OHU. Shutting my eyes, I hit my forehead on the doorframe. "Just tell me... Did it ever occur to you that I would feel the same way that you do about Jamey and his plans next year? Did it ever, at any point, enter your head that I'd want to know you were leaving? That I wanted you to stay?"

I opened my eyes to see Maggie wilt before me. "I..."

She didn't. It was written all over her face. She never considered my feelings and that I would miss her. This girl was turning me upside down, inside out, gutting me alive, and she didn't even know it.

I rasped, "They're waiting, Maggie."

Her hand rested on my chest, on the infinity link, and the touch sunk deep into my heart with the finesse of a dull blade. "You know I don't have a scholarship to Warrington next year, and you know I can't afford the tuition, Mason. It wasn't that I didn't think of you. I simply thought you already knew."

God... What I wouldn't do to keep her with me.

My hand curled around hers, holding it to my chest. "Maggie, I could—"

"Hey!" Matt appeared in the doorway, his emerald eyes going large when he scanned my face. I must be an interesting shade of pale and torment right now. "Everything okay?"

I dragged Maggie's hand off my chest and guided her inside, hurt and uncertainty straining her features. "Maggie's fine. She just needed a minute."

He nodded, chewing on his bottom lip. "Maggie, I'm sorry. I didn't mean to mess with you. Well, I did. But I didn't intend to make you think you were...uh—"

"Insane?" she said with a frail smile.

One side of his mouth lifted briefly. "Yeah, that."

I touched her back, but not long enough for her to pull away from me. "Dinner's getting cold, Sticks."

"Right. Yeah. Uh, thanks." Her chin met her chest as she padded away.

An elbow prodded my side. "Hey, you alright?"

I avoided looking my brother in the eye as I stuffed my hands in my pockets. "No."

Before he could ask me to elaborate, I returned to the dining room as Maggie took her seat.

When I helped her into the chair, she looked to me with something lingering in her eyes. Part of me thought it was residual guilt. Another part of me thought it looked like hope.

"Thank you," she offered quietly.

"My pleasure." I pushed her in the rest of the way, and then Matt and I took our seats.

Before rushing after Maggie, I had planned on loading my plate two more times. Now...I couldn't stand to see the few bites that were left. I think I left my appetite somewhere outside.

"So, Nate..." A mischievous grin graced Mom's mouth. Maybe the second bottle of wine was catching up to her. "Ashley and I were talking earlier about our nephew's upcoming wedding in three weeks. We were wondering if Maggie could join us."

Hold up.

Maggie at the wedding? Maggie with me for an entire weekend? No working? No studying? No papers to write? Three days of only Maggie and me?

Oh, hell yes!

Maggie grumbled something that sounded a lot like, "Good God, no."

Uh…

Mom continued, "It's a weekend event. Friday to Sunday in Grove Point. We'd love for her to come."

The chief finished chewing his roll and sipped his water to swallow it down. "Eve, that's kind of you, but Margaret has responsibilities at home."

"Nate, that's the weekend you're going to Robert's bachelor party in Vegas, isn't it?" Candi asked, her lips shimmering with a fresh coat of gloss.

Dad heaped another helping of potatoes onto his plate. "Even better. All of us are going, including Jamey. Right?"

Jamey nodded. "Yes, Mr. Davis. I'll be there. Mags and I can share a hotel room."

Maggie's father solemnly shook his head. "It's generous of you to include her in a family event like that, but…I'm not comfortable with this. And Margaret has Poker to take care of."

If I'd had any hope, it had just been drowned in the lake outside.

"Poker can come," Mom chirped happily. "I checked, and the hotel accepts animals. Besides, if she stays here, she's all by herself. What if she had another seizure?"

My hope resurfaced on a life vest.

Candi's nails raked through the chief's hair. "Nate, let Mags go. Let her have fun."

He sighed and aimed that colorless gaze across the table to his daughter. "I suppose that would be best. I'm sure I don't have to ask, but, Margaret, would you like to go?"

She didn't have an adverse reaction to her name when he said it, only when I did. I wasn't sure what to make of that.

Keeping her head ducked, she let silence stretch before finally speaking to her plate. "Yes, sir, I would."

A few moments passed where no one spoke before Mr. Davis scratched at his clean chin uncomfortably. He sighed once more and transferred his gaze to my parents' side of the table. "Alright, then. I'd like to get the information before I leave."

My hope was now drying off, getting toasty by the fire as it broke out the s'mores.

With dinner finished, the parents retired to the living room as the guys and I helped Maggie clear the table. On one of my trips to the kitchen, I spotted Jamey trying to have a conversation with her, but I could see it wasn't going well. Only those privy to deciphering their glares and headshakes could understand.

She really didn't get it. She didn't see how hypocritical she was about the whole thing. Now wasn't the time to bring it up, though. Things had been tense enough today, and we were making a little headway with her coming to Grove Point. No need to ruin it. We could discuss it later. Maybe during the wedding, I could broach the subject about offering to pay her tuition.

I probably should pack my cup for that convo.

After the dishes had been cleaned—or Maggie re-cleaned them after me—dessert was served with coffee. Dad had seconds of both apple and pumpkin pie, and both times, Maggie topped his plate off with an extra dollop of her homemade whipped cream.

Maggie had been quiet ever since her father arrived, but I hadn't heard her speak since dinner. While we dried the dessert dishes, I asked, "Are you okay?"

A gleam of azure sliced through the fringe of her lashes as she peeked up at me. "I thought you were mad at me."

A frown bracketed my mouth. "Irritated, but not mad."

Pleading filled her eyes, and she whispered, "I'm sorry."

Shifting closer, so our fingers touched on the counter, I noticed the sharp rise in her chest. Damn, she had no clue how much her signals were messing with my head. "What are you sorry for exactly?"

"Everything, Mason. I—"

"Margaret, it's time to go."

At her father's voice, Maggie withdrew her hand and turned to face him. "Oh. Already? I..." I knew her well enough to know that there was a checklist in her head of every task she had yet to complete.

He looked at her with regret. "Sorry. I have an early meeting tomorrow."

"Of course."

Dammit. This Operation End the Friend Zone had bombed so badly, and she was leaving. Fuck it.

"Mr. Davis," I started, "do you mind if I come over tomorrow morning and pick up Maggie? I was hoping we could go on a run before her afternoon shift at the café."

He tilted his head at me. "A run?"

"Well, she runs. I hobble after her and try not to pass out." Grinning, I adopted what I hoped was an innocent expression. "Maggie's been training me on days I don't have football practice, and I won't have any until Monday."

Something that sounded a lot like a whimper escaped Maggie, and Candi wagged her brows in approval. If Mr. Davis was aware either had occurred, I couldn't tell.

"She's been running with you. I wasn't aware." His eyes seemed to frost over a moment before softening into a powder blue as his mouth tipped up in the corner. "We want to make sure you Warrington boys stay game ready, and Margaret can definitely do that. Sounds fine to me."

One down...

I geared up, entering a territory utterly foreign to me. "I also would like to drive her to school and back home after work when I can, take some of the stress off her."

He scratched his chin, rolling that over for a long-ass minute. "That's quite nice of you to offer, son. That would be okay, too. I'm sure Margaret would appreciate it, as well."

"Thank you, Mr. Davis." The second he turned around, I folded over, lips at her little unpierced ear. "See? You just have to know how to ask."

The flash of blue flames brought another smirk to my face because, just like that, I wiggled my way through the tiniest of cracks in Maggie's shadowed world. The Friend Zone was going to be my bitch.

Then I'd get to work on Operation Keep Maggie Davis in Crescent Cove.

chapter fifty-four

maggie

The Scotts were going to be the death of me. Literally.

Good God, Mason had no idea what he had done. No one but my father and I did.

Without being told, I climbed into the back of the patrol vehicle. I jerked the seatbelt over me, clicking it in after five tries and sliding my legs to the side so they wouldn't cramp up during the drive home. I had to shift the other way when the plastic seat dug into my spine and shoulder blades. I was sure my father would take his sweet time driving home just so I'd suffer longer. He would make sure to hit every pothole on the way home, too.

Candi threw her head back, making a sound very similar to the ones I'd heard during the moonlight hours. "The Scotts sure do have some nice shit. Eve showed me around, and her closet is enormous! I could spend all day trying on her shoes. And get this. They have an espresso machine in their bathroom! Their *bathroom*! Mags, how did you land this job, and please tell me the Scotts have friends."

My father's shoulders rose higher as Candi prattled on about the house tour she'd all but begged Mrs. Scott for and each of the name brands that filled every square inch of the estate. The fact that she was upsetting my father evaded her completely.

Pulling up alongside the guardhouse, we sat waiting for the wrought iron gate to swing open. I looked out my window, a smile tempting my lips. I caught a glimpse of Bernard and his ginormous body squeezed into a chair behind a comically small desk, knees hiked up to his chest as he shoveled in a forkful of the dinner Camden had run down to him for me. He was rapt in watching what looked to be a show about runway models.

At least someone was doing this holiday right.

Candi's mouth had stopped moving as the Tahoe proceeded through the gates.

My father finally said, "I don't appreciate being manipulated like that, Margaret."

Casting my gaze to his profile behind the bulletproof glass, my stomach turned inside out. The admonishment was remarkably tame, but it wasn't something he usually did in front of anyone. He preferred to keep his scolding of me private. Poor behavior reflected poor parenting, and the great Nathan Davis couldn't have anyone believe he was bad at anything. I didn't know what to make of this or how to respond.

"Sir, I told Mrs. Scott I would speak with you later about the wedding. I think she had a little too much wine at dinner and forgot. I'm sorry. It wasn't anyone's intention to make you feel manipulated."

We both knew that wasn't the only thing he was referring to, just like we both knew my apology was bullshit. But I had to listen to his act all night, so now he'd have to play along with mine.

He was quiet for a torturous moment, head remaining forward until he looked to his side. "And, Candi, I don't appreciate you making me look like the hard-ass."

"No, baby," she cooed. "You looked like the concerned daddy that I know you are."

I suppressed the vomit inching up my throat.

"I don't want to have to repeat myself about that boy, Margaret. He's far too experienced for you. You make sure he understands there won't be anything between the two of you."

Once again, I questioned why he was pathologically paranoid about something he didn't think was possible.

Our eyes met in the rearview mirror, the unspoken part of that threat lingering in his darkened gaze. "Yes, sir."

I was going to call it here and now. Thanksgiving was officially the worst holiday ever.

Not only was my father pissed for a variety of reasons, but I had also unintentionally hurt Mason when I'd learned over dinner that Jamey had cut me out of our plan to move in together. He wasn't even going to OHU next fall. Even Poker got the boot.

I'd never felt more alone than I had sitting at that dinner table.

Maybe it was the tryptophan in the turkey, or they were just horny, but Candi and my father retired to bed early without another mention of the wedding or Mason's antics or the fact that Mason had his hands on me—*underneath* my sweater. I didn't fool myself into thinking the discussion was over, though. No amount of whiskey, women, apologies, or length of time could ever make that man forget my transgressions.

If I didn't get a beating tonight, I'd get it later.

Around seven in the morning, the engine of the electric blue Raptor rumbled through the walls of the house as it approached. I stepped out through the side door, already donned in running gear with Poker dancing on his pads next to me. Behind the windshield, Mason wore a wicked grin, pointed directly at me as if he knew he'd gotten away with something.

Which he totally had.

Poker raced toward Mason when he opened his truck door, and without casting another glance in his direction, I aimed for the passenger side.

Rude and immature? Yep.

"Mornin', boy," he said, giving Poker a rubdown. "You ready for a run?"

Poker answered by vaulting into the cab, climbing over the console, and planting himself by the back window, staring out impatiently.

"Well, at least one of you Davises is happy to see me," Mason commented.

Though I was fully capable of shutting my door, Mason appeared, obstructing the doorway. Forcing me to address him. I swore I could *feel* his arrogant ass from here.

I clicked in my belt with more aggression than necessary. "Don't give me that smug look, Mason."

Finally catching on to my level of irritation, his triumphant smile flipped the other way, his tone adopting a harsh edge. "Now I get to see you more, and your father was okay with it. Funny, 'cause it actually seemed like he didn't have a problem with me at all."

I read between the lines of that pretty damn well. Mason thought *I* had the problem. He was fooled like everyone else. How did my father have this power?

"Mason, of course, I like spending time with you. But you cornered him in a house full of people. He felt pressured to say yes to your mom and you."

He straightened, head cocking to the side. "He didn't seem at all pressured to me. Did you...get in trouble or something?"

I wouldn't tell him if I had, but it felt nice not to lie for a change. "No."

His forehead crinkled. "Then what's the problem?"

"He's the chief of police and my father. I don't like disappointing him, and a sure way to do that is by breaking his rules." Defending my father was like cleaning the inside of the café's grease trap with my tongue.

Mason shook his head like I was insane and slipped on his aviators. "Let's get out of here. The sooner you kick my ass around the lake, the sooner you'll feel better.

Well, he asked for it. My pace. Ten miles.

The following Friday, Jamey and I had plans to go to Sunset Bay for dress shopping after school. It took some convincing to get Jamey to agree on the location, but he knew I couldn't afford to go anywhere but the Vintage Shoppe.

The plan—or what I thought was the plan—involved walking to Jamey's house to borrow Ava's Focus, but as Ben met us beneath our oak tree, I realized that some silver-haired birdie had squawked me out. A silver-haired birdie currently sporting a T-shirt that read, I'M SO GAY, I FART GLITTER.

Damn Jamey.

"Change of plans." Jamey grinned at me.

"No shit."

Ben wore a matching, punch-worthy grin. "Ready to go shopping?" His hands slid together to suggest there was more to this than a thrift store shopping trip.

"Don't you have practice or a workout or a meeting or anything else to do?" I pleaded.

"Sure do." Smiling, he tweaked my nose. "Too bad I think I'm coming down with food poisoning."

I groaned. Well, two gays were better than one, right? Besides, being there was a Scott involved now, I didn't have a hope in hell of saying no. "Fine. I'm ready."

Cutting through the quad, we passed the edge of the football field. Mason was lined up with whom I recognized as Pete and Vic. The three of them charged into Matt, Camden, and Noah, each trio vying for a win.

I could have sworn Watkins screamed, "I want to paint the field with your blood!"

Huh. Probably heard that wrong.

It was either the gladiator display of muscles on top of muscles, the bright butterflies inked on those very delicious muscles, the tight jersey stretched over his muscles, or the compression pants hugging every curve of his muscles, but my lady bits had enough of this, and my brain was listening to them right now.

"Guys, just out of curiosity… If it were possible, how does someone become more than friends with another someone?"

Clutching his chest, Ben gasped, "Mags, I'm taken, and I'm gay."

He was being silly, and I knew that, but his joke only made me realize how ridiculous I sounded. Even if I didn't have a psychopath for a father, there was still the very depressing fact that I looked like Mason's late sister.

Mason Scott was a fantasy, a happily ever after that belonged only to my dreams.

"Right," I muttered, watching my last glimpse of said dreams as he disappeared under Noah with Watkins having an aneurysm above them now. My shoulders fell a few notches. I was a stupid, stupid girl.

Jamey took pity on me, sliding an arm around my waist. "You're deep in the friend zone. Way deep. Like deep throating deep."

I scrunched my nose. "Gross."

Agreeing, Ben's head bobbed. "It's tough."

"So, there's no way?" I asked. "If one were to attempt such things." I should ask my psych professor to cover masochism during our next class.

A grin spread as Ben's warm chocolate eyes glinted mischievously. "Well, one could take their clothes off in front of the object of their attraction. That should get the point across."

Jamey gripped Ben's arm, eyes wide with panic. "Shh, Ben. There are female ears everywhere and are bound to try it."

My chest felt heavy suddenly because I was sure that ship had sailed already. Multiple times. Not that I thought any less of the women on campus for being promiscuous. I probably would be, too, if I looked like them.

Ben prodded my side. "Just tell him, Mags."

I guess we were past the point of talking in code. Clearly, Ben knew I was crushing on his cousin. "He'll laugh at me. Or vomit. I do look like his sister, after all. I mean—" I sighed as we reached the Rover. "Never mind. I'm wasting your time with this. I'm wasting my time."

"No, you're not." Ben opened the rear door for me, gaze locking with mine. "I think you'd be surprised what Mason would do."

What did that mean? Would he pat me on the head and thank me?

Shaking my head, I piled into the SUV along with the boys. While motoring along, I observed that we were taking the north ramp onto Cove Highway, and my head hit the seat. The Vintage Shoppe was south.

"You guys really do suck. You know that?"

Ben and Jamey faced each other. "Oh, we know!"

Ignoring the inappropriateness, I grumbled, "Let me know when you've decided where I want to go shopping."

"Come on, Mags!" Exasperated, Jamey's hands smacked his thighs. "This is a *wedding*. Do you really want to buy second-hand shit to the first wedding you've ever been to?"

"I never want to buy—" I pinched my eyes, forcing the rod in my back to relax. "Never mind." I stopped the conversation at that point because I had said too much. It wasn't a secret that I was poor but saying it as I was sitting in a car that cost more than my house was so far beyond pitiful.

Turned out, Ben and Jamey had decided that I wanted to shop at the Promenade in Pacific Cliffs. At the boutiques that I could never afford in the Promenade in Pacific Cliffs.

I stared at the elegant signage of the boutique, just blinking at it when a hand clamped around my wrist and yanked me along.

Two steps past the doorway confirmed this was an absolute waste of time. My feet began sliding back on the light wood flooring.

"Oh, no, you don't." Another arm snagged my waist as Ben warned, "You're going in."

"Ben, I can't—"

"Good afternoon!" a cultured voice called across the shop. I tore my gaze off the swirled quartz wall behind the register to a young woman clipping over in a fitted black suit, blonde hair tied in a bouncing ponytail slicked tight to the top of her head. She was carrying a tray of drinks with cucumber slices floating in bubbly liquid. "This must be Maggie Davis."

"How—"

"It is," Ben answered. "I'm Ben Scott, and this is Jamey Hayes. We're here for moral support."

"Wonderful. The more eyes on this beauty, the better." Speaking of eyes, hers glittered with what looked like genuine delight. She set the tray down on a nearby brass table that sat between two chairs facing a lighted, raised stage backdropped with a wall of mirrors. "My name is Stacia. Please help yourself to some sparkling water. I also have champagne if you would prefer."

Champagne...?

"Water is fine, thank you, Stacia," Ben said, reaching for a glass.

"Well," she murmured, assessing me with a crank of her head. "Now that you're in front of me, I have some ideas. Winter weddings can be tricky. You want to look sexy but not freeze, right?"

I shook my head. "How—"

"She does," Jamey piped in, grabbing the glass that Ben offered.

"Good. Tell you what, Maggie. While I'm choosing some dresses for you, take these handsome men around the shop, and pick out anything you like. If the size isn't on the rack, I probably have it in the back. I like to keep the inventory minimal on the floor so as not overwhelm the eye."

"Uh-huh." Dumbfounded, I looked to the brass racks of clothes lining the stark white walls, white quartz tables showcasing entire outfits, and hanging above were several light fixtures that looked like they could impale a human fifteen different ways if any one of them fell just right. Tilting over, I didn't see a "back" to this place, and we seemed to be the only ones in here. On a Friday.

More was being said about the different sections of the store and where to find what, but I wasn't listening. Not until Stacia's heels clipped away.

Once she was out of earshot, I looked to Ben and Jamey. "What the hell?"

As in, *why would you take me somewhere that serves sparkling water with cucumber slices on a tray?*

Jamey rolled his eyes. "We made an appointment. Drink your cucumber water and get over it. If you don't like anything, fine. But at least enjoy being doted on for a hot minute."

Like Boy George was hidden in the racks, Jamey went straight to the dresses that might be suitable for a wedding. I guess. Honestly, I wouldn't know. He held one up to his body and studied himself in the full-length mirror.

Ben nudged me. "You know he's right. Come on."

Ugh. If nothing else, I'd get a laugh out of this because seeing frilly chiffon on dudes? Pretty damn funny.

Ben lifted the first dress he saw off the rack and wagged it at me. It was lovely, and before I could think beyond that, I saw the three numbers on the price tag. Numbers that were one digit away from adding a comma.

Dear God…

"It's pretty but too short."

His brows snapped together. "Mags, you've got great legs, and this blush color would be perfect on you. You're trying it on." The dress disappeared into the arms of Stacia, who I swore appeared from out of nowhere.

She nodded approvingly. "You're right. With her skin tone? Gorgeous."

"I—"

The next dress was already being shoved in my face. It was backless. Before I could shoot Ben down, Jamey said, "Too much skin. Legs are enough. We want Mason to use his imagination."

"Imagination?" I parroted with a frown.

Shifting through the racks, Ben nodded. "He's right. The less Mason sees, the more he will want to see."

"In that case." I chose something that looked more like a bedsheet with sleeves. "Wouldn't this be better?"

Jamey gasped, glaring at it and then me. "If Ms. Shag Gay could see you, she would slap you and then risk her manicure to scratch that to shreds."

By some miracle, I stumbled upon a clearance rack and dedicated all my time to it. I had no clue how much time had passed, but I wound up trying on fifteen dresses, and I found fault with everything that didn't have a red tag.

"This one." Smile fake and bright, I twirled on my bare feet, dying to itch my legs as the fabric swayed around my calves. "This is perfect." I hated everything about this frock.

From the leather chairs across from me, Ben couldn't hide his horror. "I wouldn't bury Great Aunt Matilda in that thing. She's ninety, blind, and from the deep south."

"It's…" Jamey cringed, examined the dress, and then cringed again. "Well, it's got flowers."

Ben glared to his side and hissed, "Jamey, it looks like the rejects at the Botanical Gardens threw up on her."

Leaning toward him, Jamey whispered something back.

"You can stop right there with the sidebar, boys. I'm getting it."

Sitting back and placing one ankle over a knee, Ben's chocolate orbs narrowed at me. "Fine. You have *one* dress. You need two more."

My jaw just about hit the floor. "*Three* dresses? For God's sake, why?"

Words weren't enough to explain this to me, apparently. Ben actually ticked the reasons off on his fingers for a visual aid. "There's the rehearsal dinner, the wedding, and the brunch. And, no, you are not wearing a dress more than once." Stacia swept past me with a pile of jeans and sweaters intended for my dressing room. "Plus, you need clothes to travel in." The fourth finger he threw up was in danger of getting snapped off.

I loathed to admit I needed new clothes. Well, I always needed new clothes, and it did feel nice to wear fabric that didn't have a previous owner and some kind of half-assed repair job by yours truly, but I might have a heart attack or puke on the changing room floor. How in God's name were jeans three hundred dollars?

"That's the one!" Ben bolted off his chair, shoving it back an entire foot. He aimed toward his happy helper who was holding what looked like a black dress. "She has to try it on."

"Ben!" I whined.

He kept on, only listening to Stacia comment about my hair color.

"Jamey, seriously? I can't afford—" After a quick calculation, I was already over budget with the red tag attached to me. "You have to stop, Ben."

He arched a dark brow at me. "Did you really say that? You know where his genes come from."

Frustration singed the edges of my sanity. "Why? Why would you take me here?"

He shrugged, lounging back in his chair, slinging his feet up on the matching white leather ottoman. "Because you deserve to be pampered."

I gritted my teeth. "This isn't pampering, Jamey. This is a cruel—"

"Here we are." Ben returned with a black lacy dress and a smile begging to have my foot relocated inside of it.

It was the dress I'd seen the last time we were in Pacific Cliffs when I was riding on the back of the Harley. It was breathtaking, and I had wanted it, and I had wanted Mason to see me in it. It occurred to me that I was standing in the store I had seen that dress in. And Ben had made it seem as if he were looking for this particular dress. Mason was the only one who could have known I'd been admiring it. Did he...did Mason set this up today?

"Ben, I'm getting the dress that I'm wearing, and I'd like to look at another store."

Squinting, his head slanted to study me, much like Stacia had when I'd arrived. "Okay, we can go to another store to look for more dresses, but you have to try this on first."

"Fair enough."

It wasn't fair. It was so beyond fair. This dress had magical powers to give me hips and another half-cup size even without a bra. I looked at the price tag... This one had a comma.

I dragged the curtain open to cheers and claps, and my heart *ached*. "This isn't wedding appropriate. This is what you wear to a downtown club."

Jamey scoffed. "Like you would know." He had a point.

"I've seen that dress on a lot of women, Maggie," Stacia beamed. "You do the designer proud."

This woman had to be working on commission.

"Okay," I announced. "That was our deal. The Great Aunt Matilda dress, and we move on."

Ben's mouth pursed, and I so wasn't prepared for what was said next. "No," he disagreed. "The deal was we would move on for more dresses. We're not done here yet."

"Yet?" I repeated dumbly, and suddenly, the PB and J from lunch felt like a brick in my stomach.

"You need shoes, Mags," Jamey observed. Oh, right. How had I forgotten about that?

Craning over the fitted material, I glimpsed down to my socked feet. "I...what kind?"

Ben casually sipped his water, relaxing in his chair. "Heels, Mags. You want a man, you gotta wear heels."

I gulped. "I've never worn heels."

Ben choked on his water, coughing and spitting as he gasped for breath. Stacia was so concerned she began patting him on the back. Once Ben recovered, they both looked at me, mouths gaping. Even her ponytail seemed frazzled into a state of shock.

Jamey shook his head as he stood with a sigh. Pushing me back into the changing room, he drew the curtain closed. "I know. Believe me, I know."

"You'll know what my foot feels like in your ass later, that's for damn sure," I mumbled.

I changed back into my clothes, soon immersed in another section of the store that I knew nothing about. In no time, heaps of boxes surrounded me. High and low heels, matte and glossy, straps and strapless. I felt terrible for Stacia because it was all so unnecessary. She should have booked an appointment that would be worth her time.

Once I had sufficiently demonstrated that anything hoisting me more than an eighth of an inch off the ground was impossible for me to walk in, Ben gave up and let me make another bargain. I think what I chose was something Matilda would approve of. Only because she was blind.

Ben wandered off again, and I tugged on Jamey's shirt. "I can't go to another store. This is it. I'm over budget." I waved to the floral dress and white Mary Janes that officially made me look like a flower girl from some era that came long before my birth.

Jamey shrugged. "I'll buy the rest. Consider it your birthday gift for next week."

"No!" Ben was headed toward us, and I lowered my voice. "Don't tell him I can't pay, please. It's so embarrassing."

With an elaborate roll of his eyes that put the previous one to shame, Jamey huffed.

"Now, lingerie," Ben said as he hauled me toward the back of the store.

Blood rushed from my head so fast, dizziness hit me hard. "W—what?"

Ben stopped, fully turning to me, gaze locked with my widened stare. "You need a better bra, and let's face it, you want to get laid in satin, not cotton." He pulled at my bra strap and let the elastic snap on my shoulder.

"Ben, I wasn't looking—"

"Weren't you, though?" His brow angled at me knowingly.

"I…" I took in the bras and panties surrounding us like a silk jungle. I squirmed.

From one finger, Jamey dangled a scrap of material that was printed with leopard spots. "This is a TMI moment that you need to listen to, Mags. If Mason's blood relative is any indication, you're gonna wanna open those little legs of yours."

"Yep. Too much."

Laughing, Ben hooked an arm around me and towed me in.

Stacia and my gay escorts were all too eager to have my size measured, and more cheers went around when, at some point, I had graduated to a B-cup. Apparently, misjudging cup size was a common occurrence. I wouldn't know. I had always been size *flat*.

"Jamey, why don't you take Mags over to the perfume. I'm going to see if they have a restroom here."

Once Ben was out of sight, I hissed to Jamey, "I don't want perfume!"

He stuck his tongue out at me and moseyed away. "Fine, then I'll get some." Jamey proceeded to spray himself with a stench that caused us both to gag.

By the time Ben found us, he halted, coming no closer than five feet, coughing and swatting at the air. To be fair, Jamey and I were deeply involved in trying to out-stink the other. This was why I wasn't allowed to go to nice places.

"Ready?" Ben asked.

"Yeah," I exhaled and followed Ben and Jamey while trying to come up with at least one excuse as to why I didn't want to go to any more stores. I wasn't above saying the D-word. Diarrhea was usually the end-all excuse.

At the register, Stacia waved goodbye and wished us a pleasant day. Not one item I'd chosen was on the counter in front of her. Not the flower dress, white shoes, or the strapless bra that I agreed to under duress. In fact, nothing was on the counter.

"Uh… Where is everything I tried on?"

"In the car," Ben stated, holding the front door open for me.

I blinked up at him, utterly dumbfounded. "You just put everything in the car?"

"After I paid for it." My lips parted as far as they would go, and he held up his palms. "I had specific instructions that you were not to shell out one penny. Sorry, not sorry."

I'd been right.

"Freaking Mason." I shook my head at Ben as I walked outside. "What is with you Scotts? You're all the same."

Jamey cleared his throat. "I told you. You won't be disappointed."

Over his shoulder, Ben announced, "And we are also done shopping."

Oh, God. That diarrhea excuse might turn out to be legit. "What did you do?"

A sly grin hiked up the corner of Ben's mouth. "It's what Mason did, and you can thank him later. I recommend you thank him with your vagina."

"My…?"

Ben opened the trunk of the SUV.

I swung for him. And missed.

"What's got you down tonight, Magsamillion?" Logan's soft chestnut eyes peered over his second mug of coffee. He'd been at the café for the last hour keeping me company until it was time to head over to my house for beer and cards later.

What was getting me down? What *wasn't* getting me down was easier to answer. It wasn't the new clothes hanging in my closet that did *not* include a hideous flower dress or stumpy white Mary Janes or the itchiest strapless bra ever made. It certainly wasn't the fact that I had only seen Mason in class and at lunch this week because he had team meetings before school and practice afterward, or that when I did see him, things had been strained, and we'd barely spoken. And it couldn't have been that I was missing *another* game he invited me to.

No. None of that.

"I'm not down. I'm sorry if I'm not good company."

"You're perfect company, but I prefer you smiling, and I haven't gotten one yet." He glimpsed over his shoulder to the darkened windows. "Friday nights should be for parties. Fun. Shenanigans."

"I had some shenanigans today," I said proudly. "Jamey and Ben took me shopping."

"Shopping." Echoing the word, his forehead puckered. "For what? A whole hour?"

I shifted on my feet. "More like two."

Relaxing back in his stool, he studied me. "And I bet that would include travel time." When my mouth opened to argue, he continued, "So where are Jamey and Ben now?"

I wiped up the rest of the emptied counter that I may have already cleaned three times in the last hour. "At the football game." And then going to the RAM party after.

His cup made a *plink* noise on the concrete counter, and my eyes shot to the black bands of ink scrolling down his arm. "And why aren't you at the football game?"

"I had to work."

Logan made a point to look at the empty café and drolly said, "Thank God you showed up."

I frowned at his sarcasm. "My books and supplies to Warrington aren't free. And who knows if I still have a scholarship to OHU when the rebuild is done or when the school will even open back up. I have to be prepared."

"I'm not arguing with your logic. It's just— You should enjoy your time in college, too. Take advantage of nights like this."

"There's three and a half years left."

His jaw set into a solid line. "And they're gonna be over before you realize it. There's always going to be a reason not to live your life, Maggie. You've been acting like an adult long enough. Maybe it's time to act like a kid."

Kind of a weird thing for an adult to say. "Did you go to college?"

Focusing on his coffee, his head shook. "Nah, I'm not the college kind of guy, never was. I went straight to the Corps, but I had fun and blew off steam when I could." Lifting his gaze to mine, he added, "And I still do. If you don't find a balance, you begin to lose yourself. It's not healthy." Logan sounded like he was speaking from experience.

I leaned on my elbows. "Did that happen to you?"

"Yeah. When I came home from my last tour." Logan's lashes lowered, shielding his eyes from me. "It was...difficult adjusting to life. Still is sometimes. A lot had changed in a short period of time, and I...didn't manage the stress well. But I had a family to take care of, and I had to stop being selfish. That was when I met your father, and he convinced me to join the force. I'm glad I did. I got back on track, Piper had LB, and I feel like I can be the uncle he deserves. I don't have everything yet, but I figured out what I want now."

"And what do you want?"

Logan's warm gaze lifted to mine, eyes filling with something I couldn't quite identify, but there was definite longing there, loneliness maybe. "The most important thing in this world," he said. "Someone to share my life with."

I couldn't help but smile at the simplicity of his answer. To want someone to love, something that didn't cost anything but was the most difficult thing to find. I knew something about that.

"Thank you."

Straightening, I blinked at him. "For?"

A shaved chin tipped my way, leaning closer. "Your smile."

My stupid grin only grew. "You didn't always want someone to share your life with?"

He dragged in a breath, one that spoke to him having lived a lifetime already in his young life. "The difference between what you need and what you want is a fine line. So much so that I don't think that line exists when you're younger. When you can distinguish between your *needs* and *wants*, that's the moment you become an adult. I knew that, at some point, I'd meet someone, get married, and have kids. It was just one of those inevitabilities that would happen whenever it happened, you know? But then, I began coming home to an empty house. I prepare meals for one and eat alone. I have no one to greet me when I walk in the door, call me during the day because they miss my voice, no one to take all the worries out of my head and just be with me, take the world off my shoulders when it's too much. It began to sink in how much I wanted that and wanted to do that for someone else."

Oh...

His gaze fixed intently on me. "Maggie, I was going to wait to do this, but I—"

Bright lights spilled into the dining room, forcing us to squint and shield our eyes. A cacophony of car doors slammed shut, and though blinded, it seemed as though the parking lot had filled with a horde of men in mere seconds.

My heartbeat stopped and then redoubled as the entire Warrington team burst through the doors, mutton chop free. Thank the Lord. For whatever reason, they had to wait until tonight's game was over before they shaved.

"STICKS!"

The men piled into the café with Mason at the head of the pack. As always, they were rowdy, loud, and chaotic.

I loved it.

I rounded the counter to meet them. "Did you win?" Maybe all that facial hair had been lucky after all.

"No! They crushed us!" A second later, I was hauled up in Mason's arms, pressed against his hard body, feet dangling in the air.

My hands went right to his smooth cheeks, loving the feel of them and missing the two-day-old scruff at the same time. Five days of growth was my limit, I'd learned, and we'd hit that point twenty-seven days ago.

I should thank Mason for today, for the shopping experience and buying all those beautiful clothes and shoes, but the words "thank you" seemed far too inadequate for the appreciation I felt. And with all the guys here, it would be awkward to say anything now.

"If you lost, why are you all so happy?" I asked.

The citrine bands in his eyes were alight, glimmering up at me. "Mutton Chop Month is dead!"

"So I noticed."

"It's impossible not to. Look at this handsome mug." Mason turned his face in several directions, so I could inspect it. Beard or no beard, the man was gorgeous.

I shrugged. "You'll do."

chapter fifty-five

maggie

Locking up the Scotts' front door Monday, I heard the familiar low rumble of BB's engine behind me. My heart did a happy twirl when I turned around to see Mason pulling into the circular drive, facing me. Letting the truck run, he popped out of the driver's side with a beautiful smile that took my breath away. Because his smiles were just that.

Breathtakingly beautiful.

Gaining control of my lungs, I forced out, "What are you doing home?"

As he aimed for my bike on the side of the house, I watched Mason's thigh muscles strain beneath the loose fabric of his basketball shorts and the white cotton of his T-shirt stretch taut across his broad shoulders and thick padding of his chest.

"Watkins had a doctor appointment to sharpen the stick up his ass and practice let out early." In one swift move, he had the Schwinn perched on his shoulder, tipping his head to the truck. "Hop in. I'll drive you."

I should say no, but I missed him too damn much. I scrambled into the cab, noting the passenger seat was warm along with the air pushing out of the vents. Mason's temperature control was set to cool. Soft thuds behind me in the bed forced me to turn as Mason set down my bike. A slight grin pulled at my lips. Regardless of how much he made fun of that rusty thing, he was careful with my bike, just like he was with Poker. And me.

While I worked on buckling my seatbelt, Mason hopped into the truck. He waited for me to click in before starting down the driveway. It didn't evade me that the radio remained off.

Out of the corner of my eye, I appreciated how his biceps rippled with the simple maneuver of turning the wheel as he guided the truck through the neighborhood. I inhaled deeply. He smelled like earth and sweat and all the goodness of Mason rolled into one. He still had bits of grass and dirt sticking to various parts of his golden skin, a few damp hairs plastered to the nape of his neck and forehead.

"You didn't shower?" I asked.

Relaxed behind the wheel with an elbow perched out his window, one shoulder rose and fell. "If I had, then I would have missed you."

Oh, my heart. I plucked up each of those words and wrapped them up in a cute bow.

"Besides, I know you love my man scent." He threw me a wink that on anyone else would have looked creepy. Not Mason.

"Please. Monkey poop smells better."

Oddly, there was no comeback. No idle chat after that. No interrogation. And still no music. Now probably would have been an ideal time to thank him for the shopping trip, but something seemed off with him today. It didn't feel right.

As BB pulled up to my house, I released a breath I didn't know I'd been holding. I'd made it the entire trip without having to lie to Mason.

I unbuckled my belt. "Thank you for the ride."

His gaze was fixed on the wheel, voice tight when he said, "Yup."

I was right. Something was up with him, so it was best I get gone. I plopped down into the dirt as Mason exited the truck. He had my bike on the ground by the time I made it over to his side. Poker trotted our way, and Mason gave him a rubdown plus a kiss to his head.

Mason Scott just kissed my dog's head.

"So, I guess I'll see you at lunch tomorrow?" I was surprised at how non-desperate that sounded.

Nodding, Mason stood and stared at my house. I hated when he did that. Like he was cataloging every warped piece of siding, every missing tile on the roof, every crack in the concrete. "Yeah. We have a brief in the morning, and then Coach Zawasky wants us in the gym."

Which was information I already knew, but I'd selfishly hoped it had changed from when he had updated me at lunch.

"Okay." Hiding my disappointment, I wrapped my fingers around the handlebars of the Schwinn and chirped, "Come on, Poker. Let's get you some ice cubes."

I parked my bike in the carport and had expected the truck to roll away by now. Weird how I hadn't even heard the driver's door shut.

"Sticks?"

While using my foot to lower the kickstand, I discovered Mason had never gotten into his truck. He was standing by his front bumper, brows drawn low, rubbing the back of his neck. This wasn't going to be good. Rigidity settled into my bones as I mentally flipped through my excuses before he even asked me a damn thing.

I stepped to the edge of the carport, and Mason's long legs ate up the rest of the space between us, his gaze finding mine. "I was hoping that you could come to our game Friday. The guys are busting my balls over it."

My stomach clenched around something sharp and jagged. "Mason, you know I have to work."

"I know. I thought...just this once?" Tipping his head to the side, he gave me a hopeful smile that was heartwarmingly adorable. "If the guys don't stop over after the game, then Frankie and Candi can manage the café without you, right? Maybe one of them could close for you, too?" My eyes were still locked with Mason's, but I could have sworn his Nikes were closer than they were a second ago. "There's a RAM party after, like usual, and I'd really like it if you could come. I think I should check out your dance skills so I can see what I'm working with before the wedding." Those peridot eyes sparkled with humor, and the dimples on either side of his expressive lips were powerful enough to make me forget all the reasons I should tell him no.

I swallowed each of those reasons like gulps of acid. "I can't, Mason."

"Why?" He straightened, eyes darkening a moment before returning to their bright shade. "It's one game. I mean...if you can't do the RAM party, that's okay. I get that. I'll drive you home. Hell, I'll drive you to work so you can close if you can't get the entire night off. I'm only asking you to take a few hours off to see me play. It would mean a lot to me."

My father's warnings rang through my head like a drum pounding on my temple as I felt the sting of his breaths on my bare skin, the strike of his hand when he spanked me, heard the sounds he made...*after.*

He'd never be okay with me going to the game because he knew it would be for Mason and no other reason. And if I went to that game without his permission and he came into the café when I wasn't there, or someone mentioned I hadn't been at work...he would follow through with those threats.

Maybe I should teach you a special lesson about that, too.

An invisible collar tightened around my neck, strangling my words. "I can't."

Mason's eyes turned hard, voice trimmed with ice. "You mean that you won't. Or you don't want to. Right?"

My head was already shaking. "No."

"I only wanted to spend some time with you," he gritted out.

Pressure knotted in my chest, rising in my throat. "We see each other almost every day."

"Yeah." He spat the word, looking away from me. "These little five-minute interludes are fucking great."

"I'm going to the wedding next week. We'll have time—"

His head whipped back to me, and he was so close, I doubted a molecule of oxygen could fit between us. God, there was so much anger in him. Anger that I'd seen before, but this...this felt different somehow.

"Tell me, Maggie. What happens when we come back from the wedding? Where will we be then? Here? Is this how it's going to be? Back to a quick hello before class starts? Chitchat over the Yoplait Game during lunch? Me driving you when *you* let me? Me asking you questions, only to get nondescript, bullshit answers?"

Of course, that wasn't what I wanted. I wanted *him*. But even if Mason felt the same way, I couldn't have him. My father would never allow it.

"I..."

"That's what I thought." His chin dipped back to the redwood canopy overhead, and I prayed he was counting—

His head snapped down, and that look... *Oh, God.* Unease furled around my insides, squeezing painfully.

"You know what? Forget it. Forget I asked. Forget I bothered. I'm so tired of this. I'm so fucking tired of begging you to let me in."

The world collapsed under my feet, and I was falling into the bottomless pit. My words came out in a raspy mess. "What are you...saying?"

"Fuck this, is what I'm saying."

The burn in the back of my eyes was instantaneous. "Me? Us?"

"What *us*, Maggie? There's me trying to be your friend. And there's you *not* trying. It's been four months, and I don't know shit about you other than you have a dog, and you enjoy running. Hell, I didn't even know you *had* a dog until you went out to save him in the middle of the night without even telling me that you were leaving!

"Despite asking a million times, I don't know what kind of music you like. I don't know what your favorite color is. I don't know what you think about before you go to bed or when you wake up. I don't know what would possess you at the age of thirteen to get a job and kill yourself for tips. I don't understand why you keep a get-outta-Dodge bag at Jamey's house with a shit ton of money stashed in it instead of a bank. I don't know why you use your dad as an excuse to keep me at arm's length. And I still don't know what made you cry at school that day. When you fall apart, you do it in complete silence, Maggie, and I'm starting to think that I'll never know why. That I'll never know you. So tell me. Tell me something. Anything. Fuck, just tell me what you had for breakfast today."

My bottom lip trembled, and he was going a little wavy in my vision as tears crowded their way in. "You said— You said that it was okay for us to get angry with each other, but you would always care about me."

He was seething. Ready to explode. "I mean it, Maggie."

My brain sorta went on the fritz and shut down. That was the only way to explain what I said next. "I…I'm your friend."

At that, his upper lip drew back, fisting his hair in both hands only to rip them back out. "Goddamn it! I'm such a fucking asshole. You can't even answer one of those things. You won't! You don't fucking want to."

I opened my mouth, but he cut me off.

"You didn't even tell me that you weren't going to be living here next year. We have a scholarship program, too, Maggie. You know…*you know* I would have paid if you had asked me. But you didn't ask me. And so we're clear, I didn't know you wanted to go back to OHU. I didn't know about the apartment, jobs, or the scholarship you wanted to reapply for. I couldn't because you don't fucking talk! Ever! I wanted to know, and it hurt that you gave no thought to me at all. You gave no thought to this *friendship*."

He didn't give me a chance to open my mouth before ripping into me again. "I thought… You know I really thought that—" Shaking his head, disgust contorted his face. "It doesn't even matter. You're not going to give us a chance. You threw up a wall and left me to rot on the other side. I've done everything I can think of, and it's clear to me that you were right. We are imbalanced. I've given, Maggie. I've shown you parts of me that no one has seen. I've told you things about me that *no one* outside of my family knows. And instead of doing the same, you close up and shut me out. That's not friendship, and we're not friends."

Shock rooted me to my spot, paralyzed as he stormed away. His truck door slammed in my ears, and the tires peeled in the dirt, kicking up dust and pebbles all around me. I did nothing to shield myself from their sting. It was nothing compared to the utter devastation of his words.

Minutes, maybe hours passed, and all I could do was stare at the tire tracks he'd left behind. I was gutted and numb. Why didn't I say something? Anything?

Because Mason would have demanded more. He would have gotten closer to the truth.

I had failed the last time I'd tried to push him away, and I knew I had succeeded this time.

I slunk back into the house and stood in my room, looking at my new clothes, the tags still dangling off them. My fingers drifted over the pretty blue satin, blush sequins, black lace. The three shoe boxes, sexy strapless bras with matching panties. The images of me dancing with Mason in a suit and me in a beautiful dress...all dashed away because I was a coward.

It had become blatantly obvious that the brave girl who had once said yes to Mason Scott was no longer. Somewhere along the way, I lost her to the fear. Fear that controlled me, suffocated me, drowned me.

And I'd allowed that fear to decimate my heart into a million pieces.

chapter fifty-six

maggie

Four days. Four days and Mason hadn't so much as acknowledged my existence. He hadn't been home. I'd only seen him in class as he ignored me, and he hadn't been in the quad for lunch. The most word I had received regarding our running sessions were looks of pity from the team.

After that incident with Charlie, it was no secret that Mason held grudges. And even months later, things still weren't right between them. The only reason Mason forgave Charlie in the first place was me. I'd asked him because I knew there would be a day that I would need him to forgive me, only…there was no reason he should.

I wasn't sure when I'd slept last, but it had been a while considering my hands were like mini jackhammers, my vertigo had me arriving late for each class because I couldn't walk straight, and I'd forgotten to put deodorant on today, thanks to my shit memory.

This morning, Jamey had surprised me in the quad with a wrapped gift. Regardless of my protests, he insisted on doing something for my birthday. The silver bangle inside the box coincidentally went with the new outfits Mason had bought me.

When I tried to give it back, Jamey said, "Keep it. Just in case."

So here I was, nineteen years old. I'd never been on a date. I'd been kissed once by a man who didn't remember kissing me. I'd never drive on my own. I had one friend and possibly two more by association. And I was still looking for any way out of this godforsaken town. So I was pretty much in the exact spot I'd been in this summer.

During lunch, Ben stretched out on the lawn, drawing out the cheese of his panini in one long string. "Mags? Are you…still coming to the wedding?"

Hell, if he'd stabbed me in the eye with his fork, it wouldn't have hurt as much as that question had. "No. Mason doesn't want me there. It would just be awkward and uncomfortable for everyone." No longer hungry, I slid my peanut butter and jelly back inside my lunch bag. "I've actually decided to quit the Scotts, make it easier for him."

Eyes growing large, Ben shot up. "Mags—"

"Jamey, could you help me take the clothes back?" It was rude to cut off Ben like that, but I'd made up my mind, and nothing he said would change it.

"Take the…?" Scowling, Jamey threw a fry at my head. "You are not quitting your job, and you are keeping those clothes."

"No, I'm not. I have nowhere to wear them, so it makes no sense to keep them. They were a gift, and…" As the tears crawled in, I pushed my plastic sunglasses up my nose, so the scratches lined up with my sight. Hated to admit that I detested these things, but I hadn't been able to even look at the Ray-Bans in days. "I should return them."

"Hold on. You wanted to take the next step with Mason just this week," Ben pointed out. "What happened between you?"

Too much.

"I shouldn't have—" The words got stuck in my throat, and I pinched my eyes shut. "I shouldn't have said that. I deluded myself into believing Mason could ever want me. He only wanted my friendship and nothing more. And I was okay with that. But I couldn't give him… I wasn't a good friend, and he's done with me. He should be." My voice cracked at the end, lips wobbling. After a thick swallow, I said, "Besides, I'm leaving next summer. Regardless of what you guys decide, I'm going to OHU or…anywhere that's not here." Standing on shaky legs, I grabbed my bag. "Can you tell him I'm sorry? Please, Ben? He won't care, but I would like him to at least hear that I'm sorry." Turning away from them, my heart felt like nothing more than a broken blob in my chest.

There was a rally after school that I didn't bother to stay for. I knew what they were like, and I knew Mason wouldn't look for me in the stands this time or throw a smile my way.

I didn't think I could handle being ignored by him once more.

During the week, every time I came to the café and saw the basket, I was overwhelmed with sadness, but for whatever reason, today…today, it felt more like I was in mourning. Mourning a friendship and a future I had wanted.

I wasn't sure how much longer Mason would continue donating to this project of mine. Or if he still was. People in this town relied on that basket, families who otherwise wouldn't feed their children needed that food. The consequences of what I'd done was too damn much for me to think about just yet.

As soon as I stepped inside the café, I asked Frankie for the night off. I hadn't intended to. It just sorta…came out instead of a *hello*. The team wouldn't be coming tonight anyway. Frankie was surprisingly quick to say yes, and then he gave me a hug. It was a little awkward and stiff. I didn't care. I needed a freaking hug.

It didn't slip by me that I had done the very thing Mason wanted by taking the night off. The very thing I told him I couldn't do. And if I had only said yes four days ago, I wouldn't be here. I would still have Mason. I would still be going to the wedding and dreaming of our first dance and what he would say when he saw me in a dress for the first time.

I wasn't sure what I would do with my night off, but I needed time to think, reevaluate my life. My father's control over my life. He still had the strings, pulling his puppet in the direction he wanted, punishing me, bruising me when I struggled for freedom.

Once home, I stared at my prison, at every dark corner, at every secret that had tainted these walls. This wasn't living. This was barely surviving. And I was so damned tired of it. I'd broken every promise I'd made to myself. I was everything I didn't want to be.

Weak and helpless and broken.

I hadn't told my father that I wasn't going to Grove Point yet. Maybe because I wanted to leave an opportunity for my fairy godmother to pop out of the forest and Cinderella me to the wedding. Or magic Mason to my front door.

I slipped on my running gear and took Poker to the bluffs since it was the perfect spot to think. While running along Canyon, my intention was to keep going north, but my feet swerved right onto Warrington's campus and stopped at the pinboard. It seemed like this board of cork and tacks had the power to change my life. Decisions that altered my future had been made here.

Now at my biggest crossroads, I needed that direction.

Staring at the job postings, I knew no matter what was here, it wasn't what I was looking for. I didn't want to quit the Scotts. I didn't want to push Mason away or walk out of his life.

"This has got to be fate. I can't be number three hundred and thirty-two." I turned to a familiar blond walking toward me, looking tanned and handsome in a green T-shirt and jeans.

"Hi, Brady."

He planted his hand next to where I was standing, long arm stretching out in front of me as he leaned on the corkboard. His gaze slipped over me. "Darlin', is your dog gonna help you break another heart today?"

"No. I was…" I sighed, glancing back to the board. "Looking for a job."

Brows rounding high, he nudged me with a flip-flop that probably cost a hundred bucks. "You should be partying, not working."

I nodded. "I wish I could."

As his lips pulled up on one side, those aquamarine eyes danced. "You can. Come tonight. There's a party after the game."

I know, and Mason will be there.

"I can't tonight but thank you."

"Next Friday?" he offered. "I'm not gonna stop until you say yes."

Next Friday… I didn't have to work. My father would be gone. And I wouldn't be at the wedding. This was what I was looking for, wasn't it? Freedom to do what I wanted?

"Okay. I actually could come next Friday."

"Really?" His smile stretched wide. "You mean I don't have to walk home on my knees this time?"

"Far be it from me to discourage you. A little knee-walking never hurt anyone."

He squinted, giving me another once over. "No. No, it hasn't." His grin brightened. "I'll take it. See ya then, Maggie."

As soon as Brady walked away, a sharp stab of guilt gouged out my chest. Like I was somehow…cheating on Mason, which made no sense at all. I almost screamed at Brady that I changed my mind, but I didn't. I let him walk away. He'd figure it out when I didn't show.

A tail whacked me in the back of my legs as Poker quietly whined.

My shoulders hung low, weighed down with defeat. Or was that grief again. "I know. I miss Mason, too."

A tongue hung out the side of his mouth as Poker looked behind us to the football field. My gaze followed his, to the crews getting ready for the game, painting crisp white lines on the field, setting up vendors of food and merch.

I wanted nothing more than to be there tonight. I wanted to see Mason and watch him play and cheer for him until I went hoarse. I wanted to go to that party and dance and laugh and…be with him. I wanted it so much it *hurt*.

…that's the moment you become an adult.

It was then that I knew what I wanted.

I needed to stop surviving.

I wanted to start living.

chapter fifty-seven

mason

"Tits and ass later, Cam. Get your head in the game!" Matt barked.

Cam tore his eyes away from the sidelines, grinning inside his helmet. "Addison really isn't wearing panties this time! I swear."

"Yeah, but she's wearing spankies," Jordon clarified.

"Alright." Cam cracked his neck. "Can we just lose this game already, so I can verify Jordon's intel?"

"Cam," Matt warned.

His shrug was exaggerated by all the pads. "We're so fucked. There's no way we're gonna win. Mike gave up. Why can't I?"

"He didn't give up," Ben called over from the bench. "It's called a concussion, asshole!"

Vapor curled around my cousin's mouth. "Tomato-tomahto."

I rubbed at the ache in my side. Pretty sure I had a bruised rib from the last play that tanked.

"And you, fuckwad!" A hand slammed my helmet, jarring my spine. Matt growled, "Do you think you could catch at least one pass?"

"If you can get your little girl hands to throw straight," I shot back.

Brady's fingers curled around both of our facemasks, bringing us together. "Enough of this. Whatever shit you're dealing with, handle it off the field."

Matt shoved Brady away. "How about you don't fuck up our next rush, Hale."

"Talk to your brother, Matt!" His blue eyes flashed at me, a finger punctuating every other word into my chest. "You better get that dick sucked tonight, Mase. I'm not gonna take much more from you."

Matt thrust his shoulder between us. "Fuck off, Brady." Spinning, Matt faced me, emerald eyes locked on hard. "You need to fix this with Maggie and now. He's right. You've been a bastard all week."

I shoved him back. "Are you gonna call the play sometime tonight, or should we bend over and take it up the ass?"

"Taking it up the ass would be less painful," Dylan muttered.

"You would know!" Cam laughed out.

"The Wolverines are in the tha house!" was announced as soon as we stepped inside the RAM door. I was faced with a wall of sweat, skin, and red Solo cups. Cheers bounced in my ears, and someone—or someone*s*—grabbed my ass. One would have thought we'd won the game. Hadn't even come close. It wasn't pretty, and everyone blamed me.

They were right to.

It was my fault. All of it. The game and Maggie. It was for the best, though—the Maggie part. I needed to push her away before she could do more damage. Save myself from total annihilation. The longer I knew her without *knowing* her, the harder and deeper I'd fall in love with her, and the worse it would be later.

I planted my ass in the same spot it was at every party. The bar. Girls in tight dresses pawed at me, asked me to take them to my room. However, it wasn't just my room currently. Due to Vic's unfortunate prank gone wrong with baby powder and Vaseline, I now shared my room with Pete. Pete snored and had boundary issues. Issues like enjoying porn. There was nothing wrong with watching porn; it was a healthy activity. My issue was that he enjoyed it when I was in the room.

That, and the porn starred Pete and his girl, Sienna.

My eyes flicked up long enough to scan the crowd. I sure as shit wasn't looking for a head of raven hair or Caribbean blue eyes or creamy pins or a button nose sprinkled with freckles.

Nope. Not at all.

I needed more JD.

"Mags is returning all of her clothes *and* the sunglasses," Jamey stated, sliding between stools to lean against the bar. "Thought you might be interested to know she isn't the heartless bitch you think she is."

I snapped out of my thoughts. The way the lights reflected off that platinum hair, he looked like he was rocking a halo. "Let me be clear on this. I *never* thought that about her. Ever. I want her to have all of it."

Jamey's brows flew up to his hairline. "You really think she wants to keep the stuff you bought her? That remind her of *you*?"

I twisted toward him. "I wouldn't really know, Jamey. Maggie doesn't believe in share time, so why don't you help me out here. What else did she say?"

Ben sidled up on my other side. "It was kinda hard to understand her around the tears, but I was pretty sure she was quitting to make it easier for you."

Wait...what?

"Goddamn it, Mase!" Matt's fist pounded the bar top, startling everyone. Cam swooped over to save a blonde from falling off her stool.

I looked between my cousin and his boyfriend. "She was crying?"

"All. Fucking. Week," Jamey grounded out each word.

My stomach sank and began to churn up all the JD I'd dumped into it. I had no idea she was thinking that. No idea she was *that* upset. I mean, yeah, there was a glimmer of something in her eyes during our fight, but...

"All week?"

Jamey crossed his arms over his chest. "You're such an asshole, Mason. Do you know what she asked us? How to get out of the friend zone with you. And you know why she hasn't? Because she doesn't think she's good enough for you. That you could ever want her. And yet she said yes to the wedding just to be near you. She picked out dresses, heels, and lingerie *for you*! And then you threw a hissy fit because she couldn't go to a fucking football game."

"What kind of lingerie?" Cam interjected, and Matt smacked him upside the head. Cam backed away with his palms up. "Sorry. I'll ask later."

I tore my glare off Cam and regifted it to Jamey. "The game wasn't the reason, and I didn't throw a hissy fit."

"Then what was the reason?" Matt demanded.

"The fact that she refuses to tell me anything about herself, and when she does, it's a lie. Even about the stupidest shit. She hides everything from me, and honestly, the fact that she wants to be more than friends is a little surprising since she can't be bothered with the friend part first. She wasn't even going to tell me about OHU. What kind of friend doesn't tell you that they're moving away?"

I shook the ice in my glass, trying to knock free any remnants of whiskey. "We had a fight, and I broke up *whatever* we were. Plain and simple. I asked her to tell me something real about herself, to open up to me. Just one damn thing. She refused. She shut down. She locked me out. Same as she always does. I had enough. I can't be in a relationship or a friendship with someone who won't let me know who the fuck she is."

The guys went quiet, and I was out of JD. Agitation ignited through me, burning from the inside out.

"When?" I snarled.

Ben lifted a brow. "When what?"

"When did she ask that? The friend zone thing."

"Last week," he answered. "When we took her shopping."

God… I had seen her that night. I could still feel her hands on my face, the way her smile curled around my heart, the slight weight of her in my arms. My chest felt too damn tight. I had wanted to ask her then what she picked out, but I knew she'd feel guilty and offer to pay me back, even though she couldn't afford to. So I didn't.

Fuck, I missed her. I missed seeing her. I missed her voice. I missed touching her. I missed just being around her.

"It's been going on for a lot longer than a week," Jamey muttered, reaching for the Captain Morgan.

That caused the tightness in my chest to worsen, damn near choking me. "How long?"

"Since the day she met you, Mason. You asked her out once, remember? Which was a huge deal for her. She couldn't stop talking about you—when she didn't even know your name or what you looked like. She was excited about that date, and Mags doesn't get excited. And you fucking walked out on her and broke her heart. You rejected her. On sight. Do you have any clue how that fucked with her head? And even after all of that, she still wanted you. You were never just a friend to her."

I should ram my face into the bar top. "Okay… You're right. I—" I took a breath. Then another. "I have no clue what I'm doing or how to fix this." I looked to Jamey. "Can you help me?"

Jamey's hand paused on the way to grab two tumblers. "Help you with what?"

"Get her."

"*Get her?*" Rising to his full height, he— Damn, when did Jamey hulk out? How had I missed that? "Like get up on her or get up in her? What kind of *get her* are you referring to exactly? Let me warn you, I will do neither of those."

"No, I meant—" I deflated in my seat and sighed. He was right. He was the one who had picked up the pieces after that date and every time since. Why would he help me again? "Forget it."

Jamey released a mouthful of air. "What did you mean then?"

"That you're her best friend. I can't figure her out, and I can't read her. She's…"

"Guarded," he assisted.

I scoffed. "Please. Guantanamo Bay has nothing on her."

"Did it occur to you that she has a right to be? How many times can you expect her to put herself out on a limb like that?"

I nodded, conceding his point. "Will you help me?"

Jamey looked like he considered saying yes, but then his lips pressed together. "What are your intentions with her, Mason?"

"*Intentions?*" I fought back a laugh. "What is this? The eighteenth-century?"

He leaned back over me. "Yeah. And if you're looking for anything less than 'They lived happily ever after,' I will not help you."

I considered that for all of zero seconds. I could do the HEA. Maggie was who I wanted. When I looked into my future, she was who I saw there. Poker and us in a beach house, running on the sand, spoiling her with new clothes, jewelry, shoes, kissing her every chance she'd let me…

Like a gale force wind, reality slammed into me. I may have ruined the best HEA in the history of all HEAs.

I leveled him with a stare. "That's what I want to give her. If she'll have me."

He considered me a moment longer. "Okay. But you will not speak to her tonight. You're drunk. Sober your shit up and talk to her in the morning. All you need to do is apologize, and don't be a dick. That's your first lesson. She'll forgive you. Trust me on that."

He didn't offer a second lesson, probably because of the aforementioned need to sober up first. But since it wasn't morning, I threw back a few more shots because the thought of her crying was too much to handle.

On the other side of the bar, Brady mixed a cocktail for a brunette, who for her sake, I prayed wasn't a virgin.

He slid down our way to grab the Blue Curaçao. "How are your balls, Mase? It's been what…a dickade? I've never seen you go this long. Your head is gonna explode soon. Both of 'em."

"My balls are big and shorn, Brady. Thank you for your concern. How is the virgin hunting going?"

Ignoring the disgust in my voice, he rubbed his hands together. "Since you asked...I've got something special coming next week. Literally, she'll be coming in my bed next week." A broad grin spread across his face, which in the shadows, made him look like the evil prick I knew him to be.

"Jesus." Matt grimaced. "I need to run a PSA about you. Who is it this time?"

Brady's sharpened grin should have been enough of a warning, but I never saw it coming. "A little someone I bumped into in the quad this afternoon. A lucky little someone."

No fucking way.

"Maggie?" I launched off my stool, but Matt was quick to grab me and hold me down. Probably a good thing because I was ready to tear Brady's arms out of their sockets and then use them to beat him to death.

He wagged his brows. "Looks like you're done with her, right?" Shaker in hand, Brady ambled away to go attack his new victim.

Stomach roiling, I gripped my head, things going a bit swirly. "Fuck!"

Matt squeezed my shoulder and kept me on the stool. "It's alright. Apologize tomorrow like Jamey said, and make sure she comes to the wedding. Keep her out of town next weekend, or I'm gonna have to beat Brady's dick up so he can't use it. Don't fuck this up again because that thing has diseases even the CDC can't identify."

chapter fifty-eight

mason

My alarm went off at the ungodly hour I'd set it to last night, and while I would love nothing more than to hit snooze at least ten more times, I was determined to see Maggie before Gorilla Arms did. I was sure that asshole had been waiting for me to fuck up, so he could swoop in, be the hero again. I hadn't made it hard for him. All he needed was patience, and I had a feeling he had an arsenal of the shit.

As air molecules ninja'd their way through Pete's respiratory tract, I laid in bed with my mind immediately latching onto an image of Maggie crying into Logan's chest while he held her and how those brown eyes had drilled into mine, challenging me, warning me...

I knew Logan would do right by her, and that was why my gut twisted around what felt like knives. Or maybe that was the contents of the empty bottle of JD next to me.

Sitting up in bed, the room swirled, a hammer drove into my skull, and after someone had tenderized every muscle in my body, they'd stuffed a bag of cotton in my mouth.

Why did I keep forgetting how much hangovers sucked?

Looking down at my wrinkled Henley and jeans, I thought about changing. For a millisecond. The effort that required was too much in my current state. I somehow made my way around Pete's makeshift rack on the floor without falling on top of him. I then somehow got down the stairs without faceplanting onto the marble.

I needed food to absorb the whiskey in my veins, so I ambled toward the kitchen, but a soft sniffling noise drew me to a cold stop. I twisted around to a girl coming down the stairs, Brady's brunette from last night. I'd honestly forgotten about her and the conversation I'd had with him. With another sniff, she wiped away a smear of mascara from beneath her eyes as she faltered in her steps and winced.

Damn him.

JD and Coke were thick on my tongue as I asked, "Hey, you okay?"

Snapping up her head, her red-rimmed, swollen eyes blinked at me, and then she did the one thing that really bothered me. She covered herself with her arms, trying to become smaller, hiding herself. Just hours ago, she had picked that little pink dress out of her closet and came to the party full of confidence. She should have been. Any guy would give his left nut to have a chance with that girl.

And now…?

Now she held herself like she was ashamed of wearing that dress, for coming here, for wanting to have fun, like it was her fault. I'd seen it too many times. Girls came in their sexy outfits, looking for a meaningless hookup, a man who would help them ditch the V card, maybe find a boyfriend, or let loose and dance for a few hours with their friends. Whatever brought her here, she didn't find it. No, she found something else.

Something dark and vile.

The moment she walked through that door, she was blood in the water, and Brady was the great white. He knew just how to lure them into his bed, had a keen sense of saying precisely what they needed to hear. This poor girl didn't stand a chance. He got what he wanted, and he was done with her now. All the bullshit was over, and he'd laid it out for her this morning. *Thanks, sexy. You were great. Do you mind closing the door on your way out?*

She still hadn't said anything, so I repeated, "Are you okay?"

Had he taken it too far this time? It was a fear of mine. Brady was rough in bed, and he was a sleaze, but it was always consensual as far as I knew. Legally speaking. I wanted her to tell me that she wasn't okay. That she had told Brady to stop and wanted to go to campus security, the police, the hospital.

I'd do all of that.

"Y—yeah." And this was the point that she played it off like this was normal, and that was how all guys fucked.

They didn't.

Brady was that good. Even when every instinct screamed for them to say no, *yes* was the only word out of their mouths.

"You sure?" I pressed. " 'Cause you don't seem alright."

"It's…" She shook me off. "I'm okay."

Mouth turned down in the corners, I gestured toward the kitchen. "Can I make you some coffee or tea?" I wasn't sure where we kept either of those, but I'd deal with that later.

Holding herself tighter, she stared at me as if I were an animal like Brady. In this moment, I was no different, and I couldn't blame her for that. "No. I want to go to my dorm and take a shower." *Scrub him away.*

"Do you need a ride? I'm heading out myself. I don't mind dropping you." I knew the answer, but that wouldn't stop me from offering.

Swallowing, she looked like she considered it but then ducked her chin. "No. I have an Uber coming. Thanks, though."

"Okay."

Watching her shuffle out the door, I swapped that girl out with Maggie, those blue eyes filled with shame, wincing with every step as her head hung low. God, the lines Brady would use, the way he would touch her, get her into his bed…

The urge to eat vanished, nausea front and center again.

I had to fix this. I had to say or do whatever was necessary to prevent Maggie from turning into this poor girl. I couldn't bear it.

I drove to Sands Drive, not caring that I looked like Death's uglier cousin, going too fast on the empty roads blanketed by a thick layer of fog. I pulled into the lot with four patrol vehicles parked in a row outside the café. My stomach lurched all over again. I was late, and he was here.

Gorilla Arms.

As I approached the front door, I was painfully aware that the basket on the two-top outside was empty, which was strange because I'd given Henry enough cash for an entire month of donations. Maggie could be stubborn, yeah, and it hurt to know that she wanted to give all her gifts back, but this was taking it too far.

I tore open the door, ready to tell her just that, but the scene I ran into not only stopped that from happening but also stopped all forward momentum. In a million scenarios that had played through my head on the way over here, this was not one of them. Those four cops were here, but they weren't sitting, and Maggie wasn't crying in anyone's arms.

In fact, Maggie wasn't here.

Frankie and Candi flashed me looks of concern, and so did the cops when I crossed the threshold. Logan's hand was white on his phone, and for the first time, those brown eyes weren't all I-eat-shits-like-you for breakfast.

On the front table was a large bouquet of flowers and shiny blue balloons. One balloon read, HAPPY BIRTHDAY, MAGNIFIQUE!

Birthday…?

"Where is she?" I asked breathless, still searching the room as though she were hiding behind the counter, ready to pop out.

"Don't know. She never showed up. She's never done that. She's always here. Always." Frankie swiped nervous palms down his apron front. "I saw her yesterday afternoon, and she asked for the night off. Poor kid was really upset about something, but Mags wouldn't talk about it. She promised she would be here in the morning." Looking to me, his eyes welled. "Her shakes were so bad. I should have driven her—"

Near tears herself, Candi looped an arm through Frankie's.

Robert leaned into Candi to whisper, "Did she come home after we left?"

Chewing on her bottom lip, Candi shrugged. "I don't know. We…were sleeping."

Yeah, I'll bet.

"Chief's not picking up." Logan ended the call, and though he tried to control his voice, I heard it. There was a thread of panic there, and Logan didn't strike me as the kind of dude to panic. His hard gaze flipped to me. "When's the last time you saw her?"

Yesterday afternoon from my truck when I followed her here. Since that headline was all sorts of creeper… "Yesterday at school."

Gil shook his head. "I'm calling it."

Logan slid his phone into one of the fifty pouches of his body armor. "You want me to go to the Chief's?"

Gil gave him a tight nod. "Yes. Keith and Robert, check the campus, and I'll head up a squad to search the bluffs in case she…" He closed his eyes for a beat. "In case she went for a run."

Every drop of acid in my gut hit my esophagus.

As Gil, Keith, and Robert filed out, Logan stayed behind. The door closed, those eyes on me again. "I need you to call Jamey. Ask if he knows where she is. He'll be more likely to tell you than me. If he knows anything, call me and no one else." He whipped out a card from another secret compartment in his vest and held it out.

I scrubbed a hand over my head. "I was with Jamey last night at the RAM house. He was there late—"

He slapped the card onto my chest, shoving me backward, so the entire table behind me moved. Then he was in my face with a scary ass look that promised a world of pain. "It's a goddamned phone call, Mason. It's not for me. It's for Maggie."

The death glare was still set on me, and I sucked in a shallow breath before taking the card. "I wasn't arguing with you, just explaining that it's probably a dead end. But, of course, I'll call."

He relaxed. I think. It was actually hard to distinguish between his normal posture and the I'll-fuck-you-up stance. "Good."

I stuffed the card into my back pocket, confused about Logan's request. "Why—"

A woman's voice squawked in his shoulder mic, and he didn't wait for me to ask the hundred questions building in my brain. His boots pounded all the way outside to his PPV. His tires squealed as he peeled out of the parking lot. I couldn't just sit here. I followed Logan.

Along the drive to Maggie's, I called Jamey, and as expected, he had no clue she was missing. I made a few more calls before I skidded to a stop in front of Maggie's place, parking next to Logan's PPV. Chief Davis' Tahoe was in the carport.

When I stepped out of the truck, Logan appeared around the corner of the house in a low crouch with his pistol at the ready. Where the hell did he think he was right now? A meth raid?

Panting noises drew our attention to the woods as a German shepherd leapt out of the thick foliage. It was then we both spotted his empty bowls, one turned over on the cracked concrete. Bad feelings curled in my gut. If there was one thing, and one thing only that I knew without a shadow of a doubt about Maggie…she'd *never* let Poker go without food and water.

"Chief!" Inching between the scant inches between the Tahoe and the house, Logan banged on the side door. "Chief! It's Jackson! You in there?" A cellphone blared within, and he tried the handle. When it turned at his touch, Logan paused and met my stare. "Mason, do you have your phone on you?"

I nodded, vaguely feeling Poker nudge my hand with his nose.

"Good. Stay out here until I clear the house. If shit goes down, run and hide. Call nine-one-one if you can."

My throat felt too damn dry to argue. "Okay."

He banged on the door. "This is Officer Jackson with the CCPD! Just want to make sure everyone is okay!" A pause. "I'm coming in!" Logan jerked the door open, so it hit the bumper of the Tahoe, the aluminum shades rattling against a pane of clouded glass. Using some impressive moves, he squeezed that massive body into the opening and zipped into the house. A few moments later, his voice shook the tiny shack. "Maggie! Chief Davis!"

I didn't like to think I had a death wish; however, my feet were moving forward. Maybe it was that I had never been this close to being inside Maggie's house before, but I couldn't stop myself. And though I hadn't been invited in, it wasn't like I was living by vampire laws here.

Besides, Logan was still hollering, and there wasn't any gunfire. Chances were good that all was clear.

Stepping up to the door, there was enough morning light to see the frame had warped, raw wood exposed by chips in the yellow paint, and...scratches. A shit ton of scratches. Hell. It looked like Freddy Krueger plus his entire family had a go at this thing. The wood had been gouged from my eye line down to my feet. Odd.

I looked down to my side. At the shepherd glaring intently at the door as if he could will it off the hinges. My gaze dropped to his large paws, at the black nails protruding from each pad. "You do this?"

His brow lifted as if annoyed by my stupidity. Fair enough.

Turning the handle, I tried to keep Poker outside in case anyone mistook him for a target, but that didn't happen. He bulldozed his way past me. I then somehow got my body through the minuscule opening the Tahoe allowed. Chief Davis might want to hang a tennis ball from the ceiling. Or learn how to park.

When I stepped through the laundry room, I questioned if I hadn't just gone through a time machine to the early 1970s. I thought the outside was a dump with the dirt and weeds as landscaping, the peeling wooden slats, and busted roof tiles. But the inside was worse.

So much worse.

The house wasn't dirty, but the stench of beer and something sour lingered like a thick haze. I searched for the odor, only coming up with dilapidated furniture. The brown carpet suggested it had been shag once upon a time, and the pad beneath had to have disintegrated ten years ago. A lone recliner sat on the edge of the room, and along one of the bare and pitted walls was a mismatched couch that might have been beige at some point in its existence. The bulky television required binocs to watch, and it was sitting on a rickety wooden TV stand.

A door furthest down the hall opened, Logan standing outside of it. "Chief, wake up." Whatever Logan saw made his grip tighten on the pistol, but his trigger finger stayed alongside the frame.

Panic suffused my muscles, drawing my shoulders up as my thighs tensed.

"Jackson?" Sleep coated the chief's voice, and the stiffness in my muscles eased a little. "Why the fuck are you in my house?"

Poker appeared at my side, wearing that same glare from earlier, which was now homed in on the end of the hallway.

Adopting the same glower as Poker, Logan said, "Chief, we need to talk."

There was a rough, phlegmy cough before, "What time...?" Then came a sound of irritation. "This better be good."

Logan's back straightened as he holstered his gun at his thigh. "I wouldn't be here if it wasn't important."

After a few beats and what sounded like clothes being pulled on, Mr. Davis followed Logan down the hall. At the edge of the kitchen, he teetered on his feet, eyes lined in red, hair oily and matted, tan skin leached of color. Man, he looked…wasted.

His line of sight found me unmoved on the carpet. "Mason?" I swore at my name, Poker shifted closer to me, which brought the chief's attention low. With a grunt, he cracked his neck. Eyes like chips of ice swung to Logan. "Let's hear it."

"Maggie didn't show at work today. When's the last time you spoke with her?"

He blinked hard as if that would help assimilate the information. Without answering Logan, his head swiveled, and his eyes immediately narrowed at something in the kitchen. Something he didn't like.

"Margaret!" the chief barked, then waited. Right. Like calling her name for the fiftieth time was the charm. When Maggie didn't magically appear, the chief turned as he mumbled, "Fucking lazy kid."

I… Hell, my entire body winced. My brain wanted to reject what I'd heard, but there was no mistaking it. Especially not when Logan had the same reaction as I did.

A door slammed against the wall as Mr. Davis disappeared inside one of the rooms. Shuffling and bangs followed. Something crashed as he called out his daughter's name again, but he spoke it like a ripe curse.

My fists began to curl. The house was the size of a shoebox. Where the fuck did he think she was hiding? In a cabinet?

Nearing what I would guess was his breaking point, too, Logan braced his hands on his hips. "She's not here, Chief, and I don't think she came home. Poker doesn't have food or water. And her—"

The cellphone rang again, cutting off Logan. The chief charged out of a room and swiped his phone off the counter so hard, he yanked the USB cord with it. The cord swung limply at his side as he held the phone to his ear. "Tina, call everyone in. I want two officers from North Squad and two from South to check out the hospitals, PCH and SBH. Have Harris—" On a long pause, his jaw hardened to a block of concrete. "*She did what?*" He pulled the phone away from his mouth and leveled Logan with a glare. "Did you know that she didn't work last night?"

"Not until this morning. I covered for Riggs last night and didn't have the chance to stop by the café on my break." The chief eyed the younger cop as if he were lying, and Logan quickly picked up on that. "You approved his shift change. Remember?"

Aaaand that got the chief good and pissed.

Logan continued like he had zero fucks to give. "Frankie said she came in around four and asked for the night off. As of right now, she may have been missing for fifteen hours."

A vein pulsed in the chief's temple. That glare going nowhere.

And neither was the search for Maggie.

"Brady Hale spoke to her sometime yesterday afternoon, too," I added. "He saw her on campus, but I don't know more than that. He should be at the RAM house now."

That cool stare slid to me as the phone returned to the chief's mouth. "Did you hear that? Good. Get the U Squad and campus security knocking on doors and start at the RAM house— Fine, yes. Issue an Endangered and Missing Person Alert." Whatever she said, he gritted his teeth to. "I'll get one." He hung up, using that phone to punctuate his words to Logan. "Get your ass over to the Hayeses'. You talk to Ava first before her boy."

What the hell was with these two and Jamey? Before I could ask, Logan began to say, "Chief, her bi—"

"Did I fucking stutter, Jackson?" The chief's upper lip ticked with rage, rolling his shoulders forward. "Was there something about my command that you have a problem with? I would love to hear it."

Whatever Logan wanted to say must have taken an act of God for him to keep quiet. "No, sir," he bit out. Logan abruptly twisted around, eyes meeting mine. For the first time, the secret battle between us was put on hold for a girl we both cared about, whom we were both worried for. A girl I suspected we both loved. "Backpack and bike are gone," he whispered, passing me.

Yeah, I kinda missed those clues.

The chief waited for the front door to shut and threw his phone onto the counter, the USB cord smacking a cabinet. "You can come in, Mason. I've gotta take a shower."

I blinked at that.

Who the fuck takes a shower when their child is missing? A child with epilepsy?

He knew that, right? That Maggie could be in grave danger? Did I imagine things when he used the words *endangered* and *missing*...

Dumbstruck, I watched as he marched down the hall, jerking off his T-shirt in the process. Thankfully, his bedroom door shut before the pants followed. I shook my head as my gaze drifted to the recliner I was standing next to.

I should leave, help search for Maggie, but the opportunity was here and, well, I couldn't help it. I had to know.

674 | ashlan thomas

The kitchen was around the wall, and I searched for what the chief had been glaring at earlier. Though I shouldn't be surprised considering the state of the living room, the kitchen was… Jesus.

My eyes tripped over a yellowed Formica counter lined with scrapes and stains, broken up by dingy appliances. Both sides of the chipped porcelain sink were filled with dirty plates that had been smeared in what I would guess was hot sauce and blue cheese. That explained the odor. There was no dishwasher that I could see.

The cabinets hadn't fared any better than the rest of the house, half of them without their pulls, one missing a hinge. The wooden table was covered by a poker topper and game chips, playing cards strewn over it. Six chairs that looked as sturdy as toothpicks sat on the discolored linoleum floor, the gold square pattern almost worn away. The garbage can overflowed with longnecks and two empty JD bottles. Pizza boxes were stacked on the floor next to it.

I pried open a door and lucked out to find Poker's dog food. He followed me outside, where I collected his bowls and then filled them with water and kibble. Poker trotted over, and while he Hoover'd that down, I gave him a quick once over for any wounds like Maggie would have done.

As I finished checking his last paw, I heard the pipes whine in the walls and decided to keep investigating the house. I passed a bathroom and stopped at the other door that was ajar. I flipped a light switch, and my heart…shriveled.

It was a bedroom. The most depressing bedroom I'd ever seen. *Maggie's room.* Faith's room was full of life and light with plush animals and Matt's paint strokes coloring every inch of her walls and ceiling. This looked like a prison cell. Grayed curtains hung limply over a small window that was encased by bars. The twin-sized mattress laying cockeyed on the frame was covered with a drab off-white comforter that had been stitched together a few times, and the same matted shag carpet that crunched beneath my boots was splotched with stains.

A frayed wicker laundry basket was upturned, clothes spilled onto the floor, and the closet door was open. What little clothes hung in here were now on the floor along with their wire hangers that I assumed had been the source of all the racket her father had caused moments ago. Frowning, I tidied everything up, but she had so little, it took me no more than a few minutes to get the room back in order.

As I shoved the mattress into place, the near rotted frame of her bed creaked. Maggie was tiny, but this thing was hardly big enough for a six-year-old. She had a matching nightstand and dresser, but there wasn't a desk, books, or a computer. The walls were bare with flecking paint, all accompanied by a popcorn ceiling to complete the horror of any designer.

To make matters worse, she shared a wall with her father, and I wondered if he ever had Candi over when Maggie was here. Man, that was all kinds of wrong.

I couldn't imagine what it must have been like for her to see how I lived and then come home to this day after day. I knew her home wasn't anything near what I had, but this...? I never imagined she lived like this. I couldn't fault her for wanting to hide this part of her life from me.

On the dresser was a greeting card. Singular. One birthday card from Jamey. Holding it to my chest, my throat felt thick, and shame ran so very deep. Deep enough that the back of my eyes singed with heat. *I missed her birthday*. I'd asked once when it was and she'd deflected as usual, and I...didn't ask again.

The pipes quieted as the shower turned off, and I returned to the bathroom I'd passed. It smelled like lemons but looked far from fresh. I scooted a limp curtain across the rod to reveal the caulking on the shower walls had loosened and pulled away, the tub boring deep scratches, the finish all but gone, and the towels slung over the bar were threadbare and discolored. There was one sink with rusty fixtures, a hazy mirror hanging above.

Every cell inside me was screaming to put this house out of its misery, and I'd only been in it for five minutes. I imagined a police chief's salary could afford better, but I was sure if he partied and gambled like this every week, he'd pissed his money away. This was why she had to work at such a young age. This was why she killed herself for tips and worked two jobs. This was why she hadn't told me the truth. It was too hard, it hurt too much, and the humiliation she must have felt...

I resisted the urge to put my fist through that mirror, bust the hell out of these decrepit walls. She deserved so much better.

Fucking lazy kid? He actually said that. About *Maggie*.

Hungover ramblings or not, she was his daughter. He should consider himself the luckiest son of a bitch alive to have a girl like her.

Fuck him.

Poker had finished his food, and I wasn't gonna hang around another second. I called out, "Mr. Davis, I'm gonna take Poker and look for Maggie."

Not waiting or caring for his response, Poker followed me out with a wagging tail and sped off toward what looked like a path behind the house that led deeper into the woods. I sighed.

"I'm not gonna hold my dick while you dig a hole or chase after squirrels. We have—" My words died off when I realized he'd stopped to stare at me as if he were...waiting for me.

Something, call it gut instinct, told me to follow him. Since I'd already driven on the main roads, and that was where everyone else would be searching, I went with Poker, letting him lead the way.

I followed as he sniffed along the trail, ducking his head in the thick brush and low shrubs. The further he took me into the forest, the denser the canopy became. Darkness and shadows enveloped us, the temps dropping considerably.

It was bright enough to see, but hell, Maggie could be anywhere. She could be... God, I knew not to waste the gifts that I was given. Gifts like Maggie. So what if she was only my friend? I shouldn't have pushed her away. I should have cherished whatever Maggie was willing to give me. It wasn't much, only scraps, but I...I was in love with her, and her friendship should have been enough for me.

I heard Chief Davis' patrol vehicle rumble down the road, taking the bend on Verde Way out toward Canyon. I couldn't explain why, but I felt... She was this way.

Bark! Bark! Bark!

Fear infused me as I sprinted to where Poker was, face and arms getting snagged and scratched by limbs and bushes. I came to a clearing between the crowded redwoods and firs as a fracture of sunlight caught a gleam of dull chrome in the tall grass.

Maggie.

to be continued...

The story continues with

the silent flight of a magpie

a cove novel

ASHLAN THOMAS

acknowledgments

I would like to thank you, the reader. Thank you for taking a chance on my words and trusting me with your heart.

about the author

Ashlan Thomas is a Contemporary and Paranormal Romance author, born a hopeless romantic and possibly allergic to the cold. When she isn't gardening or baking, Ashlan spends her time bringing to life snarky heroines and swoon-worthy heroes that will make you blush, laugh, and believe in true love. Ashlan and her husband live with their three children and their rescue dog, Nova, near the White Tank Mountains in Arizona.
For more information, please visit ashlanthomas.com.

methods of keeping your people were not only improper, but that we were harming them, making them worse rather than better."

"Of course," said Tyrion with a sarcastic chuckle, "the answer is always more killing. Haven't the She'Har had enough blood?"

"We have not won the argument yet," said Thillmarius sadly. "I think time is enough now, but until the elders of the other groves concede, there will continue to be matches. Every fight your children win makes the case for humanity even stronger."

"If nothing has changed, why are you telling me this?" said Tyrion bitterly. "Do you think it will make me think better of you? I still despise you."

"No," said the lore-warden. "But I thought it might give you hope, and from what I have seen, hope is a better motivator for your people than fear could ever be."

Tyrion smoothed his features, trying to hide his anger once more. "I will think on your words. Logic will rule my actions for the sake of my children, but I will not lie to you Thillmarius, my heart will always ache to burn you and your people to ash."

The Silent Tempest

Chapter 32

Before the next arena day had arrived, both Piper and Blake awakened to their powers. It worried Tyrion because they had barely two days to learn the basics before their blooding matches, but as it turned out he needn't have worried. His other children were united in their dedication to make sure that Piper and Blake were as ready as possible, and while both of them were emotionally marked by their first kills, they survived without incident.

The others performed well in their fights. Even Ian, who had embarrassed them so badly the week before, managed his match without difficulty, remaining focused on winning rather than his 'other' proclivities.

Ryan demonstrated his cleverness during his fight, showing even more confidence than before and controlling his fight from start to finish, but Brigid's match was the most spectacular of the bunch. She was fully recovered now, and her strength and the intensity of her focus enabled her to take her opponent apart with brutal efficiency.

By the end of the day there was no doubt, Tyrion's children had eliminated the other competitors without giving the opposition even the illusion that they might prevail.

He was glad they had succeeded, but their success made him even more apprehensive. He knew from personal experience what happened once the She'Har thought the matches were too easy. The young men and women of Colne were learning rapidly, and their

constant practice with each other, alongside their uncommon strength, meant their skill was increasing at a much greater pace than Tyrion's had.

At this rate it won't be long before they want them to face more than one foe at a time.

They were strong enough for that, of that he had no doubt, but the dynamics of fighting while outnumbered were different. Such fights required strong tactics and most importantly, immense confidence. Risks had to be taken. Losing the initiative in such a situation would result in the enemy combining against the outnumbered mage, and that would likely prove fatal.

Brigid was the only one he could be sure would win against such odds. The others were still developing their nerve and determination.

But he could give them advantages he had never had.

"From tomorrow on we will be changing the schedule. In the mornings you will break into five groups—three groups of three, and two groups of two. The groups of two will work on one on one tactics, while the groups of three will practice with one against two. Layla will be supervising as usual, and she will participate in one of the groups to help you get better used to Prathion tactics." Tyrion was addressing them around the evening fire as they rested after their day in the arena and digested the contents of a heavy meal.

David raised his hand, and Tyrion nodded for him to speak. "Begging your pardon, sir, but why two on one? The arena matches are always one on one."

"Normally that is true," he responded, "but while I was fighting in the arena they decided to change things when it appeared that my fights were no longer

challenging. I had to fight two at once, and by the end of my time I was routinely battling four at a time."

Piper sat at the end of one of the wooden logs, and her eyes were still haunted by the memory of her first kill. Tyrion's words alarmed her, "Four?!"

Emma remained practical in her outlook. "It makes sense I suppose," she sighed. "We'll just have to work harder to make sure we have the skill to manage it."

Tyrion gestured toward Brigid. "You have many things that I lacked. Training was unheard of then, and I was without even the most basic knowledge that those raised in Ellentrea already had. You have my experience and each other to practice with and learn from. I will also give you the tattoos that you see on Brigid's arms, those and more." He waved his hand downward, indicating the rest of his body. "The enchantment created by these tattoos will give you defenses that no ordinary mage can hope to pierce, except with weapons created by similar magic." He activated the force blade enchantment along one of his arms.

"These will make you nearly invincible, but you must use them sparingly. Draw the fights out and make them seem harder than they are, otherwise they will be pitting you against more than one opponent sooner rather than later," Tyrion explained.

Ryan whistled appreciatively, and David's eyes lit with anticipation, but Abby frowned. "Do we really have to mark ourselves with such garish symbols?"

Tyrion started to reply, but Brigid broke her silence and spoke first, "If you want to live, Abigail, then yes, you need them." Brigid rose from her seat, her slender

form casting long shadows in the firelight as she spoke with intensity, "We need every weapon possible. Someday we will face more than just weak slaves, and it takes powerful blades to cut through She'Har spellweaving."

Some of the others looked uncomfortable at her mention of the She'Har, but they didn't object. All of them had fought now, even if they didn't like the prospect. Tyrion chose then to interrupt, "Let us not speak of such things in open air, for now we need only focus on making you stronger. After the morning practices, I will spend the afternoons working with you one by one to complete the same tattoos that I have on me now. Everyone else will work with Ryan to complete the expansions to the new outbuildings. You must each learn the rudiments of enchanting, so that you can bind and strengthen the stones the same way I have done with my house."

They talked for a while longer, but when everyone grew tired and began to seek their beds Ryan approached him again. "When will we be able to send the wagon to Colne?" He was anxious to make contact and begin trading. Tyrion suspected he also hoped to see his parents.

"We can't yet," said Tyrion. "The collars make it impossible until Lyralliantha returns. She can set them to allow for travel."

"Can't you just…," Ryan gestured with his fingers as if he were holding a pair of scissors, "…snip, snip."

Tyrion sighed, "I could, but then you would be at risk again until you returned. I would also have to make more excuses to Byovar and hope that he would

do me the favor of putting a new one on you before the next arena day."

"You don't have one anymore," pointed out the boy.

He nodded, "I've been given a special privilege, and my hope is that someday you will all be able to be free of them, but that is not today."

"We really need a lot of things from there," prodded Ryan.

Tyrion took a different course, "I know you'd like to see your parents, Ryan, but have you thought of the other news you would have to deliver if you went?"

The young man's face was confused for a moment before sudden realization struck him, "You mean Gabriel, and…"

"…Haley, and Jack," finished Tyrion.

"We don't have to tell them right away," suggested the boy.

"I've told enough lies," said Tyrion. "It would be cruel to keep them in the dark."

"It will be cruel to tell them."

He shook his head negatively, "No, I've been down that road, better to get it out sooner. Let them grieve and move on."

Ryan opened his mouth and then closed it again, trying and failing to find a suitable response.

"I will make a trip this week, alone if necessary," said Tyrion. "That way I can bear the ill news. You and Tad can make the next trip, assuming Lyralliantha has returned and will set your collars as I hope she will."

"Yes, sir," said Ryan, not bothering to conceal his disappointment.

***

Two days later Tyrion made the trip to Colne, but he did not go alone. Kate rode beside him on the driver's seat. She watched the trail ahead of them anxiously as the roof of her old home gradually rose into sight.

"Are you sure you want to do this?" asked Tyrion for perhaps the dozenth time.

She nodded affirmatively even as she answered, "No, but I need to see my son."

"I could come in with you," he offered yet again.

"That wouldn't help. Go to town, take care of your business." She turned to give him a stern look, "And please, please, don't murder anyone."

He held up his hands, "I didn't hurt anyone last time."

"Only because…," her words cut off suddenly as she saw her son, Aaron. He was hiking up the trail carrying water to the house. The boy spied her at almost the same time, dropping the bucket and running toward them.

Tyrion watched Kate's face as it lit with joy, her eyes already welling with tears as she climbed down from the seat. "You don't have to come back with…"

"You be here," she told him firmly. "If you try to leave without me, I'll just walk back. I know where you live now."

He nodded but her attention was not on him any longer, Aaron had reached her, and the two of them were hugging fiercely. After a moment, the boy

looked up at him from his mother's shoulder, glaring daggers in his direction.

Tyrion looked away and flicked the reins to get the horses moving again. He ignored the boy's stare. *Don't waste your time kid,* he thought, *I've been hated by those far better at it than you.*

A little more than an hour later he rolled into Colne. The first people to recognize him got off the street quickly, shutting themselves inside their houses. A few children ran, warning others. Within minutes the town looked almost deserted, or it would have, if he hadn't been able to sense the townsfolk huddling in their homes.

Tom Hayes waited in front of his store. Tyrion had to give him credit for his courage.

"How is Tad?" asked Tom. Alice was coming out now, to stand beside her husband.

Tyrion dipped his head in greeting. "Your son is well. His magic has awakened. He will be a powerful mage."

"Is he getting enough to eat?" put in Alice.

"Actually," began Tyrion, "That's why I've come today."

"If you keep robbing me, I'll have to close the store," said Tom bitterly. "We're already in debt to every farmer and tradesman for miles around."

"I am not insensitive to your plight," said Tyrion. "I've brought iron to trade, enough to make amends for what I've cost you in the past, and more besides."

"Iron?" said Alice curiously.

"We normally trade with Lincoln to get iron," declared the storekeeper.

Tyrion pulled back the canvas that hid the bed of the wagon, displaying neat rows of heavy iron bar stock. The weight of it was such that the wagon was only half loaded, otherwise the horses would have been unable to draw the wagon. Tom's eyes widened slightly.

"That's more than Colne could use in a year. What would you have me do with it?" complained Tom.

"It was Tad's suggestion," Tyrion informed him. "Rather than trading Lincoln for iron, you could trade iron *to* them. They have a far greater need for it he tells me."

"That would upset the miners there, not to mention the foundry," said the store keeper, rubbing his chin. "How much of this do you have?"

As much as you want, thought Tyrion. *The earth is full of it.* "I could get more easily. Cut stone would be simple to acquire as well, but transporting it is even more burdensome."

"We don't see much demand for stone around here," said Tom, but his face was thoughtful.

"That might change if it were cheap and in good supply," hinted Tyrion.

Tom bobbed his head, "That might be. Come inside and let's discuss it. I assume you've brought a list of what you need?"

Tyrion smiled and patted his chest, his list was folded and tucked inside his leather armor.

The three of them talked for almost an hour. He spent some of that time reassuring both of them that their son was doing well, the rest of it was used to discuss their business plans. Tom and Alice were in a considerably better mood by the time they finished.

"I'll organize the shipment," said Tom, rubbing his hands together. "It will take at least five wagons, but I think I can borrow enough to handle it. I have some things on hand that you want, but the rest will have to wait."

"Thank you for bringing word about Tad," added Alice. She and her husband smiled at one another for a moment.

They realize I'm going to make them rich.

A knock on the door distracted them then. Mona Evans stood outside, looking anxious. Alice spoke to her briefly, trying to discourage her from entering, but the woman forced her way inside.

"Where is my son? Is he alive?" demanded Gabriel's mother once she spotted Tyrion.

He rose and walked toward her, noting the trembling in her hands as he drew near. *She's scared to death, but even that's not enough to keep her away,* marveled Tyrion. "Your son is dead," he told her sadly.

"No!" said Mona softly, her mouth forming an 'o' as her eyes widened. Her voice rose gradually in pitch as she spoke, "That's not true. Tell me it's a lie. He's fine. You said you would protect them."

He could tell she was on the verge of hysteria, but he didn't know what else to say. "He died protecting his sister," he told her. *And she died protecting her sister.*

Her knees buckled, and Mona started to fall, but he caught her. Crying, she pushed his hands away. "No, don't touch me! Murderer! My poor Gabriel, you've killed him." Regaining her balance, she backed away.

Tyrion let her go, but he followed her to the door. His magesight had already shown him the gathering crowd in the street. It was a small group of people, mainly the parents of the other children. Stepping onto the porch, he spotted Greta Baker among them.

Raising his voice he addressed them before the muttering could become shouts, "Your children are fine. They are eating and surviving." His eyes fell on Greta. "You should come inside Mrs. Baker, I have terrible news for you."

The others moved back from her, as though she might have an illness they could catch, although their eyes were filled with pity.

She took the news with more grace than Mona had, but she still left weeping.

A few hours later the wagon was loaded with the small sundries that the store had been able to provide. Tom had promised regular deliveries to be met at the edge of the foothills every two weeks. The place they had arranged to meet was only a few miles from Albamarl.

Alice put her hand on Tyrion's arm before he climbed into the seat, and he looked at her in surprise. Few people in Colne were willing to risk such a gesture.

"Take care of Tad, please," she implored him.

"You can come with your husband," said Tyrion, "when he makes the delivery. Tad will be there, but I can't promise anything for the future. Life among the She'Har is deadly."

Alice blinked, nodded, and then looked away.

"Tell the others too," added Tyrion. "I'll make sure they can see them, briefly at least. Either that or I can give them the news if…"

Tom interrupted, "Don't say it. I'm going to assume they're fine. If something happens, we'll deal with the news then."

"Don't forget about Mona and Greta…," began Tyrion.

"I won't," said Tom, cutting him off. "They'll be taken care of." Tyrion had arranged to have some of the credit for their trade agreement set aside for the families of the children he had taken.

There was no more to say after that, so he climbed up and began driving the wagon back toward Seth Tolburn's house. The sun was low in the sky, but he had no intention of spending the night in Colne. *Or at Seth's house either,* he thought.

Kate was sitting on the porch with her son when he pulled up in the front yard of the Tolburn house. She hugged Aaron once more and kissed him on the head before walking down the steps and rejoining Tyrion at the wagon. The two of them waved incessantly until the wagon had gone far enough down the trail that they lost sight of the house.

They rode in silence while Kate wiped away tears.

"You didn't have to…"

"Stop, Daniel, just stop. I don't need your constant reminders."

He shrugged hopelessly, "But Seth…"

"Is half the reason I left," she finished for him.

He glanced her way, "I thought you left because of Brigid."

"That was half of it too," she agreed, "and you were the other half."

"That's three halves," he pointed out.

"You know what I mean," she growled, wiping again at her red eyes. "Don't be difficult."

Tyrion didn't say anything for a while after that. Kate dried her eyes and seemed better, but as the sun dropped farther in the sky she began to weep quietly. Reaching out with one arm, he pulled her closer.

"I'm a terrible woman," said Kate.

Having learned his lesson, Tyrion held his tongue.

"What kind of mother leaves her twelve year old son?"

He certainly had no answer for that.

"A bad one," added Kate. "That's the sort of mother who abandons her child. I'm the worst mother in the world."

Tyrion let out a low laugh.

"That isn't a joke," she told him emphatically. "I'm serious."

"I wasn't laughing at you," he explained. "I was just thinking that I've got you beat when it comes to bad parenting. You aren't even close."

"That's true," she agreed. "But I'm the worst *mother*."

"I'd argue against that," he told her. "I can think of at least one who was far worse."

"Oh," said Kate, realizing he meant her mother. "I guess I come by it honestly then."

"You are *nothing* like her," replied Tyrion.

"If anyone could judge that, it would be you," she said with a wan smile.

He gave her a sour look, "That was low."

"I'm sorry," she apologized. "I'm feeling mean right now. I'm not myself."

"You've been keeping bad company," he said, and then he squeezed her shoulders again.

The Silent Tempest

Chapter 33

The deepening dusk had cast everything in a gloom as he stared at his old home. The lighting matched his mood.

Kate poked him. "Staring at the house won't help."

"I don't want to tell them."

"It won't get any easier if you wait," she observed.

"I've taken everything from them," he said sadly.

Kate climbed down, urging him to do the same. "That isn't true. They never would have had Haley to begin with if you hadn't made so many mistakes, or if you hadn't taken her away from her grandfather."

"Or if her mother hadn't committed suicide because of me," he added.

"Life is hard, Daniel," said Kate, taking his head between her two hands. "But it would be hard, even if you weren't in it. People die, sooner or later. People get sick, bad things happen. You aren't to blame for all of it."

He nodded, and together they walked to the door. His father answered it after the first knock. He glanced back and forth between the two of them before asking, "What do you want?"

"Alan," said Helen's voice from the interior, "Who is it?"

"It's our son," said Alan. He stepped back to allow them to enter, but there was no joy in his face.

Tyrion motioned for Kate to step inside and then ducked through the low doorway, following her. His mother was already embracing Kate, but she hurried to wrap her arms around him as well.

"Something smells good," mentioned Kate, sniffing the air.

Helen rubbed her hands on her apron. "It's just a mutton stew," she said humbly.

"We get very little meat, other than wild game," said Kate with mild enthusiasm. "There are no sheep among the She'Har."

"There isn't much left," said Helen nervously, glancing at her husband. "I wasn't expecting company."

"They can have mine," said Alan sullenly. "I've lost my appetite anyway." His eyes never left his son.

"We aren't staying," said Tyrion. "We came to deliver bad news."

"There's a surprise," said his father.

"It's Haley isn't it?" said Helen quietly. She had one hand on the back of one of the wooden kitchen chairs. Pulling it out, she sat down as though she worried her legs might fail her.

Kate nodded, a look of sympathy on her face.

"She's dead," said Tyrion. "The She'Har forced her to fight in the arena, just as I did."

"Who killed her?" said Alan, an angry intensity in his voice.

He had debated with himself for some time already, how to answer that question. "She fought several times and won, but they matched her against Brigid, and she took her own life rather than hurt her sister," he said. "She died to protect her."

"Sick bastards!" exclaimed Alan, outraged. "They're a plague on this earth."

Helen glared at him, her eyes questioning his meaning.

"The forest gods," he declared. "They're a pox. They've ruined my son, and now they've taken the only daughter we'll ever have."

"I hate the She'Har as much or more than any man alive, but you do have thirteen other grandchildren still there," Tyrion informed him. "I'm trying to keep them alive as best I can."

"*Grandchildren?*" spat Allen. "Is that what I'm supposed to call them? I barely know those kids, and most of 'em hate me for being *your* father! Haley was my daughter, because Helen and I raised her, *despite* what you did to her mother. I loved that girl, and now she's gone. Do you honestly think of yourself as a father to those children?"

He stared at his father. His face, his skin, no, his entire body had gone cold.

Allen Tennick's face showed undisguised disgust. "You're *nothing* to them. They don't even have a name for what you are, and if they did, it would be something too shameful to use in decent conversation."

"Allen!" cried Helen, shocked at her husband's tirade.

Tyrion stood in mute shock, but Kate stepped forward, and her right arm swung out, slapping his father across the cheek, *hard.* The sound of it echoed in the silence that followed.

Kate's hands were balled into fists, and she was so angry her body shook, as though it could barely contain her emotion. "*You*, don't get to say such things to *him*. You weren't there. You haven't lived through what he has. You haven't seen the things he's seen. Your son has suffered in ways you can't even understand. I've

seen him, crying over their bodies. I've seen him caring for them when they were hurt. He may not be the kind of father you were, but I've seen his heart, and you have no right to judge it!"

"Get out," said Allen. "I don't want to see your cursed face on my property again."

Kate inhaled sharply, preparing to tear into the old man once more, but Tyrion put his hand on her shoulder. "Leave it, Cat." He took a step back, pulling her with him.

There was a scuffle behind them as Helen shoved her husband out of the doorway. "Move you drunken fool!" she swore at Allen. Once she was past him, she ran to the wagon, throwing her arms around Tyrion before he could climb up. "Don't hate him, Daniel," she said. "He's been like that since they took Haley. He can't forgive himself, and he's taking it out on everyone around him. He drinks every day."

"Drunk or not, his words are still true," said Tyrion, returning the hug. "I'm sorry Mother."

"None of it is as simple as...," started Kate, but Helen held up a hand, shushing her.

"I know, dear, and he knows it too. We'll get past this, one way or another. He just needs time," said Helen.

"Take care of him," said Tyrion.

"One way or another...," Helen answered, her eyes narrowing as she looked back toward the house, "...I'll fix him." She gave Kate a stern look then, "And *you*, I can't say I understand what you're doing, but I'm glad of it. Take care of my son for me."

***

418

The next week brought another round of arena battles, but once again Tyrion's children dominated their matches. Their continued practice, and training with one another made them far more capable than their opponents, even when dealing with the special advantages that their enemies had.

Ryan's plans to expand the buildings around Albamarl were proceeding faster than anyone had expected. The fact that all of them were now capable mages was a large part of that, for it greatly simplified many of the most laborious tasks, such as quarrying and moving the stone he required for his projects.

Tom Hayes arrived in the week after that, bringing with him five wagon loads of special goods, food, and other supplies. Among those things were twenty chickens, two goats, five pigs, and even a few sheep. It wasn't enough to allow them to start butchering for meat, but they would have eggs and some milk.

Many of the parents of Tyrion's children came as well, bringing with them gifts for their sons and daughters. Much of what they brought was useless— clothing, coats, shoes, and other wearables, but amid the tears and bittersweet reunions, no one made a point to mention that to them.

There was a new feeling in the air, something that went beyond the fresh scent of new leaves and spring flowers. Tyrion's children had found new hope. Their lives had changed dramatically, something that each week's combat reminded them of, but it was not all bad. They slept in beds now, in private rooms, and they came together daily for practice and to build and expand their new home. Regular shipments of goods

from Colne had improved the taste of their daily meals, which might have produced the biggest lift in their spirits, but Tyrion believed it was something more than that.

It was contact with their parents, with the outside world in general.

Just the prospect of seeing their families occasionally had changed their outlook. Kate's son, Aaron, had ridden with the second load of goods and seeing him had brightened her mood for the rest of the week that followed.

Tyrion sat in the kitchen brooding about it one morning, watching them practice through the window. Breakfast was done, but he had stayed indoors. He was no longer needed. Looking down at the soggy tea leaves in the bottom of his teacup, he felt almost as empty as the vessel in his hand.

"Why are you so glum this morning?" asked Kate, stepping up behind him and putting her hands on his shoulders.

"I honestly don't know," he replied, turning his head to kiss her hand.

"Things are far better than you ever led me to expect they could be," she told him.

Tyrion sighed, "That might be it. I'm not used to good things."

"You said things were good for you after they let you stop fighting in the arena. Didn't you get comfortable with peace during those years?"

"Not really," he admitted. "It was quiet, but I felt as though I was living in a gilded cage, a somber imprisonment. Things were peaceful, but I had nothing. Now...," he gestured toward the window.

"…Now you have something to lose," she finished for him. Leaning over, she kissed his cheek, "That's the best part of living. You deserve to have something to lose. Worrying over it is the best sign that something good has happened to you."

"Yeah," he agreed, but he couldn't shake the feeling of impending doom.

"What about your girlfriend," she teased. "Lyrall…," she paused, struggling to remember the name properly.

"Lyralliantha, she wasn't my *girlfriend*," corrected Tyrion. "She was my owner, and yes, my lover as well, but there was never any doubt about who owned who." Yet again he found his hand at his throat, feeling for a collar that was no longer there.

"You told me that she was responsible for you being allowed to live without the collar," pointed out Kate. "That she's part of some movement to change the way the She'Har treat our kind."

"You can't weigh their actions the same way you do a person's," said Tyrion. "They don't think like we do. You've met Byovar and Thillmarius. You should have some notion now of how alien they are."

Kate nodded, "I don't understand them at all, but I do know something about women."

He laughed, "It always comes back to that doesn't it?"

"Whatever else she is, or what she thinks, she's in love with you," declared Kate with a certain amount of iron in her voice.

"And that makes you jealous," added Tyrion.

"No," she said, but then she corrected herself, "well maybe, but it's more than that."

He raised one eyebrow.

"When you had sex with Layla," continued Kate, "It made me angry, but I wasn't really jealous."

"Why not?"

"I knew you didn't love her. You were trying to punish me. It was all about you and me. I care about your heart more than any of the rest of it," she explained.

"You're saying I'm in love with her?" he asked. His stomach tensed as he said the words. He knew it was a sensitive topic for Kate, and he didn't know how to untangle his own feelings on the subject.

"Aren't you?"

"I hate the She'Har with a passion I can't even find the words to express."

Kate nodded, "Yes, but we aren't talking about the She'Har. We're talking about Lyralliantha."

Tyrion took a deep breath. "I didn't really understand her when I came here. I was young and stupid, and she was beautiful. Later I understood that she was my owner, and I thought her motives toward me were more like those of someone toward their prized pet, but what I didn't understand was the risk she had taken."

"Risk?"

"Her grove, the Illeniel She'Har, they never took slaves. Whether or not they believed we were animals or people, they didn't believe in unnecessary suffering. She risked her future when she broke their rule and put the collar on me, but she did it to save my life. Since then, I'm not sure I would have stayed sane without her. I was alone, and the people of Ellentrea were more alien to me than even she was."

Kate thought of Layla and nodded. *And she's one of the most normal ones probably,* she thought. Watching Daniel struggling to express himself, she braced herself before speaking again, "Daniel, just be honest. I won't hate you for having feelings for her. It won't be easy, but I'm not a girl anymore."

"It's different," he said at last. "She wants to learn. She has a heart, but she doesn't understand herself. More than anything, though, she's family. I think that…" He stopped, unsure how to go on.

"Just say it, Daniel."

"It isn't easy to tell the girl you've loved your entire life, that you've fallen in love with another woman," he answered, his stomach turning as the words passed his lips. "Especially when you still love that girl."

"I've been married, Daniel, and I still love Seth, despite all our fights and our problems."

"But you don't want to be his wife anymore," said Tyrion. "You don't want to live with him."

She nodded, "I had a choice, and I made it. What would you choose?"

He looked into her eyes, "If I could go back, or if I could escape all of this, I would take you and forget everything else."

"But you'd still love her."

"Part of me would," he confessed.

"That's good enough for me then," she said, reaching out to stroke his cheek. "You can't very well run away can you?"

Tyrion looked out the window, he could see Emma and Violet guarding one another as they practiced against Abby and David. "Once maybe, but now…"

"I wouldn't love you if you could abandon them. I can barely stand myself for leaving Aaron with his father," said Kate. She paused thoughtfully and then continued, "We need her."

"We?"

"You, me, your children, without your She'Har lover, none of us would have any hope. She's probably the only reason they've let you do all of this," she said, waving her arms around to indicate the house and the buildings beyond it."

"What are you proposing?"

"When she finally returns, if necessary, you should put me aside."

"I can't do that."

"You'll do what you *have* to do," she said emphatically.

"She already knows about you," he informed her. "I don't know what she thinks exactly, but it won't be as simple as that. I can't lie to her."

"You never could lie to me either," said Kate ruefully.

"No, I mean I *can't* lie to her. Whenever she touches my mind, she sees my thoughts and feelings. She already knows our past, and sooner or later, she will know about this," he explained.

"Oh."

"Yeah," he replied with equal eloquence.

Kate stood, smoothing her hair with one hand out of habit. "Nothing is ever simple around here."

"No it isn't" agreed Tyrion. "What are you going to do?"

"Start working on lunch," she said pragmatically. "Send one of them in to help, I think today is David's turn."

"I meant about the future," he clarified.

"That will just have to take care of itself," responded Kate. "Let's hope she's as understanding as I am."

The Silent Tempest

Chapter 34

A month passed as spring deepened and the world exploded with renewed growth. The arena battles had already become a matter of routine. Tyrion's children were veterans now, and one on one matches held little challenge for them. Their bodies were fully tattooed now, with enchantments that gave them both weapons and shields that made them untouchable. It was a point of pride however, that they never relied upon them.

Tyrion had impressed upon them the fact that they should improve their skills rather than rely upon their tattoos for victory. As a result they had become adept at manipulating the air and soil, at creating fine webs of aythar to detect invisible opponents, and at using impromptu shields to control the field of battle, forcing their opponents into positions more favorable to them.

The arena had become a game for them, and if they were still sickened by the inevitable ending of each match, they had learned to harden their hearts against it. The children of Colne were becoming masters of tactical combat, implacable killers without peers among the slaves of the other groves.

So it was inevitable that the She'Har would change the rules. Tyrion wasn't even surprised when Koralltis gave him the news, but he didn't expect the form that it took.

"How many?" he asked again, to make sure he had heard the arena master correctly.

"Any two you select from your own," repeated the She'Har.

"No, how many did you say they would face?"

"Six," answered Koralltis.

"They've never fought more than one at a time. That seems like a big jump to make."

"We have not forgotten your years in the arena Tyrion. The other groves are certain that they would be able to manage two at once already, even three might not be a challenge. What is not known is how they will work in tandem. The betting has grown stale, but this combination of numbers has created a strong interest. If they win, the Illeniel Grove will reap a large reward," explained Byovar, who stood nearby.

"Did you make this deal, Byovar?" asked Tyrion, giving the Illeniel lore-warden a hard stare.

"I did, but I was bound to silence," said the She'Har without flinching. "As their trainer it was deemed to be too much of an advantage for you to be told in advance."

"And what about our opponents? Were they told?"

"They have been preparing for this for several weeks now," said Koralltis.

Tyrion was furious. "My children could die. This isn't fair."

"Other groves lose slaves in the arena every week," said Koralltis. "How is this different?"

"You're stacking the odds against them," insisted Tyrion. "It's as though you want to kill them. Am I wrong?" Sudden thunder rumbled in the distance, although the sky had been clear all morning.

"The other groves will no longer wager shuthsi if they feel there is no chance of winning," said Byovar, his eyes calm.

The wind picked up, and the sky seemed to darken slightly as clouds began to form near the horizon.

Tyrion leaned closer, until he was almost nose to nose with Byovar. "Fine, if this is what you want, you'll do something for me as well."

"What?" asked the Illeniel She'Har.

"Double, no—*triple* the Illeniel bet. If my blood is on the line, I want it to be costly for the loser," he said bitterly.

"But if they lose…" protested Byovar.

"Same difference, Byovar," said Tyrion. "If they lose, then I want it to be all the more painful for the ones who put *my* children in this damnable situation."

"I don't think you realize how much has already been wagered," responded Byovar.

"I don't care," he growled. "If it were up to me, they'd have to wager it all. *My children* mean more to me than these stupid games."

"The match is supposed to start in a few minutes," interjected Koralltis. "There is no time to renegotiate the betting."

"Then *make* time," ground out Tyrion. "Otherwise there will be no match today."

"We do not have the option to refuse at this point," insisted Byovar.

"You don't have the option to go forward if you don't meet my demand," said Tyrion menacingly.

Byovar stared at him in surprise, "Tyrion, what are you implying?"

Dark clouds had covered the sun, and the air seemed heavy and foreboding despite the quickening winds. "I'm not implying anything, Byovar. I'm *threatening*." A loud rumble echoed in the distance, underscoring his words.

The lore-warden met his gaze evenly, but didn't reply. Tyrion could almost see the She'Har's mind working, calculating risks and doing the math regarding the Illeniel bets. Finally he turned to Koralltis, "Will you allow me the time to bring this proposal to the other groves?"

Koralltis eyed the encroaching storm, "You have an hour."

Tyrion smiled, "I will go select my two participants." He left the two of them and returned to where Kate and Layla were waiting.

Kate's coppery hair was being tossed by the heavy breeze. "Are we done for the day? The weather seems to be turning bad," she said.

He took a few minutes to explain the situation to them.

"You risk punishment by arguing with them," observed Layla.

Kate nodded, "At least that explains the weather."

"I'm not doing that," insisted Tyrion.

"It happens every time you get upset," noted Kate. "You either need to learn to control the weather better, or learn to control your temper."

"I haven't lost my temper," said Tyrion, even as he realized that the voice of the wind *was* playing strongly in the background of his mind. He made a conscious effort to block it out. "I forced Byovar to renegotiate the wager to give us a little time to prepare."

"There's not much you can do in an hour," said Layla.

"We can choose our two and notify them," he returned. "Give them a little while to think about how they will cooperate with each other."

"Brigid is the strongest," observed the warden. "She is also the most confident among them."

"But she doesn't work as well with the others," he argued. "She isn't likely to cooperate with a teammate."

That was a foreign concept for Layla. "You should choose the strongest and the most aggressive. Brigid is first in both regards."

Kate spoke up then, "I don't know about their abilities, but Ryan is the best planner. He has a sharp mind."

"Then send him out with Brigid," said Layla, "but I think both Sarah and David are stronger."

Tyrion agreed with Layla in that regard. In terms of absolute strength, all of his children were powerful, but Sarah and David were the closest to Brigid in raw aythar. Strength wasn't the problem though, even if Layla couldn't understand that. The two chosen had to be able to support one another.

"What about Emma?" suggested Kate.

He nodded, that had been the same direction his own instincts had been leaning. Emma was almost as strong as the two Layla had mentioned, but more importantly, she was naturally supportive. She had also proven herself to be decisive and determined even in her early battles. If anyone could work well with Ryan, it would be her. "Ryan and Emma it is then," he pronounced.

He went to Ryan's holding cell first. The boy looked up at him with anticipation, "Time to go home?" Each of them had already fought once, so it was understandable that he expected his father's next appearance to be when the arena matches were done.

"I'm afraid not," said Tyrion. "They want a special match today, but I've managed to force them to postpone it for an hour."

Ryan nodded in acceptance, appearing unconcerned. "What sort of match?"

"Two on six," answered Tyrion. "And the six have been preparing for this for weeks without our knowledge."

His son winced, "That's bad odds. I'm guessing you want me to be one of our two?"

He nodded at the young man.

"Who's my partner?" asked Ryan immediately.

Tyrion had a sudden thought, "Who would you choose?"

Ryan looked thoughtful, "Well I wouldn't have expected you to pick me for starters. Is it Brigid?"

"I asked who *you* would choose."

"Hmmm, I suppose Emma, or maybe Tad," said his son at last. "Tad and I work well together, but he's a bit more impulsive. Emma would probably be my first choice."

"That's what I thought too," said Tyrion.

"Honestly, though, you should choose Ian," commented Ryan.

"Why?"

"The odds are bad. If we're going to lose, you'd miss him the least," said Ryan with a grin.

Tyrion laughed at the morbid humor. "Stop thinking like that. You're facing six opponents who may be from a mix of different groves. They've been practicing for weeks together, and they may have a working knowledge of what you're capable of. I want you to win. You've got maybe forty-five minutes to

plan your strategy, and you won't be able to talk to Emma until I retrieve you both at the beginning."

Ryan grimaced, "Any ideas?"

Tyrion shrugged, "I'm an older version of Brigid. My solutions usually revolve around mass destruction or surprise. I chose you for a reason. You're smarter than I am."

The boy's brows lifted at that statement, "You don't give yourself enough credit, old man."

"You don't have time to waste flattering me," said Tyrion, backing out of the holding cell. "I have to go inform your sister."

Emma took the news with pragmatic aplomb, "Ryan's a good choice."

"Do you want to know why I chose you?" he asked her.

She shook her head, "Wisdom."

Tyrion frowned.

"It's obvious you didn't pick us for raw strength or talent. Brigid's better, and some of the others are stronger than us," said Emma clinically. "Ryan's the brightest, and I'm probably the only one with the wisdom and resolve to trust someone else to make decisions with my life."

Not for the first time, he marveled at her exceptional maturity. Emma had proven her inner strength more than once. "You make my point for me."

She nodded, and he turned to leave, but she spoke once more before he closed the door, "No matter what happens, Father, don't blame yourself. You made the best choice for all of us."

Startled he glanced at her once more as the door closed. He stood there for a moment looking at the wooden cell door, and his vision blurred momentarily. *She called me 'Father'.* He knew he would never deserve that appellation.

The next forty minutes passed with dreadful slowness. Tyrion wasn't accustomed to anxiety. He normally dealt with things directly and without hesitation. Even in his own days in the arena, he had learned not to worry over upcoming matches. His own life had come to mean little to him. This was different, however.

"Stop it," said Kate.

"Stop what?"

She glanced up at the sky, "That."

The weather had begun to clear up after he talked to Ryan and Emma, but it was clouding over again. Once again he was forced to close off the voice of the wind, it had snuck into his mind almost unconsciously.

"Some men bite their nails," observed Kate, "but not you. No, you have to be dramatic even when you worry."

"Sometimes the weather is just the weather," he suggested to her.

"Not when you're around," she said wryly.

He sighed. He couldn't really argue with her, since he knew she was right. Koralltis was walking toward them now.

"It is time," said the arena master.

Tyrion nodded and went to collect his son and daughter. Once they stood together, there was no mistaking their resemblance to one another; both of them were lean and tall for their ages. Ryan's sandy

brown hair was similar to Emma's mousy curls, and their eyes were almost the same chestnut shade. Emma took her brother's hand as soon as he offered it to her, and they walked together toward the arena with an air of distraction.

Layla wrinkled her face in disgust at the sight of them holding hands. "That's just not right," she commented.

Tyrion laughed, for he knew what it meant. While they had all learned to speak mind to mind, physical contact made a deeper level of communication possible. With their hands clasped together, Ryan and Emma were able to share more than just words—sounds, shapes, and mental images would be passing between the two of them. *That's something their enemies would never think to do. Their aversion to physical contact makes that sort of intimacy impossible,* he thought quietly.

"Are you ready, Sister?" asked Ryan as they stepped onto the field still holding hands.

Emma stopped a moment before stretching up on her toes to kiss him lightly on the cheek, "Always, Brother. I will protect you until the end. Win or lose, they won't soon forget this day." Together they marched toward their starting position.

Tyrion's eyes widened when he saw their opponents coming out from the other side of the field, four men and two women, all wearing brown leathers and bearing the wooden swords that marked them as wardens. "What the hell is this?!" he swore, looking toward Byovar.

The lore-warden held up his hands, "Even I was unaware of this particular."

"Dammit!" cursed Tyrion. Wardens were normally exempt from arena combat, being long time veterans of many battles. He could also see that their aythar was stronger than that of the average She'Har slave, which wasn't unusual given their experience and past successes. The wooden swords were also troublesome. Even at this distance, he could see that the weapons were unusual. A She'Har spellweave enwrapped each blade, giving them far greater cutting power. His children's enchanted shields might be vulnerable if their strength ebbed.

Any two of the wardens were enough to match either Emma or Ryan, and six—his children were overmatched.

"Ryan was right," muttered Tyrion. "I should have sent Ian." *But who would I have been willing to send out to die with him?*

"I can't understand you when you mumble," complained Kate.

"I'm just worried," he told her, and then he noticed a rough line in the dirt marking the place where Emma and Ryan had entered the field. It extended across the ground to where they now stood. His heart jumped as he realized what they meant to do. *It might have worked, if those were normal slaves. If they didn't have those swords. Now...?*

He sent his mind outward seeking to warn them, but the shield that protected the arena had already gone up, blocking any communication with the combatants. *Shit! They're going to get themselves killed.*

Kate gasped, "Daniel, you're hurting me."

He realized he had been squeezing her hand too tightly, and he relaxed his grip with conscious effort. "Sorry."

"It's bad isn't it?" said Kate.

Layla coughed, "Bad doesn't begin to describe it. They're fucked. Each one of those wardens is well known. That's Braden the Butcher, Daggoth Demonfist, Laeri the Cold, Tibbon the Terrible, Shayla the Merciless, and Hesta," she said, naming the wardens one by one.

Tyrion knew the names if not the faces. He had faced none of them before, obviously, or they would have been dead already. They had earned their current status as wardens in the years after he had been retired from the arena.

"Why doesn't Hesta have a special title?" wondered Kate.

Layla shrugged, "She has a bad temper and a habit of killing those who talk about her."

"How about Hesta the Irritable?" suggested Kate.

The female warden laughed, "I wouldn't say it within her hearing."

"Hesta the Mildly Annoyed then. Surely no one could take offence at that," commented Kate.

"Be quiet," snapped Tyrion. "I'm trying to concentrate."

"Sorry," said Kate. "I'm just nervous."

The lights around the arena changed, and the chime sounded. The match had begun.

The Silent Tempest

Chapter 35

The moment the match began, Ryan took to his feet, racing toward the six wardens. He had a tight shield around himself, and one of his arm blades was active. He kept that arm down and slightly behind him as he ran, cutting a thin line in the dirt as he ran. Emma remained behind, standing at their starting position, seemingly passive.

It probably would have worked too, thought Tyrion, *if it weren't for those damn swords.* He knew his son was making a fatal mistake. Ryan's defense wouldn't be enough to withstand all six wardens, not with the deadly weapons they carried. He and Emma obviously hoped to split the arena, using a reinforced shield to separate some of them from each other temporarily.

As it stood now, however, Ryan was simply rushing into the lion's teeth. Once he was dead, the others would simply surround Emma and wear her down. The match would be a short one.

The six wardens spread out, forming a 'v' to welcome Ryan and funnel him between them, with three on either side. Their swords were out, and some of them were grinning already.

Ryan was within mere feet of the first two when he exploded. Dirt and soil shot up and outward from beneath his feet, and in the confusion, a concealing mist filled the area. The two wardens closed on his position, ignoring the distractions as their blades swung wildly, trying to connect with their momentarily unseen opponent.

It was an aythar laden mist, the sort that Tyrion had taught them to conceal themselves from magesight, but it didn't last long. The two wardens farthest from him were summoning a wind to disperse the mist almost as soon as it had appeared.

The ones attacking found nothing to connect with, however, for Ryan's body was flying backward through the air, pulled as if on an invisible string. Emma had remained attached to him with a thin line of aythar, which she used now to jerk him back from the enemy's deadly trap.

The wardens were momentarily surprised by his sudden retrieval. Tyrion had no doubt that since arena matches were normally one on one no one had ever seen one mage fling another about in such a manner, at least not for any purpose other than to harm them. Still, something didn't seem right. He frowned as he tried to figure out what was bothering him.

"That wasn't a trap," said Layla beside him. "He was the one that flung the soil up, not his opponents."

That doesn't make sense, observed Tyrion. *Unless he knew he couldn't handle the wardens before he got to them.*

Ryan had landed next to his sister, and the two of them separated once more, this time running in opposite directions, one to either side, as though they planned to flank their opponents. They both had activated their shield enchantments now, and their armblades were out, making them each a serious threat, but if the wardens broke away to take them on, three to one on either side it wouldn't be much of a fight.

Something was wrong with Ryan, though. His shield enchantment didn't feel right. It didn't have the

proper solidity. Tyrion's magesight focused on him for a moment, and then he realized his children's ruse.

Some of the warden's figured it out at the same time. "He's an illusion!" shouted Hesta from her position on the far right.

Emma released her spell, and Ryan's illusory form vanished just as the ground shot skyward once more, this time directly in front of the two most central wardens, Daggoth and Laeri. Longtime veterans of the arena, they both understood the nature of the ambush immediately. The boy had used the distraction and the mist to conceal himself under the soil, while his sister had created the illusion to keep them from realizing the subterfuge. As the ground erupted they leapt backwards instinctively.

What their reflexes failed to consider though, was that the ground hadn't shot upward from the position where Ryan had disappeared. As they jumped back he rose from the earth behind them, armblades out and sweeping toward their backs. Laeri's shield split, and his body fell away in two pieces, but Daggoth was luckier. The two of them had been too far apart, and Ryan's right arm hadn't had enough reach to kill him. Instead he lost his left arm, screaming in pain as he fell to the ground.

Layla clucked in appreciation, "That was a three layered trap."

Tyrion nodded, amazed by their cleverness. If he had been one of their opponents, he might well be just as dead as Laeri was now.

"Remind me never to take on your son in a serious fight," added Layla.

The destruction of his shield had nearly rendered Daggoth unconscious, losing most of one arm made matters even worse for him. In a smaller match the best option would have been for Ryan to pursue his advantage and finish Daggoth before the other mage could recover his senses.

But this wasn't a small match, and the wardens knew what his most likely course of action was. Ryan created a new mist even as he started toward Daggoth. Three intensely focused beams of fire-like aythar ripped through the mist from different directions as Braden, Tibbon, and Shayla used their swords to direct attacks at Daggoth's location.

Seconds later they dispersed the mist, but Ryan wasn't there, he was fifty feet above, falling toward the ground. Daggoth was dead, having been skewered by at least one of his comrade's attacks.

"I didn't know they could jump like that," said Kate.

Tyrion was worried about something else, though. While he fell, Ryan would be unable to change directions, and the three wardens were already taking aim once more. There would be no more dodging now. *And Hesta is nowhere to be seen...*

That confused him, until his mind found her, she was at the far end of the arena. She had teleported as far as possible to the area she was least likely to be noticed during the confusion. In the heat of a battle with multiple foes, it was almost as good a method of hiding as invisibility.

Emma stretched out her hand toward her skyward brother, using her aythar to jerk him back for real now, barely in time to avoid the fresh attacks that tore

through the air where he had almost passed. She had no time to react to the female warden who appeared behind her. Hesta's wooden blade pierced her shield and tore through her back before erupting from her abdomen.

The attack had been intended for the heart, but Hesta had dropped a foot farther down after she teleported, splashing into a hidden pool of water surrounding Emma. She and her blade vanished immediately after the attack as she teleported back to her comrades before Ryan landed beside his sister. His counterattack missed her completely.

Hesta laughed, standing beside Braden now. The male warden reached out his hand, and the two of them disappeared. Braden was a Prathion by birth, although he was owned by the Mordan Grove. A second later Tibbon vanished as well.

"Tibbon isn't a Prathion," muttered Layla.

"Hesta teleported herself and Braden to him," explained Tyrion. "Now Braden is making all three of them invisible…"

"… and if she's teleporting them, they could be anywhere," finished Layla, understanding suddenly.

Ryan caught his sister as she began to crumple. The feedback from her broken shield along with her terrible wound had overwhelmed her. He was careful to avoid stepping in the newly revealed water that surrounded them like a moat for several feet in every direction. He knew he had only seconds before the wardens might renew their attack.

Even a circle reinforced shield would be of little use against whatever power the wardens were using to focus their ranged attacks, and it would put him at risk

of being stunned if his shield were destroyed, so instead he raised a thick dome of earth from the ground just beyond the water around them.

"That won't protect them for long," noted Layla.

"It's better than nothing, though," said Tyrion. Before he could say more, Hesta reappeared. She was standing close to Ryan's earthen defense, but she wasn't attacking. Instead she fell to the ground, screaming and writhing. She scratched at her legs as though she was trying to get something off of them.

Then Tyrion saw the blisters appearing on her legs in places where her leathers had started to come apart. Smoke was rising from her boots.

"I don't think that was water," muttered Layla.

"Lye maybe?" said Kate. "Where would she have gotten something like that?"

Whether it was caustic lye or some sort of acid, it was clear that Hesta wouldn't be able to focus on matters at hand. The warden was desperately trying to remove her boots and scrubbing at her legs with handfuls of dirt. The skin was coming away under the rough treatment, and her hands were beginning to burn as well, for she had gotten some of the liquid on them in her haste.

Shayla had been left unmolested for some time, and now Tyrion noticed that the Centyr mage was still standing close to where she had started. Beside her were two enormous bear-like spellbeasts. Grinning, she started across the field to join her remaining comrades; her aythar was much weaker, for she had invested most of it in her new guardians.

Given more time Shayla's aythar would recover, and with the beasts by her side she would be difficult

to deal with. Time was never a friend when facing one with the gifts of the Centyr.

"It's over," said Layla. "Ryan can't face three of them alone, especially not with those monsters in play."

Hesta was still screaming, begging her allies for help as Shayla joined Tibbon and Braden.

Tibbon laughed and mocked her misfortune. "That's what you get for trying to hog the glory, Hesta!" jeered Tibbon. Braden and Shayla ignored her completely, they had no use for a wounded companion.

Inside the earthen dome Ryan still held his dying sister. Tyrion thought he might have been working to seal her wound, but it was hard to tell and as he focused on them Ryan brought up a tighter inner shield. This one was small, encompassing just the two of them, with the deadly liquid outside of it.

The spellbeasts were tearing at the earthen dome, and Tibbon and Braden were preparing to help them. Rather than use their swords, they leveled broader blasts of aythar to help shatter and disperse the tightly packed earth.

Then the dome exploded. Ryan's will drove the explosion outward, flinging the dense earth and small stones in all directions. The strange liquid followed immediately after it. Tyrion's son had heated it to boiling, and now his power tossed it into the air as a steaming, caustic fog.

Hesta screamed even louder, clawing at her eyes. She had been unshielded, and the mist was killing her as she inhaled it.

The other three were still protected, keeping the mist from reaching them, but as they flinched away

from the assault of soil and mist Ryan followed his attack with a blow like a battering ram, shattering Tibbon's defense. The warden who had been laughing only moments before began to choke and cough as he collapsed.

Braden went invisible before a second attack could do the same to him. Shayla was backpedaling quickly, trying to get out of the deadly mist as well. The spellbeasts were tearing at Ryan's circle reinforced shield, putting a serious strain on Ryan's reserves. The mist didn't affect the magical creatures at all.

The greatest risk now was that either the spellbeasts or one of the remaining two wardens would penetrate Ryan's protective shield, letting the mist back in to kill the two young mages. Shayla was raising her sword even as she retreated, preparing to use its special ability to focus her remaining strength into an attack that would almost certainly do just that.

Before she could fire, she fell back, collapsing to the ground. A fine hole had been drilled through her head.

Tyrion recognized Emma's handiwork. She was much more capable of such precision than Ryan was, in fact it had become her signature attack in the arena over the past month. Still, he was unsure how she had managed it. Within another mage's shield, she should have been unable to attack the outside.

Then he noticed that they were holding hands once more. By joining their wills, they had somehow timed it perfectly. Ryan had opened a tiny hole in the shield just as she had sent a fine lance of power through Shayla's head.

Chapter 35

With Shayla dead and Braden in hiding, Ryan took a necessary risk. Raising a powerful wind, he scattered the deadly mist around them. Once it was gone, he lowered the circle shield and used a wide blast of aythar to toss the spellbeasts away. Before they could charge back, he stepped outside the circle and then brought the shield up again, protecting Emma and trusting to his enchanted body shield to save him from the beasts.

Long experience had taught Tyrion that Centyr spellbeasts were troublesome to deal with. They survived the death of their masters, and they were notoriously difficult to kill. Very little affected them. Most common attacks passed through their aythar bodies without harm, but Ryan's enchanted arm blades would do the trick.

Ryan moved forward to meet their charge.

Invisible and therefore blind, Braden chose that moment, by pure chance, to reveal himself and attack. He appeared some thirty yards distant and hastily leveled a sword enhanced attack at Emma's position.

The lance of power ripped through the shield protecting Tyrion's daughter, but it missed the girl herself. Unfortunately, the destruction of the shield had far worse consequences on the one who had created it. The feedback drove Ryan to his knees, and his power faltered. The spellbeasts reached him just as he lost consciousness, his enchanted body shield winking out.

Emma's return stroke killed Braden instantly.

Tyrion's children had won. The lights changed, and a chime rang out. The match was over.

But the spellbeasts didn't know or care about such facts. The first one to reach Ryan clamped down on the youth's shoulder, crushing his collarbone, while the second took one of his legs in its terrible jaws.

Emma struggled to stand, but she no longer had the strength. Her mouth was stretched wide in a feeble scream as she tried to reach her brother, but her wound made yelling impossible.

Koralltis stepped onto the field, moving placidly toward the spellbeasts as they engaged in a grotesque tug of war with Ryan's body. He would destroy them as a matter of course, but the She'Har never hurried. The boy didn't have the luxury of such a delay.

Tyrion leapt forward, but the spellwoven shield that protected the arena would not admit him. Only Koralltis could enter until the match was called, and he had given permission. Activating his enchanted arm blades, Tyrion cut at the spellweaving, but it was far too powerful for one man, even him, to destroy.

Lightning flashed, slamming down from the sky to strike the mighty shield around the arena. Once, twice, then a third time in a matter of seconds. The arena's protection shattered with a sound that rang out so loudly it seemed as though the world itself had broken. Running forward, Tyrion raced past Koralltis.

He didn't dare use his power to fling the beasts away, for fear of tearing Ryan in two, and agonizing seconds ticked past while the monsters savaged the boy, until at last he reached them. Tyrion's enchanted arm blades ripped the beasts apart, heads from shoulders, and then he cut into the bodies as well, trying to make certain he cut the central point that animated them.

Koralltis began spellweaving, sending long tendrils of vine-like aythar to wrap around Ryan's still form.

"Is he alive?!" Tyrion was shouting at the arena master, unable to help himself. If it weren't for the nature of his task, he might have killed the uncaring She'Har on the spot.

"Barely," said the arena master calmly.

Tyrion lost it then. Taking the She'Har by the throat, he shook him like a doll. "If he does not survive, you will be next!"

Koralltis studied him with wide eyes. Somewhere within the She'Har's cold demeanor lay a flicker of fear. "Let me attend to the girl. Her wound is yet mortal. She needs help."

In a rage, Tyrion lifted the She'Har and flung him bodily in Emma's direction.

Standing alone now, he raised his eyes to the crowded balconies in the god-trees surrounding the arena. The crowd was silent even as the sky grew darker. The voice of the wind was screaming in his ears, and Tyrion raised his own voice to join it, "Is this what you want? Are you happy now? When will you have enough of my blood? When will you be satisfied?" His words boomed out, louder than the wind which was beginning to move with frightful speed.

The sky above was twisting, rotating as if on some invisible axis above his head. The world had grown almost as dark as night, and the force of the gale was causing the trees to groan under its pressure.

Tyrion's mind was fading, disintegrating into the uncaring wrath of the wind. He stared senselessly

outward, but his eyes were not working. He was elsewhere, and his body was growing lighter.

Kate had run out screaming at him, but his ears didn't report her words and the wind tossed her back. She flew through the air to strike one of the holding cells. Despite the wind, she struggled to rise, but one of her legs refused to support her weight.

Somewhere, deep within, only one thought remained to him. *This is the end.* He would destroy it all, or as much as he could reach at least, and his reach had grown very long indeed. *I will scour the world clean.*

Pale hands caught his head, one on either side, and blue eyes stared into his. Lyralliantha had him now, her silver hair whipping around the two of them. A spellweaving held her firm against the rushing air, while her mind sought his.

Stop! Peace, my Love, your children are safe. Let go of your anger or we are all doomed. Her thoughts echoed through his mind as if they had passed through a vast cave.

The wind faltered, and his eyes snapped to hers. Slowly his rage began to subside, and he became aware of his own labored breathing. She repeated her thoughts, more softly now, and his mind registered their meaning with some difficulty.

"Love?" he mumbled with lips that felt strange. "You don't understand the word."

"Yes," she replied, "I do now. You are my kianthi, and the Illeniel have found love again."

Chapter 36

Kate limped as she walked from the hearth to the cutting board laid out on the counter. With each step Tyrion felt guiltier.

"Why don't you let the others take care of that for a few days?" he suggested.

Abby was already helping Kate in the kitchen, but she ignored his comment. She knew Kate wouldn't be receptive to his idea.

"I need to do something, Daniel," said Kate. "I'll go crazy if you try to make me sit down all day."

Abby nodded in agreement and gave Tyrion a look that clearly meant he should leave well enough alone.

"The bruising should get better in a few days," said Tyrion for what might have been the tenth time.

Kate pursed her lips as she began chopping onions, "You mentioned that already."

Brigid came through the front door and poked her head into the kitchen from the entry hall, "She's here, Father."

Kate nearly cut her finger. Dropping the knife, she started to smooth her hair but then realized her hands smelled like onions. "It's too early! You said she wouldn't be here until noon," she said to him in an accusatory tone.

"Relax," he said, trying to soothe her. "She's not worried about things like that. You saw what I looked like when I returned home the first time."

"Easy enough for you to say," said Kate waspishly.

"She's already met you twice now," he reminded.

Kate's expression made it plain how dumb she thought that remark was. "And both times were after you tried to destroy everything in sight with a monster storm. I'd like to meet her once without looking as though a family of rats was nesting in my hair."

"Your hair is beautiful."

"No, *she* is beautiful. Let me be, it's none of your business," said Kate.

"She healed your leg..."

"Again—not helping, Daniel," she replied sourly. "Go distract her while I wash my hands and fix my hair. Abby can you take over here?"

Abby smiled, "I'll be glad to. Brigid would you like to help me?"

Brigid cast a dark glance in Abby's direction. Cooking was her least favorite activity, and it wasn't her day to help, but if Kate was abandoning the kitchen, someone would have to step up. She nodded silently.

With his magesight, Tyrion could see Lyralliantha in the front yard, but she was making no move toward the house. Instead, she was talking to the young men and women there, moving from one to another. *What is she doing?*

Then he saw. She was removing their collars. He made his way to the door and walked out to confront her, "What are you doing?"

"Good morning, Love," she said with a faint smile. With a touch, she dissolved the collar around David's throat.

Her use of the word 'love' caught him off-guard once more. It was impossible to imagine her, or any

other She'Har for that matter, using it in such a familiar manner. "What's going on?" he asked.

"I am rectifying a mistake," she replied. Walking past him, she paused to kiss him on the cheek before removing Violet's collar next.

"Shouldn't we talk about it? Your people will not accept this."

"They already have," said Lyralliantha. "Well, the Illeniel and Prathion Groves have, but I am confident the others will be made to see the truth."

He blinked. The words were simple enough, but the meaning was hard to accept.

Lyralliantha had finished with everyone in the yard, so she started toward the house.

"Wait," he told her.

"There are still a few more."

Tyrion shook his head, "They can wait a few minutes; Kate isn't ready yet."

Her forehead wrinkled with a faint frown, "You already removed her collar."

"No, she isn't ready to meet you yet," he explained.

"We met yesterday," she reminded him. "After you broke her leg."

He sighed in frustration, "That wasn't really me. Well, I suppose it was, but I wasn't in my right mind. It was an accident. Anyway, that's not the point. She wants to brush her hair, or something like that."

"Why?" asked the She'Har with a serious countenance.

"She wants to look good, to make a good impression."

Lyralliantha's face shifted to a look of disappointment, "I thought learning love would make your kind easier to understand."

"We're somewhat more complicated than just that one emotion," he told her before adding, "She's nervous, she wants you to like her."

"Why?"

Tyrion took a deep breath, "Because she's in love with me."

Lyralliantha's face became pensive. Eventually she responded, "Does she fear me?"

"Not exactly," he replied, "but for a human it's a normal worry. She's afraid you might be jealous."

"Jealousy is not common among my people," said Lyralliantha.

"You are the first to be in love in a long time," he noted.

"Should jealousy be part of love?"

"No, I don't think so. Humans feel it when we think something we care about is being threatened."

"I would not threaten you," she declared. "Unless you were acting in a foolish way," she corrected herself a moment later.

He led her to the log benches that were arrayed around their evening bonfire spot. Offering a seat, he tried to explain, "Not a threat to me, a threat to take away what she loves."

"She is jealous of me then?" pondered Lyralliantha. "She fears I will take you away." Then she smiled, "How silly. You are my kianthi. I cannot control you." She rose and began walking toward the house. "I will explain this to her."

He started to follow, but she held up her hand, "You are not required. Let us talk alone."

Kate was surprised when she saw the silver haired woman enter the bedroom. "Oh," she exclaimed.

"Tyrion has explained your fear to me," said Lyralliantha without preamble.

"Fear?" said Kate, her eyes narrowing slightly. "I think perhaps he may not have used the best words."

"Fear might be wise," remarked Lyralliantha. "My people have not been kind to him, or to you."

"I know better than that," answered Kate, "at least where you're concerned. I need to thank you for fixing my leg."

"You are welcome," said Lyralliantha, "but I did not come to speak on trivial matters. I wish to explain my intentions, to allay your concerns."

Kate was growing steadily more uncomfortable. She barely knew the strange woman, and Lyralliantha's directness was disconcerting. There was no help for it, though. Steeling herself, she gestured toward the bed, "Would you like to sit?"

The She'Har woman nodded and took a spot near the foot of the bed, while Kate followed suit and sat as well, closer to the head. After a brief pause the She'Har began, "Tyrion is my kianthi. That will not change. Among the She'Har, this means his interests and mine are considered one and the same."

Kate flinched at the formal declaration. *She might as well have said, 'he's mine, not yours'.* She struggled with her feelings, but she had prepared for this moment. Looking at the floor she replied, "I will not interfere. I would like to stay, to help with his children, but I understand if you wish me to leave."

Lyralliantha's countenance was one of puzzlement, "That would not please my kianthi."

Now it was Kate's turn to be confused. *She's his She'Har wife, does she want me to stay as some sort of servant, or concubine?* Unsure how to proceed, Kate answered slowly, "I think, that I worry more for what would please *you.*"

"Has he explained the meaning of 'kianthi' to you?" asked Lyralliantha.

"It's something like our marriage customs, isn't it?"

Lyralliantha laughed lightly.

It was a delicate sound that immediately annoyed Kate. *No one should have such a beautiful laugh. How can I compare to a woman like this?*

Seeing the change in Kate's aura, the She'Har stopped, "I did not mean to offend. It might be easier if I could show you, mind to mind. Will you permit me?" Lyralliantha lifted one hand, palm outward, indicating she wanted to place it on Kate's head.

Kate scooted away slightly, "Wait. Will you read my mind?"

Lyralliantha nodded, "Yes, but I will also share mine."

"There are things…," began Kate, but she didn't know how to finish. "Whatever you see, please understand I want only the best for him."

"Our words are only furthering the misunderstanding, let me show you what the elders taught me," said the blue-eyed woman.

Kate took a deep breath, "Alright."

"Lie down. This may take some time. Your body will grow tired of sitting," said Lyralliantha.

She did as she was told, and the She'Har woman lay down next to her. The two of them were on their sides face to face, and then Lyralliantha reached across, resting her hand gently on the side of Kate's head, fingers on her temple.

The room vanished, replaced by a new place. A vast world surrounded them, and a red sun filled the sky. A forest stretched across the land, but it was different than the one Kate was familiar with, this forest was less uniform, more varied. Many of the trees were huge, like the god-trees she had become familiar with, but others were different, more slender, taller, shorter, and their leaves took a multitude of shapes. Somehow she knew that most of them were not She'Har. She could hear their voices through her—roots? As her awareness grew Kate realized she no longer had her old body, she was one of the trees, one of the She'Har.

The world moved around her, and the sun passed overhead with surprising speed. She was unable to move herself, but she was not lonely, for the forest was filled with voices, and she spoke with the other trees through her roots which stretched for miles in every direction. Their minds were simple, less complex than hers, but she felt a close bond with them, and through them she received messages from other She'Har, whose roots were too far away for her to reach directly. The entire forest was alive, and their roots formed a vast network that connected trees across the world.

It was a paradise of sorts. She knew when the rain was coming, for the trees shared the knowledge with one another. But it was not a perfect world. There were problems. The worst was an arthropod, a multi-

legged creature with a hard carapace. It crawled through the canopy and ate the leaves of some of the trees, but it had a special liking for the She'Har. When it found one of them it would burrow deep into the bark, wounding her people. If left unchecked, it would multiply, and soon the She'Har would die.

Most pests were easy for the She'Har to deal with, but this one camouflaged itself, hiding from their magesight. When they burrowed into the She'Har, they worked quickly, and their bodies secreted a substance that numbed the host, making it difficult to sense their presence until it was too late.

Left unchecked, the She'Har would have soon died out, and their arthropod killers with them, for the parasitic creatures could not reproduce without the She'Har to feast upon. Fortunately, there were other hunters beneath the canopy of the endless forest— large, graceful, furry beasts with long limbs and sharp claws. They had a special taste for the arthropods that plagued the She'Har, as well as for 'calmuth', the fruit produced by the sentient trees.

In the beginning, their partnership was accidental, but fortunate, and over time the She'Har grew fond of the arboreal creatures that lived with them. In their own slow way, they named the creatures that protected them, the "kianthi", but they could not speak with them as they could with the other trees.

The She'Har were different than the other trees and even the animals of that world, for they could change things. The kianthi ate their seeds and spread the She'Har, but the process was random, for the intelligence of the kianthi was limited, so the She'Har changed their seeds to benefit both themselves and the

kianthi. Now, once the kianthi ate the seed of the She'Har the seed remained with them, and it worked many changes upon their minds. The kianthi became intelligent, and the seed of the She'Har gave it the power to change the world, to manipulate aythar, as the She'Har did.

When the kianthi eventually died, the seed would germinate, and a new She'Har would emerge, growing from the earth fertilized by its host's body, but it would remember the life of the kianthi it was born from. In time, the She'Har and the kianthi became so close that they could almost be considered one race. Each tree gave its special gift to only one kianthi at a time, but the She'Har lived much longer than the kianthi. Over the course of its life, a She'Har might give rise to several offspring, while the children of its kianthi were far more numerous.

In the world beneath her branches, Kate had many kianthi, but only one was special to her, only one bore her seed within it, only one could talk to her, and she loved it. It was *her* kianthi. When it eventually passed on, she was not sad, for from it was born a new tree, and it remembered her. The She'Har knew love.

Kate opened her eyes, feeling the bed shake beside her. Lyralliantha was curled into a ball, crying. At first she was confused, both from the change in her body, as well as from seeing the She'Har woman cry, but then she understood. *She was exploring my memories at the same time.*

What Lyralliantha had experienced had been far more traumatic than what she had shared with Kate. Acting on instinct alone, Kate moved closer, putting her arms around the other woman. She made shushing

sounds and stroked Lyralliantha's hair, trying to soothe her.

Eventually they both became quiet and still, and neither moved for some time.

"You deserve better, Kate," said the She'Har woman. "He is not a punishment for you."

"I know," agreed the green eyed woman, "but it is harder to convince my heart of that."

"You have done nothing wrong. Hating yourself is not the real reason you followed him."

"My head knows that, but my heart is a mess," admitted Kate.

"We will heal it," said Lyralliantha.

Kate almost laughed, "How?"

"With love," said the She'Har woman, and then she kissed her gently.

Her eyes widened with surprise for a moment. It was a soft kiss, lips against lips, but there was nothing demanding or sexual about it. It lasted a brief moment, and then Lyralliantha hugged her tightly. Even so, Kate felt her heart speed up a bit.

An insistent knocking came from the door. Rising, Kate went to answer it. Daniel stood on the other side, looking at her with open concern written on his face.

"What?" she asked brusquely.

"I got worried," he said. "You two have been in here for over an hour."

She smoothed her hair self-consciously, realizing it must be unkempt from lying on the bed. "We're still talking. Go away."

"Why are your cheeks red?" he asked.

Embarrassed, she began closing the door, "I'll explain later."

When she turned back, she found Lyralliantha sitting up, her hair smooth and her demeanor calm and unflustered. *How does she manage that?* wondered Kate. "I still don't understand some things."

"Ask and I will explain what I can," said the Illeniel She'Har.

"Everything was different, even the sun was red," said Kate.

"That was the first world," said Lyralliantha, as if that explained anything.

"The way Daniel explained it to me, your people are grown from the trees, with the seed inside, but in the world you showed me, the kianthi ate the seed, and only a few of them got it at all. Aren't *you* the kianthi, at least the way it works now?"

"I am a child of the She'Har," said Lyralliantha. "There were no children in the first world. The kianthi were lost to us when we left, and we were forced to adapt. The elders fashioned children in the form that best suited whatever world we came to after that, and the seeds were placed within them. We no longer have predators, or kianthi. We forgot how to love, and we no longer speak to any trees other than our own. We have become cold and isolated."

"I'm so confused," said Kate despairingly. "To me it seems that you fill the same role the kianthi did."

"The kianthi loved us, they protected us, and certain of them ate the seed and eventually became part of us. I serve a similar purpose, but I was born with the seed. All children of the She'Har carry it, but we have forgotten love, and we are not special. As we have changed our life cycle, so we have changed our hearts. The seeds that were given to the kianthi then,

461

were similar to the loshti today, they gave knowledge as well as providing for a new generation."

"What is a 'loshti'?" asked Kate.

Lyralliantha smiled, "A fruit that gives the knowledge of the ancestors to the child who eats it. It is not a seed anymore, like it was when the kianthi ate it. The seeds are produced separately, within the children, like myself."

"So what are you planning to put into Daniel?" said Kate, asking her most dreaded question.

"Nothing," said Lyralliantha.

"Your...," she struggled to find a good word to describe what the She'Har had shown her, "...story, implied that if he's your kianthi, he would have to become a tree someday. Right?"

"Somehow," agreed Lyralliantha, "but I do not think it will be from the doing of my people."

"That makes no sense at all."

The She'Har sighed, "I do not understand it either, but the Illeniel Grove has a different gift than the other groves. Our elders catch glimpses of the future. That is why they refused to take slaves when we first came to this world, for they saw that it would eventually lead to our destruction. They also have seen something in Tyrion."

"What?"

Lyralliantha's face became somber, "The death and rebirth of all things, for your race and mine."

Chapter 37

Tyrion was waiting when they emerged from the bedroom. He did his best to keep his worries hidden, but he knew that, at the very least, Kate would be able to read him like a book. "Is everything alright?" he asked. "I didn't expect your conversation to last so long."

"Your mate was full of questions," said Lyralliantha, "but I learned more from her than she gained from me."

He wasn't sure how to respond to that, but Kate hugged him suddenly, her arms squeezing tightly around his midsection. Her body shook slightly as she held him. "Hey now, what's wrong?" he asked her.

Green eyes met his and then looked away, "It's just a reaction to everything that's happened. I'm relieved."

Kate was lying, even Tyrion could tell that. Something had upset her, but he had no way of telling what it was. The two of them seemed to have reached an understanding of some sort, so he didn't think it was trouble between them. Lyralliantha stepped forward as Kate released him, and he met her gaze, but he could see Kate still staring at him from beyond his peripheral vision. She had forgotten he could still see her even though his eyes weren't on her.

Why does she keep looking at me like someone who has just lost his dog?

Lyralliantha's slap caught him completely off-guard.

"What was that for?!" he protested in shock.

"That was for the way you left Kate at the dance," the She'Har woman informed him, a rare expression of annoyance on her face.

Kate began to laugh from her position behind him, but she covered her mouth quickly. Regaining her composure, she told Lyralliantha, "You didn't have to do that."

"You are too kind," said Lyralliantha, "but I will see that you get your due."

Tyrion looked back and forth between the two women, rubbing his sore cheek. He was starting to think it might have been a bad idea to let the two of them trade notes.

"You must treat your kianthi better," said Lyralliantha.

His eyes narrowed, "I haven't even seen you in months."

Lyralliantha pointed at Kate, "Not me—her. As you are my kianthi, she is yours."

"Huh?" He assumed that they had discussed his marriage to Kate, but Lyralliantha had been very clear before that marriage and the She'Har concept of the kianthi were two separate things.

"Your seed is in her."

"My…," he stopped, his mind had gone blank.

"I'm pregnant, Daniel," Kate said, to clarify what was slowly becoming obvious to him.

His magesight focused on her womb, exploring within her. It was something he should have thought to do sooner, considering their activities over the past month. It took only a moment to spot the new life growing there. "Oh!" he said abruptly, "There's a— you're…"

"You seem surprised," Kate noted in a neutral tone.

"I just—you never had any after Aaron, so I thought…," he stopped. His words weren't coming out well, and the subject of her fertility was probably a sensitive one.

"You thought I was barren?" she said, finishing the sentence for him.

"Well…"

"Things grew cold between Seth and me after Aaron was born," she explained.

Tyrion's eyes wandered, traveling over the walls around them, as if he was searching for a route for escape. Kate frowned. She had been afraid of what his reaction might be.

"If I knock that wall out, we can expand the house in the rear," he said at last, giving voice to his thoughts. "We'll need room for a nursery. Actually I've been thinking of rebuilding some of this anyway, to add another floor above. So this is pretty good timing."

Kate blinked, her eyes had begun to water suddenly.

"What's wrong?" he asked, mildly alarmed.

Lyralliantha took the opportunity to slap him once more, choosing his other cheek this time.

"What is wrong with you!?" he said, surprised. "Do I need to start shielding myself?"

The She'Har's face was serious. "That was for leaving her after you killed the warden," she informed him. "And for making her cry just now."

Kate laughed.

"Do you even know what made her cry?" he asked.

Now it was Lyralliantha's turn to frown, "No, but I am sure she had good cause. I trust her judgement."

465

Kate put a hand on Lyralliantha's arm, "It's alright Lyra, those were happy tears."

"How many more of those can I expect?" asked Tyrion.

"I am making a list," answered Lyralliantha. "I will inform you when I finish considering all the events from her memories."

Something about her face seemed off to Tyrion. "Are you—trying to make a joke?"

Her blue eyes gave away nothing, but he thought he detected a sigh. "My attempts at humor are still largely unsuccessful," she replied honestly.

Unable to maintain his annoyance he lifted Lyralliantha's chin with one hand and kissed her quickly. It was an almost unconscious gesture, but he found himself suddenly self-conscious as he considered Kate's feelings.

She put him at ease by following his example and giving Lyralliantha a quick kiss on the cheek followed by a brief hug. Her gaze turned to him then, "Don't worry. I'm not as fragile as that."

Lyralliantha watched their exchange before interjecting, "Perhaps I am jealous after all."

"Why?" asked Kate.

"When the two of you speak I find myself wondering at your meanings. Frequently you answer questions that have not even been asked. It feels as though you both speak a language that I cannot understand, or even hear," responded the She'Har. She hesitated a moment and then added, "I am also irritated that two other women carry your child while I must w…" Her words stopped abruptly.

Chapter 37

Kate's eyes flashed a warning at her, but Tyrion hadn't noticed the unfinished ending. His mind had seized up at 'two other women'.

"Wait, what did you mean by…," he began, but then he realized what she must mean. Layla was in the yard working with the teens. There was only one possible conclusion, although she was moving too much for him to resolve the inner workings of her body at that distance. "Layla?"

Lyralliantha slapped him once again, but it was milder this time, almost playful.

He looked at her ruefully. "Was that for Kate too?"

"That was for me," replied his former owner. "Kate I understand, but Layla was unnecessary."

"That's fine," said Kate. "You can count that one for both of us."

***

The next morning Tyrion was tired and grumpy. He hadn't slept well. He normally sprawled in his bed, but with women on either side of him, he had felt distinctly confined. Worse he had found himself constantly entertaining fantasies, thoughts that had ruined his ability to rest. He hadn't acted on any of them, since he really had no clue what sort of etiquette he should follow.

Kate summed it up for him.

"Sleepy?" she asked with an evil grin.

He glared at her, "Leave me alone."

"I couldn't help but notice your restlessness last night," she continued, her eyes drifting downward, dispelling any doubt about her meaning.

"I need to go talk to Emma this morning," he responded, mildly disgusted with her amusement.

Kate caught him by the arm. It was something he was unused to after his years among the She'Har. He suppressed an almost involuntary anger.

"About last night, I thought we should go over the rules," she said, releasing his arm as she noticed the look in his eyes.

"Sorry," he said quickly. "Living here has made me strange. I'm not used to some things that were normal back in Colne. Rules about what?"

"About what kept you from sleeping last night."

"Oh," he said, understanding suddenly.

"Lyra and I will decide, when and who," she said without preamble. "This is something new for all of us. Since there are two of us and only one of you, that's the best compromise we could think of."

"Shouldn't I get a say in this?"

"No."

"I thought maybe...," Tyrion found himself unable to conclude his sentence.

"Maybe what?"

"Well, since you like girls too…"

Kate began to growl under her breath, "Just because I like *you* in that regard, doesn't necessarily mean I want to jump into that sort of thing with someone else, of *either* gender. Understand?"

Tyrion frowned.

She let out a frustrated sigh, "Look, suppose you decided you had a thing for Byovar…"

"I don't like men," he snapped immediately.

"I do," she responded. "Shut up, this is an example. Suppose you liked men, and suppose you

wanted to bring Byovar back for a romp, would you expect me to join you for that?"

His cheeks flushed with sudden jealousy at the thought, "No."

"Then don't expect me to do the same with her just because I happen to have a broader past experience than you do. If something like that occurs in the future, it will be on my terms, not *yours*."

A short while later he made a diplomatic exit. Reflecting on what Kate had said, he saw the merit in her words, but he still couldn't shake the feeling that he had been thoroughly trounced. He wasn't used to losing arguments, but then, over the past fifteen years most of his 'disagreements' had been solved using violence. That was no longer an option. *I've traded one owner for two,* he thought wryly.

Remembering his purpose, he sought out Emma. She and Ryan had been returned late the previous evening. Both of them bore new scars, but otherwise they seemed largely recovered.

After a brief search with his mind, he found her in her room, seated at a small table. A short walk took him to her door, and she answered it before he could knock. Magesight worked both ways after all.

"Father," she said by way of greeting.

"Mind if I come in?" he asked.

She stood back, indicating he should sit on the bed since she had only one chair. "Asking to enter a room now—you should be careful or we might forget who is in charge," she commented.

He glared at her, irritated by the mockery in her tone, but the smile in her eyes was genuine. Taking a deep breath, he forced himself to relax. "It's a new

world for us," he explained. "I still expect obedience when I require it, but otherwise I think we should strive for a more civilized atmosphere." Studying the room he added, "I see you have a table. Most of the others are lucky to have a bed in their rooms."

Emma nodded, "Anthony made it for me while I was in the care of the She'Har healers. It's a bit rough, but I like it."

"What's that?" he asked, gesturing toward the parchment on the tabletop.

"A letter to my parents. Would you like to read it?"

He shook his head, "No, I came to ask you about something else."

She sat in the small chair beside the table, "I am at your disposal, Father."

"In your arena battle the other day, you did something that surprised me," he began. "The liquid you produced, what was it?"

Emma sighed. "My father was a soap-maker, as you know, so I grew up around caustic substances," she said, beginning to dissemble.

His temper flared, "Don't lie to me, Emma. What you did *is* possible, for a mage who understands the inner workings of the material world, but neither of us has that much knowledge. No, you did something different. I didn't feel your aythar at work, and neither did your opponents."

Her shoulders drooped, "You may think me mad."

"I'm already a few cards shy of a full deck myself, Emma, just tell me."

"Sometimes I hear things, like voices. I ignored it at first, but then things started happening…"

"Do you hear the great heart beneath us?" he asked, grinning.

"Like a giant drum," she said nodding. "I don't hear it all the time, but when I turn my attention to it, it's always there."

"And the sky?"

"I try not to," answered Emma, closing her eyes. "The voice of the wind makes me feel like I'm losing my mind."

"How about this?" he said intently, leaning forward to tap the table in front of her.

Her expression was questioning, "It's so small. I haven't thought to... oh. It does have a voice, doesn't it?"

"A small one," he said. "Everything does, so far as I know. Some of them are harder to hear than others."

"Then I'm not crazy," she said with an audible sound of relief.

"Just be careful not to show this ability in front of the She'Har," he cautioned her. "They don't understand it. It may be something new to them, and the unknown always inspires fear."

"It's the same thing you used when we first came to this place isn't it? When you made the storm..."

"They know about me now, but I don't want them to know about *you*," he told her. "Do the others know yet?"

"Just Ryan. He saw it when we spoke mind to mind," she replied. "I shouldn't have used it in the fight, should I?"

Tyrion shrugged, "What's done is done. It was such a subtle thing, I don't think anyone else noticed your unusual method."

"Layla said you went berserk after the fight was over…"

He winced, "I was foolish. I let my emotions overrule my sense, and the wind—well, you must have some idea what it's like."

"How did you stop?" asked Emma.

"Lyralliantha pulled me back to my senses, which reminds me, I want you to stay close to Ryan," he said, putting a tone of authority in his voice.

Emma nodded. "You think he could do the same if something like that happened to me?"

"He's the only one who knows. Talk to him and make sure he understands what might happen."

"I will," she said, dipping her head obediently. "Why were you so angry?"

"I have a temper," he told her. "You may have noticed."

"But you were upset because we were hurt, weren't you?"

"Don't make the mistake of thinking I'm tender hearted, Emma," he warned her. "Even evil men can love their children."

"I know," she agreed. "But I also feel some of the same things. When I was lying there, watching those beasts tearing at Ryan, my heart was filled with a black despair. Despite your best efforts before, I think that was when I truly learned to hate. You aren't alone, Father."

"Alone?"

"I hate them too," she responded. "We all do, to some degree." Emma rose from her chair and crossed over to him. Carefully she put her arms around him.

Tyrion stiffened, but didn't return the embrace. "I don't deserve this, Daughter. Someday you may wind up dead, another tool broken to feed my desire for vengeance."

"Hug me," she insisted.

Relenting at last, he put his arms around her, though he still felt like a fraud.

"*Our* vengeance, Father," she corrected. "If it comes to that, I will not feel cheated. Spend my life wisely, and I will thank you with my dying breath."

He pushed her away, unable to stand the guilt her words were building in his heart. "That sounds like something Brigid would say."

Emma agreed, "If she had the tongue for it, she probably would. You will have to watch her carefully. She would throw her life away for just the smallest taste of revenge."

"She reminds me of myself."

Emma shook her head, "No, she's even more reckless. If you ever get your chance at revenge, and you have to spend our lives to achieve it, save her until last."

Tyrion frowned. He didn't like the turn their conversation was taking, but he couldn't deny the truth of it. "Why?"

"Because she hates them more than all of us. If anyone should see the end of them, it should be her."

Chapter 38

"No more—I swear, you're trying to kill me," protested Tyrion.

"It has been months," said Lyralliantha. "I missed you."

The second sentence was something new. Since her return she had been using more language of the same sort, replete with 'want', 'love', and 'miss'. Even her attempts at humor had improved. Tyrion had begun to wonder if her past reticence regarding emotional language had been due mainly to her alien nature, or whether it was simply because he had been a poor mentor.

Kate had been a far more able teacher than he had.

The smell of something frying permeated the air, making his stomach try to perform gymnastics. It wanted to get out there, where the meat was, but Lyralliantha's hand was on his arm, pulling him back toward her. "Stay a few minutes more," she told him. "Breakfast isn't ready yet, and I promise I will let you rest."

With a sigh, he collapsed back into the bed, "Whatever she is cooking smells really good."

"You like food as much as sex," announced Lyralliantha in a serious tone, as though she were making a new observation. It might have been a joke if Kate had said it, but on second examination, he wasn't entirely sure which it was with Lyralliantha.

"Now that we have new cookware and fresh meat, Kate's been able to work miracles," he answered.

"If her secrets were revealed to my people, it would be disaster," announced Lyralliantha.

"Why?" he asked.

"They would stop eating the calmuth, and everyone would begin taking root," she said with a crooked grin.

Another joke, he realized, chuckling politely.

Changing subjects he spoke to the ceiling, "I missed you too."

"Good," she replied, a tone of satisfaction in her voice. "I will be forced to leave you again soon."

"What?"

"The loshti will be ready in another month."

"So, just wolf it down and come right back," he replied flippantly.

She patted his cheek, "It is not as simple as that."

"What will happen then?" he asked before adding, "Wait, no, tell me where this magical fruit is first. I have seen no sign of it."

"Why do you wish to know?" she asked.

"Just curious."

"It grows in my bower," she replied.

"Really?" he exclaimed. "I went there often while you were away, and I never saw it."

"It looks much like the calmuth, but this one hangs directly above my sleeping place. Its color is darker than the ordinary calmuth, but I am not surprised you did not notice it," she told him.

Her frank openness about such an important item to the Illeniel Grove surprised him. "No one guards it?"

"The other groves guard theirs, but the Illeniel need no guards. It is impossible to steal from us."

"Why?"

Lyralliantha closed her lips, she had said too much.

"You can't tell an outsider?"

"I cannot tell *you*," she answered.

Now he was offended, "That's awfully specific."

"Things are complicated where you are concerned, Tyrion," she said. "You are not an outsider, you are my kianthi, but the elders have made special provisions for you."

"They don't trust me."

"No," she said emphatically. "They trust you completely. The Illeniel will never oppose you. You need not fear them."

"They trust me, but they won't tell me why. They won't hurt me, but they won't share their secrets either. None of this makes sense," he complained.

"Rather than fret about what we cannot change, we should enjoy what we have," she told him.

Tyrion growled in frustration, but after a moment he pushed his irritation aside. "So, what will happen when you eat the fruit? How long will you be gone?"

"I will be away for a year at least," she admitted.

"At least?" he exclaimed. "How badly is this thing going to scramble your brains?"

"I should recover from the effects of the loshti within a few days. The rest of the year is merely a formality, a waiting period," she explained.

"Waiting for what?"

"To see if I've become unstable. The onslaught of so much knowledge unbalances some. The year is a period of observation, to determine if I am safe to return to the grove."

"You said, 'a year at least', how long does it take if you are deemed unbalanced?"

"I will be destroyed if I am found to be damaged," she admitted. "The dangers of an insane lore-warden are too great to be chanced."

"Just refuse it," he told her. "I'd rather not risk you."

Lyralliantha smiled, "Do not be afraid my love, for the Illeniel Grove, this is just a formality. None chosen by the Illeniel elders ever fail."

"But they do in other groves?"

She nodded.

"What makes the Illeniels so much better at it then?"

Lyralliantha looked down, "Let us talk of something else."

"More of that 'don't tell Tyrion our secrets' crap, right?" he replied sourly. When she didn't answer after a moment or two of waiting, he let out a long sigh. "Fine, you mentioned breakfast, and that reminded me of something."

Her eyes looked the question at him.

"I saw Koralltis use something he called a 'stasis-weave' on one of my children after an arena battle, but I didn't have long to examine it. Can you create one for me?"

She gave him a suspicious look, "Why do you need to see something like that?"

"I want to try and replicate it," he said honestly.

"For what purpose?"

He sighed once more, this time with feigned exasperation, "You really don't trust me do you?"

"Of course I do," she replied with a hint of anger, "but I would like to know your motives. The stasis-weave is complex and experimenting with it could be dangerous."

"You don't think I can do it," he challenged.

She rose from the bed, her movements betraying her irritation. "Why must everything be an insult to you? Breakfast is ready, we should go enjoy Kate's latest labors."

His hand fell on her shoulder, "Show me—please."

"It would be unwise."

"What if I promise to let you watch while I try to reproduce it? I'm sure it will take some time, but I won't work on it if you aren't with me," he said, trying to placate her.

"You still haven't told me your purpose."

Letting his shoulders droop he made a show of giving in, "If you promise you won't tell Kate…"

"What has she to do with this?"

"I want to make a present for her. If she had a box that could preserve meat and other things, it would be a great help for her," he answered. He kept his mind purely on that thought. That was his only motive. There was nothing else.

Lyralliantha's stance softened, "Would it mean so much to her?"

He nodded.

"Very well," she said, acquiescing. "I will create a small one, but you must only study it. Do not attempt anything unless I am with you."

Tyrion smiled, "Of course."

***

Another week passed, but unlike those in the past, the present week, and those in the future, promised many positive changes. The buildings around Albamarl were growing as Ryan's plan for expansion slowly unfolded. Tyrion's home itself would soon begin expanding once they were free to turn their attention and efforts to it.

The latest arrival of goods from Colne had included wool and some linen from Lincoln. Fiona and Dalton Brown had come along with the shipment, bringing not only the cloth, but needles and thread as well. David had grown up learning the tailor's trade from his father, and with Abby and some of the other's help he began to fashion new clothes for them all.

They were no longer slaves.

The return of clothing was a great relief to them, although most of them were already used to the nudity that had been forced upon them. It gave their small community a sense of a growing civilization. Albamarl was more than just a house now, it was a new future.

"We will be wealthy," said Tad Hayes, speaking to his father, Tom, before he left to return to Colne.

"The iron won't be enough, Son," said Tom. "There's only so much need for it in Colne and Lincoln. You've already upset the metals trade."

"There will be other things, Dad," said the young man. "We can do so much more. You'll see. The trade will make you and Mom wealthy as well."

Later he spoke with Ryan, "Have you given thought to walls?"

"They are in the plans," said his half-brother.

"Perhaps we should work on those next," suggested Tad.

"Worried about wolves stealing our animals?"

Tad glanced toward the giant trees, "Walls have other purposes."

"I don't think they'll be much use if that's your fear," opined Ryan. "You know as well as I do that in the sort of fights we might someday face walls will be of little use."

"It would make me feel better," said Tad. "We've gained so much, but it doesn't feel secure."

"The only security we have," replied Ryan, "is that they don't want to mess with *him*." He hooked his thumb in the direction of Tyrion.

Their conversation ended at that point, for Emma appeared, "Ryan, can I talk to you for a bit?"

"Sure," Ryan responded immediately, his eyes lighting up when he heard her voice.

"Again," sighed Tad, watching the two of them move away. "He spends too much time with her," he muttered to himself.

***

It was several days later when it happened.

Tyrion was outside, planning the demolition of the back wall of his house, to make way for the new nursery, when he felt their presence. Letting his magesight roam outward, he was immediately alarmed. They were everywhere, at the range of his senses but moving closer. A vast array of She'Har. *No, not She'Har alone, most of them are krytek.*

He yelled, calling to the others who were mostly in the front yard, but Emma was already moving. Her magesight was as good as his own, and she had detected the krytek as well. Everyone began running, gathering in front of the main house.

Joining them, Tyrion found Brigid already by his side. He had been so preoccupied he hadn't even noticed his dark shadow taking her place next to him. Her face held no expression, but her aura gave the impression of eagerness. *She wants to fight.*

The others were not so thrilled by the new development.

"What do we do?" said Emma anxiously.

Tyrion sighed. All his plans had come to naught. The She'Har had finally made their decision. Justice would never be satisfied. The numbers surrounding Albamarl were in the thousands, and they weren't composed of the naïve children of the She'Har, they were mostly krytek, the battle-ready creations of the father-trees.

"We die," he told them. "This is far too soon for anything I had considered."

Kate was standing nearby. "Don't try to send me away," she warned him.

He laughed, "It wouldn't do any good. There is no safe place. You will die beside me."

"Where's Lyralliantha?" asked David.

"She went to the Illeniel Grove this morning," he told them.

"She's betrayed us," spat Ian.

"Watch your mouth, boy," threatened Tyrion. "Use your brain. You'll notice that the krytek are

coming from every direction *but* the Illeniel Grove. They're the only ones who aren't involved in this."

"Could we take shelter there?" suggested Abby.

Violet nodded, desperate for any hope, "She's right! We could make a run for it."

"It's too late for that," Tyrion informed them. "There are Mordan among them, and they're within visual range of us now. Move close to the house, don't leave room for them to teleport behind us. Form a circle and be careful not to cut the person next to you."

Enchanted shields flickered into life around each of them, and their arm-blades glowed with deadly aythar as they moved to obey.

He began issuing more orders, "Brigid, stay beside me. I want you to kill anyone who enters the circle. Protect me while I work. Kate, sit with me until it's over."

Sitting cross-legged, he held Kate in front of him, kissing her cheek once more. Her body was tense with fear and anger. "Don't leave me," she said.

"What do you want me to do?" asked Layla.

The Prathion mage didn't have the tattoos he had given his children, and Tyrion knew she would be the first to die if she fought alongside them. "Lie down beside us and put a shield over us. Make it as strong as you can manage but do nothing else."

"I can fight, Tyrion," she replied, rebelliously.

"Not this fight, you can't. If you survive the early attacks, dismiss your shield and make yourself invisible. You're the only one with a chance of escaping."

"I can hide someone else with me," she told him.

"Take Kate then."

"No," said Kate. "I die with you."

He dipped his head in reluctant agreement. "I'm not sure what will happen," he said truthfully, "but I will make sure the wind finishes you before they reach you, even if I'm gone." He closed his eyes, focusing on the voice of the wind.

Before he even finished the words a krytek appeared within the circle and several others popped into being just outside it. Brigid leapt toward her new opponent with glee, ripping through its spellwoven protections before it could even get its bearings. The battle had begun.

More krytek appeared farther back as the Mordan vanguard began their assault. Strange spellweavings appeared in their hands, long tube-like constructions. Their purpose wasn't immediately apparent, until one of them leveled it at the circle of defenders. Channeling aythar along it, a deadly beam of focused power slammed into Anthony, piercing his enchanted shield and destroying his left leg. Screaming, the boy fell.

The winds were already roaring, but there wasn't time. The other krytek were aiming their new weapons, and Tyrion's children knew they were doomed. The She'Har had taken no chances, choosing to strike hard and fast, with overwhelming force and numbers.

Dozens more krytek appeared inside the front yard, and hundreds more beyond it in the field around Albamarl. The Prathion had emerged from hiding.

Faster, thought Tyrion, but the thought didn't help. The more he verbalized his needs internally, the harder it was to reach the place he needed to be. The wind

was there, but it seemed too far away. *Let me do this,* he begged. *Let me kill them all. That's all I want.*

Before the Mordan could unleash their next attack the Prathion soldiers cut them down. Their appearance hadn't been in support, they had lain in ambush. The remaining Mordan began teleporting at random, flickering in and out as they sought to avoid their murderous brothers.

Strange shapes flew overhead as the Gaelyn Grove's krytek joined the battle, followed shortly thereafter by the Centyr. Spellbeasts and strange monstrosities rushed to destroy the Prathion krytek.

"Some of them are here to help us!" shouted Emma. "Tighten the circle. Abby help Anthony while they're distracted."

More of the Mordan appeared within the circle, but no matter their size or shape, Brigid destroyed them. She moved like an evil wind, her arm blades sweeping out to divide anything that tried to oppose her. No defense could withstand her power, and when the circle was empty, she turned her will to disrupting those who fought with the Prathions beyond it.

At range, her attacks were useless against the She'Har shields. Even Emma's precise strikes were unable to penetrate their spellwoven defenses. Instead, Tyrion's children used their power to confuse and distract their enemies, knocking them off balance at critical moments or removing the earth from beneath them when they threatened the Prathions.

It was all pointless, though. The Prathions were not enough to stand against the combined might of the other three groves. Anyone with eyes could see what the inevitable conclusion would be.

The sky overhead was still and clear, but in the distance it had grown dark. A strange howling could be heard, rising in pitch and volume with each minute that passed. A massive storm was brewing, and Kate could feel a change in Tyrion where he sat behind her. Glancing down, she saw that his arms had become translucent. He was fading away...

The Mordan were desperate to press home their attack before the storm could grow worse, but no matter how many teleported into the circle Brigid cut them down before they could act. With the help of the Gaelyn and Centyr reinforcements they had regained control of the field, and the remainder of the initial strike force brought their new spellwoven weapons to bear once more.

Emma saw them preparing to attack once more, and she knew they couldn't survive the krytek's ranged weapons. Anthony was proof enough of that. On instinct alone she called to the earth, and the ground around them rose, gigantic slabs of bedrock erupting from the soil to protect them.

The Mordan beams tore through the heavy stone as though it were tissue, but the rock had robbed them of some of their power. Where the beams came through and struck one of the teens it was deflected. Their enchanted shields held. More stone rose, reinforcing what had already been reduced to rubble, but Emma knew it was only a matter of time. The Mordan were preparing to attack again, and more of them were free to help with each passing moment.

They were doomed.

Chapter 39

A second barrage ripped through their stone defenses, but now they could see that something had changed. The Gaelyn and Centyr krytek were turning to face a new foe coming from their rear, in the direction of the nearby forest.

The Illeniel krytek had entered the battle.

They came in the same motley variety of shapes and sizes—from humanoids to strange quadrupedal forms, and even insectoid designs. Their numbers were smaller than those of the Prathions, or any of the other groves, but their movements were different.

They advanced with deliberation, seemingly oblivious to the offensive power of their enemies. Where the Gaelyn She'Har directed fire against them, they simply moved, deftly dodging every attack. They moved with speed, but they were no faster than the other krytek, rather, they dodged before any blow could land.

Outnumbered as they were, they took no casualties at first, and once they were fully engaged, they began to slaughter the krytek of the other groves.

It was a strange battle. The krytek of both sides were immune to fear. They were not made to feel it. Unlike human or even She'Har warriors, they would fight until dead or ordered to cease. The Gaelyn and Centyr began organizing their tactics, combining attacks to prevent the Illeniels from dodging. It took three or four to accomplish it, but occasionally they managed to kill one of the Illeniels, but it was not enough to slow their advance.

The Illeniel force made a line for the humans and their faltering defense. Along the way they decimated the group of Mordan responsible for the assault on the humans, and once they had reached their destination, they spread out prepared to defend Tyrion and his children.

A hush fell over the battlefield as the krytek of the three attacking groves paused. Byovar stepped out from among the Illeniel krytek, and using magic to boost his voice, he addressed the enemy arrayed against them.

"Withdraw! Your goal is impossible now. Further fighting will only endanger the elders of all our groves," he shouted. It was a statement of fact.

Abby felt a soft touch, and then she heard Lyralliantha's voice in her mind. *You must stop him. We can make peace with them, but only if he doesn't destroy the groves.*

How? asked the girl.

Touch him. You must speak to him, mind to mind. Draw him back from whatever dark place his spirit has gone, before it is too late.

***

The world returned slowly, and Tyrion found himself once more in the world of flesh and blood. A voice was speaking to him in an alien tongue, ideas that meant things. They were silent, but his brain was automatically converting them into sounds. Sounds that held meaning—words.

What an odd thing, he thought.

You can hear me, Father?

The voice in his mind brought recognition. *That's Abby.*

Release your anger, calm the storm, she said, repeating the same words over and over. *Can you hear me?*

The wind was already slowing. It irritated him that she couldn't see that herself. *Of course, I can hear you. Stop shouting at me,* he answered.

Some minutes later he felt sure enough to release Kate from his grasp and try to stand. Cracked and jumbled stone surrounded them, but beyond that, his magesight showed him a multitude of krytek. Byovar and Lyralliantha stood just outside the defensive stone enclosure, and with them was Thillmarius. The krytek, excepting those belonging to the Illeniel Grove, were withdrawing.

He sent his thoughts to Lyralliantha, *What's happening?*

The beginnings of peace, she returned.

It didn't feel very much like peace. Pressing outward with his will, he pushed aside several massive stones until he they could emerge without difficulty. Thillmarius stood waiting for him, a curious expression on his face.

"Forgive me, Tyrion, we should have been more ready," said the lore-warden

"More ready? How long did you have your krytek positioned around my home?"

"Several weeks now," admitted the golden-haired She'Har. "We suspected they might try to make a pre-emptive strike, but we didn't anticipate how much force they would bring to bear."

Tyrion directed his gaze to Byovar, "And the Illeniels, did you know this would happen?"

Byovar shook his head, "No. We had only a brief warning, minutes before they came. We rushed to aid you as soon as we knew of the attack."

"I see," he said noncommittally. Addressing Lyralliantha he asked, "What happens now?"

"The elders will meet again. They have seen our resolve. We will seek an accord to formalize what the Illeniel and Prathion Groves have already decided," she answered immediately.

"Which is?"

"That humankind is sentient, deserving of our protection and respect. That there will be no more encroachment or taking of the remaining wild humans. We would have your people recognized as a part of the Illeniel Grove."

Brigid was watching him, violent energy coursing through her aura. She was ready to continue the fight. Friend or foe, it hardly mattered to her. There was a question in her eyes that needed no words. She wanted to kill the three She'Har standing in front of him and consequences be damned.

And she could do it, too, he thought proudly. *She could kill them and possibly some of the krytek still guarding us.* His other children, Layla, and Kate were watching him as well, fresh hope on their faces. Seeing them, he knew his duty, as much as he disliked it.

"If your people seek peace, make your accord, but it won't be final until we have added our agreement to the final terms," he told the three She'Har. "Tell the elders they have two days."

Thillmarius's eyes nearly bugged from his head, "Two days?! You can't make demands Tyrion. We barely held them as it was. It will take the elders months to create an accord."

"Two days," he repeated. "After that I will destroy everything for as far as my will can reach."

"Don't be ridiculous you can't…"

He held up his hand, "I can't kill you all, I know that, but I can accomplish far more than you realize. The mountains will rise, the winds will tear, and when I am done, at least half of this world will be free of your kind."

"Threats are unwise, Tyrion," said Thillmarius. "You can't win, and if you force them to war, they will eliminate humanity entirely."

"I don't care if I can win any longer," he replied. "The question is how much are they willing to lose? Two days—no more."

"But…," Thillmarius began to protest once more.

Byovar put out his hand, "Be calm, friend Thillmarius. The Illeniel are prepared, we have made ready for this. It will be as he says."

The Prathion's eyes went wide for a second and then returned to normal. He glanced from Byovar to Lyralliantha who nodded once, and then he relaxed. "Very well," he said at last.

Why does he defer to them so quickly? wondered Tyrion.

Byovar and Thillmarius left soon after that, and the remaining Prathion krytek vanished, though whether they were truly gone or just invisible was an open question. Lyralliantha and the Illeniel krytek remained.

Tyrion and his children began cleaning up the aftermath of the battle.

The chickens were gone, whether dead or alive it was impossible to say. They didn't find any avian remains. The lone pig had been the recipient of a poorly aimed blast of aythar. His body was spread across the interior of his shattered pen. They found two sheep, dead, and the rest were missing.

It appeared their days of animal husbandry were over, at least for the next few weeks.

The main house was undamaged. Its enchanted stones had resisted the few attacks that had struck it. The dormitory had sustained minor damage, and Ryan resolved that it should have the same treatment as Tyrion's home when they repaired it. It would be a lot of magical labor, but it was worth it if it meant they wouldn't have to worry about repairs in the future.

Assuming they had a future.

Tyrion pointed at one of the Illeniel krytek, a large quadrupedal insectoid with a pair of pincer like arms projecting above the main body. Its appearance was hideous, but it looked to be ideally built for clearing some of the rubble of one of the storehouses that had collapsed. "You, move those stones and stack them over there, so we can sort out what's left in there."

The creature stared blankly at him but didn't move.

He walked closer, repeating his orders in Erollith, "I said I want you to help move those stones."

"We were not made to assist in your labors," replied the krytek, dispelling any illusion he might have had that it was unintelligent.

Tyrion's temper was already dangerously short. Bringing his arm across in a sudden slashing motion,

he activated his weapon enchantment at the same time. The krytek was unprotected and unready for such an attack, but the creature stepped back and to one side before his slash could land. The timing was uncanny.

It made no move to create a defensive spellweave or otherwise defend itself. Tyrion was left glaring at it and feeling somewhat foolish. "If you're going to stand around here, I expect you to help us clean up this mess," he reiterated. Brigid was advancing on the krytek from the rear now, having noticed his angry tone and failed attack.

Lyralliantha appeared and intervened before things could go any farther. "Stop!" she commanded.

Tyrion and Brigid both graced her with withering glares.

"Were you truly planning to attack one of the krytek now guarding your home?" she asked incredulously.

"I've had a very trying day, and this obstinate, overgrown bug refuses to help us cleanup," he growled at her.

"They are not made for such labors," she replied.

"*Your* people nearly destroyed everything I've built here. The least they could do is help us straighten up their mess."

"*My* people saved you," she replied coolly. "The battle today was the doing of the Mordan, Gaelyn, and Centyr."

Irritated he shot back, "She'Har are She'Har, whatever grove they're from."

"No," she replied, growing visibly annoyed, "they are not. We are all She'Har, but they are *not* my people, they are not my race." Lyralliantha turned to

493

the krytek, "Help him with whatever he asks." The krytek nodded, and she began walking away, toward the Illeniel Grove.

"Where are you going?" he demanded.

"Home," she answered. "I need peace, and it is obvious I won't find it here."

Angry, he watched her walk for a moment before speaking to the krytek, "You heard her, start lifting."

Later he told Kate about the exchange, but rather than being supportive, she graced him with a look of disappointment. "You really can be a jerk sometimes."

"We almost died today," he reminded her sourly.

"That's not the point. You're treating the people who help you as badly as the people who hurt you," she explained.

"They're the same people."

"The five groves are separate races," she replied. "They're related, but to them they're as different from one another as sheep and goats. You insulted Lyra."

That was a fact he had never heard about the She'Har. "Did *she* tell you that?"

Kate nodded, "She showed me, visions from the elders' memories of their first world."

Stubborn, he responded, "She hasn't taken the loshti yet, she couldn't have that knowledge."

"They showed her during their councils, but speaking of that, have you considered the fact that you've driven her away when she has less than a week left before she is to take the loshti?" Her emerald eyes bored into him accusingly. "The last thing she wants right now is to be fighting with you during the last days she has before she leaves for a year."

He had no good response to that, and he had learned that his pride usually caused more problems than it solved. With difficulty he nodded at her, "I'll apologize to her—later. I'm too angry to think straight right now."

She started to put her hand on his arm, but he tensed.

"Later, Kate," he told. "I'm not good company at the moment."

With an understanding look, she turned back toward the house. "I need to sort out what we're going to eat anyway."

As soon as she had gone beyond earshot he glanced at Brigid, who still hovered nearby. "Did you see what that thing did?" The krytek in question was some yards distant now, moving the rubble as requested. Tyrion pitched his voice low for his daughter's ears alone.

Brigid nodded, "I saw them fighting the other krytek too. It took several from the other groves just to bring down one of them."

"It started moving as soon as I did. There was no delay. It was as if it wasn't reacting, it was simply acting in time with my own attack," he observed quietly.

"How could they do that?" she asked intently.

Tyrion shook his head, "I don't know." *But I will damn sure find out.*

Chapter 40

The She'Har returned the next morning, less than twenty-four hours after the attack of the previous day.

Five lore-wardens came, one from each of the five groves: Listrius, representing the Illeniel Grove; Thillmarius, for the Prathion Grove; Goldin, for the Centyr Grove; Taymar, for the Gaelyn Grove; and Mareltus, for the Mordan Grove. Lyralliantha walked amidst them, carrying a large wooden case.

They had no escort or entourage, no guards or other accompaniment.   It was a peculiarity of their race. Where a human representative might have required protection, the She'Har simply didn't bother. Their children, even the lore-wardens, were simply not that important. They could replace their children, only the trees, the elders, deserved real protection.

Tyrion met them in front of the main house, and every person living in the community they now called Albamarl, stood with him.

"I see you've returned without your soldiers," he told them curtly.

Lyralliantha advanced toward him, presenting the case, while Listrius spoke, "The five groves have come to agreement."

"What have you decided?" asked Tyrion.

"Your race is sentient, aware, and deserving of respect. Our actions in the past have been harmful to you.   From this time forward, humankind will be treated with the same regard that the five groves show to each other, and you will be considered a part of the

Illeniel Grove—assuming you agree to this accord," said Listrius formally.

Together Listrius and Lyralliantha opened the case, displaying the black tablet within. Tyrion might have thought it was made of stone, but his magesight showed him the fine almost invisible grain of the Eilen'tyral that it was made from. The tablet was densely inscribed with the hexagonal symbols of Erollith. Being written on a flat tablet, the accord was written using only two of the six axes, the past objective moving toward the future objective. It was a more practical form of writing than the usual six axes, three dimensional, sculpture-like documents.

"Where's the rest of it?" asked Tyrion after glancing at it briefly.

Listrius' brows went up momentarily. The She'Har hadn't expected the human to be so familiar with their written language. "This document contains all the practical information, but we are indeed constructing a more formal document that will contain the personal and subjective elements for posterity."

"I'll need a day to peruse this before I put my signature on it," responded Tyrion. "I will also want to see the final complete document when it is finished."

"That may not be for some months," Listrius informed him.

"I will still want to see it," said Tyrion brusquely. "To ensure the accuracy of the additional information, even if it isn't functionally relevant."

The She'Har left shortly after that exchange, and Tyrion retreated into his bedroom with the She'Har tablet. Lyralliantha went with him. She no longer seemed irritated, but Kate gave her a look of sympathy

anyway. It was obvious to her that Lyralliantha needed some support before her ordeal in a few days, but Tyrion was too preoccupied with his own concerns to notice.

Kate left the two of them alone, hoping he would take the hint.

"Read this part for me," said Tyrion, pointing at part of the text.

"All humans currently kept by the She'Har will be released," she recited dutifully. "You should have been able to read that," she admonished him.

"I just wanted to make sure I understood it properly," he replied. "I sometimes miss certain nuances. Does that mean they intend to release all the people in the slave camps?"

Lyralliantha nodded.

He chewed his lip, "That won't do."

"I thought that part would please you."

"What do you think will happen if they release tens of thousands of psychotic mages?" he asked. "They outnumber the entire population of Colne and Lincoln, and they have no inkling of how to act in a civilized society. The 'normal' human population will be overrun, tortured, abused, and most likely enslaved."

"Will they not obey you?" she replied.

"Without collars they won't obey anyone. Even I couldn't hope to control so many with nothing more than intimidation."

"How would you change it then?"

"Your people created this problem," he told her. "They'll have to keep the slave cities running. Even if they were civilized, there's no way for me to feed a

population of that size. The She'Har will have to continue supporting them."

"Then nothing will have changed," she noted.

"We'll build a city, here," he explained. "I'll make a tour of the slave cities every year and select some of the inhabitants to be released and allowed to relocate. Over time we can build and handle more of them. In the meantime, the She'Har will have to insure that their slave populations don't grow—no breeding, no more child pens."

"How long will this take?"

"Longer than my life I'd imagine," he replied, pursing his lips. "Some of them will probably die before we get to them.

Something in her expression caught his eye.

"What are you thinking?" he asked her. "You look like someone stole your dog."

"It is of no importance."

Remembering what Kate had told him the day before, he spoke again, "I'm sorry for yesterday. I was upset, and my words were rude. Are you worried about taking the loshti?"

She nodded, "In part. I am more concerned for what will happen to you while I am away."

"I will still be here when you return," he said reassuringly. "Let the future take care of itself."

Lyralliantha laughed, "But that is the duty of the Ill…" She stopped suddenly.

"The duty of the Illeniels?" he said, finishing her sentence and turning it into a question. "What does that mean?"

"It is just a saying," she replied stiffly. "My grove is known for being more concerned with the future than the others."

"No, you said 'duty', and that implies more than just a generalization," he argued. "What did you mean?"

"It is not something I am permitted to speak of," she confessed, dropping her pretense.

Tyrion's mind was quick, and several things fell into place at once. "The battle yesterday, the way the Illeniel krytek fought—how did they avoid so many attacks?" he asked.

She didn't answer.

"It's the Illeniel gift isn't it?" His eyes bored into her.

Lyralliantha nodded but didn't speak.

"And the other groves know about it?"

She nodded once more.

"But you can't tell me. That doesn't make much sense considering we are about to join the Illeniel Grove, according to this treaty," he responded.

"Let us talk of something else, my Love," she answered.

Frustrated, he growled but when she leaned forward to kiss him he relaxed. *No point in spoiling the evening over it,* he thought. *Besides, I've figured out more of their secrets than she realizes.* Smiling inwardly, he kissed her again, rising to his feet, and lifting her into his arms before tossing her onto the bed.

"Oh!" she cried, startled.

He stalked forward, the look of a hunter on his face. "Don't try to escape," he told her in mock seriousness.

"I wouldn't dream of it," she said slyly.

***

Three days later the amended treaty was signed, and the first accord between humanity and the She'Har became official. It was a solemn occasion that should perhaps, have been celebrated with great fanfare and ceremony, but the small community of Albamarl contented themselves with merely having a larger than usual dinner. The She'Har representatives remained long enough to hear Tyrion play on his cittern but returned to their groves soon after that.

All in all it was a rather anticlimactic event, despite its importance in the history of both mankind and the She'Har.

Lyralliantha was due to take the loshti the next day, so Kate left her and Tyrion alone that evening, electing to sleep in the other bedroom with Layla.

In the wee hours of the morning, though, Tyrion rose, leaving Lyralliantha to sleep alone. It was still dark when he entered the dormitory and went to one particular door. Knocking, he found Emma awake and waiting for him. She was dressed, and Ryan sat beside her on the bed.

"Are you ready?" he asked, even though the answer was obvious.

"Yes, Father," they replied together.

Leaving the dormitory, the three of them went to one of the undamaged storage buildings. Inside, they descended a set of stairs into a dark room filled with musty smells and cool earth—a root cellar built to keep food. Moving to the back wall, they stood together in a small ring.

"Don't let her go too deep," he cautioned Ryan.

"I should be fine, Father," remarked Emma. "Just make sure I follow the right course." After a few seconds her eyes grew distant, and the earthen wall in front of them opened to reveal a dark passage.

The three of them entered, and the soil closed behind them. The tunnel only extended for thirty feet ahead, but as they walked it moved with them, opening before them and filling in to the rear. It went deeper as they walked, and Tyrion kept his magesight tuned to the earth above them, marking their way.

"More to the left here," he told Ryan, giving yet another command to his son who was holding Emma's hand as they walked. Ryan silently relayed the information to his sister, and the tunnel began to meander more to the left, giving a wide berth to one of the massive roots of the god-trees.

"You're sure they won't detect us?" asked Ryan for the tenth time.

"No," said Tyrion, "but you don't feel anything happening do you?"

Ryan shook his head. Whatever Emma was doing, it seemed undetectable. The earth moved as if of its own accord.

"She's clever," complimented Tyrion. "I don't think anyone outside of us could feel the empty space where we are now."

"I feel it," said Ryan.

"Because we're in it," responded Tyrion. "I can hear the earth talking to her. She, or it, is saying that there's nothing here, nothing but more earth. I think if we were above ground we'd not even know it was here.

"I hope so," said his son.

They traveled that way for another hour, moving slowly, avoiding the great roots of the trees of the Illeniel Grove, until at last Tyrion called for them to halt, "This is it."

Ryan squeezed Emma's hand, speaking to her mind to mind; after a minute she blinked, emerging from her trance-like state. Tyrion moved to his other side and took Ryan's left hand in his own. "Focus your attention above us," he told them. "Be ready."

Emma's eyes glazed over once more, and Tyrion's face took on a similar expression. It was harder for him, for the voice he sought was farther away, muted by the heavy layer of earth above him. He found it nonetheless, and soon his mind was drifting with the wind.

In Lyralliantha's bower, far above them, a heavy dark-skinned fruit hung from a branch above her sleeping pallet. In appearance it was much like the calmuth that were to be found everywhere, but it was denser and its color different. A sudden breeze struck the branch.

It wasn't a wind strong enough to damage the branch, but within it was a thinner blast of air, moving much faster and with a razor thin edge. It neatly severed the stem holding the purplish fruit in place, and it began to fall.

Another gust caught the fruit and buoyed it for a moment, sending it gently falling to one side, so that rather than falling on the bed, it sailed out of the bower and fell toward the distant earth below. It picked up speed for a few seconds before the air began to behave strangely once more, blowing directly beneath it,

slowing its descent. When it finally touched the ground it was so softly that it hardly made a sound.

The earth received it gratefully, and the dark soil swallowed it, leaving no trace of where the fruit had momentarily lain. The loshti was gone.

In the dark cavern below, the fruit emerged from the earth to fall neatly into Tyrion's waiting hands. Pulling a heavy wool bag next to him open, he removed a strangely carved wooden box. It had a hinged lid that he deftly opened. Inside, it was lined with velvet.

Placing the loshti within, he closed the box once more and with a tiny effort of will activated the stasis enchantment carved into the wood. Time stopped inside, trapping the loshti in an eternally still moment.

An hour and a half later, he climbed quietly back into his bed, careful not to disturb Lyralliantha's sleeping form. Tyrion lay in the bed, considering his recent actions. He had sent Emma and Ryan back to their beds before storing the loshti. No one but he would be able to find it, ensconced as it was in a deep secret place within the earth.

There it would wait until he was ready.

Tyrion lay in bed beside his She'Har lover, unable to sleep, and in the darkness he smiled.

Epilogue

"Why did you stop?" said Matthew, somewhat insistently.

"I'm tired," I told him honestly. "This is a good place to let the story rest, and all of you need sleep."

Matthew disagreed, "I'm not sleepy. Just finish it."

"I've been talking for hours. Take pity on your storyteller," I said with a wan smile.

Moira tried to take my side, "I don't know if I want to hear the rest after this anyway. He's turned his children into angry killers, and now, after they created the first peace treaty between humans and She'Har, he's already breaking their trust."

I watched her carefully, "You mean stealing the loshti?"

My daughter nodded, "That's what starts the war, isn't it?"

Looking up at the ceiling, I answered carefully, "No, actually it doesn't. They live peacefully for quite a while after that—sort of."

Moira frowned, "But he stole it, won't they know who did it?"

Lynarralla started to speak, but I held up my hand to stop her. "You already know why the theft didn't create a major incident," I said to the She'Har girl. "Don't you?"

"I don't know the story, but the gift of the Illeniel elders would make it impossible for them not…"

"Ah, ah!" I said, shushing her. "You're going to spoil it for them."

Lynarralla closed her mouth quickly.

Moira growled, "That's not fair! Lynn, you can tell me when we leave."

The silver-haired girl answered seriously, "Your father doesn't wish for me to tell you."

I smiled, I had expected that answer.

Moira's rebellion wasn't done yet, though. "You don't have to listen to him, just tell me when we're alone."

"Tyrion and Lyralliantha told me to obey him as though he were my own father," explained the She'Har girl. "I cannot violate their command."

"If only my own children were so obedient," I remarked snidely.

Matthew laughed, "You wish!"

"This isn't over yet, old man," said Moira with mock scorn.

"I'm sure it isn't," I replied, "but the rest will have to wait for tomorrow."

Reluctantly, they left for bed. Silently, I made my own way to the room I shared with Penny and skillfully slid under the blankets, doing my best to avoid disturbing her. She was awake though, whether because she had been waiting or because I had been too clumsy, I wasn't sure. Her foot snaked out to slip under my ankle, letting me know she was at least partially conscious.

The contact helped ease my mind from the next part of the memories I had been following. Relaxing at last, I went to sleep.

Coming Late in 2015:

Centyr Dominance

The tale begun in Thornbear continues as Moira Illeniel begins a quest to find and rescue her father while learning the darker secrets of the Centyr legacy.

Coming in the Summer of 2016:

The Betrayer's Bane

The story of Tyrion Illeniel marches on to its inevitable conclusion. As Tyrion's quest for vengeance reaps a harvest that will devastate friend and foe alike.

For more information about the Mageborn series check out the author's website:

www.magebornbooks.com

Or interact with him more directly on his Facebook page:

www.facebook.com/MagebornAuthor

Made in United States
Orlando, FL
20 June 2022

18976745R00280

Made in the USA
Middletown, DE
15 September 2022

73293275R00411